I0561732

The Lost Heritage Trilogy

by Jenny Dee

BOOK ONE: CALL OF THE CELTS
BOOK TWO: A TUSCAN TREASURE
BOOK THREE: THE CATALAN KEY

The Lost Heritage Trilogy: Books 1-3
Call of the Celts, A Tuscan Treasure & The Catalan Key

©2021 by Jennifer Dee Communications LLC

Cover Illustrations ©2020 Chelsea Yolalan
Cover Photography ©2020 Marco Ossino/Depositphotos.com, Georgy Mayer/
Depositphotos.com, Stanislav Tarasov/Depositphotos.com, Anna Subbotina/
Depositphotos.com
Artwork ©2020 Andrejs Severetnikovs/Depositphotos.com

Print ISBN: 978-1-954687-21-9
Ebook ISBN: 978-1-954687-22-6
Printed in the United States of America

All rights reserved. The text of this publication, or any part thereof, may not
be reproduced in any manner whatsoever without written permission from
the author. Names, characters, businesses, events and incidents are either
the products of the authors' imaginations or used in a fictitious manner. Any
resemblance to actual persons, living or dead, or actual events is purely
coincidental.

Praise for The Lost Heritage Trilogy

"I just finished reading the three books. I couldn't put them down. It's been a while since I stayed up until 2AM reading. I felt like I was with the three sisters touring Ireland, Italy and Spain. I could not wait to get to the end of the trilogy to find out the secret. I can't wait to read your next book!" - Miriam S., 5-Star Goodreads review

"I love that each of your books are so different because the sisters are different. Its edginess made it a fun read. You had me trying to solve the mystery right up to the end of Book 3!" – Katherine F., Email review

"Call of the Celts is the first book of The Lost Heritage series. It is an adventurous tale full of suspense and wonder. I had it as a bedtime read and it transported me to a magical place each night. I rate it 5 out of 5, and I recommend it to anyone who enjoys a romantic historical fiction." – Maureen's Lifestyle

"An Armchair Travel Adventure. I read this on kindle while snuggled up and got lost in the travel adventure. I went to Ireland a few years ago and it was so fun to be in that setting for this adventure/ mystery/romance. It's an easy read that carried me away and provided an occasional chuckle. The writer's style is very engaging, and the characters feel like friends of mine. I highly recommend!"
- Stephanie F., 5-Star Amazon review

"Great storyline and characters. I loved the relationship between the three sisters, each different in their own ways, but close and loving. When their family history foundation is shattered by a mysterious bequeath, they go to Ireland as instructed. The trip brings more family and mystery, danger and romance to balance out the book. Can't wait for book two!" - Sheila, 5-Star Goodreads review

"I went into the 2nd book expecting to be good, but not as good as the 1st, but it truly is! I adored the story, the setting, the food, the wine, the message, and Mia's transformation was absolutely profound to read - that scene where he made her look at herself. I think that should be required reading for every woman!" – Stacey M., Facebook Review

"Mia was a very relatable character and I loved the book's body positive message. We all need a Francesco in our lives!" – Patricia L., Facebook review

"Once again, another amazing book and a great end to the series. It was my favorite one -- the twist to the plot really caught me by surprise! Clever, clever girl! ;-) I thought Marissa's character was the most interesting of the three sisters, and I loved the overall message of the book." – Leslie F., Email review

Call of the Celts

BOOK ONE OF THE LOST HERITAGE TRILOGY

by Jenny Dee

For My Nanny
The inspiration behind my own Celtic calling.
Your legacy and spirit will always live
on through me. This one's for you.

1

You live your whole life thinking you are one person, and in a single moment, your entire world changes.

Just. Like. That.

This wasn't the first time I failed to recognize my reflection in the window overlooking Park Avenue; it happened many years ago, when I swore I'd never let anyone rattle my core again. But the secrets of others have a way of exposing more than random skeletons.

Without warning, foundations can crumble to reveal your own deepest repressed truths…the ones you can no longer run away from. This was one of those moments. For my family, and for me, life was about to take an unchartered detour.

"Ms. Rossi, the printer needs to know which copy we're going with," came the interrupting voice of my overworked assistant Derek. "Ms. Rossi?"

"Yes? Oh, sorry, Derek. Please come in."

I waved the tall, lanky millennial suit-wanna-be with glasses into my giant corner office with double walls of windows and gestured for him to sit down. I wasn't in the mood for this, impatiently tapping a pencil against the glass top desk to speed the conversation up.

"We need to get this over to Wentworths in the next hour or we're not going to make the deadline," he sheepishly repeated as he handed over the two different ads for review.

My critical eye dismissed one version instantly and honed in on the fine-tuning needed for the other.

"Toss this one. I don't want to see it again. Make the font one and half sizes bigger on this one, move the text slightly to the left and for goodness' sake, please add a period to the end of that sentence," I uttered in distress. Why were good writers so hard to find?

"Tell Evelyn that if I have to correct her proofreading errors again, she'll be working in the mailroom instead."

"Oh—okay Ms. Rossi," he replied mechanically, glaring at me strangely before heading towards the door in an obvious attempt to escape my demonic wrath.

"I'm sorry, Derek," I called to him, catching myself in a weakened, unprofessional state of bitchiness. "Forget that last part. I'll speak with her later myself. Thank you for your help on this project." I managed a smile to let him know it was safe again to engage.

"Everything okay, boss?"

"Just one of those days," I shrugged off, knowing full well that if I let my emotions take the reign, I'd be the one working in the mailroom. And yet, I couldn't shake the heaviness of the last few days, as hard as I tried. So much mental clutter was taking up real estate in my mind.

The unexpected revelations, yet-to-be-uncovered mysteries and limitless questions infiltrated every cell of my brain, rendering me almost comatose in the everyday world. I grabbed my Dolce and Gabbana black coat, alerted Derek to just send the copy to the printer without my final review and left to pace the streets of New York.

In the noise, perhaps I could find some quiet away from my persistent thoughts.

How did I get here?

Growing up in suburban New York, we were a typical,

and dare I say, boring family for modern-day standards. We had our struggles and challenges, as all families do, but no tales of tragedy, dysfunction or criminal records to claim. No hint of hidden secrets locked away in a dusty attic.

Just your ordinary troupe of five—a mom and dad who loved each other, along with three sisters, who even in their obvious diversity and distinction, had an unbreakable bond.

Our dad was a good man, loved by all who knew him. Oh yes, Joseph Rossi generously handed out compliments and was the ear you turned to in a crisis. He made genuine eye contact, opened doors and gave up his bus seat for the little old lady without hesitation.

A rare man indeed, if you ask me. I don't think they exist anymore—well, at least not in my generation.

He was a travel columnist for our local paper, the *WC Review*, and even though we could read his latest write-up in the paper, it was a whole different experience to gather around the family dinner table as he regaled his stories in dramatic detail.

I'd find myself hanging on his every word. Then I'd run right to my small little bedroom to take notes in my light pink wish journal about whether I would take that particular journey or not. I kept all my dream destinations recorded in there. I remember going back and forth with Daddy, imagining the different adventures I could have.

"What would it be like to run through the Australian Outback with a koala?"

"Or feel the spray of Iguazu Falls as you walked the canyon of Devil's Throat in Brazil?"

"Maybe I will fall in love under the Eiffel Tower's night sky," I'd giggle as he kissed the golden curls on top of my head good night and wished me sweet dreams of newly explored territories.

Sigh. I wanted to be just like him when I grew up—a writer, a traveler, a dreamer. The reminder brought a brief smile back to my face before I shook off the juvenile fantasy. It had been quite a few years since I'd let myself reminisce so strongly.

I was blessed to have such an amazing father. He was so easy-going—and easy on the eyes. A twinkle in his soft browns caught the glance of every woman that passed by when he smiled and showed off those double dimples and perfectly straight pearly whites. Yet even with all that, he only had eyes for our mother.

And what a beauty she was—and is—in every way. Even though her days of pure blonde wavy locks have been joined by less-than-subtle strands of gray, and modest creases now dance around her delicate ocean eyes and sweetheart mouth, she still exhibits a youthful radiance and elegance.

I hope I will age as gracefully as she has, I thought to myself.

But it isn't her outer beauty that draws the attention of others—though it certainly doesn't hurt. She has a quiet power about her, a confidence that exists without arrogance. Natural, yet sophisticated. People listened when she spoke.

Literally. She used to be a college professor, and now enjoys giving lectures on the history of English literature. Her favorite time period, of course, was Elizabethan. In fact, we had a room in the house that doubled as her personal library and home office, filled to the brim with 16th century Renaissance novels and poetry compilations embedded into the cherry wood bookshelves.

Her favorite quote, which she playfully recited to our

dad often, was from Elizabeth I herself: *"I do not want a husband who honours me as a queen, if he does not love me as a woman."* And how my father loved that woman.

It was interesting to see my parents together, actually—the adventuresome travel columnist and the bookworm homebody. But it worked. It really, really worked. They inspired each other, and that inspired us—even up until his untimely death three years ago.

Fuck you, cancer.

I'm Megan Rossi, eldest daughter of Joseph and Alissa. Many say I favor my mom, with my naturally curly flaxen locks, aquatic mermaid eyes, curvy features and natural confidence—though I tend to be a little more assertive and outgoing about it. I was undoubtedly the daughter blessed with my father's ambitious and adventurous spirit.

Travel has always been in my blood, and although I had a childhood passion for writing like Daddy, I found that to be too whimsical a career for me to be taken seriously.

Life quickly taught me that not all dreams are meant to be a reality, and that it was every woman for herself. Thank you, middle school bullies and a corrupt administration for teaching me early on about living in a man's world. That would be the last time someone would have the upper hand over me.

So, after excelling in advanced courses and graduating with honors from Columbia University, I opted to become an up-and-coming executive, eventually staking my claim in the world as Senior Vice President for an international advertising corporation.

And I am damn good, too, I smirked as I saw the approving text from the CEO ping my phone.

Excellent call, once again. We landed Wentworths.

I love the boldness of my job. Negotiating contracts and approving (or denying) the creative team's presentations gives me a rush like no drug in the world.

I savor the control—I won't lie. There's a certain kind of exhilaration in knowing I have the power to make or break deals, and that others look to me for guidance and leadership. The long hours and travel don't bother me. Neither does the money or the ability to live quite comfortably on the outskirts of Manhattan.

I never was a city girl, so it really is the best of both worlds—a quick metro commute to my high-powered job in a culturally iconic city, while living in the suburban community of Larchmont, New York.

"We're here, miss."

I let out a deep exhale as the rideshare I flagged down during my long, brisk city walk pulled up in front of my gorgeous two-bedroom luxury condominium. I couldn't wait to strip these stockings off my body and settle down into a deeply plush couch with a huge glass of Merlot.

Grateful for the break in mind chatter, I looked around my immaculate, well-decorated home. I loved every inch of it.

I am especially fond of my second-floor bedroom porch that overlooks the harbor and lush gardens of a nearby park. It's the perfect blend of rustic nature and the waterfront—picturesque and charming, but with all the access I need to city life.

Close enough to the family, but not too close.

Although I live alone, I have no regrets about that. I have the freedom to come and go as I please, and that suits me just fine. The men I've encountered in my life have been ruthless, narcissistic and well, let's just say, as committed to love affairs as a politician is to the truth. Disloyal bastards are everywhere.

Who needs a man, anyway? Aside from sex, they're pretty useless when it comes to relationships.

Oh, don't get me wrong—I don't hate men. I quite enjoy their company and the attributes they have to offer. I appreciate a good, solid wine and dine, with great conversation and even greater nightcaps.

I'm just smart enough to know that today's men don't have the same integrity and loyalty as my father and grandfathers and ancestors before them. No need to offer up my heart to be enjoyed and then discarded like the latest tech toy.

I don't have time for those kinds of distractions, anyway, I thought, as I poured myself a second glass. I fully intend to run this advertising empire one day, and that won't happen if I'm tied up in some little house-playing scenario.

I gave up my dolls in exchange for membership in the Junior Achievement network before puberty hit, which is why I knew I needed to get my act together and stop the mental madness. Thank goodness I was level-headed enough to pull off the Wentworths win today.

An incoming group text from my sister, Mia, broke my internal diatribe.

Just a little reminder that Sunday dinner will be at Meg's house this weekend.

Whatever would I do without a second mother? I muttered to myself. I knew she meant well, though, especially after our last dinner debacle. I simply texted back a thank you with a heart.

Our tradition is to rotate Sunday family dinners between our homes—Mia's was usually the best, as she was the culinarian of the family. Our other sister, Marissa, lived in the city, in a tiny and typically unkempt, true bachelorette artist's pad. When it's her turn to host, she recommends a cool little local dive she came across, which is just fine with us.

And when it's my turn to host, I order in. I still like the dazzle of setting an elegant table and coordinating theme dinners in my home—just without all the pain of having to cook. Marissa and I weren't born with the culinary gene like Mia, though Mar can be a bad-ass baker when she wants to be.

I chortled at how different we all were. From the outside, you would never know we were sisters.

Mia is Italian through and through, with her dark, milk chocolate waves and deep brown eyes. Over the years, she has embraced her much fuller curve potential, yet her beauty is undeniable. There is a gentle, kind look to her, with a soft spot for kids and animals that seemed to have passed me by.

After falling in love and marrying her high school sweetheart, Kevin Logan, they now have three kids, two dogs, a rabbit and I think an iguana. Or a newt. I don't know—some kind of weird reptile that their son, Stephen, wanted.

Sometimes I envy Mia's ability to find and live in love so freely. The Logans are the golden family of five, with their soccer mom van and picture-perfect Christmas cards every year.

But my observant nature sometimes captures that hidden glimpse of the wear and tear it takes on Mia as a stay-at-home mom (while Kevin works all kinds of abnormal cop hours), and I don't always feel like the grass is greener on her side.

I know. I have your color-coded dinner calendar on my wall.

In came the predictably sassy response from Marissa. She doesn't particularly love being spoken to as a child, either, but lacks the wherewithal to communicate that—or anything for that matter—tactfully.

As the youngest of us, she is truly an original character. I relentlessly teased her about being adopted when we were growing up but, she's indeed our blood—a blend of us all with long, straight ebony hair and contrasting eyes of azurite. Ugh, how I wished I had that dazzling and exotic combo of looks.

Tiny frame, great boobs—and she knows it, too. Skintight clothes are her preferred style of choice, and it works for her. Like a moth to a flame.

She has no shame in flaunting her beauty or using it to her advantage. She is single like me, but much more expressive in her entanglements. At least she attempted relationships—though she gets bored almost instantly.

As free-loving as our artistic little sister is, she is equally smart—she might as well be a Jeopardy contestant with all the knowledge stored up in that brain of hers. Her problem is that she hasn't found someone with the right combination to keep her both creatively and cerebrally stimulated at the same time. Or rather, she hasn't figured out she needs both in a partner. Differences aside, I do hope she finds that great love someday.

I sometimes miss the easier days of our youth. The five of us were tight growing up—made closer by the nearby presence of my mom's parents, our beloved Granny and Pops Mahoney, who lived only a few blocks away.

My Granny had an innate fire in her that was rare for her time, but she never let society stop her. She was among the few women in her generation to voluntarily get a job outside of the home as a bookkeeper for a bookstore—which undoubtedly opened my mother's eyes to her love of the written word. Any time a new book graced the shelves, a copy somehow found its way into Mom's hungry-for-more hands.

I like to think of myself as very much like Granny—a revolutionary, a trailblazer.

"Never let anyone stop you from following your heart," she'd always say. She was living proof that a woman could do anything she put her mind to.

But aside from all her fortitude, she could easily enthrall you with her life stories and solve the most hurt of hearts with her special cups of tea. Her kindness trumped her desires.

Although Pops was a warm and friendly guy, I wasn't as close to him as I was with Granny—but we loved each other nonetheless. We were all undoubtedly overcome with deep grief when he passed away during our early twenties from stroke complications. I remember the last few days he was incoherent, and some of the things he said to my mother just didn't seem to make much sense to us about her childhood.

Like, how meeting Granny and Mom was the best moment of his life. At the time, we brushed it off as ramblings of the stroke and didn't ask questions.

Little did we know there really was something we were missing; a clue that Pops was leaving behind. One that finally made sense after this past weekend.

That fateful Sunday, dinner was planned for Mia's house, to all our delight. When we were growing up, she was the one following Mom around in the kitchen, cooking up interesting dishes and claiming that one day, she would own a chain of upscale restaurants. (You can imagine where that dream went).

It's sad, really, because she has the makings of a truly talented chef. I'd rather hop over to her house for her latest taste test than frequent any of the high-class restaurants that lace the streets of New York. Well, most of the time, anyway.

When I pulled up to her adorable two-story stone and cedar Georgian Colonial, all seemed right with the world. It was as quaint as the Logans' immaculately landscaped front lawn with white and pink tiger lilies, red roses, deliciously smelling white jasmine and endless daffodils—courtesy of my talented younger sis.

Second only to cooking, gardening was a passion of Mia's. She could be found toiling away, humming to herself, finding peace in the dirt almost daily as the flower whisperer. A new piece popped up in the garden each time we visited to add to the floral rainbow among the red mulch clouds.

What made it even more special was finding a selection of her favorites of the week as a centerpiece for our dinner table. No one's home was more warm or welcoming than Mia's.

The inside was open and airy, with pine hardwood flooring lacing the sophisticated, but noticeably lived-in dining and living rooms. She opted for earthy, yet vibrant colors, with expertly carved crown molding and handmade furniture. When Kevin wasn't busy fighting crime, my brother-in-law was one hell of a woodworker.

Mia's kitchen was her baby, though. With her love of all things food, it wasn't surprising that she put most of her time and energy into building her perfect piece of heaven.

All of the latest appliances in stainless steel sat upright among gorgeous Tuscan-style mosaic backsplashes, light-colored marble laminate countertops and terracotta tile floors. Pops of oranges, reds and greens danced around the walls with ceramic vases of fresh flowers and Italian art to complete the motif—along with vibrant lighting to keep the ambiance bright and cheery.

Her single window above the sink invited in the musical symphony of her hanging copper pots as the light breezes tangled in between them.

Walking into her home was always such an olfactory treat. We'd wager bets as we tried to figure out what she was making. By the smells of it, Indian was on the menu tonight.

"Smells fantastic. What's cooking?" I asked as I cheek-kissed my adorable little sister in her classic blue apron stained with the evening's dinner delight. Her hair thrown up in a messy bun and an oversized t-shirt and yoga pants meant that whatever she was making, she meant business.

"I thought I'd change things up and make some Chicken Tikka Masala, but with a few unusual twists, served up with roasted cauliflower rice and Naan bread," she beamed. "I think if I did it right, it should taste as delicious as it smells!"

"It always does," I smiled back at her, as I placed a few bottles of wine on the counter.

Oh, I could tell she was feeling creative—or sad. She became more adventurous in her meals when something was wrong. Out of all of us, she was the one who leaned toward emotional eating as her vice. I preferred wine.

Marissa's was sex—pretty much for every emotion.

I wondered what was up with her. I made a mental note to pull her aside a little later to do some detective work. She could typically be a bit closed off about private matters, but persuasion is my job, after all. I'd break her like a Kit Kat bar.

My greeting was shortly followed by the dramatic arrival of Marissa. She should really pursue acting instead of art; she was a natural.

Even wearing a plain, tight black t-shirt and skinny jeans with knee-high black heeled boots and her hair tossed up with chopsticks, she was stunning—like she just walked out of the latest fashion magazine.

"Oh my God, the traffic was insane today! You'd think it was a freakin' holiday with all the people on the road. Jeez!"

"Well, did you bring them?" I asked, ignoring her self-indulgent fanfare as I gave her a quick hug—and then realized my answer. I grabbed the branded box from her hand and squealed. I loved having a sister who lived close enough to our favorite bakery in Little Italy. Nothing beats their mini chocolate covered cannoli!

"Now, now ladies…are you forgetting someone? Where are my hugs?" came the sweet voice from the living room.

"Sorry, Granny," I mumbled as I hung my head in faux shame and then embraced her.

She smelled so good, like a subtle coconut-vanilla you'd find on a warm tropical island. Nearing eighty in a few short years, she wasn't walking as well as she used to these days; she recently started using a cane. But the strength behind her hugs was still as forceful and loving as always.

She hunched over slightly, with the plumpness of the most jovial of grandmas. Her all-white hair was short and wavy, and even with all her "wisdom wrinkles" (as she liked to call them), her turquoise eyes sparkled whenever she saw us.

"And how about for your mother?"

On cue, both Marissa and I ran over to sandwich hug Mom until she begged us to let her go. Her laughter was contagious—even the moody teenagers in the room who once resembled my sweet, ticklish nieces and nephew let out a chuckle.

With the Logan twins, Carly and Stephen, now thirteen and the eldest daughter, Brittany, edging towards fifteen, puberty (a natural trigger for automatic eye rolls) replaced their previous cherub-like attitudes. Every once in a while, they let down their guard and some childhood innocence slipped out…until they remembered to bury themselves back into their cellphones.

"Where's Kevin?" I asked causally. He was becoming increasingly absent from our traditional Sunday dinners. We understood why, though. He was recently promoted to detective, which meant extra hours over the last few months.

"Training. Again." Her tone was short and curt this time. Not her usual, sing-songy voice that let us know everything was perfect in her world. We knew that tone—best to just drop it and not ask again, or probe further. At least not tonight. But I had uncovered the first clue in the Mia mystery.

Damn it, Kevin, what did you do now?

"Dinner's ready."

Breaking the ice as we sat down at the table, Mom told us about a new lecture opportunity coming up.

"It's really exciting! I've been asked to be part of an expert panel on Shakespearean interpretation at a symposium to be held at King's College. You know I never liked to travel like your father did, but I am intrigued about visiting London."

"Sounds wonderful, Mom! I think you will love it there. When is it?" I asked.

"In two weeks. I don't even know what to pack, or where to go, or what to see first!"

"Oh, you have to check out the National Portrait Gallery near Trafalgar Square! You'd absolutely love its Tudor collection, from what I hear," Marissa sighed dreamily. "Will you take pictures for me? One day I hope to save up enough money to tour all of the famous galleries throughout Europe."

"You will, dear. I can feel it," encouraged Granny. She always had faith in whatever our dreams were. "By the way, have you been working on any of your own art lately?" she nudged.

She's about the only one in our family who could get away with blatant nosiness and still be adored for it.

"Well, I, um, have been a little busy and distracted. I had to pick up another gig waitressing during the day since Tony moved out."

"Wait, what?" I turned my head. Tony was her latest roomie. They were friends who decided that sharing a place and expenses would help them both save up money while working towards their prospective dreams.

"It just wasn't working out," she said nonchalantly. "It's okay, though. He was too much of a slob anyway."

Awkward silence filled the air. "You slept with him, didn't you?"

"Megan!" Mia shot me a hard glance from across the

table, only because her leg couldn't reach to kick me.

"What? I'm just saying what everyone was thinking. Look, Mar, the whole point of moving in with a platonic friend is for it to stay platonic. You know that, right?"

But I don't think she did. Marissa was known for her romantic dabbling and musical chair roommates because of it. A bartender by trade, she was still struggling to make her art dreams a reality but never could swing the rent on her own. She wanted to become a modern-day Francisco de Goya (her favorite artist), and even though she's had little success so far, she was determined to catch a break one day.

Which may explain her attempts to form relationships with men of power (sometimes women—she didn't discriminate) or even fellow artists. It's not that she intended to use anyone; not at all. She was just drawn to kindred spirits and figured if she was attracted to those who might help her out as well, then what's the harm?

But they never held her interest for long. Tony was just the next victim on her list.

Before the conversation could intensify with a snarled rebuttal, the doorbell rang.

"You expecting anyone, honey?" Mom wondered aloud.

"No," Mia said, as she cautiously rose from the table to peek through the peephole.

She had become a little more nervous than usual these days, adjusting to being alone frequently with Kevin's new position taking him away from the house so often.

"Who is it?"

"My name is Joshua Perkins, ma'am, of the Sanderson Law Firm. I need to speak with Alissa Rossi and her daughters on a legal matter. I was told I could find them here."

Confused yet intrigued, we all made our way towards

the door as Mia carefully opened it to reveal an incredibly handsome, well-dressed man holding a stylish briefcase. He was tall in stature with a well-defined build.

Dirty blonde, Ivy-League cut hair. Green eyes. Small, thin lips. A little on the pasty-skinned side. Blue micro-striped twill Giorgio Armani suit, Fendi briefcase, Rolex watch—and are those Berlutis on his feet? Damn, this guy reeked of money.

"Please, come in," Mia invited, as she fumbled with her hair and clothes, feeling embarrassingly underdressed in the moment. Not quite ready to fully let him inside, we all formed a small horseshoe in the foyer like a fierce barrier of protection waiting to see what this man wanted from us on a random Sunday evening.

"I'm sorry to disturb you at home, and at such a late hour," he started.

"How can we help you, Mr. Perkins?" Oh boy. Fluttering eyelashes as she asked. Was there seriously no one that Marissa wouldn't flirt with? And, of course, he returned the flirtation with his own coy lift of his lips that he tried to professionally suppress.

He quickly regained his composure with a clearing of his throat to deliver his news.

"I'm here with deepest condolences to inform you of your grandfather's passing, and to make arrangements for the reading of his will."

"Wait—what? I don't understand," I interjected. "What are you talking about? Our Pops died over ten years ago, and our dad's father died before we were even born. What is this all about?"

"I'm sorry for the confusion, Ms. Rossi. I'm here about your mother's *biological* father. Leigh Marino. He recently passed away, about ten days ago."

2

Stunned, the room jolted into darkness like a rural neighborhood after a power outage.

Yet even through the shockwave, I observed the guilty glance exchanged briefly between my mother and grandmother before they joined us in mock surprise—just enough to know that the assumed con man standing in front of us might actually be speaking a hint of truth.

A few awkward moments passed before Mia spoke up.

"I'm sorry, you seem to have caught us off guard. Please, come in and sit down, Mr. Perkins." As she guided all of us towards the living room, she continued to speak with composure. Graceful like Mom. "May I offer you something to drink?"

"No, thank you. I seem to have interrupted your dinner. I'm sorry. I will be brief."

Intuiting the complicated nature of the meeting, Mia nudged her children up to their rooms to give us some privacy. With a few of those famous eye rolls and some grunts, they begrudgingly moved up the stairs—though I'm pretty sure they didn't mind being excused from the adult drama that was about to ensue.

All of us now settled on her family-worn, but irresistibly comfortable plush beige couches in front of a lit stone-framed fireplace, the questions and comments came flooding in.

"Are you sure you have the right family?"

"What do you mean, *biological* grandfather?"

"Is this some kind of joke?"

"Whoa, whoa, ladies—don't shoot the messenger." Joshua Perkins became increasingly uncomfortable being the brunt of the mayhem, loosening his light blue Gucci silk tie in an effort to breathe.

"I'm sorry, Mr. Perkins," I began, trying to set the tone for a more civilized conversation. "As you can see, this all comes as quite a shock to us. We never heard of this Leigh Marino before, so perhaps you can help us understand what is going on here."

Even though I was suspicious of the man sitting in front of us, I was willing to hear him out, even if it meant learning something that clearly unsettled my mother and grandmother.

"Forgive me, Ms. Rossi."

"Call me Megan," I insisted.

"Okay, Megan. I apologize for my bluntness about your grandfather. I didn't consider that any of you would not be aware of his existence. I can certainly understand how this must come as a surprise to you—to all of you."

"Of course we're surprised. You're fucking lying and I'd love to know why." Leave it to Marissa to explode like that accidentally-lit firecracker. "Who are you and what do you really want with our family?"

She leaned in closer to him, almost all up in his face, as if to intimidate him. As much as her eyes could seduce, they could stab with a thousand knives.

"Marissa, please," begged our mother, with tears welling. "Let him speak."

She turned back to Mr. Perkins with nervous attentiveness. And there it was. The validation that what this random stranger just revealed to us could be the truth— or at least, the beginning of it. "Please, go on."

"Thank you. Again, I'm so sorry to be the bearer of bad news." He started to shift even more uneasily in his seat, wishing to be anywhere but here in this moment.

"As I understand it, Leigh Marino is your biological father," and then turning to us, "and your biological grandfather. He passed away almost two weeks ago after a long battle with pancreatic cancer."

Fuck cancer. Again. Another one of its unnecessary victims, and I didn't even know the man.

"He was diagnosed three years ago and underwent extensive treatment, but over the last two months, his health was failing fast. During that time, he was putting his affairs in order, but remained obscure about settling some of his final wishes."

On that note, he opened his briefcase to reveal a rather large, sealed, official-looking white envelope. He had beautiful hands, I noticed. Nails well groomed, too. Soft hands that would probably feel great on my body.

I shook the imagined sensation off, returning my attention to the matter at hand.

"He insisted that aside from his official will, this envelope of sealed letters was not to be delivered nor opened until his death, and not until after the official reading of his will."

He respectfully paused for us to digest just a little of what he was telling us before continuing.

"This envelope was released from his personal safety box a few days ago, with specific instructions that I was to personally find you all and schedule a reading. I am required to be in the audience of Alissa Rossi, her three daughters and Lillith Mahoney, if she is still alive."

"Oh, I am very much still alive." And in a very uncharacteristic, yet still composed tone, she uttered, "We're all here. Let's hear what the son-of-a-bitch had to say."

"Mama. May I have a moment? In the kitchen?" Mom turned to us apologetically with obvious fear and worry in her baby blues as she helped our grandmother up off of the couch. "Excuse us."

Looking at each other questioningly, we reluctantly allowed them their privacy. Although I can't read my sisters' minds, I know them well enough that I can imagine they are feeling just as betrayed and pissed off as I am.

Well, at least Marissa is. In that mind of hers, Mia was probably rationalizing it all out and figuring out a way to play peacekeeper. Typical Pollyanna.

Well, whatever they had to say, they should be able to say it to us. After all, they seem to not be surprised and we are owed some answers. I'll give them five minutes before I bust in there…

But I couldn't wait that long. I tiptoed towards the kitchen to listen in on their secret conversation. Mia tried to dissuade me, but with a single authoritative look, I hushed her immediately and held up my hand to stop Marissa from joining me, to her pissed off chagrin.

"Mama, don't you think we should speak in private with the girls before allowing this to go any further?"

"I don't know. Maybe you are right." A quick beat passed as Granny looked up at Mom. "What have I done? How could this have happened? Your father and I forged an agreement long ago to never, ever speak of this. How could he blindside me like this?"

"I'm not sure, Mama. But I think we owe it to those girls out there to tell them the truth before we get into the reading of his will. I can see the pain in their eyes. The betrayal. All they have known is about to be turned upside down."

"I'm so sorry, Alissa. So, so sorry. I should not have forced you into silence all those years ago. I only hope this secret has not cost you your daughters. Or me my granddaughters." She took Mom's hands and looked sorrowfully into her eyes. "What have I done to our family?"

I saw Mom look back lovingly at her. "So, we might have made a mistake keeping this from them. We had our reasons at the time, and they were good ones. But we will fix this. We are strong and we can get through anything together."

She squeezed Granny's hands softly. "Now, let's go back in there. We have some explaining to do."

I quickly ran back to sit on the couch as if I had never moved. Hand in hand, they walked into the deadly quiet and heavily emotional room. My mother was the one to break the silence.

"You'll have to excuse us, Mr. Perkins. We need some time to discuss this as a family. If you can leave us your number, we will be in touch to arrange another time for the will reading."

"Of course." Reaching into his inside jacket pocket, he pulled out his fancy business card and handed it to my grandmother, who was standing right next to him.

An odd look came across Granny's face as she scanned the card. "Perkins." Her eyes widened with a surprised recognition as she looked up at the young man in front of her. "Any relation to Julia Perkins?"

"Yes, ma'am," he barely got out, shifting anxiously as five strong women stared him down. "She's my, um, great-aunt."

"Interesting," she replied, not removing her eyes from his.

Then once again, the room filled with a dreaded pause (like one from a horror movie) before he smartly wished us a good evening and exited in self-preservation mode.

After the well-to-do lawyer left, the ambiance became even more intense. We all had something to say yet were too faint-hearted to start. I mean, where do you begin a conversation like this?

So, Pops wasn't our real Pops? Who was this Leigh Marino guy, and why have we never heard of him or met him? Obviously, Granny knew about this, but how long did Mom know about it? Why was it such a big secret? And what does he want with us now?

"Will one of you please explain what in the hell is going on here and how come we didn't know about some secret grandfather?" Marissa demanded angrily.

"Seriously, Marissa? Cool your jets and let them explain," I snapped back.

"Why are *you* so calm about this? You are usually a hothead, too. Or did you already know about this? Being the privileged eldest, I wouldn't be surprised."

"I don't know a damn thing. But if you shut your trap, maybe we can find out."

"Don't talk to me like I'm one of your work minions, Meg."

"GIRLS."

Granny had a way of raising her voice that elicited complete silence, and she didn't use it often. She may be old—but she was not fragile.

"Attacking each other is not going to help anything. You have a right to be angry with your mother and I, but not with each other."

She took each of our right hands and brought them together in a ceremonial-like hand holding.

"No matter what you learn tonight, promise me here and now that no matter what happens, that you will always stick together and not let this or anything or anyone come between you."

We nodded in silence.

"PROMISE ME," she ordered like a drill sergeant.

We all looked up at each other, nodded and in unison declared, "We promise."

"Good." Granny then looked over at my mother, who was a mixed bag of sadness, heartache and guilt—a limp little ragdoll of a child wishing for her favorite stuffed animal. If she could curl up in the corner with her legs pulled up to her chest right now, she would.

"Alissa, would you mind if I explained it all? It's about time I get this burden off my chest."

"Of course," Mom sighed gratefully with obvious relief and an almost instantaneous return to her normal regal composure.

Grateful for the support, Granny closed her eyes and took three deep, deep breaths. On her last exhale, I thought I saw the suppression of a tiny drop near her saddened eyes, no doubt only the beginning of a pain she was about to relive in the name of telling the truth.

"All I ask of you is that you hear me out first. I know full well that you have plenty of questions, and I promise I will be honest and answer them all. But I need to tell you all of this in my own way, and I ask for your patience and understanding as I clear everything up."

I reached out to stroke her back gently. I couldn't help but go from angry to unconditionally sympathetic towards her. For her to keep something of this magnitude a secret, it must have been sincerely painful.

"Of course, Granny. Take your time." I looked at my sisters and delivered another silent command as the eldest. "We promise to listen without judgment." Mia and Marissa bowed their head in quiet agreement.

"Where to begin?" My heart was already breaking as she looked wistfully into the distance, reaching for that elusive butterfly that was flying away.

"Even when I was young, I knew I was different from other girls my age. They were all playing dolls and house and cheerfully helping their mothers clean and learning how to cook and sew, and all the things a *proper* young lady should be learning to do in order to become a good, dutiful wife.

"But for whatever reason, that just wasn't for me. I'd watch my father come home and continue working by candlelight. He was such a kind man—not unlike your own father. Even though it was not supposed to be encouraged, he indulged my questions about his work and occasionally would take the time to teach me skills that typically only boys were taught.

"I remember him telling me, 'Lillith, never let anyone put out your fire or deter you from your dreams. Society does not define who you are. You can be anyone you want to be.'"

The memory brought a warm smile to her heart. I could see her looking back to a time when she was bouncing on his fatherly knee, transforming easily from manly provider to a child's pony. No doubt, daddy's little girl. Just like me.

"As you know, my father died just a few short weeks

before I completed school. But his words never left my heart. Against my mother's wishes, I pursued various jobs—any jobs that were willing to hire a woman at the time.

"In my heart of hearts, I yearned to be one of the few to go to college and major in criminal justice. But alas, coming from a family with little means to begin with, and with my mother left without a husband in those times, that dream was an impossibility.

"I eventually earned a reputation as a hard worker with a good work ethic—and astonished the men in the jobs I worked for with my intelligence, confidence and skills. Daddy taught me well. It was when I took my first bookkeeping job at an art gallery that I met Leigh Marino."

She took a moment for an aside. "Actually, I wasn't bookkeeping at that moment. The gallery was having an event and needed waitresses, so of course the women of the company were expected to help fill that role." She rolled her eyes gently before brushing off the sexist experience and continuing.

"I remember the moment we met clear as day. I was passing around flutes of champagne to these hoity-toity art snobs, when he accidentally took a step backward into me and my tray went flying.

"I was so angry at first—how dare he not look where he was going; he ruined my new white shirt! But then he stunned me when he just laughed as he excused himself for his clumsiness.

"It wasn't the typical condescending man's laugh I was used to, though. No, it was more of a nervous, amused, yet intrigued kind of laugh. He helped me clean up the mess, profusely apologizing while I remained irate and spoiled.

"He handed me his classy, monogrammed handkerchief

and the instant our hands touched, I knew my life would never be the same." There was that smile, the one that persuaded you to believe in true love at first sight…dare her it wasn't possible.

"When I looked up, I saw him. Truly saw him. Tall—elegantly tall in stature, with short, dark wavy hair and life-shattering aqua blue eyes that could melt an iceberg in an instant. The exoticness of the Mediterranean with the softness of an Irishman. Yes, a fascinating combination," she recalled to herself.

She looked at Marissa. "You look just like him, dear. I see him in you more and more every day," she reflected as she ran a wrinkled finger down Mar's cheek with love.

"His smile was broad and warm and felt like home. His hands were smooth and manly—but not a rough manly. A strong manly."

Granny paused for a moment, lost in the reverie. You could see her light up with the thought of love—and just as quickly as it came, it left her face.

"After that night, he began to court me. It was doomed from the beginning, though. He came from an affluent family with generations of royalty and prestige, and I was the lucky product of simple Irish immigrants who came through Ellis Island and settled in Brooklyn to find a better life for themselves.

"His family would never approve of me—and in fact, he was already betrothed to another heiress of great fortune. Money must stay with money, after all," she said bitterly.

"But—my Leigh was not like that. Not at first, anyway. He tried to fight his family and the betrothal. He asked me to run away with him, to start a new life together. He didn't care that he would be disowned. It was all so romantic and tempting. But I couldn't ask him to turn his back on his family, not even in the name of love.

"One night, he left me no choice. He packed what little possessions he could bring with him to fetch some money until he could secure a job of his own. He had already left his family and was no longer welcomed back. If I were to deny him, I'd leave him with nothing but a broken heart and no family.

"How could I turn my back on the man who lost everything to love me?

"We didn't stray too far—just enough to settle a few hours north of the city, where we would be away from the influences of his family and the high cost of living. We married the instant we found our home and declared our everlasting love. It was a beautiful life.

"He was able to find employment with a local law firm and I worked in the library. We'd both go to work during the day and come home and make endless love every night. It took quite a while, but a few years after we were married, I finally became pregnant with our Alissa. We were ecstatic and happier than any couple I had ever known. It was a fairy tale come true."

Sigh. I couldn't help but be caught up in the romance of it all, noting Mia and Marissa had the same dreamy looks upon their faces and a conflicted joy in my mother's, as I assume she hadn't heard this version of their love story all that often.

"But it was not meant to last." Deep sorrow and muffled moans erased the sentimentality in the air.

"When Alissa was five years old, Leigh received an urgent message that his father was ill and calling him home. I never thought they would have been able to track us down after all those years—or care to do so. I remember him feeling distraught over what to do.

"Ever the optimist, he thought that perhaps in his dying years, his father had come to accept his decision to love some peasant woman, as that man called me, and welcome all of us into the family.

"He wanted to rebuild his relationship with his father and perhaps reclaim his rightful fortune—which he declared would be used to send me to college to fulfill my dream of becoming a criminal justice lawyer. He said he wanted to build an even more magical life for the three of us, and even try to have more babies.

"I believed him. I believed his foolish fantasies and lovingly kissed him goodbye as I promised to watch over our precious daughter until his return. He vowed he would come home soon.

"He wrote us daily in the beginning, filling us in on how his father was so pleased to see him, but he was so ill that he had to take part in his care. He firmly believed that in doing so, he was securing our future and his place once again in the family. He wanted it all.

"But then the letters dwindled from daily to weekly and then monthly, with claims that caring for his father was exhausting beyond belief. Weeks turned into months, and those soon turned into a year. Alissa was then six and I was left, without a husband, to manage a house and family on my own. The money he sent to support us diminished along with the letters.

"Not once did he break away to visit us that entire year—not even for Christmas or Alissa's birthday or our anniversary. All we had were his letters and a false hope that he would one day return.

"He insisted that he had to let his family believe he chose them until he could convince them otherwise that we belonged there. He became consumed with their approval, not grasping that he would never truly get it—not even sacrificing us would do the trick.

"After a little over a year, his father died, and Leigh finally came home to us. But it was not the reunion I yearned for. He regretfully informed me that things did not work out the way he had hoped they would.

"His uncle—now the patriarch of the family—was pleased that Leigh chose to return and demanded that he cut all ties with me forever in order to reclaim his inheritance and place as head of the family business while he retired.

"He had never told them about Alissa. He was waiting for the perfect time, so he said—but before he could, they reinstated him with the threat that if it were to ever come out that he had a child with me, he would lose it all again—and forever this time. So, he kept quiet and led them to believe we were childless."

She stopped to take a breath, the sword stabbing through her heart once again and tears fighting to come to the surface like high tide approaching. Looking over at our mother, pale and saddened, she was that lost little girl reliving her abandonment and shame for being born. I was already beginning to understand why we were never told about this man.

"How naïve Leigh was. They had to have known about Alissa when they threatened him. If they were able to find us, then they'd know we had a child. That stipulation was a test to see if he was worthy of his fortune and where his loyalties were. It still sickens me to think about that family and the lengths they would take to get what they wanted.

"But Leigh said he did it all to protect us. His family was powerful after all—no telling what they would do in the name of preventing a scandal, he warned.

"He swore he would find a loophole though, because

he couldn't live without us. He proclaimed that once his uncle died, the reigns would be completely his and he could reunite with us—no one would be able to take what was 'ours' away from us again.

"Even though I begged him one last time to reconsider, reminding him that the money wasn't important to us, he kissed us both goodbye for what would be the last time and set off in his delusional pursuit of a happily ever after.

"I knew better than to wait for that man. He had made his decision and I was going to make mine. I knew that he would lose everything if I demanded he come back or if they 'found out' about Alissa. I had every right to be spiteful and destroy him. I was tempted to show up on their doorstep with our beautiful child and leave him no choice but to acknowledge us. But I didn't.

"He left us alone. He broke his promises and crushed our hearts; yet, I could not bring myself to betray the love of my life, even though he had abandoned us. All I could do was pick up the pieces and move on.

"I appealed to him in a letter for a divorce—something that was not easy to do in our time. By the grace of God and the power of his family's money, our marriage was dissolved. Like it had never even existed. Without an attempt to reconcile or a plea for me to just wait for him a little longer.

"He just let it happen. He didn't fight for us like I had prayed for.

"Only few months later, I saw the news about his widely publicized nuptials to the original woman he was betrothed to—a woman named Julia Perkins. Yes, this lawyer's great aunt," she added in acknowledgment to the connection.

Now it made sense why she was so thrown off guard by him. I'd save that line of questioning for another time—

there was more to that particular story, too, I bet.

"I knew all I needed to know in that moment and declared that this part of my life was over forever. I was never going to look back, and neither was my daughter. Breaking my heart was one thing. But how he could leave behind his little diamond—that's what he called your mom—I will never understand."

The heaviness in the room was all-consuming; the grief of a mother and daughter remembering the moment their life changed forever, bringing forth the memory of a man they swore to forget. My heart went out to them. No family should ever have to bear that kind of pain.

But her story had not ended there. With a few more deep breaths and a delicate tissue to her watery eyes, Granny found the strength to continue.

"It was so difficult to move on. In the back of my mind, I fantasized that this was just a nightmare and that my Leigh would come running back to my arms. That he would disown his family once again to choose our love, to choose our own beautiful family that we created together.

"But reality hit hard and I knew he was never coming back ever again.

"Now an unwed single mother, I was the outcast of the community. Its own Hester Prynne, shame and all. I didn't know what to do.

"My mother became sick only a few weeks later and I was faced with taking care of her at the same time. I had to sell her home and move her in to live with us, which helped to pay for some of her medical care and our day-to-day living expenses, thankfully.

"Her doctor would make house calls to check on us, and he eventually grew a soft spot in his heart for our little family. He'd stop by with extra food from the market or a warm blanket for the cold nights. He never judged us or our situation.

"Consumed by his profession, he didn't have the time to properly court a woman, but his heart was pure gold and he wanted a family to love. He was kind and genuine. He had a great sense of humor and could make me laugh even in my saddest times. He was no Leigh, but that was a good thing, I decided.

"I knew I could never let my heart love like that again. It was dangerous and careless and only caused grief. But I could accept the love of a good man. One who was there by my side as my mother passed away and who loved me and most importantly, my daughter, as his own. It was then that I decided to marry my Harry—your Pops—and we became the Mahoneys.

"Our community knew our story and I wanted to distance myself from the past, so we left town for a fresh start. When we came upon sweet little Armonk, we agreed it was the perfect place to begin our new life together.

"Alissa was almost eight by then and old enough to understand that although Harry was not her biological father, that he was her dad in every other sense of the word. So, to rest of the world, he became her 'real' father and no one was ever the wiser.

"He was so good to us. He loved us until his dying day—and he loved you girls as his own as well. Turns out, he was unable to have children himself, as we tried with no success, so he was grateful for the child he had in Alissa; we were all the family he ever wanted.

"When Alissa was a little older, I explained the truth in detail about Leigh and she agreed to live out the story that Harry was her father and to never reveal the identity or story of her true lineage. Sadly for her, Leigh never tried to reach out to us again. I read in the papers about twenty years ago how his uncle had died, and still nothing.

"Here he was, finally the patriarch, and still too spineless to try to find out where we were and reunite with his daughter. Never to learn about her life or any grandchildren he may have had.

"I suppose that's why I am so rattled that this young man showed up with such news today. It brings up so many questions of my own.

"How is it that he knew all of your names and where to find us—and so quickly after Leigh's death? How does he have a fortune to leave behind when he clearly violated the 'no heirs' stipulation? It both concerns me and angers me on a whole new level."

A glazed look came across her eyes as she stared off into the distance. A painful acceptance of a truth that hurt harder than the lie she told herself all these years.

"Leigh knew exactly where we were all along, all this time, but he never came back." Now she let the tears fall freely as her face fell into her hands and she began to sob with the deepest of heartbreaks. "He never came back."

3

We didn't know what to say after that. We already learned so much, and witnessed too many raw emotions, to probe any further. The agony of remembering weakened Granny physically, and with a daughter's care, our mother lifted her from the couch to grab her coat and cane.

"Mama, let's get you home."

She shot us a despondent look, mixed with desperation and a seeking of empathy, and we knew we had to put this on hold. Besides, this was a lot to absorb and we all needed time to review chapter one. Who knew how many more there were in this secret prequel?

With big, soft hugs and a bunch of genuine "I love yous," we sent them on their way. The three of us settled back down onto the couch to sort through the debris of an ancestry bomb.

"Wow." Mia was the one to break the silence this time.

"You can say that again," Marissa muttered.

A few moments passed. I'm not sure any of us could formulate a comment or question or starting point. What we had just been told changed everything we had known about our life. We had this mystery grandfather who abandoned Mom and Granny, and yet here he is risen from the dead with an enigmatic will.

"So, what do you think the old geezer wants with us

now?" Marissa's delivery not only broke the silence but gave us the much-needed breath of laughter.

"Maybe his family has disowned him after all and he needs someone to pay for his casket," I quipped, defaulting to my typical sarcasm whenever situations became intense. Awkward vulnerability was never a strong point of mine.

"Or maybe he left us a shitload of money!" Marissa hooted.

"Or maybe there is more to the story and we're about to find out." Mia's somber perspective brought us back to the reality of the situation.

"I guess there is only one way to find out," I offered, fingering the business card left behind by the alluring Joshua Perkins.

"I'll call and set the appointment if you want," offered Marissa, trying to casually steal the sexy lawyer's coveted card from my grasp. I'm pretty sure neither of us cared that he was related through some long lost connection—not like he'd be blood and taboo.

"Set the appointment—or a date? I didn't notice a wedding ring," teased Mia, who could sense the potential sister fight brewing like pungent morning coffee.

"I didn't think he'd be your type, Mar. He wore a suit, seemed to have a respectable job—you sure you want to get mixed up with that kind of hoodlum?"

"Oh, shut up," she laughed as she threw a sage green couch pillow at my head.

"Well, whoever calls him, we should do this right away. I know it must be a lot for Granny and Mom, but I have so many questions still. I don't want to wait to find out what our Grandfather Marino wants.

"I have a feeling there is more to this surprise will reading than a simple secret spoiler or inheritance announcement. Something bigger is going on. I just know it." As the wife of a cop, Mia's secondhand training had her instincts alert—and she was usually never far off.

"I agree. I can call the office now and have all my meetings canceled for tomorrow and just stay here the night—if that's all right with you, Mi."

"Of course!"

"And I don't have a shift until four tomorrow, so maybe we can get this Mr. Perkins to schedule the reading for the morning and I'll crash here, too," Marissa offered in agreement. "I'm assuming he is not from this town, so he most likely would be available and willing to resolve the matter before heading back home. I'll just give Jay a call to let him know I won't be home."

Jay, as she just enlightened us, was Marissa's newest roommate since Tony moved out; an old friend she alleges to never have slept with. We hoped for her sake, she'd keep it that way instead of playing hot potato with her new apartment pal. As her best friend of almost thirty years, we actually liked the guy and thought he was a good influence in her life.

"Okay, I'll call Mr. Perkins right now and see if I can make it happen—since I'm the only one who won't try to get a date out of it," Mia ribbed as she picked up her cell to dial the number.

The room was fraught with anxiety like a medical intern about to cut open his very first patient. No one was able to sleep a wink from either rehashing the discovery of a lost grandfather or from facing ghosts of the past.

But we were all together again—this time at Mom and Granny's. Since the emotional turmoil had the biggest effect on Granny, we thought it best to do this from the comfort of her own home.

In a place much smaller than Mia's, though just as endearing, we sat awaiting more information about Leigh Marino.

Mom moved in with Granny right after our dad died, believing that downsizing to the smaller little white ranch home would be better for both of them. The one level structure was ideal, without stairs or excess rooms to fuss about.

It was always inviting—exactly what a grandmother's home should feel like. Apple-scented lit candles, crocheted blankets on the couches and treats waiting on the counter for us, even though we were grown adults. In an instant, you could be whisked back to more youthful times.

The living room boasted a deep off-white carpet that your feet sunk into like quicksand and beautiful rose-patterned throws over the super comfortable green recliner couches. It was here that we chose to gather, rather than at a stiff kitchen table.

"Thank you for making yourself available to meet with us on such short notice, Mr. Perkins," began my mother.

"Of course. I wish our meeting could have been under different circumstances," he said as he stole a glance at Marissa, who was shamelessly wearing a tight knit leopard dress and high heeled black boots, with her long hair slicked back into a high sleek fashion ponytail.

How is it that she just so happened to have that outfit stashed in an overnight bag in her car? Maybe I shouldn't ask.

"Again, my deepest condolences to you all," he uttered with genuine sincerity, dressed sharply and expensively in black pinstripe this time, I noted to myself.

"We didn't even know the man." Closing my eyes to pray for patience, I placed a gentle hand on Marissa's arm followed by a look of *that's enough*. And she wondered why we all mothered her?

"Yes, right. Well, as I mentioned last night, we are here today as per the wishes of Mr. Leigh Marino for the reading of his will. His instructions on how this was to be carried out were very clear, if not peculiar."

"Peculiar? How so, Mr. Perkins?" probed my mother.

"Well, Mrs. Rossi, you see—Mr. Marino requested two different will readings. One for the Marino family and a separate one for the Rossi family. He thought that given the history of the family dynamics, that it would be uncomfortable to bring everyone under one roof."

"I see. How considerate of him. Or perhaps Mr. Marino is a coward even in death and cannot bring himself to tell his real family about his shameful one." Granny's words cut through the atmosphere like a butcher knife.

"Actually Mrs. Mahoney, the Marino family is aware of your existence. I cannot give you any details beyond that, but they are aware."

"Fine. Carry on," she spat as she muttered what I could have sworn were a whole bunch of Irish curse words. I didn't even know she knew Irish. Then again, as I was coming to find out, I didn't know as much about her as I thought I did.

"In addition to wanting to keep the families separate— for whatever his reason," he paused to acknowledge, "he also had additional letters and documents drawn up. There is his official will, which was read the evening of his burial to the Marino family. And it was requested to be read again once we located your family.

"After the official will is read, I am then instructed

to open and deliver the contents of this sealed envelope, addressed solely to the Rossi family."

"And *you* are the chosen one to read it to us, Mr. Perkins?" Granny asked curiously, as she emphasized his name in connection to the woman who married her Leigh.

"Yes, ma'am. I am his lawyer of record," he replied a bit defensively. "I am here—unbiased—on his behalf. However, you should know, I am only to deliver the sealed letters. I am not privy to their contents."

I could have sworn I saw him shift a little in his seat and loosen yet another expensive Gucci tie. I'm not quite sure this man was prepared for such a tough crowd—we were more intimidating than a courtroom full of witch hunt justice seekers in a murder case. But for a prominent lawyer (you bet I looked him up), he certainly was a nervous nelly behind all the hyped up glam.

"Your ex-husband was not very forthcoming about the contents of this envelope and, even as his lawyer, I have not been permitted to see them. After I read the official will to all of his heirs, as all of them must be named in the will whether they receive anything or not, I am instructed to leave this envelope—the one and only copy—with you, never to be read by the Marino family.

"Whatever this envelope contains is meant for your family and your family alone."

"Okay, then let's get to it," said Marissa as she kicked up her feet into a reclined position and folded her arms back behind her head as if ready to sun herself.

"Great. Please bear with me as I am required to read through the document in its entirety. This is going to take a while."

"I'll put up some tea," Granny offered.

"I'll grab the shot glasses and whiskey," Marissa

countered.

With everyone settled with their choice of tea or whiskey (or both), we were all ready to hear what Grandfather Leigh had to say to us all. If nothing else, perhaps this would bring some clarity and closure. It still felt surreal—was this a bona fide family mystery like I read about in my many young adult novels?

"Everyone ready?" After a room full of nods, he began. So serious, so professional. *So dang hot.*

I, Leigh Marino, resident in the City of Cobble Hill, County of Brooklyn, State of New York, being of sound mind, not acting under duress or undue influence, and fully understanding the nature and extent of all my property and of this disposition thereof, do hereby make, publish, and declare this document to be my Last Will and Testament, and hereby revoke any and all other wills and codicils heretofore made by me.

He then read a series of legal mumbo jumbo about expenses and taxes and the appointment of himself as personal representative before getting to the "disposition of property" portion of the will. I could have fallen asleep listening to the man drone on about the different properties, art galleries, restaurants and other nonsense given to these strangers—sorry, *family members.*

However, I was absolutely captivated by how damn rich this man must have been…and annoyed over the amount of crap he left his adopted son and family. He really left my mother behind for all of this?

It then came time for our acknowledgments.

To my ex-wife, Lillith Mahoney and daughter, Alissa Rossi:

Deed to Home in Charlton, New York. Also to Lillith, our gold wedding band.

We all took a deep breath as he paused and handed my grandmother a small, solid, worn-out gold band and two white, sealed envelopes addressed in old school calligraphy.

"A deed to a home?" Mia asked incredulously.

"In Charlton?" Granny could barely choke back the impending sobs as her weak fingers slid along the top of the one envelope to reveal an official deed with her and Mom's names on it.

"Yes, Mrs. Mahoney. It is my understanding that Mr. Marino had purchased and restored the original home you and your daughter grew up in. He also made arrangements for taxes to be paid for the duration of your ownership."

Wonder filled her and my mother's eyes. Bittersweet at least. A home mixed with the emotions of true love and happiness, then abandonment and betrayal. How is it that he never bothered with them, but then planned to restore and bequeath them an entire house? It's absurd.

She held on to the second envelope, sensing the privacy of its contents, already over-processing why she was left a memory-ridden old dwelling.

"May I continue?" he asked gently.

We collectively consented, wondering what the next grenades to drop would be.

To my daughter, Alissa Rossi: My mother's pearl necklace, earrings and ring set.

A plastic bag containing stunning, delicate pearls set into what I imagined were expensive cuts of diamonds was handed to her, along with her own letter. She took it carefully, almost in awe of such a valuable trinket.

"I may have been six when I last remember seeing him, but I do recall his stories about his mother. Lena, her name was. He was very fond of her and I always wished I could have met her. She felt special to me for some reason—not like the rest of Marino side," she remembered contemplatively.

Mr. Perkins continued on, growing annoyed at our interrupting commentary. Like we weren't permitted to handle this awkward situation in our own way? *Keep it shut, Meg,* I scolded myself.

To my granddaughters, Megan Rossi, Mia Logan and Marissa Rossi: plane tickets to Shannon, Ireland; Florence, Italy; and Barcelona, Spain, all three trips of which must be taken within a year of my death.

A single letter with our names on it was handed to Mia, who was sitting closest.

"Wow. That's an unusual inheritance to receive. I wonder what that is all about?" I inquired.

"I am pretty sure the letters will explain in more detail, but it is my understanding that each of these trips holds tokens for you that are in the possession of distant relatives in Ireland, Italy and Spain. They are from his mother's side, the O'Sullivans."

"The O'Sullivans?" Even Granny didn't recognize the name.

"Yes. That is his mother's maternal bloodline," he continued. "In order to leave this part of his family anything, Leigh had to work a loophole. There was a stipulation in his uncle's will about the Marino property never going to unknown heirs, should they be revealed."

"You mean to the bastards?" muttered my mother, quite bitterly. It was a side of her that was rarely shown, but we'd call it the "off with her head" Mom voice when we were kids. We knew to run for cover when the Red Queen in her came out.

"Mrs. Rossi, I mean no disrespect. I am only passing along what I learned, as much as I do know. Leigh did share with me that he had many regrets in his life, yet still had to honor his uncle's provisions.

"Even though it came to light somehow that he did in fact have an heir with Lillith, the Marino family collectively decided not to remove Leigh as head of the family. With Rocco deceased and a more modern acceptance of family skeletons, they upheld Leigh's position with the condition that this line would never be eligible for any of the Marino legacy; past, present or future.

"It was all agreed that instead of Marino heirlooms and property, he would be allowed to pass on some family trinkets from his mother's side to you, as they would not be contested by the Marino family or be in violation of his uncle's wishes. Even the home in Charlton was purchased and restored with O'Sullivan family money generously donated by one of his cousins.

"And, as per full disclosure, this was revealed at the Marino family will reading. As the O'Sullivans are part of the maternal heritage and not considered by them as their direct family bloodline, they had no objection and will not protest your receipt of these tokens. So, they are yours, without contest. The paperwork was already signed."

As if trying to make our grandfather's bequeathed gifts mean something, he added quietly, "It was all he was able to do under the circumstances."

"We understand, Mr. Perkins. Thank you," said Mia, trying to smooth over the room full of gym resistance bands ready to snap. "I am sure they are lovely. And we are grateful for such a wonderful travel opportunity."

Looking over at us in her motherly way, she cautioned, "We will have to talk about it first."

I gave her the respect of a nod, while Marissa rolled her eyes—*hmm,* I wonder where our nieces and nephew get it from.

"If you'll permit me, I am required to read the remainder of his will to completion."

Joshua Perkins proceeded to go through more legalese concerning omission, bond, the very specific discretionary powers bestowed upon him as Leigh's personal representative (which I still questioned myself), "contesting beneficiary" and so on and so forth. He ended by folding the will back up into an envelope and handing it to my grandmother to keep.

"So, question for you." Why did I raise my hand up like a school girl?

"Yes, Megan."

"When reading about the other family members, I couldn't help but notice that his stepson and step-grandchildren carry the name of Marino. Why's that?"

"Well, when he married Julia, he accepted her son David as his own. Since David's father was deceased, Leigh thought for the sake of family it would be best to legally adopt him and give him the Marino name, as he would be the only one able to carry on his legacy.

"Unfortunately, Julia and Leigh were unable to conceive a child of their own together, so the name continues to pass on through David's heirs."

"So, just like Mom became a Mahoney, David became a Marino," Mia connected.

"Exactly," he agreed.

"Interesting how some other woman's child is acceptable as an heir, but not my mother," spouted Marissa.

"It's just the way of the rich," bit back Granny. "Money forgives transgressions of money. Not to mention, having a male child is more favorable as an heir than a daughter to them. Such cavemen."

Mom looked distraught by that comment—by the whole morning.

"Oh, Alissa, I am so sorry. I should be more sensitive. I didn't mean to upset you," regretted Granny.

"Mama, you have nothing to apologize for. It's reality. It wouldn't do any of us good to pretend otherwise. I have a happy life, filled with a wonderful mother and three beautiful daughters, a kind son-in-law I love like a son and amazing grandchildren. There is nothing some estranged father could ever give me that would be worth more than what I already have."

We all came together to form a big group hug. Smiles broke out, almost forgetting that our grandfather's lawyer was even still in the room.

"I'm sorry, there is just one more piece of business to tend to. I have some paperwork for all of you to sign, acknowledging the reading, receipt of items, relinquishing your right to further contest the distribution of property and so forth. That is, unless you do have an objection?"

"I do," defied Marissa. "I'm the artist of the family. What if I want a piece of that art gallery he passed down to some distant second cousin once removed or something of mine? Aren't I entitled to fight that?"

"Marissa!" We were all dismayed by her outburst—

though why should we be? It's Marissa, after all. The kind of woman who always wanted to know why she was down on the bottom of the seesaw when others were at the top, not seeing the big picture that life is a movement of balance.

"Oh, relax. It's hypothetical." She turned to the nervous lawyer with her challenging fire. "What if I did want to protest?"

He let out a stifled laugh. "Forgive me. That felt like déjà vu. You reminded me of Leigh's granddaughter-in-law, Peggy, just now. She's married to his grandson Patrick and had the same kind of question about if they wanted a part in the O'Sullivan inheritances. She wasn't serious of course—just curious, even if characteristically materialistic by nature.

"But to answer your question, you would need to go through a whole bunch of legal channels and court hearings to fight it. In the end though, Ms. Rossi, I must tell you that due to Rocco Marino's prior will conditions, most likely you would be denied because you are a descendant of Mrs. Mahoney.

"The living Marinos have already bent the rules as it is. It doesn't make it right—it's just how it is. It's always possible to win, but unlikely."

"Of course, Mr. Perkins," said Granny as she looked him directly in the eye. "We will all"—now looking directly at Marissa—"be happy to sign whatever documents you need us to, so you can be on your way. We will not be contesting anything. We thank you for your time."

With a few quick signatures and a short goodbye, the relieved messenger boy was on his way.

While mild chatter broke out among everyone, I took the opportunity to question Granny about him in private.

"Granny, I couldn't help but notice that it bothered you

that Mr. Perkins is our grandfather's lawyer."

"Ah, my clever girl. You don't miss anything. It's nothing to do with him personally," she took my hand in hers and smiled broadly. No one else ever looked at me with that kind of pride for having a brain like my Granny did—except maybe Daddy.

"I was just taken by surprise, that's all—though I shouldn't be. Generational social circles and loyalties are still common these days in rich families. Leigh would want someone he already knew and trusted as his lawyer and advisor.

"What I am surprised about is how *gracious*," she winced sarcastically, "the Marinos were in letting us have anything at all. My Leigh was a smart one, though. I'm interested to see what kind of loophole he was able to get past his family, that's for certain."

With that, I turned to the rest of the room on cue. "I think it's time to see what these curiously classified letters have in store for us."

4

Everyone agreed that we would open our letters and read them to each other.

Although we were concerned that Granny and Mom might have more private messages they should keep to themselves, they declared that there had been enough secrecy, and that it was time to bring it all out into the open.

Ripping the bandaid off her scar, Granny went first.

My dearest Lillith,

I have no right to even call you dearest, but it is how I still feel about you after all these years. I can only imagine the shock this must bring to you. I have no desire to hurt you or open old wounds. I thought the only way you would listen to me after all these years would be through death. I only hope this letter reaches you in time.

I have thought of you and our sweet Alissa every day since the moment I left you both behind in our beautiful home. The looks on your faces burned into my mind that day and have haunted me my entire life.

I am not a real man. A real man would have denied these material demands, this pathetic attempt for approval, and chosen love. For that, I will never forgive myself.

Although this will serve as no consolation to you, I lived a very unhappy, dutiful life. Marrying Julia meant nothing—I had no love left in my heart for anyone after you requested our divorce. I vowed to never love again because I did not deserve it. Just as I did not deserve you.

I wanted to fight for us; to deny the divorce. But my hands were tied, and I was weak. There was nothing I could do but have mercy and let you go, hoping that you would live a wonderful life without me.

Many times, I wanted to risk it all to return to see our beautiful Alissa grow up; to have more babies with you like we planned and travel the world together.

I confess, I did make secret trips to check in on you both. I saw the sadness and struggle and I couldn't bear to make it worse by revealing myself. I was ashamed of my weakness, knowing I had caused all of this pain. But as time went on, I saw your happiness return. Happiness in the form of Arthur Mahoney.

I was genuinely pleased for you, my Lillith. You found a good man for yourself and our baby girl. He was ten times the man I could ever be and so I told myself it was a blessing that I had left.

After that, I kept tabs but returned sparingly as it was too agonizing to watch. The family began to wonder about my frequent trips and since I had chosen duty to them, I had responsibilities to uphold. And you to protect. I feared for what they might do to you. A coward's life, indeed.

As I near death and reflect on life, I can say for certain that leaving you and Alissa behind was my one regret. None of the money in the world or the phony acceptance of my family ever matched the depth of love and worthiness that I experienced with you.

I leave you my gold wedding band not as a mere token or a painful reminder; but as proof that my love for you never died. I looked at it every night to remember how good life once was.

You will remain forever my one true love; and in my final words, I extend my sincerest apologies for not being the man you loved, needed or deserved. I deserted you, and for that, I would never ask for your forgiveness.

Just know that for my entire life, I mourned all that I had given up and I suffered the consequences. Maybe knowing that will bring you some solace.

May what I am about to set in motion be my final act of contrition as I attempt to rectify all that I have taken from my one true family.

Farewell mo shíorghrá,

Leigh

We all sat in silence for a while, allowing Granny her moment to grieve what obviously was a deep love. Her blue eyes were more gray today, like a cloudy sky awaiting the jolt of a thunderstorm. Her hair a lighter white, a few more wrinkles around her pink-lipsticked mouth. This whole experience was aging her and her heart. After a few minutes, she finally spoke.

"I always wondered if he regretted leaving us. Now I know. For the record, I don't take any joy from his agony," she sighed, ever the compassionate human being.

"He was right about one thing though—he was not the man I deserved. But he *was* the man I loved." Tears fell gently from her glassy eyes like the beginning trickle of a new waterfall.

"Oh, Granny," I whispered as I hugged her to me. "I'm so sorry."

"Granny? What does '*mo shiorghrá*' mean?" Mia queried softly.

"Ah. It's Gaelic for 'My Eternal Love.' It is how he always signed his letters to me—even his final letter granting a divorce. I don't doubt that I was his great love. I just wish we were enough for him."

"Mama, we *were* enough. I never knew he came back to check on us."

"Neither did I."

"I still have so many unanswered questions."

"Mom, why don't you open your letter? Maybe it will answer them," I offered.

"Okay." With trembling, well-manicured hands, my mother daintily opened her envelope with a letter opener, as if wanting to preserve every last piece of what he left her.

My Little Diamond,

My, how you have grown into such a beautiful woman, just like your mother. I know you may find this hard to believe, but I have watched you grow from that spunky little girl to an even classier, bolder woman.

I admit today that I have been there through most of your milestones. From a distance, but I was there.

I was hidden in the back rows of both your high school and college graduations. I was in a car parked down the street as you posed for pictures wearing that gorgeous teal blue dress that highlighted your eyes for the prom. I had half a mind to follow you and your date to make sure he remained a gentleman, but I had a feeling you could handle yourself.

I blended into the pews at the church on your wedding day and never felt so breathless in my life as when I saw you walk down that aisle in your mother's dress (oh yes, I noticed).

I wished more than anything to give you your grandmother's pearls that day and bless your union as I handed you over to the very worthy Joseph Rossi. You chose well, my darling daughter.

When I received notification of the birth of each of your beautiful daughters, I made arrangements to pass by the nursery window off hours so I could glance at the treasures I would never get to hold.

I stood in disguise among the mourners of your dear father, Arthur, wanting to reach out and comfort you. I have been among the crowds who came in droves to hear your literary speeches. You have the brilliance and beauty of your mother—and thankfully, her courage. Your stubbornness, however, seems to come from me.

I never revealed myself because I did not believe it was my place to be intrusive; plus, I was too much of a coward to jeopardize my family arrangement. I only wanted to be a part of your life, in whatever way I could be, yet honor my agreement with your mother and my uncle. But I just couldn't live without watching my precious diamond grow up.

I know you will come to hear about my stepson, who I adopted and gave my last name to. Out of no disrespect to the fine young man that I helped to raise, giving him my name was not the same as giving you life.

You must know, my daughter, that no child on this earth ever replaced you. You still remain, to this day, my one and only baby. The child born out of the only love I ever had to give; the best piece of me will live on in you.

I never once forgot about you, sweetheart. I loved you with all my heart and soul and became a broken man when I left you. Know that you never did anything wrong. You did not deserve a father's abandonment.

But also know that even though I never reclaimed you, I never truly left. Though I am not sure that will bring you any comfort for what I have done.

I am so proud of you. You are beautiful, smart, kind, graceful— everything a father could ever wish for in a daughter. You have undoubtedly passed those traits on to your own daughters— courtesy also of a very good man. Had things been different in life, I would have been proud to have called him my son. I am so sorry you lost him so young.

I cannot take away your pain. I cannot give you back the years together I stole from you. I cannot make up for lost time or apologize enough for not being a good father.

All I can do is leave you with the only promise I never broke: I loved you every second, of every minute, of every day since the moment you came into this world. And the truth is, your sparkle never left my heart.

With all the love I have,

Your Father, Leigh

Mom carefully folded back the letter and delicately placed it back into the envelope as if it could shatter like glass if mishandled. We allowed her time to digest what she had learned.

"That was…intense." Marissa spoke for us all after a

few moments had passed.

"Mom, how do you feel about all of this?"

She looked over at Mia sullenly in response. There was no shortage of crying today, as these letters were gut-wrenching. Mom straightened up in her chair to gather her thoughts before she spoke.

"It's a lot to take in, actually. The fact that he watched me grow up and was really at all those milestones, but never approached me, is quite a shock."

"Kinda creepy though, isn't it?" I couldn't help but nudge Marissa after her ill-timed insensitivity. Really? No filter at all?

"I can see how it would seem creepy to you girls," she managed with an amused smile, used to Marissa's antics. "But to me, it's not. It's actually endearing—and also angering. How I wished he would be there for all those special occasions in my life and then to find out he really was, but never let me know? It's going to take a while to sort it out."

"Of course, it will," Mia pulled Mom's hands into hers and stroked them. "A whole lifetime of beliefs has just been uprooted. It is going to take time for you—for Granny, for all of us—to come to terms with everything we have learned over the last few days."

Sensing the emotion of the room, I decided we needed to take a break.

"You know what? Why don't we talk a walk down to the water? I think we could all use some fresh air—and I do love those cranberry-orange scones from Julio's Bakery. Come on, it will be good for us."

My sisters immediately perked up at the idea, but Mom and Granny were hesitant.

"You know what, dears?" started Granny. "Why don't

you go on without us? I think your mother and I could use a few minutes alone to work through our feelings and grief. How about you bring us back some scones and we'll put up some tea?"

I smiled big at her, understanding perfectly. "You betcha, Granny. I'll even pick up a few of those chocolate raspberry petit fours you like, just for you."

Our walk down to the water was eerily quiet. The waves were practically still as we approached the worn, wooden dock that surrounded it. We found some equally tattered benches to sit on, feeling the warmth of the sun and the slightest of breezes blowing through our hair.

A hint of spring teased us, as we patiently waited for the winter cold to subside. The only sounds were that of a few delicate wave crashes and some pesky seagulls chirping for food. A solemn moment, indeed.

"So, that was something," said Marissa, breaking the silence.

"I can't even imagine what Mom and Granny are going through right now," Mia said with her usual empathy. "I mean, to first live with the pain of the abandonment, then to live with a suppressed lie, for it all to come out unexpectedly and change everything they ever thought to be true. I'm heartbroken for them."

"Me too." I let a beat skip before revealing what had been swimming like salmon upstream in my head for the last hour. "Hey, did you guys pick up on what he said at the end of Granny's letter?"

"The Gaelic thing?" Marissa wondered.

"No. The part that said something about 'may what I am about to set in motion be my final act of contrition' stuff. Don't you think that was cryptic?"

"Yeah, that *was* kind of puzzling. What do you think it means?"

"Maybe he just meant how he acknowledged us in the will or brought our presence to light after being hidden all these years," Mia offered.

"No, I don't think that's it. I think there is more to this story. Something is tugging at me. I feel like our little trips have something to do with it. Call it a hunch."

"Well, speaking of the trips," began Mia. "I don't know how feasible it is for the three of us to take all of these trips. Especially within the course of a year."

"Mi, you are getting ahead of yourself," I cut her off, not wanting to endure her maternal perspective on why this may or may not be a good idea. "We don't even know the details of this just yet. Maybe it is one trip per person. Or maybe they are weekend jaunts or one after the other over a simple week or two. Let's just wait and see what our letter has to say." I was anxious to read it, but I knew the others needed some space and time to absorb the new information.

Still, I couldn't help but feel my heart soar with excitement in between the chaos. Ireland? Italy? Spain? It's like a dream to me to be able to explore all these wonderful places; I already had my bags packed in my head.

Although I have been to a number of foreign countries through my corporate travels, including Italy, it was always quick and too business-like to be able to truly enjoy the cultures. Sightseeing was never on those agendas. Though I did know London inside and out like a second home.

My workaholic personality prevented me from truly living in the moment or unearthing all that the journeys had to offer like my father so often did. This was a once-in-a-lifetime opportunity to make some bucket list wishes come true and I was going with or without the agreement of my sisters. Though, I was pretty sure that Marissa also had stars in her eyes.

"Well, I for one am intrigued by it all," she said as if reading my mind. "Do you think we gave them enough time? Maybe we should have brought the envelope with us."

"No, that wouldn't be right. We promised to read our letters in front of each other. After hearing and seeing how vulnerable Granny and Mom were with theirs, we owe it to them to stay in this together."

"Mia's right. Though it is getting a bit chilly. I think it's okay for us to start heading back. But—bakery first!"

With decadent pastries in hand, we walked back to our beautiful family home. We shared so many wonderful memories here. Granny still had the old-fashioned tire swing on the tree, where we would twirl each other until we were dizzy.

Then there was the worn-out mini-house in the backyard that Daddy built with his bare hands for whenever we visited our grandparents—a tree house was too dangerous, he told us, so he made one on the ground.

We even bought a mini toy kitchen set to go inside. Oh, how we loved to play in there for hours. I'd clean, Mia would cook and Marissa would pretend to decorate. Now all tattered and weathered, full of cobwebs, dirt and insects, it still had a magical charm to it. My, had life been so much simpler then.

We arrived to find Mom busy in the kitchen gathering everything for tea, while Granny was sitting at the dining room table simply looking out into the distance through the large bay window. It was melancholy inside their usually energetic house. Faces worn from weeps, eyes weakened from emotion, it was clear that this whole situation was weighing heavily on them.

Even though I was dying inside to read our letter, I didn't want to be selfish. It had been a hard day already and who knows what other surprises were waiting to pop out like a jack-in-the-box.

"You know, why don't we just read this another time? We've had enough for one day."

"Nonsense," said Granny, though the words came out as barely a whisper. "Just because I am a bit sad doesn't mean that we have to call it quits. Now, just sit yourselves down. Let's have some tea and scones while we have a listen to what good old Leigh had to say to three granddaughters he never met."

On cue, Mom entered the room with her crème-colored Lenox teapot with matching sugar bowl, creamer, teacups and saucers. She was always so stylish when serving— even when it was just us sitting around casually like this. She brought in an assortment of herbal teas, knowing our tastes were as unique as our personalities.

Mia followed suit, presenting our scones daintily on yet another matching Lenox tray, accompanied by whipped butter and some orange marmalade Granny always kept on hand from a local farmers market. I added the rich petit fours as promised to the platter.

After settling down with our teas and desserts, the awkward silence ensued.

"Let's see what our mystery is all about, shall we?" Marissa nudged Mia.

"Meg, as the oldest, why don't you go ahead and read

the letter to all of us?" Mom suggested.

Obliging, I took the letter from a willing Mia and carefully opened it, inhaling sharply. I somehow knew that whatever I was about to read would change our future. Maybe not in this exact moment—but our lives were never going to be the same.

My Darling Granddaughters, Megan, Mia & Marissa,

I know all of this might have come as quite a shock to you, hearing about some old grandfather who abandoned your mother and grandmother. Why would you care about my death when you never knew me in life?

I would not blame you for your anger or confusion, but I ask that you allow a dying man a final wish to help set things right.

I loved your grandmother and mother with all of my heart— so much so, that I left them because I believed they would be better without me. I lived in great sorrow day after day, regretting my decision.

But that is neither here nor there. I cannot change the past or your impression of me. I have watched you grow into strong, beautiful women and I know your loyalty runs deep. You all remind me of different parts of my own grandmother, Alessia— my mother's mother—and it is through her spirit of love and family that I write to you today.

In my will, I bequeathed you three trips to be taken within a year of my death. These trips are more than just for your travel pleasure, though I do hope that they bring you great joy. They are about reclaiming your own lost heritage, one that is not associated with the patriarchal Marino clan, but that of your ancestral O'Sullivan line.

I knew that there would be no objection to the will for trips or tokens left to you three because they are from O'Sullivan blood. But what is unknown to the Marinos is the depth of treasure that the O'Sullivans (and extended family branches) hold.

It was a sacred secret held onto through the generations as a result of family shame—one that could only be passed down to those worthy of knowing without judgment or betrayal.

My mother withheld it from my father; he never knew her family's true legacy, nor did he care. He was too absorbed in protecting his Marino name. On her deathbed, not too long after my father's own passing, she called to me and revealed the truth of her lineages.

Now as I am on mine, I will pass on the legacy and history to you. But first you must make these journeys to meet with your rightful kin. Awaiting you in each country is a sacred family heirloom that has been in the possession of my maternal relatives, kept safe for the moment I was ready to bequeath them to you.

All three of you must journey together to each place and learn your heritage as a family. You will find that the gifts you receive will suit each of you quite well.

You will first go to County Mayo, Ireland where you will be welcomed into the home of Colleen O'Sullivan. Colleen is my first cousin and the last of the O'Sullivans, aside from you all. In her possession is an ancient Celtic ring that belonged to my great-grandmother, Elena, though it traces back much further than her generation. This ring shall be passed down to our aptly Celtic-named heir, Megan.

You will then travel to Florence, Italy where my mother's cousin, Sister Maria Bianchi, awaits you. As she is nearing 100 years of age, should she predecease me or your arrival, her lawyer, Francesco Marchesi, will greet you. There awaits a special Italian carved wooden jewelry box to be given to sweet Mia.

Finally, your journey will conclude in Barcelona, Spain. There my distant cousin, Edward John Rubio, will bring the final relic: a rare statue imagined to be sculpted by Francesco de Goya, which shall be presented to the fiery Marissa.

Insert squeal of delight from Marissa while I shot her a quick glare of warning to let me finish.

In order to claim your inheritance, you must follow what I have asked of you. All three together to all three locations within the year. My overseas relatives each have further instructions and information on pre-paid arrangements for your accommodations, meals, travel and spending money during your time away from home. You will need for nothing.

This plan was also designed with the utmost secrecy. In order to protect our legacy and yourselves, I ask for your discretion as well until all is revealed. I cannot emphasize the clandestine nature of this request enough.

May these journeys bring you blessings you never dreamed of and may you remember that your lineage extends far beyond the poor judgment of a selfish man; there is a fantastic ancestry to discover and it is my wish that you embrace it—and life— wholeheartedly.

With love and admiration,
Your Grandfather, Leigh

I put the letter down and looked around the soundless room. Everyone was dealing with the information in their own way. Granny sat straight up, her wrinkled lips puckered in a combination of intrigue and annoyance. My mother was faking a smile—I knew she was genuinely happy for us, but her heart was still too shattered by it all.

Marissa was jonesing to get going—I could see the newly wound up grandfather clock gears turning. I was keeping it together like a professional, but my insides wanted to jump out in childish excitement. Mia looked a bit distracted and downhearted, avoiding eye contact with any of us. I decided to break the ice.

"Well, that is even more mysterious sounding than before I read this. If it's just a ring, statue and jewelry box, can't they just ship it to us? It *is* the 21st century."

"Are you kidding me? Why are you looking a gift horse in the mouth? This sounds like a once-in-a-lifetime *dream*," cried Marissa.

"I agree. It's not every day you receive a gift like this." Mom then smiled affectionately, as if captured in a memory. "I feel like your father would be behind you on this. Almost as if he played a part in making it happen for you."

"You're right. It is pretty exciting! I can't wait!" I turned to Granny. "Would it upset you if we fulfilled Grandfather Leigh's wishes? Just say the word and we can leave this behind."

Granny looked over in a bit of a shock. "My sweet girls," she started, as mini pools formed in her sparkling eyes. "I have waited all my life for Leigh Marino to show me the kind of man he could be. If he wants to right his wrongs through you, there is nothing that would make me happier than to see your own dreams come true."

Without skipping a beat, Marissa started with the plans. "I hated my job anyway. I'm going to march on in to Greg tomorrow and tell him where he can shove it! I'm ready to travel the world on this grandpa's dime! And I'm sure Jay wouldn't mind having a bachelor pad for a while, as long as I can still kick in the rent."

I laughed and joined in the fantasy. "I have accrued so much vacation time over the years of non-stop working, I'm pretty sure I might even have months available! For sure, I have enough to get us started on Ireland as soon as you ladies would like."

"How wonderful!" Mom exclaimed. "Oh, it does my heart good to see you girls be able to do something together. Although I grew up without siblings, I know there is no stronger bond than that of sisters."

"Is there anything in there about how you find these tickets or what the next step is?" Marissa asked.

"I didn't see a P.S. or anything." I checked the envelope again. "Wait…something is in here."

I pulled out a travel agent's business card. "Bingo! I'm guessing Ms. Veronica Ashford of Legacy Travels might have the answers we are looking for."

"Do you want me to call her?"

"Nah, Mar, that's okay. I think we can all agree I am the planner of the family. I can work on getting us all organized. You can research the weather and area and let us know what we should pack and sightsee. And Mia, you would be perfect for figuring out some must-dine restaurants. Oh my gosh, this is so incredible!"

I felt like a little girl about to meet Mickey Mouse for the first time. But Mia didn't look like she wanted to go to our inherited Disneyland; she shuffled on the couch quietly, still avoiding eye contact.

"Mia, honey, what's wrong?" gently probed Mom.

The room quelled, giving Mia a chance to collect her

thoughts. She cleared her throat a few times, trying to speak but couldn't, and then started crying uncontrollably into our mother's arms. Mom held on to her tightly, stroking her hair in comfort while looking up at us as confused as we were.

"I'm sorry. I'm so sorry," she sobbed.

"Sorry for what, sweetheart?" my mother crooned, trying to help settle our distraught sister. I joined them on the couch, rubbing Mia's back in sympathy.

Once she calmed herself a bit, and accepted some tissues, she was ready to let it out.

"I'm sorry that I am going to ruin everything for everyone."

"Mi, how could you ruin everything? If you don't want to look for restaurants, it's okay, we can wing it."

"No, no, it's not that." She took a deep breath. "I just—I can't go." And with that, more guilt fell from her eyes like an unexpected storm.

"Why can't you go?" Marissa asked in a soothing, tender voice, as she knelt before her sister.

Shifting moods quickly from sad to indignant, Mia snapped. "You're joking, right? Why can't I go? *Why* can't I go?" She paused a moment, inhaling sharply. What were we missing?

"I have children and a husband to think about. I can't just up and leave them. It must be nice to have your single lives where you can do whatever you want, but I actually have a family to consider. So, I'm sorry to let you and your dreams down, but I'm not going."

"Mia, I—" I stopped myself. We didn't think about her position before getting all worked up. She had a valid point. It was too much to ask of her.

"Mia." Granny turned to face her full on. "Our sweet

Mia, always putting everyone ahead of herself," she said as she stroked a piece of hair off her rounded, tear-stained face. "Do you really think you are alone in this?"

A little calmer and more composed, she answered, "Yes, actually, I do."

"My dear, when it comes to dreams, there is always a way. Let this be a lesson to you," she advised grandmotherly. "Your mother and I discussed this possibility while you stepped out to go down to the water and we already called Kevin and filled him in. He is on board with whatever you need to do.

"Mom and I will take turns staying at your house in the guest room to make sure the kids are dressed, fed and taken to school and all of their activities."

"We will take great care of them," Mom chimed in. "You can be at ease, knowing that they are in good hands without disrupting Kevin's schedule, either."

Quietly she whispered, "I can't ask you to do that."

"You didn't ask, now did you?" said Granny. "We offered, knowing what it is like to have that family you do everything for. Knowing that you always put yourself last. Well, now that all on the home front will be taken care of, it is up to you whether you decide to do this or not. For yourself."

"Mi, I am so sorry I didn't think about how difficult this would be for you to get away. It was selfish of me," I began. "But you do also deserve this break. You have a beautiful home and family, one that you postponed your own dreams for because they mean the world to you. Forget me and Marissa for a second. Do you want to go on these trips?"

"I—I would really like to. I just—I don't know if I can leave my children, even in good hands. I've never been away from them for more than a day or two."

"They are not little babies anymore, Mia. I think they would be inspired to see their mother do something so cool," Mom prodded.

She pondered that for a moment. Nervously twisting her tendrils between her fingers, you could tell she was torn.

"I have an idea. Why don't we give you some time to think about it? We have a whole year. A few days or so won't make a big difference," I gestured.

"You know what?" she considered. "No. You are all right. I haven't done anything for myself in years and my heart is so intrigued by this. To learn about some history we never knew about, meet some cousins and see the world? This chance doesn't come along—ever. I would be a fool not to go on an adventure with my sisters."

She coyly grinned and Marissa and I tackled her for a big sister hug, laughing all the way.

"Okay, then. I will call the travel agent tomorrow morning and get it all started. Now, who's up for Chinese food delivery?"

5

"We will now begin boarding for Flight 452 to Shannon, Ireland," announced an overly chipper attendant over the loudspeaker. Didn't she realize the roosters weren't even awake yet?

"That's us! Are you ready, ladies?" Did Mia realize it? How can anyone be so cheerful in the morning? Even my breasts weren't as perky as she was.

"I know I am," said Marissa, as she quickened to reapply her ruby red lipstick before putting her makeup bag back into her huge black Coach purse. You would think she was about to go to a concert instead of on an eight-hour overseas flight.

Did I mention it was *really* early in the morning?

Mia and I, on the other hand, went for a more casual approach with our flight ensembles. Since it was just the beginning of April, it was still chilly out. The arrival of "spring" meant little to the Northeast region—and even less where we were headed. I was so impulsive in booking the flights, I had forgotten to consider we were headed towards the rainy season in Ireland (well, rainier than normal). Too late to change plans now.

As we boarded the plane, we could barely contain our excitement.

"Can you believe how rich dear old Grampy was? First class tickets and all!"

"I know, Mar! We are certainly going to travel in style." Yes, luxury definitely suited me quite well. With my frequent traveling, I was already used to it, so I was relieved not to be relegated to coach seating on our trips. Sorry, not sorry. I become, shall we say, *particular,* when I travel.

Anyway, as soon we settled onto the plane, I was ready for some celebratory champagne. We took our complementary flutes as we sat in oversized recliner seats and relished in our good fortune.

"Ladies, what should we toast to?" asked Mia.

"To an adventure of a lifetime," I said.

"To the mystery of it all!" chimed in Marissa.

But Mia said it best. "To sisterhood."

We all yelled *Sláinte!* and drank down what must have been a very expensive reserve. The bubbles danced on my tongue before they smoothly tingled the back of my throat. A good reserve, indeed.

The flight was long but made wonderfully relaxing by our first-class accommodations. Personal feather pillows, fleece blankets, eye masks and dedicated televisions were only the tip of the iceberg—the food was spectacularly delectable.

We elected to share a cheeseboard for starters, along with a Midleton Mule with Jameson for Marissa, a Guinness for Mia and a Bailey's Mint Martini for myself. We then ordered one of each of the main dishes so we could savor them all: honey and whiskey grilled salmon with rosemary roasted red potatoes; mustard-crusted pork loin with apple-cabbage slaw; and lentil-mushroom shepherd's pie.

Of course, no smorgasbord was complete without the assorted mini scones served with jam, clotted cream and tea. If this is a sample of what's to come over the next two weeks, I should figure on gaining about ten pounds.

When we arrived at the airport's baggage claim, we were greeted by a big "Rossi" sign, held by a stout little woman with curly gray hair that playfully exposed a few subtle traces of fiery strands. She was wearing long brown pants and a colorfully stitched Galway sweater, but nothing was as bright as her beaming smile and elfish green eyes.

"Are you cousin Colleen?"

"That I am! My goodness! Look at ya—you're as beautiful as deities! C'mere and gimme a hug." She wrapped her big, strong arms around the three of us in a joyful embrace. I loved her instantly.

"Is that all you be taking, is it now?" She had a small baggage trolley alongside her and started to put our bags on it as we tried to object.

"Oh, no. We still need to wait for our luggage. This was just our carry-ons," explained Marissa.

"I tasked Marissa here with letting us know what to bring. Big mistake," I laughed, motioning my thumb over to my sister for easy identification. "I'm afraid we were coaxed into bringing something for every season."

"Hey, you never know!" she giggled.

"I'm Megan, by the way. And this is Mia."

"I'll try to keep ya straight. Do any of you have to go to the jacks before we head out? Long journey ahead, don'tcha know."

"The jacks?" Marissa asked in confusion.

"The ladies room," I offered. Turning to Colleen, "I tried to brush up on some common Irish terms before I got here."

"Ah, aren't you something!" Her big grin was contagious. Over the next few minutes, we did find a "jacks" to freshen up in, then grabbed our bags, loaded up the trolley and headed out to this huge minivan. Thankfully it was roomy—we had a lot of luggage with us.

"Thank you so much for letting us stay in the family home. It's very generous of you," said Mia.

"Ah, sure look it! It was your Granda Leigh who went through all the trouble, ya know. It's the old O'Sullivan gaff down in Louisburgh. I'm up a bit a ways in Newport myself. No one actually be living there in Louisburgh at the moment. I have Mr. MacGovern tidying it up every week for me. Such a good man." She nodded in agreement with herself.

The view from the car was breathtaking—even if we were a bit unsettled driving on the opposite side of the road through millions of roundabouts. This place certainly earned its reputation as the Emerald Isle. The hills of such perfect greenery were like a painting, as we passed several pastures rotating between free range sheep, cows and horses along the way.

The depth of color was only heightened by the contrast of silver-clouded skies in the background. You would think that the rainy season would make it all dreary, but the lush green popped even more enchantingly like an emerald shining through a cave enclosure.

There was something so familiar about it. Like I had been here before. Almost as if I could take over the wheel and know exactly where I was driving. Such an odd sensation, since I had never been to Ireland—except in my dreams.

I know I have passed this landscape before, I ruminated in my head. I remember that goat farm in the distance, and that sharp curve in the road somehow. I even remember the debacle of having to reverse the car all the way up the road we just traveled on so a bus could pass on this narrow, one lane street. Déjà vu?

My trances along the trip were often interrupted by our dear cousin, who we quickly found out had a gift for gab. I mused to myself how she must have kissed the Blarney Stone many, many times.

"Now, where we be at now is in County Clare. That's where you'll be finding the touristy stuff. Are you planning on doin' some sightseein' at all?"

"Oh, yes! Definitely," squealed Marissa. "I want to explore as many ancient buildings as I can while I'm here and see art museums like the Hunt. I find that all so fascinating."

"I heard the Bunratty Castle has an extraordinary medieval dining experience that I signed us all up for," inserted Mia. "I booked an extra reservation for Saturday night if you'd like to join us, Colleen."

"That'd be fierce! I do love going on the lash!"

"Having a night out," I whispered to my perplexed sisters.

"So, you best be planning on stayin' down south for a spell. I have your spending money from Granda Leigh that should cover things like that. I'll be givin' that to ya when we get to the house.

"Where you'll be resting is in County Mayo. It originated from *Contae Mhaigh Eo*. That's Gaelic for 'plain of the yew trees.' It's a grand place. Right upon the Atlantic Ocean with its own treasures indeed. You might want to be checkin' out Croagh Patrick, too—that's an ancient pilgrimage site. Quite lovely.

"Oh and Clare Island," she continued without inhaling. "I haven't been there in donkey's years but 'tis a grand sight. You just take the ferry crossing from Roonagh Pier. It is rumored to have been the home of the Pirate Queen

Grace O'Malley, don'tcha know."

"It all sounds so wonderful, thank you! I am typing this into my phone so we remember."

Mia's affirmation made Colleen beam even brighter. What a kind, sweet woman she was. The remainder of the two-and-a-half hour drive to our destination was filled with similar conversations of where we "must go" all along the coast—that is, both western and eastern coasts. She had us taking a train cross-country to Dublin, warning us that we best not leave until we see the Guinness Storehouse.

When we arrived at the O'Sullivan home, it was that brief point in time right after sunset where you can see all the hues of the sun mix with the impending darkness of the evening sky. As we drove over the bridge and through the entrance, I noticed the town had an unusual setup. I never saw connected buildings mingling both homes and stores in a single unit before—at least, not outside of a city. Usually, I see either a storefront or series of townhouses. But there we were, in the heart of the town, learning that her dear friend Ellie Walsh lived in the light yellow house in between the post office and pharmacy.

Our family home happened to be situated around the corner, next to another home with a diner on the other side of it and a hotel across the street. Interesting, to say the least. It reminded me of a Monopoly board.

But the house was simply charming. A tan two-story unit with a light brown roof hovering over three shutterless windows and a lower floor bay window aside a cobalt blue front door. Since the home was situated on a corner, it boasted a lovely lush side garden, full of glorious bushes and flowers, most likely native to the area. I bet I'd find Mia here every morning.

Oh, yes. There was a small, white wood porch on the

side, too, with just enough room for a single, weathered rocking chair. I could feel the years of work stress fade away just by looking at this serene place.

"You must be all flogged after such a long trip. I'll wet the tea and see what dear MacGovern rustled up for us for supper. Ah, grand! He left us his mum's lamb stew. I'll heat that up with some of this nice sliced pan here.

"Now, I'll be having a rest here with you all tonight and be making a hearty breakfast to welcome ya properly. I do have to crack on to Newport in the afternoon, so you won't have a car. It'd be best that you don't try driving on these Irish roads, now, with the left and the right being all mixed up and the troublin' roundabouts, as you Americans seem to think.

"You have a bit o' money, plenty to help with transportation, and I got a few chums that can help as well. You'll work it out," she assured us.

"Oh—make certain to stock up on some messages, ya hear? You don't want to be pissin' away your cash on eating out all the time. Plenty of tools right here in the kitchen for ya."

"Mia's on food duty. She is the family cook—her food is amazing!" Mia smiled at Marissa's compliment.

"Well, well, isn't that something? I'll be happy to sample whatever you cook up one of these days. For now, rest up. I'll take care of tonight's supper and then tomorrow we can chat some more. Oh, feck! I almost forgot to give you a tour."

After she put up the tea and set the stew for heating, she walked us around our new living quarters. It was just as darling on the inside as it was out, in an old-fashioned kind of way. The bottom floor was covered in old, tattered pine hardwood except the kitchen, which had a worn-out white tile with a few cracks here and there.

Alongside the living room wall was a built-in bookshelf housing an assortment of books, photographs and knick-knacks that must have dated back centuries. The taupe-painted walls were adorned with various Celtic totems and magnificent nature paintings that complemented the rich colors of the house. Further adding to its history was a gorgeous woven Celtic-designed throw rug in vibrant colors of green, rust and gold.

Off to the right side, like an L-shaped turn, was the "setting area," as she called it. This was a more cozy space, with a gray leather loveseat and two matching high-back arm chairs adorned with light blue velvety throw pillows and matching Irish woolen blankets.

The seating was arranged in a semi-circle fashion around the brick fireplace and solid wood mantle—certainly not the cheap fake gas fireplaces of modern times. Stacked alongside of it were freshly cut pieces of wood and cast-iron pokers.

Above the mantle was a fascinating painted portrait of a man and woman—and if I didn't know better, I'd swear I was practically looking at the male version of myself.

His hair was golden, a gentle mop of blonde curls that stopped right above his shoulders. Underneath a light gray suit jacket, he wore a royal blue collared shirt that highlighted his deep, penetrating blue eyes—I'd venture that they were even more vibrant than this decades-old painting could reveal. A matching light gray bowtie finished his ensemble—no, dare I say, his smile did, with the single dimple on his right cheek playfully revealing itself.

The woman beside him was just as lovely, with exotic chocolate wavy locks rolling down the sides of her face and curling at an end right above her breasts. Atop her head was a veil-like hat of white with small pink roses weaved into it. Her demure white lace blouse had beautiful pearls sown into the bodywork, all accentuating her beautifully Mediterranean skin tone and dark brown eyes.

Again, the familiarity struck me, as I could see our Mia in her reflection. In all her sweet rambling, Colleen had not revealed who they were, but I made a mental note to ask her when she was done with her stories.

Moving on past the setting area was the very small but functional combination kitchen and dining room. A solid dark pine wood table sat close to the edge of the wall with two matching benches on the long sides and two head chairs. The table set-up and centerpiece had a country feel to it—warm, welcoming and homely.

The yellow painted walls, pine colored cabinets and rustic decorations added to the country feel, offset by only a few modern touches of a granite countertop and relatively new white appliances. Off towards the back was a tiny room that she told us held a basic washer and dryer and some storage space.

At least we wouldn't have to wash our clothes on a washboard in a local stream, I joked to myself. That's how old this place appeared to be.

She stopped for a moment to brew our tea—never stopping her chatter, however. As it steeped, she led us up a narrow red-carpeted staircase by the front entrance that opened to a tiny hallway. Upstairs held a series of three bedrooms—one modest master and two relatively smaller rooms. I immediately called dibs on the master as the eldest, to my sisters' disappointment.

The master was a lovely shade of lilac with accenting floral curtains that made you feel like you were about to rest in a meadow. A queen-sized bed sat at the center of the room with a matching purple floral duvet ensemble and assortment of fluffy pillows in all shades of violet.

The dark mahogany bedpost was complemented with matching nightstands, dressers and a velvety lounge chair with a tall reading lamp. So cozy and inviting. The full-mirrored door inside opened to a long, deceivingly deep closet. Not the huge walk-in I was used to, but it would do for now.

Right outside of the hallway bathroom was a dangling string that presumably led to the attic…calling to me like a treasure map pointing to the big "X" marks the spot.

As Colleen ventured down to check on our dinner, we brought up our luggage and settled into our respective rooms. We took turns freshening up quickly and quietly, as we took it all in.

"Well now, don't you look all comfortable." Colleen greeted us with a beautiful bowl of steaming stew, glasses full of a local red wine and a teapot ready for post-dinner enjoyment. *Hmm,* I didn't realize how hungry I was.

"This is absolutely delicious!" Mia exclaimed. "My compliments to the chef!"

"Well, I won't be takin' any credit for that. Maybe if you see that Mr. MacGovern around here, you could be so kind as to let him know for his mum."

We continued dinner with some small talk, clearly feeling the drain of the day. We offered to help Colleen clean up the kitchen before settling down in front of a fire with a nice cup of Barry's Irish tea…and a few scones, of course.

"Colleen, who is that couple in the portrait?"

"Ah, now that would be your great-great grandparents, Cian and Alessia O'Sullivan," she said. "Quite the love story, ya know. Star-crossed lover stuff. But that would be a story for your ancestors in Italy to tell. We each were given our specific tales to tell you."

She lowered her voice in a frustrated aside. "Though I don't know why it has to be so prim and proper and all with the way of the tellin'.

"Here, you'll be learning about your great-great-great grandparents, Elena and Baran. There be much to say, but best be savin' it for another night. We've got plenty o'time."

She paused, but only for a moment. "You should be goin' up to rest your weary bones now. Like I said, I'll be gettin' up early in the mornin' to rustle up some breakfast before I'm on my way. We can chat some more then."

We all hugged good night and went up to our rooms. Colleen had already told us she planned on sleeping on the pull-out sofa, refusing to accept any of our offers to stay in one of our rooms for the night.

As the house went still, my mind started racing with questions. Star-crossed lover ancestors? Who were they really and why couldn't Colleen divulge any info? What story *was* she able to tell us? What should we do first— stay here and learn more about our heritage or explore like tourists? Why is everything so familiar to me?

After what seemed like hours of internal mental inquiries, I finally drifted off to sleep in the comfort of a home I somehow already knew.

6

When I finally woke up, the sun was bright and peeking in through the cracks of the blinds in the bedroom window. On top of my resistance to being an early bird, the jet lag made it even more difficult for me to turn over and check the time.

Ten o'clock? Wow, I guess I was more tired than I thought.

I took a few deep breaths as I gazed upon my surroundings, soaking up the nuances of the room that I missed in the evening light. My nose caught the scent of bacon and my stomach responded in turn. I would rather have lulled around under the covers until I felt ready to rise, but a hungry growl was pushing me out the door like an excited little puppy.

Down in the kitchen, my sisters were already up and chatting away with Colleen, who was setting the table with the last dish. As she removed her breakfast-stained, red-checkered apron, she was a vision in a bright yellow and green floral dress with flat loafer shoes.

"Perfect timing!" she exclaimed. "I just made the last of it. What's your fancy?"

"I'll just have some tea, thanks." I wasn't big on coffee. I just couldn't get used to the taste. My palate enjoyed a nice, relaxing cup of tea in the morning to get started. Though I did appreciate the smell of a freshly brewed pot of java.

From what I gathered, Mia was already on her third cup. She couldn't function without it and since she was probably up before the birds, it was a safe bet it wasn't her first go-round. Nope, already dressed with her hair done perfectly up in a bun, I'd say she'd been awake for quite a while.

Marissa was probably nursing her first cup—black. It was interesting how she would either drink just straight black coffee or fancy frappuccinos, but nothing in between. Like me, mornings were more challenging for her, as evidenced by her open robe and light pink silk nightie.

A breakfast feast welcomed us to the table: scrambled eggs, crisp bacon, pork sausages, a little unusual muffin-like thing I came to find out was black pudding (which didn't taste anything like pudding or a muffin), hash browns, fresh fruit, some rye toast and assorted jams and lemon-poppyseed scones. You'd think she was feeding an army with all this food.

"Everything looks delicious, Colleen. Thank you again for all your hospitality," I said.

"Ah, it be nothing, lass. Eat up now. I won't be 'round for another day or two, so you'll be on your own with the cookin'. I take it you slept well?"

"Oh, yes, thank you," said Mia. "This house is lovely. Very comforting."

"That's grand. Now I was thinkin' you should stay here at least one more night before you go out on the town," she said in her 'I have your itinerary all planned out' kind of way.

"I agree. I was planning on walking through the town, going to the market, things like that."

"Oh Meg, if I give you a list, would you mind picking

up a few things for me for dinner? It's been so long since I have been without a husband or kids, I would really love to just stay here, sit on that side porch and read a book. It would be so nice to have a day without running any errands."

"Of course, Mi! I think that's a great idea. Mar, how about you?"

"If you don't mind, I was going to research some more places to check out while we are here, so we can talk about where we want to go and make a plan later. That cool? Or do you need help?"

"I think I can manage a few bags of groceries."

"This be a local town, so there won't be a trouble if you brought a basket home with you and returned it later. Not sure about the trolleys though. Best be bringin' some coins if you want for one of them. Ah, and in the cubby over there be some bags. Cost extra now if you don't bring some with you.

"Now, the Gala Market is in the center of town, about half a kilometer down the road on the left towards the bridge."

"Wonderful, thank you! I am excited to explore the town."

"Well, I'll be crackin' on now. You have my number in case you need to give me a ring. I already let them nosy neighbors know who's in here so they don't call the Garda on you. Though I suppose you should be prepared for some popover greetings from them. Grand crew, though. Lovely people.

"Enjoy your time here. Oh—and don't be worrying about no crickety sounds. That just be your relatives peeping in on ya from time to time. I reckon that cod brother o' mine Shane be curious to see who's shacking up here himself."

"Shane? Isn't he—" Marissa broke off midsentence as Colleen shot back a wink and left us on that note.

"Great, ghosts. That makes me want to take a shower right now," I said sarcastically as we shivered at the very idea of being in a haunted house.

A little freaked out about the thought of some dead cousin watching me undress, I jumped in and out of the shower, opting for piling my hair on top of my head in a wet, messy bun and throwing on a pair of faded blue jeans and the first sweater I saw—a light blue cashmere.

I kept the makeup light as I was on vacation and didn't see the need to get all dolled up for a walk to the market, especially since I was all bundled up under layers anyway. Just a touch of foundation and light mascara would do. With purse in hand, I was ready to go exploring.

The houses along our street were basically on top of each other, with nothing but a cement sidewalk as the front yard and little space for privacy. It reminded me of a city, yet with the quiet movement of the suburbs.

So much community. Kids playing ball in the backyards; families bringing in grocery bags from their parked cars; a big, burly man standing outside smoking a cigarette; and a nice elderly couple sitting together in their own side garden at the opposite end of the block—she was knitting and he was whittling wood.

No doubt everyone would know everyone else's business around here. As much as I was a private person myself, the thought of that neighborly closeness didn't bother me for some reason. *Strange*, I mused.

As I walked on, I came across the stretch of town that held most of the shops and very few homes. So many adorable window fronts—hand-woven rugs, knitted sweaters, whipped ice cream, Celtic jewelry, a pharmacy, a toy store, about four different pubs—I definitely need to come back down here just to investigate these little shops some more.

But first, I was on a mission to find the grocery store.

Ah, there it was. Nothing too different than the local little retailers I was used to, I suppose. I took Colleen's advice and went with a basket. I was only picking up a few items for a day or two until we had a game plan.

Stepping inside, it was like a farmers market with an abundance of fresh fruits and vegetables right up front. The shoppers were all so friendly, chatting with each other and sharing recommendations on this product or another. Just in a foreign language that was supposed to sound like English, I observed curiously. Accents are thicker than bacon around here.

There was such a peace and happiness to my new surroundings, though. Everything was easy and simple. Ha, simple. The exact opposite of my chaotic life. Since arriving, I've fought the urge to check my emails or return messages.

I had a few texts from Derek, but thankfully, by the end of the unreturned message thread, he had figured it out. Still, did he need me to double check the copy anyway? No. I told the team that I was going to be unreachable and I was going to keep that promise to myself to let this be my time. I deserved a break, damn it.

I've spent countless years and nights burning the midnight oil at that place. Picking up the slack for incompetent but cheaper staff members. Budget cuts can be such a nightmare.

Or maybe it really was my expectations. I set the bar so high sometimes that even I can't reach it. But how else would we land such high-profile clients? "If you want something done right, you have to do it yourself." The motto of my clichéd life.

But now, in this moment, I had to choose to let go of the reigns and trust that my people were good enough to hold down the fort. Besides, if they don't do a great job, then that only validates how much I'm needed.

Holy shit. Did I really just think that?

Since when was I insecure about my job or my abilities? Is that why I chose all these years to work non-stop, so that I would make myself somehow irreplaceable?

What was going on at work right now? Maybe they were making changes while the control freak was gone. Am I going to come back to a completely altered career that no longer values me?

You're being ridiculous, Megan. Get a grip. You are a hard worker and good at what you do. They can get by without you, but they thrive with you. Let it go and—

Smack!

Lost in conversation with myself, I didn't notice anyone behind me as I backed up looking for the carrots Mia requested.

"Oh my goodness, I am so—" I looked up, stunned at the gorgeous man in front of me, barely mumbling out, "Sorry."

"Not a worry, miss," he said in a sexy brogue. Before me stood a 6-foot tall deity with a handsomely chiseled face. He was like a work of Irish art with his long, raven hair that waved just above his shoulders, his green-blue gaze and some dark stubble around his broad chin.

He was sporting ripped jeans and a green, blue and white flannel over a dirtied white t-shirt. His entire essence oozed sex appeal like I imagined a Celtic God would.

And this is why you should always put makeup on before going out, Megan, I chided myself.

"Are you alright?" he broke my nomadic thoughts, which were probably written all over my face as I continued to stare at this poor man like a psychopath.

"What? Oh, yes. Yes, sorry. I'm—grand," I managed to respond, as I nervously fussed with my hair—as if I could make a messy bun look fabulous.

"Grand, are ya?" He had a hearty, yet pleasant enough laugh that I could imagine was contagious. Well, it sucked me in. "So, an American lass is tryin' on some Irish, is she now?"

I blushed. Blushed? Oh my God, what is wrong with me? I've never turned to jelly in front of a man like this before. I'm an empowered, independent woman!

Buck up Megan, before he thinks you are a complete idiot, I warned myself.

"Well, when in Rome," I said, lamely attempting a joke, though judging by his confused face, I'm pretty sure the Irish aren't familiar with that saying. "I'm Megan. I'm here with my sisters visiting a cousin and this is my first time in town."

"Well, *céad míle fáilte*, Miss Megan. A thousand welcomes," he winked as he extended his hand to shake mine. Who ordered the lightning bolt? "I'm Kieran. And who might your cousin be?"

"Colleen O'Sullivan." His eyes raised in recognition and his lips in a semi-smirk.

"Do you know her?"

"Lassie, this is a small town. Everybody knows everybody around here. Colleen O'Sullivan happens to be one of my favorite old mots. A darlin', she is. Chatty little nugget, but as kind as they come. How long will you be staying?"

"Well, we are here for a few weeks. My grandfather, who I didn't even know was a grandfather, left us this mysterious will about traveling to three countries to find our heritage and I'm supposed to get some kind of ring here, which I know nothing about and—"

I looked up to see an amused expression on his face. Oh God, I was rambling—and rambling about something that was supposed to be a family secret.

What the hell, Meg?

"I'm sorry, I'm going on and on and probably boring you to tears."

"On the contrary. I'm finding our conversation fascinating. A secret granda and mysterious ring? It's the stuff storybooks are made of. Lucky you for getting to live it."

"I guess so." Awkward silence passed, as I tried my hardest not to stare into his swimming pool eyes. I didn't realize they even made men this perfect anymore. And something about that accent was making me weak in the knees, like some high school girl whose crush just said "hi" as he walked past her locker.

"Well, I best be on my way. My mum's waitin' on me to bring her some messages. It was grand meeting you, though I dare say my left foot mighta been a bit bruised in our scuffle." He chuckled warmly.

"Sorry again. It was nice to meet you too, Kieran." I succeeded to even more awkwardly put out my hand to shake it, secretly hoping to feel the electricity again. To my surprise, he lifted my hand up to his lips and gave it a gentle kiss with his soft, thick lips as he stared straight into my eyes—into my soul.

"I'm sure to be seein' you again, Miss Megan." And off

he went, stopping once to turn his head around and smile as I stood there, lifeless.

Thank goodness Mia had written everything down that we needed because I felt like I just had a lobotomy. I was complete mush. Jeez, how long has it been since I'd been with a man?

Oh right, just a few months ago I had ended it with Eddie Birkens, an associate in our sister organization that I met at a recent trade show in Vegas. Nothing happened in Vegas since we were professionals, but the second we got back to New York, the sex was on. It was a good tumble for a few months, but it wasn't meant to be much more than that.

I got bored—and not because he wasn't attractive or because we didn't have great physical chemistry, but I was left wanting more. Although a well-respected peer, he lacked the level of intellectual stimulation I required in an ongoing relationship. I need someone not afraid to challenge my mind, and he was a man of very few words and insights.

Running into this Kieran guy was more than that. It was a spark I hadn't felt since my first long-term relationship in my twenties. Back then, I thought Scotty and I would have been married with a few kids by now.

Unfortunately, his wandering dick squashed that delusion and I resolved instead to put my whole heart into my job. Sure, there were a few decent men along the way, not all straight-up sex, but none had been the right one for me. No one compared to Scotty or to the feelings that I had for him. He was my one and only prince-charming-gone-wrong.

The man who single-handedly ruined the girlish notions of romance for me.

Yet, one single encounter with Kieran seemed to stir that all up. My stomach fluttered and my heart raced. How is that possible? I just met the guy and barely talked to him. More like rambled at him. I can't explain these funky emotions—just like I can't explain the familiarity of Ireland. I felt instantly drawn to him as if I had already known him.

And I just let that man walk away.

Would I ever see him again? I wondered. *What is going on with you, Meg?* I had to shake off all this drivel. Setting my head back on straight, I finished my task at hand and gathered up our groceries—all while occasionally looking around to see if I could spot my new Irish crush again.

He vanished as quickly as he showed up. But his musky scent and sparkling eyes accompanied me as I walked back to the O'Sullivan house.

When I arrived, Mia was relaxed with her cute red reading glasses on, sitting in the rocking chair, completely submerged in her book. Marissa was chatting away on her phone near the garden of white lilies in the back of the house and hurriedly said goodbye to whoever she was talking to as she saw me approach.

"Who was that?"

"Oh, it's just Jay. Checking in on us," she replied a little too quickly. I'm guessing by now their relationship had crossed that line—I mean, he *really was* one sexy guy. I wouldn't be able to resist him. No use in pressing her for details, though. We'll find out as soon as it's over. "How was the market?"

"Interesting. It was difficult to find everything because my logic didn't seem to match up with theirs. But it was adorable and friendly, just like the rest of this town. You should check it out with me next time. There were some great little shops I saw where we could get some souvenirs for Mom and Granny and Kevin and the kids."

I decided to leave out my interlude with Kieran for now. I needed time to recover from my out of body experience. No, correction—to put it behind me because it was one of those one-time-only destined moments. No use even bringing it up. I'll just tuck it away in one of my private memory archives.

"So, Mia, what are your plans for all this stuff I got for you?"

"I was thinking of trying my hand at shepherd's pie. It's a simple dish to make and easy enough to have for leftovers tomorrow so I won't have to cook every night."

"That's smart. This is your vacation as much as ours and even though we'd love to be spoiled with your cooking, we need to be fair about it."

"I agree with Marissa. Maybe we should come up with some kind of chore chart. I mean, we will be staying here in this home and need to upkeep it and feed ourselves. If we all rotate some meals and clean-up, we can make sure it's fair. And since Marissa and I are better suited for breakfast and lunch duty than dinner, we can take some nights off from home-cooked meals and dine out in style, thanks to our grandfather's little trust fund."

"Brilliant idea. Why don't you take care of organizing that? I'm good with whatever you assign me," said Mia.

"Me too. And while you work on that, I am finishing up a sightseeing plan for us. I have some really cool ideas on how to fit it all in. I, too, can be a wonderful organizer," Marissa declared with pride.

"Perfect. Let's get to work and then talk about it over dinner tonight."

I did everything I could to pull a chart together, but

between my wandering mind and the glorious kitchen smells, I was easily distracted. I could still see those exquisite baby blues looking at me with great humor. I felt the rush of embarrassment flush back into my cheeks in recollection of my girlish reaction.

What was it about this international lad that made me instantly giddy? This is not how a professional Senior VP acts! Where was my composure?

It didn't matter anyway. It's not like I'm going to see him again. I'm not one to really believe in all that destiny and serendipity crap. Like that was some kind of love at first sight moment and we would magically meet up again, fall in love and live happily ever after.

Grow back up, Megan. Get real.

Oh, who am I kidding? Deep down in my soul, as much as I resist it, I am a sucker for romance. Fine, I admit that when I am alone on the weekends, I watch those diabetically sweet and predictable television chick flicks and secretly wish for the iconic love story to enter my own life.

Thanks to my idyllic cable addiction, the idea of running into this beautiful stranger again in such a small town ignites fireworks in my soul. For too long I have suppressed the inner romantic in me, living in the reality of a man's world and jaded by the decline of gentlemen in my path.

I let my imagination wander about how it would feel to be held in those super strong arms and touched by those manly hands. Kissed by those full, satiable lips.

I could write a novel about this kind of once-in-a-lifetime experience. American girl meets Irish boy and he changes her life. She gives up her ambitious, corporate ways to choose love over power and prestige. Classic tale, but like all stories, they can be recreated with unique twists and turns. Before I knew it, I somehow had my laptop open and just started composing.

It had been years since I let myself write something other than a business report or ad proposal. A lifetime ago, I would have indulged in imaginative prose that brought me laughter and joy. It was a passion I subdued in pursuit of a better life for myself; one in which I could provide a solid foundation that I could be proud of.

But what had I sacrificed along the way? And why am I all of a sudden questioning my life decisions?

My queries were interrupted by the call to come to dinner. Quickly finishing up our chore distribution, I made my way down the creaky stairs.

"I found so many places that we can explore over here on the west coast," began Marissa, while I stepped in to help Mia serve what was undoubtedly going to be a fantastic dinner.

"I think our best bet is to sign up for one of these guided bus tours down the southwest coast," she continued. "It's five days long but will cover hot spots like the Cliffs of Moher, Galway City, the Hunt Museum, historic abbeys and the Blarney Castle. A little something for each of us."

"Five days is an awfully long time to just travel when we only have two weeks. We're here on a mission," Mia reminded her. I couldn't help but laugh—even now, she was such a mom.

"Yes, but I spoke with Colleen earlier today and she will be tied up for quite a few days. Something unexpected came up with her other cousins up in Newport and she told me we should do the tourist thing now," Marissa explained.

"If we are unable to get any answers, we might as well take advantage of this opportunity in front of us. I worked it out where if we leave tomorrow, we'll end up by the

Bunratty Castle for our dinner on Saturday and Colleen can meet us out there. At that point, we can wrap up our trip and head back with her."

"I think that sounds like great plan, Mar. We could all use the brainless activity before we get into whatever it is that really brought us here. I'm in!"

Mia looked up from serving the steaming shepherd's pie onto the dishes and smiled at us. "Okay then, count me in, too!"

We all turned to each other with a group high five, ready to take on Ireland.

7

Ireland was every bit as breathtaking as we imagined. Our first stop was in Connemara, known for representing true authentic Ireland heritage. On the border of counties Mayo and Galway, the wild, untamed landscapes were a vision to behold.

Here we experienced Killary Harbour, Ireland's only fjord. We opted for the 90-minute boat tour around the majestic scenery. Words could hardly describe the beauty of the countryside, which ebbed and flowed in an incredible range of colors—between the lush green hills, the naturally carved glacial shale stone edges and the glistening of the water.

We met a lovely couple, Eric and Daniel, who were from California and celebrating their honeymoon. Together we dined on the native mussels that were farmed from the harbor as we gleefully spotted a few otters and seals playing hide and seek in the water.

After our sea excursion, we indulged in the land's perspective of the harbor by taking a pony trek around the beaches and hills of Connemara. Although we were not avid horse riders, thankfully our ponies were mild and tame as they skillfully took us on a gorgeous seaside expedition.

It was a dream come true. Whoever would have thought in a million years that we would have a rich grandfather who would want us to indulge in this kind of life experience? As

I breathed in the views, I no longer felt guilty for doing so; I felt immense gratitude.

After spending the night at a traditional little bed and breakfast in a nearby fishing village, we ventured on further south with a stopover in the cultural destination of Galway City. We instantly fell in love with its artistic charm, which held a different intrigue for each of us.

I adored a medieval walking tour honoring historic Galway; Marissa was mesmerized by the Spanish Arch; and Mia couldn't get enough of the street markets and musicians as we tasted our way through the city.

We ended up at the iconic Cliffs of Moher a few hours before sunset, stumbling upon the most stunning vista I have ever witnessed in my entire life. We hiked up the South Platform, where we were able to see the acclaimed puffin colony on Goat Island and a strikingly clear panoramic view of O'Brien's Tower at the opposite side of the cliffs.

Fueled with energy and awe, we trekked on towards Hag's Head. There, up against the jagged edges of one of the resplendent cliffs overlooking the Atlantic Ocean, I could feel several lifetimes merging at once. The memory of it all blasted at me as hard as the winds that nearly knocked us over the cliff.

The magic in the air was undeniable. Rushing back to me were the ancient myths I remembered reading about when I was younger, during a time when I was so enthralled by everything Celtic. I'd read book after book about the legends and deities associated with the Emerald Isle.

At this very spot, it was said that the Tuatha Dé Danann fled on horse and fell over the edge, dubbing this the Leap of the Foals. Then there was the story about a fisherman who discovered and fell in love with a mermaid here. Or, my personal favorite, how beneath the sea sits the Lost

City of Kilstiffen, a kingdom that is said to return to its former glory once the golden key to the castle is found. I felt equally lost as I felt found right here in this very spot.

"Meg, are you okay?" Mia asked, breaking the silence. I had no idea that in my daydream, tears had started streaming faintly down my cheeks. I brought my finger up to touch one as I turned to face my two sisters.

"Oh! I guess I was so touched by it all, I hadn't even noticed I was crying! This place is just so—spellbinding. I feel like it isn't even real."

"I feel the same way. It's like you are transported to another space and time," Marissa agreed.

"Yeah. Exactly. I mean—this is going to sound odd. But do either of you feel like you have been here before?"

Marissa and Mia quickly exchanged puzzled looks. "Not really," said Marissa. "Why, do you?"

"Yes, and I can't explain it. I know it's crazy. But I feel this sense of home, this air of peace, being here in Ireland. It's the complete opposite of everything I am, all the hustle and bustle of a corporate life, always on the go. All of this makes me just want to stop and—I don't know—breathe it all in. Like all of this is enough."

"I don't think it's the complete opposite of everything you are, Meg," replied Mia, as she reached out to touch my arm. "I've known you all your life, remember? You are a strong girl with a tough outer shell of ambition, but you've hidden your true self behind that.

"The Megan I know inside is the sister who had a vivid imagination and who would write the most wild stories as a child. She stargazed with Daddy about exploring unknown worlds and loved storybook fantasies. The woman who doesn't even realize it, but purposely lives outside of the city and commutes because she can't live 24/7 in that crazy urban vibe."

She paused a moment, unsure of whether or not to continue her retrospect, but decided to do so soothingly.

"I know Scotty hurt you. I know you thought that you would spend your fairy tale life with him. When that jackass broke your heart, the only way you knew how to survive was to become tough. Don't you think it's time to let that hurt go and allow the inner Megan to come back out? Maybe that's why you feel at home here. Because when I see all of this, I see *you*."

I sunk down to the ground, the waterworks falling endlessly in hearty sobs as my sisters gathered around me and held me until I could weep no more. Mia knew me better than I knew myself.

Scotty had plunged a hole in my heart that I hardened and blocked through a career. Work never disappointed. I thrived at my job. There, no one could hurt me or take me down because I knew my worth. They'd never let me go because I was too valuable. They'd never replace me.

Or would they? Here I was in the stunning country of Ireland and one of the first anxieties to pop into my head was, what if they could carry on without me? What if they found out I *was* replaceable?

Scotty thought I was. He had no problem moving on with Bethany, marrying her within six months of us breaking up and starting the family I envisioned having with him.

Oh God, have I really been carrying this inside of me all this time? Did I turn myself into a workaholic not for power or prestige, but so that I wouldn't feel?

The realization clobbered me like a baseball bat to the head. I had given up my passion of writing because it would stir up emotions that I needed to keep buried. I cut myself off from the world and from love so I couldn't feel that pain ever again.

It was so overwhelming to bear this all at once. I had felt bits and pieces emerging ever since we landed, but in the solitude of the present moment, I was forced to face the entire puzzle of my life, whether I wanted to or not. The pain was being exorcised and I had no control.

I had no control.

That frightened me even more than heartbreak. I was all about control. I decided when, where, how. Emotions included. But now I was as vulnerable as I'd ever been in my life. I felt broken, the glass within me shattering. Completely fragmented.

"Oh Meg, I am so, so sorry. I should not have been so blunt. I don't know what came over me," Mia expressed regretfully as she sat alongside me.

"Please don't apologize, little sis." I squeezed her and Marissa's hands lightly. "You were only trying to help. And you were right. Everything you said was true. I have been suppressing it for so long that it had to be said. God, what a horrible sister I must have been this last decade."

"Eh, we got used to it," Marissa joshed. "But in all seriousness, I get it. Love is hard. We grew up watching a real-life Cinderella story in Mom and Dad, and for you and me, it hasn't panned out like that. I know Scotty really did a number on you, but he did it to us, too. He was like a brother to me and for him to walk out on all of us dealt a blow that I haven't quite recovered from either."

I looked up at her with a compassion I haven't had in years. I had such a low tolerance for this sister who was so unlike me, only now to realize that we have the same heart after all; we simply expressed our grief in different ways. I reached out and embraced her.

"I'm so sorry, Mar."

"It's okay. Maybe this is what we needed. Maybe this is what the trip is really about. Sure, you might get some cool ring at the end of this, but like we questioned before, it could have easily been shipped to us. Or you could have traveled here to recover it on your own, while Mia went to Italy and I went to Spain.

"We were meant to travel together on this adventure—an adventure designed to bring us closer together. Maybe even learn more about ourselves and support each other along the way. Maybe Grandfather Leigh really did have an inkling into who we were and what we needed in order to become the women we were meant to be—and Ireland is your place to discover you."

"That is uncharacteristically deep of you," I joked to break the uncomfortable heaviness of the moment as she rolled her eyes. "Kidding. I know how smart you are, Mar. And it's true. There is definitely more to this journey than an heirloom and a mystery."

"I'm just glad that you are the one to go first!" she countered.

With a burst of giggles, my sisters helped me up off the ground. We linked hands in an unbreakable bond, walking back down the cliffs as the sun set into gorgeous streams of red, orange and yellow.

As everyone from our group began the walk back to the bus, I asked my sisters to go on and leave me for a moment. I stood there in that mystical place, closing my eyes and taking a vow.

Here, I will leave behind the pain of the past. Here, I will release my broken heart and melt the ice that keeps the warmth away. Here, I will say goodbye to the dream of Scotty, who was not meant to be mine, and say hello instead to future love. Here, I will let the shell of control-freak Megan go and set my true self free.

It's time to honor who I am and fearlessly live the life I was meant to.

"A round of pints for everyone!" shouted Marissa, as she plopped down a wad of cash on the beer-soaked pub counter. Turning to us with pints of Guinness, she gleefully declared, "Tonight, we have earned the right to get knackered!"

It only took us four days before finally getting ourselves to an authentic pub. After the long, emotional day, I was certainly grateful for the change in atmosphere and some brain numbing. The music and crowd were lively and loud, as was expected for an Irish tavern.

Beer was splashing, laughter was roaring all around and people were dancing and cheering like life was the grandest thing on earth. It was hard not to fall into the easygoing charm of it all.

"What should we drink to?" Mia asked.

"Living in the moment," I responded.

They nodded their heads in agreement and with a raising of the glasses, we exclaimed, "To living in the moment!"

We found a somewhat quiet little corner nook to settle down with our beers and order some food, since we were absolutely starving. I decided on classic fish and chips, while Mia delighted in ordering an oak grilled salmon and Marissa a burger—which she never had a chance to eat because she ended up dancing with some hot Irishman who was bedazzled by her exotic looks.

Before we knew it, she was running over to let us know what room she was going to be staying in that night—

instead of with us—and warned us to make sure to get her in the morning before the bus left. *Ah, Marissa.*

Left alone with Mia, we enjoyed our meal while being surrounded by the liveliness of the scene. Oh how we relished the dancing, the drinking and the jolly good cheer of contagious laughter. The Irish really know how to live in joy, and it was inspiring.

I hoped that I could keep my vow to let that part of me back out. But I could feel the weight of the emotional release taking a toll on my energy level and knew I wouldn't be able to hold out much longer. My battery was draining quicker than a car whose headlights were left on.

"You know, I really am sorry I said all that earlier. But I am glad that I was able to see a glimpse of the old Meg back there. I just want to see you happy again."

"I know. I do, too. When you went back to the bus, I stood there and made a promise to myself to let go of past hurts and open my heart again. There's just something about this place that makes it seem easier to do than when I'm home."

"That's good! And who knows, maybe you will be the next one to meet a sexy Irishman!"

"Well…" I broke off, not meaning to drop the hint, but in my fatigued, alcohol-induced state, it just came out.

"Megan! What do you mean, 'well?'"

"Well…okay. I didn't really want to tell you guys about it, because it was nothing. It's so silly, really. Not exactly like taking off for a tumultuous night of passion like Marissa just did."

"Oh shut it, Meg and tell me!"

"Okay, okay! You win." I took a deep breath—why was I so nervous about telling the story?

"When I went down to the market the other day, I ran

into this really good-looking local—literally, as in I ran over his foot. Oh my gosh Mia, he was absolutely dreamy, like out of a Gaelic *GQ Magazine*. I don't remember the last time a man made me so nervous!

"I was trying to figure out where everything was and I ended up backing into him. I then fumbled all my words and couldn't speak. Me, speechless! Imagine that."

"Uh, actually, I can't. Wow—so what happened?"

"I managed to get out a few audible words as these piercingly magnificent eyes stared right through me. Mia, I can't even describe it—I felt like I was back in high school when Scotty first walked by, but even more intense. Plus, he was funny and kind and made me feel comfortable even in all my gibberish."

"Ooh, sounds sexy. So, did you get his name? Are you going to see him again?"

"His name is Kieran. I highly doubt I'll ever randomly run into him again. Plus, he's probably married or has a girlfriend, anyway. It was just some chance encounter at the market and memories to keep me warm for a few days. That's all.

"But it was really nice to feel butterflies again. I haven't felt that in a while. It's what placed me onto this emotional rollercoaster of mixed feelings right now."

"Okay, so we need to go back and find this Kieran fellow then. Meg, you can't just give up!"

"Don't be silly. What am I going to do, track down every Kieran in the country until I find the right one? I can't get caught up in silly impulsive illusions."

I held my hand up before she could speak. "No. I can't do that to myself right now. There is a difference between me realizing that I need to heal the past and open back up for love versus going on a wild goose chase after a mystery man I just met."

"Okay, fine. But would it hurt for you to explore the men here in the meantime? You don't need to worry about me. Go out and enjoy yourself tonight."

"Thanks, but I'm not in the mood. There's more to what I'm feeling than casual sex. I don't want a random fling anymore that leaves my heart cold long after he leaves my bed. I actually want to meet someone sincere for a change. Like I'd rather have no one instead of a wrong one. Know what I mean?"

"Actually, I do." She said, kind of pensively. Now is my chance to dig deep and find out what was up with her before we were all interrupted that Sunday evening.

"Hey, we've been talking so much about me on this trip that I haven't asked how you've been doing."

"I'm fine. You know, same old."

"No Mia, don't pull that shit with me. Do you really think I didn't notice your mood before Joshua Perkins knocked on your door and dropped this mystery on us? Spill it. What's going on with you?"

"Nothing really. Just frustrated with Kevin always being out of the house with his new promotion and training. I mean, I am happy for him, of course, but I'd be lying if I said I wasn't a little bit jealous."

"Have you given any thought to opening up your restaurant like you always wanted to?"

"I have, but not sure what good thinking about it will do me. With Kevin out of the house so much now, the kids rely on me even more to get them back and forth to color guard and soccer and math tutoring and all that. I barely have time to read a book, let alone think about starting a new business. I just don't think it's in the cards for me."

"Why not? Why should you have to put your life on

hold forever? The kids are older now—surely there are carpools you can get involved in or they can Uber to where they need to go."

Mia rolled her eyes at the mere thought of the children being inconvenienced in any way. "Yeah, right. As if!"

"Well, if there is anything I can do to help, just let me know. I'm here for you."

"I know and I appreciate that. There is just a lot I need to work through. It's not just the restaurant thing. I've actually come to terms with that. It's just that I'm feeling more and more like a single mom instead of a married woman." I couldn't believe she was opening up like this— that this was repressed inside her all this time. God bless Guinness. Why do we do this to ourselves?

"I do everything to keep the house running and my family satisfied, but no one is around to spend any time with me. Like I'm just their servant. The kids are always out with their friends or at after school programs and Kevin is always working. I can't even remember the last time we spent a night together."

She looked up at me as the embarrassment rushed to her face. My heart was breaking for her.

"I'm so sorry, Mi. I had no idea things had gotten so bad. I guess I'm just so absorbed in my own little world, and imagine you and Kevin have this perfect life, that I don't check in with you enough." I reached for her with a big bear hug.

"I'm really sorry and I am going to do better. Anything I can do for you?"

"No, but thank you. I really needed this trip. I didn't grasp how much I did until I got here. I am so glad you all pushed me to go. Maybe I can find myself again like you are finding yourself."

"No doubt you will. We are all in this together. Have you talked to Kevin about this—about how you feel?"

"I try, but he is always so exhausted when he gets home that he just wants to eat and go to bed. It's like I need to make an appointment with my own husband to even ask, 'How was your day?'"

"Well, maybe when you get back, you should insist on taking a day for you both to spend together. I'll volunteer to run the kids wherever they need to go and you both can just go out on a date and talk."

She smiled big. "I might just take you up on that offer. I think we would both like that.

"Okay," she added. "Enough about our sorrows. Let's grab another drink and get out on that dance floor before we call it a night, shall we?"

Early the next morning, we met up with Marissa at the bus and the smirk on her face told us all we needed to know. She wasn't too forthcoming with the details, but she did say she enjoyed her night and that she was easily falling in love with Ireland.

That love was deepened the moment we stepped off the bus and onto the pavement in front of the Hunt Museum in Limerick—flood lights couldn't compare to the brightness in her eyes. Her enthusiasm was contagious as she lovingly dragged us from exhibit to exhibit, oo-ing about the European medieval statues and ah-ing over ancient Egyptian artifacts.

Then came the squeals of delight as she entered the worlds of Picasso, Renoir and Moore; she could have stayed in there for hours looking at a single painting. Although art is not my thing, I did find myself in awe of the grandiose masterpieces that stood before me. Such heartfelt innovations preserved with such care.

The tour of the museum wouldn't have been complete without a stop in the gift shop to purchase a few framed prints that would look great in her living room, a series of Picasso cards and an oversized ceramic mug for her morning coffee. After grabbing a quick snack, we headed back to the bus to continue south to County Cork.

Since there is so much to do and not enough time for us to dig deep into everything we wanted to see, we decided to stick to either the classic touristy places or indulge in a unique experience. So in Cork, instead of seeing more museums, we opted to take a few smaller excursions throughout the city to encounter the culture.

With tons of energy, we started off with Mia's choice of exploration—a four-hour walking tour through the English Market, where we tasted our way through the city with cheeses, fresh oysters from the Atlantic Bay and sinfully-rich chocolates. We ended the jaunt with a full gourmet meal and local brew, which left us completely stuffed, but happy.

It didn't take much for Marissa to then nudge us onto a quick beer and whiskey tour, where we witnessed the brewing process and enjoyed world class samplings.

Although the amount of food we ate diminished our energy into a walking coma, I guilted my sisters into joining me on a fun ghost story evening stroll through an old part of town. Nothing like spooky tales to get you ready for bed—especially those laced with a bit o' truth (or so they say).

By day four of our journey, we were starting to feel the fatigue from being on-the-go so much, but how could we not absolutely love all that we were experiencing? Today was declared "castle day"—one I was very much looking forward to. The itinerary called for a tour of the Blarney Castle in the morning and then the long trip back up to Bunratty Castle for dinner.

Blarney holds such rich history and legend. The moment I began walking through the Garden of the Seven Sisters, I was enchanted. I didn't expect to ever be so fond of a single place on earth.

I was especially drawn to the lore of the witch who was said to inhabit the Rock Close area of the castle grounds. Rumor claims she is trapped within the large stone alongside her kitchen, tasked with granting the wishes of those who travel up and down her bewitched stairs. As a sucker for legends and magic, I took on the dare by my sisters to re-enact the wishing ritual.

I walked all the way up and then, quite awkwardly, all the way down the stairs backwards with my eyes closed, focusing only on the silly old desire of my childhood: to meet my own prince charming and live happily ever after.

Smiling at the thought, I winked at the bottom of the stairs as a challenge to the witch to bring forth my intention within the next year. I knew that it wasn't possible, but it was a nice change of pace to allow myself to be so innocently lighthearted. I could stand to lose some of my seriousness.

The energy of the ancient witch and Druid lore was all around. Exploring the different areas, we came upon the eerie Druid Cave, colorful Fairy Glade, the creepy Sacrificial Altar and the legendary Witch Stone, where I placed a few pennies in homage, as I wished for her own release. I could have sworn her apparition swirled around me in a ghostly hug.

We then walked through part of the majestic gardens,

which could only be touched upon in the short amount of time we had left to spend there. We decided to stick to the Bog Garden area, enjoying the views of its two waterfalls, 600-year-old yew trees and a willow tunnel at the end of the path's boardwalk. I could tell this was where Mia wanted to venture for hours.

I didn't even know this kind of beauty existed in this world. There was so much more to see, but not enough hours to see it all.

We ended our time at the castle with—you guessed it—the climb up the steps to the infamous Blarney Stone. Now, there was no way that I was going to lean backwards over an edge (even if now safely enclosed with an iron railing) to touch my mouth to that bacteria-festering icon, but Marissa was game.

We encouraged her to go for it, as out of all of us, she was the one who could certainly use the promised gift of eloquence. That comment got me a playful punch as she conceded in agreement.

A light picnic lunch in the gardens ended our time in County Cork before we began the over four-hour trip back up towards Bunratty Castle. It was an unusually tranquil ride for us. Marissa had fallen asleep, Mia was reading her book and I found myself staring out of the window in reflection of all that had happened over just a few short days.

Mostly, I was in awe of how serene I felt. How at home I was. How enraptured by everything I had just witnessed in my mini circuit of this beautiful country. I could feel the magic in my veins, coursing through like a moonlit lake of fairy dusted potion.

Something in the air had awakened the essence of my soul and it called to me to play. My inner child couldn't help but want to run out in the middle of a meadow and sing; to stop and smell the unique perfumes of the flowers; or to write stories about the forbidden romance locked within the history of the castle ruins. Without my laptop on me, I settled for a journal I had in my bag and just let the words flow through me.

We arrived at Bunratty Castle just before sunset. It was as glorious a fortress as I could have ever imagined—right out of one of the childhood books Mom used to read to me. Structurally sound and well preserved, it was hard to believe that this was originally built in the early 1200's.

Oh, I just couldn't wait to get in there and experience the food and the music—and the renowned honey mead. What a great way to end our first little trip.

My thoughts were interrupted by Marissa's phone ringing. A few moments later, she rejoined us.

"That was Colleen. She'll be here soon—she's running just a bit behind. She's bringing a friend so she didn't have to drive up alone, which delayed her a bit. I already worked out an extra ticket, so that's taken care of."

"Oh, I'm glad. I was a bit worried about her making the trip. Though I suppose she is a pretty strong woman who can take care of herself," said Mia.

We walked over the stone drawbridge towards the Irish palace, checking in at the entrance and sneaking a peek at the neighboring gift shop. We then were escorted through the gardens to the castle itself, where we patiently waited outside as instructed until Colleen and her friend could join us.

I was overwhelmed with the historical architecture of this ancient structure and imagined what it would have been like to grow up as a princess in these halls. What marvelous balls they might have held. What scandals lived within the walls. A few minutes later, my reverie was broken by the excited babbling of our beloved cousin right behind us.

"Well, if this isn't a wonderful sight! Blessed be! Did you all have a grand time? I'm delira ta hear about all of it!" We all stepped in to hug and kiss her, excitedly starting to talk over each other about our favorite parts of our expedition, not noticing her friend coming up from behind.

"So, these must be the American cousins you have told me all about," he interrupted in introduction. My heart stopped instantly—I knew that voice.

"Feck, I am such an eejit! Forgive me my manners. Yes, this be Marissa, Mia and Megan, though I still have difficulty sometimes rememberin' which is which. Cousins, this lad here be my good friend, Kieran MacGovern," she said fondly. "He be our prince charmin' tonight, that he will."

With a wickedly playful smile that showed off his chiseled cheekbones, he turned to take my hand to raise it up to his soft lips and kiss it before bringing those extraordinary eyes back up to meet mine. "Hello again, Miss Megan."

With one look, I immediately felt starstruck and at home all at once. If ever there was a time to believe in Irish folklore, this was it. *Damn, that Blarney witch worked fast.*

8

"Ay, so you know each other already? Fancy that! What's the story?" asked Colleen, as our entire audience watched us, locked in the moment like a frozen computer screen.

Still in shock, I was grateful that Kieran answered for us.

"We met the other day down by the market, when she backed up and over my foot with the trolley," he chuckled in remembrance, which only made me fluster even more.

"I'm so sorry, again," I managed. "How is your foot?"

"I'm no worse for the wear, lass."

"Would ya get outta that garden! Kieran, ya real cute hoor. All this time ye be knowin' Miss Megan would be here and you never let on? Quite the clever man, this one is. Is that why you was slyly askin' about whether me cousins were taken or not?"

Now it was his turn to flush slightly. Colleen was not one for subtlety, that's for certain. Did he really know I would be here? Did he come to see *me?*

I wanted to throw up. Thankfully, Mia stepped in to rescue us all from the awkward silence.

"Colleen, why don't you come with me up the stairs to the Green Hall? I bet you know the best spot to view the pre-show. Marissa, why don't you head up first to make sure the stairwell is clear?" she hinted.

Marissa started to protest, but then caught the glare of her older sister beckoning her to join them. With a confused look back up at me and Kieran, she obliged, though I could hear the questioning whispers as they walked away.

I looked up to see Kieran smiling down at me. I didn't realize how even a few inches could make a man appear so much taller, towering over me like the Empire State Building.

"I believe I told you I'd be seein' you again."

"Did you really know I'd be here?"

"I did. When Colleen told me all about your little adventure to the castle and then droned on about how she had to drive up here all by her lonesome, I offered to accompany her. I'm sorry if I've made you uncomfortable, *a ghrá*."

My love? The Irish sure were friendly and free with their endearments. And yet, it made me melt faster than global warming.

"No, not at all. Just—surprised. I didn't think we'd ever meet again." Something about his name sounded familiar though, I realized. "MacGovern? I've heard that name before."

"MacGovern I am. I'm after taking care of the house you are stayin' in. Perhaps you heard a bit about my mum's cookin', too."

"Yes, that's it! So that explains why you knew Colleen when I mentioned her and were so confident you would see me again. And here I thought it was some kind of destiny," I teased.

His laid-back mannerisms made it easy to begin to relax around him. The edginess I felt was slowly dissolving away into a sense of comfort.

"Maybe it *is* destiny," he replied, looking back at me

intently—my comfort slowly fading away again. How can anyone have this kind of intensity in a single look? It could inspire the earth to rumble and quake.

My sister's call broke the spell again as I landed back on my proverbial feet.

"We're all set. Follow me!" announced Marissa, who didn't miss a beat in sending me a wink now that she was obviously all caught up. I'll have to remember to thank Mia later for saving me the repeat conversation and Spanish Inquisition.

"Shall we?" Kieran asked, as he placed his strong hand on the small of my back to lead me up the very tight, winding stone staircase to the Green Hall. The mere touch of him sent shivers down my spine as heat rose up throughout the rest of my body like ascending lava.

We were greeted by the dinner hosts—the Earl's butlers and ladies of the house dressed in medieval garb—with a glass of honey mead, the sweetness and strength of which made my head spin just a little bit more than the intoxication of Kieran's presence. I'll admit that it was so good, I snuck an extra mug of it when no one else was looking. Liquid courage was on my menu for the evening.

The beauty and intricacy of the Green Hall's carved walls left us feeling astounded. The colors of the fabric tapestries were richly gold with designs of reds, greens and purples—truly royal hues. The stained glass windows, expertly hand-designed furniture pieces and photos of ancestral stories brought the heritage of the castle to life.

As I closed my eyes to snap it into a photo in my mind, I could hear the pre-show music playing. I imagined I was back at some ancient royal gala and instinctively started to sway. Marissa was the one to catch me before I bumped into a stranger.

"You okay?" she wondered in amusement.

"I'm grand," I smiled back. "Oh Mar, isn't this place so amazing? I could have been a princess in this very castle in a past life. Could you imagine?"

"You being a princess? Yes. Finding you like this, all silly and carefree right now? No. But it is nice to see," she added with a rub to my back. "You deserve to be happy. Maybe your story is just beginning," she said with a blatant nod over to Kieran.

We both looked across the room, watching him laugh heartily as he greeted and interacted with strangers like he'd known them forever. His mere existence lit up the hall, not just for me, but seemingly for anyone who met him. Not unlike how Daddy could charm a room, I noted.

The air was bursting with joy and camaraderie unlike any event or party I'd ever been to. Kieran glanced over to catch us watching him and before I could blush, he raised his mug of honey mead with a wink and Cheshire cat smile before greeting another passerby with Gaelic glee.

It was finally time to gather around our table for the banquet to begin. The hall was set up with rows of long wooden tables and benches surrounded by the magnificent décor of feudal times, whisking me back to another time and space.

Kieran, clearly a gentleman, escorted all of us women to our bench seats before strategically taking his place beside me. We chitchatted with other out-of-towners who were seated at our table until the festivities were ready to start.

A group of young college-aged friends were backpacking through all of Ireland on their spring break. A mother and daughter were celebrating a very special birthday. It was extraordinary to hear the stories of how others were brought here this very same night.

The Earl welcomed us with great fanfare while castle nobility sang and entertained us as we enjoyed our four-course feast (without silverware!). The tables were lit solely by candlelight for a truly antiquated, intimate feel.

It was a wonderful evening of mirth as we were serenaded by the famous Bunratty Castle Singers. I could feel the emotion rise to my eyes as I heard their angelic voices harmonize *Danny Boy* with such grace and beauty.

I felt Kieran reach for my hand under the table and give it a squeeze. I didn't even have to look at him to know he was equally moved by the musical synchronizations. I let my hand fall naturally into his as we enjoyed the show in between dinner and dessert.

From time to time, he would turn to me and we would talk about how he came to know Colleen, or I'd share some of my favorite adventures from the past few days as a tourist. Kieran seemed to get along rather well with my sisters, too, taking an interest in learning about Mia's children and enduring Marissa's gushing over her Hunt Museum experience and lifelong dream to become an artist.

If he only realized the true way to a girl's heart is through her sisters, then he'd know how sweet this moment was for me.

I didn't want the night to end. Not only because it was one of the most captivating dinner experiences I ever attended, but because of Kieran himself. A certain level of mystique was added to the evening with him being there beside me, secretly holding my hand out of view like we were forbidden lovers.

Yes—I was the countess and he was just some peasant man who stole my heart. I'd sneak out of my stone tower to meet him by the creek for a starlit night of passionate kisses. If I believed in past lives, I could imagine we did in fact live another story together.

Saddened that dessert was over, I wasn't ready for the fairy tale finale quite yet. I enjoyed playing pretend in my mind; a pastime I had long forgotten in exchange for cunning advertising and ruthless advancement.

"That would be a fierce performance! I enjoyed that I did, I did! Thank you for invitin' me. We best be off, though," Colleen said as she grabbed a complimentary coffee on our way out of the castle.

"So soon?" Mia asked on my behalf.

"Colleen here has her Sunday mass early in the morning. I promised to get her home for a decent night's rest," Kieran replied.

He turned to each one of us girls and kissed our hands. "Thank you for allowing me the pleasure of your company. I hope to see you again," he added, lingering a bit longer on my hand before the electricity turned back to darkness with his departure.

I wasn't going to get any sleep that night with all the thoughts and feelings rushing through my head— or Marissa's demands to fill her in completely. So, we extended our night by making the customary post-banquet stop at Durty Nelly's for a drink and sisterly conversation.

"Mia only filled me in enough to understand what was going on. Now dish it!"

Laughing, I told her the story until she was satisfied that she heard enough.

"So, you had no idea he was the caretaker when you met him? How sweet of him to try to see you again. I was watching him—he seems smitten with you." Mia observed in her cop-like way.

"Smitten? What are we, in grammar school?"

"I'm just saying that it's not in a way most guys look at girls these days. You could tell there was an attraction, but a respectful one. Not one of 'I want to get in her pants' but one of 'I'm intrigued by her.' Smitten seems to fit the bill.

"Plus, Colleen confirmed he was single and contrary to his looks, not a ladies man—except when it comes to charming old bitties, as she put it," she teased.

"I have to agree, Meg," Marissa chimed in. "He is quite the gentleman, though I'm pretty sure he wouldn't mind getting in your pants," she corrected. "I liked him very much."

"He does seem like a decent guy, doesn't he?"

"So, what's next?"

"I don't know. I mean, let's be real. We only have a little more than a week left here and then we're home and I'm back to the grind. I'm not sure I want to make a big deal of this. Maybe I should just accept this as one magical night and let it be."

"You could play it safe like you always do, sure," chided Marissa. "But what if you just let yourself take a chance for once. Who cares if you never see him after this trip?

"Why can't you just let down your guard and allow yourself to enjoy the romance of it all? Why do you have to see where this fits into your perfectly laid out future? You are here right now. The present moment is all you have—for once, just make the most of it."

"I know. I did just make a promise to myself to open up more and take new risks. I'm not going to chase him down, though. If our paths cross again, then I'll just take it from there."

"Oh, your paths will cross again. I know it," reassured Mia, like she had access to her own personal crystal ball.

The next morning, we found the road back to County Mayo to be relatively uneventful. The bus made a few stops along the way for some last-minute sightseeing, including to the pilgrimage sites of the Holy Mountain of Croagh Patrick and Our Lady of Knock—a famous shrine citing that Jesus, the Blessed Virgin Mary, Saint Joseph and Saint John the Evangelist once appeared there. I couldn't imagine ever having enough time to truly see all the wonders this country had to offer.

After what seemed like countless hours on a bus, we finally arrived back at the house shortly before dinner, grateful to settle into something more familiar and less over-populated. We were greeted by a handwritten note left by Kieran, welcoming us back and letting us know that his mum's colcannon fish pie need only be heated up for dinner tonight.

I was more than a little disappointed to have missed him and that there wasn't a personal touch to his note. Maybe it was just going to be that one charming evening after all.

We unpacked, ate the delicious dinner left for us and engaged in some light conversation about the highlights of our trip. We were pretty worn out from the travels but were looking forward to finally getting down to business.

Colleen was supposed to come over the next evening to begin sharing some of the family stories and the purpose of us being here. I admit that I had forgotten all about it on our cyclone of a tourist tour.

I chose to sleep in the next morning, awakening to the sounds of Mia humming in the backyard garden below. I peeked out the window to see her happily pulling up the very few weeds that existed, smelling the flowers in her path and selecting a few for what I could only guess would be for tonight's table arrangement.

Marissa was further back towards the end of the yard in what appeared to be a flirtatious phone conversation, fingers twirling through her dark, loose tendrils. Curious. I wonder if that was her new little country lover or maybe Jay. Well, whoever it was, she was happy, and I was happy for her.

I strolled down the stairs to find a still-hot pot of coffee and kettle of water awaiting me. I chose a traditional black tea alongside a blueberry muffin with butter for breakfast. Not wanting to disturb my sisters or my solitude, I snuck outside to sit on the rocking chair, journal in hand, to get lost in some writing.

About an hour or so later, Marissa and Mia found me and shared the news that Colleen would not be able to meet up with us for another few days, as a house emergency came up that she had to tend to; something about her wretched plumbing.

Marissa wanted to take the opportunity to check out Clare Island for the next few days and booked a room at the Lighthouse, not knowing when we'd get the chance again to do more exploring.

"It is supposed to have the most spectacular sights! Since we've been so busy, I selected the spa relaxation package so that we could enjoy the tranquility of the scenery while we are there."

"I'm not up for another adventure just yet. Would you mind if I stayed behind?" The thought of traveling again was unsettling, even if it was a promise of a retreat. So much had happened in the past few weeks—so many emotions and revelations—that I craved some time alone to review it all.

"Of course," said Mia. "We are leaving this afternoon and will be back Tuesday night. If you change your mind, just let us know and you can always meet us there."

"That's a great idea. Maybe I will do that. I just need some time to myself. A lot to think about."

"We completely understand," Marissa agreed. "Oh, by the way, while I was walking this morning, a neighbor of ours—Mr. O'Dooly I think his name was—stopped to say hello. He was saying something about being a longtime friend of the family's and that he would be happy to check on the house while we were gone. Is it me or are people overly friendly and up in everyone's business over here?"

"Seems to be the way here," I chuckled. Every local was a town crier.

"Yeah well, just be careful, Meg," she cautioned. "He seemed harmless enough but was a little too interested in knowing why we're here and mentioned something about unusual activity in the neighborhood lately. Just stay safe."

"I will. I promise."

With a big bear hug from each, they were excitedly off to pack for their next escapade. I realized that meant I would be on my own for the first Sunday dinner in a very long time, but there were enough ingredients around for me to toss together something simple. I'd have to go back to the market tomorrow, but I had plenty to hold me over for today.

The thought of going there sent a whole garden of butterflies coursing through my stomach again. *Does Kieran go to the market every day? Would I run into him?*

Nonsense. I can't spend my entire time in sanctuary thinking about this man and wondering if fate would bring us together again. I actually had plans for something else while the girls were away—to dig into that attic.

I couldn't wait until Tuesday for Colleen—Mr. O'Dooly wasn't the only one curious about why we were here. *I need some answers now,* I said to myself as I looked up at the hauntingly beautiful portrait of my great-great-grandparents.

The house was unnervingly still with only the sounds of the rickety floors. It was a moment mystery novels thrived on, which made it all the more spine-chilling yet exciting at the same time. To calm my nerves, I pretended it was good old cousin Shane just checking in on me.

I found a large flashlight in one of the kitchen cupboards and armed myself with it as I ventured upstairs to the attic. It was just as I expected: dark, full of cobwebs and with treasures waiting to be discovered.

There were boxes of papers, a few old trinkets collecting dust here and there and some old, worn-out clothes. I wondered to myself why this stuff just wasn't thrown out or given away instead. I did happen upon a few exquisite dresses and hats that I imagined were quite the fashion back in the day.

Being a child at heart, I decided to try one of the dresses on. One was a royal blue, long-sleeved satin gown with intricate white lace overlaying the heart-shaped, form-fitting bodice. White sheer fabric flowed over the sleeves for an air of elegance. The bottom of the gown fell slightly past my ankles, trimmed with more lace in a whimsical floral pattern. Built-in ruffles underneath gave the dress volume and I felt like I was ready to go to a grand gala.

Needing to check my reflection and verify my newly

imagined life as courtier, I carefully managed to get myself and this massive gown down the attic stairs and into my bedroom to take a peek in the full-length mirror. I decided to undo my ponytail so that my natural curls flowed over the shoulders of the dress freely.

I have to say, I couldn't help but admire how I looked in the medieval fabric. The coloring brought out the deepest hues in my eyes and its shape hugged my curves in all the right places.

Feeling noble, I twirled and curtsied, holding my hand out as if the imaginary prince standing there was waiting to kiss it and ask me to dance.

"Why, I would be honored to have this dance with you," I said out loud as I embraced an invisible lover in my arms and began to waltz. He twirled me around like the wind scooping up the fallen leaves.

I jumped when I saw Kieran standing in my bedroom doorway with an amused look on his face.

"You scared me half to death! What are you doing here?" Hand to my heart, I made my way over to the bed to catch my breath.

"I'm sorry, I didn't mean to frighten you. I didn't know anyone was here. Colleen told me you went off to Clare Island, so I'm after finishing up some work on the deck out back. I heard some noise inside and I thought I would come check it out. Seems like I interrupted a very important dance lesson," he said, suppressing a chortle.

"I was—um—I was up in the attic and found this dress and guess I just got caught up in the moment. I can't even begin to tell you how mortified I am." Still standing leaned up against the doorway, he traded his playfulness for a more serious, temperate tone.

"Don't be. You're not the only one to be found caught

up in the moment. I thought ye an *aisling*."

"What's an ash-ling?"

"A vision. Megan, I didn't know if you were real until you started dancin'. You are the most beautiful woman I have ever seen."

He cautiously yet purposefully moved into the bedroom towards me. I was completely frozen as if trapped under ice. He stood just an inch away as he ran his fingers through my hair and caressed my cheek. He took my hand in his to lift me off the bed until I was only a breath away.

"I haven't been able to stop thinking about you and those eyes since that day at the market, *a ghrá*. You are unlike any woman I have ever met."

"I am?"

"Indeed." We locked gazes for a moment and the world stopped. He gently weaved his hand through the back of my hair to draw me closer as his lips touched mine. They were soft and full with the strength of a man but the restraint of a saint.

He lingered ever so lightly, letting me set the pace and intensity of our first kiss as he never once took those mesmerizing eyes off mine. With all the passion I never knew was inside of me, I drew him closer and gave him all of me in that single kiss.

I could feel the roughness of his unshaved scruff against my skin, heightening the raw desire within. The smell of his pure masculine muskiness played with my senses, driving me to the brink of insanity. I pressed my body up against his, feeling the hardness of his chest muscles even through the layers of dress that separated our skin from touching. I ached for more.

Our lips parted, allowing our tongues to intertwine, seek, explore—setting off tiny explosions within my body.

The heat rose between us, the natural voltage uniting more than just our lips. His hands, no longer tangled in my hair, took my face as he pulled away gently, pressing his lips to my nose and then tenderly to my forehead.

Why was he stopping? I didn't want it to ever end. As if he could read my mind, his broken, spent voice whispered, "Slow *a ghrá*, and let us savor this. 'It takes time to build castles.'"

I recognized the old Irish proverb from one of Granny's many teachings. How romantically clever of him. Pausing only to run his fingers through my hair and kiss my cheek once more, he started to turn away.

"Where are you going?" I asked, breathless.

"I think it best that you get yourself out of that dress before I do it for ya, lass. Meet me downstairs when you're ready. I want to show you something."

Obligingly, I grabbed a pair of jeans and a form-fitting green sweater from the top of the dresser drawer, fixed my hair and makeup and went down to the back door where Kieran was waiting for me. He took my hand and led me towards the back of the yard, where an enormous peach and fuchsia-colored rosebush was the spotlight of another well-groomed garden I hadn't yet noticed.

"I grew up hearing stories of the legendary love between your great-great grandparents, Cian and Alessia. One of them was this here rose bush that they planted together. Now any true gardener can tell you a good solid rose bush can last only up to thirty-five or forty years, but not this one.

"Over a hundred years this one would be. Tended with love by the families that followed, stowing blessings upon the caregivers. It's become its own folklore around here."

"It's so beautiful. I've never seen roses that color

before. They're so unique. Do you really think they are the original roses planted?"

"Ay. Love has a way of making things everlasting. Even if this bush here was actually replanted in secret several times over the years by new generations," he hinted, "it blooms nevertheless in the same sacred spot. Its magic has already taken hold."

"This entire country seems magical," I said wistfully. "How much do you know about my ancestors?"

"Not much. Just a bit here and there. From what I do know, there is rumored a scandal behind their love story— quite the holy show. I've always had a bit of curiosity about it, I have, but too much respect for the O'Sullivans and Collins' to be nosy about their business."

"Collins? Who's that?"

"Oh, that be Colleen's mother, Mary Collins, who married the old Banan O'Sullivan III. That's who she be living with now—her cousins on her mother's side. Ain't nary an O'Sullivan left, aside from Colleen and you all. Her dear brother Shane and his family tragically died in a boating accident off the shore of the Atlantic about ten years back. Nearly drowned herself in tears with grief. Which is why I reckon she was so tickled to learn of your existence."

"How horrible! To lose a brother and his whole family like that? The more I hear, the more I realize I have yet to learn. That's why I was up in the attic before. I thought maybe I could find something to tell me a little bit more about our family history before Colleen has the chance to fill us all in.

"I feel so drawn here. I can't explain it Kieran, but I feel like I'm home, like I'm already part of the story."

"I find that enthralling. Say, would you like some help

up there digging around? The deck can wait a bit more. If it's not an intrusion," he added considerately.

"I would love that, thank you. There were some boxes that were a bit on the heavy side for me. From what I can tell, you seem to have strong arms," I said, suggestively running my fingers down his shoulder all the way to his fingers.

I entwined them with mine as I smiled wickedly, feeling my confidence around him beginning to grow. "Let's go unravel a mystery."

9

Having someone who knew the ins and outs of the house was coming in fairly handy. Kieran scored another flashlight and an extension cord that let us light up the attic better with a small lamp. Amidst the dresses I had found earlier were more boxes—old kitchenware, some clothes bins and quite a few heavy loads of books.

I'm not sure what I was looking for—and even less sure of what I had gotten myself into. We spent a good part of an hour just looking through some of the box contents, sharing a few laughs about what we found but nothing that stood out as anything special.

That is, until I came across this one particularly small box marked "AO" in calligraphy. I opened it up to discover a bunch of old photos.

"Check this out."

"Ah, that be the same couple as photographed above the mantel. Quite the beautiful pair, for sure. You have his eyes, you know."

"I thought so, too. So, that's Cian and Alessia. And then here's Cian with another blonde man who looks just like him—do you know who that is?"

"I'd venture to say that's his older brother, Banan Junior—Colleen's granda."

"And here they are with a little girl—I think that might be my great-grandmother, Lena. Grandfather Leigh's mother."

"I'd wager you're right."

"She's beautiful. She reminds me of Mia." I turned over the back to read the inscription and froze.

"What is it, *a ghrá*?"

"Nothing. Just that it says Mama, Papa and Diamond. That's what our grandfather used to call my mother before—before he took off and left her."

I couldn't control the bitterness that crept up inside me. All this heritage and we never knew about it. Heritage that our mother missed out on all these years.

"What do you suppose…" he asked as he pulled out a weathered leather-bound book from underneath the photos.

"It looks like a journal. Do you think it's okay to look at it?" There was something unsettling about finding someone's private thoughts in an attic—even if the ancestor died close to one hundred years ago.

"I don't see the harm in it." He handed it over to me so that I could open it, revealing a cover page with the name Alessia Bianchi originally written on it, but the Bianchi was crossed out and replaced by O'Sullivan. The first page was dated March 19, 1892. I couldn't help but stare at the perfection in her handwriting.

"You know what? Why don't we bring this box downstairs and get outta this manky attic? I'm famished— let's grab a bite before we dig into this, shall we?"

"That sounds like a good idea. I know we have some ingredients on hand to whip up an easy pot pie. I'm not much of a cook, but I can definitely handle that."

"Sounds grand. I'll grab a bottle of wine or two. Looks like we might be needing it tonight."

The evening was an unexpected pleasure. While I was preparing dinner, Kieran had taken it upon himself to lay out a beautiful place setting with some white lace mats and napkins from one of the cupboards. Wine glasses were already filled with the souvenir honey mead we picked up from our Bunratty adventure.

Two single, tall-tiered candles sat upon silver holders giving the room a soft glow. In the background I could hear the sounds of Celtic instruments crooning their love songs. It made me wish my dinner itself had the same kind of amorous flare.

"My, aren't you talented at setting a mood," I teased. "No doubt this is how you get all your women to fall madly in love with you."

"To be honest, it's been a long time since I've wanted to go to such lengths to please a woman. I guess you be bringing out the best in me." There was that irresistible smile before he gently kissed me again on the lips. "Dinner smells delightful."

"I wouldn't be complimenting me just yet. Cooking is not my forte," I laughed.

"Well then, it be a good thing we have plenty of mead to wash it down with."

The conversation throughout dinner was light and spirited. He told me all about how he learned to play the piano and guitar as a young lad and how it inspired his love of music. I shared my stories about my father and all the places I wanted to visit, though I doubted anything could ever measure up to the beauty and awe of Ireland.

"It suits you just fine, ole Éire."

"I feel like I belong here. Work is constantly stressful, and my life back home is so hectic. But in Ireland, I am a completely different person. Calm and at peace. Does that sound crazy?"

"Yes."

"Really?"

"I'm just codding ya, lass. It's not crazy a'tall. I think whenever we're outside our environment, we feel a freedom to just be ourselves. It sounds like you've lost a bit of yourself back there. Well, I don't know *that* Megan, but I will say that I am completely beguiled by the Megan sitting in front of me."

"You're pretty charming yourself, *prionsa*."

"Prince, eh? Well, *mo banphrionsa*, shall we retire to the setting area to take a gander at that journal?"

Before I could respond, we heard a loud bang outside. Instinctively throwing the light on, Kieran made his way to the back door to investigate. Flashlight in hand, he did a quick scan of the yard, lingering in the bushes to make sure nothing was hiding there. Satisfied that there was nothing to see, he protectively double locked the door and checked the front to make sure we were nice and secure.

"Was prolly just a critter trying to get into your trash. 'Tis a bit cold around these parts still and they'd be looking for something to eat. Here, let me set the fire and get us all warmed up. There's a blanket in that drawer if you can grab it and I could do with a bit more drink, if you don't mind."

Within minutes, he had the fire blazing and we settled down on the sofa with our glasses of honey mead and the journal. Not that we needed the warmth or the excuse for closeness, but the heavy wool blanket bound us tightly together. It felt so natural to nestle into the grooves of his chest as he brought his strong, protective arm around me and held me close.

How could it be that I already felt such a familiarity

with a man I literally met a week ago?

We read the first few pages together and I suddenly realized how helpful it was to have my own personal translator. Fortunately, Kieran already knew the Italian language well; much better than the few courses I took in college. Although I could get the gist of what Alessia was writing, some of the references and slang she used were beyond my American comprehension.

After reading a couple of her initial entries, I lost hope in this being the juicy tell-all I had envisioned.

No, it was simply some young girl's daily dream-doodling about her chats with girlfriends, an unrequited crush who ignored her and an annoyance over a teacher's dismissal of her academic abilities. What was crystal clear was her fiery spirit and love of life, however.

Page after page we read on, hoping to find something, anything that might give me insight into the mystery of why we were here; what this secret heritage was really all about. Before I knew it, I sensed myself being carried up the stairs and placed into my bed.

"What—what are you doing?" I asked groggily.

"You're completely shattered, *a ghrá*. You fell asleep mid-sentence. Why don't you get some shut eye and I'll check on you in the mornin'? I'll lock up and leave a light on downstairs."

Too tired to fight, I allowed him to cover me with a warm blanket and darken the shades in my bedroom. He set the journal—earmarked on the last page we read—on the dresser before coming back over to the bed.

Bending over to caress the stray piece of hair from my face and place a gentle kiss on my forehead, I heard him whisper gently in Gaelic what must have been the equivalent of good night, as I drifted off into a peaceful slumber.

Was it all just a dream? I woke up feeling dazed, but when I saw myself still in the clothes from the day before under the blanket, I knew that the evening with Kieran was as real as the sunlight beaming in through the window.

Shivers and goosebumps ran down my body as I noted that the warmth that was once Kieran was no longer surrounding me. The sensation of hope traveled back into my heart when I saw a text message from him waiting on my phone.

Good morning, a ghrá. Hope you slept well. Need to grab some messages for Mum this morning. See you at noon? Your Kieran.

My Kieran. I smiled at the thought of that. Wait—what am I doing? I can't get caught up in all this mushy stuff after one day. I can enjoy my time with him, indulge in some kisses and attraction, but pretending it can be anything other than a brief interlude is insane. Still, I couldn't resist sending an equally saccharin message back.

Good morning, prionsa. I'm heading to the market myself this morning. Noon is perfect. Until then, Your Megan.

With that all settled, I jumped into the shower and decided on a bright floral dress and white sweater. I let my hair hang down to dry naturally into waves, knowing the fresh air would do a better job than a blow dryer would (especially since I forgot the electrical converter to plug it into). Grabbing my bags and the basket I forgot to return last week, I set out for the market on an unusually warm day—possibly the warmest we'd had since arriving.

Enjoying the glorious morning, I waved to each local as I passed them by. All I could think of was meeting up with Kieran again and reading more of my great-great-grandmother's journal. I was so lost in the tunnels of my mind that I hadn't noticed the shadow behind me.

I thought maybe I was being followed, but as I turned around, I only saw the friendly neighbors I had just greeted. I cautiously continued on my way, glancing back occasionally to check, but finding nothing. Still, I just couldn't shake the eerie feeling.

You watch way too many suspense films, Meg.

I made it in and out of the market without incident this time. And since I had some extra time to spare, I decided to pop into a few of the shops to do some souvenir shopping. I came upon a traditional wool store and settled on matching pink sweaters for Mom and Granny. I also found some matching eggshell-colored woolen glove and scarf sets that my nieces and nephew might actually not be embarrassed to wear—teens were so hard to buy for.

I also stopped by a little jewelry store and picked up three matching Celtic bracelets to commemorate our sister trip to Ireland and purchased an extra trinity pendant for myself. There were some pretty earrings I found for my nieces and engraved money clips I thought Stephen and Kevin might like. Pleased with my shopping experience, I made my way back home.

Home. Who would have thought some old little house in the Middle of Nowhere, Ireland would feel like home. Smiling at the thought, I grabbed Alessia's journal and settled into the side garden.

It was more of the same boring teenage diatribe for a while. Here and there, I found juicy nuggets relating to her relationship with her family (thank goodness for Google's online translation assistance), including how strict her father was about the men she was allowed to date—"no one outside of her kind." I could see where that was headed. Finally, a hint into this alleged scandal.

She also talked about her lack of respect for her mother's constant fear and siding with her father over everything, from manners to societal expectations. And how her parents were so much easier on her two younger sisters, putting more pressure on Alessia to marry well and bear heirs as the eldest since there were no sons to continue the family business.

I deciphered that she wasn't all that fond of her younger sister, Dominica, who broke every rule known to man and got away with it. To paraphrase: a party girl who loved her men but still presented herself to elders as the perfect noble lady that parents could be proud of. I could hear the resentment in Alessia's voice as she spoke about the unfairness of it all.

She did seem to speak affectionately of her meek little sister, Concetta. At least there seemed to be someone in the poor girl's corner.

The morning passed quickly, and right on time, my sexy Irishman strode up to the side of the house to greet me with a kiss and a bouquet of gorgeous pale pink and purple heath spotted-orchids, native to County Mayo.

"They're beautiful, thank you. I'm not sure I am going to survive all this spoiling."

"'How can a woman be expected to be happy with a man who insists on treating her as if she were a perfectly normal human being?'"

"Oscar Wilde. Well done," I said, acknowledging his poetic reference. "'The very essence of romance is uncertainty,'" I countered with another Wilde quote. He lifted his eyebrows in acceptance of my matching wit.

"Ay, is that a challenge? I shall mind myself to not become predictable then."

With those words, he grabbed me into a heated embrace, not waiting for my permission before his lips and tongue were exploring mine in rushed desire. His right hand holding my face locked against his as his left started to smoothly explore my back, inching lower towards my waist so that he could pull the full of my body against his.

For a moment, we were simply lost in this passionate hold that paused the orbiting of the universe—until I had to pull away, realizing that we were outside for any passerby to see.

"What's wrong, *a ghrá*?"

"Nothing. Just that there are neighbors all around and—"

"This be Ireland, lass. Nobody minds witnessing grand expressions of fondness, especially when the lovers are in one's own garden. Gives 'em something new to gossip about anyways," he proposed.

"Still I—" I broke off, embarrassed, frazzled. I didn't want the kiss to end. But if I didn't end it, I would have given in to the deep hunger I felt right there on the spot.

Pull it together, Megan. You're treading in dangerous territory.

Sensing my hesitation, Kieran respectfully pulled back.

"I have an idea. Why don't you grab a sweater and we can take a walk down to the creek? Get some fresh air. Then you can tell me all about what you've been reading in that there journal. I brought a few sandwiches and whatnot with me and we can have lunch at the park if you're hungry."

"That sounds really nice. I saw a wicker basket in one of the closets. I'll grab that and a blanket for the ground.

If you could grab some wine and glasses and maybe a few snacks from the kitchen, we can have ourselves a picnic."

"A bit of a romantic yourself, are you now?" I was perilously worshipping that smile of his—the perfect balance of boyish grin and manly warmth. He didn't need words when his mouth expressed it all. Now I was even more grateful for choosing to stay behind while my sisters went off on their spa retreat.

Since the creek was further down past the shops and over the bridge, I enjoyed the new scenery as we explored more of the village. Along the way, I noticed a small brick church with stained glass windows—the kind that looked like it could have doubled as a schoolhouse back in the day. I adored the antique character of this town.

There was another stone structure nearby that was in complete ruins, which Kieran explained was an ancient wedding altar—an extension of the church. Those who were wed in that very spot were said to be supernaturally blessed in their unions by the presence of goddesses, fruitful in their procreation of children and in their lifelong trades.

Legend had it that a forbidden couple secretly exchanged vows there, but when the young woman's betrothed found out about it, he brought a small army of friends and weapons to destroy the altar the next day, setting a curse upon the lovers.

Now it was reduced to rubble and overgrown weeds, but I imagined if someone really wanted to, they could properly restore it to its original splendor. Yet still, even in ruins, it was not an eyesore but an intriguing bit of history that hid a whimsy of enchantment that felt an awful lot like the energy surrounding the Witch Stone.

Along the way, I filled Kieran in on the passages I had

read in the journal and the conclusions I formed about Alessia and her family. He agreed that it sounded spot on, recalling that he had heard her union with Cian was not one her father approved of and that she had left her family to live here in Ireland, where the folks were a bit more accepting.

We finally came across the little creek, its clear water trembling over natural gray, mossy rocks with a few strategically placed man-made stepping stones. Before it lay an open, lush green meadow of land and a small forest of pine trees—the kind Bambi would've surely frolicked in.

We set out the blanket upon the grass; the morning dew dried up by the daycs sun. Kieran poured some of the leftover honey mead from last night into our glasses while I set out the spread of food. We toasted to a beautiful day, to the company and to the mysterious journey we were on. I inhaled the truth of where we were.

"So, this is truly where I came from. My ancestors not only lived in that very house, but as children, they must have come down to this stream to play. If I close my eyes, I can see Alessia washing out some knickers as Lena takes off her socks and shoes to go wading and splashing right here. Cian's in the background, sitting on the ground with a pipe enjoying the sight of it all."

"You have quite the imagination there, Miss Megan. Ever put it to good use?"

"As a young girl, I loved to write stories. Then as I grew older and realized there wasn't much stability to be had in such a fly-by-night field, I turned to advertising. I was still able to write and create, but in a different way. I turned out to be very good at it—being able to take a client's vision and turn it into their reality."

"But what about your visions, *a ghrá*? Sure it's grand to bring their dreams to life, but how do you express yours?"

"I was—*am*—fine with it. I infuse my ideas into theirs. It's natural for me and I've gained a lot of respect and credibility as an executive because of my work. Having that control, prestige and stability was enough for me, so I put my writing on the back burner.

"I'm my own woman because of it, Kieran. A woman I am proud of, who can fend for herself and thrive in a man's world. Sometimes, childhood dreams have no place there."

"Creation is like a heartbeat. Without it, you slowly die until the heart stops beating completely."

"Whose quote is that?"

"Mine."

Overlooking the water rushing down, my tears started matching pace with the realization that he was right. All these years, I'd been gradually fading away until I no longer recognized my reflection. When those middle school boys grabbed at my matured breasts and the school did nothing about it, my spirit hardened and it changed the softness of my baby face.

When Scotty shattered my heart, I closed the door to love and affection, further aging my soul and darkening the sparkle of my eyes. Fighting man after man on my way up the corporate ladder, weathering sexist advances and countless hours seeking validation, I continued to erode inside and forget the young girl who used to dream up a much more positive expectation from life.

Alas, life was not a fairy tale I could write away.

Daddy dying was the nail in my coffin; no longer would he be there to argue with me in an attempt to help me see and release the light of my soul that I was burying away. Every year, I burrowed another foot under the ground. He died before he could save me. I now understood the angst I'd see in his eyes when he'd look at me; like he had failed me.

But he didn't. He never could. I was the one who failed myself.

I felt Kieran come up behind me and gently wrap his arms around me, kissing the back of my head before laying his chin on my shoulder.

"When I look at you, I see so much passion inside. I'm not just talkin' about your physical fire that's hard for me to resist, mind you. I see the fiery spirit of a woman who indeed is independent and strong but is also witty and playful and yearnin' to tell a story of her own making.

"Your mind is not limited to executing the dreams of others, *a ghrá*. You can still run with the wolves of men and be the inspired woman you are inside. I can feel your true essence, Megan, and it moves me to share mine."

"I want to write again," I whispered, finally admitting what was truly burning in my heart. "I do feel alive when I let it out on paper. It feels right." I turned to look at him, feeling the fear bubble up inside as I considered how following my heart would turn my whole world upside down.

"But how can I just throw away an empire I helped to build? How can I turn my back on everything I have worked so hard for and risk losing everything?"

"No one is saying you have to give up your job. You can still kick arse in advertising and be that woman. But maybe cut back on the hours you spend making others happy and invest them into your own passions instead. You don't have to make that choice—you just need to follow what calls to your soul."

"That's the problem. I don't know where my heart

begins and where my head ends. I can't figure it all out right now and it scares me. I had a plan, Kieran. That empire was my plan.

"But the more time I spend here—the more time I spend with you—it feels empty. But it's all I know. Work is all I have been able to trust in and rely on, except for my family of course. I'm terrified of not seeing how the future unfolds. I used to be so certain and now, I can't even see past tomorrow."

"All we have is this moment, today. It's all we ever have. But that's the beauty of following creation. It brings us the future. We don't have to design the unknown. That's God's work. Our job is to simply live."

"That's an awfully tall order for a control freak," I admitted nervously.

"Then let someone else take the lead for a change," he responded as he leaned in to kiss me. The slow graze of his lips burned into a more zealous yearning to dive in deeper. He laid me back onto the blanket smoothly, moving his kisses from my lips to my neck and then to that sweet spot right under my ear. With a tug of my lobe, my body responded with an aching desire for more.

He moved to my side and still lingering around my neck with his hot breath and mischievous bites, I could feel his warm, slightly rough hands move down, under and into the bodice of my dress to cup my breast and tease my nipple ever so slightly. My back arched in pleasure, willing him to continue his exploration of my body.

I moaned at his touch, reaching my hand under his shirt to feel the power of his own tight, hot chest, prompting him to sit up and remove it completely. The way the sunlight circled around him and the fervent gleam in his eyes as he looked at me—only me—made him the most exquisite man I had ever seen. Yes, he was definitely a Celtic God reincarnated on earth.

We locked gazes for only a moment before his mouth was back on mine and the weight of his body consumed me. I couldn't resist running my hands up and down his muscled back, feeling him shudder as I teased with some light scratching of my fingernails.

He pulled up and off me slowly, running his hands through his hair as he blew out a hurricane of hot air.

"I think it best we take this somewhere more private, lass. And swiftly, because with the way those incredible blues are shining up at me, I just might hafta take you right here and public be damned."

Agreeing, I promptly sat up and gathered everything together in the basket as he pulled his shirt back on. I fussed to throw my hair back into a respectable ponytail and straightened my dress, though anyone looking at us could tell that we were recently engaged in more than just conversation. Hand in hand, we walked back in contented silence towards the house, as if words would shatter the beauty of the moment.

10

I reached for my key as we neared the door, only to find that it was wide open.

Bizarre, I could have sworn it was locked before we left, I thought to myself.

Oh well, maybe Mia and Marissa came back a day earlier than expected. Or maybe Colleen was able to stop by sooner after all. Frustrated at the idea of entertaining anyone other than Kieran, I pushed my way into the house with him behind me as I called out their names.

But we didn't find anyone there—what we walked into was a completely trashed house. Papers, blankets, pillows, books and artifacts were all over the floor. Not completely broken; more like tossed aside. Drawers and pantries were opened and emptied.

I froze in place—who would do such a thing?

Kieran immediately called the Westport Garda, bringing me back out to the sidewalk in front of the house in case the perpetrator was still inside. Luckily, the Irish police were on site within ten minutes to check the place out, though we didn't see any sign of someone moving about the house or leaving since we had returned. Everything remained still.

"What a haymes! Do you know who's wantin' to be doing this to you, or what they were looking for?"

"No, no idea," I whispered as I answered a bunch of routine questions. After they did an initial clearing of the house to make sure no one was there and dusted for evidence, they let us back in to see if I noticed if anything was missing. I told them it was hard to tell, since my sisters and I were only guests, but looking in our rooms, it appeared as if nothing of value was taken.

Strange—why didn't they take any of the jewelry we brought from home or any of the clearly valuable artwork that was placed throughout? As far as I could tell, nothing was missing; just ruffled.

I felt violated. It wasn't my home, but I was staying in it, so it was a personal betrayal. Did they know I wasn't there? What if I *was* inside? What if they were armed and I was in the wrong place at the wrong time? And then I remembered back to earlier this morning, when I felt as if I was being followed.

"You never mentioned you were being followed!" Kieran accused as he ran his hand in frustration through his hair. "Why didn't you tell me? Feck."

"I'm sorry, I just didn't think anything of it. I thought it was my imagination. I kept looking back and didn't see anyone, so I thought it was just a critter again."

"Ah, my money's on that not bein' a critter last night, neither."

"Marissa did warn me about a Mr. O'Dooly who was overly interested."

"That old coot? He's an odd one for sure, but harmless. I'll check it out, though. Wait right here with Commissioner Brady. I have a few calls to make."

Nodding my head, I sank down into the living room armchair. Another neighbor from down the street stuck her head in to find out what the commotion was all about and knowing her well, Commissioner Brady allowed her inside to sit with me.

"Hi dear. I'm Ellie Walsh from just a few doors down. I seen you and your sisters here with Colleen. She filled me in on your visit before you came. Here, I brought you a cuppa tea," she said sweetly as she handed me an insulated mug of chamomile and honey.

A plump old woman, no doubt close in age and best buddies with Colleen, she had a full head of wavy white hair and a heavily wrinkled face that couldn't hide her soft, green eyes of kindness.

"Thank you," I managed. "I don't know who could do such a thing."

"Don't you be worrying about that. Our Garda boys here are as good as they come. They're after catching that dosser, they are. It's a small town and someone musta seen somethin' around here. We see everything," she winked with a knowing smile that made me turn red.

"Nah, don't you be needin' to turn scarlet about that, neither. Our Kieran is a fine thing, he is indeed, a good honest fella. With that face he could be havin' lots o' mots but his mum raised him fine and proper to be a gentleman. I reckon he is sweet on you the way he is being all protective."

"He's a very good man," I agreed. "I wonder where he went, though?"

On cue, he came in through the back door and headed straight for me. "Good day, Mrs. Walsh. Thank you for looking out for my Megan."

"Ah 'twas not a thing. I best be going now but glad you're all right. I am down in the light yellow house now if you need anythin' a'tall."

"Thank you again for the tea. It was lovely to meet you." And it was. Her presence was soothing, like her tea. Like Granny's tea. It made me really miss home and my sisters.

"I have to call Mia and Marissa and tell them what happened."

"Wait a minute, lass. I called Colleen and we agreed to let your sisters be for the day. It would only cause more chaos to bring them home right now. I've spoken with the Garda and after they help us clean up the place, they'll be leaving an armed guard here for the time being."

"An armed guard? Am I in danger?"

"I don't know, *a ghrá*. This kind of thing doesn't happen often 'round here. We'll be takin' every precaution we can. And I won't have any arguing about it, but I'll be stayin' here with you until your sisters return. I won't get a wink of sleep unless I know for myself that you're all right."

"Okay." Everything was happening way too fast; the room started to spin like a tilt-a-whirl at an amusement park. I felt Kieran pick me up and mutter something to the Garda about taking me up for a rest. This was becoming a habit it seemed, him carrying me lifeless to bed.

When I woke up, the house was tranquil, and the sky had darkened. Everyone must have left. That is, everyone except Kieran, who was resting comfortably in the lounge chair beside my bed thumbing through Alessia's journal.

"Good evening, sleepyhead. How was your rest?"

"Good. What time is it?"

"Half past seven. You've been asleep for quite a while."

"Have you been sitting there this whole time?"

"I have. You're just as beautiful asleep as you are awake, ya know. Like an angel." I blushed at the thought of him watching me, and at the thought of him staying by my side for the next 24 hours.

"How's the house?"

"Most of it is cleaned up. It's just this room and a small part of the setting area that we didn't get to yet, but we can tackle that tomorrow. Hungry?"

"Starving. I picked up some food today. Or we can just reheat some leftover pot pie."

"I promised the boys to thank them for their help today with a pint. Let's get you out of this house for a spell. I know a great place," he winked as if he knew a secret I didn't.

"Sure. Let me just freshen up and I'll meet you downstairs."

The house was exactly as he said—you wouldn't have known that only a few short hours ago, it was completely in shambles. Still, I could feel the anxiety rise as I walked through the living room and spotted an officer standing guard outside of the back door. I was instantly relieved by the thought of getting out of this place, though I worried about what would happen again when we left.

"Billy and Horace have this place under tight watch," he said, reading my mind. "Not to mention your do-good neighbors who are on alert. There ain't nobody who'd get at it again. You're safe with us."

I smiled meekly up at him, letting him lead me to his truck. Before opening the door, he took me tightly into his arms and kissed me tenderly. "You look mighty pretty, by the way."

Finally noticing him through the fog of my thoughts, I saw he changed his clothes from earlier and had his hair slicked back. He donned a black leather jacket and ripped black jeans with matching work boots, looking sexy as hell.

The smell of his cologne wafted through my nose, setting off little twinges of longing throughout my body. Was it even possible for him to look more gorgeous in the moonlight than in the sun?

"You clean up well yourself, handsome. Where are we going?"

"To my favorite little pub. Great food, great music and I know the owner pretty well. Fantastic guy," he said, grinning mischievously.

A few moments later, we arrived at a place called Gov's and I looked at him curiously. He only smirked as he opened my car door, took my hand and escorted me into the loud, rowdy pub. Celtic rock music was blaring from the band on stage, laughter filled the air and you could smell the Guinness in pints all around.

"It's quite busy for a Monday night," I yelled over the din of the crowd.

"At Gov's, every night is Saturday night," he beamed.

Recognized by a table of officers and other guests, a raucous cheer and raising of glasses announced Kieran's arrival. We went over to greet his fans, introducing me as "his" Megan, the American lass who stole his heart. It earned him some teasing, but they were all so goodhearted in nature.

"Quite the place your Kieran has, doesn't he?" said a short, rotund little rascal affectionately known as Tuggs.

"Wait—this is *his* place?"

"It is! I reckon, who did you think Gov's belonged to?" The lightbulb went on. Of course. Short for MacGovern. I made my way over to a smaller table of guests where Kieran was now obviously playing host to. After a quick introduction, he excused us to a more quiet space in the room—though anywhere you went had you yelling just to be heard.

"Why didn't you tell me you owned a pub?"

He boyishly shrugged his shoulders. "It just never came

up. It was me da's, and when he passed away ten years ago, it was his wish for me to carry it on. I have, with the help of a few partners. But they know better about the running of the business, for certain. Me, I'm in it for the music and the people. You'll have to excuse me for a moment though, because I'm gettin' the eye that I'm late."

"Late? For what?" I tried to ask as he kissed my cheek and carried himself off towards the front of the pub.

I looked around for a few minutes trying to find him. Good old Tuggs passed by and noticed I was without a pint, so he graciously bought me one and asked me to join him and his buddies at their table at the front of the room.

"Do you know where Kieran went? I can't seem to find him."

"Look up, lass. He be right there on the stage." And so he was, standing behind an electronic keyboard. Within moments, the band started playing and the energy level of the room went through the roof.

The lead singer had a sultry, sexy voice that crooned rock lyrics, while the two guitarists, drummer and Kieran on keyboard all took turns with their musical solos. It was hard not to dance and get into the feeling of the music, song after song.

I would catch glimpses of Kieran looking over at me while he performed, but it was when he looked away and released himself to his music that I knew exactly what he meant when he said he could see my essence. That was pure Kieran. Musical, lyrical, free.

Was I absolutely, completely falling in love with this man I just met, against my better judgment? Or was I just getting wrapped up in all this elated giddiness? Then I remembered my promise to myself to just let go and be in the moment.

When the set ended, he made his way through the crowd to come find me. Drenched with sweat, he exuded pure, raw sexiness. I threw my arms around his neck and jumped up to circle my legs around his waist, planting a hot smacking kiss on his lips.

"That was amazingly hot!" I exclaimed, hearing the room break out in applause over my amorous greeting. I turned all colors of crimson as I jumped down onto the floor. Kieran simply laughed and raised his fist up in the air in triumph.

He led me to a small table in the corner of the room while a waitress, as if trained in the art of serving Kieran, instantly brought over two pints, two burgers and a bucket of fries to our table.

"Thanks, Lily!"

"You betcha, boss!" She turned to me with a wink. "You know, this one's a keeper. If I weren't already madly in love with me own fella, I'd be tryin' to steal this man's heart away. But from the looks of it, there ain't no other girl in the world the way he be lookin' at you, so it'd be a fool's wish."

Kieran shot her a glare of warning. "Just musing, that's all," she muttered as she went to her next table.

He was right about Gov's—the food was delicious, as was the music and the ambiance. It was definitely what I needed to feel better after today. Just being around all the elation was enough to lift the poorest of spirits up.

"How about getting out of here?"

"But don't you need to stay and take care of business or play again?"

"Beauty of being the boss. I call the shots and I call it a night off with my girl. Besides, my crew has it all under control. Best a man could ever ask for."

Returning to the house brought reality all back. In my mind, I knew we were well guarded, and it did make me feel better to know that Kieran was staying with me, too, but I just couldn't put away the disconcerting feeling. I sat down among the disheveled mess that still waited for us in the setting room, trying to understand why this all happened. What was this person looking for?

"Here, *a ghrá*. Have some of this." He handed me a shot of whiskey, which I took willingly, as he sat down beside me.

"I just don't understand. Who would want to do this?"

"I don't have an answer for ya. I've been trying to wrap my head around it myself." I let my body fall back into his arms as we silently watched the fireplace flames flicker. I caught the chill of the poorly ventilated house and shuddered.

I felt him move my hair slightly so that he could press his warm lips to my neck and squeeze me closer. The chills came rushing back, but they were chills of excitement. His lips and hands traveled together, touching, feeling, exploring.

I turned my head and moved my body so that I could take his full lips on mine. I could taste the faint whiskey mixed with his own exotic flavor that I'd come to crave. The tenderness subsided and passion soared through our bodies, daring us to give more of ourselves than we ever had before.

He lifted me from the couch and carried me up the stairs. He stopped as he reached my bedroom door and just smiled.

"What's the matter?" I asked, perplexed.

"Nothing a'tall. It's just nice to have you conscious as I carry you to your bed for a change."

We laughed as he set me down and took a step back to close the door. He just stood there, barely a shadow in the darkened room. He grabbed a lighter from the dresser and lit the lilac candles that were part of the bedroom décor.

Moving back towards me, he never took his eyes off mine for a second, not even as he expertly unbuttoned my blouse and removed it. Pleasantly surprised to find a delicate pink camisole instead of a bra, he let his fingers trace the contours of my breasts under the lace as his teeth erotically pulled the straps down off my shoulders.

His lips nuzzled back into the groove of my neck, finding those subtle places that drove me to the brink of ecstasy. His hands disposed of the camisole, returning just as swiftly to feel the softness of my breasts and the tightening of my nipples exposed in the cool air.

I returned the favor by pulling his shirt off over his head, placing my hands on his bare chest and then around to his back. It was my turn to explore the pleasure spots of his neck and shoulders, feeling more aroused by his manly moans.

Our lips found their way back together as our hands began unbuttoning each other's pants. We both glided out of our remaining clothes, our two naked bodies being all that remained in the moonlight, aching to be joined as one.

Kieran tenderly led me to the bed, but I decided to maneuver his body under mine instead. I wanted to savor every part of this man, this beautiful man, who had not only revived my sexual passion but also my heart and soul.

I could feel him wanting to fight me, but I simply shook my head and let my persuasive eyes beg him to let me have my way. He obliged, after first pulling me down by my hair in a long, hard kiss. The pure touch of our bare bodies made my insides pulse, but I didn't want to rush this moment. I was so used to hard and fast goodbyes that I wanted to savor this relatively new experience.

I pulled my lips away from his and began my journey. I started at the base of his neck, a spot I found to be one of his weaknesses. My lips and hands headed south, licking, biting and kissing my way down his hairless, toned chest. I could feel his back arch slightly, which only deepened my desire to please him.

As I lingered my tongue around his pecs, I allowed my hand to wander down to wrap around his hardness. Stroking lightly, groans escaped and I could feel his need to rebel against my control and turn me over. I ignored his pleas, pushing aside his hands as I let my mouth travel further to where it yearned to go, enjoying every taste of his sinfully delicious body.

Unable to wait anymore, he overturned me so that the weight of his entire body pinned me down like a wrestler. Using a single hand to raise my arms above my head and restrain them, he grinned wickedly as he frustratingly did nothing but look at me for a while. "My turn."

He began by sensually taking one of my fingers into his mouth and kissed his way down my arm, and back to my neck and ears. It didn't take long for him to find my nipples waiting for his mouth to consume them and raise them into even more hardened mountainous peaks. Rushes of electric waves raced through me as he nipped them, escalating the sensations throughout my entire body.

With his mouth content where it was, his hand traveled down to discover the rainforest of wetness that awaited him. His mere touch triggered fireworks. He found my throbbing clit and began his expert massage, heightening all of my senses to madness.

Just when I thought I couldn't take any more, he

released his hold with a look of warning that I was not to move and I obeyed. I could feel his tongue travel over my stomach and downward, finding me again and bringing me to the edge of orgasm. I felt the explosive rush take over, the pureness of ecstasy exposed—but he wasn't done.

He expertly glided inside of me, his hardness a perfect fit. Grabbing onto his back and winding my legs around him, I took him in deeper. With each thrust, we moved in sync like the harmonies of his rock band. I could feel the build rising again, wanting more, yet forbidding its end.

Gentle at first, the thirst quickened to uncontrollable desire until our mutual release left us both spent and completely satisfied. I could feel the weight of his body relax onto mine, not yet ready to pull out and disconnect us from the moment.

When he did, he rolled to the side to take me into his arms and plant a sacred kiss on my forehead.

"I know we've only just met, but I need you to know that I've never felt for another woman what I feel for you. I don't know what you're doin' to me lass, but you're suddenly stealing all of me." He intertwined his fingers with mine and moved in closer so that I could feel his breath on my neck.

"I'm not sure I can quite find the words to describe how I feel right now either."

"Then I guess I will just have to settle for you showing me," he suggested, as he kissed me into an endless night of lovemaking.

11

Waking up in the morning beside Kieran felt right; like he belonged there. Our naked bodies curved into each other like the perfect puzzle pieces. I carefully pulled free of his grip, noticing how one of his hands found a comfortable spot cupping my breast as he slept. It pained me to remove myself from him in any way, but I was hungry from a long, active night and wanted to surprise him with breakfast.

I managed to leave the bed without disturbing him, and as I looked back over at him, I understood what he meant when he said I was beautiful when I slept. He was a magnificent vision at rest, his dark hair a tousled mess; his face nestled sideways into the pillow.

Ah, we have a snorer here, I chuckled quietly to myself as I heard the muffled sound escape. At least it's not too bad—I hope. *Could be a deal breaker,* I thought humorously.

Grabbing a robe out of the closet, I made my way down the stairs to see what I could rustle up. I settled on making some scrambled eggs loaded with cheese, bacon and tomatoes atop rye toast. Fast and easy. As generous as I felt in making breakfast, I wasn't in the mood to make a big spread.

I was tired—believe it or not—of daily scones and endless carbs, so I had picked up some fresh berries for a mixed fruit salad.

Standing there over the stove, I realized that I had no idea if he was a coffee or tea person or if he was even a morning or night person. There was so much yet to discover about him.

I decided on making a large fresh pot of coffee anyway and added more ingredients to the pan to offer breakfast to the two officers standing guard outside. They were both grateful for the sustenance, as they were growing weary waiting for the shift change. Apparently, there was one already during the night—every eight hours—and no one had recorded any activity or disturbances, which made me feel more at ease.

Turning back to work in my little kitchen, I started washing and preparing the fresh blueberries, strawberries and raspberries for my fruit bowl. I remembered a recipe from a friend that called for adding some slivered almonds, coconut flakes and a touch of honey, so I thought I'd experiment a little like Mia does—and hope for the best. As I began mixing it all together, I sensed my lover coming up behind me.

"Well, what do we have here?"

"I made you a hearty American-style breakfast. Hope you're hungry!"

"Ravenous," he said, as he bit the back of my neck. "But I could use a meal as well."

He didn't care that I was busy, turning me around to face him so he could kiss me good morning. I lost track of what I was doing, instantly responding to his seductive invitation for a different kind of breakfast. We were both startled enough to pull apart when I dropped a spoon on the floor, bringing me back to my task at hand.

"Behave yourself, Gov," I warned. "Let me finish this

or we'll die of starvation."

"It'd be a grand way to go," he smirked.

"Still. Oh, what do you drink in the morning? I wasn't sure if you liked coffee, tea, juice?"

"Coffee, black. Usually just a single mug of it to get me goin' after a long night. Sometimes two." Walking over to the back door, he waved at the guard, noticing he got a head start on the chef's breakfast. "What's the story?"

"Duke said that everything went smoothly and that nothing happened. It was a boring night."

"Maybe for them," he teased. "I'm glad. Hopefully the eejit will keep his or her distance from here."

"I hope so, too. But I feel pretty safe right now."

With breakfast practically finished, I made my way over to the table to set it. I started humming one of the band's rock tunes that got stuck in my head from last night. It was more of a ballad and something about it just tugged at my soul.

"Ah, *Dream Rose*. You liked that song, did ya?"

"I did. It was hauntingly beautiful, with such heart."

"Out of the shadows and into the light
Dream Rose, she appeared
No longer a vision at night
Just a touch away, I feared
That I may sleep to watch her disappear

My heart and my life
How could I ever carry on
Without my sweet Dream Rose
Forever here by my side"

Stunned, I could only listen in awe as his pure sultry tone sang the words to the music that played repeatedly in my mind.

"I had no idea you could sing. You have an incredible voice. Is it one of the covers your band plays?"

"No. An original."

"Wow. Your band wrote it? Whoever knows how to put words and music together sure knows what he or she is doing."

"It was me. I wrote it the night I came home from the Bunratty banquet," he said with a rare vulnerability that touched me. "I wrote it about you. You're my own Dream Rose, like one from the magical bush out yonder. Life hasn't been the same since you ran over my foot."

I was speechless. No one had ever written a song about me, let alone sang it to me. I could only respond by walking over to him and kissing him with all the tenderness I had in my heart. Breakfast be damned, I was going to show this man once again exactly how he made me feel—right there on the kitchen floor.

Although breakfast wasn't as good reheated, we managed to fuel ourselves and take a break from our obsessive lovemaking to get down to business. We still had some cleaning up to do before my sisters got home and I did want to go through more of Alessia's journal.

There wasn't much to tidy up in my room, aside from refolding a few clothes into the drawers and reorganizing my shoes and luggage in the closet. Doing a second check, I noted that nothing at all seemed to be missing or damaged—even my souvenirs were intact. Kieran volunteered to finish up downstairs in the setting area. He was still working on putting things back in place when I joined him.

"Anything missing from down here?"

"Not a thing, *a ghrá*. It's baffling. If they were looking for a person and got frustrated, they woulda just rummaged a few things on the way out the door. If they were lookin' to rob you, there's plenty worth taking to pawn for money. No, it was something specific on their mind, and I'm venturing he—or she—didn't find it."

Curious, indeed. But what Kieran said made sense. At least if he was right, that meant that we shouldn't be in any physical danger from the intruder. Looking around, it seemed like he had everything all back in place, until I saw the box of pictures I had brought down from the attic were overturned under the sofa. I took them out and started to assemble them back into the box, noticing a few were missing.

"Kieran look at this. Some of the photos we were looking at the other day aren't here anymore—like the one with Cian, Alessia and Lena. Do you think—"

Midsentence, he cut me off with a raise of his finger and rushed up the stairs to the attic. I followed him, understanding his hunch, already knowing what we would find. Sure enough, the tiny little loft was beyond trashed. Papers were everywhere, trinkets broken, boxes smashed. Someone was on a mission—a mission that involved a legacy I still didn't know anything about myself.

There was a hint of Irish temper boiling beneath his surface like a slow burning hotplate. He grabbed my arm forcefully and led me out of the attic and back down the stairs.

"Kieran, you're hurting me." He apologetically loosened his grip and moved his hand down to hold mine more gently, still moving rapidly to the setting area. He motioned for me to sit while he began pacing and mumbling a slew of what were probably Irish curses. He sounded a lot like Granny a few weeks ago.

"It's time, Megan. Call your sisters and have them come home. I'll get on Colleen and see when she can get here. There is a reason you are here and it's time she did the telling of it. I'm not liking this one bit. Not one bit, I tell you."

He walked towards the front door to have a word with the guard by the side garden and then called Colleen. Without alarming them, I convinced my sisters to come home early under the guise that Colleen was ready for us and after a long trip, didn't want to be up too late tonight.

Kieran came back in, still as wired as he was when he went out.

"I have some things I need to take care of right now, *a ghrá*. I need to check in on Mum, plus I need to have a little chat with the Commissioner to fill him in on what we learned. You're safe here with the guards. Colleen is on her way. I should be about two, three hours most. Did you get a hold of your sisters?"

"Yes, there is a ferry leaving in an hour that they can hop on. I told them Colleen was coming here earlier so they wouldn't be suspicious."

"Atta girl, good thinkin'. I hate leaving you like this, but I want to take care of business and return in time for the story. I don't mean to be intruding on your family business. But I can't protect you if I don't know all the facts."

"It's okay, I know. I want you there with me. My sisters will understand—they won't have a problem with it. You go ahead. I'll be just fine. I'll see you later." Moving a loose tendril of hair aside from his cheek, I leaned up to give him a kiss goodbye.

"I'll be back, Dream Rose," he said with a more relaxed tone, closing the door behind him.

I was grateful for the few hours to myself, truth be told. So much had happened over the last 48 hours—the last week—the last month! All my intentions to sift through my brain clutter had been tossed by the wayside in a tornado of unexpected events.

We learned about an unknown grandfather who abandoned our mother and grandmother. His dying wishes led us to Ireland and soon to Italy and Spain, on a wild goose chase for a few mysterious relics left to us in his will, and on a captivating mission to learn the legacies of our family's past. And now—with the break-in and missing photos—the stakes were seemingly higher than ever.

So much had been stirred up since coming here. The moment I stepped foot onto this sacred soil, I have felt both at home and lost. In the silence and peace, I have been challenged to find myself again and to finally heal the hurts of the past—to let go of the person I had let myself settle into.

Do I dare risk it all to write and travel and let those deepest dreams become a reality?

And then there is Kieran. Sweet, fierce, loving Kieran. I am carelessly getting swept up into this international intrigue that has to inevitably end, but I don't know if my heart can take the agony of letting him go. Oh dear God, am I falling in love with him?

How can that possibly be? I poke fun at those incredulous dating shows that end in engagements after only a few months and shake my head at real-life proclaimed happily ever after stories. Yet here I was, knowing a man for a single week and considering the word "love" when I think of him.

It's absolutely ridiculous. I must be confusing lust with love. Idyllic romance with love. In my vulnerability and realization about Scotty, were my broken-down walls just grasping onto the first nice man who came my way?

How could I turn what is clearly a random holiday affair into something of substance? I barely know him. I just found out he likes his coffee black today, for goodness' sake. I only learned that he owned a pub last night and that he has a sensual singing voice this morning; one that he used to sing a song for me—a song that he wrote about me, no less.

Am I simply following his delusional lead? How could he possibly have the same deep feelings for me? Is he equally captivated only by the idea of being with some American girl on an enigmatic trip?

I knew I would drive myself crazy if I kept letting my mind ask all these questions. I don't think I am quite ready to confront this just yet. Yup, classic Meg avoidance. I decided to take out the journal again and distract myself with the love woes of an ancestor instead.

About an hour later, I heard the welcome sounds of my sisters bantering as they entered the house. *Hmm,* didn't they notice the armed guards outside? I took a quick peek to see Billy and Horace diligently hiding out of sight. I bet Kieran had something to do with that.

Happy to be surrounded by their familiar faces, I ran to the front door to greet them with big hugs.

"Hey! How was your trip? I want to hear all about it!"

Tropical storm Marissa was eager to spill the details. Leaving her luggage right near the door, she plopped down on the couch in excitement. Mia resigned to do the same but was more cautious about it.

Uh oh, her CSI antennas were up—damn it.

I put on my best game face, bringing in tea and some of the fruit salad I had made from this morning as I listened to Marissa gush about their Clare Island experience.

"It was fantastic! Oh, I wish you would have been there with us! We stayed right within the lighthouse in this adorable little room with a view overlooking the sea. It was so tranquil, unlike anywhere I've ever been! Everyone dined together like a big family each night. The service made us feel like royalty. And then we went to the yoga center and got all zen.

"Oh, we split up for some alone time too, so I went on one of those bike hikes while Mia traveled down to the town's shops and then I think spent most of her day in the lighthouse's library, right? It was great to get away. I feel rejuvenated," she ended with a big sigh to indicate she was done and ready to come up for air.

"That does sound amazing and relaxing." I looked over at Mia, who was growing more anxious and uncomfortable by the minute. "What's wrong, Mia? Didn't you enjoy yourself?"

"Oh, I did. Very much. It's not that."

"Then what is it?"

"You tell me," she said accusingly.

Nervous, I shifted in my seat and took a sip of tea. *Shit, I knew it.*

"What do you mean?"

"Come on, Meg. I'm not stupid. You call us to cut our trip short with some story about Colleen needing to meet us earlier—she's a pocketful of energy, late owl type, so what's the big rush all of a sudden? Plus, you've been jumpy since the minute we walked through the door.

"You think I don't notice the officers standing in the

back of the garden? Give me a little credit. Wife of a cop, remember?"

"Can't get anything past you."

"No, you can't. Now tell us—what the hell has been going on around here?"

"Okay," I took a deep breath, not knowing exactly where to start. I led them through the first day when I decided to go up to the attic and found the box of photos and diary. I filled them in on what I learned about our ancestors so far. I left out the part about Kieran joining me for now—I'd get to that later.

Then they sat wide-eyed and worried as I recounted how I felt like I was being followed when I went to the market and then after taking a walk to the creek, how I found the house in shambles.

"Wow, who would do such a thing?" asked Marissa incredibly.

"Well, Kieran and I seem to think that it could be related to our family inheritance, since a few pictures were the only thing they took."

"Wait—how does Kieran fit into all this?" Mia caught on quick.

"Well, that's the other thing," I relented, ready to spill the beans. "We've gotten closer."

"How close?" They asked almost in accord, like a staggered echo.

I started my next round of storytelling, hardly able to contain the pure bliss of finding my own pot of gold. Knowing they'd somehow get it out of me anyway, I told them everything their hungry little ears wanted to hear about our delicious entanglement.

"I'm so happy for you—and relieved he was here to help!" said Mia, with Marissa concurring.

"Me too. I honestly don't know what I would have done without him here. He's the one who set up the guards, helped me translate some of this journal and is now working on who knows what to keep us safe.

"If it is okay with you," I began nervously, "he'd like to come back and hear what Colleen has to say to see if it helps him figure out some pieces to the puzzle. I know this is a private family matter, but he's all wrapped up in this now. But only if you are on board with it."

"Of course," obliged Mia. "I like the fact that someone local is here to look out for us, especially when we have no idea who or what we are up against."

"Yeah, sure," said Marissa quietly, but I could tell there was a hesitation in her voice. I dismissed it, knowing her well enough to recognize that the little hint of jealously over my special overseas adventure played a part in it. I knew she was genuinely happy for me, but she would be happier if she had her own love affair going on at the same time. Weird—because I thought she did.

"Thank you. He should be back in another hour, about the time I expect Colleen to arrive. I'd like to read a little more in this journal first. Do you want to join me?"

"Actually, I'm feeling unsettled from hearing all this and need some time to think. You know how I get—I'd really like to go lose myself in the kitchen and make us all a wonderful dinner before we talk. We do have some food in there, right?" I laughed at Mia as I nodded my head in consent.

"How about you, Marissa?"

"Same with me. I think I'd like to take a walk."

"I don't think that is a good idea with everything going on. We should stay together where the guards are until we know we are safe."

Reluctantly, she agreed. "Fine. I'll just go out and walk around the backyard for a bit—in the guard's view," she added.

"Hey," I called to her, as she turned around in obvious frustration. "I love you, Mar."

She smiled meekly, but it was at least a smile. "I love you too, big sis."

12

The air was filled with the scents of Mia's Guinness beef stew and soda bread. I could hear my stomach rumbling before it unceremoniously turned to flutters when Kieran walked in.

"It smells grand in here!" he exclaimed with hungry enthusiasm as he made his way towards me, then hesitated.

"It's fine. They know."

Relieved, he pulled me in for an affectionate kiss hello. Time did him some good—he was back to his agreeable self again. He greeted both my sisters and then Colleen, who arrived only a few minutes earlier. She was busy in the kitchen helping Mia set up as she rambled on about her latest crisis, glad to have an ear in my sympathetic sister.

"What have you been up to?" I asked him.

"I promised Mum to help her run a few errands. She's getting on in the years and though she can't be kept from her kitchen, she's having a hard time with the keeping of the house and whatnot. Her friend Gerty popped over for a visit, so she scooted me out—but not before she yanked some info out of me about where I'd been," he grinned. "She hopes to be meeting you before you leave."

"That would be nice. I'd love to." Meet his mother? The panic moved through me like the oxygen masks had unexpectedly popped down in a turbulent airplane. Not sure which life-risking situation I'd rather be in right now. This was moving way too fast, like my brakes were tampered with and I couldn't stop the speeding car.

"Dinner's ready!" came the call from the kitchen to break my panic attack.

She had outdone herself again, I thought, taking a bite into a tender morsel of beef. Dinner was full of frivolous conversation, sharing our tourist tales, learning even more places that we "must see" according to Colleen and hearing all about the pub locals from Kieran.

But underneath it all was the underlying tension of what the evening was really all about. When dinner was done, it was Colleen who was the first to break the silence.

"Shall we retreat to the setting area? Kieran, be a good lad and get the fire goin', would ya?"

Sat and settled, not even a creak from the old house dared to break the hush that fell over us as we anxiously awaited what our cousin had to reveal.

"Now mind you, I'm only allowed to be tellin' you about the ring legacy. Still don't understand the way of all the tellin', though," she muttered to the side.

"Anyways, the story of the O'Sullivans dates way back, quite a few generations where they be of royal blood livin' just outside the Pale. That'd be Dublin," she advised.

"Now over many a donkey's years, wars and whatnot pushed our ancestors to settle across the way in County Cork. Though they were no longer in line for the crown, they were still mighty noble with all their riches, they were. Many lived on in peace and prosperity for a good yard of time as such.

"Back in those days, there was no mixin' of the blood, as they would call it. That would have been a holy show for sure! Had to be pure Irish through and through, they did. That is, until your great-great-great grandparent's generation.

"Banan O'Sullivan was the babe of seven children and hardly an heir, but still all posh enough, as it were. One day, his da—that would be James O'Sullivan—met a Spanish nobleman, Eduardo Rubio, whose family had just fallen from grace, thanks to his dosser of a father. That eejit cost the Rubios their honorable status. Didn't have the full shilling, if you know what I mean," she hinted as she circled her fingers around her head in a "cuckoo bird" motion.

She then paused to reprimand herself for not sticking properly to her intended narrative. "Of course, the story of the Rubios has to be the tellin' of *someone else* when you get to Barcelona. All these rules with the tellin'. Egads."

"It's fine," I said as I placed my hand on her arm and smiled. "I love the way you are telling your chosen story. Please continue."

With a grand grin, she resumed her tale to tell.

"An arrangement was made for Rubio's youngwan, Elena, to marry our Banan so that she would be well taken care of and not livin' in bits. Being that Banan was the youngest of seven, who he was hitched to made no matter to his da. Jammy for Rubio, indeed, the lucky bastard.

"It was reckoned a fierce match, though the two forced lovebirds were not so tickled to lob the gob and join in marriage. Elena had to give up all she had known in Spain to move here, she did.

"They were both given a savage fortune for the deal, though. Since staying with his four older brothers on the O'Sullivan family land would be biscuits to a bear, they decided to move away and settle in County Mayo—landing right here in this very gaff.

"It was a purely rural area back then, but Banan—that

cute hoor—had the means to build their home upon this land, along with several other homes and businesses. It's how the chancer made his own fortune, don'tcha know. Of course, those properties have since been sold off to pay for various debts of certain gammy heirs, mind you," she lamented.

Hmm—so I wasn't far off about this town being built like a Monopoly board, with our multi-great grandfather being Uncle Moneybags. Interesting.

"After a while of the marriage, Banan and Elena formed a proper kinship and were rather taken with each other. It is said they were a lovely couple; kind and generous to all. They got on brilliantly—had a grand life, ya know. Well, she bore him two lads: Banan Junior and Cian.

"I'm goin' to just call him Junior so there's no making a haymes of the two Banans," she pointed out, as we nodded in appreciation for the clarity.

"When Junior was born, Banan the elder presented Elena with his mum's treasured ring, which he himself had received in secret upon her death. The story goes that Agatha O'Sullivan had a mighty big soft spot for her wee little one, and so he became the chosen one to inherit the sacred family jewel.

"One of them original Claddagh rings from the 1700's—a one-of-a-kind, never-made-again type. The *Legacy of Love Claddagh*, it be called. Here," she said, handing me an old, tattered picture she took out from her purse.

"It's striking," was all I could muster to describe what I saw. It was a gold Claddagh-style ring with a Celtic knot braid around the band and a solitary emerald sitting upon its center in the shape of a heart, a border of tiny white diamonds caressing its delicate outline.

Not particularly a jewelry person by nature, I fell in love with the exquisitely designed sphere. It called to me just like everything else in this country. Passing the photo around the room, my sisters were equally impressed.

"It was said to be branded in the name of love, it was. But more on that later. Let's not stall the ball," she gestured hastily, eager to carry on.

"So, Banan Junior got the ring from his mother, Agatha?" Marissa asked, perplexed by the complicated history.

"No, no, that wasn't the way of it. Let me back it up. Now, follow along.

"Agatha got the ring when she married James O'Sullivan, who inherited it from his mum and so on. And since Agatha's babe, Banan *the First*, proved to be a dear fella to his foreign betrothed, Elena Rubio, she felt it right to pass it on to him above the others. When Banan *the First* realized his love for Elena and their newborn son *Junior*, he was buzzin' to make it hers. It was then Elena's jewel for keeps."

Colleen courteously paused for Marissa's light bulb of acknowledgment to go off. "Got it."

"Now, as I said, there be two boys from them. Junior and Cian. Well, Junior was a bit of a spoiled scallywag, if you ask me. Entitled little twit, I heard. And I could believe it, because he be my own grandfather—and not the warm type neither.

"He married into another rich family, takin' Kira Callaghan as his wife. Another prize if you ask me. Snooty grandma. I hated when my da made us pay a visit. Sorry, I'll carry on. They had Banan III—me da—and Teagan O'Sullivan, me auntie. All these Banans—I'll just call me da 'Three.'

"Are you keepin' up with me, lasses?"

"Actually, I think so." She grinned when she saw me writing away in my own journal like a *New York Times* reporter covering a big scoop.

"Ah, now that's smarts. Well done, cuz. You found yourself a good match, Kieran, if you don't mind my saying."

He beamed warmly as he pressed his lips into the top of my head. "I did indeed."

Colleen continued with her elongated diatribe about how Junior was a "wile slabber," causing trouble wherever he went. As the rumor goes, he was envious of his younger brother, Cian, whose somewhat better looks and even better disposition earned him a lot of respect in the community—until his dalliance with Italian-born Alessia Bianchi.

Junior tried to use the scandal to his advantage to nudge his baby brother completely out of the way, but his parents would have none of it. Colleen apologized for getting ahead of herself again, cursing that she had to stop the story there because she'd never get to the "real of it" if she kept going off on her tangents.

She resumed the family tree lineup: "Three," her da, married a lovely woman named Mary Collins and had Colleen and her brother Shane. The Collins were with whom she lived with now, as they were the only family she had left after her brother's passing.

Her auntie Teagan also went on to marry well—to a man named Harry Walsh. Tragically, she could not have children. So Colleen, who had never been married or had children herself, is now the last in that line of O'Sullivans, she explained.

On the other O'Sullivan line, Cian and Alessia, despite all the protest and shame they faced, married and had Lena, who then married the wealthy and ambitious Antonio Marino for money.

"Poor lass," Colleen bemoaned. "Her heart was broke to the bone by Ian McDonough, her true love, when he honored his da's wish for an arranged marriage to another mot."

Colleen then revealed how Lena was so crushed and devoid of faith that she ultimately gave up on love and chose to marry for money instead—despite Alessia's attempts to steer her daughter back towards her heart.

But Antonio was madly in love with Lena, and perhaps his inability to take no for an answer wore her already weakened heart down to submission. She subsequently bore two sons, Leigh and firstborn Antonio Jr., who sadly died at the tender age of seven from smallpox.

From there, Leigh married Lillith, and supposedly had no children before divorcing her and marrying his original betrothed, Julia, and adopting her son as his own.

"I always thought I was the end of the O'Sullivan line—aside from Leigh, of course. I thought my cousin was slaggin' me when he called me about the ring and confessed about his Alissa. Scarlet I was after giving him some lashin' for lyin' and then it bein' the bang on truth after all.

"But there you have the whole of it."

Feeling satisfied that we were all caught up on the family tree, Colleen then shifted back to the history of the ring, saying that because of Junior's poor behavior and the difficulty the scandal brought upon the star-crossed lovers, Elena bequeathed the *Legacy of Love Claddagh* ring to Cian and Alessia instead. She supported their love and their fight to be together and believed the ring represented everything their marriage stood for.

Apparently, that didn't sit well with Junior, who protested but lost the fight in the end. He instead was satisfied with many other riches that weren't as sentimental in value, despite his wife Kira's continued objections.

"I remember Grandmum Kira eating the head off Granda one day, saying he was a right moran for not nabbing some ring out of Great Auntie Alessia's bag. I happened to be earwiging under the kitchen table, and they didn't even know it. I did that a lot," she chuckled mischievously.

But the ring remained in Cian and Alessia's possession, Colleen attested, until it was ready to be passed down to Lena as their love child. Even though Lena did not live with love for her husband, the purity of her love for her children and her loyalty to her family made her worthy enough in Alessia's eyes to inherit it—with the promise to keep it secretly away from Antonio and the Marino family. She had faith in her daughter's heart, and that was enough.

Lena held onto the sacred band, hoping that her son would be the one to once again honor its true symbolism, given its rich history and meaning. By then, she had regretted her own life choices and vowed to restore the deep meaning of love back into this legacy.

She secretly cheered with pride as her son, Leigh, ran away to marry his true love Lillith, even against the family's wishes. However, she was not convinced of his strength to keep his promise to stay away from the family, and so kept the ring a secret.

Lena originally intended to bequeath it to Colleen as a true O'Sullivan, but with no family to pass it onto herself, Colleen had no objection to it all working out this way.

"Fair play, it is. All is as it should be," Colleen declared before she explained how it all went down.

When Lena was dying, as Leigh told Colleen, he had

confessed everything to his mother about his love for Lillith and the secret daughter they shared. It was then that Lena revealed the existence of the ring, and an accompanying letter that tells of its origins.

She finally believed he was ready to receive his rightful treasures and keep them safe—all of them.

She urged him to continue to keep the ring silent from the Marinos—made him take an oath to pass it along to his true family when the time came. That was one vow he did not break.

He never told the Marinos of this ring, of its meaning or of its value. Designed for royalty, today it was worth hundreds of thousands of dollars.

"How can that be?" Marissa interrupted. "I didn't realize that emeralds could be worth so much."

"Oh, that ain't no emerald, lass. That be a rare green diamond."

The room became more silent than a Charlie Chaplin movie. A few minutes passed before I spoke.

"Where is the ring now and why would our grandfather pass it down to me and not to Mia, if it's a ring that represents love? She's the married one of the family. Or better yet—why not to our mother?"

"Ay lass, I wondered that myself. When Leigh and I spoke, he was acting the maggot, saying that he had other plans for his Alissa. He crafted quite the deadly strategy for this legacy after studying you all since you were wee babes. It wasn't haphazard, I can tell you that. Blows my mind to think of all the planning involved. Fine thing, he was."

Her voice was filled with genuine awe.

"Anyway, he knew that you had the romantic spirit of his grandmum. You were undoubtedly, to him, the rightful

Celtic *dúchas* and being such, he knew it would be meant for you."

Looking from me to Kieran, she commented, "By the looks of it, sure seems he placed it in the right hands."

I blushed and could feel Kieran heat up a bit as well. Were we really that transparent? It was just an affair, for goodness' sake. Not something worth earning an extravagantly expensive ring for. Holy crap—hundreds of thousands of dollars.

"It be held in a lockbox down in Dublin. You'll be needing to take your next trip there to see Quinn Clark, who will be doing all kinds of verification stuff before sending you to the bank for the lockbox."

"Colleen, may I ask why there is all this mystery surrounding the ring? I mean, why keep it a secret and have us go through such lengths to pass it down through the generations?" asked Mia.

"It be richer than millions, lass—in legend more so than even money. It carries with it a blessing of love and there ain't nothing richer than that in this world. In the wrong hands, it could be melted down to nothing and sold. In the right hands, it will live on, as will its legacy."

"I promise to treasure it always. I will protect it and pass it along to the right person when my time comes," I said, choking up. "I am so honored to be chosen for this."

Marissa interrupted the moment to remind us of something important: did this ring have something to do with someone breaking into the house and stealing the photos?

"That be a mystery to me, for sure. As Leigh told it, I was the only one he was tellin' the truth to about the ring—not even his family or his lawyer. It was just a trinket to them, he supposed, so best be leavin' it that way so you'd get no push back.

"I didn't know anything about it a'tall until Lena reached out, except like I said, I did sometimes hear Grandmum Kira rumble about a ring that was rightfully hers not bein' hers, but that didn't last too long. Lots of baubles later and I'm sure she got over it. And I'm the only one left on this side for the O'Sullivans, so there be no put off ancestors over here."

"Do you think there could be any unknown heirs in your line who might know about this legacy? Or maybe even—who was the first lady again? Oh, Agatha. Perhaps there is someone interested from her side of the family; the one before she married into the O'Sullivan's."

"I suppose there could be," she considered thoughtfully. "I suppose we could even join in Grandmum Kira's line if we wanted to, if she kept rattlin' on about it. But remember, this ring has been a secret in our family for generations and as I heard it, swearings of secrecy accompanied the tellin' of it. Though not sure how much coulda been leaked from me grumpy old grandies, so anything is possible, I'd wager. I can write up my own extended family tree if it helps."

"It would. Thank you," I replied.

"Do you remember when Mr. Perkins told us that one of the family members—oh what's her name?—was curious about protesting this?" Marissa recalled. "What if she is behind it?"

"Peggy Marino? Patrick's wife? I guess we shouldn't rule out anyone at this point. We can have Kevin check in with the authorities at home," I said. "It seems like the more people who are exposed to this legacy, the more suspects to consider."

"Which reminds me," interjected Colleen. "All of you

in this room, including you, Mr. MacGovern, breaking the rules as an outsider—you must vow that you will not speak of this to anyone beyond these here walls. The next person to hear this story, Megan, should be the heir of it."

"I understand. But what about my mother and grandmother? They are part of this heritage. May I share this additional information with them?" I thought it would only be fair, since it should have been in their possession all along.

"Ay of course, but just be careful in the tellin' that it ends there. Never know who be earwiging out there, lookin' to start trouble."

"I promise, I will be very careful. Only my mother and grandmother. No one else."

"Right then. I'm a bit flogged. Would ye be mindin' if I stayed over the night?"

"Not at all. You are welcome to stay as long as you'd like," said Mia. "And please do not fight me on this—I insist you take my room tonight. I can stay in with Megan."

"I won't be fightin' you tonight, lass. Thank you."

"In fact," I announced, "I think we should all be turning in. We learned a lot tonight and we should just sleep on it. We can figure it all out in the morning—including our trip to Dublin."

Nodding in agreement, we pitched in to tidy up the kitchen before retiring. I hated seeing Kieran leave after knowing what it was like to wake up in his arms, but I knew this would be for the best. Besides, I thought as I kissed him goodbye, we could both use a night of *actual* sleep.

Early in the morning, the preparations for Dublin

began. We each took our parts—Mia on transportation and hotel duty and Marissa on touristy must-sees. I called to make arrangements to meet with Quinn Clark later in the afternoon.

This whole trip was turning out to be one big tumultuous journey. Part of me was looking forward to going back home to normalcy. Thank goodness we already planned to wait two months before taking our next trip to Italy. I was exhausted just thinking about it.

With not much time to spare, we boarded the train to Dublin after bidding Colleen a sad goodbye. I had to settle for a "see you in a few days" call with Kieran, sullenly realizing that I only had four more days before I left him for good.

Oh, how my heart and body ached for him like the desert for water. I wish he had been able to join us, but I knew this was a sister trip and I needed to honor that. These were going to be the longest two days of my life until I saw him again.

But maybe that was a good thing—maybe I should cut the ties now since I was leaving soon anyway. Go cold turkey. Just let that one amazing night be the best memory of my life and not complicate it any further. It would be better that way, I decided. It had to be that way, for both of our own good.

The train ride was humdrum, with my sisters and I remaining relatively quiet except for a few whispered exchanges of insight into what we had learned about the ring and our family history. I was more anxious than anyone to find out what kind of verification Quinn Clark needed and what awaited us in Dublin.

Kieran made his objection to the trip without him or police protection known, but we assured him that we were three strong women who would be fine. We let him arrange for a guard to take us to the train depot and then had one awaiting us at Dublin to escort us to our hotel. I was starting to get annoyed with the whole macho overprotective thing.

How did I ever survive life without it? I sarcastically questioned.

Dublin was a bustling city—the complete opposite of that old-world little town in County Mayo. After we checked into our hotel rooms, we realized we had a few hours before my meeting with Mr. Clark, so we decided to lighten things up with some sightseeing.

We stopped in the National Gallery of Ireland for Marissa, who was particularly enamored with the Monet and Italian painters exhibits. Of course, in the gift shop, she found several books on Goya she just *had* to have.

After exiting the museum, we strolled through the city's famous Merrion Square. I grinned broadly when I saw the dedicated Oscar Wilde statue in one of the park's corners and nodded in credit to the powers that be for sending me their not-so-subtle sign in the form of the very quote Kieran first seduced me with.

I took a picture of it and sent it off to him to let him know I was thinking of him.

Quinn Clark's office was tiny but meticulously kept, a single suite on the third floor of a large Dublin office building not far off from the Square. He was a short, stout man, balding with a thick mustache and ruby red cheeks. A genial character, he greeted us warmly, exclaiming how he was awaiting our arrival.

"May I offer you some tea?" asked the young, red-haired beauty with emerald eyes and perfectly manicured hands. I assumed it was his assistant.

"That would be lovely, thank you," remembering that

here, it is more polite to accept than decline.

"Please come sit down," offered Mr. Clark. "It's a pleasure to meet you all. Now which of you be Megan Rossi?"

"That would be me," I said, extending out my hand in welcome before sitting down. The visit was rather routine; he simply needed to check my passport to confirm I was the correct sister, take a sample of my DNA with a swab of the inside of my cheek and have me sign some papers releasing the lockbox to me.

He told me that he should have the approval by morning and would then provide me with the bank's address after exchanging the proper clearances.

"That went better than I anticipated," confessed Marissa. "I half expected another riddle to be solved before getting to the damn bank."

"We haven't gotten there yet, so don't jinx us," I kidded. "Well, we have plenty of time to kill this evening and probably in the morning before we hear back. What's your fancy?"

They looked at each other with a signal of agreement. "The Guinness Storehouse!"

We made it into the Storehouse right before closing, as luck would have it. We had just enough time to go on a self-guided tour, learning how to pour a perfect pint before enjoying one on the house. The free sample took us way up to the seventh floor to the Gravity Bar, a circular room with wide-open glass windows revealing a 360-degree panoramic view of the city.

We were so engrossed in the moment that we failed to notice a man hidden among the crowded lounge area watching us carefully.

"Ladies, I don't know about you, but this has been the

experience of a lifetime. I'm so glad to be sharing it with you both," said Mia as she raised her glass in a toast.

"Oh, it's been a dream come true. All this art and history—it makes me sad to see it come to an end soon," shared Marissa.

"Me too," said a familiar voice. I turned around to find Kieran standing right behind me with his own pint and that sexy smirk.

"Kieran! What—what are you doing here?"

"That was all me," said Mia with pride. "I asked him to come here to be with you. It didn't seem right for you to be apart with so few days left here."

"Not that I am not thrilled to see you," I said, then turning to my sisters, "but this is our family adventure. It's supposed to be about us."

"It *is* about us. But it is also about *you*," Mia pointed out. "This is your particular journey, in Ireland, with this ring. Every experience you have here is a part of the big picture. That includes Kieran."

"Excuse us a moment?" I pulled Mia to the side, leaving behind a confused Kieran and a perturbed Marissa.

Whispering, I began to scold her. "What are you doing? You have no right to meddle in my business like this. It's unfair to Kieran. It has to stop."

"Why, Megan? Why does this have to stop? It doesn't take a genius to see that he is genuinely crazy about you—and you about him. I have not seen you glow like this, like ever—not even with Scotty. Are you telling me that you are okay with just walking away from this—from something you may never find again for the rest of your life?"

"Yes. No. I mean, I don't know. I'm so confused, Mia."

"I know, I get it. I didn't mean to push. But don't you owe it to yourself and to that man over there to honestly see what this is?"

I tossed her a slight head bob as a gesture she could be right.

"There's a reason I booked separate rooms for us all tonight. I suggest you take advantage of it," she advised in that maternal, no-nonsense tone of hers, walking away back towards the rest of our group.

"All settled," Mia announced in cocky triumph.

13

It took less than a minute after closing the hotel door behind us before Kieran began ravishing me. Clothes fell to the floor in rushed desire—the kisses were hard and zealous instead of the gentle, loving ones leading the way on our first night together.

"Not being with you last night drove me crazy."

"Tell me about it," he whispered hoarsely. "I must have taken a dozen cold showers."

He continued to kiss me hard, deeply, as he grabbed my breasts and began toying with my nipples to stir me up. I curved under his touch, bringing his body closer to mine. His hand moved rapidly down my side and into me, satisfied to find me moist and ready for him. He slipped inside so naturally, his thrusts hurried with mutual longing.

"Not so fast," I smiled naughtily, turning him over so that I could take control. I wanted to know what it felt like to ride him like a Harley Davidson, to feel that rush of adrenaline against my open road. I decided to start out slowly, moving ever so seductively and building up the intensity between us.

I ignored his pleas of wanting more, yearning to go faster, but that made it all the more exciting for me to take my time. When I knew neither of us couldn't resist any longer, I moved more forcefully, skillfully rocking with increasing speed. With each passionate lunge, I could feel both of us rising to the heights of ecstasy until we simultaneously exploded into an orgasmic wonderland of love and lust.

I held onto the electric shivers that coursed through my entire body, pausing to let the release flow through me completely into an uncontrollable shudder before curling up in his sweaty, loving arms. I knew then it would be another delightfully sleepless night.

Morning came too soon, and the hint of sunlight from the window reminded me that this couldn't be some lazy day in bed—there was a lot to be done. Looking over at my beautiful man lying there asleep, I soundlessly left the bed so I could get into the shower. Not long after, Kieran had awoken and snuck in to join me, distracting me once again from my mission in the most pleasing of ways.

We finally were able to pull ourselves apart and get dressed. He ordered up some breakfast, which I had forgotten about, while I checked my phone to see if there were any messages from Mr. Clark. I was hoping the results would have been in by this point. Not realizing that I was being watched, I looked up to find Kieran staring at me with an amused smile.

"What?"

"Do you know how incredibly adorable you are when you pout in frustration?"

I could only shake my head at him, moving over to the bed to sit on his lap for a full body embrace and kiss. Although I was laughing, I noticed he became a bit more thoughtful and the air in the room shifted from playful to serious.

"I could hold you like this for the rest of my life, *mo shíorghrá.*"

My body immobilized in place. Freezing superseded

fright or flight, leaving my instincts clouded as to what to say or do next.

"What did you just call me?"

"*Mo shíorghrá*. It means—"

"I know exactly what it means," I interrupted crossly as I leapt off his lap and walked over to the other side of the room to let my brain take over for my foolish heart.

'My Eternal Love.' What Leigh called Granny. His broken promises, her crushed heart and the end of a true love all came rushing back to me. Just like Scotty and his own empty words. Another sworn road that led to nowhere.

It was the wakeup call I needed that this had gotten too serious, too fast, and that it needed to end now before it went any further. I should have fought harder against Mia's suggestion to live in the moment and insisted that Kieran return home. Look where it's gotten me now.

I've been lovestruck stupid. *This* is exactly why I tried my damnedest for years to rid myself of my own quixotic nature. It's a drug that pulls me in and makes me hopelessly delusional.

I am only here for two weeks; it's not real. This is not some simulated sentimental movie I'm starring in. It's just some overseas flirtation. *Jesus, Megan. Are you that daft?*

I know better than this. My vow be damned—I was in over my head with this butterfly transformation of soul nakedness. This is not what I committed myself to on those cliffs. His seemingly harmless sweet talk reminded me that I was only conning myself that we could play the role of everlasting lovers.

"Whoa, Megan—why are you so angry?" He looked truly bewildered.

"I'm not angry—I'm just—I'm just frustrated. Mostly with myself. Kieran, we've known each other, what, a week? And you are dropping endearments of eternal love? Come on, Gov."

"It's how I feel, Meg. What's gotten into you?" I saw the look of pain in his eyes and had to turn away.

"It's just—" I paused for a moment, not knowing what to say. Usually so composed, I couldn't find the right words. "This is not a fairy tale, Kieran. Flowery language may have gotten me into bed, but it's not going to keep this, whatever this is, going. It's so—trite sounding," I blurted.

Looking utterly baffled, I could see a bit of temper flaring beneath his volcanic surface. "Sorry, I don't just drop meaningless flatteries to get a woman into bed. That's not who I am, and you should at least know that by now. I meant every word I've ever said to you."

"Yeah well, that's what Granny thought too before my grandfather up and abandoned her. I won't be another victim of Irish blarney."

"Ah, so that's the story, is it? It's about your granda? You gotta be kidding me."

"No, I'm serious. Who's to say that you wouldn't do the same thing to me the second I board the plane?" As soon as the sassy words came out, I knew I hit a nerve, but held firm to my defiance. I had to cement my mindset.

You are in a meeting with Jones and he is trying to usurp you, I told myself, recreating an old work adversary scenario. *Gain your emotional balance and rise above his persuasion. You are the influencer. You call the shots.*

Full on angry now, Kieran marched over to where I was, grabbed me by the arms and looked straight into my eyes with fury as he spat, "I am not your grandfather. Don't ever compare me to another man like that."

He stood strong, holding on, as we matched fire with fire. Finally, he released his grasp when I let a wince sneak out, but he didn't budge from his place right up against my face.

"Fine, then let's just talk about you—this," I gestured, pushing him back to give myself space. I couldn't look at him any longer. My resolve was diminishing quickly, and I knew I had to be strong for my own self-preservation. One of us had to be logical about all this. Guess that would have to be me.

What good would this relationship do when I returned to New York? That was the fundamental question that had to be addressed. That's what this ultimately comes down to. Time to face what we were both in denial about.

"This has all been wonderful, but I think this has gone far enough," I finally said matter-of-factly. "I'm leaving in two days, so there is no point in dragging this out, Kieran. It's time to end this little love game, don't you think?"

Stunned at the change in personality, he mumbled something inaudible before addressing me.

"What game? Who's playing a game? Have you lost your mind? Who *are* you?" he asked as he exasperatingly ran his fingers through his hair in disbelief. He legitimately looked taken aback. "I'm not playing any games here, Megan. If anyone be playing at something, it's you, out of nowhere. I don't even know this woman standing here in front of me."

"Well, it's time you met the *true* Meg, then. The smart and sensible one. Not the scared, helpless, silly girl you seem to fancy."

"Believe it or not, I fancy *all* of you," he barely managed through gritted teeth.

"No, what you love is the drama of it all. Since the day we met, it's been non-stop romantic gestures and surprises and all kinds of courting. For what? We shouldn't be talking and acting like it's love when we just met because truthfully, it's not going anywhere.

"Can't we just call it what it is, some really great sex, and move on?" I felt the scorpion sting go right through his heart, instantly regretting the words.

"Feck, woman, really great sex? Is that what *you* think this was?"

I might have gone a bit too far. I couldn't backtrack now, though. What's done is done. I had to be the director and call end scene. Now or never—before my nerves of steel dwindled.

Still, it killed me inside to see him hurting like this; to know I was the one hurting him. I'd be lying to myself if I said this felt right. It didn't. But ending this now was the only thing that made sense in the big picture. Clearly, he wasn't on the same page.

"I didn't ask to meet you. I didn't ask to fall in love with you. I didn't ask for any of this, Meg. But here it is, clear as day and I can't stop or control what I feel."

"You just met me. It's not real. It's just—lust," I barely managed, still trying to convince myself more than him.

I started to weaken. I was fighting so hard against the feelings, against my own growing love for him, but it just can't be. We're from two different worlds, literally. I live in another country, for goodness' sake.

"Don't you dare tell me what I mean and what I don't mean, lass."

He grabbed me and kissed me more vehemently than he ever did before. My body couldn't help but override my mind and respond, feeling the heat that was so natural between us, mixed with the sweetness of two souls that were connected by more than just kisses.

"Does that feel like just lust?" he pleaded in a raspy,

broken voice.

As I stood there fighting against the tears, speechless without a sharp comeback, his temper took a backseat. He gently lifted my chin up for our eyes to meet, with sincere concern and even the threat of his own tears lining his eyes.

"Do you mind telling me what this is really all about, lass?"

I took a moment to gather my scrambled thoughts.

"I feel like I am all caught up in some girlish love fantasy and I don't need this complication in my life right now." Perhaps straight up honesty might be the ticket to get me off this merry-go-round.

We sat in silence for a moment until I felt stronger to resume. He was giving me the chance to explain myself, which made him all the more difficult to resist. Ugh. How am I going to get through this sensibly with those eyes on me?

Be resilient, Meg. You can do this.

"I have worked my ass off to get where I am in life. I have fought against a corporate America where men are more respected, and I have had to claw my way with as much dignity as I could to earn half the respect. I am independent and can take care of myself, Kieran. What we have enjoyed has been truly fantastic, but it's not this Disney-esque love affair that needs to extend beyond this trip.

"Although I appreciate your concern, I also don't need some man protecting me as if I can't handle myself. I hate who I have been, feeling like this feeble female needing some knight on a white horse. I'm a strong woman, damn it, not a victim. And I certainly don't need to fall into the arms of a man and forget who I am. I won't lose myself ever again—not for anyone."

He paused for a while, taking in everything I said before he got up. His back stiffened, standing away from me, inhaling deeply. He sensed I was not going to budge. He then turned around and spoke sharply.

"I love you for exactly the woman you are, Megan Rossi. I love that you're independent and can take care of yourself. I love that we can match wits. I love your fire and everything that makes you, you. The bad-ass executive and the whimsical writer.

"I love *all* of it. So much so that I wanted to keep you safe. Not to be sexist and diminish your strength, but to preserve it. I love you, against my own wishes, feck it, but I do. It was truly instant for me. Why can't you accept that?"

"Because it can't be," I concluded in a defeated whisper. "We got swept up in the moment. It's time for us to just let it go before either of us gets hurt."

"Too late. Forgive me for misreading your signs that you felt as strongly for me as I felt for you. But if a fling is all you wanted, you got it. Thanks for the great sex," he hissed back bitterly, as he walked out the door and slammed it.

All I could do was just sink down into the corner on the floor, dumbfounded.

What have I done? What the fuck is wrong with you, Megan?

I then let the sobs fall out until I was a completely crumpled ragdoll of a mess.

Gratefully, my pity party didn't last too long. Mr. Clark called soon after with the news that I was cleared to pick up the ring from the bank. I took a few minutes to pull myself together, covering up the evidence that I had a long morning of crying before seeing my sisters.

I also had to come up with a good cover story about why Kieran was no longer there—I just didn't have it in me to listen to them rattle on about their own fantasies about us. I'm not sure if they bought the story that he had to go back to his mum to help her out, but it was enough to keep the questions at a minimum—at least for now.

The trip to the bank was surprisingly just as smooth as our meeting with Mr. Clark. With some simple identification, I was handed the keys to the safe deposit box and led to a private room for us to view its contents. Inside was a small metal fireproof box that had certainly seen some wear and tear over its many years.

Opening it up, we were collectively stunned at the pure exquisiteness of the ring I held in my hand. The picture had not done it justice. Although it could use a bit of a cleaning, you could tell it was well preserved over the many generations.

"The *Legacy of Love Claddagh* ring. Wow. It's absolutely stunning," I whispered in awe.

"I'll say. Try it on—does it fit?" Marissa asked.

"It's a little loose. I guess I'll need to get it fitted, though I'm not sure I'm really worthy of wearing it, despite our grandfather's faith in me."

"Why would you say that?" Mia asked.

"Kieran didn't really go home to check on his mum."

"We already suspected that," confessed Marissa. "Are you ready to tell us why he did leave?"

"We got into a fight. He called me *mo shíorghrá* like Leigh called Granny and I don't know—it just triggered me. All the pain came rushing back from Scotty falsely promising to love me forever and seeing Granny's broken heart and thinking about the impossibility of living in two different countries—I just—I couldn't let all this nonsense go on. So, I put an end to it. It didn't end very well."

"Oh Meg, I'm so sorry." Mia gave me a big hug. Marissa, on the other hand, was just staring at me incredulously.

"So you mean to tell me, that after all this time, you find someone you could actually love, who loves you like crazy back, and your response is to run away?"

"Marissa!" scolded Mia.

"No. Don't chide me like I'm the one in the wrong here. Meg, we have watched you struggle for years to get over Scotty. And then we saw you have this wonderful epiphany at the Cliffs of Moher and watched as our sister came back for a brief moment in time, remembering that she was worthy of love.

"That love miraculously came along in the form of a truly wonderful man—and right at the moment you were tested to see if you believed in that love, you failed. You failed miserably, Meg. Not only have you hurt your own heart, but you undoubtedly broke one of a man who so plainly and genuinely cares for you.

"What the fuck is wrong with you?"

"I don't know," I said, as the waterworks started up again. After this trip, I was certain I'd run out of tears for the next one hundred years.

"I—I just don't think it makes any sense to pursue something that inevitably has to end. How would we make it work? We live across the Atlantic Ocean from each other. It's complicated. Am I supposed to just believe that somehow things would work out?"

"Yes, damn it. It's called taking a risk—and it does happen outside of your little advertising world. Maybe you are right—maybe it will blow up in your face and it won't last. But for crying out loud Meg, what if it can work out? What if what you've been looking for your entire life is right in front of your face?

"Are you really ready to just walk away from it? Do you think that we get so many chances at love that it's worth rolling the dice and hoping you'll find another perfect man close by in New York City? Seriously?"

I let the air fill with silence as I absorbed everything Marissa just said. I could only stare at this ring in my hand, remembering its significance and how it was bequeathed to me.

"Oh my God, what have I done?"

"Nothing that you can't fix," said Mia gently, lifting me up from the floor and handing me a tissue.

"How about we take this ring back to the hotel to keep it safe and then take one last go around Dublin. When we get back, you can call Kieran and work it all out. I'm thinking he will need the day to cool down, but I have no doubt he'd rather be with you than without you."

"I really hurt him, Mi. You should have seen the look on his face."

"Well, then it's up to you to bring the smile back. Fight for love, Meg. You deserve it."

"Thanks. I don't know what I would do without either of you." I embraced them before Marissa let out one of her perfectly timed cynical comments.

"You would make a complete mess of your life."

Back at the hotel, we decided to each freshen up before heading out for lunch in the fair city of Dublin. My mind was racing with how I would apologize to Kieran and ask for his forgiveness.

What a mess you've made this time, Rossi.

I took out the ring one last time for inspiration, noticing

a note inside of the box. We must have missed it tucked inside the back corner while admiring the sparkly jewel at the bank. Seeing as it was a bit weathered itself, I carefully opened it up, curious about what it would say. I figured it was probably the legacy letter that Colleen mentioned came along with the inheritance.

As I read the words, a smile came over my face and I knew exactly what I needed to do. I protectively pocketed the tattered piece of paper, leaving the valuable ring locked safely back in the box and on the nightstand before meeting my sisters in the lobby. It was time to take a break from all this drama.

Lunch was outstanding. Mia had somehow managed to get us in to the 1592 Restaurant—a dining establishment not even open to the general public. I had to give it to her— she was craftier than I gave her credit for.

It was an adorable little place, more traditional in style than the city splendor that surrounded it. Knowing this could be the last fine dining experience of our trip, we decided that good old Granda Leigh would not be disappointed in our indulgence.

We each ordered something different so we could share plates, selecting from marinated chicken breasts, baked cod and sirloin steak, accompanied by mushroom risotto and buttered asparagus—and of course, a Bailey's Irish cheesecake to top it all off.

I decided to tuck my troubles away and just enjoy this time with my sisters. We chatted about the diary and the mystery, and they filled me in more about Clare Island. We imagined what our trip to Italy would be like, teasing Mia about what mishaps she would drag us into on her journey.

As we were already on campus, we explored Trinity College, admiring all the history it held, from books and literary exhibitions to an ancient harp and beautifully manicured gardens.

"Mom would love this place," Mia mused, as we agreed.

So would Daddy, I thought. *What would he think of the disaster I've made of my life today?* I wondered.

Our tour coming to an end, we decided it would be best to pack up our stuff and head back to the west coast early. We only had two more days and with the ring in hand, we could spend the rest of our time just relaxing in our ancestral home.

The moment we arrived back at the hotel, our plans were thwarted. Seeing my door slightly open—forcibly so—I quietly tiptoed backwards so as to not be heard by an intruder, and then ran straight to the lobby to report the break-in. I didn't know if anyone was still in there, but I wasn't about to be one of those crazy suspense knuckleheads who tried to go inside and check it out by themselves.

Mia and Marissa met me in the hallway by my room as the hotel manager and security guards rushed from the elevator. They had already called the Dublin Garda, who were on the way. Stepping aside, we let the armed security guards enter first, to find no one inside. Waving us in, I gasped to see how wrecked my room was.

"Just like the O'Sullivan house was," I whispered.

"Sorry?" asked the guard.

"We were staying at our family home in Louisburgh and had a similar break-in earlier this week. Everything was disheveled, but nothing was taken. Same here, except—"

I froze. The box! The lockbox was gone.

"Meg, what is it? What's missing?" prodded Mia.

"The ring. They took the ring."

"How could they take the ring? Didn't you lock it in the safe?" Marissa demanded.

"I wasn't thinking, I guess. I figured we were only going to be out for a little while and I had the privacy sign on the door so housekeeping would not come in, so I thought it would be fine right here by the bed."

"Can you describe this ring to us, miss? I'm also gonna be needing a formal statement," said the lead officer, who had just arrived. I went through the motions, explaining everything I knew, showing them the picture from Colleen that I happened to bring with me.

Mia and Marissa had their turn speaking with the Garda, noting that their rooms were undisturbed. We gave them our contact information and they said they would be in touch after reviewing the security footage and conducting their investigation.

When they were done in the room, they left us to gather our things so we could head back west. One of the guards remained outside of the door and planned to escort us to my sisters' rooms to retrieve their luggage, and then to the train station to ensure our continued safety.

All I could do was stand there in disbelief before starting to pack.

"I can't believe it. So, someone must have been after the ring the whole time. But who?" Mia asked.

"Beats me. Like Colleen said, not many people knew about it. I'm guessing we should do some digging into who might know about it within different extended family lines. So much for preserving its secret," I muttered.

"I'm so sorry you lost the ring, Meg. I hope they find it and put the jackass behind bars."

"It's okay, Mar. It's just a ring."

"How can you be so calm about this? Someone has

broken into your space—twice—scared you half to death and stolen your inheritance worth over a half million dollars."

"Whoever was following me has finally gotten what he or she wanted. Now, maybe we'll be left alone in peace. Let them have it—there are more valuable things in this life than an old ring. We are safe and no one was hurt. I have everything I need in front of me."

"Not everything," Mia reminded me.

"Almost everything."

14

As expected, both Colleen and Kieran were waiting at the house upon our arrival—as were our favorite armed guards. Mia had forewarned me that she called Kieran to explain what happened and softened him up enough for him to join us.

Just seeing him set off rockets of different emotions, from fear and shame to pure joy and relief. He could barely look at me, I noticed. Colleen, oblivious to our tension, rushed over to us in mad worry.

"Oh my dears, I'm so glad you're not hurt! I feel terrible for my part in this. I shoulda told Leigh this would be too dangerous and to keep you out of it. Bound to be someone sniffin' around after a rich man's funeral, I told him, I did."

"It's okay, Colleen," I told her softly. "Everyone is safe now. They got what they wanted. Hopefully that's the end of it."

"Well, now that I know you are all safe here with the guards, I'd best be on my way," said Kieran.

I impulsively grabbed him by the arm. "Wait. Please."

He just turned and looked at me with a mix of anger and pain, driving a knife into my heart. Peering around at the other company, I used my eyes to plead them for a little privacy. Mia took the hint and escorted Marissa and Colleen to the bedrooms to unpack so we could have our space.

All I could do when we were alone was look at him with such regret. I stood there, all the words I rehearsed in my head gone. I just didn't know what to say.

"What do you want with me, Megan? I thought you said everything that needed to be said."

"I know you are angry, and you have every right to be. Can—can we sit down for a minute?" I motioned towards the sofa that held the memories of our passionate embraces. Begrudgingly, he followed my lead.

"I'm sorry, Kieran. I am really, really sorry. I was so scared, and I didn't know how to handle my feelings about leaving you and I just—I blew it."

"Blew what? It was just a fling, remember?" Ouch. I flinched like he had just hit me in the head with a ceramic vase. I deserved that.

"No, it wasn't. It's not. I've tried to fight it, but I can't. And I was wrong, so incredibly wrong, to act as if it was nothing—like *you* were nothing. Being with you is something I have never experienced in my entire life.

"I let myself fall into this abyss where I lost control of my emotions, let myself feel completely free—and when the reality hit that my time here was coming to an end, I went into default mode and hardened out of fear.

"I had to protect my heart. I'm so frightened of what I feel and the fact that I can't control it, that I can't for certain say that I know how it will all work out—it just paralyzed me."

We sat there speechless for a moment. He was softening, but I saw I still had some work to do. I could feel him demanding my vulnerability at all costs—at the cost of his love.

"It's not easy for me to be so open, Kieran. This is new territory for me. I don't need to divulge my deepest sentiments in a client meeting or with a random lover. But with you, it's different. You make me feel so unbelievably loved and beautiful and accepted fully for who I am—all of me.

"I'm terrified of losing control of my life, of letting my heart take over and lead the way. But, I'm even more terrified of losing you."

Pausing, I took a deep breath. I moved my hand over his and instead of flinching, he took it in his, waiting for me to finish.

"I love you, Kieran. God help me, I am so completely and unreasonably in love with you. I know I have to stop being so cynical and trust myself and my heart for once in my life. I don't deserve a second chance after what I said to you, but I'm asking for one anyway. Can you ever forgive me?"

"I suppose so," he said with a slight smile. "But is this really what you want, Meg? Really, truly what you want? I need to know for certain. It's not easy for me to lend my heart out for the risk, either, you know."

"Yes. I want you. I want us. The second you walked out the door this morning I crumbled. I—I don't know if I can truly live without loving you. But I also don't know how it could work. I mean, truthfully, I don't know where to go from here."

"You're getting in your head again, *a ghrá*. We'll sort it out."

"You seem so confident about it. How can you be so sure? We live in two different countries, lead two different lifestyles. I try not to be in my head, but how could I not be?"

"Have a little faith. You're not the only one with inheritance money, you know. I have plenty to use for a few trips to New York. We can make it work, but *a ghrá*, sometimes it takes a bit of effort. It's not always an easy road. But it's worth a try, isn't it?"

"If it means having you love me, it's worth more than just a try." With that, I reached over to tenderly kiss him. A kiss never felt so wonderful, because it meant that all was right with the world—our world.

Our full-on reconciliation was interrupted by the chuckling of a few recent eavesdroppers.

"I guess it's safe to come down now?" Marissa teased.

"It is," I laughed.

"Well done, you two. I'm glad you be back together and all, but can we get down to the business at hand? What are you be going to do about that ring of yours?" asked Colleen.

"Well—" I smiled sheepishly.

"What is it, Meg?" asked Mia.

"I actually have something to tell you." I paused for effect. "The ring wasn't stolen."

"What are you talking about? Of course it was—we were right there with you when you realized it was gone," stated Marissa, confused.

"Actually, that was a decoy ring. The original ring is hidden safely somewhere else. Here—read this." I took the folded note out from my pocket and handed it to Marissa to read out loud.

To the heir of this magnificent ring,

Though we do our best to preserve this family secret, many a greedy fool will try to gain possession of this treasure. To keep it safe, I have created this mock ring in its likeness. Let it be revealed as true; and then once safe, the faithful jewel can be found in the protection of Our Lady of St. Mary—at the very church down the road from the O'Sullivan family home.

Ye need only ask for the head priest, who has vowed to hold this secret in the confidence of this church until the rightful heir comes to claim it. There, ye shall find the legacy letter and the many blessings that accompany it. Honor and cherish this mighty band as I did and do right by your heritage in the name of love.

Yours, Lena O'Sullivan

"Wow," Mia said. "So, you knew this whole time that only a fake was stolen, and that the real one was here? No wonder why you were so cool when it all went down!"

"Why didn't you tell us?" asked Marissa, disconcerted.

"I thought it was best I told everyone at once. Besides, I didn't want any of the Garda to know until I had the real one in my possession and was out of the country.

"They can close the case or pursue it when we are gone; but for now, I didn't want anyone at all to overhear us or get wind of it and chance them finding the true ring. I liked knowing, at least for the moment, that we were all out of harm and wanted to keep it that way."

"Smart lass, she is, she is!" declared Colleen. "So, you'll be going to get it in the morning then, will you?"

"Yeah, it's been a long day. We can take off after breakfast and finish our journey here once and for all."

"Actually, I think Marissa and I should stay behind. I think you and Kieran should do this together—without us." Marissa returned her consent.

"But this is your inheritance and legacy as much as mine. We are in this together. I can't do this without you," I contested.

"Meg's right. I shouldn't even be here to begin with. This is your family journey. I shouldn't have any part in it, other than to just love on this one as much as I can before she leaves," Kieran argued.

"That's exactly why you *should* be the one to go with Meg. Look, we appreciate you thinking of us, but it isn't our place to be there. The heir of the ring should be joined by her love and read the legacy letter together. We can read it when you get back," Marissa added.

"Okay, then. Kieran, are you okay with this? Can you go with me in the morning?"

There was that warm dimpled smile I missed so much. "There's nothing I'd love better. But on one condition."

"What's that?"

"That at some point tomorrow, you come meet my mum before she cuts me head off."

"Deal," I laughed. "So, what do you all say we sit down and order in a nice quiet family dinner?"

"That sounds lovely," replied Mia.

"Actually," proposed Kieran, "I have a better idea."

A night at Gov's was exactly what the doctor ordered after another long day. It was the perfect way to lift our spirits, dining on a hearty meal, chatting with our new buddy Tuggs and other locals, and watching my beloved fall into his soul as he played his keyboard with the band.

It was nice to sit back and indulge in some small talk and laughter. Mia updated us on some humorous mini disasters Mom and Granny were having at home with juggling the kids' schedules and attitudes. Kieran and I talked about where I would bring him when he visited in a few weeks and prepared him for the investigative questioning he would undoubtedly receive from the rest of the family.

We also admired a new Celtic ring Marissa was wearing—a Claddagh of her own, which she claimed she purchased at a souvenir shop while we were paying for merchandise in another. We all agreed we had plenty of keepsakes racked up over two weeks that would fill one suitcase alone.

Not wanting to make my sisters or Colleen uncomfortable in the small house with thin walls, Kieran invited me to spend the night at his place instead. Bidding adieu to my approving sisters and cousin, off we went to his cottage.

It was hard to see the details in the dark, but it looked as sweet as I imagined it would be. His mum was already asleep in her room, thankfully on the first floor and far enough away from Kieran's upstairs bedroom for plenty of privacy. I never loved on a man with such heart and soul as I did that night.

In the morning, we were greeted by a tall, striking elderly woman with gray-black tendrils, familiar blue-green eyes and a delicate china doll face. I half expected his mother to be another little Irish bitty, but she was not the withered, sick old lady Kieran had led me to believe she was. She smiled at us coming down the stairs—a smile that quite clearly she handed down to her son.

"Well, I'll be! Is this the mysterious Miss Megan that has stolen me lad's heart?"

"It is," Kieran beamed proudly. "Morning, Mum." He went over to give her a peck, then brought me over to be formally introduced. She wrapped me in a big bear hug and I loved her instantly.

"I was just about to make breakfast. You hungry?"

"I can make breakfast, Mum. Why don't you sit down?"

"I'll have none of that, lad. You know I am perfectly capable of making breakfast."

Turning to me, she asked, "Is he this bossy with you too, lass? Thinks just because his mum hurt her hip a while back that she's incapable of living. I still have me arms, ya know."

I couldn't help but laugh as he shook his head. "I tried Mum, but Meg here has already set me straight on her being an independent woman and all."

"Well done," she said approvingly.

We enjoyed a simple family breakfast getting to know each other. I could tell that he got more than his smile from his mum—he had her innate kindness and generosity, along with her stubbornness. I loved witnessing their own little family dynamic and grew even fonder of him, seeing how much they adored and looked out for each other.

"Well, we best be going now, Mum."

"Where are you off to?"

"Meg has some family business to finish up this morning and then I thought we'd just head back to the O'Sullivan house and spend some time together before she flies home tomorrow."

"Oh, darn. I was just getting to enjoy your company and now you're going. Safe travels, lass," she said with an embrace. "You are welcome back here anytime, you know. Any time a'tall."

"Thank you. It was a pleasure meeting you. Say— would you like to come over for dinner? My sister is an outstanding cook and we would love for you to join us on our last night."

"That sounds lovely! It would be grand to take a night off meself and enjoy another's home cooking. Kieran darling, just give me a ring when you have the time and I'll get myself all ready. How delightful!"

In the truck, Kieran leaned over and gave me a long, hard kiss. "You just made my mum's whole life with that invitation, you know. She's quite fond of you, I can tell."

"I'm fond of her, too. You made her seem like some elderly old woman who could barely walk. She seems perfectly healthy to me."

"Ay that she is, I suppose. I guess I need to work on my overprotective skills," he relented. "Oh—wait a minute. I almost forgot something."

He jumped out of the truck and ran back into the house for a moment.

"What's wrong?" I asked when he came back winded.

"Never you mind. Are you ready to go get that ring?"

"Let's do it!"

We agreed that we would park his truck at the house, go inside to say a quick morning hello and change my clothes, and then take a walk down to the church. It had been raining all night and the overcast sky threatened to open up again, but he assured me that we would be fine.

I told my sisters and cousin I had invited Mrs. MacGovern to dinner, which pleased Colleen immensely. I was going to miss our bubbly old cousin, but we already agreed to monthly video calls to stay in touch.

While my sisters began to pack, Colleen offered to gather up the remaining old photos and journal to take home with us, along with a few other trinkets from the house that she was happy to part with.

The plan when we got back to the house was to enjoy the afternoon and evening quietly as a family before our flight first thing in the morning. It was bittersweet to see our trip come to an end, saying goodbye to the wonderful people we met, but we were ready to go home.

Boy, did we have some stories to share!

But first, I had a mission to complete. With Kieran's hand in mine, we set off for Our Lady of St. Mary's to claim the genuine *Legacy of Love Claddagh* ring.

The inside of the church was just as picturesque as the outside. Old, refurbished wooden pews lined the small room leading the way up to the altar, which was adorned with white and gold fabric, tall gold candelabras and fresh white floral arrangements on each side.

Above the altar in honor of the church was an intricate sculpture of the Mother Mary built into the wall, hands spread out as if blessing the congregation. The stained glass windows that lined the side of the wall depicted various religious symbols and stories, wrought with detail and sacred meaning.

Although I was not much of a churchgoer, I couldn't help but find myself enamored with the tiny cathedral. From behind a starch white curtain came an elderly priest, perhaps well into his eighties, donning a pristine white and gold robe and holding a Bible to his heart.

"Ah, welcome, my children. May I help you?"

"Good morning, Father. I am looking for the Head Priest of this church."

"That would be me. I'm Father Joyce." We bowed in his presence.

"It's nice to meet you, Father Joyce. My name is Megan Rossi. I am Colleen O'Sullivan's cousin and descendant of Cian and Alessia O'Sullivan. Have you heard of us by any chance?"

"I have indeed. I have been waiting for you, Ms. Rossi. I believe I have something precious of yours in the back here. Please wait right here a moment."

"Wait," I stopped him. "Don't you need some kind of identification or proof of who I am or something?"

He had a somewhat toothless, yet lovable grin. "My child, I would know a daughter of the O'Sullivan line anywhere. You look just like old Cian from the photos I've seen. Your family is legend in this town. There be no doubt in my mind that you are the rightful heir."

Within minutes, he was back with an absolutely beautiful, dark Kelly green Fabergé egg with an intricately designed trim of golden Celtic knots. He presented it to me, gesturing for me to open it in his company. Inside was a stunning statuette of a green and gold Claddagh symbol, and within the empty space of the Claddagh heart were the tied strings of a small black felt bag.

My heart pounding, I opened the bag to reveal the *Legacy of Love Claddagh* ring—its brilliance blinding like the sun. The decoy had nothing on the original. Unlike the fake version, this band happened to be a perfect fit as I slid it onto my right ring finger to embrace it with all its glory.

Father Joyce then motioned to a small latch under the stand of the egg, which when opened, revealed an ancient piece of parchment paper.

"The legacy letter," I deduced. I delicately opened it up, making sure to preserve its integrity and protect it from ripping. I looked up at Father Joyce and thanked him for watching over our family legacy.

"It has been an honor, Miss Megan. Would you mind doing an old man a favor, though?"

"Of course. What is it?"

"This egg has been under the church's protection for over fifty years—thirty under my sole care. It would warm my heart if I could share in the reading of the legend. I vow to never speak of it to another soul. I should know better than to be intrigued by worldly possessions such as these, but I can't help but to wonder about the story behind it all."

"Of course, Father. I can think of no better place than to read it right here." Beaming like a little boy on Christmas morning, the priest took his place on the bench to my left, while Kieran joined me on my right.

THE LEGEND OF THE LEGACY OF LOVE CLADDAGH

In the year of 1682, a noble king, King Padraig II, asked young silversmith Duncan McGuinness to fashion him a unique ring intended for his new bride. He had given the lad a rare green diamond, the richest jewel in all the land.

When young Duncan asked the name of the king's intended so that he may bring her spirit into his creation, he was heartbroken to learn it was his own Maeve Flanagan.

Although from different upbringings—Maeve's of nobility and Duncan's of simple silversmiths—the two younglings had a fondness for each other as children, sneaking off to play in the woods and spend days by the creek.

As they grew older, fondness turned to love, and they planned to run away so they could be together. But as Duncan found out that very day, Sir Flanagan had promised his daughter Maeve to the king and that ended all dreams of being together.

Woefully broken hearted, Duncan decided to leave his Maeve one last piece of himself to remember their love. So, being in his truest of heart, he forged the ring with the green diamond in the symbol of the Claddagh, created a band in the likeness of the trinity knot and added a drop of his blood to the branding fire as it closed the hands around the heart.

The king was quite pleased with the one-of-a-kind ring and when presented to his almost bride, it was said she could feel the presence of love within the exquisite band. She asked to be taken to its maker to thank him for his gifted work, unbeknownst to either that the silversmith was indeed her truest love.

When she found out it was Duncan, and he acknowledged that it was his blood within the ring he designed for her out of his own love, she agreed to follow him into their special woods for a final moment together before accepting her fate as future queen. There, they made love for the first and only time, with Maeve giving him the gift of her innocence and the ring symbolically set firm upon her left hand.

After they were joined in sacred love, the Goddess Danu came upon them and blessed their union and the ring forevermore.

Angered that fate was to keep them apart, Maeve declared that she would no longer wear the ring if she was not with her true love, for it would break its spell. She henceforth lied to the king about the ring being stolen and hid it where it could never be found by the kingsmen: in the nook of the tree where the lovers joined.

Shortly thereafter, on the eve of their wedding, Maeve found herself to be with Duncan's child. The king was none too pleased to find out he was betrayed and that his bride was not his virgin to take.

But fearing ridicule of his people and the shame if the truth were told, he forced Maeve to claim the child as his and they wed before delivering the happy news to the kingdom. The king then had Duncan hunted down and killed, ending the love affair forever.

Crushed, she gave her body to the king to do what he wished

with it, knowing she would never find joy again—until her love child, Aine, was born.

She went on to have other children with the king, proper male heirs to his pleasure. When the king died and the first son took over, the queen Maeve was then free to disclose the truth to her Aine alone, along with the ring and its legend—with the promise that only her rightful heirs who mirror the value of her heart and share the truest of loves would know the truth and the blessing of this treasure.

Maeve then went back to the forest where she and Duncan made love and took her own life to finally be with her beloved, the ring once again upon her finger. As Aine returned to that very spot to honor her parents, it is said that they both appeared over their daughter, ring now on her finger, and sanctified the magical love that it possessed.

It did eventually bring Aine great true love, and so she carefully dictated this story and passed on the secret blessing to her firstborn daughter, Fiona. And it is I, Fiona, who have written this tale of love for my heirs to witness.

May he or she who is blessed to carry on the legacy of love live on in consecrated bliss with their beloved, as my mother, Aine, and her daughters after did. For there be no truer jewel of love than the one forged with the blood of a sacred lover, consecrated by the goddesses and blessed by the original paramours in death's reunion.

Go gcuire Dia an t-ádh ort.

"That was a mighty beautiful story. Thank you for sharing that with me, child. Allow me before you part to bestow a blessing upon you."

He brought me up to the altar, dipped his fingers in holy water, granted me a special blessing of devotion and affirmed the sacred powers of the ring would carry out its loving intention in the name of God. I was touched by the gesture, already feeling stronger in love than before I walked in.

We thanked him for his help and the blessing. Knowing how conspicuous carrying and packing such a valuable Fabergé egg would be, we asked him to keep it in the church's possession to help preserve the protection of the ring.

Stepping out of the church, I felt an enormous sense of relief. Finally, I had my family heirloom safely in my possession, the immediate danger suspended by a clever faux ring. I now had a critical piece of knowledge not only about my ancestors, but also about the heritage behind this extraordinary jewel.

But what relieved me most was that my heart had finally opened to love, and he was standing here, right beside me, and he wasn't a dream. I didn't need Father Joyce's blessing—I was already blessed. I turned and smiled adoringly at my own beloved, taking his hand in mine so that we could walk back home united.

"Meg, wait a minute. I have something for you." Curious, I followed his lead as he took me over to the ruins—to that sacred altar where lovers used to marry.

"What is it?" He reached into his pocket and pulled out a gorgeous pendant, surprisingly a replica design of the *Legacy of Love Claddagh* ring—right down to the green heart in its center.

"A few days ago, when I was running some errands for Mum, I took a picture of your ring down to my jeweler friend and asked if he could forge a matching pendant with an emerald. Don't worry though, *a ghrá*; I told him that I found this random photograph on the internet—he was none the wiser about its origin."

"It's the most beautiful and thoughtful gift anyone has ever given me. Thank you."

"Without knowing the content of that letter, I had this forged under the same kind of love—except for my blood, of course. Be it a symbol of how I feel about you, to remind you that you are my own one-of-a-kind jewel, even when we are apart.

"I love you, *mo shíorghrá*. I don't know where the road will be taking us, but I hope it takes us together. As the proverb goes: 'The future is not set; there is no fate but what we make for ourselves.'"

I decided to accept his unconditional love with a proverb of my own remembrance. "'You for me and I for thee and never another. Your face turned to mine and away from all others.'"

Then right there, upon the sacred ruins, we pledged our eternal love and sealed it with a kiss. Our life together had just begun—there was no knowing where it would lead, but for once in my life, I was going to follow my heart.

O'Sullivan Family Tree

O'Sullivan Family Line

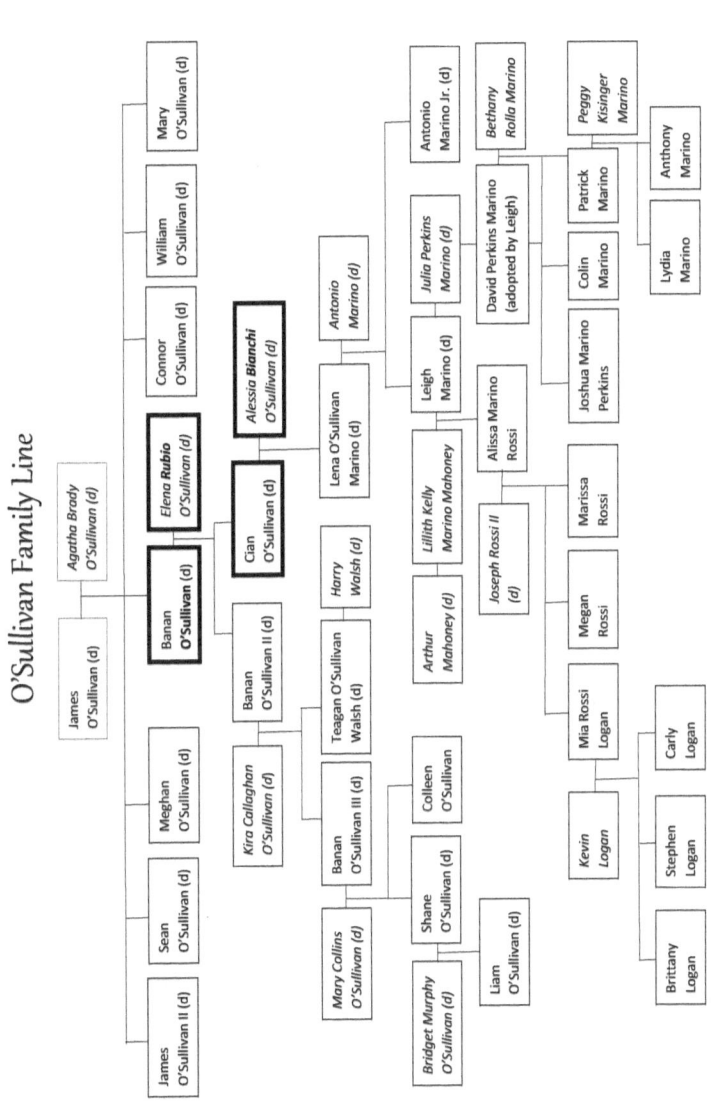

A Tuscan Treasure

BOOK TWO OF THE LOST HERITAGE TRILOGY

by Jenny Dee

This one is for my sisters, who have stood by me through thick and thin. We have an unbreakable bond and I love you with all my heart.

It's also for all the women out there who struggle with loving themselves just as they are. You are beautiful, lovable and worthy of everything your heart desires.

Never forget where your true beauty lies.

1

Well, that certainly wasn't the welcome home I expected, I thought as I settled deeply into my soft sable couch after a long, trying day with an enormous glass of Cabernet.

Normally, I love a silent house. When the kids are asleep or quietly hanging out in their rooms. When my husband Kevin is working. When the house sparkles and chores are done for the day. It's what I live for—some quiet, reflective "me time."

But not tonight. Tonight, I feel broken. Empty. Wishing this house was full of its normal vibrancy once again. Oh, I'd give anything to have it all back.

After our wild adventure to Ireland and a rather long and stressful flight home (I hate flying), I was looking forward to having some much-missed family quality time. But when I got home, no one was even there to greet me.

Where were my kids? Apparently, they had plans with their friends and would be out for the night at sleepovers. Long gone are those days of innocent childhood when my sweet dancer, Brittany, and my double trouble twins would have normally made a huge, messy *"Welcome Home, Mommy"* sign for me—complete with dried finger paint caked into the kitchen table.

Heck, I would have settled for a grumbled *"Hi, Mom"* as they barely looked up from their phones.

But no. It seemed like no one even remembered I was due to come back home today. Clearly, Kevin didn't. Otherwise, I wouldn't have walked upstairs to find him having sex with some random woman I never met.

Chloe. I will never get the moan of her name of out my head. Or the sight of how he touched her in ways he hasn't touched me in years.

I dropped my double blue canvas suitcases, making a loud thud as I cleared my throat. It took every last ounce of strength I had not to let the tears come out. No, weak Mia was not going to be invited to this party. Not until I was alone.

"I'm sorry, am I interrupting something?" I asked, oh-so-innocently.

Stunned, Kevin and this Chloe girl stopped mid-thrust, jumping off of each other and grabbing my favorite red satin sheets to cover up, as if I didn't already see everything. Some waif-thin yet muscular young girl—couldn't have been more than twenty—tried to hide behind both her straight purple and blue hair and my big oaf of a cop husband. I could have snapped her in two like peanut brittle.

"Jesus, Mia! I had no idea you were coming back today."

"Obviously." I stood there calmly in place, not raising my voice. Just staring at them. I lifted my eyebrows as if cuing him to continue speaking and daring him to work his way out of this one.

"It's not—"

"It's not what it looks like? Is that what you were going to say? I think we are well past that, don't you think, Kevin?" I turned to the girl now.

"I don't know who you are, and I don't really care. But

give me some last moments with my *husband* and then you can live in sexual bliss together, honey, because he'll be all yours."

Chloe looked over at Kevin, dumbfounded with her purple-tinted contact lenses and then stared right back at me like the guilty little lamb child she was.

"Did you hear me? Get your clothes on and get out of my house before my peaceful demeanor fades," I uttered ever so coolly with a forced smile.

I never saw anyone scurry so fast. She didn't even get fully dressed. She picked up her clothes, threw on her long black Imagine Dragons t-shirt, mouthed *"what the fuck?"* to Kevin and then ran down the stairs and out the door.

Alone, I just stared at Kevin Logan. Him and his receding dark brown hairline with a few touches of gray that I thought made him look refined. His clean-shaven, aging tanned face that still had a boyish charm.

His bold, intricate lion tattoo wrapped around his well-toned left arm and shoulder—the one I used to love running my fingers and tongue over in our younger, more intimate years. His chest full of matching thick, dark hair that was evidently well-groomed for the occasion.

He was still in decent shape, priding himself on daily workouts and lean protein meals, with just a small little pouch developing that I didn't mind because it made him less flawless. But all the sweetness of those tender brown eyes I fell in love with as a high school girl had been replaced by a worn-out, unaffectionate louse of a man.

His overall attractiveness diminished forever by his act of betrayal.

Who was I to judge, though? Here I was, all slobbed out from a long plane ride in black yoga pants and an oversized black sweater—the darker the colors, the better to hide what was really underneath. I wasn't as toned as dear Kevin—and certainly not as svelte as "Little Miss Chloe."

My hair was a tangled mess of dark brunette waves tied up in a disheveled ponytail above my bare, naturally olive face with those blessed dark circles under my deep brown eyes, courtesy of traveling sleep deprivation.

Signs of the thirties and approaching forties were starting to make some marks on my whole body (and let's not talk about what two pregnancies—one with twins—did). Despite my haggard appearance, my soul felt refreshed and rejuvenated from my sister trip—that is, until this moment when my entire world came crashing down from life's latest wrecking ball.

I don't know where the strength came from, but I remained stoic as I confronted my now-dressed husband.

"How long has this been going on?" I asked him point-blank. No use in playing cat and mouse. I wasn't big on long-winded conversations, anyway. I'm a get-to-the-point, blunt kind of girl—when I'm not avoiding conversation all together.

"I never meant for this to happen."

"Oh yes you did, you son of a bitch. Your dick didn't just fall into her. You just never meant to get caught. I'll repeat: How long has this been going on?"

"It was only this once, I swear." He couldn't even look me in the eye. *Liar.*

"Are you kidding me right now? How stupid do you think I am? I am your *wife.* I've known you since we were fourteen years old. Please, at least give me the courtesy of your honesty if you can't keep your vow of fidelity. Don't I at least deserve that?"

Finally, he found the guts to look up at me. Since when

was Kevin Logan a coward?

"A few weeks. But she really doesn't mean anything. I was just—lonely."

Oh, here come the pathetic puppy dog eyes. The ones that usually make me melt and forgive. Not this time. After twenty-something years, I've built up an immunity to their power over me. Especially now that I'm scorned.

"Oh, I see. Poor Kevin's wife abandoned him to go to Ireland and he needed some comfort. You deprived soul. How difficult life must have been for you."

"Actually, you have no idea how difficult life has been. This promotion is killing me. I feel like all I do is work and then I have to come home to a demanding wife who wants me to do more work around the house or help with the kids. I can't catch a break. Jesus, I'm overwhelmed, Mia. I made a mistake."

"A mistake? I could forgive a one-night stand as a stupid mistake—maybe. But not a few weeks' worth of mistakes. How many others have there been?"

"None."

"I don't believe you."

"Believe whatever you want. You don't give a shit what I think, anyway."

"You're right. I don't. In fact, I'm thinking those long hours of overtime and training were bullshit excuses for you to get time away from this house to do whatever you pleased with whomever you pleased."

He looked down at his feet and I knew, right then and there, that I was on to him. He couldn't even deny it.

"Can you blame me? This house feels like a prison. A man should be able to come home to his own house and be able to relax and unwind after a long day."

"Oh, and that's my job? To make sure I am the dutiful

wife who has the house all clean and presentable with a hot dinner and your fuzzy slippers and evening newspaper ready for you, darling?"

"Well, you're the one who wanted to be a stay-at-home mother. I've worked my ass off all these years to give you exactly what you wanted."

"You have *no* idea what I wanted," I finally screamed, holding back the tears but not the emotions. I was not going to break, but I was headed towards volcanic eruption.

"You never asked. You *assumed* when I got pregnant with Britt that this is what I wanted. Did you forget about all the years together when we'd talk about our dreams? Did I ever once mention I wanted to be a fucking housekeeper for a sexist pig of a man?"

"Well, whose fault is that? How about you use your voice for a change and tell people what you want? You expect everyone to be mind readers. Me, the kids, your family, your friends. It's like we have to pull a conversation out of you, for Chrissake."

"How would you know? You are never around. You work non-stop and when you come home, you barely acknowledge me. How am I supposed to have a conversation with you? I am stuck in this house all damn day with no one to talk to. The kids are always with their friends and everybody has their own busy lives to lead."

I was fuming. Everything I've wanted to say for years just started spewing out of my mouth, and there was no stopping it.

"I do everything you want me to do and yet it is never good enough. *I'm* not good enough. I have nothing to call my own because I have sacrificed everything to make you and the kids happy. You at least have a job to go to, people to interact with—and clearly, people who care enough to have sex with you. I don't have any of that. You haven't tried to even touch me in over a year."

"You know Mia, I'm tired of your sainted act. The perfect wife, the perfect mother. The most selfless human being on the face of this planet who can do no wrong. The only person who has made sacrifices.

"If you had to live with you and all your standards of perfection and judgment, you'd go crazy too. I can't take it anymore. I can't even look at you without feeling like I am living with my mother. And no one wants to fuck their mother, Mia."

His words were a knife in my heart.

"Is that really what you think of me? Like a mother? Really, Kevin? Who else was I supposed to be? Who else is here to take care of the kids, the home, *you?* You can't even do a damn load of laundry or make a simple meal. You don't even do anything around the house to the point where I'm either begging you for your help or being forced to hire someone. I have *no* support from you whatsoever. If anyone has made me into your mother, it's *you.*"

"I don't do anything around here because by the time I get home from work I am too tired to be bitched at about how I'm doing something wrong. Who works overtime to pay for you to *still* sit on your ass every day even though the kids are old enough to take care of themselves? Who let you go off on some fantasy trip to Ireland with your sisters for two weeks?"

"You asshole. Who *let* me? My mother and grandmother and dead grandfather did—not you. Don't you dare try to take any credit for that or deny me the right to have some kind of happiness in life. It's been years since I've felt this alive, like my life meant more than being just a wife and a mother."

"If I make you that unhappy, then maybe we shouldn't be married anymore."

Deadening silence filled the room. He finally said what we both knew this was leading to. The signs have been there for years, but neither one of us had the nerve to say it until now.

"Fine. I hope you and Chloe are very happy together." Broken-hearted and dejected, I needed to get one last jab in. But he was the one who left with the final gut-punch as he slammed the door on his way out.

"And I hope you are happy with Ben and Jerry. They're in the freezer waiting for you to stuff your fat face with."

So here I am with my glass of wine, box of Kleenex and yes, pint of ice cream. I swear I have better, more meaningful conversations with those ice cream Gods than I've had with my husband in at least five years.

They understand me in ways human beings can't— they give me the sweetness I crave and the companionship I lack. No wonder the scale tips close to the 220-pound mark. Sometimes I feel like they are all I have in this world. Pathetic, right?

I needed to get my mind off the events of the day before I dehydrated from the endless weeping. I forced myself to remember Ireland and how wonderful that time was with my sisters.

Oh, how I needed a break away from it all. The beauty of the land was something I had never seen. All that wondrous greenery and the adorable herds of sheep and cows roaming free. I just wanted to get out of the car and play with them!

I wondered what it was like to be so unrestricted;

to wander the earth with no responsibilities and pure acceptance. To look and feel like all the rest of your kind. To be amidst that type of unspoiled nature day in and day out. It must truly be an extraordinarily simple and wonderful existence.

Next life goals.

The majestic Cliffs of Moher and stunning Killary Harbour fjord were settings out of an enchanted painting. I could have watched the colors of nature that danced off the sea and sky for hours. So serene—it was like the angels stopped the earth so that we could experience what heaven would be like.

I absolutely adored the gardens at the Blarney Castle; I could have spent an entire week wandering through all the diverse flora. Attending an authentic medieval dinner in another real-life castle was a once-in-a-lifetime experience that will forever have me smiling whenever I hear the song *Danny Boy*. We were able to see so much in such a short amount of time.

Going to the spa with my younger sister, Marissa, and getting lost in the library on Clare Island was heaven-sent. How blissful it felt to fully relax knowing I wouldn't hear my name being called to run someone somewhere or asked what's for dinner. I was able to read an entire book in one day! I thought I was in a dream—and I promised myself that I would take the time to pamper myself more often.

But the highlight for me had to be all the food (of course). Oh, how I still dream of opening up my own restaurant and creating wonderful dining experiences for my customers.

Forgetting about what it does to my figure, I genuinely have such a divine love of food—I appreciate the different flavor profiles and textures of so many culturally-diverse meals. I am fascinated by the distinct regions of the world, and how they each blend different ingredients together to create their own signature dishes that reflect their heritage. I, too, love to experiment with various herbs and spices to bring my own personality flavor into my meal infusions.

Needless to say, Irish fare was not something I was accustomed to—very meat- and potatoes-style, but with a few unexpected surprises thrown in. The diversity within the various counties in Ireland taught me that not even a country's cuisine can be pigeon-holed into a stereotype.

In fact, on the Killary Harbour cruise, we dined on the most fresh, exquisite mussels farmed right from the fjord itself and cooked in a white wine, cream and onion sauce. Who knew?

The Galway Market—what a cornucopia of scents and flavors! From sizzling fresh sausages and home-baked breads to fresh fruits and imported cheeses, we didn't know what to eat first. Traditional Irish breakfasts were interesting—I think I was the only one who actually enjoyed the black "pudding." (I believe in giving everything a fair try!)

And of course, nothing compared to the honey mead and pints of Guinness to wash the food down with.

It was also something special to be able to spend time in our ancestral family home. It was so warm and inviting. I adored our feisty Celtic cousin, Colleen O'Sullivan, the keeper of our Irish relic. Boy, was she a trip and a half! She could talk your ear off, that was for certain. But I'd never met a kinder soul.

And Kieran MacGovern—sweet, handsome Kieran who stole the heart of my older sister, Megan. He is a dear one. I was grateful he was there to watch over and protect us all when the break-ins were happening. We still haven't had any leads on who ransacked the house or stole the fake *Legacy of Love Claddagh* ring, though. I made a mental note to check in with Meg tomorrow about it.

Even though it wasn't my particular keepsake, it was easy to get caught up in the romantic love story behind the ring and the mysterious heritage of our grandfather, Leigh Marino. A man we never knew about until a lawyer by the name of Joshua Perkins showed up at my door to tell us of his death and will, compelling my mother and grandmother to reveal an old family secret.

We have since learned so much about our ancestors dating back several generations and how their stories are entwined into ours today.

It's been an interesting journey, that's for sure. With Ireland under our belt and the true *Legacy of Love Claddagh* ring on Meg's finger, our next stop is Italy—a destination that is meant for me and an old jewelry box. In two months' time, we needed to be ready to learn the next part of the story.

But I can't even think about that right now. As my Ireland reverie faded away, I returned back to the present moment. Back to the sunken couch that fit every one of my weighted curves to perfection. As I dug my spoon about halfway down to a stuck chocolate chip cookie dough ball, reality hit hard.

It was over.

Not just the trip. My marriage.

Oh my God. My marriage was over.

For better, for worse. Worse has arrived!

For richer, for poorer. Well, maybe a lottery-worthy jewelry box was waiting for me in Italy to support my meaningless stay-at-home mom life, as Kevin seems to see it.

In sickness and in health. Instead of helping me fight my depression or loving me unconditionally through the ups and downs of my weight battle, he turned to someone more happy and healthy.

Forsaking all others. *Right.*

Kevin was my first love. The love of my life.

I just found the love of my life in the arms of another woman. *Fuck, me.*

How did we get here? When exactly did it go wrong? We were so blissfully happy when we started out. The poison crept in so slowly—how did we not notice the arsenic-laden downward spiral? When did we both stop caring and fighting for *us?*

There was no use questioning it all now. It was over. There was no coming back from this. The damage had been done—to both of us. Years of ignorance had led to the inevitable.

All I could do now was figure out how to pick up the pieces of my broken life and move on.

2

The last month had been one of the most challenging of my entire life. Telling the kids that their parents were getting divorced was heartbreaking. Going through endless meetings and discussions with Kevin and lawyers about living arrangements, custody of the kids, alimony, child support and division of assets was painstakingly real.

We were doing this. We had been together for over twenty years and soon it would become a faded memory, like the tattered pictures of our ancestors. I thought he was my forever.

So did the kids. My personal pain is nothing compared to watching their heartache. I wish with all my being that I could wave a magic wand and turn our family back into a happy and whole one—for their sakes.

My own family has been incredibly supportive since I broke the news, with each of them stopping by at different times to check in on us. They have truly stepped up to be my source of strength with comforting conversations, distracted bouts of humor and assistance with the kids.

But Sunday dinners, when we are all together, have been much more intolerable for some reason. The first week was nice and simple at Mom and Granny's with just pizza; we opted for easy comfort food and light conversation about Ireland.

I survived that just fine, mercifully. Everything was too

raw for them to want to broach the subject with me or the kids. They let the elephant have its undisturbed place in the corner.

The week after was at Marissa's in the city, which is always at a restaurant because my little sister can't (or rather, *won't*) cook. But I was grateful for that—in a restaurant setting, it's easier to be invisible and detached from the conversations, especially since the ambiance is so loud.

Last week was thankfully canceled because Meg had a work conference and Mom was invited to a baby shower, so Marissa and I just grabbed a movie, which meant I didn't have to talk much then either. She isn't much of a prober anyway, so I didn't mind her company.

This week is supposed to be my turn and I'm not sure I'm up for it quite yet. I know it sounds selfish, but I don't want to hear about all the good stuff happening in everyone's life right now.

Although I am happy for Meg and her newborn relationship with Kieran, it's painful for me to be reminded of what I just lost. I've agonizingly listened to her stories about their plans for the future—how they talk daily, their back and forth visits between New York and Ireland, her increasing bond with his mum and hints of a wedding in the not-so-distant future.

Even Kieran himself has a new project in the works, inspired by my sister. It's a Celtic rock album featuring his band, with—you guessed it—the song *Dream Rose*, the one he wrote for Meg, posed to be its first released single. Finally recognizing that his father would want him to pursue his dreams instead of fulfill a family obligation, plans are in place to transfer his father's pub, Gov's, over to his business partners so he could have the freedom to build his career and his life with Meg.

Yes, the future MacGoverns were well on their way to establishing their happily ever after.

Life also seemed to be going well for my younger sister ever since Jay moved in. Marissa's latest roommate is an old elementary school friend of hers that we always liked. She swears their relationship is platonic, but she has that sparkle in her aura that indicates some kind of romance is blossoming for her. Any day now she'll make the dramatic reveal.

Even Mom has a new man in her life—a retired lawyer named Bruce Bennett, who she met a few weeks prior to the whole grandfather revelation at one of her literary conferences in Boston. He had approached her after a workshop one day and asked her out for a drink. They found out they both lived close to each other in New York and well, they hit it off.

When all the drama surrounding Grandfather Leigh went down, she thought it was best to wait to tell us about Bruce until after we returned. Now a few months into the relationship, she is obviously radiant and glowing. We have yet to meet the man, but somehow I get the impression that he's here to stay. It is truly wonderful to see my mom so happy after all these years since Daddy passed.

But I guess now I know how they all felt when they were alone and I was "ecstatically" married.

It certainly was a melancholy evening. I didn't even get dressed—I remained in plain, cheap oversized gray sweatpants and a matching sweatshirt with my hair in a braid. I knew I would stick out like a sore thumb, but I also knew my family understood. I didn't need to impress them.

One by one, everyone arrived. Mom was looking as

sharp as ever in a black and white pantsuit and stylish checkered heels, her white-golden curls piled atop her head. Granny was in her Sunday best, a darling light blue Windsor jacket dress with gold buttons that accented her stunning turquoise eyes and comfortable, cushion-soled beige flats upon her feet.

Then came sophisticated Meg, with her classy black lace camisole and black slacks, gorgeous mane of blonde curls dancing around her porcelain face and killer oceanic eyes. The last to arrive was our fashionably late supermodel-like baby sister Marissa; an exotically dark-haired, light-eyed goddess in a skintight yellow leather dress and matching stilettos—no doubt dressed for an after-party later tonight.

Needless to say, I felt even crappier about my appearance after looking at this crew of beauties.

Usually excited to dabble with cooking, I couldn't bring myself to be the adventurous Mia in the kitchen everyone looks forward to. No, they would have to settle for quick and easy lasagna and store-bought garlic bread.

For the first time since I could remember, I forgot to cut some fresh flowers from my prize-winning garden for the table. In fact, when was the last time I even watered my flowers?

My mood unfortunately set the tone for everyone else. I looked at my solemn kids sitting around an eerily quiet dinner table.

My eldest, Brittany, has become a full-fledged teenager, hell-bent on blaming me for the divorce. Her anger clouds her gorgeous chocolate eyes—oh how she looks just like her father. She has his shade of dark brown wavy hair, his more bronze complexion and the Logan family's feminine curves. Daddy's little girl in every way.

To her, he is perfect, so the divorce is naturally my

fault. We are at each other's throats constantly over her too-revealing choice of clothing, curfew and everything else imaginable that I set a rule for. My favorite is when she threatens to go live with her father because she hates me so much.

I will give Kevin this much—he at least backs me up and tries to help keep this wild one in check.

Then I look over to see how torn my younger girl Carly is; a budding 13-year-old tormented by adolescent awkwardness. Mousy brown hair that she wears in a braid because it's too frizzy, and big, hazel-brown doe eyes hiding behind thick eyeglasses. Though I think they are quite stylish and sophisticated, she is counting down the days until she can wear contacts and be free of her eye cages.

She is most like me in spirit—more reserved and introverted. She's my mama's girl, but she also looks up to her big sister for approval and feels like she needs to defend her dad as well.

None of my kids should feel like they need to defend either one of us. It's not a contest, yet they can't help but feel like they have to choose, no matter how many times Kevin and I try to convince them otherwise.

Then there's my sweet boy, Stephen; Carly's other half. I'm so grateful they have this special twin bond that will help them get through this. Once a chubby little cherub, he is currently going through a long and lanky phase—but I can see so much of my dad in him.

He has his handsome features, including a dazzling smile with double dimples. He doesn't even realize the charisma that he has; any moment now the girls will be flocking to our door. I just hope he doesn't let thinking that he has to be the man of the house get in the way of him living a normal childhood. I love how he is so protective of me, but I don't want him to take on that burden.

For what seemed like an eternity, the only sounds you could hear were the clinking of the forks against ceramic plates and a few mouths crunching into garlic bread. It was Meg who finally broke the silence with an update about the ring theft.

"Kieran said that the Garda finished going through the hotel's surveillance footage and conducting interviews of the other guests who were there that night. Unfortunately, they didn't get a clear shot of the individual, but did catch that they were Caucasian with blonde hair.

"No way of telling male or female or seeing any other identifying features, though. And no one had any additional information to offer, so it looks like a dead end for now."

"I guess whoever did this knew what he or she was doing," Mom commented.

"Yes and no," Meg replied. "There's more. Although there has been no further activity by the house, the priest at St. Mary's Church where the ring was held was contacted by a male voice asking about a Fabergé egg they once saw at a service.

"Knowing that the egg was never on display during service and figuring that this person meant to cause trouble, Father Joyce told them that the original family was donating it to a local charity. He then called the Garda and made arrangements to actually donate the egg to keep the church safe."

"Someone knows an awful lot about something that's supposed to be highly confidential," noted Granny.

"I agree. Well, let's think about who knows about this legacy," Meg suggested. "There's all of us here at this table—immediate family. Plus, Kevin and Kieran."

"I highly doubt Kevin would have said anything to anyone, even with everything going on. He's a cop; he knows better. I think he just told people I was on a sister trip," I offered.

"Agreed," Meg nodded. "Kids, have you said anything to anyone about it?"

"Like anyone would care about some stupid inheritance that wasn't theirs," responded Brittany, as the twins simply shook their heads no.

"Brittany, don't speak to your aunt like that. A simple 'no' would have sufficed." *Lord, give me strength.*

"Whatever. Can I be excused?" Not wanting to start another fight with her in front of the family, I simply nodded my head and waved her off.

"You guys can be excused too, if you wish," I said to the twins. Stephen jumped straight up with a smile and an unspoken "thanks" to head up to an evening of video game playing. Carly stayed behind.

"Is it okay if I stay? I like hearing the stories."

"Of course, honey." Her sweetness just warmed my heart.

"Okay, so that covers that," Meg continued. "I trust Kieran—he even lied to his poor mum about it all. And the Dublin Garda know a little bit about it, but I'd like to think we can trust them, too."

"I hope you are not angry with me, but I did share some of the story with Bruce—not details, just that my birth father had passed away and that his inheritance to you girls was the trip. Nothing about the heirlooms or what has happened though, I promise," said Mom.

"That's okay, Mom. You are part of this and we trust your judgment. Do you think Bruce has kept this silent?" I asked.

"I do," she replied.

"Well—I, um. I told Jay," Marissa confessed.

"I'm sorry—you did *what?*" flamed Meg. "Why on earth would you tell *him?*" Cue the battle. Almost every Sunday, without fail.

"What's the big deal?" Marissa countered. "I didn't realize it was a crime."

"This is a family matter, Marissa, and he's not family. Wait—oh my God, you're sleeping with him now, aren't you? I knew it!"

"Ugh! Why do you always think the worst of me? I'm not sleeping with Jay," she insisted, as Meg rolled her eyes in disbelief. "And how come it's okay for Mom to tell some new boyfriend we never met, but it's not okay to tell Jay, who I've known almost all of my life?"

"We don't need to question *Mom's* judgment," Meg chided.

"Oh, like you are an amazing judge of character! Do we need to review *your* track record? And how about Kieran? You only met him like two seconds ago. How do you know you can really trust him and that he wasn't behind the Ireland break-ins? His timing of coming to your rescue was all too convenient, don't you think?"

"Would you both just stop it?" I couldn't take it anymore. Ever since childhood, they have always been oil and water, but I wasn't in the mood for their infantile antics tonight. I had enough of that on a daily basis as a *real* mother. But of course, it was up to me to restore the peace.

"You *both* have a point. It's true—we shouldn't tell anyone outside of our family circle because it increases the danger and we've taken a vow to protect our legacy. But we should also give Marissa a chance to explain. Marissa, why *did* you tell Jay?"

"Look, I thought since he lived with me, he deserved to know that his life was potentially in danger and why. I'm sorry. I know I shouldn't have, but I was scared one night and he wouldn't let up until I told him what was going on. I tried not to give him too many details."

"It's okay, sweetie. We've known Jay a long time and he's practically a son to me. I'm sure we can trust him," Mom said to relieve Marissa's anxiety and soothe Meg's nerves.

I was grateful for Mom stepping in to douse the dynamite as well. Although I could support Marissa's reasoning for telling Jay, I did tend to agree with Meg on one point—this only confirmed my own suspicion that he was her newest fling. Even so, I highly doubted he would be the one to cause any trouble. He really was like a brother, and he never personally gave me any reason to doubt him.

"Fine. But just watch what else you say to him," said Meg, needing to get the last word in. These two were insufferable at times. How was I going to survive Italy with them?

"Okay, that's settled," I concluded, giving both of my sisters a look of warning to not continue one-upping each other with their verbal jabs. "Continuing on—there is cousin Colleen. I know she has a gift for gab, but I'm certain she's bound by secrecy and honors that vow."

We all nodded our heads in agreement before Meg kept running down the list. "There's also our cousins in the other countries who we have yet to meet—but Grandfather Leigh would have chosen them for the same ability to be discreet.

"Odds and ends—Father Joyce, Mr. Clark and the bank manager in Dublin. Anyone who is helping our cousins in Italy and Spain right now. There's Joshua Perkins the lawyer and the entire Marino family—including Peggy, who we might need to keep an eye on," Meg considered thoughtfully.

"Colleen also mentioned a few disgruntled grandparents that may or may not have passed the secret down to their generational lines," Marissa added.

"Wow, I guess there are many more who know about this than we realized," I pointed out. "It could be just about anyone at this point. One harmless comment to someone outside of our circle could have set this all in motion."

"I suggest we continue to proceed with caution," advised Granny. "I'm not sure this legacy chasing is a good idea anymore. Not if it puts your lives in jeopardy."

"I'm sorry, but I am not giving up this once-in-a-lifetime opportunity just because some jealous lunatic wants a piece of the pie," objected Marissa.

"I hear what you are saying, sweetheart, but I have to agree with your grandmother. Nothing is more important than your safety," said Mom.

"If it helps, Kieran suggested that we all upgrade our house surveillance systems and contact the police forces in Italy and Spain as extra security measures when we travel. I think we should look into this as soon as possible," Meg advised authoritatively. Always the executive in charge.

"I'm sure Kevin can hook us up with the latest technology. I'll ask him the next time we meet," I offered.

"That's all well and good, but I still don't think traveling to Italy next month is smart considering we don't know who is after the inheritance and why. So far, you've only experienced harmless break-ins. But you don't know what this person could be capable of. I don't like it one bit," said Granny, worried.

"I'm okay if we skip it altogether. I don't need some old jewelry box," I confessed, seizing the opportunity to end it.

This could be my ticket out. I had no desire to continue this journey. I'd be happy to just be left alone to figure out my life—not relive the lives of ancient ancestors or keep my sisters in line when they decide to butt heads on foreign soil.

"Well, I'm not okay with that," Marissa cried out. "I don't have much and the thought of having a real, rare Goya statue means the world to me. You can't give up on me. Please," she pleaded.

"Mom, I think you should go," Carly spoke in a hushed tone. "I wish I could go on an exciting journey like this. I'd love to see that jewelry box and what makes it so special."

Everyone just looked at Carly and grinned at her innocence. I could just imagine this is exactly how Meg dreamed as a child whenever Daddy would tell us about his latest travels.

"We'll talk about it," I said, scanning the room with my eyes to inform everyone that this was to be put on hold.

Mom, sensing I had enough for one evening, smartly prompted the others to start leaving. "It's getting late and the kids have school tomorrow. Why don't we continue this conversation next week after giving it some thought?"

I was so grateful for her support. Everyone willingly got up and began their goodbyes. I saw Mom pull Meg and Granny aside and then caught a knowing glance sent my way from the three of them.

What were they up to?

It didn't take long for me to find out—Meg was asked to take Granny home so that Mom could stay behind to talk with me. The last thing I needed was a lecture from my mother, but it looked as though she wasn't going to give me a choice.

"Mom, I'm really tired. Can we do this another night?" I asked as she sat down on the couch beside me.

"Mia, I'm worried about you. You've been through a terrible ordeal."

"I'm fine. I just had a long day and want to get some sleep," I argued defensively.

"That's all you seem to be doing these days. I know this hit you hard. I know you are depressed. You have every right to feel how you are feeling."

I appreciated how she was trying to empathize with me like a good mom does, but I just didn't want to listen to her. I sat there without responding. I figured, let her say what she came to say and then hopefully she would get the hint and leave.

"I hate seeing you this hurt. I wish I could take your pain away. I am so sorry for all that you are going through—as a mom, my heart is just broken for you. But what is worse than seeing you in pain is seeing you on this downward spiral.

"You haven't worn anything but sweats since you got back from Ireland. You take no pride in your appearance and that's unlike you—you love doing your hair and makeup to even go out to just the grocery store. And I've never known you not to be excited over hosting a family dinner.

"Mia, look at me."

She took my hand in hers and it felt warm and soothing. She gently lifted up my chin so that our eyes could meet. I could feel the burn of the tears edging out to roll down my bare cheeks like flickers of fire as I saw her lovingly look back at me.

"Don't you think it is time to start putting some of these pieces back together, sweetheart?"

And then they came. The uncontrollable sobs; the anger; the frustration; the defeat—all rolled up into a tornado of emotions that whirled around me, leaving devastation in its wake. I couldn't help but start yelling all my stormy thoughts and feelings at her.

"Don't you think I want to feel normal and happy again? Do you think I like looking like this? You have *no* idea what I am going through. You don't know what it feels like to look like me—or to feel the deepest kind of loneliness knowing that your one true love is gone and that no one will probably ever love you again—at least, not looking like this."

I bawled as she wrapped me in her arms like I was her newborn babe once again. I even curled up into a fetal position in an attempt to resist this adult pain. She let me just cry until it turned to mere sniffles before she spoke again. I could see the tears in her own eyes that she was fighting so hard from releasing.

"My beautiful Mia. You are right—I cannot fathom what it's like to go through your particular struggle. But baby girl, I do understand what it's like to feel abandoned. I know what it's like to lose the love of your life and not know how on earth you could ever face the world without him."

Daddy. That's right. She put on a brave face for us but deep down she was inconsolable when we lost him to cancer. And her father left her and Granny when she was just a young child. Maybe she did really understand what I was going through.

"How did you get through it?" I barely managed in a

whispered croak. "How did you find the strength to live again?"

"It wasn't easy, baby. At first, I pulled myself together because I still had you girls and Granny to look after. You all needed me and that got me through the initial devastation. Your kids need you, Mia. They need to see their mom healthy and strong and resilient—which you are."

"You're right. I've been so wrapped up in my self-pity that I haven't been sensitive to what they are going through. No wonder my daughter hates me." I started to weep again.

"She doesn't hate you, sweetheart. We all grieve and react in different ways. She feels safe to take it out on you— that's a mom's job to be a punching bag, unfortunately." She let out a little chuckle to lighten the mood a bit. "But sweetie, you can't just do it for the kids. You have to heal for yourself."

"I don't even know who I am anymore. I've just been Kevin's wife since we graduated high school and then a mother. I wouldn't even know what to do with myself."

"Give yourself time. Start out small. You don't have to have it all figured out today. Get dressed and put makeup on tomorrow. Give yourself a chance to feel better by taking care of yourself. Go out and get a new book—you love to read. Get lost in a story; someone else's life drama. Look up a recipe for a new dinner for the kids.

"Slowly, but surely, you'll start to find your footing by getting back into a routine. You'd be surprised at how quickly you can bounce back once you add some structure into your life."

"That does make it less overwhelming," I consented. "I think I can start there."

"Now, I'm not saying it's going to be easy. You are going to have days that will tear at your heart and that's normal. But also let some good days come back as part of the normal." Still exhausted from all the emotions, I simply nodded my head in agreement.

"I know you are tired and need to get some rest. I just want to leave you with one last thought."

"Hmm?"

"Don't be so quick to dismiss the trip to Italy. Forget what Granny and I said about the danger; we are just being overprotective old bitties. I know you girls will figure out how to stay safe.

"I have a very strong feeling this journey might be what you need to regroup. Do some soul searching in an environment that doesn't remind you of Kevin and daily life. Just promise me you will at least think about it before shutting the idea down completely."

"Okay Mom, I will." I gave her a hug and a smile. "Hey, thanks for not letting me push you away tonight. I guess you knew what I needed better than I did."

"Baby girl, we are all here for you. Your sisters want to do anything they can to help, too. Marissa even offered to take Brittany for a weekend. You know how close they are—she thinks she can get through to her in a way that you and Kevin just can't right now. Meg is happy to pitch in and help with whatever you need, too. We all love you so much."

"I love you guys, too. I'm really blessed to have you all in my life."

With a kiss on my forehead goodbye, she left me to sit in stillness with my thoughts. It was time to move on and accept what life had to offer me—the good, the bad and the unknown.

3

Mom was right. It did help to do something as simple as get dressed and put some makeup on. Even the kids were more easygoing in the morning as they got ready for school—it was as if their energy instantly reflected my own. At least it's a start.

I decided to take the day to just pamper myself. I wasn't going to do any chores, make any phone calls or run any errands—except for a trip to the library.

As I rummaged through my regular section, I quickly realized that it wouldn't suffice. Romance novels were a sore spot, and even crime stories would remind me of Kevin. Too raw, too soon.

Instead, I found myself drifting over to non-fiction. My first instinct was to hit up the recipe books—but I knew all too well I'd spiral into a world of baking that would not work for my current figure. As I passed through the food section, I noticed a wonderfully vivid Italian cookbook, and that's when the idea came to me.

I walked over to the foreign country section and began my search for the perfect book on Italy. I wanted to at least heed Mom's advice and consider going on our next trip. Maybe if I could bury myself in a book all about it, I could be inspired once again for the journey.

I found a few different selections—one in particular about Florence and another about the Tuscany region in general. I thought they would be good places to begin.

Instead of returning home to an empty house, I decided to take my new books to a local park. There was an arboretum right up the block that featured the most beautiful botanical gardens. Lush lilacs, wild orchids and various colored lilies surrounded the wooden benches nestled into wondrous solitude.

I love gardening second only to cooking. I find such tranquility sitting within nature—which only reminded me that it was time to tend to my own gardens back at home.

Yes, little by little, my life would get back on track. There was more to it than grieving over a divorce. It was time to remember all that was good about life.

As I sat amid the scented red, yellow and peach rose bushes, I opened my first book. Florence. The photos of the colorful capital city of Tuscany possibly couldn't do the different Renaissance and Gothic architecture justice. I bet the palaces and churches are magnificent sights to behold.

Meg would certainly love the majesty of it all. And Marissa—well, what a dream come true it would be for her to visit the Uffizi Gallery. I myself wouldn't be able to resist the Boboli Gardens or a walk through the leather market with its sights and raw scents.

The more I read, the more I realized that I had to go. I needed to fulfill my portion of the journey. It was apparently my new birthright, and by gosh, I was not going to succumb to this pity party and deny myself—or my sisters—this epic opportunity.

As if reading my mind, Meg called. I couldn't wait to tell her the good news, but something in her voice warned me that this was not a social call.

"Hey Meg, what's up?"

"Can I meet you at your house in twenty minutes?

Marissa is already on her way. I have an important update I need to talk to you both about."

"Of course. What's wrong?"

"I'll tell you when I get there. Oh—and please don't say anything to Mom and Granny about this just yet. I'll explain it all later."

"Okay, Meg. See you soon."

Those felt like the longest twenty minutes ever. Marissa showed up first in her normal chaotic style, complaining about how this better be good because she didn't get to finish her manicure on her only day off this week. Thankfully, Meg showed up not too much longer and got to the chase.

"I found this in my mailbox this morning." She handed me a typed note and nudged me to read it out loud.

Did you bitches really believe you could fool me with a fake ring? You think you are so clever. You'll be sorry. Watch your backs. I'm coming for you and your "lost" heritage.

We sat there flabbergasted for a moment.

"Did you call the cops?" I asked.

"Not yet," said Meg. "I wanted to show you first before it was taken into possession."

"Who do you think could have written it?" inquired Marissa.

Meg could only shrug her shoulders. "I don't know. I think this clarifies that our suspect does have a vested interest in our bequeathed keepsakes, though."

"Hmm, but who exactly?" I wondered aloud. "I mean, I would think that the Marinos would be satisfied with whatever they got from Grandfather Leigh and leave us to our trinkets—which is what I *thought* he led them to believe that's all they were."

"Maybe there is someone who didn't get what they wanted out of the Marinos. Maybe there is a black sheep we are missing who is disowned and thought his or her ticket would be through this legacy instead," suggested Marissa.

"Could be," agreed Meg. "Mr. Perkins did say that Peggy seemed miffed about this other line of inheritance. But that doesn't explain how she or anyone else actually knows about the true value of this ring—or its existence. Why would they question the zirconia as a fake? If they were led to believe the items were not of intrinsic value, why the doubt?"

"Great questions." My cop wife goosebumps started tingling. "There is definitely more to this story. Someone knows more than we realize and is now angry we happened to stay one step ahead of them. It's like Great-Grandmother Lena foresaw it when she left that note in the box with the decoy."

"Do you think she knew exactly who would go after it?" Marissa contemplated.

"Perhaps. But so much time has passed—if she did, then that would make it a different legacy; one where outsiders have been trying to claim it for generations." And with that comment, it all clicked for me. I continued.

"And if that was the case, then maybe it was Colleen's grandmother, Kira, after all. She—or rather, her descendants—appears to be the most likely scenario right now."

"True, but that doesn't explain the break-ins in Ireland and then this note here in New York. Unless there is more than one person orchestrating this."

"Could be, Meg," I agreed. "But my gut is telling me that this is one person following us around. Something is just tugging at me that they are from around here, and then followed us to Ireland and back. He or she may be soliciting help from others so that we can never get a clear identification, but I believe there is one mastermind."

"That sounds so creepy," said Marissa as she wrapped her arms around herself and cringed. "I don't like this at all."

"Me neither. Which is exactly why I didn't want to get Mom and Granny involved right now. They worry enough as it is. When the time is right, we will fill them in. Until then, let's keep it to ourselves."

"Agreed," said Marissa and I in unison.

"So, what do we do now?" Marissa posed the perfect question. *What does this all mean for us?*

"I'll take this down to the station and file a report and have them connect with the Ireland authorities to see if they can piece anything together," said Meg. "Maybe they can pick up traces of fingerprints or DNA on the note. I'll also ask my neighbors if they noticed anyone suspicious in our area."

"I think Kieran's suggestion to get security cameras is a good one. I can call Kevin this evening and ask him to help us out immediately," I offered. "We'll have to get them installed at Mom and Granny's too, but since they already know we were thinking about it, they won't suspect anything."

The room went quiet. No one wanted to address the obvious, so Marissa took us on a detour instead.

"I made something for you both," she said quietly, reaching into a flat pink carrying case she brought with her. She pulled out an absolutely gorgeous series of paintings and presented one to each of us.

"I was inspired to capture a piece of Ireland for all of us. I don't know what hit me, but all of a sudden, I just couldn't stop painting. Just like Meg was thrust back into her writing, I was called back to my art."

"They are stunning, Mar," Meg said with tears welling up in her eyes. "It's the Cliffs of Moher—where I had my epiphany. You portrayed that moment so poetically. I'll treasure this always."

Equally emotional, I gazed upon my mural of the Clare Island Lighthouse with awe, reminding me of my peaceful days there. "Oh, thank you, Marissa. This is so touching."

"I also made one for me, and another for Mom and Granny. I'm glad you like them," she beamed. Then suddenly, her face dropped, and she became teary-eyed herself.

"What's the matter, Mar?"

"It's just—I'm glad we have this memory, and I'm glad Meg has her ring. I'm just sad that it has to come to an end, and that I'll never get to see what's waiting for me in Spain. I know that sounds selfish. I'm sorry."

"Don't be sorry," soothed Meg. "I think we are all disappointed. But maybe it's for the best. Maybe if we explain the situation to our other cousins, they will forfeit the rules and just send you and Mia what you rightfully deserve."

"Maybe." That prospect seemed to bring a small smile to her face. "Though I was looking forward to another sister trip. It really meant a lot to me to spend that time with you both."

"I know what you mean. We don't have to let this stop us, though." I had to speak up. I couldn't let this be the end of our journey—dangerous or not. We were three tough, strong, savvy women. Why should we sit back to the side like helpless females because of one little note?

"Huh?" My sisters looked at me dumbfounded and confused.

"Just hear me out. I've given this a lot of thought over the last few days, and I realized *I* can't be selfish and make this just about me. This is an incredible gift, and I'm not going to stop us from enjoying every moment of it."

"Mia, I'm so glad you're feeling better about all of this and are willing to see this through. I'm relieved to see your spark coming back. But don't you think it's a bit careless of us to put our lives in jeopardy again?"

"I agree with Meg—as much as I don't want to. These legacies won't mean anything if we're dead."

"So, we ramp up our defense and be more cautious. We get the cameras installed in our homes. We hire bodyguards using the extra money left over from Grandfather Leigh's Irish traveling trust fund. We alert our contacts in Italy to have security measures taken upon our arrival, during our stay and afterwards, to keep them safe as well.

"I'm not letting some stupid note-writer stop me from finding out the truth. Someone out there doesn't want us to have our heirlooms, and I want to know who it is and why. This is about more than a jewelry box or even a sister trip—I will not let another person bully me into submission again. We're going and that's final."

"Well, I'm not going to argue with her. Count me in!" Marissa didn't hesitate to jump on the opportunity.

"I don't know, you guys. I don't think it's a good idea," said Meg cautiously. "But—I won't be the one to stop us, either. I'm in."

"Good. Now let's get planning," I instructed. "We have less than a month away and lots to do. I've been researching some places to see—you are going to love Florence!

"Meg, I'll give you the short list and you can begin some itinerary planning for the days we have to ourselves. Mar, you can figure out what we need to pack and let Meg know of any other must-sees on your list. I'll get the ball rolling with Kevin on the security here and contact our cousin in Italy."

"Wow, sounds like you have it all under control! It's like you're my mini me. I'm so proud," Meg playfully teased.

"Why, thank you—I think! Oh, and one last thing. Let's keep this hushed. The less we say to anyone, the safer we'll be. No more going outside of the family, just in case. Agreed?"

"Agreed."

Over the next month, the preparations started coming together. We never did tell Mom or Granny about the note, but we did reveal that we wanted to be on the safe side for this next leg of the journey and filled them in on the extra precautions we were taking. They were satisfied with our prudence and blessed our adventure, albeit with knots in their stomachs.

No additional messages were sent, and the police didn't find any trace of DNA evidence on the note (aside from ours), so the trail's gone cold. But we remained vigilant. Kieran had come for a quick visit to help Kevin out with coordinating all the security cameras—plus, he enjoyed any excuse to see his beloved Megan again. It was obvious they were still as much in love as the day she departed Ireland.

Kevin and Kieran seemed to hit it off really well; it

made me sad to think that had things been different, this would have been a wonderful family dynamic.

Though I must say, things have gotten better on the home front. Kevin and I are no longer at each other's throats. In fact, I'd venture to say that since separating, we're much more relaxed and at ease together; a natural friendship of respect and civility was forming.

At first, I thought it was for the sake of the kids, but it feels genuine. I mean, we still have some outstanding disputes when it comes to all the legalities, but for the most part, it is quite amicable, and he has been very generous with the alimony proposition.

Of course, that will only take me so far. As a newly single mother, I can't just rely on that money to carry us, especially now with two households to support between us. I'd have to enter the workforce once again—something that both excited and scared me.

I was looking forward to getting out of the house and rejoining society. To work alongside new people I could maybe call friends and build a social life. What frightened me was the lack of skills I had; it's been almost twenty years since I've worked outside of the home, and with all the modern technology, I wasn't quite sure where I'd fit in.

It's a whole new world out there—and I still had to figure out how I would juggle work, the house and taking the kids back and forth to their activities.

I had faith it would all work out, though. Things were looking up, and I knew we would be okay.

The kids were old enough to take on more responsibility, including making dinners and cleaning the house. Carly was turning out to be quite the little chef; she's been observing me in the kitchen and even took it upon herself to start watching the cooking channel and read junior chef books from the library.

Stephen has been an amazing young man of the manor—he learned so much from his dad over the years that he was able to jump right in with some yardwork, mowing and even fixing the little things that needed work around the house. Plus, he surprised me with how well he can dust and mop. He can make my floors shine better than I can sometimes!

Even Brittany has been more willing to put in her share of the work without complaining. In fact, ever since her weekend at Marissa's, she's come back much less angry and more accepting. Our relationship seems to be back on track; who knows if that will change, but for the moment, I am so grateful for whatever Mar did or said to bring my daughter back to me.

Plus, Kevin has been helping Britt on weekends with learning how to drive, so soon that will be one less child to run errands for. She even offered to help take the twins wherever they needed to go when she got her license.

Yes, things were looking up in the Logan household.

We had one last family dinner at Megan's before our trip to Italy. Her place was absolutely beautiful and her table was always so elegantly set. Tonight, she opted for a big Mexican spread of tacos, enchiladas and quesadillas— and even attempted her own empanadas!

Now that she has more time on her hands, since purposefully cutting down her hours at the office, she was starting to experiment a little more with cooking instead of always ordering in. *Not bad,* I observed. *She's got potential.*

In fact, both my sisters seemed to have made positive life changes after our trip to Ireland. Not only was Meg writing more—and less of an executive workaholic—she's since made time to quickly visit Kieran and his mum, take a cooking class and even redecorate her living room with a hint of Celtic flare.

It was wonderful to be a witness to her transformation. For so many years, she kept the pain of the past stacked within a wall of bricks that hardened my once whimsical sister. I have no question that although her healing came from her own soul searching and reconnection to who she truly is, Kieran had a lot to do with her change.

He's the type of man who supports her every dream and every need. He encourages her to follow her heart as a writer, while acknowledging the part of her that still needs that executive control in the boardroom (and undoubtedly, in the bedroom). They are a sweet match. And as much as it hurts to see their love blossom while mine wilted, I'm genuinely happy that they have finally found each other.

And Marissa? She pleasantly surprised us all when she painted those Irish scenes. What's more, she's continued to both sculpt and paint things that inspire her. She still tends to the bar for income, but the light of creativity has been sparked again.

I'd venture to say that she's matured a bit since our sister trip. Even her ability to keep Jay as a roommate has lasted longer than expected.

Perhaps it's because she finally revealed that she's been in a relationship with Tony, her former roommate. It all makes sense now —that would keep her from sleeping with Jay and validate her insistence that he was not her current lover. Who knew how long it would last with Tony, but she seemed genuinely happy at the moment.

As for me, I still have some work to do. I'm hoping that Italy will do for me what Ireland did for Meg—open up doors and epiphanies that changed her life.

Sitting down to dinner, we took turns updating each

other on our planning process. Security cameras now installed at every house, I felt less anxious whenever I heard movement outside. I admit that's when I miss Kevin the most. I knew whenever he was around, I was completely safe.

At least he coordinated armed guards to accompany us to the airport here and to keep watch over our houses while we were gone. Mom and Granny were going to stay with the kids again, but Kevin decided he would be more comfortable staying at the house with them instead of at his new apartment. We all appreciated that gesture and agreed.

I shared how I had several conversations with our Italian cousin, Sorella (Sister) Maria Bianchi, along with her lawyer, Francesco Marchesi, and that everything was set on their end for our arrival. Meg had a loose itinerary ready for us, and Marissa informed us about must-have packing essentials.

She even picked up an electronic translator to help us speak and understand the language. It sure would be different than traveling through English-speaking Ireland!

Although we could all feel the nerves about our next trip, we knew we did all we could to keep ourselves safe. We were ready to find out what the Bianchis had to tell us about our heritage—it was Italy or bust!

4

"**B**uongiorno! *Benvenuti in Italia!*" came the greeting over the loudspeaker as the plane touched down on Italian soil.

It had been a long 10-hour plane ride; one that I was glad was over. Not a fan of being high up in the sky—where I could easily plummet to my death—I must say that having first class accommodations again surely made the experience easier.

Of course, since our plane was destined for a quick layover in France before arriving in Florence, we took full advantage of the fine international dining. We shared delectable meals of Parisian-inspired cod in a Basque chorizo crust, quail stuffed with foie gras and a vegetarian truffle risotto.

The meal ended with individual mini boxes of petit fours that melted in your mouth. And of course, the wine—oh the wine! *Note to self: a Tuscan winery must be on our to-tour list.*

But that was for another time. Business would come first on this trip. We were quickly greeted after customs by Francesco the lawyer, as our cousin, Sorella Maria, was too weak to make the journey to the airport and back. She was almost ninety-eight, and although she had her health and wits about her, walking long distances was a challenge.

Instead, we were greeted by this perfectly-chiseled,

handsome 52-year-old gentleman—and I only know his age because that's what I was told. Before us stood a God of a man, with a Mediterranean tanned face that made his pearly whites shine even brighter.

His deep, rich coffee-colored hair sported some strands of gray, an attractive combination matching the close-shaven beard that framed his manly facial features like the sculpted artwork that he was. His chestnut eyes simply sparkled with warmth as his ring-adorned hands lifted up each of ours to kiss them in greeting.

Meg and Marissa were welcomed first, saving me for last. "*Ciao, Bella,*" he said as he took my hand. "You must be Mia. It's a pleasure to finally meet you."

"*Ciao,*" I managed to verbalize. "It's nice to meet you, too."

This man had style. A smoky topaz Gucci suit with a starched white button-down shirt—the first two unbuttoned, of course, to reveal his generous bouquet of chest hair. No tie, all casual. Hot chocolate-colored Italian leather dress shoes completed the ensemble. Yup, he was a lawyer, all right. Just missing the briefcase.

"Come. I'll help you with your bags," he said with a thick, rich accent made of sensual suede and leather—well, if they made a sound, it would be his voice. "We'll get you all settled into your townhouse before joining Sorella Maria for dinner."

As he explained it, our cousin lived in an assisted living community right on the outskirts of Florence, a complex of adjoining rooms exclusive to the retired nuns of the region. As visitors, we would be staying nearby in a locally furnished townhouse-like apartment, previously arranged by our grandfather.

The quaint town was called Fiesole, known as the "sky

above Florence." True to its claim, the ancient community sat upon its cloud of twin hills that overlooked the earthly city of vibrant colors—a view you would only dream of seeing on a postcard. Like a Thomas Cole painting come to life.

Many a celebrity and scholar were known to frequent this pretty town that stole their hearts. It surprised me to think that a nun would be living in one of the most affluent areas in the region, but Francesco explained that where she lived was one of the earlier built structures that stood well before it became such a fan favorite of the rich and famous.

Plus, it was close to where her mother's childhood home was, and even though it had been taken over by her aunt Dominica's family line, Sorella Maria wanted to live out the remainder of her years near those treasured memories.

He mentioned that Sorella Maria was a spirited one— she once told him she had already put in her service to God several times over, so now she would appreciate all the comforts the earth provided until He called her home. Not exactly what you would expect from a lifelong holy sister who gave up all worldly possessions, but she did present a valid argument.

I had a feeling we were all going to adore her.

The photos and descriptions I saw in my books did not do the actual scenery justice. As we drove up, I found that I was holding my breath to take it all in—the inexplicable familiarity of it all. I now get what Meg meant when she said Ireland felt like home to her. That's exactly how I felt about this very spot.

We arrived at the townhouse he arranged for us to stay in and understood why so many were enchanted by the area. The neighborhood was nestled among blossoms of wild white orchids, fragrant pink magnolias and tall cypress and lemon trees. I'd made a mental note to pick a few of the riper pieces of fruit for some freshly squeezed lemonade.

Situated within the heart of the main community garden was a weathered white stone fountain surrounded by a circle of lush greenery. It was guarded by stone statues of goddesses and wild animals that I could imagine coming to life at night and playing within the sanctuary.

I noticed a few wrought iron benches off to the side of the red stone walkway, surrounded by all this gloriousness—no doubt somewhere I would lose myself in a book.

Walking up the worn-out stone path to the front entrance, I noticed even the outside was an authentic, rustic Tuscan peach-textured exterior, with light gray shutters and terracotta plant holders filled with flowers of purple, red and pink. Simply charming.

Inside was just as delightful. Immaculate and stylish—a striking contrast of modern against the exterior antiquity feel. The floors were a dark stained wood and the walls a modern eggshell with high wood beamed ceilings.

Comfortable light beige sofas with multi-colored checkered throw pillows in shades of browns, reds and blacks greeted us as we entered, surrounded by elegant glass tables topped with artificial orchids in sheer blue glass vases.

The open-air layout of the living room area gave way to the kitchen, which was decked out in clean white appliances and marbled counters. An elegant bouquet of fresh magnolias sat upon the dining table as a centerpiece, welcoming us—along with a bottle of the very expensive Masseto wine and a decorative gourmet food basket.

I was delighted to see it was filled to the brim with

almond biscotti, crushed pepper crisps, herbed olive oil, aged balsamic vinegar, black olive bruschetta, marinated artichoke hearts, prosciutto and provolone-stuffed peppers and amaretti cookies—all the makings of a delicious mini snack feast. I didn't realize how hungry I was until my stomach grumbled in response to my eyes.

Right outside of the kitchen through sliding glass doors was a small balcony with a white patio table and chair set, and a red brick walkway to a semi-private outdoor pool. Even that was sinfully landscaped with colorful flora and a stone waterfall that released waves like a woman in ecstasy.

On the second level were our bedrooms; three huge rooms with king-sized beds featuring goose down pillows and duvets you could sink into like divine quicksand. The furniture was of a rich antique-carved cherry wood with rounded bronze knobs, which matched the nightstand lamps and wall sconces. Everything was thoughtfully and immaculately designed, I thought.

Two bathrooms completed the upstairs level; one with a red, gold and brown mosaic-tiled shower and the other with an oversized jacuzzi-style luxury tub. The kind you'd soak in with a large glass of wine as bubbles soothed away your troubles. Sounded blissful to me.

The largest bedroom—the master—was gifted to me as this was "my" journey. Francesco had already brought our luggage up to our respective rooms before departing, leaving us a few hours to unpack and rest until dinner. I took advantage of the downtime to admire my surroundings.

I don't know how I missed it during the tour, but my room gave way to a second-floor balcony—one that led to the most exquisite panoramic view of Florence. This all couldn't possibly be real.

I decided to sit outside on the balcony for a while before

joining my sisters in freshening up. So many emotions were stirring inside me. The colors of the country made me feel alive and vibrant—like they were the fuel I needed to reboot my life.

The hospitality not only of the wine and gift basket, but of the delightfully charming Francesco himself, made this trip even more endearing. I couldn't wait to see what was in store for me in the beautiful land of Tuscany.

"Mia, are you ready yet?" called Marissa from the hallway. Oh my, I had completely lost track of time.

"I'm sorry—give me fifteen more minutes to pull myself together. I got distracted." I called back.

Wanting to look my best for my first night in Italy, I pulled out a casual yellow sundress with white sandal flats. I didn't have enough time to fiddle with my travel-tousled hair, so I scooped it up into a loose ponytail and added a small yellow flower to pretty it up.

Happy with the reflection looking back at me given the short time I had, I was ready for a great evening.

My sisters looked absolutely gorgeous, of course. Meg was wearing a short black skirt with a red blouse and matching stiletto heels, her golden mane falling gently over her shoulders. Marissa, the bombshell, was stunning in a black leather dress and thigh-high black boots with her pin straight hair. Suddenly, I felt way underdressed and ashamed.

It's an automatic reflex, triggered even more so when I am around my naturally beautiful sisters. How I wished I had their bodies and good looks. Oh well, this will have to do for now. I tried not to make my self-disappointment too obvious and faked a smile as I walked down to greet everyone.

A stylish Francesco picked us up wearing navy blue trousers and a light blue long-sleeved raglan jumper sweater. He had a sensual leather-esque smell to him that stirred up something in me, which was odd, considering I haven't felt any attraction towards a man since, well, Kevin.

Have I been a corpse for the last twenty years?

"Well, here we are," Francesco announced as we pulled into a tiny little neighborhood. He explained that the elderly tenants who lived here shared a common kitchen, and that he had arranged for a private after-hours meal for just the family.

We walked into a little hall lined with long, rectangular tables that seated ten apiece. They were adorned with a rich red linen and lace overlay. The napkins completed the table, wrapped in a gold-trimmed mosaic-tiled napkin ring that was quite elegant. The tableware was a simple golden yellow ceramic with copper tumbleware; practical, yet stylish.

"Ah, there's my favorite girl," said Francesco as a young female orderly escorted our cousin into the room. "Sorella Maria, allow me to introduce you to your American cousins, Megan, Mia and Marissa."

"*Piacere, cugine.* Welcome, cousins."

Her smile could light up the darkest of skies. She was a short, rotund woman with a short mop of curly white hair. Her face was weathered from wisdom, and the warmth in her hazel eyes was undeniable, even from behind wireframe coke-bottle glasses.

Clutching an oak walking cane and wearing a modest dark gray church gown and black cardigan sweater, she made her way over to the table towards us.

Cued by our savvy escort, we bent down one by one to kiss each of her cheeks in a ceremonial greeting. Francesco pulled out a chair for Sorella Maria, and then after she was seated, did the same for each of us.

It was a lovely dinner. The dining hall chefs had prepared a wonderfully juicy Florentine steak served with traditional panzanella. Our cousin spoke remarkably good English, with very little translation required by Francesco. Turns out, her mother had her learn it from childhood so that she could speak fluently with her Zia Alessia and Zio Cian whenever they would visit from America.

We were all grateful we wouldn't need to worry about deciphering her words, though she did like to intertwine some of her favorite Italian sayings every now and then. It was intriguing to hear all about her side of the family.

"Nonno—my grandfather, Dominic Bianchi—was a very kind and gentle man, as was Nonna Ginerva, my grandmother. I used to love going to their house every Sunday for homemade almond biscotti while the adults enjoyed their espresso and played cards.

"Now, they had three children—Alessia, the eldest; Dominica, who was named for her papa; and my mamma, Concetta, *la bambina.*

"Alessia is the one who married your great-great-grandfather, Cian. She was a kind woman who sadly found herself disgraced by her family. I'll save that tale for another time, though," she winked. "I'll focus on the Bianchi family background for now.

"Her younger sister, Dominica, was awfully ambitious," Sorella Maria began. "She intended to make a name for herself in society, especially after the shame Alessia brought on *la famiglia* Bianchi. She ended up getting exactly what she wanted, marrying the very wealthy

Vincenzo Moretti and moving into the family home when both my grandparents passed.

"The Morettis had three children, my *cugini* Dominic II, Camila and Matteo, all of whom married and had their own children and grandchildren. Nonno's namesake, Dominic IV, continues to own and live in Casa Bianchi today," she paused to acknowledge.

"Sadly, Dominica was such a jealous person. Fearful that her sisters would one day try to take it all away from her, she cut ties with Alessia and my mamma. You see, Mamma was also quite scandalous, having me out of wedlock. My papa had abandoned her when he found out she was with child, and she never saw him again; I never even met my father.

"So, Mamma passed on her own name to me, who the Morettis refused to honor as a true Bianchi. It was all Dominica needed to substantiate her disownment of Mamma and me. *Boh. Aveva le mani nella pasta.*

"*Scusi.* I mean that Dominica should have minded her own business and let my mother be—not put her hands in the pasta, as the saying goes. She is the last one to talk about righteousness. I didn't even have the chance to know my own *cugini* or see Casa Bianchi ever again because of the Moretti's hatred towards us.

"But my Zia Alessia was much more accepting. She and Mamma had a wonderful sister bond—much like yours—that carried on through the years. I was able to meet and know my *cugina* Lena quite well, which is how your own Nonno Leigh knew to entrust me with his quest."

"That was absolutely fascinating, Sorella Maria. Thank you for sharing that history with us," said Meg. "To tell you the truth, I am not surprised over your mother's relationship with your aunt Alessia. I must confess that I have an old journal of Alessia's, and she speaks quite fondly of Concetta. Not so much about Dominica, however."

"*Che meraviglia!* How marvelous. I should love to look at that one day. I didn't get to see her often, but I loved my Zia Alessia very much and would be delighted to read about her life."

"Of course. I would be happy to bring it over the next time we visit."

"*Scusami,*" said Sorella Maria, excusing herself as she started to rise. "I must retire now." She motioned over to another orderly for assistance. "It was darling to meet you, my sweet *cugine*. I'll look forward to our talks again. *Buona notte.*"

We took turns giving her great big hugs goodnight. I instinctively stood up to help clear the table, but Meg reached out her hand to stop me.

"No, Mia. Not this trip. You are always the one to cook and clean for us. I want you to relax and enjoy every moment without having to take care of everyone else."

"I don't mind helping, Meg. It makes me feel useful." That came out a little snippier than I intended. On cue, Francesco broke the ice with an offer I couldn't refuse.

"Mia, why don't you let Meg and Marissa take this turn? There will be plenty to clean up over the next few weeks, no? Would you care to join me for an evening walk around the grounds?"

I looked over at both my sisters, who were shooing me away with their eyes and heads. "Like Meg said, we've got this. Go have some fun."

"I don't want to leave you alone," I protested. There was safety in numbers, and as beautiful as this country was, with all of the potential danger surrounding this trip, we could never be too careful.

"Mia, have you not noticed the guards keeping watch outside of the door? I have also arranged for more to monitor your townhouse while you are gone, and I have instructed them to alert me of any disturbances. I have taken every precaution necessary to keep you all safe. I can even have one of the guards follow closely behind us, if that would make you more comfortable," Francesco offered.

"Mia, just go. We will be fine," urged Marissa.

"Okay, if you think it is safe," I hesitated.

I decided to trust being in the company of Francesco alone and declined the offer of a guard. I wanted to make sure my sisters had the added protection. Plus, it was difficult enough knowing someone was watching our every move; it would be nice to have a break from that shadow behind me.

It was a beautiful evening outside as Francesco escorted me through the fragrant foliage, intertwining his arm with mine like a grapevine. My, how friendly the Italian gentlemen were.

The velvety atmosphere was clear, the heavenly stars proclaiming their rightful spotlight in the ethers above. The illumination from the city lights below tried to answer the challenge with their dancing colors. Like the invisible line in between, the wind made its chill presence known; enough so to make me shudder.

"Here, take this," Francesco said as he removed his jacket to put it over my shoulders.

The warmth was immediate, and I became much more relaxed. *Mmm,* I thought as I inhaled his earthy, yet spicy, masculine aroma infused deep into the fabric wrapped around me. His sly arm now curved around my waist, I was thawing from the inside out in multiple ways. I admit, I enjoyed soaking in all this rare male attention, for whatever it was worth.

We remained walking in silence for quite a while, just taking in the city backdrop. When we neared the edge of the garden, he stopped us to sit on a nearby bench.

"Everything okay, Mia Bella?"

"Hmm, what? Oh. Yeah, sure. Why?"

"You've seemed distracted all evening. You hardly touched your meal and let your sisters and cousin do all the talking."

"Oh, I'm just tired." I feigned a smile. I really didn't want to get into it with a stranger. I don't even open up all that easily with my best friend Lucy.

"Yes, you have had a long journey indeed. But it is more than being tired. I can tell."

"How could you tell something like that? You just met me," I replied defensively.

"No need to be upset, Mia Bella. I mean no harm. I am just an observant man."

Curiously—and uncharacteristically—I probed. "And what is it that you think you observed?"

"I met this woman at the airport today who was vibrant and full of life, enamored with all the new wonders around her. The moment she found herself surrounded by lush gardens, I saw her taken away to another world—one of bliss and magic. I left that woman inspired to explore and touch and learn everything there was to know about her surroundings.

"Tonight, that fire burned down to a flicker. A wall has gone up where an open window stood earlier. Not even weariness can douse that kind of light. Silence has replaced curiosity, and insecurity reigns over confidence. The reason for such, I have yet to figure out. But I am happy to listen with an open heart and mind to what troubles you, *cara.*"

I was stunned at how easily he read me. All I could do was look up at him, speechless. Part of me wanted to unburden all that was buried deep in my heart—my hurts, my jealousies, my wishes.

The other part of me demanded to remain private, reserved. It wasn't his business whether my light was on or off. Sensing my hesitation, he backed off.

"Okay, Mia Bella. On your own terms, in your own time. Just know that I am here whenever you need me."

He then took me completely off guard by reaching over and pulling me closer to him. My head lay against his chest, where I could hear his heartbeat and steady breathing echoing in rapid harmony.

My body was nestled under his rather muscular arm and I could smell his earthiness even more. He placed a tiny peck on the top of my head, soothing my hair gently with his smooth hands. It was comforting in a way that I had not felt in a very long time—and not intrusive in the least.

As a small tear escaped down my cheek, I realized that it was more than sex that ended a long time ago with Kevin. It was affection; just a simple gesture, a touch, a tender kiss to let me know I was still loved. That I was still beautiful in some way.

I held onto this moment as tight as I could, not knowing when I'd ever experience this affection again.

Next thing I knew, his finger lightly grazed my cheek. I had gone lifeless right there on the bench in Francesco's arms. Suddenly, I felt flustered and embarrassed by the whole situation.

"I am so, so sorry. I did not mean to fall asleep on you

like that. Forgive me," I said, as I quickly pulled away and up off the bench to start walking briskly. "I think we should head back now."

I needed to get as far away from this charmer as quickly as I could before I became completely unraveled. He already discovered too much and it unnerved me. How could I expose so much of myself to a stranger? How could I be so careless as to trust him after a few phone conversations and an evening stroll? Repression was stirring within me, begging to rise like untamed boiling water and it had to simmer down.

"Whoa, wait a minute—what is your rush, *cara?*"

He caught up to me and took me by the arm to bring me to a standstill.

"Mia, relax. You have no reason to be ashamed. You were only asleep for a few minutes, and I thought you could use the rest. It wasn't a chore to spend some extra time outside on this beautiful night, with a beautiful woman."

Beautiful woman? Was he not seeing the same disheveled hair, black-bagged eyes and mid-section dinner rolls that I saw? What was the deal with this guy? Now I really felt the urge to return to the dining hall. I was ready to sprint a 5K away from this uncomfortableness.

"Still, I need to get back to my sisters. They must be wondering where I am."

"Okay, *cara,*" he responded with a dimpled smile and half laugh. "Let's take you home."

5

Early the next morning, we received a call from Francesco that Sorella Maria was feeling under the weather from all the excitement last night, and that she needed a day or two to recuperate. We agreed that the best thing to do was to give her time to rest—we had two weeks to learn what we needed to, and her health was most important.

Of course, with the free time that was just gifted to us, we would make the most of it by starting to check some tourist to-dos off our list! When in Florence…

Before arriving, we decided that we didn't want to tour the entire country like we did in Ireland. The Emerald Isle was small enough to explore some of the regions' major highlights, but here, in Italy—where would we begin? Which cities would we go to, and which would we forsake?

There were too many choices and differing opinions that we thought it best to stay local and truly get to know and appreciate the single region of Tuscany; Florence in particular.

Today, we were going to simply stride through the city. If there was a specific church, palace or landmark we wanted to explore further, we'd do it on the spot.

Maybe we'd pass a farmers market and sample juicy, ripe tangerines or shop at the infamous leather bazaar. Maybe we'd find an interesting local dive to eat lunch in or indulge in a picnic in a park. Whatever we decided, we wanted to do it with ease and with presence in the moment.

Our first venture took us towards the famous Piazza del Duomo, where—you guessed it—we ended up booking a 3-hour guided tour. *Ugh, Meg.*

Even after all that careful "planning" to be carefree, she somehow convinced us to relinquish control and sign up. No wonder she was a top influencer in the advertising industry. I must say, however, that it ended up being worth it. I don't know how we would have been able to uncover or see all the treasures this one area held if we had just walked by it casually.

We began at St. John's Baptistery, one of the oldest buildings in Florence. We learned that St. John was the city's patron saint, said to be chosen as its protector as far back as medieval times. You could tell that he was a figure of importance here.

In fact, our timing could not have been more perfect, as the end of our trip coincided with Florence's annual *Festa di San Giovanni* held in his honor. We made a mental note to be a part of that spectacular celebration before we left.

St. John was widely celebrated throughout the city's architecture, with this dedicated building—St. John's Baptistery—constructed during the times of the Renaissance in what would become known as a "Florence Romanesque" style (I wasn't sure who knew more about it, the tour guide or Marissa with her FAQs).

It was uniquely shaped as an octagon with intricately designed bronze-casted doors and marble statues adorning the ancient landmark. The inside was a rich dark green and white marble with carefully crafted religious scenes designed into a stunning mosaic ceiling. It truly amazed me to think about the time, creativity and patience it must have taken to build something of this magnitude.

Next, we were taken to Giotto's Campanile—the Bell Tower. More than just offering an unbelievable panoramic view of the city, taking the over 400-step trip to the top exposed us to beautiful life-sized art statues, carvings and the tower's seven bells.

I must say that the trip was a struggle for me; thankfully, my sisters and other tourists were kind enough to have patience with my frequent breaks to catch my breath. But I was super proud of myself for not giving up. It actually inspired me to want to get in better shape, or even sign up for hiking.

Okay, maybe that was taking it to the extreme.

We were then escorted to the gorgeous Cattedrale di Santa Maria del Fiore (the Florence Cathedral). Simply looking at the exterior of this 19th century Gothic Revival gem was breathtaking. I never knew that architecture could so fascinatingly intertwine such colors as white, green and pink into a marbled masterpiece.

The Brunelleschi's Dome itself was truly iconic, before even stepping inside to witness the frescoes and stained glass windows. How could so much history and art be found in one relatively small section of the entire world?

The guided tour ended with a visit to the Opera del Duomo Museum. Now normally, I am not a museum person. Although I can have an appreciation for history and art of all kinds, I'd much rather lose myself in a botanical garden or arboretum. However, the hues of Florence's architecture and the masterful art throughout was enough to draw me in to its man-made blossoms.

Works from Michelangelo, Donatello and Pisano were not overrated. The Gates of Paradise were spectacular. The Altar of St. John and other cathedral reconstructions, statues and medieval art were overwhelming—we weren't able to see it all on this short little tour. I wondered if even a full week would be enough time.

So did Marissa, who wasn't the least bit thrilled about Meg pulling her away from her elongated moments of art adoration. Fortunately, the end of the tour diffused that brewing argument so I didn't have to.

Famished from our Piazza del Duomo exploration, we headed towards the Piazza San Lorenzo marketplace. We ate our way through the two levels of assorted fresh cheeses, cured meats, stuffed pastas, wood-fired pizza and this wonderful Chianti wine booth.

In between the samplings and food purchases (I was already planning a wonderful dinner for one night!), we couldn't get enough of the leather, pottery, clothes and potential souvenirs.

Thankful for our Grandfather Leigh's generous spending fund, we took advantage of our good fortune and treated ourselves to a mini shopping spree. We didn't have to look far for amazing mementos to bring home, either. A genuine leather vendor was like a one-stop-shop for me.

I found a killer red leather skirt for Brittany, which was sure to earn me some "cool mom" points for a change. Oh, and a nice brown leather belt for Stephen—and a cute little black leather jacket I thought Carly would like.

Beautiful handbags were the perfect choice for Mom and Granny, and even a nice wallet for Kevin with his initial on it. Hey, just because we were getting divorced didn't mean I couldn't still be thoughtful. He remained surprisingly supportive throughout this journey; the least I could do was acknowledge him with some gratitude.

My sisters each came out with their own handbags, gloves, jackets and skirts I knew they would look striking in. I found a nice bag for myself, and they somehow coaxed me into buying a stylish brown leather jacket that fit nicely.

I also found some beautiful Italian scarves and bracelets along the way, plus a few other tchotchkes that I couldn't pass up. But what caught my eye the most was this little bookstore tucked away in a side alley. It looked all cozy, and I knew that when I got some free time, I'd be coming back here to immerse myself in a corner with a cappuccino and novel.

It had been a long day already, but it was still only afternoon. Coaxed by my relentless, energetic sisters, I somehow found the energy for more exploring.

We realized we were close to the Piazza Santa Maria Novella, one of the main city squares in Florence, so that became our next destination. There, we came upon its famous Basilica, asserted to be one of the oldest churches in the Dominican order. Matching the beautiful visions of the other city architectural sites, it declared a mix of many different styles. A little bit Gothic, a little bit Renaissance and a little bit Romanesque—quite beguiling and unique.

Underneath the nearby train station were hidden gems of shops and yet another bookstore I could easily find myself lost in. How I wished I could steal away from my sisters and enjoy some quiet time there. Although I loved this time with them, I had yet to escape for some much-needed solitude. Thankfully, with only a few more purchases in hand, they were ready to call it a day and head back to the townhouse for a rest.

"I'm beat—but also famished! What should we do for dinner?" Marissa asked.

"I'll cook something. We picked up so much stuff at the market that it would be a shame to let it go to waste!"

"No, Mia," Meg protested. "We told you—this is about you, and we want you to enjoy yourself. Not work."

"But don't you see, this isn't work to me," I pleaded. "We have all week to eat out. I love to cook—you know that. It's like therapy for me. I love nothing more than to take random ingredients and make something delicious out of them.

"Besides, I feel inspired and creative. I'd go crazy if I were eating out somewhere else knowing that all these fresh foods were here, dying to be made into something special."

They both looked at each other and smiled. "Well, if you insist—"

"I do," I affirmed. "So, you just kick back and relax, and I'll have something whipped up before you know it!"

They gratefully indulged me and left me alone to my fancy new kitchen while they poured themselves some wine and talked about what tomorrow could bring.

Content with a glass of Chianti from a bottle we picked up in the marketplace, I set my sights on the fresh ingredients in front of me. For starters, I had the makings of a caprese salad, courtesy of the fresh buffalo mozzarella, vine-ripened tomatoes, garden basil and our welcome basket's bottle of balsamic vinegar. Light and refreshing.

I then had difficulty deciding between a meat dish or a vegetarian pasta dish. This is where I could waste hours being indecisive! We did nosh quite a bit as we walked through the marketplace, so I decided to go with an easier dish and save the meat for a bigger dinner at another time. Maybe one we could invite Francesco to.

Where did that come from? I wondered as I shook the thought off. I did find my mind wandering over to him rather frequently throughout the day. *What was he up to?* Probably working. He is a successful lawyer, after all.

I cleared my thoughts to return to the task at hand. What

shall it be? I looked at the handmade pasta, Parmigiano-Reggiano and truffles in front of me and it came to me—Tagliolini con Tartufo! Simple, yet flavorful. I thought this little bit of chef work would be just enough for a wonderful home-cooked meal, without tiring me further.

I could feel the jetlag setting in as I stood there over the gas burning stove. I was relieved that we planned on staying in for the evening. After dinner, I'd change straight into my pajamas and curl up with a book before heading to bed early.

Knowing my sisters, we had another jam-packed day of city hiking ahead of us, and I needed to be able to keep up.

I was right—this time, we would be sightseeing near the Arno River. Our first stop was the Ponte Vecchio, which literally means "old bridge." It's a historic bridge that survived World War II and a relatively recent restoration, providing pedestrian passage over the river. It's also home to several little jewelry and artsy shops. Charmingly medieval.

We then moved on to Marissa's dream stop: the Uffizi Gallery. Knowing how popular an attraction it was, she had pre-booked (yet another not carefree) tour to make sure we would be admitted. Marissa made a point to tell us that she would be visiting here again, with or without us, because the tour would simply not be enough for her to capture everything.

I couldn't blame her. How difficult it must be for her to have to follow along; to watch Meg and I go on our legacy adventures while hers was not for another two months. Not to mention, Meg's restrictive travel planning style was probably weighing on her free-loving desire to explore all this amazing art on her own terms.

I could tell she wished she could abandon us if only for one day to let her heart soar, but at this point, Marissa would take advantage of whatever time she did have with these masterpieces—and we knew better than to deprive her of this experience.

Begrudgingly, we followed along and tried to keep pace with her energized enthusiasm. I wondered if the bodyguard assigned to watch over us these past two days shared my restlessness. Even though it felt creepy to be watched at times, it was also reassuring to have such protection.

There was no denying the exquisite works on display by the ever-so-gifted Leonardo da Vinci, Michelangelo, Raphael and more. Seeing the *Birth of Venus* by Botticelli, *Medusa* by Caravaggio and other famous pieces I thought I'd only see in books cannot even be described in person. I at least managed to have a deep admiration for the artistic beauty that surrounded me.

But I would be lying if I said I just wasn't feeling the tourist thing today. Maybe the time difference change is catching up to me. Maybe it's all this physical exercise and the rubbery feeling in my untoned legs.

Maybe all of the emotions I have been feeling and suppressing are surfacing. For whatever reason, they were a lot less intense when I was in Ireland. But everything was beginning to take a toll on me all at once right now.

And yet, we continued on, my discomfort unnoticed. I had become good at hiding my feelings over the years, so my sisters' ignorance didn't surprise me. I knew when to smile or interject a comment at just the right times to make it look like I was engaged. I had almost perfected it.

Almost.

As we sat down for a quick bite for lunch, Detective Megan Rossi began her inquisition.

"You seem a little...off today, Mia. Everything all right?"

"Yeah, I'm just tired. I just don't think I am adjusting to the jetlag as easily as I did when we went to Ireland." I hope they buy that. I'm really not in the mood for their investigation of my feelings.

"Are you sure? I mean, I can usually tell the difference between you being worn out and when something is wrong. And I know part of you is tired—but it feels like there's a little more to it."

"I'm fine, Meg. Really." I tried my hardest not to be armored in my responses. But realizing that they were not going to accept "just tired" as an answer, I had to give them something plausible enough so they wouldn't keep digging.

"I guess all the walking is getting to me a little. I'm not as active as you both normally are, so I'm just trying to adjust to it and not hold you back."

"Why didn't you say something, silly?" Marissa asked. "We can definitely slow it down or mix in more relaxation. To tell you the truth, I'm starting to feel a bit overwhelmed, too. We have so much time; we don't need to cram this in all at once."

"Thanks, but you don't need to say that to make me feel better."

"Since when have you known me to do that?" Marissa snorted in truth. "I mean it. So, why don't we do this? We'll enjoy a nice, quiet lunch now. Then we'll see the Palazzo Vecchio for Meg since it's right here. And then we'll just go back and chill by the pool or something."

She had a good plan. I felt better about not cutting the day short on them and comforted to know some downtime was coming much sooner than expected.

"That sounds perfect. And I have so much more food left over that I can make another quick dinner for us tonight."

"Oh, I forgot to tell you," Meg interrupted. "I spoke with Francesco last night after you both went to your rooms. He made arrangements to take us to some local restaurant for dinner tonight. He thought that with Sorella Maria being under the weather and all, he could fill in a few of the blanks for us."

"That sounds fun! Did he say how she was feeling?" asked Marissa.

"He said she was doing better. It's really just her age and all the excitement getting to her. She needs to go at a slower pace—but he warned me to never repeat that to her or she'd whip him," she said with a giggle.

"What if we suggest that we see her for breakfast or a late morning lunch instead? Maybe if we talk with her earlier in the day, it might not be too taxing on her afterwards," I offered.

"You are always so sweet and thoughtful," said Meg. "I think that's a great idea—I'll text Francesco and let him know. Now, let's eat!"

After finishing off our delicious Tuscan ciabatta pizza, it was Meg's turn to be enamored with the Palazzo Vecchio. An imitation of Michelangelo's famous David statue sits right out front for passersby to admire. Yet another tour *(good grief)* was booked so that we could see the most popular rooms in the palace, including the Hall of the Five Hundred.

An avid reader as well, Meg had always wanted to

visit this particular place (and many other landmarks in Florence, as she kept reminding us) since reading and watching the movie adaptation of *Inferno*.

Satisfied with our tourist adventure for the day, we were ready to return to our Italian landing pad and let ourselves rest for a while.

Sitting by the pool was more relaxing than I ever expected. It was a nice, warm day with a few gentle breezes playing through the cypress trees. From my blue cushioned lounge chair, I could see the entire view of Florence. I decided to fold down the bright yellow table umbrella so that my skin could soak in some of that brilliant Tuscan sun.

Comfortable with only my sisters around, I was able to wear my solid black one piece without shame. Marissa, of course, was scantily clad in a leopard print bikini. Meg was a little more conservative in an aqua blue tankini, but it still showed off the attractiveness of her curves. Of course, that prompted layers of insecurity to surface.

What did I ever do to deserve this body? Why couldn't I have their physical gifts? Life would be so much easier if I didn't always feel the need to hide myself away.

Just look at them. They are so playful and uninhibited in the water. I wondered what it would be like to be comfortable in my own skin instead of constantly checking around to make sure no strangers were approaching or that the guards weren't sneaking a peek at us.

If I caught a glimpse of anyone besides my sisters, my cover-up and towel were ready right by my side to quickly pull over my protruding stomach and thick thighs. *As if that really worked—like no one could tell what was underneath, Mia?*

Since the divorce, I was becoming more self-conscious than ever. Maybe because with Kevin, I felt safe enough not to care what I looked like. I was lovable exactly as I was.

Yet in reality, I wasn't. I had let myself go. That *had* to be the reason Kevin stopped touching me and sought comfort in the arms of women like Chloe. I wasn't the tinier little teen he fell in love with. I never recovered physically after two pregnancies and found it difficult to make love unless we were completely in the dark.

I couldn't bear to let him see those flaws. I couldn't even look at them myself.

Even behind clothes, I can't hide what I've become. I know I'm not morbidly obese, but it feels that way sometimes. When you see all these perfectly shaped women around you, and men paying attention to them, it makes your flaws all the more real and raw.

A mirror doesn't lie like your sisters do.

Even when married, I would go home and cry into my pillow after a girls' night out, feeling rejected as I watched the men gravitate to the skinnier women. I tried to tell myself it was my wedding ring that deterred them—but I knew the truth. Wedding ring or not, I was no longer desirable. It was a hard truth I had come to accept.

But a harder truth to face was that I was now truly alone, and I probably would be for the rest of my life. Who would ever want to be with me now?

Grateful for my sunglasses to hide the few tears that trickled, I let myself get lost in a suspense book to forget all about my sad, pitiful existence.

6

My mood didn't change much as I was getting ready for dinner. I really didn't want to go out, especially not feeling like this. I struggled with finding an outfit that didn't make me feel uncomfortable. But I knew I had to make my dutiful appearance. And I had to change my attitude—fast.

I fought the two opposing wolves within me until I decided I wasn't going to allow my self-pity to take over. I was in Italy, for goodness' sake. Depression or not, I was going to enjoy as much of it as I could. I needed to shove these insecure feelings deep down into my internal grave.

When the doorbell rang, I could feel the butterflies flock to my stomach. But why? This man was over a decade older than I was, and I'm still a married woman (technically). Italian men are known for their charisma, and I just had to remind myself that his paying attention to me was no more than his typical, natural magnetism to everyone.

Still, I found myself wanting to look prettier than usual for him.

I walked down the stairs to open the door since my sisters were oblivious to his arrival. There he stood, all casual in black with a matching leather jacket and hair slicked back. Damn, was he sexy for his age. I remembered when I used to think men in their fifties were considered "old," but I was slowly changing my mind about that. I believe he would be what my grandmother's generation called debonair.

Since I had yet to verbalize a hello, he made a gesture to let himself in.

"Mia Bella, how wonderful to see you again. You look lovely," he smiled as he kissed each of my cheeks and entered the living room.

"Thanks," I managed, unsure of how lovely I could really look. I was only wearing a simple green maxi dress and my hair was curled up into a basic ponytail. I reminded myself to stop the head chatter and compliment him back.

No self-pity tonight, Mia, remember?

"You look amazing yourself."

I called up to my sisters that Francesco had arrived, and they both yelled back in unison that they needed ten more minutes. Great, ten minutes alone with this man. My palms started to sweat, and I could feel the panic setting in.

"Let's sit on the patio while we wait, shall we?" he offered.

With a hand on the small of my back, he guided me towards the door and pulled out a chair for me.

"So, how is your tour of Firenze so far?"

Oh, I could do this. Small talk. Perfect.

"It's stunning. I saw photos before I came, but they didn't do the city justice. I'm positively enamored with the colors and structures. I'm not usually into architecture— I'm more of a nature girl—but the beauty is undeniable."

"Ah, so have you been to the Boboli Gardens yet?"

"No, not yet. I think that's our next stop," I said as I rolled my eyes, imagining my sisters ruining my long-awaited experience with another crammed school of fish-like tour.

"Tired of our beautiful city already, *cara?*"

"No, not at all. Just tired in general. I feel like we are rushing through everything, and I haven't been able to keep up." I felt the shame rising up like mercury in a thermometer without warning. He simply shook his head in what seemed like disappointment.

"There is so much to see, and visitors spend too much time with tours and checklists, in my opinion. *Non tutte le ciambelle riescono col buco.* Not everything in life needs to be a plan."

"True, and I'm the last one to argue that point given my last two days here. But shouldn't there be some kind of plan in life? How would anyone reach their dreams or even get anything done?"

"Mia Bella, there is a difference between making a plan and living a plan. You can make a plan to see something or do something your heart desires. But once the plan is made, let life take the wheel."

"I'm not sure what you mean." He was confusing me beyond belief—plan, but don't plan—and yet he appeared amused as I tried to decipher his cryptic escape room message in my brain.

"You Americans always with your having to figure life out. Let me give you an example. You saw Ponte Vecchio today, no?" I nodded, listening intently.

"And crossed over it as you walked on to your next destination—let me guess, the Uffizi Gallery and Palaccio?"

He paused for effect as I nodded again.

"All wonderful places, indeed. Top places for tourists to visit. But—did you happen to catch a glimpse of the Bardini Garden on your scheduled way from place to place?"

"No, I didn't."

"Ah, many do not know they were recently revitalized,

so it is one of our best kept secrets. It is a magnificent place for a quiet stroll, filled with floral terraces and sweet-smelling blooms, with birds chirping in the distance and butterflies waving hello.

"Had you decided to go to the area and choose to observe your surroundings yourself instead of booking tours, you would have most definitely come upon this little piece of paradise. You would have let life take you somewhere even better than planned."

My mouth transformed into a thoughtful grin at his way of thinking and agreed. After all, we weren't supposed to take tours—the intention actually was to have this carefree journey, exactly as he described.

"I see what you mean, and now I am sorry I missed such a place. I'll have to make a note to go back there—but without a plan," I added to let him know I heard his wisdom.

"Indeed—but there is even more to behold in our great city. Let her guide you to her most treasured sites. That's where the true magic lies."

"So, we shouldn't take the Chianti vineyard tour?" I teased.

"Absolutely not!" he responded with full on laughter, a deep, hearty roar that had his eyes sparkling like glittery confetti.

"I forbid it. In fact—I must insist on being your personal guide. The only way to experience the heart of Tuscany is through the eyes of a true Tuscan. When were you thinking of going?"

"I'm not sure. I think in a few days."

"Well, I will look at my calendar and clear a day for you ladies. Someone needs to make sure you have a proper wine experience while you are here. *Pfft*—vineyard tour."

"We would love that, thank you," I accepted.

He reached out his hand to touch mine and for a moment, I could sense his soul. His chocolate eyes were rich and warm, inviting me in to see more as they glistened along with his smile.

Our gaze was broken by the shouts inside that my sisters were finally ready.

"Shall we?" he asked as he led me again with his hand on my back through the door to join the others. Instead of getting my normal goosebumps when he touched me, I started to feel more at ease.

Dinner was outstanding. He introduced us to a local eatery where we were exposed to the truest of Tuscan dishes while he taught us some basic Italian along the way. We began with a simple unsalted bread, which we dipped into pure, herbed extra virgin olive oil. *Yum! More, please!*

Our *primi,* or first plate, was a delicious sampling of ribollita (vegetable and bread soup), ravioletti (ricotta and spinach-filled ravioli) and trippa (cow's stomach lining in tomato sauce). I thought my sisters would be sick on the spot when they found out what it was; but as for me, I enjoy trying local delicacies. I thought it all had wonderful flavor.

For *secondi,* or the main course, we were presented with a trio of entrées: ossobuco (braised veal shanks), salsicce e fagioli all'uccelletto (pork sausage with cannelloni beans) and fagiano arrosto (roasted pheasant). For *contorni,* or the side dish, we delighted in carciofi fritti (fried artichokes).

Not knowing how it was possible to have room for dessert, Francesco insisted that we try the castagnaccio, which was somewhat of a dense fruit and nut cake. Top this all off with never-ending glasses of wine, and it was the most extravagant meal I think we'd ever had.

Talk in between courses was light, mostly about our travels so far and his family. He has one younger brother, Lorenzo, who is also a lawyer in their family business. Their parents sadly died close to fifteen years ago in a car crash, leaving their entire fortune to both of their heartbroken sons.

Busy with the business, neither had time to settle down, but his brother *did* father 18-year-old Felicia, a nurse-in-training who everyone adored. You could see Francesco's eyes light up when he talked about his compassionate niece. I had found his Achilles heel.

While we waited for dessert to arrive, Francesco filled us in on what was happening with Sorella Maria. Now well-rested, she was looking forward to seeing us again—and it was agreed that earlier in the day would be better suited for her.

"Sorella Maria did give me permission to share a little bit of history with you," he said with a sly grin. "However, I am under her dire warning—*acqua in bocca!*—that there are some things I may not reveal as they are stories for her to tell.

"So, if I am not forthcoming with answers to your questions, it is because I am afraid of our dear sister striking me with her ruler."

He pretended to cower in fear over what she would do to him. Sweet, actually, how much love and respect he had for our cousin.

"As you can tell, the Bianchi family has a complicated history. As the eldest, Alessia was to be granted the sacred family jewelry box that was made by her grandfather, Dionisio. How the box came to be is the story to be told by Sorella Maria," he noted.

"Dionisio had two sons: Dominic, the eldest, and Luigi.

They were close, the brothers; no bad blood existed between them ever. Dominic went on to have three daughters, and Luigi had two sons, so essentially, Luigi's line is the one to officially carry down the Bianchi name.

"All the children grew up together in harmony and great family love: Alessia, Dominica, Concetta, Matteo and little Luigi. It wasn't until their teenage years that the family started to drift apart and begin their new lives.

"Luigi Senior had an opportunity to build his own fortune up north near Milan, so he and his clan left Florence and the family business behind, knowing it would be in the good hands of his older brother. Time and distance weakened the bonds of the cousins, as the two families went their separate ways—but with no ill will.

"That left the three girls as heirs to the Bianchi architectural empire started by Dionisio, and Dominic in possession of the jewelry box. Now, as the eldest, it was expected that Alessia find and marry a suitable man who would be trained by Dominic to carry on his and his father's legacy.

"And a suitable man was found; Vincenzo Moretti was chosen to be her husband."

He paused, waiting for the name recognition to set in. Meg was the one who figured it out first.

"Wait—isn't that who Sorella Maria said married Dominica?"

"Yes—good, you were paying attention!" He continued on, pleased that we were following along so well.

"Alessia wanted no part of the Moretti family or their money. She found Vincenzo to be arrogant and condescending. She was too much of a dreamer to be tamed by the likes of such a…"

"Pompous fool!" Meg interjected. "I remember reading

about him in her diary. She never referred to him by name, so I never realized the connection. She sure had quite a few colorful words to say about him."

"I think we need to get back into that journal again, Meg," suggested Marissa. She was right, of course, but I was so fascinated by the story that I didn't want them to go off on a tangent.

"Agreed," I acknowledged, then turned to Francesco. "Please, go on."

"All the while Alessia protested her betrothal to that *pompous fool*," he added with dramatic emphasis, "a devilishly handsome young Irishman by the name of Cian O'Sullivan had crossed her path. That, my loves, is all I can say about that for now as well."

Hearing our groans of frustration, he admitted he could tell us just a little bit more. He shared that the ensuing scandal opened the door for Dominica to step in and win the heart (and wallet) of Vincenzo—and her father's approval.

That was how the Morettis have since come to take possession of the Bianchi family business and home. The jealousy that Dominica had for Alessia was borderline obsessive, and she set out to destroy her older sister—as well as her younger one, who she felt betrayed her by remaining loyal to turncoat Alessia.

With Alessia self-exiled in Ireland, Dominica wanted to make sure that no one else challenged her position as head of the family. She reveled in the fact that Concetta was chastened an unwed mother and continued to ostracize her and her sweet daughter, Maria, from the family completely.

Fueling her fire was the fact that Concetta had the audacity to pass on the Bianchi name to her "bastard" child, so Dominica denounced both of her sisters forever. Neither were permitted to come near her, her family or the family home ever again.

Although they lived a great distance away from each other, Alessia and Concetta always remained loving and close. It is why when Alessia's daughter, Lena, wed into the corrupt Marino family, she originally bequeathed the jewelry box to young Maria instead, to preserve its intended heritage.

Alessia already worried that she made the wrong decision about giving her daughter the Celtic ring and didn't want to chance another intimate heirloom falling into the wrong hands. Even though she knew Lena had the right heart at her core and would remain obedient to her oath, she was concerned about what the Marinos would do—or discover—about their treasured family secrets.

A ring was much easier to hide than a wooden box.

Since Dominica had removed herself as a sister, she had no idea about this transaction, nor would she care about a simple jewelry box or its meaning. It remained a secret between the two sisters.

As Sorella Maria grew older and chose a life of sisterhood, she contacted her cousin Lena—as her aunt and uncle had since died—to share that she wished for the box to be passed back down to Lena's family when the time came; she did not want it in the greedy hands of her Zia Dominica's kin. Sorella Maria, however, agreed to safely hold onto it until the perfect heir could be identified.

When Lena was ill and Leigh had confessed to her about the existence of his daughter, Alissa, it was then that Lena connected her son with Sorella Maria to orchestrate the gifting of the jewelry box. Originally, it was intended to go to our mother, but our grandfather had a grander scheme in mind as he neared the end of his life.

"It was clearly meant for his granddaughter, Mia,"

concluded Francesco.

"What do you mean it was 'clearly meant' for me? I don't understand."

"You will, *cara*. All in good time."

As his story came to an end, we individually absorbed the information as we indulged in the flavorful dessert and post-meal espresso that was just served. Our legacy was becoming more complicated with each trip—and this was just one grandparent's side!

I could only imagine what we would find if we investigated Granny's lineage or our dad's family tree. There was so much to take in—yet it also provided more clarity about the family dynamics of our roots.

It never dawned on me to question how Francesco factored into all of this until Marissa made the connection.

"Please do not take this the wrong way," she began. "But if this is supposed to be our sacred family secret, how is it that you know so much about our history?"

"That's a fair question. You see, my grandmother, Mina, and Sorella Maria were best friends growing up. Lifelong friends—sisters, even. Neither had any siblings, so they formed a close bond that was never broken.

"My grandmother died young, only a year after my grandfather, leaving my mother orphaned just as she entered adulthood. Sorella Maria, not having a family of her own, took my mother under her wings as if she were her own child. So, naturally, when my parents met, married and had Lorenzo and I, she became our adopted grandmother.

"I can't remember a time when Sorella Maria was not a part of our family," he recalled fondly. It explained why he was so warm and affectionate towards her.

"When Leigh approached her about making arrangements for the jewelry box to go to Mia, she was concerned over her failing health and ability to carry through his wishes—especially since she was so much older in age than he.

"So, she took me into her confidence, with Leigh's blessing, to protect your legacy. And it is with the greatest honor that I do so," he added. "I love Sorella Maria with all of my heart. I would do anything for her."

"Please forgive us for questioning you, Francesco," Meg chimed in. "There have just been too many shady encounters throughout our journey, and the more who know about this, the more we feel like our lives are in jeopardy."

"Of course, *cara*. I am not offended by your questioning at all. I think it is smart of you to be cautious. I can assure you, I have no desire to harm you or take what is yours in any way. I am sworn to protect you—and that is what I will do as long as you are in my care."

We all thanked him for the lovely evening, and for the insightful information. We looked at each other knowingly; he was someone we could trust without a doubt. If our Godly cousin had faith in him, then that was good enough for us.

7

By days four and five, we were grateful for the opportunity to sleep in. We spent an entire day at the house, resting, swimming and keeping it low-key. Meg was avidly reading through Alessia's diary, Marissa was sunning herself by the pool and I lost myself in a good book.

It gave us some time to catch up with each other as well. Being in a new country with a somewhat refreshed spirit, I was more open to hear about the newest developments in my sisters' lives. Although I assumed that all was magical in their worlds since they were in relationships, I found that not everything was as sugar-coated as it seemed.

Kieran's mum had taken another bad fall and found herself in the hospital with a cracked rib. He had to put some of his record producing on hold to care for her once she returned home, and I could feel the tension in Meg's voice as she worried about her Irish family. Although she would never admit it, I knew she was torn between being here with us on this journey and being there for her love.

But, Meg being Meg, she would honor her promise to us above all else, which made her inner conflict all the more difficult to witness. It was probably why she was all gung-ho about the guided tours; the more structure, the less her mind could wander. I wished there was a way I could release her from her assumed obligation, but she would never allow it. Her loyalty to us was one of the things I admired most about her.

It was then Marissa's turn to fill us in on how tough it was for her to be separated from Tony. She did seem to have a different air about her when she talked about him. Her melancholy was evident—had a man successfully stolen our little sister's heart and surrendered her into commitment? It was a new side to her we had never seen before, and I could only imagine the turmoil that it caused within her.

Plus, she finally confided how she was feeling increasingly frustrated with having to wait her turn for her heirloom—our impulsive little sis was never one for much patience and it was beginning to show. She couldn't help but carry around the fear that something else would happen to keep her from Spain, similar to how the warning note almost kept us from Italy. Meg and I reassured her that no matter what, we would make sure she'd get her bequeathed statue, yet Marissa was hesitant to hold onto hope. No doubt it's why she wanted to escape into her world of art so badly.

As we chilled by the pool, I found it easier to open up about how I was feeling about the divorce, and how it affected the kids. I told them how grateful I had been for their support; I honestly don't know how I would have gotten through the last few months without them by my side.

It was cathartic for all of us to express our woes and remember that we were there to lean on each other. I know for myself, a little bit of weight was lifted off my shoulders just from being able to verbalize what was inside of me, and then being able to listen to them unload. It reminded us that we truly were in this together, and that above all else, our sisterly bond would get us through anything.

The remainder of the day was much more easygoing. We took a short walk down the block for some wood fired pizza and gelato for lunch. Not having much of an appetite by evening, we munched on leftovers and basket goodies while we curled up on the couch and watched an old rom-com (with subtitles) together. It felt amazing not to have anywhere to go or anything to do in particular. I think we all needed that regrouping before heading off to bed.

We planned to meet up with Sorella Maria later the next morning, just before lunch. Typically an early riser by nature, I uncharacteristically kept the window blinds down so that the sun did not wake me up as it rose before me for the second day in a row.

I snuggled down into the comfort of my pillow and blankets and allowed myself to simply rest. Another day of no responsibility. No children to get up and make breakfast for. No errands to run. No tours to go on today. No, today was just going to be about seeing our cousin and then spending the rest of the day in more solitary luxury. Maybe I could even figure out a way to escape to one of those bookstores by myself.

When I finally arose to greet the day, I felt refreshed. Many of the emotions and fatigue that had been plaguing me a few days earlier were swept away with my dreams. Today was a new day. I couldn't help but open the doors to the balcony and simply smile at the view in front of me. How could anyone be miserable when surrounded by so much enchantment?

I was excited to hear more about the Bianchi story today. Francesco had dropped hints about a secret behind the jewelry box and teased us about an ancestral scandal, just like Colleen did. After years of being married to a cop, the inner detective in me couldn't wait to piece this mystery all together.

I popped down the stairs to see a well-put together Megan in jean shorts and white button-down shirt and a still-groggy Marissa in a green and white nightie. They were gathered on the couch with their coffee and tea, with an extra mug waiting for me.

"Good morning," chirped Meg. "I'm so glad you're finally up. I wanted to share something I came across in Alessia's journal."

Since finding it in the O'Sullivan attic, Meg had sporadically read through the pages to try to unearth more information about its author, Alessia Bianchi O'Sullivan. She didn't find much in the beginning—just some normal teenage frustrations and sisterly dissonance. I'm guessing after spending a day and night of reading it, she had finally discovered something interesting.

"Since hearing Francesco tell the story, I couldn't help but wonder if there were more subtle clues in the diary that I missed before. I've been reading through this for hours now, hoping to find any kind of juicy nugget.

"She went into her anger over the betrothal to Vincenzo, though she only irritably referred to him as *Bischero*—Italian for idiot—and how she caught Dominica propositioning him several times. She wished that she could be released from this arrangement so that her wicked sister could marry him instead, since they deserved each other," she laughed.

"Then there were a few lapses in time where she wasn't writing in her journal at all; it appears she had stopped for a while. There were a few entries referencing meeting an Irishman, who I could only assume was Cian. Lots of lovey-dovey references to him being her soulmate, and a few of the memories she captured about their nights together. Juicy, but nothing too revealing in terms of a scandal. But then I came across this."

She pulled me down to join her on the couch, so that she was sandwiched between me and Marissa. Her Italian interpretative skills were impressive, as she paraphrased what Alessia wrote in the journal. Since leaving her Italian-studied boyfriend, she invested in an electronic translator to help her navigate some of the foreign phrases she couldn't decipher.

No matter what Mamma says, I just can't walk away from the man I love. I won't. How can I forget the way he looks at me with those ocean eyes like I am the only woman in the world? How his kisses make me feel alive, and how feeling him inside of me completes my very soul?

I don't care if I am a sinner. I don't care if Papa calls me a disgrace and spits upon my love. I'd rather die than live a life without him, for without him, life is death anyway.

Tomorrow, I will run away to Ireland with my Cian, and we will live out our days in love. Curse the Bianchis. Curse Mamma and Papa. Curse that Dominica. She can take what's supposed to be mine. I don't want any of it, or any of them.

I will make my own family, and there will be so much love to feed me that I will never hunger a single day again.

"I assume that mommy and daddy were not thrilled to find out about her Irish love," Marissa snarked.

"Is there more?" I asked. Meg nodded and continued, noting that this post was written later on in the evening.

My beloved Cian leaves in a few short hours for home. His trip here is done, and he must return. I told him that I intend to come with him, but he denies me this. He denies me a life of love. Tells me that I would regret leaving my family; that family is important.

Well if family was so important, they would not be making me marry a man I do not love. To be a dutiful wife to a greedy, mean Bischero who is only in it for the money and power? That is not for me, I told him. He was the only man my heart will ever love.

So I will go to him. I will go to him tonight and never look back. I have all that I need packed. I have some clothes, some photos in Nonno's box, some food and this journal. I need nor want for nothing more than this; than my Cian.

He cannot turn me away; he must not. I will not accept anything but his arms around me as we start our new life together. To make all his promises come true. Oh, I cannot wait to be just his and leave this restricting world behind. I shall breathe life in once again.

I will leave a note for dear, sweet Concetta, promising that I will send for her when I am settled. I will leave a note for Mamma and Papa, telling them that I love them, but that I cannot live the life they chose for me. I will leave my country behind forever.

And I know in the deepest part of my soul, that I will never regret following love. I am sorry, my family. I hope one day you can forgive me for my betrayal.

"Wow. So, she really did leave her family behind for love." *How romantic,* I thought.

"There's more, I'm sure, but this is as far as I got. I'm hoping that Sorella Maria has more insight into what happened during those missing pages that prompted her to leave. From what she told us, our cousin adored her grandparents. That doesn't exactly sound like the kind of people who would shun their own daughter. There has to be more to the story."

"Speaking of—we should get ready to go. It's almost ten-thirty," Marissa prodded.

When we arrived at the retirement home, our cousin greeted us with more spunk and energy than she had the first night. Dressed in a lovely stone blue dress and light brown jacket, her smile was radiant, and her natural kindness welcoming. She made arrangements for us to talk privately in their communal sitting area, where freshly brewed cappuccinos and biscotti awaited us.

"How wonderful it is to see you all again. Praise God for bringing us all together," she began.

"It is delightful to see you, too. How are you feeling?" Meg asked.

"Much better, thank you, my dear. I just get so tired at night. Besides, I love nothing more than a good *chiacchierata*—chat—in the morning."

We sat down upon the red cushioned armchairs arranged in a semi-circle. The dark wood table was set with a silver platter of assorted biscotti and four steaming mugs.

That answered my question as to whether or not Francesco would be there. I oddly felt a surge of disappointment. As if she could read my mind, Sorella Maria explained his absence.

"Francesco is working on a case today," she mentioned. "He said something about needing to tie up loose ends so he can take three beautiful women to a vineyard this week?"

"Oh, yes," I replied, turning to address Meg and Marissa. "I forgot to tell you. He offered to take us on a drive through the wineries. He said it was a much better experience to explore with a local than to take a tour. I hope you don't mind."

"Of course not! That sounds amazing," said Meg.

"As long as I get some wine, I don't care who takes me," chuckled Marissa.

"*Bene.* Now that's all settled. Where shall I begin? *Non avere peli sulla lingua,* as they say—I'm not one to mince words. I will tell it to you straight. Francesco was kind enough to give you some history, yes?"

"Oh, yes. He told us all about the family tree, including Luigi's family and how they moved away and that Dominic retained the family business. He mentioned how Alessia was betrothed to Vincenzo but chose to run away to Ireland with Cian instead, leaving Dominica free to marry into the Moretti family instead.

"But he also said he wasn't allowed to tell us about Alessia and Cian—and neither could our cousin Colleen in Ireland. Why is that?" I asked.

"When your Nonno Leigh came up with the plan for each of you, he was very particular about how everything was to be revealed. It was quite clever and took a great deal of time. He was rather rigid about who would tell what, so that everyone would have an equally rich story to tell. We *cugini*, bound not by actual blood but by honor, all consented to fulfill his request.

"*Ogni morte di Papa*—at every death of a Pope, or 'once in a blue moon' as you Americans would say, there is a great love story to tell. The love between Alessia and Cian is rare, and I was the one sanctioned to share it with you.

"As you now know, when Alessia was a young girl, her parents arranged for her to wed Vincenzo when she came of age. Alessia was not fond of the idea from the beginning. She never wanted to be a wife to anyone. She was a headstrong young woman with dreams of being a grand herbal healer—but her parents dismissed the idea of their daughter practicing 'the devil's work.'

"Alessia ignored her parents' wishes and began studying with a local *strega*—witch—who would teach her about herbs, potions and homemade remedies. My mamma told me she was a natural at it, as oftentimes her older sister used her for practice. Luckily for Alessia, Mamma was a bit *maldestra* and always getting hurt."

You could tell Sorella Maria was envisioning her clumsy mother in that moment, and how the two sisters would play nurse and patient.

"As her teenage years passed, Alessia continued to rebuff any advances made by Vincenzo—and he would make them. He would taunt her for being so virginal, as she was to be his wife and he had the right to have her whenever he wanted her. *Bischero,*" she said with disgust.

"Right before turning eighteen, Alessia was walking to the *mercato* for some ingredients for her latest herbal experiment. It was there in the piazza where she came upon a lost young man in need of directions.

"I know this, because this is all written in a long letter she sent to my mamma after she left," she said as an aside. "Remind me to give it to you before you leave; I would love for these histories to be passed on to your own children," she said before continuing.

"That blonde-haired, blue-eyed rascal was named Cian, and it is said that *erano incantate*—they were enchanted the moment their eyes met. Alessia was well-versed in English thanks to her rich education, so it made communication seamless between the two strangers. She directed him to his destination, but he would not leave until she promised to meet him for dinner that evening.

"They talked into the wee hours of the morning about hopes, dreams, their families—everything.

"Cian was a man with a heart of gold. Alessia was a woman of many dreams. They were a perfect match. The friendship was as instant as the *passione*. They had both kissed others before, but nothing like this. They were quickly swept away in each other.

"Within the three short weeks he was in town, they fell madly in love and were practically inseparable. She lost her innocence willingly to him and claimed that he was her *anima gemelli*—soulmate—in every way. He supported her dream of being a healer; she challenged him to follow his own heart to America. Together, they believed they could do anything.

"Their time together in Firenze was short, but intense. She would sneak away to see him, knowing that her parents would never approve. Unfortunately, their secret did not last long. Her vengeful sister Dominica had been following them for a few nights and eventually led their parents to catch them in the heat of passion, right in il Giardino Bardini."

I smirked at the mention of the Bardini Garden, and how Francesco pointed out this particular place as easily missed, but a treasure to behold. I wonder if he knew this part of the story and that connection.

"There is a saying in Italy: *L'affetto verso I genitori e fondamento di ogni virtu.* It means you shall honor your father and mother. In those days, that commandment was not negotiable. So, when Alessia was caught and then confessed that she had been seeing this Irish boy Cian behind their backs, it was considered a great sin and betrayal—not only to her betrothed, but to her parents and her community.

"What made matters worse was that he was not Italian, which made him an unsuitable match for the heiress to the family business. Dominica had made sure that Vincenzo was aware of Alessia's duplicity, which made the Moretti family furious at the breach of agreement and forced Nonno's hand.

"Elder Vincenzo Moretti was a powerful man, and this did not bode well for anyone. Nonno luckily convinced the Morettis to allow him an opportunity to make amends; after all, it was still in the Morettis' best interest to marry into the Bianchi family for the extra fortune.

"To preserve Vincenzo Jr.'s pride and not brand him a cuckhold, it was agreed that no one would ever speak of Alessia's affair, and all would believe that she still was his chaste intended.

"Although by nature my grandparents were very loving and understanding people, they had a reputation and code of honor to uphold. What a difficult decision Nonno Dominic had to make. If society ever found out about this dalliance, *la famiglia* Bianchi would be shamed and they would lose everything. Elder Vincenzo had threatened to see to that.

"Nonno forbade Alessia from ever seeing Cian again. In fact, he was the one who arranged for Cian's sudden departure and threatened that if Cian did not break it off with his daughter, that he and his family would live to regret it. But as they say, *i frutti proibiti sono i più dolci*— forbidden fruit is the sweetest.

"Alessia could not stay away, and so defied her parents to meet with Cian one final time. He told her of his need to return to Ireland—without her. It broke her heart. She refused to believe him, even when he tried through tearful eyes to claim that he used her for fun; that it was just a game to him.

"Alas, *l'amore domina senza regole;* love does not play by the rules. He loved her so much that he could not lie to her, and so he faltered and told her of her parents' demands. But he also told her that he believed they were right; they did not belong together, and that her place was with her *famiglia*.

"Alessia was too strong-willed to allow anyone to make this decision for her—she was leaving with him whether anyone liked it or not. They were going to decide their own fate, she declared.

"And so, in the middle of the night, with a small sack of belongings and her most treasured items—the jewelry box from her Nonno Dionisio included—Alessia risked it all to join Cian in Ireland, leaving nothing but a letter for Mamma and my grandparents, professing her love and begging forgiveness."

"What happened when she left?" Meg was not the only one curious to know more.

"Well, it created quite the scandal when it was discovered that she had left. To save face, her father had to declare Alessia 'dead' to the family, and announced that his more dutiful daughter, Dominica, was promised to the Moretti family instead. And so, on the day of her eighteenth birthday, Dominica wed Vincenzo Moretti and took her loyal place with great satisfaction.

"Everyone believed that Alessia was cut out of *la famiglia;* it was what Dominic and Ginevra promised. And that is the story that has been passed down.

"But I know better, because Mamma confided that my Nonna Ginerva secretly sent letters to her beloved daughter. Even though she and Nonno disapproved, in their hearts, they knew Cian and Alessia were made for each other, despite their different backgrounds and family expectations. Ultimately, they only wanted their daughter's happiness.

"But Dominica was a force to be reckoned with by then, and if anyone ever found out, she would destroy them all—even her own parents. *Acqua in bocca*—it was never spoken to anyone, and Alessia was free to live out her life in peace, knowing she still had her parents' love."

"Sorella Maria," Meg interrupted when our cousin paused for a moment, "we came upon an entry in Alessia's diary that I was hoping you could shed some light on. She wrote how when she left for Ireland, she promised Concetta that she would send for her. I know you said they kept in touch, but since you are still here in Florence, I am wondering if she ever kept her promise."

"Ah, she did indeed, child. When Cian and Alessia arrived in Ireland, it did not take long for them to build a happy home and even happier life. After they wed and *bambina* Lena came along, they made plans to follow Cian's dream to move to America.

"They decided to transfer the family home over to Cian's nephew Banan—I believe that was Colleen's papa—and it was then that my Zia Alessia reached out to Mamma to join them.

"Alas, by then, Mamma was with child and she did not think she would survive the trip across the ocean. She managed to find a small home for us here instead, and my grandparents took care of us as best they could until their deaths.

"Nonna died first from *il colpo d'aria,* an illness from which she never recovered. It is said Nonno died only four months later from a broken heart." She paused to remember the despair she experienced from losing them as a young girl of only eight.

"Left with no one but a bitter older sister, my mother wished then that she had followed Alessia to America. Dominica quickly turned her back and left poor Mamma with no one. She said to her: *Hai voluto la bicicletta? Allora, pedala!* If she wanted a bike, she had to ride it. Meaning my mother had to live with the consequences of her own choices.

"Dominica took whatever money my grandparents left for Mamma away and refused us shelter when we could no longer afford our home. She took over the Casa Bianchi, and we were never permitted to see it again. Her grandson, Dominic IV, owns it currently. How I have missed it," she added wistfully.

"After being ostracized by Dominica and the society she controlled, Mamma found comfort in the nuns of Santo Rosario, who took us in and cared for us. Cian and Alessia reached out several times to bring us to New York to live with them, but we were happy in the simplicity of our life here.

"It is growing up in the convent that led to my calling to serve God," she informed us.

"That Dominica sounds like quite a piece of work," Marissa commented.

"That she was. I am glad I never had the chance to meet that horrible woman. I met Zia Alessia a few times, when she, Zio Cian and Lena came to visit during the summers. She was every bit as *bella* as they said. You look a lot like her, Mia," Sorella Maria mused.

"Me?"

"Yes, you. You have her eyes, hair and kindness. I

sense fire in you; a fire worthy of powerful dreams. You may not see or feel it, but I can. It's in you and is why you were chosen for this journey."

"Can you tell me more about it?"

"I'm afraid we will need to leave that story for another time," she said wearily. "*Scusami,* but I must rest now."

"Of course," said Meg, as she helped the elderly woman rise from the chair and take hold of her cane. "Thank you for sharing this history with us. It's all fascinating, and we look forward to hearing more again soon."

An orderly came to escort our cousin back to her room, leaving us to discuss our next steps over a now cold cappuccino.

"So, what do we do now?" Marissa asked.

"I say we find Casa Bianchi and pay it a little visit," I said mischievously.

8

"Can I help you?" asked the young, dark beauty, clearly making it known that we had disturbed her. She couldn't be more than sixteen and her vampire-like bite made Brittany seem like an amateur teen. I should count my blessings.

"Is this the Moretti residence?" I asked.

"Yes. Now, what do you want?" I could tell which bloodline ran strong in this one. Still, I wasn't going to leave without fulfilling my mission.

"We've been tracing our family roots and one of them led us here. Our great-great-aunt Dominica used to live here."

"Whatever. No one is home," she spat as she started to close the door. I gently stopped it from shutting all the way.

"Oh. I'm sorry to bother you. Could you just tell me if your grandparents still live here, and when they might be home?"

"Listen, lady. Nonno died ten years ago and Nonna isn't in her right mind. Sorry, can't help you."

"Wait—could you at least take down our number and have your Nonna or even one of your parents give us a call back? It would really mean a lot to talk to them."

Rolling her eyes, the ingrate grabbed a notepad and pen to jot down my name and my phone number. It was probably a lost cause, but worth the effort anyway. She quickly closed and locked the door the second I finished my number without even saying goodbye.

"Wasn't she charming," Meg commented.

"Yeah," said Marissa, in a far-off daze. It looked as if she had seen a ghost.

"Mar, what's wrong?"

"Nothing. I—I thought I saw someone I knew come from the back of the house just now. But it couldn't be," she shook her head in disbelief.

"Who was it?" I investigated. She looked instantly uncomfortable, and I could tell that the next words out of her mouth would be a lie.

"It was probably just one of the guards. Let's go," she said as she walked back towards the car we rented for the day.

Meg and I just looked at each other in joint uncertainty, not knowing whether to pursue this conversation now or later. We decided to put it on hold until Marissa was in a better frame of mind. It was obvious she wanted the subject changed.

"So, why did we come here again?"

"You'll see. I have a special surprise in mind for a special someone," I hinted.

"Francesco?" Meg asked with a sly smile.

"Wait, what? Why would you think it was him?"

"Oh, I don't know. Maybe because you get these goo-goo eyes whenever you are around him," she teased.

"Don't be absurd. I'm a married woman and he's basically twice my age. I'm not here for a romance like yours, Meg."

"Whoa, girl. Don't be so defensive. First off," she started, "you are in the middle of a divorce. Any day now you might get word that it is finalized, so there is nothing wrong with a little flirtation. Second, he is not twice your age! He may be older, but he certainly is attractive and sexy as hell."

"I personally enjoy older men. They are more— attentive in bed, let's say," Marissa revealed.

"Oh my goodness, would the two of you stop? He is just our cousin's lawyer. Nothing more."

"She doth protest too much, eh Mar?"

"Methinks so, too. Listen Mia, relax a little. Loosen up. We know you have been through an incredibly rough time with your divorce. We are not saying that this is your Kieran or anything."

"Then what are you saying?"

"We're saying, take down your walls," Meg said gently. "Let the man charm you and pay attention to you. He clearly adores you, *Mia Bella*," she emphasized.

"We might as well not be in the room when you are there."

"That's absurd. No man has ever wanted to be with me over—" I stopped. I could feel those emotions bubble up. Nope. Time to shut it down.

"Never mind. It's silliness. Anyway, I was thinking of cooking again tonight—we have the makings for peposo alla Fiorentina."

"No, Mia. No way. What were you going to say?" Marissa prodded while I stayed silent. "Don't do this. Don't do what you always do and shut down."

"How come it's okay for you to do it? Why don't you tell us who you thought you saw just now?"

"Nu-uh. We're not going there—you are not going to turn this back around to me. That was literally nothing. Something is boiling here, Mia. Spit it out."

"She's right, Mi. You haven't been yourself this week

and we know something is up. You pushed me in Ireland, remember? Now it's our turn to push you." Great, now Meg was conspiring to harass me, too.

"Why can't you just leave it alone? It's not really any of your business."

"You're right. It's not. But whatever it is, it is eating you alive inside and we just want to help. Why won't you let us in?"

Meg was pleading with me at this point. Sitting in the car, on the side of the road next to the big, old Bianchi house, I was trapped like a cat in a shelter cage. They had me cornered, and all my feelings started to surface. They wouldn't go back down, damn it. *Not now. Why now?*

I tried to choose my words carefully and calmly.

"Because you wouldn't understand."

"Try us," Marissa said, as she reached her hand from across the backseat to touch my shoulder with a small squeeze. That simple touch was all it took to release the floodgates. They let me cry for probably a good five minutes straight, giving me tissues and holding space while I emoted.

When I felt like I cried my last tear, I thought maybe I should finally let them in. It would be nice to talk to someone about it, even if they couldn't possibly relate.

"I'm having a really hard time right now. I'm trying to fight my sadness and anger, but they have taken a hold over me. I just lost the love of my life. That's nothing I can just 'get over' easily. I never thought I'd face a life without him. But here I am, alone—and fat."

"Mia, you're not—"

"No, don't." I snapped. "Please don't tell me I'm not fat, or that beauty comes from within me. It's easy for you to say because you are both physically flawless. You can look at any man and they will melt and come right to you. I've seen it. It's been my whole life, watching from the sidelines, the third wheel to the otherwise beautiful Rossi sisters. It hurts. It hurts so bad."

The tears came again in violent typhoon waves. There was more inside, oh so much more.

"I envy the both of you more than you know. More than your prettiness and ability to attract men. You both have this natural confidence to go after what you want. You reach for your dreams, and even if there is a challenge or you might fail, you do it anyway.

"I don't have that in me. I don't have any dreams, any purpose, anything to look forward to in the future. All I am is a mom, and now a divorced, unlovable nobody. And it's not that I don't love my kids—they are the best thing that has ever happened to me, and I am proud to be their mom. But it's like I don't have an identity for myself.

"I'm probably going to end up a crazy old fat cat lady." I was exasperated at the thought of what that would look like.

"Mia Lillith, you listen to me, and you listen to me carefully," Meg began after some time, pulling out the big guns just like Mom would by adding my middle name.

"You are not a nobody, and you will not be some crazy cat lady. You have no idea how envious *I* am of *you*. I always thought you had a beautiful home, a loving husband, wonderful children—you seemed so naturally happy all of the time. I always thought you had the perfect life and it was what I always wished for with Scotty.

"I had no idea you were in so much pain, and how deeply hurt you have been all this time. I'm so sorry I have not been more attentive to your needs over the years."

"Me too," added Marissa. "But Mia, you are not

destined to be alone. I don't want to dismiss your feelings about your weight, but if you could see what we see, all we see is our beautiful, loving, compassionate sister. Do you really think that you have nothing going for you?"

"Yes," I managed to squeak out. Meg lifted my chin up so she could look into my eyes with a love only a sister could have.

"Girl, you have some sexy curves going on, and an exotic look. But beyond that, you have passion. I see it when you cook. I see it when you decorate your home and tend to your gardens. You make these masterpieces and bring so much life to everything you do. To your kids, to us—to everyone. Any man would be crazy not to find that irresistible."

"And, if I might add, you do have a future," Marissa insisted. "Yes, your marriage is over, and that really sucks. But like you always remind us, there is always a silver lining.

"I have never known you to not take a positive spin on anything thrown your way. You make the impossible happen. You have just forgotten who you are, that's all. You are strong and brave. You know you have dreams in your heart that you gave up in order to raise that amazing family of yours. But maybe—just maybe—the silver lining in all of this is that you get to rediscover who you are and follow your dreams again."

"I don't know what it is about these trips that make her so profound all of a sudden, but Mar's right," Meg giggled as Marissa playfully punched her. I was grateful they were there to break the heavy mood. I'd even take one of their classic fights to shift the focus away from me.

"You know what?" Meg asked aloud. "I have an idea. Just like I spent some time alone in Ireland, I think our dear sis here could use some time to herself for reflection."

"What are you suggesting?" I asked through red puffy eyes. Ugh, I hated how I felt after the weeping was done. All I wanted to do now was sleep it off.

"Well, Kieran's mum is still feeling ill, and although he didn't come right out and ask, I am sure they could both use my support right now. And, to be completely honest—and selfish—I really, really miss him. This across-the-ocean falling in love thing is harder than I expected," she admitted.

"We have the time to spare before we meet up with Sorella Maria again, so maybe I can book a flight to Ireland the day after tomorrow for just a few days. Not that I want to abandon either of you on our sister trip, of course. But, maybe we could each use a personal break to regroup before we learn any more about our Italian heritage."

Picking up on Meg's cue, Marissa was relieved to suggest her own plan. "I think you have a good point, Meg. I'm starting to feel overwhelmed, too, and could use some space to sort some things out—since we have a few days to ourselves now. It's not easy for me to navigate this love stuff with Tony, and I think being away from him, and on my own, might help me clear my head.

"Plus, I really want to go on that multi-day immersive art experience while I'm here. No offense, but being limited to those tours with you two dragging me away all the time is not exactly how I pictured my international art tour dream," she bashfully confessed. "So, why don't I sign up for that while Meg takes a trip to Ireland?"

"That sounds perfect, Mar. Then Mia, this will give you some time alone to do whatever you want, whenever you want."

"Time to myself sounds really nice," I admitted. "As

long as you both are feeling the same way and not offended if I take you up on the offer. But—what about our safety in numbers pact?"

"I'll be safe in Ireland with Kieran, and one of the bodyguards can watch over Marissa while the rest continue to stand guard over you and the townhouse. It'll be fine."

"Okay." I was instantly warming up to the idea of having some "me" time. Not having to follow someone else's schedule, take another one of those damned history tours or answer questions about how I was feeling—that definitely sounded appealing.

"You convinced me."

"Great! When we get back to the house, Marissa and I can make our arrangements. Could you do us just one favor though, Mia?"

"Sure, what's that?"

"Can you see if Francesco can give us that special wine tour of his tomorrow before we go? I think a nice, relaxing sister day without any more of this legacy stuff would do us all some good before we split up."

"I like how you think! I'm on it."

It *would* be great to have unrushed quality time with them before we parted, though the thought of having Francesco join us admittedly made me anxious. I warmed inside like a brewing tea kettle at the thought of spending a whole day with him in wine country.

9

"**B**uongiorno, signorina," said a handsome middle-aged man who looked amazingly like Francesco. He had the same deep toffee-colored eyes and golden skin, but was a bit younger and less built than his brother.

"*Buongiorno.* You must be Lorenzo," I greeted. "I'm Mia. It's wonderful to meet you. My sisters will be right down."

"I've heard so much about you, Mia. You are as lovely as my brother said." Oh, that smile definitely was genetic, sending electric waves through me as he took my hand and kissed it. What was it with these Marchesi men and their magnetic charm?

His hair was slightly darker with less grays, and his face softer without the beard; not as chiseled as Francesco's, but just as dashing. Dressed in a pink polo shirt and khaki trousers, he had the aura of being a ladies' man. I had no doubt he had unclaimed children somewhere all over the country.

Sensing me wondering where his brother was, he motioned to the stunning red Fiat® 124 Spider convertible waiting outside with Francesco waving from the driver's seat. An older version of the man before me, he was sporting a bright teal polo shirt that looked amazing against his olive skin.

I felt a bit embarrassed now that I wore practically the

same color dress, though I had hoped no one would notice. He motioned for me to come towards him, and Lorenzo encouraged me to go on while he waited for the others.

As I approached the car, I realized it was only a two-seater. Parked in front of Francesco was another gorgeous vehicle, a black BMW® 4 convertible that belonged to Lorenzo. He would be escorting Meg and Marissa while Francesco had the "pleasure of my company," he said.

When I asked him why two vehicles, he insisted that there was no other way to enjoy the Tuscan countryside, and that squeezing all of us into one car would ruin the experience.

I could hear my sisters squealing as they approached the cars with Lorenzo, already pleased with how much better a drive through the country would be with these fine gentlemen, instead of an overbooked bus tour.

"So, where are we going?"

"Mia Bella, leave the destinations to us. You, *cara*, are instructed to simply enjoy the journey. Lorenzo, *'ndom!*"

Since we left at the crack of dawn, we witnessed the sun beginning its ascent, bringing a blaze of vibrant tones to the otherwise clear blue sky. It was thrilling to let myself go and enjoy the open air as Francesco sped along the slow, winding country roads with the roof down. The wind whipping through my hair, I felt a surge of freedom course through my body.

I didn't think I could find another country as breathtaking as Ireland; yet here I was, enamored by the Tuscan countryside with its own luxuriant landscapes. There were countless hilltops and open fields, garnished with bales of hay and free range animals, and a plethora of olive groves, cypress trees and vineyards. The fields of sunflowers were extraordinary; so much so, that the brothers pulled over briefly so I could touch, smell and revel in their gloriousness.

The Marchesi brothers promised us more than a vineyard experience—and they did not disappoint. The first stop was a beautiful little medieval village called Collodi. It is said that the author of Pinocchio grew up in this small town, taking its name as his pseudonym.

We visited its featured Parco di Pinocchio, an adorable tribute to the book brought to life through children's rides, a museum with a virtual library, workshops, an ivy maze and more. Though time was limited, we did get the opportunity to enjoy a real puppet show, and it brought me back to the days when my sisters and I would put on a show for our parents and grandparents.

I don't remember the last time I laughed with such childlike abandon.

We then took a moment to stroll through the village's Garzoni Garden and Butterfly House. Wow, how it left me speechless. More than just pretty terrains of countless kinds of flowers, the garden was laced with manicured walkways, baroque statues and festive fountains. Magnificent.

Tropical butterflies filled a greenhouse with their flamboyant wings—one even landed on my shoulder to pose for a quick picture with me. Oh, I could have spent my entire day there.

Seeing this small little village, barely even mentioned in my books, made me realize how much of the world is truly unseen because we rush or plan. As I stood at the steps where the water cascaded gently down its rock foundation, I felt his presence surround me before his arms followed suit.

Placing them around my waist, he leaned his head in and rested it against mine, chin on my shoulder, so that we were cheek to cheek. Normally, I would flinch at a stranger's touch, but I found myself just allowing the natural gesture to envelop me.

"You seem light and happy, *cara*. It's wonderful to see you this way," Francesco said softly.

"I feel like I am in heaven right now. Words cannot even describe what I see with my eyes or feel in my soul. It's pure magic."

"I chose this spot just for you," he said, as he continued to hold me against him, catching his own breath at the views in front of us.

"I come here myself whenever I need to decompress or just be reminded how grand the world can be. The moment I found out you shared my love for landscapes, I knew I had to take you here. Not a person comes here who doesn't appreciate its splendor. But only certain visitors feel that uncontrollable pull that brings us beyond earth and into the infinite wonder of the universe."

"I had no idea you loved nature so much," I responded.

It took me by surprise to find that this strong, masculine lawyer had a soft spot for Mother Nature. It was instantly endearing and made me feel even more connected to this man.

"We are not always who we appear to be, Mia Bella. We all have our walls and masks that we wear. But when we let ourselves open up and share our loves and dreams and even hurts within us, it is then when we see the true beauty and essence of a person.

"I enjoy getting to know you, *cara*. You have surprised me as much as I have surprised you today. It pleased my heart to hear you laugh so playfully at the puppet show and to see you throw your hands up in the wind with abandonment as we drove fast. To let me hold you like this without resistance," he added in a whisper, as I started to tense up at his acknowledgment of the embrace.

"Don't, Mia," he pleaded softly. "Don't ever turn away from being in the moment. I want nothing more from you than to merely stand here and gaze at our world. You are safe with me."

I believed him. He wasn't trying to be smooth or seductive; I could sense that. I was safe, and so I let myself relax back into him. I could actually feel his smile rise against my cheek, followed by a quick squeeze of my middle. He then took my hand as we all walked back towards the cars and on to the next destination.

Only a little more than an hour later, we found ourselves at the smaller and lesser-known wine region in Livorno called Bolgheri. Lorenzo explained how this was the place to go if you were a true wine lover—affectionately known as a "Super Tuscan."

It was yet another site to behold, with views of an ancient castle and the Tyrrhenian coast, where you could watch the whitecaps battle it out against the sand. There, we were treated to a glorious glass of Sassicaia—a wine known to rival even the Bordeaux. I can attest to that claim, as the superior taste was nothing like I had ever experienced before.

The men had yet another surprise for us—not only were we getting a personal tour of one of the vineyards in the area, but we would also be going horseback riding! Could this day be any more of a dream come true? I always wanted to own a horse ranch one day, filled with tons of animals.

All these childhood dreams and wishes were flooding back to me. I had forgotten how much fantasy resided in my heart. I wondered to myself about the possibilities of a new existence.

Could I really make some dreams come true at this stage of my life?

I was introduced to my horse, Miele (Honey in English), and we instantly connected. I ran my hand down her apple cider smooth mane and forehead, cooing and telling her how beautiful she was. She whinnied in gratitude and accepted me gracefully as I mounted her leather saddle.

I caught a glimpse of Francesco looking over at me in amusement.

"What are you smiling at?"

"Another layer unraveled," he responded as he prodded his roasted coffee-colored companion, Forza, to begin the trail. As I watched him take off to lead the way, my two sisters came up behind me on their own gorgeous steeds.

"You seem to be enjoying yourself today," Meg said sweetly.

"I am. This has been amazing so far—and it's not even lunchtime! I could not have planned a more perfect day if I did it myself."

"Seems like someone has been paying attention," Marissa winked as she took off behind Lorenzo.

Riding Miele was undoubtedly a highlight of my day. She was patient and gentle as I guided her and stroked her soft mane. The path we took led to the most stunning land tapestry of open fields, forests and farmland, once again taking me through what I had thought could only be created in a painting.

At times, we trotted, and I'd laugh as Marissa's horse had a bit of an attitude and decided to gallop instead. Lorenzo was more than happy to come to her rescue, I observed.

As we ended our ride, we realized how famished we

were and decided to hit up the town for some lunch (and more wine for us ladies). We came across a local small-town restaurant and took our time dining and talking. No one was in any rush; we just let the day take its course.

We feasted on cured meats, rich cheeses, fresh baked breads, native olives and more, complemented by an assortment of white and red wines. We were joined by the owner, who took great pride in explaining the characteristics of each glass as we learned the nuances between the different grapes, methods and blends used for each. It was captivating to learn the depth of art that went into making a single flavor profile.

The next two hours were spent driving through more of the countryside. It was exhilarating on the open roads—and with nary another vehicle in sight, Francesco and Lorenzo pretended to race each other as us girls roared in laughter at their brotherly competition.

In between contests, Francesco and I would listen to music and make light conversation about the views and where we were passing, places he used to go in his youth and the fond childhood memories I had. I was free to be my unbridled self; more so than I had allowed in a very long time.

The whole trip was planned to be an entire loop of the Tuscan region; one big circle from start to finish. Our final stop before "home" was supposed to be another vineyard, but we caught Lorenzo gesturing at us to pull over. Francesco exited the car to chat with his roguish brother and soon returned bright and breezy.

"We are going to take a slight detour," he explained. "After talking with your sisters for the last few hours, my little bro realized there was one more place along the way that you all would appreciate. We'll be there in about ten minutes."

We exited for Lucignano, another little medieval-like village hidden within the more popular tourist towns of Siena and Arezzo. Lorenzo led the way to the Municipal Museum, located within the Town Hall.

"I have a feeling you are going to love this," Lorenzo proclaimed with pride. "After spending the day with these lovely ladies, I've learned that Meg is a hopeless romantic and Marissa is an art connoisseur, so there is no more perfect place to show you in all of Tuscany."

The museum featured various works of art from the Renaissance and Middle Age period. Marissa was in awe as she walked through the ancient frescoes and historic religious paintings.

"It blows my mind how so much art exists in this world that is either unknown or not recognized as some of the greatest pieces of work in history," she mused.

Our self-guided tour of the museum led us to the Audience Hall, which revealed the real purpose of our stopover: the famous Golden Tree.

Made in the likeness of Gothic jewelry, the tree-shaped shrine was the only one of its kind in the world, Lorenzo explained. Set within a protective glass case, the exquisite design of the magnificent tree was truly unique. Twelve symmetric branches were covered with vine leaves and medallions of crystal. The top was adorned with a crucifix and pelican, which Lorenzo explained signified self-sacrifice in the name of love.

"The whole tree is symbolic of Christ's life. Its golden root represents His birth. The branches growing off of the trunk embody His teachings and life's work. If you look closely, you can see that the ornaments depict different prophets," he pointed out. "The crown is His crucifixion and glory."

"It's incredible," Meg uttered in awe.

"Ah, that's not all, *cara*. You, most of all, will love this part," he said, smiling at Meg.

"The Tree of Love, as it is called, is known to bring good luck to lovers. It's an ancient local tradition for lovers to promise themselves to each other in front of this shrine, as it signifies eternal love. It is believed to bestow the couple with luck and eternal happiness."

"I love it! Thank you so much for taking us here to see this. I must make it a point to bring Kieran here one day," she said with her big, romantic, goofy love face.

"He may not be here now, but since we are, I'd like to believe that its good fortune is not for lovers alone," Francesco proposed. "Meg, as you stand before the tree with your whole heart and thoughts of your beloved, may your union with Kieran be blessed forevermore."

"Thank you, Francesco, I am so touched."

"Marissa, may the love you have with your Tony also be blessed," he continued.

"Thanks." She managed a polite smile, but I could tell she was uncomfortable with the blessing. She had a fear of commitment that she was still working through, so wishing for her eternal happiness with a single person undoubtedly made her writhe on the insides. Bless her heart.

"And Mia Bella, as you stand here in front of the Tree of Love, may you also find and embrace what it is your heart desires. My wish for you is to love yourself as others love you, and for life to be full of all the dreams you deserve."

Blushing profusely, I managed a small "thank you" and started to turn away. But I stopped myself, and decided to return the kind gesture instead.

"And to Francesco and Lorenzo, our wonderful tour

guides—may you also be blessed with love, luck and happiness wherever you go."

"*Grazie,*" they responded in thankful unison.

A short while later, we found ourselves at Italy's oldest wine estate, Barone Ricasoli. Known to be the "founder" of Chianti, the winery had a rich history that dates back over nine hundred years. After seeing Lorenzo chatting with one of the workers, and then with who appeared to be an owner or manager, he came strolling back with a big grin on his face.

He told us he just managed to negotiate a special treat: a private, immersive experience that would teach us about the culture and creation of some of the wines—and we would even be allowed the rare opportunity to make our own vintage!

These brothers can really be persuasive and influential, I thought.

What an incredible (albeit messy) experience that was. We were invited into a small area of the vineyard, where we were asked to remove our socks and shoes. We then rolled up our pants and skirts to mid-thigh level, washed up and slid into sanitary paper slippers to walk over to where five individual bins of grapes awaited us.

It was supposed to be straight forward, but of course, I had to ask questions about what each grape was, and then if I could mix and match a few into my bin to create my own unique combination. Hey, what's the point of creating your own wine if you had no say in the flavor profile?

After removing the slippers and stepping into the bins, we had a blast stomping the grapes into oblivion as the goo encased our now-sticky toes. It was super cold, too! I thought the ripened fruit would be room temperature, but they were actually close to freezing—we had to stomp quickly so our feet wouldn't ice over. I shuddered at the thought of anyone losing a hypothermic toe to the wine making process.

During our squishing task, the guide explained how the foot crushing helped to accelerate fermentation, and that the addition of acid, sugar and alcohol would kill any of our human germs, assuring us that our wines would not taste like feet. We all had a great laugh over that, as I'm pretty sure we were all thinking it, if not saying it.

When we were done stomping, they labeled each of our bins with our names and told us that when the fermentation process was complete and the wine was ready, we would each get our own personalized bottles mailed to us.

We were even able to design our own branded labels, which was fun—especially for Meg, whose advertising background had her masterfully whipping up a professional looking wrapper. Marissa's was more artistic of course, and mine, well—I think when my kids were kindergartners they could draw better.

But at least my culinary talents meant I'd have a better tasting wine, and I'd take that over a fancy label any day.

After cleaning up and taking a leisurely stroll through the vineyard, we elected to enjoy a gourmet dinner on the winery grounds. The restaurant itself was elegant, with windows displaying a clear view of the surrounding rows of luscious grape vines.

Famished, we opted for the a la carte menu over the tasting menu, so that we could pick and choose what we wanted to share among us. For appetizers, we enjoyed a selection of beef tartare and poached eggs with mustard-marinated escarole. For the first plate, we decided to keep it simple with one selection: the outstanding potato gnocchi with peas, mint cream and cheese fondue.

For our main course, we shared rabbit terrine with pistachios, Tuscan squab and venison with cherries and chocolate. The looks on Meg and Marissa's faces were photo-worthy when they heard Francesco order for us.

Surprisingly, they both found something they enjoyed and were warming up to the idea of trying new foods. Of course, the meal wouldn't be complete without the vintage Chianti from the estate.

"What shall we toast to this evening?" Lorenzo asked.

"To the most extraordinary day with the most beautiful women," Francesco responded.

"To our gracious hosts, who gave us the experience of a lifetime," I countered.

"*Saluti!*" we all exclaimed, raising and clinking our crystal wine glasses together.

Throughout dinner, we each shared stories of what happened throughout the day, commenting on the funniest moments and the touching ones, and everything in between. The night was filled with laughter and friendship, in true Italian style.

As our evening drew to a close, the waiter demanded that we not leave until we sampled their featured dessert: raspberry ice cream with a twelve-spice infusion. We obliged, each intending to only try a spoonful, but ending up devouring the entire portion between us. It was the perfect finish to the perfect day.

The drive home was subdued and quiet, our bellies and hearts full.

"Did you enjoy yourself today, Mia Bella?"

"I truly did. Francesco, this was one of the absolute best days of my life." I placed my hand on one of his legs and he briefly took his eyes off the road to look at me. "Thank you for today."

He smiled and took one hand off the steering wheel to hold mine for the majority of the drive home. The cold air from the convertible sent shivers down my spine—or was it the company? I settled down comfortably into the seat as we drove with nothing but the sounds of the night and the stars in the sky.

Returning home late after a wonderful 14-hour journey, we were all completely exhausted, yet energized internally from the experiences we had.

While both Meg and Marissa quickly packed for their morning departures, I decided to crawl into the softness of my bed instead of trying to figure out what I would do over the next few days. Taking a page from the Marchesi book, I would let the next day lead me to where it wanted me to go.

10

The next morning, we said our goodbyes as we split up for the next three days. Meg was set to fly out to see Kieran and his mum, with our best wishes for her speedy recovery. Marissa was on cloud nine, ready to take her multi-day, skip-the-line art excursions through the multiple Florence art galleries.

Since it was an integrated experience, complete with workshops and meals, she would be staying with her group at a local hotel. She declined the need for a bodyguard, assuring us that in a structured group setting, she felt she would be more than safe. I didn't agree, but there was no changing my stubborn little sister's mind.

By ten o'clock, I was left alone in the solace of the townhouse. Ah, the peace and quiet was certainly welcoming. I debated on whether to stay in to enjoy the luxury of silence, or follow my curiosity to the special nooks of the city. Curiosity won out, and I found myself headed to that little bookstore in the Piazza San Lorenzo.

I ended up chatting with another tourist at the bookstore's bakery counter, who told me about this 5-hour cooking workshop she recently attended that was purely indulgent. I determined right then and there that this was an experience I wanted to have, so I immediately used my phone to register for an open spot that happened to be available for the next day.

By the time it was my turn to order, my culinary adventure was all set. I couldn't be more excited! It was already turning out to be another great day.

I had a hard time deciding which delicious pastry would be the perfect complement to my cappuccino, so I settled on two: a fedora, which was a delectable orange sponge cake with cream and chocolate, and sfolgia, a light puff pastry filled with ricotta cheese and caramelized pears.

I resigned myself to gaining weight over this entire trip—and every morsel had been worth it so far.

Nestled into a corner chair exactly as I had envisioned, I began reading the new romance book I had just purchased. As I sat there to open the book, I realized with pride that I was reading a romance; the very type of book only a few weeks ago I couldn't bear to look at in the library.

Why, Mia, I believe progress has been made, I thought to myself with genuine satisfaction.

Engrossed in the paperback lovers' story (or so I thought), my mind wandered over to Francesco. We made plans to meet up nearby after lunch, as he said he wanted to show me a few more local sites I might have missed during my first tour of the piazza. It made me eager for lunch to come and go so I could finally find out the surprises he had in store for me today.

I admit, it was quite nice to have a man be so attentive to me. I can't remember the last truly thoughtful thing Kevin did for me. Come to think of it, I'm not sure he was ever the type of man to make small gestures to please me.

Yet, that's what Francesco did. Even though some experiences yesterday could be considered "over the top," it's not that they were necessarily extravagant. They were meaningful every step of the way. Some cost money, others cost Lorenzo some kind of negotiation.

But all were designed with me and my sisters in mind, and it meant the world to me that they went through that kind of trouble.

I looked at my phone to check the time and realized that I had missed a call from New York. My heart sank and my stomach dropped. It was my lawyer, and I knew exactly what he wanted.

Deciding to get it over with and not procrastinate, I returned his call to find out I was right: the divorce papers had been finalized and were ready for my signature when the trip was over.

The news hit me harder than I expected. I was gut-punched. Being in a public place, I couldn't exactly bawl my eyes out like my body wanted me to, so I closed my eyes and took a few deep breaths.

It was actually over. Twenty-plus years of true love dissolved with a simple piece of paper. Memories of sneaking out as teens to make love, a dream wedding, romantic vacations to the Caribbean, welcoming the birth of our children, supporting each other through deaths of loved ones and other life hardships—all of it now confined to a small memory box in my mind, closed and sealed with the stamp of failure.

That was a lot to process. My peaceful demeanor was immediately replaced by great grief and sadness. I was promptly brought back to that place of anguish, feeling the loneliness and insecurities creep in. All I wanted to do was crawl back under the covers and fall asleep into the darkness.

Well, why couldn't I? I asked myself. This was my time to do whatever I wanted. And life was leading me back to bed. I'd load up on some pastries I passed on earlier so that I'd have something sweet to eat later on, and then I'd just have leftovers for dinner. I'd have no need to leave the house. Yes, that is exactly what I'm going to do.

At that moment, the phone rang. It was Francesco, no doubt on his way to meet me. I was not in the mood for him. I didn't want Italian charm or great experiences. Not now. I wanted my pillow and blanket and teddy bear. I ignored the call and then shot him back a quick text to be polite.

Sorry, have to cancel. Not feeling well. Talk soon.

I quickly gathered up my stuff to leave, surprised that he didn't respond immediately. Too bad if he was mad and his male ego wounded. He'd get over it.

As I went to the counter to pick out an assortment of sweets, I saw Francesco stroll into the bookstore with a concerned look on his face.

"Mia, are you all right?" I was so angry that he was there—that he ignored my text and came looking for me instead.

"What are you doing here? I told you I had to cancel," I snapped, annoyed at him.

"I was already here, a few doors down and I figured if you were in the piazza, that you would be close. A hunch told me to check for you in the bookstore, and here you are. You said you were not feeling well. I wanted to make sure you were okay."

"I'm fine. I really don't want to do this now."

"Well, I am here, and you are not leaving until you tell me what's wrong. Sit," he commanded, pulling out a café chair and motioning for me to take a seat.

The stubborn ass in me wanted to tell him to fuck off and then leave anyway. He had no right to make demands of me or question why I was canceling. I had every right to make my own choices. But there was something in his eyes that told me he was worried, and I figured the least I could do was give him an explanation. Maybe then when he understood, he'd leave me be as I'd asked.

"I just got the call from my lawyer. The divorce is final," I said matter-of-factly. "I appreciate you coming here, but I'm not in the mood to be a tourist. Can I go now?" I rose to get out of my chair, but he rather forcefully sat me back down.

"No, you cannot go now," he spat back in a hushed tone, trying not to make a scene.

"I know you are hurting and angry and rightfully so—but do not take it out on me, *cara.*"

Ouch. He was right. But still—I'm an emotional basket case. Even if it was my own sister sitting in front of me, she'd be knowingly signing up to be target practice if she didn't have the good sense to depart. Like, right now.

"I'm sorry. I just have a lot to process. I—I don't have it in me to fight today," I admitted with defeat. His presence was wearing me down.

"Come with me," he said soothingly. He got up out of the chair and lifted me up out of mine. He took my hand to lead me out the door, but I resisted. What part of "no" didn't he understand?

"Please, just trust me."

Reluctantly, I obliged, allowing him to walk me down the street, hand in hand without a word spoken, towards an obscure little park off to the side of the road. We walked until we reached a large grassy area, where no one was in sight—I honestly don't even know if the bodyguard was around.

He then took me into his arms and held me in a tight

embrace. I tried to push out, but his embrace was strong and firm, his hands soothing their way down my hair and his lips whispering, "Let it out."

We stood there for what seemed like eternity, until they came. First one little stream down the cheek, then the rest followed like dominos until I was weeping in his arms. He didn't say a single word; he only held tight to comfort me as I expelled the pain from my soul.

When I felt spent, he released me and guided me to sit on the grass. He placed his hand on my curled up legs and looked down, saying nothing until I was ready to speak.

"Thank you. I guess I needed that more than I knew."

"Sometimes we know what is best for ourselves; sometimes others do. I did not mean to force or pressure you without your consent. But I could not let you be alone like that, holding onto all those emotions as if you didn't have them.

"I care for you, Mia, and it hurts me to see you in such pain."

"I appreciate that Francesco, truly. And I am grateful that you want to help me. But I am a private person. I don't like to cry in front of others. It's my pain, not theirs, and it's unfair to burden anyone with my problems."

"The only problem you seem to have is thinking you are a burden to others," he responded. "The people you love will never think of you like that. They want to help you; they want to give you the same love back that you give to them. It is okay to be private and selective in who you confide in. What is not okay is choosing *no one* and keeping this all to yourself."

I remained quiet for a while, hearing what he had to say.

Once the door to my emotions were open, I could

feel every fiber of my being raising its hand for a chance to speak up. There was something bothering me about a comment he made yesterday, and I wondered if now would be the time to address it. I looked up to see his eyes on mine and then quickly looked down, deciding against it.

"What is it, *cara?* I can tell you want to say something. You can say anything to me," he reassured. "Please, free it from your mind. Not for me—for yourself."

"Okay," I exhaled a big, deep breath before I took a plunge off this diving board. "Yesterday at the Tree of Love, you wished for me to love myself," I recalled.

"Yes. Did that bother you?"

"Yes. No. Well—both. No, because it was a kind gesture and meant with the best intentions. I know that. But it was unsettling at the same time." I took a deep, deep inhale before blowing out the fear of what I was about to verbalize. "Can you really tell I don't love myself?"

I started to tear up again and wasn't sure if I could control it, especially when I knew he would be nothing short of honest with me. That's what scared me the most right now—the truth.

"At times, yes," he said in a gentle tone, treading lightly. "Yesterday, I could not. Yesterday, you were free— without whatever chains you put on yourself. You exuded confidence, joy and peace—that is when you are accepting of yourself and your aura shows it.

"But now, today? Your grief is your grief—there is nothing I can say or do to take it away. It is your own process and will be healed on your time and terms.

"However, beyond that grief, I sense the self-deprecation. Every negative thing you feel about yourself. Taking the blame as if the situation was one-sided. It is that, *cara,* that must change. You will never be truly happy until you accept yourself the way you are."

"I can't," I replied, fighting back a second round of waterworks.

"Yes, you can. I will show you. Come," he said, lifting me off the ground.

"Francesco, I can't do this today, I told you. Thank you for talking with me and letting me get some of this out. I really do feel a little bit better. But I just want to be alone."

"I know you do. But I ask for your faith right now. Come with me now and spend the day with me. If after an hour or two you are not enjoying yourself, I will take you back to your townhouse and leave you to your peace until you are ready to talk again. I promise.

"But give me at least one hour of your time before we part. Can you do that?"

He was hard to resist. I don't know if it was his charm or his sincerity, but I agreed to his terms. I was exhausted and just wanted to sleep; but a part of me thought maybe being distracted might be a good idea after all. He hasn't let me down yet—and I did have his word that I can split in an hour if he did.

The persistent Italian led me down this little dirt path that revealed an adorable garden of assorted roses and lilies of glorious colors. He gestured for me to pick some fresh wildflowers to create a bouquet for myself. The perfume was intoxicating, and I could feel it lift my spirits to be surrounded by the natural essence. Maybe this wasn't such a bad idea after all.

Continuing along our path, we came across a poor, old homeless woman, sunken down low against a magnolia tree. Seeing her put my own life into perspective. How shallow I was being, wallowing over a lost love, when I am on this extravagant vacation, thanks to a rich grandfather. There are people in this world who literally have nothing.

I was compelled to go over to her and give her my bouquet of flowers. Greta, her name was, instantly lit up and thanked me for my kindness. But flowers would not be enough. I reached into my purse and handed her a few of the hundred dollar bills I had from the vacation fund and told her if she would still be here this afternoon, that I would be back with more.

Touched by my sentiment, Francesco didn't hesitate to reach into his own wallet and give her money as well. He took it a step further by making a phone call and arranging for her to have shelter that evening. It felt really good to put my own problems aside and help someone else.

She was so grateful as we walked with her into town and to the shelter. She couldn't thank us enough as her eyes filled with appreciative tears. Now, those were the kinds of tears worth crying.

After escorting Greta to a safe haven and making a generous donation to the shelter itself, we continued on our way towards the leather market again. I admit that the thought of going to that market after helping only one person was still showing entitlement, and I told Francesco just that.

"Mia Bella, what a generous heart you have. You should use some of it on yourself sometimes."

"I have no problem spending money on myself," I replied.

"I'm not talking about buying things for yourself just for the sake of buying. I am talking about making purchases with intention. I will show you."

"Okay, but it still doesn't change the fact that it is

selfish," I countered.

"If it puts you at ease, *cara,* then make a commitment to use whatever money you have to donate to causes that touch your heart. You have that power."

He was absolutely right—I could actually do some good in this world. I had the means to do it, and as soon as we got home, I thought that volunteering my time and newfound money would be a wonderful way to make good use of my freedom. I would add it to the new goals list I started creating a few days ago.

"I see a smile—does that mean we are ready to continue on?"

"Yes," I said, albeit hesitantly.

He led me to the main street market, and then right to the owner of a silk dress stall. They exchanged the traditional double cheek kiss greeting before he introduced me to his strikingly exotic friend.

She was right out of the movies. A dark-skinned, dark-eyed, dark-haired beauty with an unbelievable body dressed in a green form-fitting, ruffled trim linen dress and black stiletto heels. Wow, this woman had legs for days.

"Ana, may I present to you my American friend, Mia. Mia, Ana is a very old friend from school."

"Not that old," she winked as she reached out to kiss my cheeks in welcome as well. "Pleasure to meet you. What brings you to Italy?"

"I'm on a trip with my sisters visiting our cousin," I responded politely, trying not to let the green-eyed monster do the talking for me.

"I see," she replied, obviously confused since she sensed more than a family connection between Francesco and me.

"Their cousin is Sorella Maria," he added, bringing the

lightbulb of recognition to Ana's face. "They all decided to take a few days to themselves, and I have the pleasure of escorting Mia around today."

"How delightful! Sorella Maria is a wonderful woman," said Ana with a tone of deep respect.

"She is," I agreed, still feeling insecure being around this woman, who was not only pretty, but kind as well. The whole package. I noticed her eying up Francesco and wondered how "friendly" they really were.

"Well, what can I do for you today?" she asked.

"We are in the market for a lovely silk dress for Mia, and you are the best," he charmed. "Something that would accent her natural beauty."

"I have just the thing. Wait right here."

Only a few moments later, she returned with a stunning paisley dress of gorgeous browns, golds and reds that I would normally only wish I could buy. It was low cut with spaghetti straps, and looked like it would form against my waist before flaring out.

There is no way that would look good on me. Only a supermodel like her could pull something off like that. I excused us, pulling Francesco aside.

"What are you doing? I cannot wear a dress like that."

"Why not, *cara?* It looks like it was made for you. Besides, I trust Ana's instincts."

"I bet you do," I mumbled under my breath.

"*Scusi?*"

"Nothing. I'm not getting that dress."

"Okay. Then I will."

He walked away and towards Ana, who wrapped up the dress and added in a beautiful dangling red pendant necklace with matching earrings and bracelet. Not wanting to be rude, I thanked Ana graciously and then proceeded to give Francesco the silent treatment after walking away.

"Why are you so angry with me, Mia Bella?"

"You just wasted your money. Francesco, there are just—certain things I can't wear. I'm already feeling like shit. Why would you do something that makes me feel worse about myself? I thought your mission was to make me feel better."

I stopped and looked at him.

"It is. Mia, you have not even tried the dress on. You don't know how you will look in it."

"Oh, but sexy skinny girl would?"

"Yes, she would. Do not belittle her because of her looks. She cannot help her body frame as much as you cannot help yours, and it does not define who either of you are."

I looked down feeling somewhat ashamed for my attack on another woman, who was nothing but kind to me. He made a good point; judging another unfairly is no way to make myself feel better.

"Ana is an extremely talented designer," he continued. "She works with models of all shapes and sizes. She made that dress with her own hands. I assure you, if she thought you would look good in it, it's because she has had another model sample it with your quite pleasing curves."

He lifted up my chin so that he could look into my eyes.

"You do not have to try it on until you are ready. But promise me that one day when you are feeling good about yourself, that you will allow yourself to appreciate how this dress might make you look.

"I don't know why you Americans have such poor body images. Why you resist accentuating your full, delicious shapes and being proud of every inch."

"You really want to know what's going on in my head?"

I was getting so angry having to defend myself all the time. First my sisters, now him. Fine, he wanted the truth? He was going to get it. Pandora's box had officially been opened, baby.

"Yes. Tell me."

"All my life, I have had this battle, Francesco. It's not going to go away overnight. I've lived in the shadows of my sisters, who attract men just by existing. I walked in on my husband having sex with this young, anorexic-like woman after refusing to make love to me for years.

"I don't look like all the supermodels who can wear anything and look amazing. It is a real struggle, damn it, and you and they know nothing about it.

"None of them know what it's like to have to buy a dress that needs to be just the right looseness to cover up stomach rolls—one that faultlessly gives the deceitful appearance of having a flat stomach just so that I can feel better about myself.

"Or how I have to go into a dressing room with three different sizes just to see which one hides back fat the best, praying that I really don't have to end up with the largest size I brought in to try on. To have to go to an actual store and not be able to shop online because the cut and fit is never what it looks like on the screen. To not wear sleeveless dresses without some kind of jacket to cover up my flabby arms.

"So, stop suggesting that what I feel is silly and all in my head. It's not as easy for me to walk up to a market and ask for some sexy dress without trying it on as it would be for others who simply know it will fit their body type no matter what.

"Every day of my life is a struggle to figure out how I am going to hide the obvious, and I just want to look thin and attractive again like I did in high school. Your false compliments are not going to change my reality."

Somehow, I managed to get through all of that without a single tear or stutter. Anger and frustration fueled me like solar power, which was then met by Francesco's growing eruption. He threw his hands up in the air in utter exasperation, grumbling to himself in pure Italian before turning back to me.

"I wish you could see yourself like I see you. It's not just words and charm. I speak the truth. There is no reason for you to hide anything about yourself, Mia. Forget comparing yourself to your sisters or to women like Ana.

"Forget your *bischero* of a husband for not appreciating the quality woman he had and turning to superficial lust. Forget Hollywood and all the advertisements you see," he urged.

"That is not true beauty. Here, in Italy, we embrace all bodies. The skinny, the voluptuous and everything in between. It is all gorgeous to us, because it is only a body; a mere vessel that holds the real attraction of a woman: her soul.

"What will it take for you to realize you are already perfect just as you are, Mia?"

"Losing weight," I said honestly. "I'm uncomfortable in my own skin. I can't help that."

"We'll see about that," he said, shaking his head in defeat. I could see he knew that he was not going to get anywhere with me, so he let it go. He sighed as he took my hand and began walking us back towards the marketplace.

"Like I said, when you are ready, try it on. Okay?"

"Fine," I consented, knowing full well I had no intention of ever putting that confidence-killer on my body. Ever. I would just stick the dress in my closet and if by some miracle I felt like looking at it again, I would. Most likely I would donate it.

I took his lead to let the conversation end. I didn't want to pursue it any further or let it ruin the rest of this already awful day.

"So, what would you say to some matching shoes? Surely you do not discriminate against shoes the way you do dresses?"

I caved and gave him a look that said shoes were definitely in the safe zone—and a welcome addition to the divorce retail therapy I decided I needed. Once I found these absolutely to-die-for pair of dark brown leather high-heeled boots, everything became right again with the world.

11

Francesco stored all of the shopping bags in his parked car while we continued our mini-tour of the city. He was kind enough to check in on my feelings to see if I was up for more, and surprisingly, I was. I hate to admit that the guy knew what he was doing when it came to lifting me out of my funk.

I agreed to walk with him through a less busy part of the city towards a restaurant he claimed was one of the best dives he had ever dined in. Along the way, we came upon a quartet of street musicians playing the most angelic instrumental sounds.

A small crowd formed around them; some dancing, some cheering and others merely dropping some money into their collection hats as they walked by. The next thing I knew, Francesco was twirling me around.

"Dance with me, *signorina*," he requested whimsically.

I couldn't resist being caught up in the allure of the moment, despite our earlier argument. He brought me close into his arms and led us in a slow dance. I could feel the heat rising up through every inch of my body as I felt his pressed against mine. He was staring intently into my eyes, and I couldn't help but release a nervous laugh.

I forgot what it felt like to slow dance with a man. Every so often, Kevin and I would be invited to a wedding, and instead of asking me to join him on the dance floor, he'd sit at the table looking at his phone while I'd jealously watch the happy couples waltz from afar.

I should have known then that things were headed downhill. All the signs were there in hindsight.

Still, I had to let go of those memories. They wouldn't bring Kevin back to me or fix the damage that had already been done. I was faced with the sad truth that we had simply grown apart—and that we were better off this way. Resigned, I realized there was no use in focusing on the past and trying to figure out what went wrong.

The best thing I could do was live right here, in this moment. In the arms of a man I was growing quite fond of.

"Where were you just now, *cara?*" he whispered into my ears with his lips so close I thought he might be able to taste them. I wished he would and found myself wondering what his mouth would feel like on my body. It gave me the shivers—the good kind.

"Nowhere important. I'm here now," I replied as I let myself move in closer to lay my head against his shoulder. I felt him pull me into a tighter embrace so that our hearts beat against each other, our inhales and exhales working towards unison.

When the music ended, the crowd clapped, and I couldn't help but redden at the mere thought of being in this handsome man's arms. I wasn't used to such public affection, and yet, there was something invigorating about it at the same time.

Francesco once again took my hand as we continued on to dinner. It was a small and private place in an alley off the main street, the inside illuminated by only a dim light and the natural glow from the candlelit centerpieces.

Classical opera music played lightly in the background and the wait staff were dressed in tuxedos. I was already impressed.

As our meals were served, we made small talk. He discussed some of the non-confidential details of the interesting cases he was working on, and I told him all about the culinary class I planned for tomorrow. I casually invited him over for dinner afterwards, since I knew that I would want to experiment right away with what I had learned—and would enjoy the critique (and company).

"I'd be delighted. Your sisters have told me you are quite the chef."

"I don't know about that, but I certainly love to cook."

I'm not sure what was making me so nervous about being here with him all of a sudden, but I found myself ordering glass after glass of a Brunello di Montalcino reserve. I felt giddy, lightheaded and unguarded for a change. Plus, it helped drown out the reality that my divorce was final, and I wanted to think about anything but that.

"What is it that you love about cooking?"

"Food is fascinating to me. All the different flavors and textures and the unlimited number of combinations you can possibly create. I want to be part of the art of bringing ingredients together to make people happy. I've always wanted to own my own restaurant, you know."

"Actually, I did not know that. That's wonderful, Mia. Is that something you wish to pursue when you get back to New York?"

"I haven't given it much thought. I would love nothing more, but I'm not sure it's realistic right now. I still have children to take care of, and that's an awful lot of responsibility. I need a job first and to settle into life as a single mom. I can't just nonchalantly decide to follow some girlish notion."

"Let's say you could." I looked at him quizzically. "Let's say you had the means to open a restaurant. Would you reconsider?"

"I mean, maybe. But there is so much more to it than money. There's planning and hiring and training and marketing and execution and operating and a whole world more that would need my attention. I wouldn't have the time for all of that."

"But it's a maybe?" he nudged. "Opening up your imagination and removing all mental obstacles—if you had a team and resources behind you, would you finally chase your dream?"

"In a perfect world? Of course."

"What would it look like?"

"*Hmm.* Funny enough, I had always envisioned an Italian restaurant. But there are so many in New York, that I wouldn't want it to be any commonplace establishment. I'd want to experiment with new dishes.

"Come to think of it, as I've dined in and around Florence, I've been so inspired that I've kinda been creating menu ideas in my head."

"You should write them down. Even if the timing isn't right for your vision now, it doesn't mean that you can't create goals and record ideas as they come to you. There's nothing stopping you from imagining it all, is there?"

"I guess not," I considered. "It would be fun to conjure it all up on paper."

"Exactly. You have so much passion for it—it would be a shame to leave it locked up in that pretty little head of yours."

He just looked at me and smiled.

"What?"

"I just can't help being in awe of you, Mia Bella. When

you love something, it is without boundaries. There is this spirit about you that is simply irresistible."

I could sense my temperature rise and couldn't tell if it was his eyes or the wine that made me feel so flustered. I ordered more, welcoming the further intoxication so my mind would stop thinking. As soon as I got up from the table, I swooned right into Francesco's grasp.

By then, I was full on drunk with a massive case of the giggles. He somehow managed to get me to his car and then to my place, and like the gentleman he always is, he escorted me to the door and into the house.

"Thank you for making me go out instead of coming back here for a pity party. My husband—wait, ex-husband now—is such a jerk. Good riddance, bastard," I yelled to the pretend man in the corner of the room.

"Will you be all right?" Francesco broke my imaginative conversation with his concern.

"I don't get it. Why wasn't I good enough for him? I gave him the best years of my life and three really great children—and instead of loving me, he wants to fuck little girls like Chloe? Why did he do that, Francesco? Why do you men do that?"

"Not all men, Mia. Your ex-husband does not represent all of us. What he did was wrong, and you deserve better than that. Come, let me help you to your room. You've had a bit too much wine tonight."

"I don't deserve better. I was a bitch. He said I was like his mother. Did you know, his exact words to me were that 'nobody wants to fuck their mother, Mia.' Well, no one wants to fuck a no good prick," I yelled back to the Kevin ghost as we wound up the stairs.

"And then—then he told me as he abandoned me to go be with Chloe that I should stuff my fat face with more ice cream. Wasn't that nice of him?"

I could feel Francesco tense up in anger, before setting me down on the bed and helping me off with my shoes. He then looked at me with as much composure as he could gather, while I could barely sit up straight.

"That was a cruel thing to say, Mia, especially from a man who vowed to love you for the rest of his life. None of it is true. That *bischero* is lucky he is not here in front of me right now. No wonder you struggle with yourself," he said as an aside and with a sadness in his puppy eyes.

"He's right, though. If my own husband can't love me, then who can?"

"Mia, look at me." He lifted up my chin so that our gazes met.

"You are one of the most exquisite women I have ever met. You *are* lovable just as you are."

I don't know what made me do it, but I awkwardly leaned in and surprised both of us by kissing him. Initially, he responded with intense passion, but then pulled away.

"Mia, I can't. I'm sorry." He stood up and made his way towards the bedroom door, hanging his head down low in conflict.

"Why not? You said—all night you have told me I was irresistible and beautiful and lovable. I don't understand." The faucet of tears was filling up my eyes.

First Kevin, now this guy? Rejecting me tonight, of all nights, after the emotionally connected day we had just spent together? What the actual fuck? Did I read all the signs wrong? Is he just pitying me? That's it, he was! He just felt sorry for me. Poor little chubby Mia who just got dumped by the love of her life.

"Mia Bella, don't cry. I meant all of it. It's just not the right time for me."

Then it hit me. Of course—how could I be so stupid? That was even worse than pity! He was a scoundrel who was just trying to get into my pants, and then suddenly developed a conscience at the last minute.

"Oh my God. You're married, aren't you?"

"No, Mia, I'm not."

"You have a girlfriend?"

"No, *cara.* It's not that."

"Then what is it? Why don't you want me?"

"Oh, *bellissima,* I very much want you. In fact, it's taking every ounce of my fortitude to resist you. You are drunk, *amore.* I'm not the type of man to take advantage of vulnerable women, especially those who are intoxicated with a broken heart.

"Now, let's just get you into bed, and we'll talk tomorrow at dinner before either one of us has had any wine."

"You're uninvited, you phony. You're a liar just like the rest of them," I cried into my pillow as I turned and felt him put the covers over me and give me a small kiss on the forehead.

I heard him leave the room and then lock the front door before I passed out on a tear-stained pillow, reminding myself that this was my destiny to live out the rest of my life alone and unloved.

The next morning, I barely made it up in time for my cooking class. I debated not going and just wallowing away in bed, angry at Francesco for leading me on, and angrier at myself for falling for it. But I wasn't going to let another man bring me to my knees. Especially not some fake, charming Italian man who thought his words of "I really do want you" would soften the blow of rejection.

Besides, it was all about food and cooking, and what better comfort to drown myself in than that?

I shook off my wounded pride and got ready for the 5-hour food market and cooking experience. Our teacher, Chef Luigi, was a well-known chef from six different restaurants throughout the city. He had planned to take our small group of eight down to a local market and teach us how to select the best ingredients.

This was truly fun, as we met different farmers, butchers and bakers, sampling all along the way as we (tactfully) discerned the higher from lower quality selections. It was the ultimate distraction. After my experience last night, I passed on the wine complements offered to us, not wanting to repeat the hangover that was currently plaguing my head.

Once we were finished, we brought back our goodies to the teaching kitchen, where we learned various authentic Italian cooking techniques. I was completely immersed in the experience, practically forgetting all of my problems.

I released rage as I chopped fresh-from-the-farm vegetables to make the bruschetta. Frustration dissipated with every massage and rolling of the scratch-made pasta. And sadness gave way to joy as I pulled it all together for a delightful meal shared with the new friends I made for the day.

Throughout the morning, I ignored the texts coming in from Francesco trying to check in on me. I should have been more logical now that I had my wits about me.

I embarrassingly recalled the prior night's events and how I unceremoniously uninvited him to dinner. In the light of a sober day, I could understand his supposed excuse of not wanting to take advantage of me in that condition, but my feelings were still hurt. I was too raw to get into any more of those in-depth conversations he kept insisting on having.

Hopefully he took my rescinded invitation to heart, even if I was drunk. I had no desire to see him again tonight. I needed a break from everyone and everything. That was the whole point of this respite—to be *alone.*

But a peaceful evening was not what life had in store for me. I returned home to find a plain white envelope that must have been slipped under the door. I assumed it was Francesco's way of trying to reach me since I had only texted him that dinner was canceled for tonight and refused to return any of his other phone calls.

I threw the note on the table while I put my leftover ingredients in the refrigerator and changed into something more comfortable now that I was in the privacy of my own space. Part of me wanted to ignore the note entirely, yet another was pulled to read it.

Finally, I decided to just get it over with and see what he had to say. It was something I never expected.

"Raul! Luca!" I yelled out frantically to the guards assigned to the night shift. Hurriedly, they both approached me at once, but then decided that Raul would stay behind to continue guarding out front while Luca responded to my call.

"What is it, Signorina Mia?" he asked.

"Who left me this note? Did you see them?" I asked, shaking as I handed him the folded-up piece of typed paper.

"*Scusi?* I never saw anyone come to the front door. I don't know how this is possible," he fumbled.

"Well, it is. How could anyone get past you?"

Recollection crept over his face, as did embarrassment.

"*Fanculo,*" he cursed. "We heard a disturbance in both the pool area and side garden, so we went to check them out. He or she must have slipped this through the front when we left those posts. We did come back and conduct a full search and found nothing, so we thought it was a wild animal or wind or something. I'm so sorry, *signorina.*"

He immediately dialed into his two-way radio to alert Raul of the situation and called for backup to secure the premises. Two additional guards arrived on site within a half hour for further protection, along with a face that I had not wanted to see that night.

"Mia, are you all right?"

"What are you doing here?"

"The guards called me the second they secured reinforcements. I needed to make sure you were safe."

"I told you I didn't want you here." I was starting to see why my family referred to me as the stubborn Italian of the bunch. I showed no mercy.

"Well, I'm here, and you are just going to have to deal with it. I'm not here to talk about last night, so table the attitude. I want to see the letter." Italian obstinacy matched, point, set.

Realizing that there was no way I could get him to leave, I let him inside and brought the note to him.

Give up while you still can. If you get in my way of that jewelry box, you will live to regret it—or not.

"*Porca miseria!* Who would write such a thing? Where are your sisters now? Have you contacted them?"

"Yes. Meg is safe with Kieran at his house and the Garda is on their way to keep an eye on them. Marissa said she is back in her hotel room and that the front desk authorities assigned a guard to her floor and will be vigilant of any newcomers.

"I called Kevin and he has the kids, my mom and grandmother under his watch, so they are safe as well. Raul made sure to also beef up security at Sorella Maria's complex, and as you can see, they assigned two more guards here for the night. You can go home now."

"You called *Kevin?*" he asked incredulously.

"Of course I called him. No matter what, he is the father of my children and would do anything to protect our family. Does that bother you?" I hope that stung like I meant it to.

"What I feel doesn't matter. What matters is that you are protected, and I am not leaving until I know you are."

"I'm fine. Like I said, you can go."

"No, you are not fine. I can tell you are shaken up."

His voice softened. As much as I wanted him to leave, I felt safer knowing he was there, inside the townhouse with me. Though, of course, I couldn't admit that to his face.

"Please, let me just sit awhile with you. We don't even have to talk."

"Fine. But I'll be in my room reading. Feel free to hang out on the sofa down here," I said as I walked up the stairs away from him.

An hour passed, and the house was eerily still. I don't remember hearing him leave, I thought to myself. *Good, glad he finally got the hint.*

Just when I thought the coast was clear, I heard rustling outside my bedroom door and then the water running. Even though as a cop's wife I should know better than to investigate such crime-inducing noises, I peeked my head out of the door to see Francesco coming out the main bathroom.

"The house was so quiet, I thought you left."

"No, I've been talking with the guards trying to find any clues. Seems like it had to be at least a two-person team," he said.

"Really?" That made me nervous. Thinking it was only one psycho was digestible. More than one made me edgy and scared. The sound of the water pulled me back from my wanderings.

"What are you doing?"

"Mia, you have been through one hell of an ordeal. I'm drawing you a bubble bath. It will do you good."

I had to confess; a bath did sound wonderful. I stepped inside to see the lights dimmed, with rose-scented candles lit and a large glass of wine sitting on a small tray on the floor. Bubbles with the essence of lavender filled the oversized tub and the sounds of soft classical music set the luxurious mood.

"Where will you be?"

"Downstairs if you need me. Enjoy, *cara*." He said, gently closing the door behind him.

Once again, he knew what was better for me than I did. I could fight it, or I could indulge—and it was way too tempting not to dive right in.

12

I removed my clothes and slid into the hotter than normal, but ideal temperature, world of bubbles. I could feel the lavender oils already soothing my worn-out body and soul. I took a sip of the wine left for me and closed my eyes, envisioning I was floating on a cloud of lily petals.

Breathing deeply, I just let myself soak without moving.

A few minutes later, I thought I heard the bathroom door open. Jumpy at first, I soon realized it was only Francesco—naked. He stood there for a moment as I stared at the exquisiteness of his toned body. As "old" as he was, not much about him was aged. He was every bit as masculine as I remembered Kevin. He left me completely speechless.

He slowly approached the tub, not saying a word. Instead, he just moved the tray of wine from aside the tub and knelt down next to me. My heart pumped harder and my insides tingled. Still, not a word was spoken as he gently took my head in his hands and tenderly kissed me.

I can't even describe the appetite for lust that stirred up inside me, feeling his lips against mine, his tongue parting them to join us in a deeper kiss. It was slow and sensual and breathtaking. He pulled away to just look at me with that face I've come to take such comfort in.

"May I come in?" he asked.

I was dumbfounded. Isn't this the same man who

rejected me last night? I hope he didn't feel like he hurt my feelings that badly that he had to force himself to want me. I wasn't that desperate.

"Francesco, please. I don't want your pity," I pleaded, lowering my head.

"Pity? Take a good look at my body, Mia. Does this look like pity to you?"

I glanced up as he rose. Right at eye level was his evident hardening. I was caught so off guard that I found it difficult to speak. "No," I barely made out.

"That's because it's not. I'm very attracted to you. I'd like to show you just how much if you'd let me."

Oh, how I did want him to join me, and yet, I was petrified. The only man I had ever been with was Kevin, and all kinds of fears coursed through my veins.

"I—I don't know. I don't know if I'm ready to show my body to another man," I admitted shyly.

"I know, Mia Bella. That's why I made you a bubble bath. This way I can still touch you without you feeling uncomfortable around me."

"You planned this?" I asked incredulously.

He grinned seductively. "How else could I get you naked—sober?"

He laughed as he bent down to kiss my forehead.

"I do very much want to be with you, Mia Bella. Now that you are in your right mind, you can make a conscious decision. But the choice has to be yours. Say the word, and I will leave."

He stood there patiently, waiting for all my wild thoughts to process. How my body ached to be touched by a man again. But would I disappoint him? Oh, man. Something else I hadn't considered until that very moment.

He must have been with so many women in his life,

how could he expect to enjoy sex with a one-man-only housewife? He sensed my hesitation, and with a slightly saddened face, took a step back.

"This is too much for you. I'm sorry—I'll go."

"No—wait." He stopped and turned back around. "Don't go."

Slowly, he re-approached the tub, where I remained lifeless and scared. Putting his hands lightly on my shoulders and back, he guided my body forward so that he could join me from behind. I adjusted to let him fully in, feeling the sensation of his hardened body against my bare skin.

Once he was settled, I made sure the majority of my body was covered with the bubbles. I felt him move my wet hair over to one side so that he could kiss my neck, ear and shoulder on the other. I shivered at his touch, so he began washing my back with the now tepid water, all the while lingering his lips near my ears.

"You are beautiful to me, whether you believe it or not, Mia Bella."

I loved the way he called me that. I moved so that I could turn my neck to see his face and kiss him. His hands now free, they traveled to the front of my body where they found their place on both my breasts. He toyed with my hardening nipples, sending rippling sensations down to the lower parts of my body. Oh, how I missed this kind of touch. Ached for it.

He gently turned my head back around so he could kiss my neck once again, finding out quickly that it was one of my most favorite spots to be touched. He then repositioned our bodies so that he could easily hold and play with one breast, while allowing his right hand to move slowly down.

I shuddered as his fingers unintentionally tickled my

side, then moved down and over to my thigh. His fingers explored until they found what they were looking for, and with a skillful movement, were split between being inside and rubbing my clit.

A small moan escaped as he continued touching multiple erogenous zones at once. I kept trying to stop so that I could pleasure him back, but he denied me, whispering that this was about me and that he'd have his turn later.

Asking me not to resist him, I relaxed back against him and surrendered to his exquisite strokes. With every verbal and non-verbal affirmation I released, I felt his own arousal and desire to push me to the brink of madness escalate with intensity and dexterity.

I ascended to places within my soul that hadn't be accessed in years, allowing the build and climax to obliterate all my senses. When it was over and I was completely spent, he kissed my neck once more as he shifted to get out of the tub.

"Where are you going?" I asked, not understanding his need to kiss and run instead of snuggling me into his arms.

"Not far," he winked. "When you're ready, come find me in your bedroom." Oh. This wasn't over.

I remained in the tub for a few more minutes, trying to absorb what had just happened, and the invitation that awaited me. It felt so natural and right, and yet, I still couldn't shake my nerves. He was clearly an expert on women's bodies; how could I ever make him feel as good as he just made me feel?

All I knew was that I wanted to try. I wanted to give back to the man who had given me so much this week. His time, his ear…his fingers. Steadying myself, I rose, put on my robe and walked towards the bedroom. This God-like man stood naked near the balcony as the moonlight illuminated everything about him. Hearing me approach, he turned to welcome me.

"How do you feel?"

"Amazing." I practically giggled like a little girl. *Get a grip, Mia.*

"That was only the beginning," he promised.

He moved towards me and brought his hands up to the tie that held my robe together. I looked over in a panic to the exposed balcony, and thankfully he caught my eye movement. He went over to close the door, along with the room darkening curtains, and I immediately felt a sense of relief.

Only a single candle lit the room, just enough so we could find each other's faces.

"I'd prefer to see more than your face, but we'll do it your way for now," he said, as he quickly de-robed me.

Once again, his hands were back on my body, but this time exploring with a freedom the tub did not allow. He pulled me into a deep, heated kiss, moving his fingers down my back to eventually squeeze and rub my behind. I could feel his re-hardening as we stood skin to skin.

He moved me slowly over to the bed, laying me down in the middle and kissing me once again. His lips trailed down, moving ever so gently and slowly over my breasts to suckle them, then over my stomach, where I tried not to wince with shame. He didn't seem to mind any part of my body, as he continued the descent, spreading my legs apart with his muscular arms and pleading with me to let him taste me.

His tongue found me waiting for him, wet and willing to receive whatever attention he wanted to give me. He masterfully massaged and sucked on my clit as his fingers moved rhythmically inside of me, doubling the pressure that wanted to cry out in sweet release. I couldn't help but to cry out his name in maddening ecstasy, shuddering from another explosion within.

I felt him rise up, wondering where he had gone, until I heard a ripping sound and realized he was getting a condom. *He's both sensual and safe,* I thought, relieved to be with a man who intended to protect me in every way. It made me want him even more.

He was soon back on the bed with me, resuming our passionate kissing and touching. He finally allowed my hands to do some of their own investigation across his solid chest and downward. I loved the feel of his manhood in my grasp—so much so that I took my time to arouse him, delighting in hearing him groan my name.

It didn't take much longer until I could feel him parting my legs once again and entering me gently. Wincing with slight pain, he asked me if I wanted him to stop— embarrassed, I confessed it had been so long that I was tender there. He reassured me that I had nothing to be ashamed about, claiming my tightness was excruciatingly pleasurable for him in ways he couldn't describe.

He took his time until I adjusted, and soon we were moving in a fervent rhythm. My body naturally responded to his, and our kisses intensified with each thrust. He moved in a way I never knew a man could move before, making sure that I was heightening to orgasm along with him. When we both finally came, he collapsed onto the other side of the bed, as breathless as I was.

He turned to give me a peck on the arm before he got up to take care of business, and then returned to the bed to hold me. Neither one of us felt the need to speak, as we drifted off into a blissful sleep wrapped in each other like a blanket.

In the morning light, I looked over to see Francesco soundly sleeping.

He truly is a gorgeous man, I thought as I moved a tendril of hair from his face. I felt refreshed, rejuvenated and a whole bunch of other things I hadn't felt in a long time.

Realizing the sun was bright and shining, even from behind the thick curtains, I carefully got out of bed so I could put my robe back on—all while trying not to disturb him.

"What are you doing, *cara?*" I heard him ask sleepily.

"Oh, good morning. I'm sorry, I didn't mean to wake you."

"Come back to bed," he grumbled, lifting up the covers to show me why.

"I don't think that is a good idea," I said nervously.

Frustrated, he sat up in bed and ran his fingers through his hair as he puffed out a sigh. He then jumped out of bed and made his way to the bedroom door, locking it and guarding it so I could not get out.

"What are you doing?"

"We're going to put a stop to this nonsense once and for all," he said commandingly. "Do you trust me or not?"

"I do, but you know—"

"I know what you have said. And we're going to change that. Right now," he said in a stern tone, clearly frustrated with my sense of modesty, until he noticed my automatic flinch. "Come," he said more gently.

He took my hand and brought me over to the closet, which doubled as a full-length mirror, and stood behind me after opening up the curtains to let the light in.

"Francesco, what is this?"

"It's a mirror," he replied sarcastically. "I'm asking you

to trust me right now, and you said you did. I'm about to make you very uncomfortable, but in a good way. I will not hurt you, and I will not do anything without your consent. I promise," he added, kissing the side of my neck to reassure me that I was safe.

I had no idea what he had in mind, but I was already freaking out on the inside.

"I want you to look at the woman standing in front of this mirror. Tell me, what do you see?"

"I see a ragged thirty-something-old lady with smeared makeup and bed head," I laughed, trying to make light of the situation.

"Fine. What else do you see? I want you to look carefully at her energy. Take your time."

I didn't know where he was going with this exercise, and it was clear that he was not going to let up. I could choose to fight him, or just go along with it and get it over with. So, I did as he asked, and took a long, hard look at the image standing in front of me.

"I see someone who feels peaceful this morning. Satisfied—more than satisfied." I thought I saw him blush himself, with pride for a job well done.

"Good. What else?"

"She's actually happy. For the first time in a long time, she feels attractive and desirable. I really had such a wonderful—"

"Stop," he cut me off. "Focus on the woman in the mirror and what she is feeling in this moment. You said she feels attractive and desirable?"

He moved my hair to kiss the back of my neck as I croaked out a yes.

"Do you feel that way right this very moment?" he asked as he moved his hands over my robe, rubbing my breasts through the thick terry cloth fabric.

My back arched as again, I conceded yes.

Then without notice, he removed the belt from around my robe to open it. I began to protest and he stopped—but pleaded once again in a whisper to trust him. Anxious, I let him proceed with removing my robe slowly, tossing it behind us and out of my reach. His moves were so loving and gentle; I knew whatever he had in store for me, he would not hurt me.

But he was right about the making me uncomfortable part. There I was, standing completely naked and exposed, my entire body illuminated by the sunlight. Without flinching in horror as I imagined he would, Francesco continued to stand behind me, perhaps even admiring what he saw.

I turned my head so that I couldn't see myself, partly angry for letting myself be exposed, and partly ashamed that he could see all of me. I wanted to cover myself right back up, yet there was a part of me that didn't want to fight him—the part that didn't want to hide anymore.

"Why are you doing this?"

"I want you to take a good look at that woman in the mirror. This woman is the same exact woman a few seconds ago that said she felt desirable and attractive. Nothing has changed."

"How can you say that?" I whispered hoarsely, now wanting the game to end. Letting him see me completely nude was one thing; making me have to look at myself was another.

"I see nothing but beauty when I look at you. Every inch, every curve, every so-called flaw you think you have. My attraction to you has not disappeared; quite the contrary. I want you more now than I've ever wanted you before."

A tear trickled down my face as I turned to face myself in the mirror, trying to see what it was that he was seeing. Did we have two different sets of eyes? How could he possibly desire all of this? And yet, clear as day, there was his arousal staring back at me in the reflection and against my behind.

"Tell me what you love when you look at yourself. Any part, even the tiniest feature."

I squirmed, feeling even more uneasy, just like he promised. He wasn't going to let up. Finally, I answered with something obvious and simple for me—my hair. He responded by running his fingers through my unkempt mane, agreeing that it was silky and smooth and wonderful to grab onto in the throes of passion. He tugged on it ever so slightly to demonstrate, enough to start the foreplay.

"What else?"

"Um, I guess maybe my lips, ears, I don't know. This is silly."

But my natural defense mechanism didn't stop him from acknowledging both my ears and my lips with the sensual movement of his wandering tongue—starting with baby nips with his teeth and then full on contact of his luscious mouth on mine. Just when I thought the kiss would end it all, he pulled away and resumed his position behind me.

"Next. Give me something else you like about yourself."

"I actually think I have pretty hands and feet," I offered, struggling to find something left that didn't make me cringe.

He took my hand and kissed it gently, then took ones of my fingers into his mouth and seductively sucked on it. He then laid down on the floor and told me to hold on to the wall while he repeated the gesture with one of my toes. I laughed and told him to get up, but I found myself oddly stimulated by the sensation. I could feel the wetness building up within me.

"Anything else?" Now catching on to his intentions, I naughtily told him my breasts weren't too bad.

He returned my wicked smile and instructed me to watch myself in the mirror as he joyfully cupped both my breasts, taking one of them into his mouth. He tantalized my nipple with his tongue before nibbling it and sending a sharp, but electrifying sensation through my body.

I did as he asked and found myself being aroused even more as I watched my own reaction. I was beginning to like this exercise after all and was ready to tell him exactly where to go next when he threw me a curveball.

"Now, tell me a part of your body that you are ashamed of."

"Wait, what?"

"I'm not done here. I need you to tell me where it hurts to love yourself."

I was not expecting this. I was just on the verge of succumbing to sex in the daylight—after having been brought to near ecstasy watching him savor the best parts of my body—only to suddenly shift gears to focus on the parts I longed to hide. Instinctively, I went to cover myself up.

"Mia, please. Talk to me. I have already seen all of you. I accept you just as you are—now let me help you accept yourself. Tell me what upsets you so."

"My stomach rolls," I said, starting to cry softly.

He gently lifted my head back up so that I could look at myself again. He then brought his arms from behind me and caressed the entire surface of my belly, tracing its outline and each mortifying stretch-mark. He then came in front of me and knelt down so that he could place kisses all over it as if he revered it.

"Do you know what I see when I see your stomach? I see proof that you created the universe's greatest miracle. You carried and grew *life* inside of you. Do you know how powerful and sexy that is? How erotic that is to the very core of a man, since our primal reason for sex is ultimately to procreate?"

"I never thought of it that way," I admitted as he moved my hands so that I could touch my own belly.

"Do you remember how it felt when they were growing inside you? How proud you were—so proud that you probably couldn't stop rubbing or touching this very same belly?"

I smiled weakly at the thought of it. Oh, how I loved holding my little ones that were blossoming in my womb. At the time, I did see my stomach as a miracle holder and not rolls of flab.

"This is that same belly, Mia. You should be as in awe of it now as you were of it then. Do you think maybe you can be a little less harsh on your stomach considering all the hard work it has done?"

"Maybe."

"All right. I'll take a maybe. Give me something else."

"I've had enough. Please hand me my robe."

"Just one more," he begged. "One more and then we can stop and you can wear an Eskimo suit for all I care."

"Fine," I relented. "I hate my ass."

"Really? Well no offense Mia, but your ass is my favorite part of your entire body."

"It is?"

"*Mmm-hmm.* See, most men don't want a scrawny little ass. At least, not this man. I love how supple yours is, and how I can grab onto it as I enter you."

With an athletic coup, he had me bent down on the

floor in doggie-style position. Pausing to make sure I was okay, he then spread my legs and first inserted his fingers to happily find me wet and ready for him before sliding his hardened cock inside. Before thrusting, he turned my head so I could see us in the mirror.

"I want you to keep watching, *cara*. Watch me make love to you."

I obeyed as best I could, looking into the mirror as he grabbed on to my behind and masterfully moved inside of me. Occasionally, he would spank me, not so hard as it would hurt, but enough so that the surprise sting would heighten my orgasmic awakening. If he took it too far, I was to simply let him know, but I couldn't help but yearn for more. I unexpectedly enjoyed it a little rough.

Kevin would never get this experimental with me, and I realized there must be an untapped reservoir of sexual fantasies buried deep within me that this man was bringing to the surface—without shame.

I watched his movement, witnessing his face full of pleasure, then saw mine, loving every single moment of the eroticism. I couldn't believe how much I delighted in watching myself have sex. How my nipples remained erect, how fascinating it was to see a man move inside of me and how my body tensed and released in response. How skilled he was at holding me in place with one hand while stroking my clit with the other, a perfect harmony of thrusting and pulling his way to yet another joint orgasm.

When his own final thrust came, he grabbed tightly onto my ass and playfully slapped it as he let out a satisfied animal growl and withdrew.

He then handed me back my robe to indicate he was done with his little lesson, but instead of rushing to put it back on, I just let it sit there crumpled on the floor beside me.

"That was—unbelievable," I gasped, as I lay there on the floor stunned.

"Did you watch like I asked you to?"

"Yes."

"Did you see how your body reacted to my touch and to the pleasure you were receiving?"

"Yes. It was fucking—hot. I didn't expect to feel so—turned on."

"See Mia Bella, your body already knows it wants and deserves that kind of pleasure. It doesn't have requirements for its size or shape in order to receive its natural right to orgasm. It will never discriminate. So, why should you allow your brain to override the wisdom of your body?"

He made a good point. God, how did this man come to know so much about a woman's body? Nope, never mind. I didn't want to know.

But what he said gave me a lot to think about. I did refuse attention and desirable advances from my husband because of my insecurities. Although I don't condone his cheating, I can understand how Kevin might have become frustrated with me and forced to pull back. I shut him out. He didn't deserve that—and neither did I.

Having sex with Francesco had been one of the most liberating experiences of my life. I didn't ever want to shut this part of me down again. I couldn't promise myself that I could fully embrace my body like he did, but if it meant having that kind of pleasure in my life, no matter who it was with, I was willing to give this self-love thing a try.

"There's just one more thing before I go down and make us some breakfast," he said, interrupting my thoughts.

"Oh no, there's more? Haven't I been a good student?"

"Straight A," he said, leaning in to give me a kiss. "But

I have some homework for you."

"Was I that bad?"

"Absolutely not, Mia Bella. You know exactly how to satisfy a man in every way. Make no mistake that you have innate talents in this department that make me never want to leave this bedroom," he reassured me mischievously.

"What I have in mind is more of an exercise on how to please yourself more. I've enjoyed exploring your body and finding the areas that stimulate you the most. But I want you to feel comfortable enough to tell me where and how you want me to touch you. Don't be afraid to tell me exactly what you want me to do with my hands and lips."

"I don't know. I never really gave it much thought before."

"Oh, Mia. What kind of a man were you married to all these years?" He just shook his head in surprise and muttered a few Italian curse words in disbelief.

"So, your assignment is this: learn what it is that turns you on. Touch yourself and get to know your own body. Masturbation is a wonderful way to connect to yourself."

I colored at the thought of it. My sisters and friends talked about it all the time, but it's not something I really got into because I was married and well, didn't think I needed to. I sheepishly told him okay, I'd give it a try. He suppressed laughing at my innocence and put his clothes on.

"Where are you going?"

"To make breakfast. I've worked up quite an appetite. Unless you would care to be so kind as to whip up something hearty for this famished man?"

"I'm definitely hungry, but not for food," I responded seductively, as I surprised us both in leading him back to the bed and letting my newly released sexual tigress out to play.

13

Thankfully, Francesco had to leave right after breakfast to get to his office, otherwise I wouldn't have been able to do anything today; though part of me wishes we could have spent the entire day in bed. I felt like I was on my honeymoon all over again, where all we did was make love. Not to discredit Kevin, but this was ten times more amazing than sex with him ever was.

But, as I reminded myself, I couldn't get all swept up in the experience that I'd forget about the important things in life—like checking in on everyone back home.

It was great to hear those sweet voices of mine, letting me know how school and their activities were going. Brittany was chosen as one of the leads in her summer ballet recital and went dress shopping this weekend with my mom for an upcoming school dance.

Stephen went on an overnight camping trip with the boy scouts and his dad and apparently learned how to kayak, which admittedly tied a few slipknots in my stomach at the thought of it.

Carly was so proud that she got an 85 on her English test after struggling for a while and told me how she and Granny baked cookies from scratch. Chocolate chip—her favorite kind.

According to Mom, Granny and Kevin, all was quiet on the homestead. There were no disturbances around any of the houses, and everyone was well-guarded. The police back home were in communication with the force here to see if they could trace any similarities between the notes that could lead to a genuine suspect. So far, this person had been successful in flying under the radar.

I missed everyone back home. I did love my adventure in Italy, especially last night. Oh, how I loved last night—and this morning (even the weird, but erotic self-love exercise Francesco tormented me with).

But I missed my children. There was no doubt that they were the lights of my life; the "accomplishment" I was most proud of. If I do nothing else, I'm honored to have been blessed with the gift of raising such wonderful human beings who get to call me mom.

Even chatting briefly with Kevin to see how things were going made me nostalgic. Maybe I was imagining things, but he seemed to have a sadness in his voice as we were talking. I'm just glad that after our huge blowup, we have simmered down to amicable status and can get along for the sake of the kids, and for each other.

There is nothing sadder than a divorce that ends in a lifelong battle after two people had loved each other so deeply. I was truly grateful that we chose to maintain a friendship when all was said and done.

With my phone calls completed and a whole day set out in front of me, I wondered how I would spend my time today. Still sitting in my robe, I debated even getting dressed, especially since I was put on notice not to leave this townhouse unless there was an emergency.

I get it—if someone could get past the guards only yesterday, it would be best if I didn't venture out into public for now.

Thoughts of Francesco rushed back to me as I lay on

the cushioned sofa trying to watch television. The way he handled me, the way I stroked him, the way we moved together like well-oiled gears of a clock. How he smelled like raw, leathered sweat and how the sound of his thick accent diminished into a weakened huff as he called out my name.

Just remembering made me start to tingle again. I blushed at what he suggested I do to learn more about my sexual hot spots. Dare I say, it was less of a struggle to accept his homework challenge when the mere thought of him already made me hot and wet.

And no one was around, so…*why not?*

At first, I felt awkward and nervous. It felt so weird to be anxious about something so personal and supposedly natural. I started with verifying some areas where I knew I liked to be kissed or touched, based on my experience with the only two men I'd ever been with my whole life.

I caressed those areas with the tips of my fingers and confirmed, yup—those are definitely trigger spots for me. I could tell the difference thanks to the automatic writhing of my body.

I was driven to study myself more, wondering what kept me from the art of masturbation for so long. The heat within me intensified, and newly discovered pleasure zones made me squirm ever so slightly. I removed my robe and navigated towards where the two different men both loved to concentrate on, feeling even more awakened as I understood why.

God, how amazing the female body truly was.

How my breasts filled into my hands, providing my fingers with easy access to my tightening nipples. I found that tugging on them triggered instant sensations down below. I stayed there for a while, captivated by the sexual control of a mere pull. Oh, yes, keep those electrical pulses coming.

Not wanting my breasts to selfishly get all the attention, I moved downward and into my own body, experimenting with different pressures, areas and speeds—all while trying to touch and caress my clit at the same time. That was a bit of a challenge; one that I reminded myself I could easily master with some practice. *Mmm,* I can and would repeat this assignment as often as I felt called to.

I was unbelievably comfortable all of a sudden with my own power for pleasure, and felt in awe at how my body responded to the various stages of arousal. When I had finally brought myself to orgasm, it was a different kind of rush than it was with a man; an inexplicable satisfaction of knowing I regulated my release on my own.

And Francesco was right—I would have some new insight to share with him, hopefully tonight.

Satisfied with how I just spent my morning, I hopped in the shower, daring to explore a little more and generate my own kind of steam.

I decided to remain comfortable in a pair of sweats I brought along with me, and as I looked in the mirror at my reflection, I noticed something very different about myself.

I looked cute in these sweats today.

They were no different than the last time I wore them, curled up on my couch at home with a pint of ice cream watching some awful reality television show. Back then, I felt like a slob, choosing this outfit because I didn't care about my appearance one bit.

And yet, standing here today, I didn't see myself like that. I saw a woman who cared about her appearance and perceived the outfit as purposeful coziness instead. How extraordinary to have that kind of epiphany!

Cute and comfy, I ventured down to the kitchen. I was in the mood to play around with some of the random ingredients left to see what I could come up with.

Before I knew it, I had five different dishes that I ended up serving to the guards because, well, who else would eat it? Plus, they appreciated the home-cooked meals after such long, arduous shifts and it made me feel good to thank them in some way for keeping me safe.

One hour led to another, and the next thing I knew, I had a mock menu designed for my "restaurant." I even designed what the inside would look like, drawing how I wanted the tables arranged, the types of chairs I'd have, the wall colorings and even the décor accents.

But that wasn't enough. I went online to pick out table and serviceware. Fabrics and centerpieces. Lighting fixtures—no, not that one. Yes—*that* one.

The ideas came rushing out of me like I was channeling some restaurant-designing goddess. Pages of paper were filled with scattered thoughts, but when I looked closer at them, I could see the cohesive plan within the pieces.

Shit, did I just design my dream?

I couldn't stop. I reorganized my thoughts so that they made sense, and then kept on creating. What would the wait staff wear? What kind of music would be playing in the background—would I have live music nights? What kind of promotions could I run to drum up business, and who could help me get the board of health and liquor licenses?

It was thrilling to unleash it all into a real blueprint—for when I was ready, of course. I did have to be realistic about it all.

But I had goals. Real, definable, future goals for the restaurant I've always wanted.

All that inventing had me yearning for a break. The sun was setting, and the pool was calling me. Even with a slight chill in the almost-summer air, I felt rebellious. God, what did that man do to me? Something in me was unleashed, and I liked it.

Peeking around to make sure the guards were not looking my way, I stripped away all my clothes and jumped straight into the pool. I had never been skinny-dipping before, and it was categorically cathartic.

The cool water was refreshing against my skin, and I enjoyed the freedom to move around without the restriction of a suit. I finally related to the unabashed sovereignty I imagined my sisters felt in their bikinis—and it had nothing to do with what they were wearing.

I was at home in the water like this. I wondered if I was a mermaid in a past life. I laughed at the thought of it, and of me being buck naked in some outdoor, semi-public pool where anyone could walk by.

"Well, you seem to be enjoying yourself, *cara*," came an unexpected voice by surprise.

I jumped, my initial reaction to cover myself up. He simply laughed heartily.

"I think we are well beyond playing shy, don't you think?"

I joined him in his laughter as he walked over closer to me. "Feeling frisky, are you?"

I simply nodded my head, and within seconds, he was out of his clothes and up against me in the pool.

When we were done fooling around, we got dressed and went inside to sample the smorgasbord of food I had prepared earlier in the day. Between his moans and facial expressions, I could tell he thoroughly enjoyed my cooking—at times, I couldn't tell if he was more aroused by my culinary skills or by my bedroom moves.

Excited about my dream downloading, I showed him what I had been working on all day. He was genuinely impressed at the thoroughness of my imagination.

"Busy girl today?"

"I was. A lot of dream making and exploration," I hinted. "How did your day go?"

"Pretty stressful actually. I have this one client who is so damn difficult, and I just wasn't getting through to him today. Frustrating as all hell. If he wasn't paying so much money and the case wasn't open-and-shut in his defense, I'd kick his ass to the curb," he disclosed with complete irritation.

"I'm sorry. Anything I can do to make it better?"

"Actually, I did have something in mind. Yes—*that,*" he acknowledged as I gave him my seductress eyes. "But first, I wanted to take an evening stroll somewhere in the city. Let the fresh air reboot my system. How does that sound?"

"Absolutely delightful. Let me just change and I'll be down in a minute."

The evening air was crisp and the sky clear. You could see stars for days and the moon was near full. We parked near Ponte Vecchio and I had a feeling I knew exactly where we were headed. Instead of ruining his covert operation with my excellent detective work, I just let him set it all up his way. He was so damn cute when he did things like this.

I was right—he led us straight to the Bardini Garden. I smirked when I saw the entrance, but covered up to feign shock. "Where are we?"

"The Giardino Bardini—the one I told you about,"

he replied excitedly. "I know most people enjoy this site during the day, where you can fully see its colors and vibrancy. But there is a certain magic in the air at night."

That there was. Walking through the iconic wisteria tree tunnel was like moving through a fairyland. The wind blew the branches, almost making a song in the night. Fallen petals stirred upon the ground, and not another soul was in sight. We stopped in the middle of the tunnel to sit and listen to the native melodies around us.

"Not many know that this is a place for lovers," he said, breaking the silence.

"So I've heard. Did you know about my ancestors being caught making love in this very spot?"

My question took him off guard, and though I couldn't see him clearly in the dark, I could've sworn he was embarrassed that I had entrapped him. He let out a nervous chuckle and took my hand in his and moved in closer.

"I did indeed."

"It's a shame they couldn't finish what they started."

"It is."

"Then let's just hope history doesn't repeat itself," I said with a smirk. I boldly took the initiative to heatedly kiss him and unbuckle his sexy leather belt as the wisteria petals closed their sensitive eyes. This time, he was going to be mine, and I'd be doing the pleasing.

I loved waking up in his arms for the second day in a row, briefly saddened by the thought that my sisters would soon be returning. He did need to go back to work again, so I spent the remainder of my time collecting my thoughts and returning them to the task at hand: we needed to figure out who was following us and learn more about this jewelry box.

Meg and Marissa arrived back at the same time, since Mar's hotel was near the airport and they could safely travel via public transportation together to get here.

Marissa went first, telling us all about the different masterpieces she saw, and how she took a sculpting class and won first place for her *Statue of a Lonely Waitress,* as she named it. She had a special radiance about her—I was so happy that she was able to take this opportunity to indulge in her passions and reignite her artistic creativity.

She said she was also able to put her relationship with Tony into perspective, promising herself that she would work on opening up more and not be so afraid to love him. It warmed my heart to hear that, knowing how hard love has been for her.

Meg shared that Kieran's mum was faring much better, and that her prognosis for recovery was favorable. She thanked us for letting her go—she needed peace of mind and Kieran needed the support. It also gave them a chance to work through some of the next steps of their relationship; to figure out a better game plan for ultimately being together. She came back glowing as well.

It seemed like there were three happy sisters all around.

I then took my turn to share how my three days without them went—leaving their mouths agape with excitement. I didn't even tell them the details of our erotic mirror scene, or how I finally discovered masturbation, or the skinny-dipping, or me riding Francesco like a stallion under the Bardini Garden's wisteria tunnel.

They didn't need to know everything. The bathtub and couple rounds of bedroom sex were enough for them to squeal in joy for me and allowed me to answer enough questions to keep their curiosities satiated.

I then told them all about my restaurant planning—inspired by my cooking class and Francesco's words of wisdom—and they were even more happy and supportive over that development. They offered to help me with time, money, babysitting and anything else I needed to make my dream a reality. I really do have the absolute best sisters in the world.

But then we had to address the elephant in the room: the note that got past the guards.

"Did you notice anyone following you at all in Ireland, Meg, or you, Marissa, on any of your tours?" They both declared a definitive "no," which led us to believe that our stalker hones in on one sister at a time; whoever was to receive the next gift.

We all agreed that we had to proceed with caution for the rest of our trip.

After taking the day to recuperate from traveling, art tours and hours of lovemaking, respectively, the three of us were excited to find out more about our Bianchi legacy. We were ready to meet up again with our cousin the next morning; this time, to discover the whereabouts of the jewelry box and instructions on how to retrieve it.

"*Buongiorno, cugine!*" she greeted with great enthusiasm. We returned her effervescence with hugs and kisses, settling back down into the sitting room armchairs.

"I've heard you've had quite the adventure," she began.

"It shook me up a little, yes," I replied. "But we're not backing down. We are well-protected and eager to hear more stories."

"*Eccellente!* Now, where did I leave off, again?" she wondered to herself.

"You finished telling us the family tree story, and then were going to tell me why I was chosen for this particular journey."

"Ah, yes, that's right. I've decided to wait on that. I'd like to share those details when you have the actual box in your hands, if you don't mind. It will give it so much more meaning."

I smiled warmly at her. "That's fine. Whatever you think is best."

"*Grazie,* then that's what I shall do. Today, I will tell you where you can find your treasure, of course, but I would love to hear more about you three girls and your lives. I've done enough talking! *A tavola non si invecchia*—at the table, no one gets old. That's our saying for let's enjoy our time as a family."

We broke bread with Sorella Maria for a few hours, learning all about some of her mischievous days as a young girl and her most precious works of service as a nun. We each shared about our family, our homes, some of our own unique adventures and more. It was a morning filled with pure laughter and joy as we built a new family bond.

She then sent us on our way, wishing us *in boca al lupo,* which we learned meant good luck. We were armed with the information we needed to retrieve my family treasure.

Since the pickup location was near the Pitti Palace, and there was no rush, we decided to do some impromptu sightseeing. Once again, I was reminded of the genius that went into building Florentine architecture.

Since Marissa had just returned from an art tour that included the palace's museums, we were mercifully spared from having to go through the extensive artwork exhibitions. Instead, we chose to stroll through the grounds, admiring the courtyard with its statues and fountains.

I was ecstatic to finally be visiting the famous Boboli Gardens. There was something for each of us to enjoy here. Marissa fawned over the Neptune fountain and white marble statues strategically placed throughout the gardens, as well as the fascinating stalactite artwork built right into the Grotta Grande.

Meg was enamored with the exquisitely manicured amphitheater, its symmetrical perfection of greenery and stonework. I, of course, adored the meadows and the geometrical maze flowerbeds of reds, whites and pinks. It was all so remarkable.

Famished from our self-guided tour, we decided to have a late lunch in a small coffee shop within the nearby Bardini Garden. In the sunlight, it was even more extraordinary and enchanting. I suppressed a wicked snicker as I passed the purple canopy once more, Meg noting how romantic of an area it was. Oh, if she only knew how much so!

Some simple, yet delicious paninis were all the fuel we needed to discuss our plan of action for getting the jewelry box. I looked over at the guards, who bobbed their head in acknowledgment that they were still with us and that we were safe.

"I can't believe we are so close to getting the jewelry box," Meg said. "You must be so excited."

"I am! And who would have guessed it was in the old Casa Bianchi attic all this time?"

"So, what's the plan? We can't exactly show up unannounced like last time. Not with 'Little Miss Sassypants' answering the door," Marissa reminded us.

"It might be difficult to make this happen, when after all these years, the Morettis might not let go of something that is technically in their possession."

"I know," I admitted. "But Francesco said he already

made a deal with the family. They have agreed to dig it out of their attic and meet us in the morning. They said something about this random trinket being of no value to them, and that they would be more than happy to get rid of the piece of junk."

"Oh perfect!" exclaimed Meg. "Then if that is all settled, why don't we just take the rest of the day to enjoy ourselves some more within these picturesque gardens?"

"Sounds like a plan to me!" Marissa agreed, and I nodded.

We sat for a few minutes longer, making small talk over some delicious pastries and coffee. A few minutes later, I heard the beep and looked down at my phone to see the incoming text and smiled wide. I winked at my sisters to indicate it was time to go. The trap was set, and our stalker took the bait.

It was time to go to the jewelry box's real location and claim it before he or she was any the wiser.

Arriving at the very old convent-turned-hotel, we were astounded to think that once upon a time, this was a religious sanctuary. Many of its original relics still lined the walls of the lobby, however, adding to its charm.

Approaching the front desk, I asked to speak to the manager, Giovanni Destino. When I told the sweet and bubbly concierge who I was and showed her my identification, an air of recognition came across her face.

"Signora Logan, we have been waiting for you. Just a moment. Signore Destino will be right down. Please, have a seat and make yourselves comfortable."

Five minutes later, a kind-faced, elderly man approached us. He was accompanied by a much younger version of himself, a strapping young boy carrying a black lockbox.

"I am Giovanni Destino and this is my grandson, Giorgio. This box has been in our safekeeping for many years. It has been my family's honor to guard it for Sorella Maria, Signora Lena, Signore Leigh and now you, Signora Mia."

"Thank you for protecting it for so long, sir. May I?"

"Oh, no. Not here, my dear. Please, come with me to my office, away from wandering eyes and ears," he said, walking us towards a small little office down the hall.

"Giorgio, you can leave that right on my desk for now. *Grazie,*" he said, kindly dismissing his kin so that we could be alone.

"No one, not even I, know the contents of this box. We've had very strict instructions regarding how to guard over it until the rightful heir was ready to claim it. It is now yours. I will bid you *addio* so that you may open it in private. I presume you have the actual key?"

"I do, Signore Destino. But you do not have to go. You have honored your promise to keep it secure all these years, so surely you can be trusted, no?" I hinted, seeing the old man's face light up like a Christmas tree. "It would be my honor if you would join us as we open the box."

"Oh—oh! I would be *cosi felice! Grazie!*"

I don't know why I was so nervous to open the container to see the box, but I was. I wasn't sure what to expect. Was it like the one I had as a little girl, pink and flowery with a little dancing ballerina on the inside? Was it spooky like a jack-in-the-box? Was it just plain wood with nothing inside?

It was none of those. What came out of that locked black box was something so extraordinary that it took my breath away.

A solid chestnut rectangular chest served as the base for this intricately carved wonder.

The sides were grooved into a symmetrical vine and leaf pattern with a masterful overlay of glittery gold.

The top depicted a single raised, carved red rose. It barely looked weathered; an indication of its preservation or perhaps a somewhat modern restoration by our dear great-grandmother.

A majestic red ruby adorned the rose's center. The outer rim of the chest was trimmed with delicate circle-cut diamonds, the jewels adding a hint of richness to an otherwise basic wooden box. It was truly a masterpiece beyond my wildest imagination.

"*Che squisito*," marveled Signore Destino. "It is exquisite. I have never seen such a work of art. It must be worth a pretty penny."

I was speechless. No wonder why this was kept locked up tight for so long. And here I jealously wondered how a jewelry box could measure up to Meg's Celtic green diamond ring. There was no doubt now that they were of the same rich history and worth.

"Mia, this is gorgeous. This is no ordinary box—it looks like it was handmade," Marissa determined, examining it from all angles. "It's exceptional."

"It truly is," agreed Meg. "But we don't know how much time we have before we are followed again. We need to get this back to the house undetected."

"You're right. Thank you again, Signore. I will forever be grateful to you and your family," I said, giving him a big hug.

"Let's get this box locked back up safe and sound."

14

"Where are you?" came the frantic voice on the other end of the line.

"Driving back to the townhouse. What's wrong, Francesco?"

"The guards lost him. We don't know where he went."

"Him?"

"Yes. It was a man who was following you, but somewhere between the Bardini Garden, and then figuring he would go straight to the Bianchi house from there, he slipped through their fingers. I just wanted to make sure you were all safe."

"We are. Raul is driving, and Luca, Benny and Matteo are in the car behind us. What do you think happened?"

"My guess is that he went to regroup and will try to break in tonight. We have extra guards stationed near the Bianchi house, out of view from the already well-secured premises. We don't want to alarm their own security, so they're using the house across the street as a stakeout. Luckily, it's a timeshare, so any movement there would appear like just another round of tourists."

"Okay, good. So, what do you want us to do?"

"Go back to the townhouse and pick up a few things— and make it quick. The guards have seen no movement so far, and we want to get you ladies in and out of there before there is any. We have no way of knowing if or when he figures out we duped him. Meet me at Sorella Maria's in an hour. Be careful, *cara*."

How sweet the concern was in his voice. I know Meg hates when men try to be overprotective, but I didn't mind it at all. It was comforting to know someone was looking out for us.

We did as we were told, taking only what we needed for the night and the next day, and successfully left without being noticed. Two guards remained behind to keep watch, while the double duty followed us to Sorella Maria's. All gathered together—except for our napping cousin—we tried to figure out what our tracker's next move would be and devised a strategy.

"My guess is that he will try to break in tonight, obviously with no success. I believe you will all be safe— at least for this evening—especially since he thinks the plan is for you to recover the jewelry box from the Bianchi house tomorrow," Francesco presented. "But, we are talking about someone who has alluded the authorities in three different countries already. I'd rather not assume and take chances."

"So, what do you suggest we do?" Meg asked.

"His first instinct should be to go to the townhouse, so that's why we cleared you out of there. Meg and Marissa will stay here in the retirement home with Sorella Maria. The local authorities will help to monitor the entire grounds and be stationed around the perimeter of Sorella Maria's and your guest rooms.

"Mia and the jewelry box will be coming to my house. I already have surveillance cameras, and two of the new guards will keep watch. Though, since you have never been to my house before, I'd like to think this character doesn't know where I live, nor would he consider going there."

"How convenient," responded Marissa with a stifled giggle. I shot her a hard look that said, *quit it,* but it was too late; Meg caught it and laughed while both my and Francesco's faces flushed. He cleared his throat.

"Moving on—does anyone have any questions?"

We all shook our heads and became somber. This was not a game; this was getting dangerous. Some lunatic was after us and a jewelry box, and had yet to be identified. I didn't want to leave my sisters behind, but I knew that they would be safe. Someone did have to stay with our dear cousin and make sure she was protected as well.

Francesco and I decided to leave right away, so that we could avoid being seen by our follower if he made his way to Sorella Maria's. I was sad to be missing a nice family dinner and a stroll through Alessia's diary with my cousin and my sisters, until I looked over at my handsome escort.

No, I thought. *Not that sad.*

His home was bewildering; like a mini-mansion in the hills. A large, wrought iron gate, opened only by a special code, made way to a winding forest-like road that led to the front of his modern Gothic-style, two-story house. Off white columns lined the entrance to the dark red front door with gold trim.

Stepping into his "lobby" was like stepping into one of the palaces. White marbled floors contrasted against dark green walls adorned with brilliant works of art. The first room we walked into must have been the living room, with deep cushioned, light gray sofas placed in front of an unlit white brick traditional fireplace.

Did they really use logs? It was a far cry from my flip-a-switch gas version at home.

Even in all its elegance, there was an air of homey comfort. From the looks of the outside, I expected it to be stuffy; but instead, it was inviting and cozy. I looked over towards the hallway on the right, which he mentioned led to the main kitchen.

When my eyes lit up like a child in anticipation, he gently told me that he wanted to get me all settled in first, and then he'd be happy to give me a grand tour and let me loose in there.

Up a spiral winding wooden staircase were a series of bedrooms, bathrooms, offices and hall closets. He gestured for me to look inside one of the "smaller" rooms—a guest room decorated in shades of purple that he said his cousin Sophia loved to stay in.

"This will be your room, *cara*. Do you like it?"

I looked at it, disheartened that I would be staying in a guest room. I had assumed when he summoned me to stay with him, that it would be *with* him, in his bed. I tried to hide my disappointment as best as I could; after all, he was being a most gracious host and keeping me protected.

"It's lovely," I managed. "Thank you."

All of a sudden, he was roaring with laughter.

"Oh, Mia Bella, you are so innocent and sweet sometimes," he purred. "I was kidding, my darling. There will be no guest room for you," he added, stopping to take me into his arms and kiss me enthusiastically. I responded by wrapping my arms around him and pulling him into me tightly. *Mmm, does this man know how to kiss.*

He had to force himself to pull away, saying that there would be plenty of time for "that" later. First, he wanted me to unpack and unwind after the long day. He also admitted that he was anxious to see this jewelry box he's only heard stories about for so many years.

I acquiesced, joking that I didn't blame him for being more interested in a diamond-studded box than me.

Responding to my subtle challenge, he swiftly picked me up and carried me to his bedroom to affirm which of the two he treasured more.

As we lay there in the afterglow, my mind began its incessant chattering. I realized there were only a few more days left before I returned home, and I felt like there would never be a good time to address what was going on between Francesco and me.

Normally, I would shove it down and not deal with it; the inevitable end would come when it wanted to and I'd deal with it then. But feeling more self-confident and empowered recently, I wanted to be clear on where things stood. *Where to begin?*

"Francesco, can we talk?"

"Of course, *cara.* What is it?"

"I—uh—hmm. I'm having trouble forming the right words."

"Whatever it is, just say it. Surely you know by now you can say anything to me," he said soothingly.

"I know. I just—okay, here it goes." I closed my eyes and took a deep breath. Being open and upfront. New territory. Scary as fuck. But a new Mia was emerging, and I liked her strength.

"I've loved these last few days with you, truly. You have opened me up to so many things. Like, how I should look for the hidden gems in life, rather than let tours or structured plans guide my experiences. How I should accept myself a little more and open the door again to my dreams. How—how I should embrace sex and everything about my own sexuality."

"It's been my pleasure to do all of those things for you, *cara.* I have also relished my time with you. You have been a wonderful teacher as well."

"I have?" *What could I have possibly taught him?*

"You have so much passion and creativity inside of you, that it inspires me. I am a lawyer; that's not the most creative and fun job, you know. You've brought me back to remember the simple things in life that I adore—nature, wine and fantastic company," he said, sweeping a piece of my hair off my face and letting his fingers wander through my thick, tousled mane.

"That's all this is, right? Fantastic company?" I asked sheepishly, walking through the door of the conversation I knew we needed to have.

"Oh, *cara*. I did not mean it like that," he said as he took my face in his hands and kissed my lips gently, yet fully. "I care very deeply for you. You have to know that."

"I do. And I care deeply for you, as well," I admitted. "Very much so. But I also just, I don't know, want to clear the air about what's happening between us."

I paused briefly, not knowing how he would take what I was about to say next. *Just be blunt, Mia.*

"This ends in a few days, doesn't it?"

I looked up at him with sad eyes, the reality of leaving him behind nailing into my gut. My candor took him by surprise, and I could see the genuine regret in his eyes.

"Mia, I am sorry if I have confused you or misled you in any way. It was never my intention."

Part sad, part relieved, it was actually the answer I was hoping for.

"Oh no, Francesco, you didn't. Not at all. I never thought this would go beyond my trip here."

I could see him start to breathe easier again, being reassured that he had not just broken my heart into a mosaic of tiny pieces.

"I figured this was just a fling for you and nothing more.

I'm still technically married until I sign the papers and I have a lot of soul searching left to do. I wouldn't have the energy for another relationship. I was just afraid of hurting your feelings by not wanting to try to figure things out after I left, like Meg and Kieran did."

"*My* feelings? You were worried about *me? Che dolce.* No, *cara,* my feelings are not hurt. I'm relieved that we are on the same page. Be it known, however, that this is not a 'fling' for me, as you called it. What we have here is very special to me. I will always care for you, as you are engraved into my heart.

"But ours is one of those encounters that is meant to be only for a reason. Destined to teach us or enrich us in some way and then move us forward. Would you agree?"

"Yes, exactly."

I gazed warmly at him. He spoke the truth in the most elegant of ways. This *was* destiny, but that did not mean it was intended to last forever. Although I could lie in his arms for eternity here, and parting would be bittersweet, in my heart I knew that he would live on as a sacred memory.

"So, do you feel better now that you got that off your chest?"

"I do, thank you."

"Good. Because I'd like to pick up where we left off before we go down and take a look at your other magic chest."

I didn't want to leave the bed, but he urged me to head downstairs to see the kitchen and join him for dinner so that we could replenish our tanks. The room—if I can even call it something so insignificant—was more amazing than I imagined it could be, with mosaic tiling, marbled counters, stainless steel appliances and a row of copper pots hanging just like in my house. We were so alike in so many ways, I noticed.

He offered to whip us up something quick, but knew better than to get in my way. I asked him to show me where he kept his ingredients and made him leave me to my culinary creations.

After dinner, we retreated to the living room area, where I carefully removed the jewelry box from its container. He was just as in awe of the work of brilliance as we were. I was also grateful for the opportunity to finally be able to take a good look at it myself after being rushed out of the convent-turned-hotel.

The details were perfection; whoever carved this did so with a great deal of skill and care.

"How do you open this?" I wondered aloud, realizing that it was completely sealed shut.

I turned it every which way and couldn't seem to find any kind of opening. Yet, I could hear the rattling inside of it. Something was in there. Francesco simply looked at me with a Cheshire cat smile, as if he knew the answer to my riddle.

"Not everything is as it seems, I suppose," he taunted.

"You know, don't you?"

"I might," he hinted. "But," he said in a more serious tone, "that is for your cousin to tell you. For now, let's put the box away for safe keeping and turn in for the night."

"If you insist," I responded, knowing full well what his true intentions were for the remainder of our evening alone.

As the sun peeked through the slits in the window blinds, we awoke to the sound of his phone ringing. It was from one of the guards stationed at the Bianchi house. I let him finish his call uninterrupted, even though his side of the conversation was frustrating and left me curious as to what was happening.

To keep myself from going insane, I checked in on Meg and Marissa, who said they had an uneventful evening with a delightful nun. He finally hung up the phone and had a disturbed look on his face.

"What is it?"

"It's the strangest thing. I mean, it's great that there was no attempt to break into the Bianchi house last night—no one there was put in harm's way. The only sightings were the mail carrier, a few high school girls and some suit who must have had an appointment with Moretti. Nothing unusual."

"Okay, so do you think that he will attempt today? Maybe he decided to wait until we went and actually had the box in our possession before he would make a move."

"I would have thought you were right. But he's already made his move."

"What do you mean?"

His face was white as a ghost.

"What are you not telling me? Francesco!"

I pushed him when he refused to say anything. He was shaking and tears were forming in his eyes.

"It's a good thing we got you out of the townhouse last night," he muttered with a broken voice. "Two guards were found unconscious this morning and the place was completely ransacked."

"Oh. My. God. Are they okay?"

"Thankfully, yes. Benny has already been released from the hospital and is at home resting with his wife, suffering only a mild concussion. Matteo is being kept overnight for observation since he was hit harder, but is projected to be sent home in the morning. The polizia are on site gathering evidence as we speak."

"I'm so sorry we brought all of this danger here."

"Mia Bella, it's not your fault. Before this, it was only harassing notes and harmless break-ins. There was no way for you to know that this would turn violent. They are smart and determined. That's for sure."

"They? I thought they only identified one man?"

"They did, but he must have had help. How could one man take on two guards, at two different times, otherwise? We may be looking at one mastermind and some lackeys to do the dirty work. This is serious, Mia. Someone is out for blood."

He continued to shake, his mind racing and heart pounding.

"You're keeping something from me. I can tell."

"How can you tell?"

"Cop's ex-wife," I smirked. "Now, out with it—and don't bother to sugarcoat it."

I could tell he did not want to talk further, but I persisted. Finally, he took a deep breath before revealing that a note was left behind.

I'll kill you bitches before you steal another one of my fortunes.

We immediately left Francesco's estate to go get Sorella Maria and my sisters from the retirement home. Francesco insisted that it was no longer safe there either. Even if the perpetrators found out what we were doing and tracked us back to his place, he assured us that no one would get through those gates or near the house undetected; it was a fortress.

With all of us safe and sound back at the Marchesi

compound, our nerves were shot. No one knew what to say or do next. Sorella Maria was escorted to one of the guest rooms so she could lie down, and my sisters brought their bags up to two other rooms to settle into.

Out of respect for the nun staying with us, I moved my things into Sophia's favorite purple guest room after all. Neither of us felt comfortable "living in sin" while she was staying with us.

We all elected to take some time to rest, think and otherwise chill out before rejoining for dinner. Meg and Marissa took a tour of the grandiose house, finding themselves in the downstairs billiard room challenging each other to a best two out of three game to relieve their stress. Francesco was pulled away into critical conference calls for the next few hours in his home office, leaving me to have uninterrupted time to myself.

Unable to concentrate on my latest novel, my mind went into overdrive about the note left behind—about everything that had gone down since the moment we found out about Leigh Marino. So much had happened since then, and we had pushed our luck too far this time.

What would it take for us to be safe again? I wondered. Ugh, I just wanted to get rid of the damn jewelry box. Nothing was worth losing our lives or having innocent guards harmed.

This was out of control, and someone needed to put a stop to it. Just then, an idea flashed through my mind—oh yes, that someone was going to be *me*.

I instantly got on the phone and began making calls. I knew exactly who I could turn to for help while I was stuck in the fortress, our two minds collaborating magnificently. After about an hour of formalizing a solid game plan, I was satisfied with what my new partner and I had just set in motion.

Now, all I could do was wait to see if it would work in the limited time we had to pull it off.

Please God, let this work to keep my family safe, I prayed. *And let justice be done. No one messes with my family and gets away with it.*

There was nothing else I could do but have faith in my co-conspirator and the good Lord above. It was out of my hands now. Knowing that I'd go crazy if I didn't distract myself, I forced myself to dive into the suspense of someone else's drama until dinnertime.

Dinner was a much-needed respite from the anxiety; some small talk acting as a band-aid for the emotions we were all experiencing on the inside. Lorenzo had come over to join us, bringing in a wonderful array of takeout so that no one (me especially) had to cook.

Sorella Maria engaged us with more stories of her youth, bringing her mother, Alessia, Cian and Lena to life through her memories. By the end of the evening, they were no longer characters in a storybook, but real people whose lives gave birth to ours.

"When I was eleven, I remember there was a neighborhood party during one of the O'Sullivan visits. Oh, it was such a *grande affare*—grand affair. Lena and I got to wear matching floral dresses that Zia Alessia bought us from America and I felt like such a princess. Mamma also looked beautiful that day in a red dress and her hair all curled and wavy," she recalled.

"I'll never forget how right in the middle of the festivities, Zio Cian whipped out his violin and started playing some music. How fun it was to hear him play some Celtic tunes. Zia Alessia decided to teach us the Irish jig, too. Oh, how we all loved to *danza!*

"It was also magical to watch Zia and Zio dance in each other's arms and look into each other's eyes. The love they shared lit up the sky brighter than the stars.

"Zio Cian was a very special man," she continued. "This one time, right before church, Lena and I snuck out to go play by the pond and I accidentally fell in. My dress was completely ruined and I began to cry. *È stato orribile*—it was horrible.

"I just knew Mamma would be angry with me about it. But Lena ran to go get her father, and he came back, so gentle and kind. Zio Cian picked me up and snuck me into the house so I could change my dress and fix my hair before Mamma could see. He said, *'non preoccuparti piccolo'*—don't worry, little one. He wasn't going to tell Mamma, he promised. She never even noticed I was in a different dress until after we came home from church.

"He was the closest man to ever be a papa to me," she said wistfully. "I wish I could have spent more time with them. The last time I saw Zia Alessia, she gave me this beautiful little sapphire necklace. I have treasured it all of the days of my life. And now, I'd like to give it to you, Mia."

"Oh, I couldn't possibly—" I started, looking at the delicate pendant she pulled out from her pocket. It was a simple, pear-shaped sapphire on a solid gold chain.

"Nonsense. What's a 98-year-old *sorella* going to do with this necklace? Give it to your little one—Carly, right? From what you have told me, she would love to have a piece of this mysterious heritage of hers."

"She would indeed," I smiled and accepted the necklace graciously. "Thank you."

After our cousin was done sharing her stories, Lorenzo and Francesco also got in on the fun, telling us what it was like growing up with Sorella Maria. How if the boys behaved themselves during mass, she would sneak them lollipops when their parents weren't looking afterwards. How she brought them into the church gardens to teach them how to plant and tend the soil—which explains where Francesco first discovered his love for nature.

We then took our turns talking about our family and the trouble we would each get into as young girls (Marissa most of all), and how our father was the most magnificent man in the world and would have loved all of this. The hours of storytelling were exactly what we all needed to lift the burden of fear from our hearts.

Unfortunately, the spell broke when Lorenzo had to excuse himself to head back to work on a case. A box full of leftovers in his hands, he winked at me on his way out the door. *Always the Lothario, that one,* I mused.

After the trying day, we all decided it would be best to turn in early and get some rest. Luckily, everyone else was agitatedly preoccupied enough themselves to not notice my heightened state of apprehension. That is, everyone but Francesco.

"What is it, *cara?* You have been in another world the whole evening."

"It's nothing. Just overwhelmed with what happened today."

"It was a difficult day, indeed. But there is more. I can sense it," he observed. Once again, this man had a solid read on me. I hated lying to him, but I had to throw him off my scent. I had to go undercover with my emotions to satisfy his craving to solve the mystery that was me.

"I can't get anything by you," I admitted. "It's just that I'm starting to feel sad about leaving so soon; that this adventure is about to come to an end and real life will be waiting for me back in New York." Well, it wasn't too far from the truth, anyway.

"Mia Bella, life will be whatever you make of it. It is not your location, but how you live your life with intention, that defines it."

I smiled up at him and his endless wisdom. "You're right. I'll try to look at it from that perspective. Thanks for always knowing how to make me feel better." I reached up to give him a warm hug and light kiss.

Pleased he had uncovered and appeased the recesses of my anxiety, he bid me good night as I settled into a lonely bed, without Francesco by my side. I had no intention of sleeping, however. My mind struggled to come to terms with missing his presence and contemplating what tomorrow would bring.

The next morning, we gathered around the breakfast table for some pastries and coffee. I couldn't help but pace back and forth. I hadn't heard a thing about my plan and was starting to wonder if I was in over my head. Maybe it wouldn't work after all.

What if it made things worse? I questioned. *Well, too late to turn back now, buttercup.*

"Mia, what is with you? You're going to wear a hole into this antique throw rug," Meg noted.

"I guess I'm just on edge."

"We all are," Marissa said. "Maybe Sorella Maria can tell us a little bit more about the box." Just then, my phone dinged.

"Hold that thought," I said, smiling in relieved victory. *Yes! It worked!*

"Uh, *cara,* what is going on?" Francesco asked.

"Have a seat, everyone, and I will tell you all about it."

15

"The plan was brilliant, if I do say so myself," I began, with an audience of suspenseful eyes watching me in curiosity as I weaved my story of deception. I was so enthralled to be the author instead of the reader this time, and I was going to enjoy narrating how my plot unfolded.

It all started after we were forced to gather here at Francesco's house; practically prisoners at the mercy of some game player who wanted what was rightfully ours. I decided that we were not going to cave in to this threatening coward and give up our legacy as easily as our grandfather gave up his family (no offense, Gramps)—but that didn't mean we could continue to put ourselves in real danger either.

So, I explained how I took a page out of Lena's "book" and created a decoy—except I kicked it up a notch to make it much more believable than a zirconia knock-off of Meg's ring. I confessed that I made a phone call to Lorenzo yesterday morning, who was more than happy to help us trick the perpetrator, especially since we were all confined here anyway, and he was our best connection to the outside world.

"The little devil," Francesco bit back with bewilderment, as I smiled mischievously and held up my hand to indicate that there was much more to be told. He nodded in respect for me to proceed.

"After Lorenzo and I brainstormed about the resources he had and the plausibility of our plan, he went down to a local antique shop to find any kind of wooden jewelry box with a carving on it. Luckily, he found a few different options, sent me the pics and I chose the perfect smokescreen," I revealed.

I went on in detail about how Lorenzo then visited the Marchesi family jeweler, Roberto, who carefully embedded a number of small, but real, diamonds and a few rubies into the etching. He also had an old 18-karat gold, diamond and peridot Buccellati brooch that we added into the box to sell the idea that this was the real deal.

It just so happened that Roberto owed Lorenzo a favor and he was able to cash in on a particularly slow day for the businessman. And, just as fate would have it, the respectable jeweler had received a shipment in that morning with the pre-cut stones, making pulling off an adorned chest within a few hours a real possibility.

"Lady luck was definitely on our side—or perhaps, it was Lena and Grandfather Leigh who sent the Gods our way," I mused out loud.

"Sounds like it," agreed Meg. "But where did you get the money for all of this? It seems awfully expensive."

"Well, this decoy cost us a six-figure loan from our grandfather's fund, but I thought it was worth it. I'm sorry I didn't ask you guys first if it was okay, but I had to act fast," I admitted with a little bit of guilt. "But once this stalker has everything appraised, and sees its worth, he would have no reason to question its authenticity. I'm counting on it being the perfect set-up to hopefully appease the greedy thief."

"I'm good with it," praised Marissa. "So, what's next? How do we use it to trap the bastard?"

"Well, there's more," I said, and continued with my story.

While Lorenzo was busy playing alchemy with the fake box, I decided to add an extra-special touch to our plan of deceit. Remembering a recent project with Carly that involved making paper appear old, I soaked a sheet in hot tea and let it dry until it had the ancient consistency I was going for.

I then used my impressive calligraphy skills I learned as a young girl to craft a short but sweet love note from Dionisio to his unnamed love—since I didn't know her name—telling her that even though she shined brighter than the jewels on this box, it symbolized the depths of his love for her.

Lorenzo already had the box prepared in his trunk before making his way to our old place to pick up the remainder of our things. We were banking on the townhouse being watched, praying that the perpetrators would end up following Lorenzo to Francesco's house to begin the entrapment.

"When Lorenzo came to dinner, I slipped him the old note to add to the box later on, along with our note of surrender. Using my own handwriting, I asked that they please leave us alone, claiming that they won and to just take this jewelry box and never bother us again; it wasn't worth getting killed over."

I paused, not sure whether or not to share the rest, but thought it would be best to come clean.

"I also might have promised that when Meg returned, we could somehow orchestrate handing over the ring without getting the authorities involved," I meekly confessed. "And, um, I might have also suggested that the best way to get Marissa's statue would be to let us go to Spain in peace to retrieve it and then release it to him as well."

"You did what?"

"You said what?

"Mia, are you crazy?"

In came the rush of inevitable scoldings.

"I know, I know," I relented. "I'm sorry. I shouldn't have taken it so far, but I just wanted this to work so badly."

"We'll circle back to this later, *cara,*" Francesco warned sternly, looking displeased. "Go on. What else did you and my little brother concoct?"

Begrudgingly, I went on to explain how we knew once Lorenzo was spotted here, at Francesco's house, that he'd be followed when he left—and he confirmed that he was. Luckily, as he exited through the driveway gate, Lorenzo had been able to convince our guards to pull back to let the jackasses tail him. Lorenzo promised that he was a sharp-shooter; adequately armed in case he was attacked.

"He was ready for anything and was rather disappointed that he didn't get some target practice in," I shared with a giggle. Francesco did not share my humor, as a growl made its way to the surface. I swallowed hard and returned to the plan.

I explained how we had to make sure the perpetrator took the bait to follow Lorenzo, so he left the house with the leftovers disguised as a questionable box—hopefully to convince anyone watching him that it contained the jewelry box. Lorenzo further set the scene by acting all suspicious and looking around to "make sure no one was following him."

And it worked like a charm. After he left, he led them straight to the retirement home, as planned, where he would drop off the faux jewelry box at Sorella Maria's. We knew they would never believe we'd bring it back to our townhouse. It was risky, but we alerted the local authorities of our plan and surprisingly had their full cooperation—with some regulations, of course.

After pretending to interact with the polizia about the jewelry box and showing his identification—all part of our master scheme—Lorenzo was permitted to place it on Sorella Maria's back porch. He then added my note on top, in an envelope marked "we surrender" on it.

The guards were positioned on site to allow anyone to approach and take the box, and then they would move in and catch the culprit—and his potential henchmen—when the time was right.

Lorenzo left the scene, watching carefully until he knew he was alone, and was instructed to wait for the phone call from the station once he safely returned home.

With our plot in motion, all either of us could do was wait. And now, Lorenzo was on his way over—confirmed that no one was following him—to tell us how it all went down last night.

"That was pretty ballsy of you, Mia," Marissa said. "I'm impressed!"

"Me too," said Meg. "But why didn't you tell us about this earlier?"

"Same reason you didn't tell us about the ring decoy," I replied. "There was no need for anyone else to lose any sleep last night. I was up all night praying that I did the right thing, and that this would work. I hope you're not angry with me."

"The only reason I'm not angry is because you had the good sense to involve my brother," said Francesco. "That sneaky little fox. I *knew* he was up to something last night!"

"I couldn't have done it without him. And we didn't

want to bring you in on it either because, well—we didn't want you to worry and take control and be all protective big brother about it. You tend to do that, you know."

"Sadly, you're right," he admitted. Just then the door opened to a very tired little brother, who jumped back when he saw the whole room turn to stare at him.

"Guess you filled everyone in?" he asked me.

"I did. But they will wait patiently for the rest of the story until I get you a hot cup of coffee first."

All seated quietly with freshly brewed coffee and tea, we were ready to hear what transpired last night.

"Well, after I had texted Mia, they took the bait," he began. "About an hour after I left Sorella Maria's, a man casually walked past the guards under the guise that he was visiting his aunt. Of course, he made a slight detour and went straight for her back porch. He took the box as planned, but before the polizia could grab him, he had snuck the box through a taxi's passenger door window and the car sped off. My guess is that during that one hour window of downtime after I left, they hatched a plan to sneak it out, knowing how guarded the retirement complex was," he added.

"So, they got away?"

"Not exactly, *cara*. The *box* did, yes. As did who I believe is probably the mastermind behind all of this. But, the polizia successfully captured one of his minions, Horatio—the one who stole the box—and brought him into custody.

"They offered him a reduced sentence if he'd give up the name of his boss. Having no loyalties and wanting nothing more than to save his own skin, he squealed like a little pig and gave up the name Jordan Kissinger."

"Jordan Kissinger? I have never heard that name before

in my life. Have you?" I asked my sisters, who both shook their heads with the same perplexed look on their faces.

"Well, apparently he must be the one after your treasures. The good news is—he believed the decoy was real," he said with a big, satisfied smirk.

"How do you know?" asked Meg.

"Well, the car got away with the box, but didn't notice that the polizia had captured this Horatio guy in the process. So while Horatio was in custody and the station had his phone, the text came through from a contact, 'JK,' that said:

Jewelry box is legit. Real diamonds and expensive heirloom confirmed with letter inside. Let the bitches be for now. Money transferred to account. Headed to airport in morning. Don't contact again.

"So, what now?" asked Marissa.

"Well, the lead *Questore* contacted the Florence airport, who verified that a passenger by the name of Jordan Kissinger was in fact booked for a flight to New York this morning. Customs at both airports are on high alert for anyone declaring the jewelry box and expensive brooch. With any luck, we'll get this guy before he even boards the plane today, and this will all be over."

"What a relief that will be!" Meg exclaimed.

"So, do you think we are out of harm's way?" I asked Lorenzo.

"For now, I think so. One of his men is locked up, and I'm sure if he told this one to back off, he told any others to as well. I'd bank on him being on that flight home—or in jail by the end of tonight. None of the polizia have noted any disturbances anywhere since last night, so breathe easy."

"Still," Francesco warned, "we are not relieving any guards of their duty until you are safely home, and I know that Sorella Maria and the sisters are protected as well."

As if on cue, Sorella Maria made her way down the stairs to join us after a nice morning nap. We spared her any of the details of the true danger or the plan I put into place.

What she *did* think—because of the "harmless" first note—was that we all wanted to be together at Francesco's, just to be extra cautious. There was no need to upset the poor old woman.

"Oh, *buongiorno,* everyone! I'm so pleased to see you all again."

We took turns greeting her, then led her to sit down in the most comfortable armchair with a green and red checkered throw pillow. She asked if we had the jewelry box, indicating she was ready to see it for herself and tell its enchanting story. Her timing could not have been more perfect.

"*Che magnifico!*" she exclaimed. "No wonder the ancestors guarded this so carefully. *Bellissimo.*"

She took it into her wrinkled, fragile hands to admire it up close, reviewing every groove and sparkle. I put out a bowl of fresh berries for everyone to snack on while she revealed the mystery of this delicate treasure chest.

"This jewelry box was built with the very hands of my great-grandfather, Dionisio. He was such a daydreamer I heard, always with his head in the clouds," she began with her own dazed look, lost in the reminiscing.

She went on to explain the legend in great detail. How our family's heritage was of meager roots; mere farmers who tilled the land and worked long hours. Wealth was not something the Bianchis were born into, but like in all families, it was expected that the sons would continue to cultivate the land as they came of age.

"But that was not enough for Dionisio," she proclaimed. "Although he never minded the hard labor and helping his family, his dream was to be a great architect like those who built the city's most iconic landmarks. His father would not support his dream, reminding him that he came from nothing, and would never be accepted as anything but a lower-class farmer."

And so, she revealed, Dionisio grew to become the laborer he was trained to be indeed. Yet, he could not extinguish the dream inside of him. Night after night, he would sneak out of the house and into the barn with only an oil lamp to light his way.

There, he would spend most of his nights whittling away on old pieces of wood not suitable for the fireplace. He carved until his masterpiece was finished—the prototype for a new building he intended to construct one day.

That following spring, he met a lovely young woman, Luciana, and she changed his life forever. Her family came from money, but that did not stop them from kindling a courtship. Her parents were openly opposed, forbidding their daughter to fall in love with a simple farmer. That was no life they wanted for their only daughter.

That did not stop them, of course. We were sensing a pattern in our grandfather's lineage when it came to love matches.

"After a few months of courting against her parents' wishes, Dionisio brought Luciana into the barn to show her his design. She was so moved by his intricate work that she insisted he bring it to her father at once."

Sorella Maria continued to explain how Luciana's

father made his fortune as an architect, and he couldn't help but be impressed with the young lad's work. He opened his mind to speak more with Dionisio, asking him if he could design blueprints for a small church that was planned on a new piece of land he acquired. He never expected to be so pleased with Dionisio's vision and talent.

Willing to give the young lad a chance to prove his worth, Luciana's father did something rare, crossing class systems and taking the poor farm boy on as an apprentice. His architectural concept for the church exceeded all expectations, and from there, Dionisio's dream to begin a new family dynasty came to life.

His parents were so proud of him—his father eventually apologized for doubting him and freed him of his family's farming obligation. As Dionisio's reputation and wealth grew, he helped his two brothers to secure their land and future success by employing outside workers and paying off all the taxes.

Instead of letting his ambition tear him away from his family, he chose to strengthen those bonds. He was a good man, they said; known for always donating to the poor and investing in those less fortunate.

"By this time, Luciana's parents had grown fond of the young boy, and granted him their blessing to marry their daughter," she said. "On their wedding day, Dionisio presented Luciana with a hand carved jewelry box he had made just for her. That, and a heartfelt letter explaining its origin."

Sorella Maria still had that very note and handed it to Francesco to read aloud, so that he could translate from Italian to English for us all. He was careful not to rip the very old, fragile piece of paper, taking his time to preserve it.

My darling Luciana,

I began carving this box the day we met. You are the one who has captured my heart and now lives in my soul forever. You believed in me and made me believe in my dreams.

This chest symbolizes that whatever we wish, whatever we desire, will come true because we make it so. We are the creators of our own destiny.

The vines symbolize the harvest and bounty of our united soul's labor; together, we can do anything and turn our dreams into gold.

The rose represents your beauty—not only your face, but your heart to see the man beyond the farmer.

The diamonds sparkle bright to light our way through our journey.

The ruby is our one heart, forever etched for generations to witness and know where they came from.

Let this chest serve as my gift to you today, my love. And to our future children who choose to follow their dreams as passionately as we did.

My love forever, Dionisio

The room went still with sentimentality. Some were moved by the romance; others felt pride and awe over his bravery and conviction. The jewelry box became even more precious now that we knew how it came to be.

"I am so honored that this was passed down to me," I said reverently. "But I'm still not sure why."

"Ah, my sweet *cugina*, because you are the dreamer of the family. Your Nonno Leigh was very astute; he could tell there was a passion in your soul that could not be subdued forever. In granting you this gift, it was his hope that it would unlock your heart to pursue what it is you truly desire."

"I don't know what to say."

"Mia, as we Italians say, *una buona mamma vale cento maestre;* a good mother is worth a hundred teachers. You have done well by your children and your family, and by that token, you have already earned this box. Just as you still need to learn how to open it, you are tasked with unlocking the mystery of your own heart. For my dear, it is not in a man, but in your dreams, where the key lies."

"So, there's more to it? Now we need to find a key? This never ends," Marissa moaned.

"The chest itself is for Mia, as the ring was for Megan and the statue is for you, Marissa. But that is not the end of your inheritance. Once you have it all, all will be revealed."

"Will we know then how to open this? I have been wondering if it was a solid box or simply locked. I hear something inside, though I can't find any indication of a keyhole."

"That is not for me to share, *cugine.* I've said too much as it is. Best to leave you with only this: the secret lies in Spain, and it will be up to Marissa to find the missing piece that brings it all together."

She said it so sternly that we knew better than to argue or probe the nun further. As sweet as she was, the ardor was in her to take you down if you disobeyed her. Instead, we thanked her and then turned the subject over to how we would celebrate the remainder of our time in dear Firenze.

That's when I got the call I was waiting for. I hung up with immense satisfaction.

"Who was that?" asked Meg.

"You'll see," I hinted.

"You are full of surprises, *cara.* This one isn't dangerous, too, is it?" Francesco asked, lifting his eyebrow at me.

"Not if we move quickly," I replied with a wink. "Sorella Maria, how would you like to go for a drive?"

I could not have expected her reaction to be any more heartwarming. Eyes bright as a child, wetting with tears, she reached out her hand as if she was seeing a mirage.

"This—this is my Nonno's house. Casa Bianchi," she said, her heart heavy and yet light.

"It is. Dominic's wife, Gloria, just called to let me know her children are all out with friends, and her husband will be at a lunch meeting for a few hours. She's agreed to let Sorella Maria see the house one last time. But we have to hurry," I urged.

"How could I ever thank you, Mia? Your heart is as true as they come. God bless you."

Gloria greeted us at the door with a warm embrace, helping to bring our cousin through the threshold of a home she once loved so dearly. She stood in the doorway, grasping onto every inch—the changes, along with the sacred details that seemingly withstood time.

"Right there, in that very corner, is where Nonna Ginerva would bake treats with us," she reminisced.

"And over there—on that wall, there used to be a huge deer head. Glad that's gone; it gave me such nightmares as a girl!"

Sorella Maria guided us from room to room, Gloria graciously allowing us to roam free. I thanked her for making this dream happen, while Sorella Maria continued to touch and feel her way through vivid memories.

"It is my pleasure," she assured me. "I never understood why families must be torn apart by such silliness and harbor resentment for generations. I guess I have a soft spot for those targeted by Dominica, as I've heard the stories from my kind grandmother-in-law about how Dominica made it her mission to disparage her every opportunity she got for marrying her beloved son.

"Her reign was not a gentle one, and it shaped generations of bitterness, entitlement and cruelty," she explained, shaking her head in sorrow. "I'm so glad you left your number, Mia. How sad it must have been for Sorella Maria all these years."

"I can't imagine. I truly appreciate you calling me. I didn't think your daughter was going to pass the message on to you, to be honest."

"Ah, that one. Teenagers. Got an air about her like her father, I'm afraid. He can be kind when he wants to be—which is what lured me into his web—but *only* when he wants to be."

"I hope we're not causing any problems by coming."

"Not at all. She has every right to be here. This should have been her home as much as it is ours. But, I must say it is getting late, and I am concerned my husband will return any minute," she cautioned.

Understanding, I gently prompted our crew to finish up the tour and get ready to head out. Just as we completed our goodbyes and were walking down the driveway, in pulled a hot red Ferrari with who I assumed was Dominic Moretti IV behind the wheel.

"What have we here?" he asked coolly from behind designer sunglasses and a hardened smirk.

"Francesco Marchesi," replied my handsome lover, putting out his hand for a macho handshake.

"And this is Meg, Mia, Marissa and Sorella Maria."

He nodded as Francesco pointed to each one of

us. Thankfully, Gloria came up from behind to play peacemaker.

"They're your family, sweetheart," she explained. "I invited them. Sorella Maria was a child when she was last here in her grandparent's home, and Mia thought it would be a nice gesture to let her come by and take a look at it, for old times' sake."

He was hardened, but slowly eased the tension in his body, removing his sunglasses and forcing himself to be courteous. I could tell it pained him greatly.

"Of course. I would never refuse such an honorable request. How did you find it, Sorella?" he asked, his voice dripping with repressed disapproval.

"It was ever as wonderful as I remembered it. Thank you for your kindness. It meant so much to me to remember my Nonno and Nonna like this," she said in her natural, loving way. She looked at him with a fondness. "I know your eyes. They remind me of my mother's."

He grunted a *"hmm"* in response, and I could tell he had enough of the pleasantries. Charmer.

"We must be going now," I prodded, as my sisters and Francesco began escorting our tired but happy cousin to the car. "Thank you again, Gloria."

We hugged and she made her way back towards the house. I prayed that she would not be retaliated against behind closed doors for her generosity.

"Oh, Mia—did I remember that correctly? Mia?" Dominic called, lightly grabbing my arm and pulling me to where the others couldn't hear.

"Yes."

"A little friendly…family advice," he sneered.

"What's that?"

"Watch your step when dealing with the rich and

powerful. You're out of their league, *bambina*." And with that, he let me go and walked towards the house with cocky arrogance, never looking back.

16

Although it unnerved me, I shook off what that prick Dominic had to say to me and refocused my attention on the car full of loved ones. We were making plans for dinner and decided to go back to Sorella Maria's since she was exhausted from all the excitement.

Everyone thought it would be safe enough to let her return home, as the polizia were still on site and would remain there until we left the country. No one wanted to harm the nun, we were certain; they were looking for us and knew we would be at Francesco's. As long as we left after dinner, all would be fine.

We made a quick stopover to pick up her overnight bag from Francesco's house, checked in at the now abandoned townhouse to ensure Lorenzo really didn't leave anything behind (good man, he didn't!) and then we were on our way to Sorella Maria's.

While our cousin returned to her room for a rest before dinner, Lorenzo pulled us aside to share the latest update from the authorities.

"I hate to tell you this, but it looks like this Jordan Kissinger somehow got away—again," he said, shaking his head, baffled. "The flight to New York was never canceled and he checked in online, so everyone was on high alert at both airports. But he never actually got on the plane."

"So, he never left?" Meg asked incredulously.

"That's just the thing," he replied. "He did. After they found no trace of him boarding or deplaning, they did a natural sweep of the surrounding airports. Turns out, he is more clever than we anticipated. A passenger by the name of Jordan Kissinger bought a last minute ticket out of Pisa to Boston, paid in cash.

"Since we were so certain he would be on the Florence to New York flight, no one ever contacted Interpol to watch the other airports, and he cleared right through customs without being tagged suspicious. *Stupido,*" he muttered.

"Is it verified that he landed in Boston?" I asked.

"His boarding pass was scanned as being on the plane and the flight attendants confirmed it was a full flight with no seat unattended. Boston customs confirmed a jewelry box and brooch matching the description as declared, so although anything is possible, it seems as though he is there, yes. Or rather, *was*. Probably rented a car or took public transportation to get home."

"At least we know his name. We *will* catch him, right?" I thought even if he escaped us now, there had to be a way to track him down.

"That's the other thing—we can't find a trace of someone named Jordan Kissinger based on the other identifying information we have. No DMV record, no social security, no passport on file—looks like he had dummy identification. Until he makes his next move, the trail's gone cold. I'm so sorry," he concluded.

"I wonder if the Morettis played a role in this," I said aloud.

"What makes you say that?" asked Marissa.

"As I was leaving, Dominic pulled me aside and gave me a warning that we were 'out of our league' trying to beat the rich and powerful."

"Why didn't you say something earlier, *cara?* If I get my hands on him—"

"Relax, Romeo," said Marissa, pulling Francesco back. "Go on, Mia."

"I just thought he was being a shit because we brought Sorella Maria to the house. But, it is curious how it was never broken into—nor was there an attempt to—when we laid such a good trap and whoever was following us instantly took the bait."

"That's true," agreed Meg. "I wonder if whoever it was, was already in contact with Moretti and called him to see if the jewelry box was really there or not. Obviously, he would learn that it wasn't and that we attempted to fool him. That would explain why he went to our place instead."

"Well, whatever the case, I will be keeping a close eye on that family," Francesco declared, his brother nodding his head in agreement. "If they are involved, I'll find out."

"So, are we able to be out in public yet? Or do we hold up in this mini-mansion until our flight leaves?" Marissa had an excellent question. So many unknown variables now, reminding us that we'll always have to watch our step until we find out who is behind this.

"*Signorine,* I believe you are safe to enjoy your final day tomorrow," said Lorenzo with conviction. "I believe Mr. Kissinger, or whatever his real name is, is in fact in the U.S. He has the fake box, the value of which he has verified according to his text, so there is no reason for him to doubt its validity—yet. His narcissism will convince himself that he has succeeded in scaring you all into submission while alluding authorities.

"His next move will be on New York soil, waiting for the ring that Mia promised him," Lorenzo added, shaking his head towards me as if to say that I took things a little too far. I should have listened and let it rest with the box for now.

"Besides, the text Horatio received while he was being interrogated is reassuring that the danger has been put on hold," he added. "The police have not seen any more incoming texts, except from a cohort who informed Horatio that he had also received a message saying the project was over and that he would be destroying his burner phone—though thanks to that text, the polizia were able to track him down and take him into custody as well before that happened. Both separately corroborated that it was only the two of them helping Kissinger, so I'm confident no one is available to do Kissinger's bidding at the moment.

"And thanks to Mia, again, she planted a bug I gave her in Moretti's home office while you were there, and a private investigator friend of mine is monitoring for any contact or plans made against you. So far, all he's heard was a conversation between Moretti and who he assumes to be a U.S.-grounded Kissinger, telling him that he was on his own now; Moretti didn't like you snooping around his family and wanted no further part in his plan. That's reassuring enough for me to believe the danger here has been lifted for the remainder of your stay.

"Not to mention, you still have your bodyguards—and us—so I don't see any reason why we can't enjoy the *Festa di San Giovanni* tomorrow."

"I agree. For now, the threat is minimized. Let's live for tonight and tomorrow and enjoy the wonderful company we keep." Francesco raised up his water glass in *saluti* as we agreed that was a splendid idea.

Dinner was bittersweet, knowing it would be our last with Sorella Maria. We exchanged more stories, dined on the oh-so-delicious Florentine steak one more time and filled the room with love and laughter. We said goodbye to our wonderfully kind and spirited cousin, as she would not be up for such a grand adventure as the festival the next day, and there would be no time to stop by again before our flight.

She thanked me profusely for giving her one of the greatest gifts she's ever received—the chance to see her grandparents' home once again. Then she performed a special blessing over me before we departed for Francesco's.

"*Comincia, che Dio provvede al resto.* All you need to do, child, is take that step towards your dreams, and God will see it through."

The evening at Francesco's around the fireplace was somber. We were all worn out from another two-week marathon of emotions and adventure. Lorenzo bid us farewell for the evening, followed by Meg, who wanted to call Kieran to see how his mum was faring. She not so subtly nudged Marissa up to her room as well, leaving only Francesco and me around the kitchen table.

I was grateful for that, as we had a red eye to catch the next day after the festival, and this would be the last chance for us to be alone together.

"Why so quiet, Mia Bella?"

"I'm always quiet," I joked.

"Yes, true. But more so tonight."

"My mind is in overdrive. A lot to process. The jewelry box meaning. This Kissinger guy getting away. Leaving tomorrow. I feel like even though a lot of good things came from this trip, I just didn't have enough time to digest it all before heading home."

"So stay."

"Stay? I can't stay." *Was he nuts?*

"Why not?"

"First, because I already booked a flight for tomorrow night. Second, I need to get home to my family."

"Well, first, you can always change your flight and extend your trip a few days. And second, doesn't your family deserve to welcome home a clear, 'processed' Mia? Just give yourself two more days here."

"You'd like that, wouldn't you?" I smirked.

"I would," he admitted. "But I am also fine with saying goodbye tomorrow as planned and letting you have the time you need to yourself without distraction. Even though I'd be tempted to track you down," he said sensually.

"I don't know. I mean, I guess two more days won't hurt, but isn't that unfair to my mom and Granny and even Kevin to have them keep watching over the kids while I spend two more days here in the lap of luxury?"

"Okay, we're going to forget about Kevin and how this might disrupt his life, after all he's done."

I went in for a rebuttal but he shut it down instantly with his raised palm.

"Mia, don't defend him. Yes, it takes two, and we know how it goes, but the truth is, those fantastic children of yours are not your sole responsibility in this world. You also have one to yourself. And I am sure Kevin is capable of managing being a single parent for a few more days before you take back over."

"True. He is."

"All right then. And so now you don't have to worry about your mother or grandmother, because he is a big boy and can handle it. Plus, your sisters are returning home and they can help if needed. You know they would support you on this."

"I know they would. You're right. I really do need

this," I said, pleading more to myself to let it happen, but also looking to him for the right answer.

"You don't need *my* permission. Consider this the new Mia—make your own choices, *cara,* and take control of designing the life you want. You don't need anyone's permission but your own."

"Do I need your permission to do this?" I asked slyly, seducing him into a heated kiss that had him dragging me willingly up the stairs and into his bedroom.

I wanted to cherish this moment, remember for one last time what it felt like to be so thoroughly touched and completely ravished by a man. Who knew when the next opportunity would arise, so I made sure to take my time tasting every morsel of his being, and giving him every ounce of mine.

We were going to make this night count.

Going to the *Festa di San Giovanni* on our last day was the perfect send-off. We didn't have much time in the morning for sexual distractions, so after I came out of the shower, I forced him into it before he could rip off my towel like the naughty imp he was.

Not fully packed, I perused the few dresses I left out in his closet, not knowing what to wear to this kind of an event. No, not this one. Or this one. Maybe…oh. I reached in and took out the garment bag with the dreaded silk dress from Ana.

I stared at it. *Do I dare?*

After arguing with myself for what seemed like an eternity, I figured, *what the hell?* At least if I tried it on and it looked awful, I could leave it behind with no regrets on my part, and no hard feelings on Francesco's. I had become much more confident in myself that a lousy fitting dress would not tear me down so easily. At least, I hoped it wouldn't.

But when I looked at my reflection in the mirror, I was shocked by what I saw. It actually fit as flawlessly as he promised; Ana was a genius designer. It hugged my curves in all the right places yet veiled my undesirables. Not in an oversized shirt "hide me" kind of way that I was used to, but in a flattering outline that accentuated every uniqueness of my shape.

The form-fitting brown leather jacket my sisters coerced me into buying, along with Ana's gifted jewelry set and those sexy brown boots, made my ensemble complete.

I really am beautiful just as I am, I thought to myself with tears in my eyes. I finally was able to see how others saw me, and it was the most exonerating feeling in the entire world. I was ready to love myself—all of me—and I vowed to never say a hateful, negative word to the woman standing in front of the mirror ever again.

I could hardly believe my transformation—and neither could Francesco as he stood motionless in the bathroom doorway.

"You look—stunning," he stuttered. "I'm—I'm at a loss for words. You take my breath away, Mia Bella."

I thanked him and allowed him a single sensual kiss; stopping us before we went too far. As much as I wished we could make love in this poignant moment, we had people waiting for us downstairs and he still needed to get dressed.

"You were right about this dress—right about a lot of things, actually. I'll never forget you, or this," I whispered with love, blowing him a kiss as I left the room to join the others.

After checking in on Sorella Maria and reporting that she was well, but tired, Lorenzo met up with our motley crew just in time for the festivities to begin.

We were fully entrenched in the Tuscan culture, awed by its colors, sounds and tastes. It began with a parade through the city—starting at Palazzo Vecchio and ending at the Duomo, where the brothers recommended we capture it.

Marchers dressed in bold gold, blue and red carried banners, played music and presented the traditional candles to the Archbishop as a nod to the ancient heritage of the city and its patron saint.

At the conclusion of the parade, we united with the citizens of Florence and its many tourists to attend the reverent mass at Santa Maria del Fiore. It was as if you could feel the presence of God looking down over all of us with pride and love as we paid our respects. It was humbling—reminding me not to forget to keep God in my life and as my strength.

We then spent the morning walking through the great city, where most businesses were closed but hot food stands lined the streets. We indulged in our favorite treats as we listened to the competing sounds of the talented musicians and watched the compelling acts of street performers.

We took a break from all the festivities to sit in an outdoor café and capture the moment like a Polaroid in our hearts.

"I'm going to miss this place," sighed Marissa.

"Me too," agreed Meg. "Although Ireland stole my heart, this is definitely a close second."

"Well, Florence has mine," I said reflectively, knowing that my life has forever changed. The time was right to share my decision to stay a bit longer.

"In fact, I've decided that I'm going to extend my trip here two more days. I need some time alone to reflect on everything that's happened. I've already changed my flight and worked it out with Kevin. I hope you're not upset with me."

"Why would we be? I think that's a great idea." I could always count on Meg to be supportive. "Take all the time you need. I guess this is as good a time as any to tell you that I actually changed my flight as well. I'm going to be spending the next month in Ireland with Kieran. We still have some stuff to sort out, and with his mum recently recovering, it's best that I go there."

"But what about your job? And Mia, what about the kids?" Marissa asked with her childlike pout. "Why am I the only one going back home?" We couldn't help but laugh at her dramatics.

"Sorry kiddo, but I've put my job before everything else for too long. I need this time to see if we can really make this relationship work."

"And I need to gather my thoughts so that I come home feeling sure about myself and ready to start my new life as a single mom—with big dreams to fulfill. Don't worry, Mar; your time is coming. In two short months, we'll be spending the end of the summer in Barcelona on *your* adventure."

"Yeah, you're right. But patience really isn't a virtue of mine," she whined. "I'm happy for you both. Just sucks for me to be going home alone on that long flight."

"We know. But maybe you need that space to yourself as well. Both Mia and I have gone through life-changing journeys, and I would expect nothing less to be waiting for you. Think about what matters most in your life and what you want next," Meg offered.

"Thanks, Meg. I guess always being surrounded by people, I'm just not used to being by myself. You're probably right. A little quiet time wouldn't hurt, would it?"

"It's why I'm staying. I need it right now more than anything else," I explained. They both looked at me with those suspicious sister eyes, and I knew exactly what they were thinking.

"No," I smirked. "I am not spending them with Francesco."

I looked up at him and we both smiled at each other with great affection.

"Mia Bella needs her time, and it's important that I am not there to distract her, as much as it will pain me to know she is still in the same city—especially looking like this," he said, playfully hanging his tongue out as if he was a drooling pup waiting for a dog biscuit.

"But alas, I have arranged for her to stay in a hotel, which will be well-guarded, as will she, just as a precaution. Tonight, we will bid farewell." He took my hand and kissed it sweetly, looking deeply and tenderly into my eyes.

"So, if you won't be with this hunky man, what will you be doing?" asked Marissa. I think she was baffled by my decision to choose solitude over great sex.

"I'm not sure yet. I know I'll end up in a garden at some point, but I think I am just going to take the moments as they come."

Ending our meal on that note, we had just enough time to attend the Calcio Storico game before my sisters' flights that evening. Apparently, the men we were traveling with had extensive connections throughout this entire city and were able to hook us up with an entrance to this sold-out fan favorite.

It was one of the most fascinating events I've ever

attended. Not being a sports fan, I was surprised at how intrigued I was by the players dressed in full medieval garb in what was an interesting combination of soccer, rugby and wrestling. I think what surprised me most was their ability to move around in their getups, let alone play a sport!

When it was over, we began making our way over to the airport, with Lorenzo taking his leave for the evening to go on a first date with a woman whose name we learned was Loretta. Tears, hugs and well wishes abound, Meg set off for her month-long romance and Marissa was ready to head back home, promising to keep an eye on Brittany so that I would return to a still-happy mother-daughter relationship.

Our sister time in Italy had come to an end, but I had one last evening before I was ready to go it alone.

There was no better way to enjoy our time together than by taking a boat ride down the Arno River to watch the celebratory fireworks display. Warm tears stung my eyes, knowing that the time I dreaded was finally upon us; we were at the end of our journey.

"I'm going to miss you," I barely hushed in a breathless tone.

This man had helped me access my vulnerability and embrace it. To accept myself, and dare I say, even love myself just as I am. To give me that little nudge I needed to follow my heart and fervently want to pursue my dreams of opening my restaurant. He gave me so much more than a sexual awakening; he blew open the doors to reveal the very essence of myself.

"I will miss you, too, Mia Bella. I hope you will remember all that you learned here. I hope now that you have found yourself, that you will never close your heart up again—not to love, not to dreams, not to yourself. I wish nothing but a life full of love and joy for you, my beautiful Mia."

Not knowing it was possible to have a kiss so deep, passionate and tender all at the same time, I lost myself in his sincerity and his exploring tongue. Feeling his hands holding my face and his fingers caressing my hair, I joked that if *this* was how he was going to kiss me goodbye, then he shouldn't be surprised if I *do* end up on his doorstep one last time before I left—something he acknowledged he would not mind at all.

In fact, he still wanted the pleasure of removing this silken dress off my body after one final nightcap tonight, and then he promised he would let me go on my solitary retreat. It didn't take much to convince me to spend one more evening with this glorious man.

We then needed no more words, falling into each other as we gazed towards the sky's horizon.

As vivid colors lit up the heavens like an exploding rainbow, we sat in silence with my body against his in an embrace, licking our salted caramel gelato cones. I felt warm, comfortable—content. Yes, this trip had changed me in many ways. It made me realize that our Grandfather Leigh truly knew what he was doing when he set this whole plan in motion.

These journeys really were about more than just family treasures—they were about *us*. Meg opened her heart to true love. I opened mine to myself.

Bianchi Family Tree

Bianchi Family Line

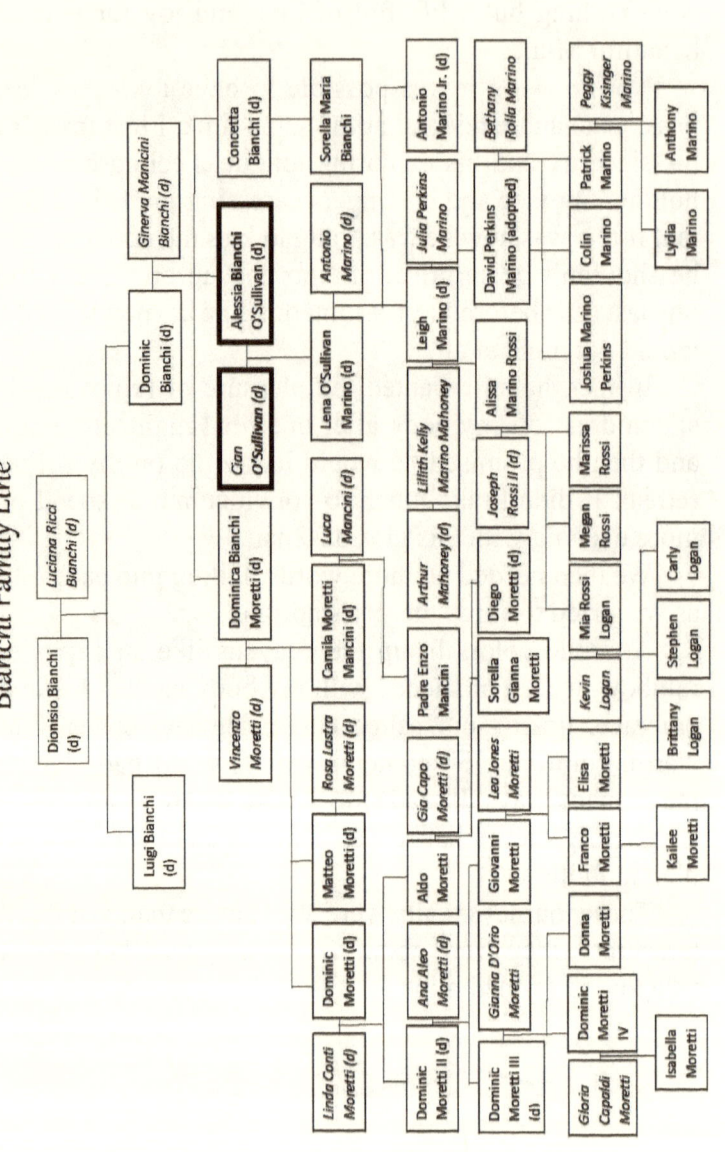

The Catalan Key

BOOK THREE OF THE LOST HERITAGE TRILOGY

by Jenny Dee

To every woman who ever doubted herself; we are all the dark and the light. May we find peace with our flaws and embrace our authenticity.

We are perfect just as we are.

1

"**D**on't stop," I moaned, as the dripping of the hot wax made my chest flinch. I looked into the eyes of my lover, who knew exactly what I needed to feel better.

Knew how when I was feeling angry or insecure, the best thing to do was to fuck it out.

Now, don't go judging me. I'm not like my pretentious, perfect oldest sister, Megan, or my girl scout of a sister, Mia. I never saw how living the "good girl" life was any fun. Besides, someone needed to be the rebel of the family.

It's not like I am necessarily a "bad girl," either. I don't do anything hardcore. I've dabbled with some drugs, but I grew out of that phase, realizing pot was all I needed to soothe my nerves. It was cleaner and quicker than a trip to the beach. I didn't need to chant with my feet in the sand to make life better.

Combine a good high with my love of sex, and it made life super pleasurable. After all, isn't that what we are here for on this planet? To enjoy it?

I fully intend to live life to the fullest until someone has to cart me away in a wooden box. Preferably laced with diamonds.

The way things were going, I was on my way to having everything I've ever wanted in life. Soon, I'd be going to Spain to claim my lost heritage and have all the money I could ever need to build my art gallery and buy a beautiful house like both my sisters have.

Looking over to the man who just made me orgasm multiple times over the last four hours (thank you, roomie, for having a business trip!), I also knew I had found the one who finally understood me and accepted me as I was—the flawed, yet gorgeous human being I am.

I have no problem admitting I am hella sexy. I am proud of my exotic, Mediterranean looks, my long, dark jet black hair that loves to be pulled and my luminescent blue eyes that call, 'come hither, my love.'

My body has made the boys swoon my entire life, following after me like a puppy dog begging for a bone. Put on a tight leather dress and stiletto boots that ride my legs like a biker on his hog, and I can pretty much get anyone I want.

But this one—this one actually wants more than that from me. He gives me everything my body craves yet stimulates my mind and heart in ways I never thought possible.

I finally feel supported in my dreams of becoming an artist. I'm not put down over my "choice" of a bartending career as I fight for my rightful place in the creative community. He knows that it takes time and the right opportunity, and with his connections, he's working on getting me more exposure for my recent canvases of Ireland and the ones in my head of Italy I've promised him.

Even though those trips were more about my sisters and their journeys and not mine, I was still inspired by them to go back to my craft. Long hours trying to make ends meet didn't leave much time for sculpting or painting or even doodling; but after witnessing the pure beauty of those Irish landscapes, I couldn't help but be called to capture them with my watercolors.

Those majestic Cliffs of Moher where Megan had her epiphany and remembered who she was; how the curvature of the mountain resembled the profile of an old woman, earning its name as Hag's Head. How there was no beginning nor end to the sunset-layered sky, melting into fiery reds and oranges imprinted in my memory.

Then there was the fascinating, weathered lighthouse at Clare's Island. Just Mia and I took that trip for an absolutely amazing few days at the spa. I made a painting especially for her, knowing she found her serenity in a book, miles away from the challenges of home. I had hoped that it would symbolize lighting her own way, no matter how dark it got.

For Mom and Granny, I recreated an image of our ancestral home, so that they could look at it and feel like they were a part of our journey, even from across the ocean. Within it, I etched the imagery of the ring that Meg received as a family heirloom to make it truly a meaningful, O'Sullivan family painting.

Damn, was that rock stunning, by the way. Green diamond? *Of course, meant for Meg,* I thought sardonically. Whatever. Moving on.

Me—I was so captivated by the art galleries and culture that I ended up sculpting a few smaller pieces of art...a mini Spanish Arch, the Blarney Castle's Witch Stone and a pint of Guinness, which secretly represented my own little love affair in the Emerald Isle, I recalled bashfully to myself. My sisters weren't the only ones to have some fun, you know.

I'm very proud of my work. So much so, that as soon as this sex marathon is over, I'll get back to creating my Italian inspirations.

I happened to like Florence just a tad bit more than

Ireland, though they are both so culturally unique that it would be unfair to compare them. After taking the long, half a day's worth flight back home all by myself, I had more than enough time to start brainstorming sketches of the scenery.

I definitely needed a vineyard painting—a beautiful scene filled with intertwining grapevines in the background, with an elegantly set table with glasses of wine off to the side, and a bin of partially crushed red and purple grapes front and center; maybe with a foot walking towards it to represent our cool, make-your-own-wine stomping experience.

Oh, and somehow I'd love to weave in Mia's expertly carved jewelry box. Or, make that a different painting. To be determined. Wait—I got it—the Bardini Garden with its wisteria tunnel and the box lying on the ground with a simple ray of sunlight that escaped in through the trees to highlight it. Yes, I liked that imagery very much.

Speaking of gardens—wow. All the statues in those beautifully manicured estates—those heavenly white marbled carvings of wildlife and deities joined together in play and protection; they took my breath away.

Not typically much of a gardener, I was suddenly inspired to design a landscape that I would have once I purchased my new home. Mia can help me with the floral arrangements (and maybe keep them alive), but the statues would be of my own creation.

I can hear them now, the visitors...*oh Marissa, these are exquisite! Where did you get these?*

They are one-of-a-kind Rossi originals, I would reply. *I'd be happy to create an inspired piece for your own garden, if you'd like.*

Oh, yes please! they'd demand.

I'd perhaps make some for my own art gallery; the one I will open up by the end of this year with good ole Grampy's inheritance (I hope).

Though I will admit that the greatest piece of work that I am inspired to conceive somehow—not sure yet if by paint or clay—will pay homage to the Tree of Love that the Marchesi brothers took us to see in a small, random town, with its intricate branches and symbolic medallions. Now that was something to admire.

Although, I did kind of cringe when they bestowed a blessing of eternal love and luck on me while standing in front of the enchanted tree. At that time, I knew I was falling for the amazing man lying beside me, but given my track record, I'm hesitant to believe anything in my life is meant to last.

I usually end up sabotaging it and pushing people away. But then again, they are usually assholes and when I finally get their number, out the door they go.

But looking over at my love, his naked body glistening from the sweat and indications of fatigue forming around his beautiful emerald green eyes, I knew there was something different about him. He had been there for me through this entire journey, supporting me even when I felt left behind while Meg and Mia had their special adventures.

Why am I always the last one? Does it always have to go in age order?

I know, I do have a little (okay, medium-sized) green monster living inside my head. She's ugly, too. Who could blame me, though? These so-called amazing "sister" trips never turn out as planned. I'm pushed to the side like some tag-along so they can go "find themselves."

And now both my sisters have exactly what they wanted and decided to leave me behind (again) to come back to

New York alone. At first, I wondered how they could do that to me, but then I realized it was nothing different from normal.

Well, at least not for Meg, who has always been self-absorbed. It's not that I begrudge her love—I am truly happy she has finally found someone and opened her heart to Kieran. I can't help but really like him and think he is exactly what she needs in a partner to keep her from being so serious all the time.

I just wish her new love and Ireland-inspired transformation would have returned her to the sister who used to remember that I existed and paid a little more attention to my life.

But it's actually Mia who surprised me the most. She always cares about everyone and checks in on me more than anyone else bothers to. I guess she deserves time to think about herself and stay in Italy a few more days, but still. Ugh. I'm not good at doing this alone thing.

The only thing making me feel a little better about all of this is knowing my time is coming two months from now. But I'm not exactly the patient type.

Yes, I'm complicated. I'm up and down with my emotions and opinions. I love and hate equally. I can be extremely impulsive, stubborn and feisty. Sometimes irrational. I think with passion instead of logic.

I can't help it, but looking over again at my hot and sexy boyfriend, I can finally say I hit pay dirt.

Joshua Perkins.

Who knew that the moment he walked through that door to tell us about some unknown grandfather, that it would be more than an instant attraction? Yeah, I know I've been lying to my family about dating my old roommate, Tony.

As if. He couldn't find my G-spot if his life depended

on it.

But Joshua—oh my God!—we clicked like a key in a lock.

At first, I thought he had a pull towards my big sister, but he told me that Meg was way too proper for him. As the youngest in his family, he could relate to that feeling of never being good enough, so he was able to see me for who I really was, and not just my looks—the only thing everyone else seemed to care about.

It started with mind-blowing sex. Jesus, how he was open to my kinky side. Not that I am a crazy sadist, but I didn't mind a little game of bondage, a little light whip or a nipple clamp here and there. He indulged my sexual fluidity by allowing another woman to join us so I could still experience the sweetness of the female touch and taste.

He even didn't mind when I invited another man to devour me while he watched.

Don't worry, I am always safe. I may be sexually adventurous, but I'm not stupid. No man (or woman) will be giving me any kind of disease or getting me knocked up, thank you. Kids were not for me. Not at the moment, anyway. I had a career to jumpstart first and didn't really think I was the settle-down type.

At least, I wasn't until Joshua crossed my path. Now, as I lie here in his arms and think about how he has been there for me all these months and how deep our feelings have grown for each other, I've realized that maybe I could have my own happily ever after, after all.

I've struggled with telling my family about him, even though he's told me from the very beginning that I should just be honest with them; that there is nothing to hide. Unfortunately, my relationships don't tend to last, so I hold off on admitting to being in one until I know there may be a chance it could work.

I also just can't stand the judgment that oozes out of the eyes of my loved ones. Just like when Meg deduced that Tony wasn't my roommate anymore because we slept together. Like she was so virtuous.

I'm not going to get into her private life, but on the outside, she pulls off the perfect lady illusion and enjoys a detached sex life behind the scenes—well, that was before Kieran, anyway. Funny how when we were listening to the story about our wicked ancestral aunt Dominica appearing one way to society, but another way privately, I unfairly matched her to Meg. I know, my sister isn't that bad. I love her. But it doesn't mean I can't stand her sometimes.

Back to me, though. It's frustrating to hide who I am so that I'm not looked down upon all the time. Especially by my "perfectly" behaved family.

I love sex. I don't know why that is such a problem in today's world. Women get such a bad rap for pursuing it and enjoying it, and that's bullshit. Our bodies were made for pleasure just like men, and you don't see them branded with vicious names like slut or whore.

But if that's the label you want to slap on me, go right ahead. I'm still going to do my thing and not apologize for it.

I might have to apologize for keeping Josh a secret, though. Sure, they've been fine with me not saying anything until things got more serious in the past. But I'm not so sure they're going to be okay with me having lied about his identity and making them think it was Tony. Or letting them alternatively think it was my current apartment pal, Jay. After all, he's my best friend and it would have made more sense.

I have my reasons for pretending, though. I really didn't

think it would get so—complicatedly real. But I had to cave and reveal my lover's "name" at some point because my caring, yet perceptive sisters could tell I was getting something more than a good roll in the sheets. Apparently, I was glowing.

I didn't mean to lie. It just came out. I knew that Josh's connection to our grandfather's family might hurt Granny's feelings. After all, he is the great nephew of the woman who married our grandfather. After everything she had been through, I wanted to protect her. I didn't want to be the reason she had a heart attack or something; she has already weakened physically since having to relive this experience.

But now I was at a crossroads. I never expected to fall in love with Josh, and I was pretty certain he had deep feelings for me, too. I knew I had to come clean.

Maybe that was part of my new journey—to not be afraid of disappointing my family anymore. To live my life without apologies and have everyone just accept me for who I am. Maybe now that it's my turn, the focus would *finally* be on me and *my* happiness.

"There seems to be a lot going on in that beautiful head of yours," his sultry voice spoke, breaking my deep thoughts. "What's going on?"

"Nothing. Just thinking."

"What about?" He turned so that his glare could burn right through me with kindness and love. I adored how his cat-like eyes sat glowing within his rounded, whiter-than-an-Irishman pale face, with a sharp nose and thin lips that curved into a mischievous smile.

He had a killer body, made possible by his gym addiction

and perhaps acrobatic-like sexual performances. His arms were solid, as was his six-pack. And I was certainly not unhappy to see the package waiting underneath his boxers for me the moment our clothes first hit the floor.

This man was fucking fine. And, he genuinely cared about my feelings, making him even sexier to me. He was so easy to open up to. It was a bonus that he came into this situation already knowing about the heritage journey, so he was instantly protective from the beginning.

Plus, he never once probed; he always respected my grandfather's request that the contents of the letters remained a secret. Whenever I wanted to share, he would stop me and say that he couldn't betray his professional oath—even if he was curious. I really respected that about him.

Trust has never been easy for me, but I found myself able to share whatever was in my heart so easily with Josh, knowing that he would never judge me.

"Pretty much everything, I guess. How my sisters are still off gallivanting through Europe while they left me on my own to come back here to nothing."

"So, I'm nothing now," he teased, faking a stab to the heart.

"No, silly. That's not what I meant," I said as I gave him a light pull of his dirty blonde, messy head of tousled hair. "You know exactly what I mean. They are off in their brand new rich lives after having wonderful, meaningful adventures and I'm just stuck here waiting for my turn."

"Your turn is coming, my love. Spain is only two months away. Then it will be all about you, just like you like it," he joked.

I ignored his mocking. I was trying to be serious. Wisely, he caught on and stopped kidding around.

"Marissa, just have a little patience. If your journey is anything like your sisters', then you are in for one hell of a ride. Enjoy the moment, babe. Don't rush through it."

"You're right, I guess. I just hope that it will be as amazing for me as it was for them."

"It will be. I promise."

"How can you promise something like that?"

"Because I see your heart, and I know what you deserve. Your grandfather orchestrated this so that each one of you had a special heirloom—and an awakening to come. He never met you face to face, but it seemed as though he did a psychically flawless job of understanding exactly what your sisters needed and represented; I have no doubt he knows the same for you."

His perspective was always insightful…and usually on target. Damn it, I hate a man who's right all the time.

"Thank you for saying that," I responded, before my mind wandered off again to the clouds.

"Now where did you go? Come on. Talk to me," he urged, gently stroking back a loose tendril of hair from my face.

"I—I just wonder what's in store for me. You said that my grandfather would know what I needed, but that's just the thing. What is it? Meg's journey was about love—isn't that something, as a single woman at the time, he would wish for me to have?

"But then Mia's journey was about following her dreams—yet again, isn't that what I have been struggling to do for years? If it's not love or success for me, then what is it?" I couldn't help but ramble on now that the emotional flood gates had opened.

"Meg has always been the smart, ambitious one. She has gotten everything she's ever wanted in her life. Granted, she's worked hard for it—but even the moment she wished for real love, *poof!* Her wish was the universe's command—or rather, some Blarney witch's spell manifested.

"And Mia has always been the kind, good-hearted sister who people adore, and now that she wants to pursue her childhood vision of opening a restaurant, no one questions her and we're all supposed to be completely on board to help in any way we can. I can't help but feel like it won't be the same for me.

"I've always been the impulsive, black sheep of my family. I know they love me, and I don't doubt it for a second. But it's always Meg with her condescending 'wow, that was actually a deep thought' shit and Mia with her patronizing 'one day it will happen' crap that gets me.

"I don't want to wait anymore, Josh. I don't want to live beneath their expectations—or mine. I am smarter than they give me credit for, kinder than they see and more determined than ever to get exactly what I want."

"And what is it that you want?" I thought long and hard before answering that one.

"Respect. And I'm tired of trying to earn it."

"Well, you already have mine," he smiled as he looked at me, running a finger down my reddened cheek.

"I see who you are, Marissa. I see the brilliance. I see the hard work ethic and the passion behind your recent artwork—they are outstanding and full of life and emotion. You have a golden heart that has sucked me in without warning.

"I love you."

I did not see that coming. I mean, I felt it, at least on my side, but I didn't know that he would actually return my feelings. Suddenly, I felt extremely uncomfortable and started to rise from the bed. He gently stopped me and pulled me back down so that our naked bodies were warm against each other—but it was a different warmth than sexual afterglow.

"Did you hear what I just said?"

"Yes," I squeaked out.

"I love you with every ounce of my soul. I knew it from the moment I laid eyes on you. And not just your smoking body, which I am very much fond of," he added seductively before turning back to genuine.

"I love every part of you. The woman inside—the insecure one, the fiery one—even the bitchy one. But most especially, the one who takes me as I am, listens to me and makes me feel like there is no other man in the world." He hesitated, looking down, almost afraid to make eye contact for a moment.

"Am I alone in this feeling?" he finally asked, before raising his head up once again to look into my deer-in-a-headlight spooked eyes.

He let me take a few moments to catch my breath and formulate a response. Usually, I can drop the "L" bomb like no big deal even after a few weeks; it was so easy for me to fall in and out of love. But this man—this man right here had changed the game on me.

I really, truly, sincerely, without a doubt, love him. And that scares the shit out of me. Because this time—this time when I say it, my heart means it.

"These last few months have been absolutely amazing, in so many ways. No one has ever been as supportive and on my side as you have—without judgment, without chiding me, without ever making me feel less.

"You've inspired me, challenged me and accepted me for everything that I am, the good and the bad. You don't know how much you being here has meant to me. I've never experienced anything like this before.

"I do love you; I love you, Joshua Perkins, with every cell of my being."

He then leaned in for a slow burning kiss, one that was not of rushed or dramatic lust; but of a gentle, soul-deepening, heart-melting connection. We then made love—*love*—in a way that I had never experienced with a man before.

It was then that I decided the charade was up. I loved this man, and he loved me, and it was time to stop living in the shadows.

2

With Meg still out of town and Mia sick from traveling, both unable to attend for what would typically be our traditional Sunday family dinner, I thought it was the perfect way to break the news gently to Mom and Granny first—instead of to a whole crowd of watchful eyes.

I decided I would announce that I was seeing (and in love with) Josh, and that he would be joining us for dessert so they could get to know him better. By the end of this evening, my secret would be out, and I could finally live life in the open.

But first, I had to get through this day. I had hours before dinner, and my mind was racing through all of the different scenarios. Would they accept him with big, warm Granny hugs? Would they go into inquisition mode? Would they be happy for me or tell me I was crazy? Oh God, make it five o'clock already so I can get this over with.

I had to find something to do to pass the time, so I started baking. Now, Mia was a chef extraordinaire in the kitchen but baking—that was my jam. No one came close to my confectionery delights; I was in high demand around the holidays for my scratch-made cookies, cakes and pies.

But what to make for Sunday dessert in the summer? Oh, I know—they love my fresh fruit tarts. I'll make mini portions and fill them with different favorite fruits. Raspberries for Granny, banana cream for Mom and a tropical mango for Bruce, my mom's new boyfriend.

I liked Bruce well enough, but he was another one who always seemed to be questioning me as a human being. He was kind, funny and polite. Yet something was off; I couldn't put my finger on it, but there was this vibe about him that made me edgy.

No use in telling Mom about this though. She was head over heels for this man, and I am the last person on earth who would want to take her happiness away—especially since it took her years before she could even look at a man after Daddy died. No, I would have to trust her judgment and hope that he really was the good person she claimed he was. Even though I think at heart, she is way too innocent a person to be an intuitive judge of character—especially with men. Time will tell, I guess.

I secretly wished he would not be there tonight so that I could talk with Mom and Granny alone, but maybe it wouldn't hurt to have another male body around as I introduced Josh to the tigresses. He could help run interference—I was pretty sure I could at least count on him for that. You know, male solidarity and all.

While kneading the dough for the crusts, I realized my unfocused anxiety was shredding my delicate tart bases and I had to start over. Maybe using a rolling pin wasn't such a good idea. I thought blondies might be safer, so I was happy to find some white chocolate chips in the cabinet. *Good, I don't have to make a store run*—my decision was made.

While the blondies were cooling, I began pacing again, trying to find the right words to use tonight. Why was this so difficult? Why couldn't I just come out and say it? Since when was I shy about telling anyone what was on my mind?

Because I loved him. Because it was real. Because I

never brought home a man to my family I believed was "the one" who would last. For once, I was really frightened over whether or not I would get their approval. I think I just bit my last decent nail off.

Turns out, I had nothing to worry about. Seated at my grandmother's Lenox-set kitchen table, dining on her famous meatloaf, the words just naturally came to me when they asked what was new in my world.

"Joshua Perkins? You mean that lawyer who read us my father's will?" asked Mom incredulously.

"Yes," I said sheepishly. "I wanted to tell you earlier, but I was afraid to hurt Granny's feelings, since he, well, you know—is Julia's family."

"Oh my darling, Marissa," Granny began, looking at me with her pretty blue eyes that matched her pants suit. "I wish you didn't keep this a burden all to yourself. You poor thing. All this time, worrying about *me* and wondering if I would be okay with it?"

I looked at her with rare tears in my eyes and simply nodded my head.

"My beautiful girl, you do not know me very well at all," she advised with a kind smile. "I would never judge a man based on who his family was. If that were the case, then you would never exist, now would you?"

She made a valid point. The Marinos were assholes, and yet she fell deeply in love with my grandfather. He turned out to be an asshole as well, but at least he was a good enough man to admit it in the end.

"Besides, I never had a problem with Julia herself," she explained. "I never met the woman, obviously, but I do remember Leigh telling me about her when we ran away to get married. He felt bad about leaving the woman he was betrothed to behind with the society of wolves, saying she was quite a lovely and nice person.

"And when Joshua was here—under attack from all of us, I might add—he held his own, and was very sympathetic and patient as we grieved and learned all about Leigh's plan. I would very much like to meet him under different circumstances and get to know the man who has stolen our girl's heart."

"I agree, sweetheart," added Mom. "It brings me such joy to see a sparkle in your eyes and love in your heart. We should have him join us next week for dinner."

"Well," I began, "I already invited him for dessert tonight. I hope that's okay. He'll be here in about an hour."

They both looked at each other and smiled. "Perfect. We can't wait."

I was so relieved that they were supportive instead of angry with me. This was going to be a great night after all—I think. But I noticed Bruce sitting back in his chair, tall, dark and sophisticated like the lawyer type that he is (yet much more stuffy than my Josh) with an air of disapproval on his boy-next-door face.

I wanted to ask, *What's wrong, Bruce? Sad that you are no longer the only Alpha male of the group?* But my Mom, who must have noticed his distance herself, beat me to it.

"You're awfully quiet, my dear. What's wrong?" He managed a fake grin as he looked into her eyes to respond.

"Nothing at all. You were having a family discussion. It's not my place to butt in," he said, but then turned to my direction. "Not that it is my business, but I think it is wonderful that you have found someone that makes you so happy."

If he had a bridge to sell, I wasn't about to buy it. Did

my Mom and Granny really fall for his faux blessing? Not wanting to let this jackass ruin my good mood, I excused myself so I could call Josh to let him know the good news—that they were waiting to welcome him with open arms.

It was a delightful evening. Everyone—including stodgy Bruce—managed to interact swimmingly and all get along. Although I noticed a few awkward exchanges between the men, for the most part, it was easygoing and lighthearted. I couldn't have asked for a better night.

As we were getting ready to leave, Mom pulled me over to the side.

"I am glad you finally told us, baby girl. None of us really believed it was Tony," she hinted.

"You didn't?" She just laughed her 'you can't get anything past your mom' laugh.

"Not for a second," she replied. "But I did think it might have been Jay, so you got me there. I knew you would tell us when you were ready. As long as he makes you happy, I am thrilled for you, my sweet daughter."

"I am really happy, Mom. I've never felt like this before. It's kinda crazy."

"Good. It's supposed to be a crazy adventure, this love thing. Have you told your sisters?"

"Not yet." Even though I knew deep down they would support me, I couldn't help but fear the inevitable taunting.

"Well, next week, Meg will be calling in for dinner and we can leave you and Mia to speak with her alone before we all join around the table. I'd expect that you'd want to bring Josh every week?"

"I haven't thought that far ahead, Mom. I can't—if I do, I'm afraid this will all blow up in my face."

"Oh my girl, if there is one thing you must learn, it is that you deserve the happiness in front of you, and that it can last. Don't be so caught up in fear that you push joy away," she warned. I looked at her with my little girl eyes full of terror and nodded in consent. I was so not comfortable in this unchartered territory called love.

"It will all be okay," she soothed as she drew me in for a big mama bear hug. God, how I loved this woman.

"That went surprisingly well," Josh said as we sat in the car in front of my apartment.

"I know," I replied. "I didn't expect that."

"I really like your grandmother. She's hysterical."

"Yeah. She seemed to like you, too. I can tell," I beamed.

"Not sure about your mom's boyfriend, though," he noted.

"I noticed you giving each other looks all evening. Do you know him?"

"Not quite. Our firms cross paths on occasion, so I know of his reputation. Excellent criminal lawyer, from what I hear. We sometimes get involved behind the scenes when contested wills or nasty divorce settlements come into play."

"Oh." He was hiding something. I could tell from the way he shifted his eyes uncomfortably.

"What?" he asked as I stared him down.

"Why do I feel like there's more to this story?" He hesitated, huffing out a huge breath of frustration.

"Listen, Mar, I just met your family. I don't want to cause any problems."

"If there is something I should know, then spill it. We promised to always tell it to each other straight, remember?"

"Okay. But promise me you won't go storming off in a

fit of rage when I tell you."

"I wouldn't—okay, I promise," having to swear an oath because he was right. I might be a little bit of a hothead.

"I've never met Bruce personally, but I have heard of him. Rumors only, though. Nothing verifiable."

"Rumors about what?" I nudged.

"I don't know how to tell you this," he started off, procrastinating all the way. I sat cross-armed in the car staring him down like a drill sergeant, waiting for him to stop being so damn theatrical about it and just tell me already.

"His now ex-wife had brought him up on charges of physical assault, which led to their divorce. His name was cleared, but whenever you hear a story like that, it makes you wonder if he is guilty and used his connections to get off, or if he really is innocent."

I just sat there, the pissy-ness growing instead me like an oak tree from an acorn. The anger was mighty and he knew me well—I was about to explode. I *knew* something was off about him. If that man even *thinks* of laying a hand on my mother…

"Babe, I didn't tell you to upset you. You asked. I just met your mom and she seems really nice—and vulnerable. He could very well be harmless. But if I kept quiet and something happened to her, I would never forgive myself."

I started to come down from a boil to a simmer. Just his presence was the soothing force I needed in my life to bring me rationality before impulse. Plus, the fact that he was wearing a green polo shirt that matched those crazy intense eyes of his didn't hurt to distract me from my semi-murderous thoughts.

"How credible are your sources?" I asked in a monotonous, no feeling tone.

"It's an actual case. Public record. No evidence to support her claims, though, which is why it was dismissed. She could have been after his money and made it up. Don't rush to conclusions," he advised.

"All I am saying is to watch your mom for any signs of distress and to monitor him for any signs of a suppressed personality. I'm sure she can handle herself. She doesn't seem like the insecure type to be with a man who would abuse her in any way."

He made a valid argument there. My mother wasn't one to allow any monkey business; the first sign of anything off and she'd be out of there. Naïve or not, of that, I was certain.

I decided I would just catalogue this nugget of information in the recesses of my brain and keep a close watch on this Bruce guy. I'll give him the benefit of the doubt for now—but one wrong move, and that man will wish he never crossed my path.

The next Sunday, Mia and I arrived earlier to video chat with Meg and Kieran before Josh and Bruce arrived for dinner. We were having it at Mom and Granny's again because the kids caught Mia's cold and her house was festering with germs. And my apartment was out of the question because Jay already had plans for friends to come over to watch a baseball game.

I told them about Josh, and they were much more encouraging and excited for me than I expected. In fact, I was waiting for Meg's chiding about how she thought she would be the one to land him first, or joke that he was just the next victim in a long line of broken hearts, but she surprised me by saying she noticed the immediate chemistry and was genuinely thrilled that I was in love.

Mia was a little more cautious, with her motherly and ex-wife of a cop questions, but I think I answered them all to her satisfaction as she enveloped me in a big sister hug. I can't even begin to describe the weight that has finally been lifted off my shoulders. I should have never doubted my family's love and support for me. Sometimes I really do think I have them built up in my head all wrong.

As Mia was setting the dining room table with Granny, and I helped Mom place the pot roast into serving dishes in the kitchen, I thought it was the ideal time to check in on her before the men showed up.

"So, how are things going with Bruce?"

"Very well," she beamed. She looked exceptionally pretty today in a mauve-colored sundress with harmonizing sandals—even her fingers and toes matched. I loved how her style was always so complementary and precise.

"I really like him, Mar. He is so thoughtful. The other day I mentioned that I had a little pink parasol as a child for whenever I was out in the sun, and next thing you know, I had one in my hands before he took me on a sunset stroll," she said dreamily.

"That's sweet. So…he's good to you?" I investigated, not so subtly. She was visibly taken aback by my detective-like tone, jerking up to a straightened back, defensive position.

"Yes, very good. He is one of the kindest, most gentle men I've ever known—aside from Daddy. Why are you asking me this?"

"Well, Mom, you can never be too careful these days," I alluded. But she's a smart cookie. She knew exactly what I was talking about, and somehow, I was reassured by that.

"I assume you heard about his ex-wife's allegations?"

she said, turning back to wipe off some of the gravy drippings that fell onto the counter with double annoyance.

"Yes, but only because Josh thought we should know," I defended. "He didn't want to cause trouble, but he thought it wouldn't be right if he kept the information to himself. He didn't want anything bad to happen to you in case the rumors were actually true."

"Honey, I'm not mad at Josh," she said, cooling down her almost-temper at having to defend the man she loved. "I think it's sweet how he looks out for you and was worried about me. It's endearing. But neither of you have anything to worry about."

"Are you sure?"

"Yes, baby. Bruce was upfront with me about it from the beginning and we have had long talks. The allegations were just that—he never laid a finger on Eleanor. And I believe that. He has never given me any indication he is capable of violence, ever."

"That's good to hear," I exhaled with relief. "Just promise me that you will be careful, though, anyway. I love you, Mom."

"I love you, too, baby. You do the same," she counseled, her mama spidey-senses tingling as an automatic reflex.

With everyone seated around the table, it felt great to be all together again as a family. Even the men appeared to put their questionable dislike for each other aside for an evening of pleasant conversation.

Meg and Kieran were only on the phone for an hour before they had to go to bed (it was way into the wee late hours for them) but they filled us in on how well his mum recuperated from her rib fracture and how they were settling into domestic, yet temporary, bliss.

Kieran finally finished recording his Celtic rock band's

first album, and in just two more months, it was set to be released to the public. Gov's, his father's bequeathed pub, has now been sold to his business partners and he was free to live life as a romantic nomad. It suited him, that kind of existence.

Meg, completely enamored with her new life, was contemplating leaving the advertising world altogether—something I never expected her to do in all the adult years I've known her. Instead, she wanted to pursue her lifelong dreams of traveling and writing, and planned to continue her exploration of the world well after our trip to Spain.

Mia shared about her last two days in Italy, surprising us with the fact that she did not see Francesco after that night, keeping to her intention of having alone time. She spent one of her days entirely in an off-alley bookstore, wrapped up in a novel and indulging in cappuccino and decadent pastries.

On her last day, she went back to the Bardini Garden, where she sat and reflected on her journey and how much her experience in Florence healed her heart. Nature soothed her soul and reminded her about the important things in life. She came home refreshed and ready to juggle double duty as a single mother and restaurant owner—something she planned to jump on after our trip to Spain. Since we offered to help, she already had an idea of how we could all pitch in, too.

Great, I thought sarcastically.

Mom received another lecture opportunity, this time in California, and announced how she and Bruce would be taking this first trip together as a couple to Los Angeles. She radiated with joy, and with the way he looked at her, I could tell it was mutual. It made my heart soften a bit for the guy. I guess I could lighten up where he was concerned—only until he gave me a reason not to. He wasn't completely off the hook yet.

Granny was ready for her own adventure. Inspired by our journey, she joined a senior citizen traveling group, which took day tours to different museums, historical landmarks and even casinos. This weekend's trip was at the Museum of Modern Art in the city; a place I have visited so much that I practically had the blueprint memorized. She was so excited to be having lunch inside the museum with a few old girlfriends of hers who would also be joining her on this trip.

"Maybe next time I go, Marissa, I will see one of your paintings on those walls," she mused with pride. Granny had so much faith in me—much more than I had in myself.

As I looked around at my loved ones sitting at the table, I realized that everyone was in such a great place in their lives—including me, now that I was free to love Josh in the open.

But of course, that fragile sense of peace can never last long in this family; an incoming call from Mia's ex-husband, Kevin Logan, quickly changed the mood from serene to anxious.

When she heard he had news to share about Jordan Kissinger, the maniac who has been terrorizing us since we started this adventure, she put the call on speaker so we could hear for ourselves straight from the cop's mouth.

"They got them, Mi. They caught the bastard—and his accomplice. Allegedly, the Marinos were behind it all along."

Shock filled the room. Could it be true? Could this nightmare finally be over? Kevin waited a beat before continuing so we could catch our breath.

"After we failed to find a Jordan Kissinger spelled

traditionally, it wasn't that hard to find an alternate that fit the description of the perpetrator. Apparently, a J-O-R-D-E-N K-I-S-I-N-G-E-R has quite the rap sheet—and a connection that gives him a motive." Pause for effect.

"He's Peggy Marino's older brother."

"I knew it," I pointed out. "I knew this had to be connected to one of them."

"You were right," he continued. "Did some checking into this guy to see what he was capable of. Never had a violent record before, though. Petty theft, drug possession. But sometimes in these cases, it escalates to more. Maybe he saw dollar signs and a way out.

"But that's what the authorities will hopefully get out of him. He's in custody now. So far, he is pleading innocent, but the evidence is stacked up against him. He wasn't at work the last three weeks—claiming he needed to take a leave of absence for mental health reasons. We're still investigating his whereabouts in April.

"Found the phony passport matching the traditional spelling of the name used at the airport and a crumpled up boarding pass in his glove compartment. Guess from where to where? Oh, and along with some cocaine, of course."

"Wow. So, who was his accomplice?" Mia asked.

"Peggy herself. She is also in police care. It started out that we were just going to question Peggy and the rest of the Marino family as standard procedure.

"Turns out, one of the officers who questioned her noticed the brooch she was wearing matched the description of the one Mia planted. While he stalled her, the team got a warrant to search the house and lo and behold, they found the fake jewelry box in her room.

"She is claiming her brother mailed it to her as a gift last week, and that she didn't know it was connected to

Leigh's maternal family heritage. Kisinger's protesting that he never left her the box; that he's never even seen it.

"They are quite the pair—turning on each other to save their own ass. Very common in these kinds of situations; always happy to sell the other out to get a better deal."

"Do the police think there is any chance they are telling the truth?" Bruce queried. I thought he didn't get involved in family matters?

"Not likely with all the evidence, but we're keeping the investigation open. We can't rule out a setup—we never know if someone outside of the family is trying to make it look like it was an open and shut internal job. We have to consider all possibilities still at this point.

"However, a couple of the other family members— except her husband Patrick—confirmed Peggy's belligerence at the will reading and then weeks of her complaining afterward about not knowing anything about this inheritance, touting that her husband legitimately has a right to it.

"We've questioned Patrick, and although he seems to check out as not being involved in the scheme, we've advised him not to leave town. We're not letting anyone off the hook just yet," he warned.

"Good," I spat. "I want them to pay for doing this to our family. Whatever it takes to make them rot in jail, Kev, do it."

"You know I'll do what I can, Mar, but I can't get emotional about it. I have to follow the rules and thoroughly investigate this. That means I need my officers to speak with each one of you again—plus Kieran, Jay and your cousins. Everyone who knows anything."

"Of course," we all said in layered unison.

"One last thing," Kevin warned. "Keep your guards up.

This isn't over. Even if it turns out Jorden and Peggy are guilty, we still don't know what lengths they have gone to already. For all we know, they could have a contingency plan in case they got caught."

"Like enlisting Dominic Moretti again," Mia pointed out.

"Well, the bug planted at Casa Bianchi is still in effect, so we are monitoring that as well to make sure that family doesn't get involved again. We're making sure to cover all angles," Kevin explained as he wrapped up the call. "Just stay safe, everyone, and call me if you have the slightest concern or uneasiness."

Thanking him for the information, we all promised we would be careful and keep him informed. One way or another, this mess was about to come to a conclusion soon.

3

Walking into my apartment after a dramatic family dinner and a short nightcap at Josh's, I found Jay passed out on the couch surrounded by crushed bags of chips, almost empty bowls of salsa and guac and bottles of beer all over.

As sweet as this guy was, he certainly was a pig. I knew he would eventually clean up after himself, but sometimes I would love for the house to stay tidy for just one day. Who needs kids when you have Jay?

My entry must have startled him awake, as he jumped and grabbed a beer bottle in defense at the sound of my keys clinking onto the counter.

"It's just me," I said, muffling a giggle.

"Ugh, Riss. You scared me," he grumbled sleepily.

"Why are you always so jumpy?"

"Gee, I don't know. Maybe because you are mixed up in some crazy family adventure with stalkers and potential murderers out there."

Okay, I know—I shouldn't have told him about my family secret. I already had this argument with Meg several times over. But it's Jay. I've known the boy since the third grade and I trust him with my life. Even if he was a big weirdo at times. Besides, he has a right to know if his life is in danger—what if the psychopath came to our front door?

At least with Jay here, I felt a little safer. His black belt ass could karate chop the life out of an intruder.

"Not anymore," I revealed. "Seems like they caught the jackass. And his sister—that Peggy Marino woman who wanted to protest the will."

He looked at me confused—I wasn't sure if it was because he was still coming out of a deep sleep or if he really wasn't catching on. He insisted that I take him through the whole story and by the end, he finally understood that we were no longer in danger.

"So, the jewelry box was a fake?"

"Yup. Mia had the brilliant idea to create a decoy to throw them off track. Oh, and she also added a real, expensive old lady brooch and a fake legacy note inside so the idiot would buy its authenticity, at least initially. Turned out better than we could have ever imagined, since it brought upon their downfall."

"Interesting," he responded, becoming more hushed and contemplative. I could tell that brilliant academic mind of his was turning its gears.

"Kevin told us, Josh and Bruce tonight that he'd have more questions for all of us. You, too, since you know about it. He just wants to make sure all angles are covered."

"Sure. No problem," he paused. "Wait—you mean Josh was there?"

"Yeah," I nervously confessed. "I finally told my family and brought him to dinner. They loved him."

And there it was. The disapproving look—Jay's own little green monster. We were twins in that way, equal in tempers and envy, though he covered it much better than I did (most of the time). He did have a kinder overall disposition—always a gentleman holding open the doors, chatting it up with the little old ladies at the grocery store and otherwise charming even the grumpiest of bosses. He reminded me of my dad in that sense.

Currently a traveling salesman by trade, he was a struggling artist like me, waiting for that big music break. He could sing the most poetic verses while skillfully running his fingers over the strings of a guitar, his eyes closed and lost in the moment. Like he could be in a crowd yet only need to play for his party of one; his soul.

He really had a gift, not unlike Kieran and his keyboard, but more alternative and acoustic in nature than my soon-to-be brother-in-law. I looked over and saw that vulnerable musician mixed with grumbled irritation.

I didn't understand where his jealousy was coming from, though. We were always friends; never crossed that line. He was like a brother to me. Guess that's what it was. He's just overprotective. Especially with everything that has gone down lately.

"Happy for you," he managed with a forced smile as he got up to walk towards his bedroom.

"Why don't you like him?"

"I like him just fine," he said defensively in his pseudo-Puerto Rican accent. "I'm just tired of listening to you guys have sex all the time while I'm not getting any. Thanks for giving me a break and going to his place tonight, by the way."

"I don't get it, Jay. Why *aren't* you getting any?" I questioned. "You are hot. Any girl would want to be with you."

That was the truth. With his Latin roots, his hair was as dark as mine with luscious curls that twirled around his striking face and heartbreaking sapphire eyes. He was a bit on the tall and awkward side, yet there was something about the way he carried himself that exuded pure sexiness. Must be that tropical blood of his.

Looking at him just now, it made me wonder why we were never more than friends…

"I don't want just any girl, Riss. You know that's never been my style."

"I know. You're too good a catch to pass on, though. Get yourself out there and find that woman!"

"My heart's not ready to move on just yet," he sighed heavily as he waved me good night and closed his door to indicate he was done talking about this.

When he first moved in with me after we realized we could help each other financially, he had mentioned being in love with a woman who just wanted to be his friend, and it was hard for him to just settle for someone else.

It amazed me that a man this good-looking was a one-woman type of guy, instead of living up to his womanizer potential. Meg loved to tease him, calling him a hopeless romantic.

He confessed he thought he needed to earn more money so that he would be "enough" for this woman. He joked how he would have to find some kind of pyramid scheme to get involved in, since he didn't think he'd be winning the lottery anytime soon—and especially since no surprise legacy was waiting for him with a rare green diamond ring or jewel-adorned mini treasure chest.

He would do anything just to give her the world, he said. Now there was a broken-hearted puppy dog if I ever saw one. If only he could reset himself with a one-night stand, he might be able to move on.

The next morning, I found him still brooding on the couch, his hair a wet mop after a fresh shower. I could tell something was bothering him, so I sat down beside him as he instantly blushed and turned away.

Oops! I quickly looked down to see a nipple had fallen out of my black nightie and tucked it back in with a nonchalant apology. Nothing he hasn't seen before.

"What's wrong?" I asked. Clearly irritated, he got up off the couch and made his way over to the kitchen for some more black coffee.

"Nothing. I think I need to take a ride to clear my head."

"Give me a minute to throw clothes on. I want to come," I pleaded. I had missed our motorcycle rides while I was in Italy. It was "our thing" ever since he got his first bike in our early twenties.

"Riss, not now," he tried to deter me. I know he needed to ride to get space, for whatever his broody reasons, but did he not know me and my persistence by now?

"Why not?" I looked up at him with the eyes I knew he couldn't resist. One way or another, I was going to cheer my second favorite fella up. Reluctantly, he leaned back against the counter and motioned for me to hurry up and get dressed before he changed his mind.

Sliding behind him onto the back of his Harley always gave me the goosebumps. The way his masculine body fit into his leather jacket and tight jeans—and how his hair tucked into a helmet with a few tendrils peeking out—was just like out of a cologne photo shoot.

I loved putting my arms around his waist and feeling him tense up at my touch. Even though we were just friends, there was something electric about it all (though not in a disrespectful way to Josh).

He smelled exceptionally good today, too. The fresh rain shampoo mixed with my jasmine body wash (guess he ran out of his) and some musky aftershave was an interesting combination to say the least, but for whatever reason, I was digging it. It kind of suited him—*tough, yet girly on the inside,* I snickered to myself. Totes appropriate.

He barely let me get on before he sped off onto the highway, cuing that even though I was there, he still wanted silence to think. I put my chin up against his shoulder and let the wind pass through both of us, tangling my hair into a delightfully knotted mess.

Exhilarating, liberating, adrenaline-pumping. Every single time I got on this bike with him I was transported to another world of danger and freedom. And he was pushing it to the limit this time, rushing carelessly around curves and jutting in and out of lanes. I loved every second of the thrill.

When we finally got back to the house, he quickly jumped off and went straight inside, still not speaking to me. I followed quietly in after him, removing my helmet and placing it onto the table next to his. I just couldn't let it go—against my better judgment.

"Jay, what the hell is going on with you? You've barely said a word to me all morning." He turned and looked at me in a way he never had before. Heated. Angry. Desperate.

"Let it be, Riss," he clearly warned with such raw emotion.

"No, I won't let it be. Why are you so worked up?"

"Having a shitty day. That's all," he insisted.

"No, that's not all. You've been moody since last night— ever since I told you about the Marinos being captured and Josh coming over for dinner. What's the deal?"

He stood there, his jowls throbbing in and out as he tried to soothe his own temper. I was not helping matters with all my pushing, but I thought he needed to talk and let it out. Sometimes we all need that prodding.

"Jay! Fucking talk to me already. I'm your best friend.

Is this still about some stupid girl you can't seem to get over? She's not worth it."

That did it. I'm an insensitive shit who speaks before she thinks and is a master at hitting a nerve. But I didn't expect such a volatile reaction.

Without warning, my typically calm and gentle friend moved over to where I was standing near the front door, pinning me against the wall with his palms surrounding my head and his legs spread out blocking mine so that I couldn't move.

His body was so close to mine, not even a half inch away from touching, but even in his anger, I could tell he'd never harm a hair on my head. Yet still, there was contained rage brewing.

He just stared into my eyes with an intensity that scared me, intrigued me and aroused me all at once. His breath was a second away from my lips, his face right up against mine. I found it hard to swallow, waiting for him to spit out what I felt him longing to say.

"I said, let it go." He meant business. He refused to move from his stance, his eyes searching and pleading for me to either stop or figure it out myself. I could feel the burn from inside him as his body heat rose between us, and I admit, it was a little alarming.

"Release me," I whispered angrily. Shocked at his own actions, he apologetically freed me from his body cage and cursed himself as he moved away.

"I'm sorry, Riss. I didn't mean to lose my temper like that," he said, looking over at me with genuine regret.

"I can't help you if you don't tell me what's wrong," I softened, sensing he didn't need my matching temper. I walked over to him and embraced him in a hug instead. He clung to me as if for dear life before gently pushing me away. At least he was much calmer now; even soft spoken.

"I can't do this anymore. I tried, but this isn't working. I—I have to go. I'm sorry."

"Go where? I don't understand. I want you to talk to me," I practically begged him to open up and let me in. "Please. I don't want you to go."

"I just think it's for the best that I move out," he said as I glared at him in disbelief. Where was all this coming from?

"Listen, Riss. I haven't been completely honest with you, and I haven't always done the right thing by you. I need to set things right," he rambled. "Besides, you have Mr. Moneybags to take care of you now, and I'm sure he doesn't need some male *best friend* hanging around," he pointed out sarcastically.

That stung, but he was right; him living with me was a source of ongoing contention between me and Josh. Yet still, I didn't want to lose this man from my life. Even if he did just insult me by inadvertently implying I was a gold digger…

"Jay—wait," I tried, but he just shook his head and walked away. I watched him, baffled, as he went to his room, threw a few things into a bag and walked towards the front door.

"I'll make sure you have my half of the rent until you find a new roommate, though I think we both know where that's headed. I'm going to crash at Dave's until I can figure things out. I'll grab the rest of my things once I land somewhere."

He looked back at me remorsefully, almost pausing as if not really wanting to leave. I couldn't find the words to stop him, but the confused tears that began falling spoke volumes.

"I never meant to hurt you, Marissa. Or anyone else. I hope you can forgive me." And with that, Jayson Rivera walked out of my door and possibly out of my life, without notice or explanation.

I didn't think I would feel this saddened over his departure. The apartment felt empty—not like when he went away on a weekend business trip. I always knew he was coming back. But he wasn't this time, and I still had no idea what the hell he had gotten himself mixed up in or what made him want to leave me; leave *us*.

He was my best friend—next to Josh, of course. I hadn't realized how much I missed him in my life until he sauntered back in earlier this year with a proposition I couldn't refuse. I had just lost Tony as a roommate because I made the mistake of sleeping with him and needed a replacement, stat.

I knew I couldn't repeat that mistake for a fifth time (yeah, habitual issue—and yes, one of them was a woman, so it's not like it matters whether I get a male or female roomie). I made that clear to Jay when he signed up to be my new co-tenant and begged him as my oldest friend not to let me screw this up; to stay strong if I got weak.

But luckily, Josh entered my life around the same time, so even if I were tempted to fail yet again, I was rescued by my new lawyer lover. It seemed to have worked, and despite his messy habits, Jay and I really got along well. I had no idea that something "wasn't working."

He just completely blindsided me. It made me wonder if I really was the problem after all—and if it wasn't just about my sexual habits like I had thought. What if I was simply intolerable as a roommate?

The thought scared the hell out of me, considering I was in love with Josh and had already started dreaming of us moving in together one day. I had even thought for a brief moment that this could be a sign for us to take the next step now that Jay moved out.

Apparently, Josh did, too. When I told him what went down, he immediately suggested that I move in with him and let Jay keep the apartment to himself. The idea terrified me, and I told him as much.

"I'm not sure I'm easy to live with," I admitted.

"You think I haven't figured that out already on my own?" he teased. "I know exactly what I'd be getting myself into. And I'd love every minute of it. Waking up to those beautiful eyes every morning, kissing those lips every night. It will make the rest of the day bearable," he joked.

"Cute, real cute," I laughed. "I'm serious though. I'm like a magnet for living arrangement destruction. What if you fall out of love with me?"

"That could never happen, Mar. I know you've had bad luck with roommates—but that is all they were. I love you and am willing to go the distance to be with you. I want to spend the rest of my life with you."

He leaned in to kiss me and instantly I felt reassured. I was still hesitant about making such a big move, though. I would be giving up the apartment I'd lived in for four years, and I'd be on his turf. Knowing him, he wouldn't let me pay a dime towards rent (ask me how often I've paid for anything on a date). So…

In addition to being with the man I loved, it could be exactly what I needed to bartend a little less and focus on my art a little more. No, I wasn't really a gold digger. But if my love wanted to support my dreams, how could I refuse his generosity?

"Okay," I said cautiously. "Let's do it."

I began packing up my things immediately and planned to move in by the end of the weekend. Jay was not happy when I told him, but he really had no say in the matter, especially since he was the one who left me. He did, however, agree to move back into the apartment and re-lease it in his name, only until he found another roommate.

Things between us were tense for a while, though after almost thirty years of friendship, we didn't want things to end on a sour note. He even sent flowers and a housewarming gift to congratulate us. It was a start, at least. Although he refused to confide in me about what was going on with him, he still wanted a place in my life and said he would always be there for me. I believed him. I needed to believe him.

Everything fell into place after the move. It all happens for a reason, they say. Josh had an extra office that I was able to use as an art studio, and I went to work on my Florence-inspired paintings and sculptures. Oh, how I loved bringing my visions to life.

I was able to cut back on my hours at the restaurant so I could focus on my creative work, thanks to Josh's financial support. Besides, since we lived in uptown Manhattan, the commute was now much longer and sucking precious time out of my day. Josh suggested that I quit altogether and wait until I returned from Spain before I found something else closer to home.

Home. I was in a home—*our* home. Family dinners continued each Sunday, and I was excited to be able to finally host one in a beautiful dining room when it was my turn. Since my apartment was too small, I had always arranged for us to dine out locally. Convenient, but never cozy.

Now, I was able to put out my own fancy dinnerware and try on a chef hat—after all, how much different from baking could cooking possibly be? A few recipes later and I was ready to be Martha Stewart.

Yes, I could get used to this kind of happy life, especially now that we no longer had our stalkers to worry about.

More evidence was found against Jorden and Peggy; enough to keep them locked up and away from us all. Police had found paper in Jorden's office desk that matched the type he used when leaving us threatening notes in both New York and Italy; the blurry image from the Dublin hotel matched his body build and hair color; he could not vouch for his whereabouts in April (an undocumented "business" trip); and the shipping package retrieved from the recycling bin at Peggy's house confirmed the jewelry box was sent from her brother.

Not a peep has been heard or a disturbance recorded anywhere since they were arrested. With Meg now back in the U.S., there have been no attempts to retrieve her ring, or to find the real box now that Mia's decoy was exposed as a fake.

No more threatening notes about those or about finding our final piece in Spain, and believe me, security has been monitoring us 24/7. We had every reason to believe we were in the clear.

The only sadness we experienced over the last month was hearing of our dear cousin Sorella Maria's passing. A grief-stricken Francesco said she went quietly in her sleep; in fact, that very evening she had claimed how her life was complete now that she was able to see her grandparent's home once again and fulfill her promise to our Nonno Leigh.

We held a candlelight procession in her honor at Granny's local church and grieved her over a traditional Italian dinner courtesy of Mia. We will never forget the blessing of meeting her and learning all about our Italian heritage.

But now, it was time for us to focus on our next, and final, adventure: Barcelona, Spain.

4

The Spain trip was going to work a little differently than the previous two. Our cousin connection there, Edward John Rubio, is actually an American citizen living in New Jersey, and we arranged to meet up with him this Saturday. He was going to fill us in on some of the backstory before joining us on our journey to his ancestor's country.

Edward John—EJ as he insisted we call him—was an eccentric little character. Named for his great-grandfather, Eduardo, he had been born and raised in America after his father, Matteo, moved here and married his sweetheart, Gloria. An only child whose mother passed when he was five from a fatal car accident, he proudly carried on the Rubio name.

Dedicated to his career, EJ didn't marry the love of his life, Rodney Anderson, until they were well into their fifties. He admitted that they thought they were too old to consider having surrogate or adopted children themselves, yet found joy in spoiling all of Rodney's nieces and nephews, of which there were many.

Though his grandfather's brother had married two different women and was thought to have illegitimate children all throughout Spain, none have been officially documented—until recently when those ever-popular DNA ancestry tests revealed a surprising family match.

However, as the current heir and a lover of the whole

legacy idea and meaning behind the statue (yet to be revealed, he declared), EJ was more than happy to pass it on to his distant American cousins as requested. He agreed with Leigh's assessment that it should go to a fellow art connoisseur.

"Are you an artist as well?" I inquired.

"You could say that," he hinted, his cherub-like smile taking over his chubby European, pink-colored face with hazel eyes and balding brownish-gray hair. He's considered a young cousin in my grandfather's generation, though none of us could figure out what number or how many times removed he would technically be.

He had an inventive, unique style—wearing a casual short-sleeved, totem-printed, button-down shirt with weathered jeans and colorful oxfords. I should have guessed what his profession was.

"I'm actually the owner of the Rubio Art Gallery in Manhattan," he said with pride.

"Oh my gosh, how did I not make that connection before?" I gasped. "I love it there! The *Haunted Beings* sculpture exhibit is daring and marvelous!"

"Why, thank you. It's one of my favorites, as well," he replied. "I hear you are quite the *artiste* yourself." I blushed at the thought of someone actually calling me an artist.

"Not exactly. I've done a few paintings and sculptures in a home studio, but nothing on display."

"Since when are you so modest, Mar," Meg teased. "Her work is beautiful. I have no doubt she will have her own exhibits on display one day." I smiled at the thought of my big sister being proud of my creations. Maybe she has turned a new leaf and is paying more attention to my life, after all.

"I would love to see your pieces sometime. Perhaps

when we get back from Spain, we can talk about bringing in some starters as a seasonal exhibit to gauge public response," he proposed.

"That—that would be amazing," I gushed. "Thank you."

"Very well, that's settled. Now, shall we talk about what's in store for you in Catalonia?"

He went on to explain that although considered part of Spain geographically, Barcelona technically belonged to an autonomous region known as Catalonia. In fact, many of its citizens spoke the dual languages of Spanish and Catalan—a dialectic blend of Spanish and French. Looks like my high school studies may not be enough, after all, though I think a few common phrases I've picked up from Jay's family throughout the years might help me with some lingo.

I thought I'd need to invest in another translator, but EJ assured us that we could get by with basic Spanish and even some English. Although he didn't live there, he was brought up speaking the language and would be there by our side to help us navigate the glorious city.

He mentioned how he had only been to Barcelona a handful of times throughout his life—more recently over the past year after Leigh approached him. Our grandfather had asked him to help bridge the gap between his Spanish heritage and the family's immigration to the United States, and EJ was more than willing to oblige.

He understood how Leigh wanted to keep the legacy alive, and that it would be best if the journey took us abroad to experience it firsthand. EJ himself was enthralled with the mystery, and painstakingly took on his self-appointed role as "Heir Master," he proclaimed.

"Leigh didn't miss a thing," he revealed. "He even

knew about our DNA discovery and located my lost cousin, Teresa Balles. Although Leigh didn't tell her about the legacy per se, he did form a relationship with her so that she would be willing to sublet her Barcelona house to her American kin—like a timeshare. Such a convincing little devil," he chuckled.

Once EJ heard of Leigh's passing and our projected timeline for arrival, he enacted the plan to provide Teresa with an all-expense paid, two-week trip to her dream destination of Australia in return for the Airbnb-type trade. She was more than happy to accept the generous offer, and invited EJ and his husband to stay with her a few months ago when he traveled there to set our adventure in motion.

He said she was a delightful, mousy bookworm of a woman who was surprisingly thrilled at the thought of spending time in the Outback. Her home was impeccably tidy, everything in its place—and as long as we promised to keep it that way, she had no problem with the arrangement. She did hope to meet us one day as well, she said.

Perhaps she would end her trip a day early and join us for the planned family celebration.

Oh yes, part of the plan was to bring all of us together in the end—us sisters, Mom, Granny, our loved ones, our country-hosting cousins—everyone was invited to the grand reveal party in Barcelona on day thirteen.

Though I think for Teresa, he made arrangements for a family brunch on our final day instead to preserve the secrecy of our trip. Either way, it would be nice to meet the woman who generously put us up in her home.

"Will Rodney be joining us as well?" Mia asked.

"Oh no, cuz. He's offered to hold down the fort while I go on this little adventure. He's a bit jealous, of course, but super supportive. I promised him a place at the party table, and we'll spend a second honeymoon there after that's over, so he's tickled pink over that idea. Just you and me, ladies!"

"So, how will this all work?" Meg asked, always the planner.

"Well, I'll be flying out with you and getting y'all settled into the house. We'll do some touristy stuff and then I have to take care of some business—you know, statue stuff," he winked at Marissa, "and then we'll get right down to it. No use in playing cat and mouse too long, especially with all the trouble that seems to be following you."

"Actually, that's been resolved," Meg informed him. "They have charged our grandfather's paternal relatives with all related crimes as of right now, and there have been no further threats or trouble."

"However," Mia interrupted, "we'll still have bodyguards and want to make sure the local authorities are monitoring the house we are staying in. I'd rather be safe and vigilant," she asserted.

"Smart cookie. I agree—I don't need the beets kicked out of me protecting some statue, as gorgeous as he is."

"He?" I poked.

"Ha, never you mind, cuz. All in due time," he warned playfully. "Point is, I agree with Mia and would rather be careful. You never know who could be lurking around in the shadows."

We all consented, then parted ways. With only a few days left to go before our final trip, the girls and I had some initial planning to do and lots of packing left. I was becoming more excited by the day. I was finally going to embark on my mission.

I couldn't decide what dresses to bring, or what to leave behind. The weather was sure to be balmy, with its

Mediterranean breezes and sweltering end-of-summer sun. As I was trying to decide between a basic black tank dress and a silky red floral one, I felt his warm arms come up from behind me and smiled.

"I wish you were coming with me this time," I pouted.

"We've been through this before. You need this time with your sisters, and I have a case that I need to wrap up. I'll be there for the party. I promise," he cooed as he kissed the side of my neck.

"It's just not fair. Meg got to be with Kieran, and Mia with Francesco. Why must I go lover-less? Why must you torture me so?"

"It will be torture for me as well, babe. But I'd just want to keep you locked up in a room and you'd never see the sights of Spain or do your legacy thing. Besides, I hear absence makes the sex grow stronger," he implied, bringing his hands from behind his back to stroke my taut breasts.

He pulled me into a luxurious kiss, the dresses falling free of my hands so I could draw him in against my body to feel his full heat. His hands skillfully unbuttoned the front of my blouse, which carelessly fell to the ground in a slump—soon followed by my skirt, stockings and lace slip.

I purred as his hands wandered to my already hot and wet insides, pulsing me in preparation for what was to come. He tossed my suitcase and belongings from the bed so that he could lay me belly down and ass up, asking me to continue fingering myself while he watched and stripped off his own clothes.

He removed my hand from its frenzied state and licked each one of my fingers as he effortlessly glided into place. I could feel his fullness inside me as one hand reached around my left nipple to squeeze it and his other grabbed my ponytail.

Oh, this was not going to be slow and gentle, I noticed as he forcefully pounded me into rapid ecstasy before collapsing on top of me. He got up quickly though, throwing on his pants and shirt. I hated that he had to go back into the office instead of going another round.

"Oh, by the way, I just found this in the mailbox," he said as he grabbed a small, sealed blue envelope off of the dresser. "I was tempted to open it since it had your name on it…" he broke off, waving the note above my head humorously so that I couldn't reach it.

I think he just enjoyed seeing my naked body jiggle trying to get it. He finally relented, and what I read sent shivers down my spine.

"What is it, babe? I hope it's not from some secret lover you've been seeing on the side," he teased.

"Nothing. Just a thank you note from EJ," I covered. Thankfully, he was in such a rush to get to work that he believed me, giving me a kiss on the forehead on his way out the door, claiming he'd be home in time for dinner.

After he left, I took a good, long hard look at the note again.

Watch your back. I'm not done with you bitches yet.

I froze, not knowing what to do. I thought the Marinos were in custody. I thought this was over. Who could have sent this? Do I tell my sisters? Do I call Kevin and the cops? Why didn't I just tell Josh?

Questions were spinning through my head. I didn't want anyone to worry. I knew I should keep everyone informed, but what if they decided that it was not safe to go on this trip? Fuck, no. No one was going to keep me from this. No one.

We were going to still have guards, so we'd be safe. *Yes, we would be fine,* I convinced myself.

I wasn't going to fall into the same trap of fear everyone else gave in to. I was just going to tuck this into the tiny zipper of my luggage, just in case, and pretend it never happened.

As far as I was concerned, I'd watch my own back. If anything else happened, then I'd bring everyone into the loop. But not until I set foot on Spanish soil. I was going to get my statue come hell or high water.

At our last Sunday dinner before the flight, I was on edge. I'd like to think I had a good poker face, but I was beginning to doubt that. Josh had been questioning my uneasiness all week, but I chalked it up to just being nervous about what awaited me in Barcelona. No one questioned it was nerves.

I tried to let myself get caught up in the small talk and discussions over the landmarks we planned to visit while we were there. Even EJ and Rodney joined our family dinner, bringing quite the colorful conversations to the table. We all instantly adored them and their playful banter with each other. You could tell that they were meant to be.

As the evening drew to a close, I found myself alone in Meg's kitchen putting dishes in the sink when Bruce walked in. He had been quiet all evening, saying very little and faking a smile or polite response from time to time to seem engaged. I would say he was more of a people watcher than a contributor this evening.

"Are you all set for the big trip?" he asked, finally trying to make small talk.

"Yup. Packed and ready," I replied shortly.

"Marissa, I don't pretend that there isn't a distance between us. I'm hoping when you return, we can get to know each other a little better. For your mother's sake," he added.

"Sure," I responded, not taking my eyes off from rinsing the dishes. He stepped up beside me and turned the faucet off, waiting until I faced him.

"Do me a favor, please."

"A favor?" I barely knew this guy and he had the nerve to ask me for a favor?

"Yes. I know it seems like you are out of danger. But please, promise me you'll watch your back. Your mother couldn't take it if anything happened to you girls."

I cringed at the words—and at his grin that accompanied them. All color drained from my face, but I quickly turned back to the sink as if what he said wasn't a big deal. *Could it be?*

"Of course, I will. I'd never let anyone hurt me or my sisters," I informed him matter-of-factly with a cold stare down. Getting the hint that the subject was closed, he sighed and slowly exited the room.

Was that a veiled threat? Did he leave that note? Was Bruce somehow connected to all of this? He did appear to come into the picture and Mom's life at an all-too-convenient time: when Grandfather Leigh died. I wondered how much he really knew about our legacy.

But should I tell someone about Bruce—or the note? was the bigger question. I should probably alert the family cop, but Kevin might turn around and warn my sisters, and then Spain would be shelved for sure. *What should I do?*

"Ready to go, love?" came the familiar, welcomed voice from the doorway, breaking my distressed mind chatter.

I took a deep breath and decided it was best to just shake it off and forget what Bruce said. I was going to Spain. They would stop me if I mentioned anything, I'm sure. And would Mom even believe me if I told her Bruce was a threat? I know Josh would, but I couldn't start a family argument right then and there. Maybe I'd alert my ex-brother-in-law once I landed so he could take the necessary steps through the police force.

But first, I was getting on that plane and getting my damn statue.

"I am," I replied, turning around so he could see my bogus smile. "But I need to make a stop at my old apartment first. I left something there I need for the trip."

"No, you didn't," he protested. When I tried to negate him, he just held up his hand to stop me.

"Mar, it's okay. I know you just want to see Jay before you go. It's cool with me," he assured me, and I immediately felt better. In fact, he had a better plan than my fly-by goodbye.

"Why don't I do this? I'll drop you off so you can spend some time there, and you can just take a taxi back," he suggested, handing me a fifty-dollar bill.

I loved how he knew me so well. I did want to see my old friend and make peace with him before I left. Even though we texted now and again, I could use a cup of coffee and a chat with my sort of-maybe-still a bestie. It made me love Josh even more that he encouraged my visit, knowing how my two men were at odds with each other. Maybe even after all of this, they could learn to tolerate each other for my sake. At least, this temporary waiver of jealousy was a step in the right direction for Josh.

The door opened to a very surprised Jay wearing nothing

but an old pair of gray shorts, the beads of perspiration covering his tightened chest and dripping from his hair. Obviously, I had interrupted an in-home workout.

"I'm sorry. I should have called," I said as I turned around to leave.

"No, Riss, it's fine. Come on in. I was just finishing up anyway." He opened the door fully and motioned for me to enter with a geeky, awkward smirk. "Sit down and make yourself comfortable. Mind if I grab a quick shower though? Do you have time for a visit?"

"That's why I'm here," I smiled at him. I could tell he was just as anxious as I was to have our first real conversation since our separation.

"Is Dave here?" I asked. His friend had agreed to move out of his studio apartment to move in with Jay, instead of the other way around. From what I've heard, things were working out really well that way.

"Nope. He's working. Hang on, I'll be right back. Grab a beer if you want," he offered while he scurried to the bathroom.

Not even five minutes later, he was out and more fully dressed in jeans and a black tank. *Wait—was he still using my jasmine body wash that I left behind as a stinging reminder I used to live here?* I chuckled to myself as he sat down on the couch beside me—though not too close. He was clearly keeping his distance.

"So, what brings you here?" he asked to break the ice.

"I'm leaving for Spain tomorrow. I thought it would be nice to catch up before I went."

"I'm glad you stopped by," he admitted with that beautiful smile of his. "I've missed you, Riss."

"I've missed you, too. Can we start over?"

"No need for us to start over. Let's just simply start a

new chapter," he replied, always with a hint of poeticism in his outlook. True markings of a musician.

We chatted for a while; he filled me in on his latest escapades with Dave and the boys, and I shared what my sisters and I planned for Spain. He got a kick out of my description of my newest flamboyant cousins and wished he could have been there to meet them.

Although he still avoided confessing what he was truly up to, he mentioned that he had been cleaning up his mess and apologized again for leaving me high and dry.

We agreed to put it behind us and look towards the future. He even sat there as non-judgmentally as possible while I updated him on my relationship with Josh; he sweetly continued to wish me nothing but happiness, even though it pained him to do so. It gave me some hope.

It was like old times again, comfortably falling right back into place with each other. So much so, I felt like I needed to confide in him. He was the one person I could unburden my soul to; I knew he would have my back and do pretty much whatever I asked to make up for him abandoning me.

"Hey, can you do me a favor?"

"Name it."

"Can you keep an eye on my mom for me—well, more like on Bruce?"

"Of course. Why's that?"

I wasn't sure I should say anything further, but I knew I needed to get it all off my chest. If one person knew what was going on at least, I could rest easy knowing my family here was being watched over.

So, I told him about the note, and what Bruce said. Jay swore to keep it a secret, though he tried to convince me to alert the police and tell my family, practically pleading with me not to leave. But he knew me better than that.

And I knew him better—he was not going to let me go without promising that I would check in with him every single day and keep him informed of everything that was going on. Every last detail, he demanded.

"Or else," he warned with a serious look. "Don't make me get on a plane to Spain and track you down."

I had no choice but to concede and place my trust in him. I would do as he asked, and I knew he would keep me and my loved ones safe. *Please don't let me down,* I thought as I hugged him goodbye.

5

Holy shit, I'm in Spain, I thought to myself excitedly as we exited the gate and made our way to baggage claim. *We made it!*

I was bursting at the seams, unable to contain my glee. My sisters were equally joyful as we waited for EJ to get our rental car and drive us to our distant cousin Teresa's house.

"Can you believe we are finally here?" I squealed.

"This is it, Mar," Mia responded with fervor. "It's time for you to claim your heirloom and finish this for us!"

"I for one can't wait for this to be over, though," Meg added, evidently tired from the trip already. She was lagging behind and not her usual energetic self.

"Not that I'm not excited for you, sis," she quickly added, seeing my bubble burst a little. "I don't mean that at all. I just mean for this to be all over and we can settle back down into a normal life again."

I knew what she meant. Still, it was frustrating that she was ready to give up before we even started. Why couldn't she have the same enthusiasm for me that she had for Mia? But, I couldn't let her bring me down. I've waited too long for this.

The drive over to the house was your typical busy city commute. Traffic, honking cars—yet here, the profanities were either in Spanish or Catalan. I still wasn't trained enough to know the difference. Thank goodness EJ was already a master at navigating us through the foreign city.

Even though we were told we'd be staying in Teresa's house, I assumed that meant an apartment in a Barcelona complex. Boy, was I wrong, as we pulled up to a 5-bedroom luxury Spanish villa not far from the beach, in the southwestern neighboring coastal town of Sitges.

Located only about a half hour from the city center, the artsy town was famous for its beaches, renowned Carnival celebrations, historical museums and motor racing—all of which intrigued me. It's as if the village was designed just for me.

Teresa's home was simply gorgeous, with its pristine white, modern 4-floor structure, multiple viewing windows and palm trees bursting out in greeting. Walking up the terra-colored stairway, the front porch was enclosed in crystal clear glass panels to protect us from falling while gazing upon the Mediterranean Sea drawn out in front of us.

I found myself lost in the blue and white crystals as the sun beamed its light down to play. I closed my eyes to inhale the salted scent of the sea and imagined the warmth of the water engulfing my body in bliss. I couldn't wait to dance within the waves that called to me.

Continuing on our tour, the inside of the villa was just as incredible as its exterior. Contemporary Ibizan style all the way—its whitewashed walls, polished floors and colorful paintings accenting the purity. Aside from the front door and lobby area, the first floor seemed to only house a master bedroom suite and bathroom.

I walked into the dream knowing this would be my personal space, separated from everyone else. A large king-sized canopy bed welcomed me into its soft white embrace, colored only by a couple of red throws and pillows.

It seemed undisturbed and unused. Did Teresa even sleep in this room? Sigh, if only Josh could be here to indulge in the privacy of it all. I guess it was for the best considering this was a stranger's home after all, and we shouldn't disgrace her bed. But oh, the things I imagined we could do in here...

Moving on to the next floor, we found the living room with its spacious, comfortable yellow leather sofas (finally, some color in this place!), a family-style dining area and a kitchen that left Mia gasping as if she was having an orgasm on the spot.

Yeah, we would be dining on her interpretation of Mediterranean cuisine this week, that would be for certain. I saw the wheels of creation turning and the desire to shop rush through her very soul.

Off to the left, there was a smaller master bedroom with its own half bath, a room we agreed would be best suited for EJ as our not-so-humble host. He made even the most boring of house tours entertaining.

As forewarned, everything had its place. It almost made me afraid to walk around for fear of breaking one of Teresa's blown glass figurines on display. Small ballerinas and flowers, colorful animals and a large, intricate crystal village most certainly must have been imported. A quick check at a small green and yellow snake confirmed at least one of these was from Venice.

The third floor housed the remaining three bedrooms, which although not masters, were still luxuriously big with an adjoining bath. Obviously meant for Mia and Meg, they happily placed their suitcases on their respective beds and shrieked over their panoramic balcony views of the coast.

I noticed the third bedroom door was closed, however.

Sneaking a smirk, EJ took my arm and guided me towards the room, gesturing for me to open it. Standing in front of me was an open room with only a desk in the corner, hidden by a huge easel, basket of paints and sculpting tools. I was speechless.

"Do you like it?" he asked. "Teresa barely uses this room, so when I approached her about setting it up as an art studio for you, she was delighted to oblige—as long as you leave behind a piece of brilliant artwork for her home, she requested."

"Oh, it's fantastic, thank you! Thank you so much!" I was so overwhelmed with emotion that I ran over to give him a great big bear hug.

"I already have an idea to paint a mural of blown glass images for her!" Pinch me! A studio just for me? This place was a *dream*. How was I ever going to leave here? Oh—by being dragged by the arm to keep moving, that's how, as I was quickly reminded by Meg.

We weren't done with the tour just yet, apparently, leaving the fourth floor as the *pièce de résistance:* a rooftop pool with a 360-degree vista of the city. Surrounding it was a huge lounge area filled with red striped cushioned chairs and white umbrellas—enough for a party of at least thirty. Noticing the barbecues and bar over in the right-hand corner, I was guessing that this would be where we'd have our final family party.

EJ suggested that he take his leave to freshen up and that we all do the same, leaving me to jump right into painting, Mia to probably read and well, Meg to do her planning.

We had a few hours before dinner, and I decided that I'd rather dine as an unkempt mess from traveling than give up the opportunity to feel those brushes in between my fingers.

Gazing at the perfectly primed white canvas in front of me, I let the paint colors take me away. Since I already knew what I wanted to make for Teresa, I started there, knowing that once I saw the city, I'd be distracted to capture a different visual.

I think that's why I haven't really been featured as an artist yet—I was never focused long enough to finish something. Truthfully, my Ireland series was the first I had ever completed in one sitting. Even Italy was still waiting for my final touches.

Before I knew it, Mia was gently knocking on the door to give me a 30-minute warning in case I did want to shower and change before we left. Grateful for her interruption, I decided that I was satisfied with my progress and could use the break.

Instead of driving, EJ guided us towards the super convenient public transportation that took us into the heart of Barcelona. There, the bustling of the nighttime filled my senses with exotic excitement, urging me to join in its dance of life.

He took us down to the famous Las Ramblas (or was it La Rambla? No one could give us a straight answer), a pedestrian promenade lined with trees, shops and restaurants of all kinds. The pavement swirled like waves with bright, colorful mosaics—from what we could tell in between the breaks of the crowds' feet.

I recognized one style of mosaic and EJ confirmed it was, in fact, a genuine Joan Miró. Holy crap. I was standing *on* greatness.

This place certainly was a hopping nightspot. Thankfully, EJ had already done his homework on prior trips and sourced out the best places to go. He first took us to a hidden gem—a cava bar—where he insisted that we needed to pre-game to kick-start our trip.

With no room to sit, we each ordered a glass of the champagne-like bubbly spirit and stood shoulder to shoulder. The sparkling wine was so refreshing, we insisted on buying several bottles to keep at the house for future dinners.

Next, we strolled down the boulevard, stopping here and there at souvenir shops, though we decided it would be best to come back another time for that, as we were already lugging around bottles of cava. This most definitely was a unique, cultural area: the live musicians and performers I expected; what I did not expect were the human statues and an erotica museum.

Note to self: come back when I'm on my own to explore that one.

We finally ended up at our destination, a little outdoor tapas dive café. Pitchers of red and white sangria filled the center of our table, as did an assortment of Spanish appetizers, ranging from patatas bravas (potatoes in a spicy sauce) and chicken brochettes, to grilled calamari and a platter of Spanish ham and manchego cheese with toasted bread dipped in a tomato and olive oil mixture. Everything was so delish.

We were so engrossed in our food and sangria that we almost forgot why we had come.

"So, which story would you like to hear first, my dears? Our American migration, or how my prestigious family fell from grace?" he ribbed.

"Ooh, let's do the juicy scandal," Meg selected, obviously feeling her peach and white wine beverage go to her head.

"All right then, the scandal it is!" EJ concurred.

He clearly savored divulging every salacious detail of his family's historic drama. He began with how we were really connected—our thrice-great-grandmother, Elena (the one who received the ring from Banan I when she married into the O'Sullivan line, he noted), was sister to Eduardo Rubio, EJ's namesake and great-great-grandfather.

"We were descendants from the royal House of Bourbon, albeit quite a few lineages removed from the throne line. Think of it as daughters with second born sons having second born sons multiple times over. Still of noble, royal blood and prestige, yet nowhere near being heir apparent," he explained.

"Elena and Eduardo were children of a younger son in that generation's family, Horace Rubio. Now, Horace was an ambitious one, always trying to figure out how he could wedge himself in line for the throne somehow. Unmistakably, that was an impossibility, but that didn't stop the devil from trying.

"He schemed and plotted and planned downfalls, even murders and attempts to impregnate the queen-to-be," EJ dramatically and deliciously acted out for us.

"He eventually was caught and charged with treason, shaming his family's name and stripping away all of their fortune. At the end of it all, he was left with no family or heritage; nothing but an old dragon statue his mother gave him as a token of his now deceased legacy."

He mentioned that he'd go into the history of the dragon statue at another time—but I was ever so intrigued to finally know what the statue's likeness was.

A dragon! How cool!

EJ continued on with his fascinating story, as if he were performing a Shakespearean play.

As a result of his treachery, Horace's family was forced

into middle class living, something so unfathomable to the old man, that he took his own life. In doing so, he left behind his wife and two teenage children to suffer his consequences.

Young Eduardo successfully found employment as a fisherman, earning him back some of the respect that was lost through his father. He was a hard worker, determined to provide his mother and sister with a strong foundation. Since Horace died before being able to arrange for his almost-of-age daughter's betrothal, that task now fell to Eduardo.

While working on the docks one day, he met an astute businessman from Ireland by the name of James O'Sullivan (husband to Agatha and father to Banan I, Meg reminded us). James had taken a liking to young Eduardo, admiring his work ethic and kind spirit.

He spent the better half of a day with the young lad, and when he learned of his family's disgraced legacy and his dilemma over his sister, it was James who proposed to join Elena and his youngest, Banan, in marriage.

It was a sad day for the Rubio family, as Elena did not want to be torn from her family; especially not from her sickly mother. But it was the only solution to make sure she was well provided for. Eduardo knew he would be responsible for his own wife and family one day and could not care for his sister indefinitely. This seemed like the best option for all.

Since the fallen Rubios had very little dowry to give in exchange for Elena, James and Agatha had mercy upon the young couple and gave them enough to live out their lives without struggle. Even though her immediate family was no longer of royal status, Elena was still a noble enough woman herself, with all the mannerisms and upbringing that would be appropriate as young Banan's wife.

Although there were a few gossips and whisperers, the Irish townsfolk respected James enough to honor his decision for the union, never questioning his reasons. Eventually, the young couple moved away to start a new life and fell in love.

"And you know the rest of the story from Colleen, if I'm not mistaken?" he concluded.

"Yes, thank you! That was an amazing story! Sad, but poignant. What a wonderful brother Elena had," Meg mused.

"Indeed," EJ agreed. "There's more to that story, too, but for another time I'm afraid. I'm wiped. Shall we retreat back to that superb villa for the night?"

We all agreed, feeling the grogginess set in. On our way back, EJ reminded us that he needed a few days to set everything up before Marissa could actually retrieve the statue—he first needed to go through an identification and clearance process, and while that was in progress, he had an overseas art transaction to attend to.

He'd be giving us the next three days on our own, though he did mention that he'd probably still crash at the villa a night or two in between. He suggested that we take full advantage of his absence.

Settling into the cushy bed, I looked over at my phone to see the light go off. I smiled as I saw the incoming text from Jay. I glanced at the clock and realized it must be close to dinnertime in New York.

How was your first day?

Incredible. This house is ridiculous. First floor master suite to myself. Third floor art studio. Rooftop pool. I mean, come on!

Sounds chill. Everything still cool?

No notes or weirdos. All good here.

Good. You forgot to text me when you landed.

Are you my dad now?

No LOL. But I'll be like one if you make me come out there to check on you. You promised me, Riss.

K. I'll text every day. Promise.

U better. Get some sleep. Love ya kiddo.

Right back atcha doll xo

I smiled, putting down the phone. I loved how we were back to our normal selves again. I was also glad I finally confided in someone about the note and about Bruce's spine-chilling words. I knew Jay would have my back, and I always liked the feeling that someone was protecting me. Not in a creepy way, but in a caring way.

Speaking of, I realized I should probably text my boyfriend good night!

I wanted to leave Josh a little love note so he'd know he was the last person I thought of as I went to sleep. I figured he'd be busy with work, but he quickly responded to tell me how he missed me and how cold and lonely the bed was without me.

Our exchange turned into a wonderful delay, as he FaceTimed me from his bed with a provoking visual.

Completely naked with a hard-on, he coaxed me into joining him in a little nighttime phone play. Not the same as the real deal, but it was still a pleasurable way to fall into a deep slumber after watching each other masturbate and orgasm. God, I couldn't get enough of this man.

After a wonderfully sound sleep, I awoke in the later part of the morning to a quiet, darkened room. I almost forgot where I was, thinking I was in a dream surrounded by all the softness. It felt amazing to just sleep in without having to get up and go to work at a pain-in-the-ass snob restaurant.

Based on our experience from our past two trips and bouts of jet lag, my sisters and I already agreed that we would take this first full day to relax and adjust, rather than jump right in to sightseeing. After all, who could resist a day sitting poolside on a roof overlooking the Med coast?

Lounging on a float in the pool and drinking a cava mimosa instead of my normal black coffee, I felt the warmth of the sun penetrate through my skin. Mia had already been up for about four hours, taking a walk around the grounds and finding a little nook to get lost in her latest crime novel.

Meg had the same idea as me, lazily sleeping as long as she could before venturing out to join me at the pool.

"This place is ridiculously amazing," she said. "I thought I was sleeping on a cloud."

"I know, right? This new relative certainly knows how to live in style!"

"What are you drinking?"

"Oh, this? It's cava with orange juice. There's one with your name on it right over there on that table."

"That's my girl! You're the best," she smiled as she grabbed another floating lounge and joined me in the pool. By then, Mia had made her way up towards us, sensing that we were past the morning cranky stage and ready for her early bird perkiness.

"This was such a great idea to just spend the day here," she mused. "I hope you don't mind, but before EJ left, I had him run me to the store to pick up a few items so I could make brunch and dinner here tonight. Figured I'd whip up a Spanish tortilla in a little while, and then try my hand later at paella."

"Sounds perfect, Mi. But before you do that, why don't you just relax and join us?" Meg invited.

I saw her hesitation—I knew that she had come a long way in having more self-confidence since leaving Italy, but she still struggled with her body image slightly. Even being twenty pounds down since then, I could tell she hated the idea of bathing suits and pools when anyone else was around.

"Come on, Mi. The water is warm, the sun feels incredible and I'd love to just chill in the pool with my sisters," I encouraged.

"Well, when you put it that way," she relented, finally disrobing to reveal what must've been a new leopard print tankini set—a huge leap from her regular, dowdy one-piece cover-ups.

"You look amazing!" I exclaimed and whistled. "What a hottie." I loved making her blush every now and then. She just needed to own her inner seductress, though I sensed there was more to my sister than she let on in that department. I saw the sparks between her and Francesco in Italy, and there's no way they tangled in lame missionary lovemaking.

For a few moments, the three of us floated around in silence, sipping our drinks and letting the sun beat down to form glistening beads of sweat on our bodies.

"So," began Meg, "how are things going with Josh?" Now it was my turn to blush. I wasn't used to having such conversations that left me giddy and childlike.

"Surprisingly perfect. I thought for sure I would have

screwed things up by now. But, he's different. He accepts me for who I am, and I don't have to pretend to be someone else to earn his approval."

"That's wonderful, Mar. So, he is treating you right?" inquired Mia. She'd never stop being the wife of a cop, divorced or not. Too many years of training.

I simply laughed. "Yes, he is. He's been footing a lot of our expenses so I don't have to work as much in the restaurant, which lets me focus on my art. Not that I'm in it for the money, but it really is a nice change of pace to not have to penny pinch."

"Seems like things are getting serious," Meg deduced. "I was surprised at how quickly you moved in after Jay moved out."

There it was. I knew sooner or later the condescending monster would rear its head.

"How come it's okay for you to live in another country with someone you just met a few months ago, but it's not okay for *me* to move in with the man *I* love?"

"No need to get defensive, Mar. I'm not judging—I'm just making an observation. There's a difference," she explained in her obnoxiously uppity tone. "All I meant was that you have never lived with a guy on purpose, with the intention of being more than a roommate. You are usually skittish of commitment. I just want to make sure you are okay, little sis. That's all."

"Oh." I guess I do have a tendency to defensively jump to conclusions, especially around her. "I get it. It surprised me too, to tell you the truth. Jay left so suddenly that it made me wonder why I could never hold down a roommate. I mean, I never slept with Jay, so I don't know where things went wrong."

I caught Meg and Mia exchange a joking glance, like

two high school girls who knew gossip that I didn't.

"What?"

"What?" Mia asked. "Girl, are you really that dense?"

"Dense about what?"

"Jay!" Meg replied.

"What about him?"

"Seriously, Marissa? The guy is obviously crazy about you," Mia suggested.

"Wait—Jay? No way. He's like my brother. He would never think of me that way."

"Oh, no?" Meg challenged. "Have you ever caught him blushing as you paraded around in one of those silk nighties of yours? Have you noticed how protective he is of you? How about how damn jealous he is of Josh, and pretty much every guy that ever entered your life since you were kids?"

"Yeah, but that's because we're best friends."

"Okay, you keep telling yourself that," Mia laughed and dropped the subject to shift to another uncomfortable one. Bless my sisters and their persistence.

"So, how does Josh feel about you having a guy for a best friend?"

"He's fine with it." They both glared at me with a "yeah right" kind of look. "All right, so he's not thrilled about it. But now that we live together, he doesn't feel so threatened. He even let me hang out with Jay for a little while before I came here."

"Let you?" Mia questioned, perplexed.

"Not like that. I didn't need his permission—I think you both know me better than that. I mean, he willingly suggested that I spend time with Jay because he knew how much it would mean to me. He was cool about it. He's a great guy."

"He seems to be," Meg agreed. "I'm really happy for you, Marissa."

"Me too," said Mia. "But if he ever hurts you, he will have to answer to me."

"I hope you've said the same thing to Mom," I let slip.

"What do you have against Bruce?" Meg asked quizzically.

"Well, I found out about his ex-wife's claim of abuse, and even though he was found innocent, it still unsettles me. And I see the way he and Josh are leery of each other. I don't like the way he looks at me, either. He's always been kind, I guess, but there is something peculiar about him that I can't put my finger on. So, my guard is up."

"That's understandable," reassured Mia. "After so many years, we are all protective of Mom and want to make sure she is okay." Sensing this could probably turn into an all-out battle and ruin our day, the family peacekeeper once again steered the conversation in a different direction.

"I say we cherish this time we have together. Jorden and Peggy have been charged, and we have had no indications of any further threats. No notes, no stalkers, no disturbances. I believe we are free to enjoy this trip without worry, so why don't we do that? I'm going to whip us up a delicious tortilla and then we can talk about where we want to go tomorrow," she stated cheerfully.

"Let me know if you need help! I'm going to go hop in the shower," Meg responded.

I just nodded, hiding my guilt-ridden face behind big sunglasses so that it wouldn't reveal my suspicion that our danger wasn't over. But Mia was right about one thing—it had been quiet since arriving here in Spain, and hopefully it would remain that way.

6

A new day dawning, I couldn't wait to go out and about to explore the charms of Barcelona. Today was going to be "museum day," a trip to paradise in my book. I knew my sisters were not the biggest fans of art exhibitions, but they were totally accommodating of my need to take in as much culture as I could.

We started out at Museu Picasso de Barcelona, where—you guessed it—the entire building was dedicated to the works of Pablo Picasso, spanning a 20-year career. Of course, I was enamored with the display of Cubist paintings he is famous for—oh my God, to see them live, in person, was indescribable. The imaginative and daring play of lines and colors, turning an ordinary portrait into a genius defiance of traditional technique. Awe-inspiring, to say the least.

Even more fascinating than his late works were the primordial sketches of his youthful beginnings as an artist. They were more conventional in style, and it was an experience to see the transformation of his people-inspired art. He captured their essence in *Man in a Beret;* portrayed the reality of living on the streets in *The Wait (Margot);* and then completely recreated human beings in a new light when he painted one of his dearest friends in *Portrait of Jaume Sabartés.*

But there was so much more to see. His ceramic

pieces were exquisitely unique. I was equally enthralled with the personal photos of him that were donated by his photographer so that we could catch a glimpse of the man behind the masterpieces during the final years of his life.

If it weren't for my sisters urging me along, I could have spent the entire week digesting all of this wonderfully rich history. *Why is it that I am the one always rushed? I should be able to call the shots a little more on my journey, shouldn't I?*

Well, I didn't want to leave, but we had two more museums to fit into the day, they reminded me, so I acquiesced to finishing up my first tour. On our walk over to grab the metro towards the Museu d'Art Contemporani de Barcelona, we briefly stopped at a little local bakery for a light snack of Spanish hot chocolate and traditional Catalan xuixo: a sugary-topped, deep-fried pastry filled with scrumptious custard cream. *Muy delicioso!*

Bellies full and happy, we made our way to MACBA, as it is known, to wander our way through the "short century," featuring works from the early 1900s to today. Abstracts, colonial interpretations, modernism and decades of political debate in art form lined the great halls. This was diversity at its best—allowing perspectives from all over the world to blend together in harmony for the public to appreciate and admire.

Perhaps that is what magnetized me so passionately to art. There was an unspoken acceptance of individuality, and it gave me somewhere to belong.

Satisfied with MACBA, I then tormented my sisters for another hour as I gawked through the Joan Miró Foundation, perhaps one of the most beautifully designed museums in all the world. With its clean and contemporary shapes and colors, the designer, a friend of Miró's by the name of Josep Lluís Sert, clearly captured his essence by combining art with architecture.

Throughout the exhibitions, I grew increasingly inspired by the man's diversity in styles, ranging from cubism and poetic women to his darker surrealist and political exposés.

Of course, I couldn't be completely selfish and make it all about me, even though I wanted to. So, along our tour of the city, we stopped by the famous Park Güell for Mia, which was fine with me, since the grounds were a colorful mosaic tribute to naturalist artist, Antoni Gaudí. I was relieved to see it was much more than just some pretty flowers to look at.

I especially loved his *El Drac* creation, a multi-colored dragon/salamander that welcomed us into the park. It made me think of how EJ said my statue-to-be was in the form of a dragon, wondering what the significance of this mythical creature was in Spanish culture. I felt oddly connected to it. Like the dragon was my true spirit animal.

We strolled through the perfectly manicured gardens, Mia especially relishing in its biodiversity, from olive, oak and almond trees, to the aromatic native flowers and bushes of rosemary, lavender and magnolia. The colors danced within its vivid greenery, and the scents tickled our noses with soothing essences.

We stopped for a while to take in the serenity of our surroundings, hardly believing this peaceful gem resided in the heart of a busy metropolis.

Meg seemed to be more tired than normal on this trip, having to sit out a few exhibitions during the day and opt for metro rides instead of walking. She thought the jet lag was really getting to her since she'd been flying back and forth to Europe so often, but promised that she'd find the energy to keep exploring.

At her request, we visited the absolutely breathtaking and iconic Basílica de La Sagrada Família before the long afternoon drew to a close. The Basílica itself, still in progress, was a continued reflection of the work of Gaudí, magnificent to behold. We were able to enter one of the towers, from which we held our breaths to look out over the impressive view of Barcelona.

There also happened to be a special performance there of the acclaimed drama, *Misteri de la Selva,* written in an ancient romance language but easily understood through the beautifully expressed players. I have to admit, it was quite moving and touching.

Romance isn't really that bad, I mused to myself, thinking of my dear Joshua and how very much in love I was with the man. I can see why Meg was such a sucker for a great love affair.

Wrapping up the evening at a little nearby café, we indulged in more sangria and tried new tapas. We quite enjoyed these smaller dinner samplings in contrast to the fancy, multi-course banquets we indulged in while in Florence or the hearty meals in Ireland. Yet all of these trips have been incredible experiences I will never forget.

Tucking myself in for the evening, I looked forward to checking in with my love.

"And how was my girl's museum adventure today?"

"Oh my God, you would not believe everything I saw! Picasso, Miró, Gaudí—and so many contemporary artists. The colors, the textures, the symbolism and emotional portrayal; I couldn't get enough of it. Like I was whisked away into my own kind of fairy tale—a darker one, mind you, but another world altogether where I just felt, I don't know, at home. Understood. It really was a dream come true today."

"Good for you, baby. I am glad you are enjoying every moment." I heard something off in his voice as he said it. In fact, his whole tone was foreboding ever since he picked up the phone.

"What's wrong?"

"Don't worry about it, love. I want you to just focus on yourself right now."

"Cut the crap, Josh and spill it," I demanded.

"Okay," he acquiesced slowly. "Have you talked to Jay lately?" With a sense of remorse, I swallowed hard before answering.

"Yes. He made me promise to check in with him daily. I hope you're not mad."

"No, of course not. At least, not at you," he reassured me. "Not sure why he would make you promise something like that when I'm your boyfriend and he's not."

Ah, the resentful jab. That was familiar at least. I didn't bother to address it. I wasn't up for a male ego boxing round tonight.

"Say, have Bruce and Jay ever met?" he continued when I refused to acknowledge his petty comment.

"Hmm, not to my knowledge. I mean, they know of each other, but I don't think we've ever formally introduced them. Why do you ask?"

"I—I saw them together at the coffee shop on that corner by your old apartment earlier today. I didn't get close enough to hear what they were saying because I didn't want them to know I was there. They were rather intense. It just seemed so odd. I thought maybe you would know why they'd be meeting."

"That is pretty unusual. I'll have to ask him."

"Don't, Marissa. I'd rather you not talk to him at all, actually. I don't trust him."

"Josh, I have known him my entire life. If he was meeting with Bruce, I am sure there was a damn good reason. Maybe he was just keeping an eye on him like I had asked."

"You asked—never mind," he stopped himself from scolding me, knowing with my growing terseness that he had to tread lightly. "Okay, but you didn't see them, Mar. They were mighty cozy for two grown men who had never met before. They are up to something. I can feel it."

"I think you might be overreacting."

"Seriously, I want you to stop talking to Jay for the moment until I can figure it out." So much for treading lightly.

"I'm sorry, did you just forbid me to speak with my best friend of over thirty years? What are you, a caveman?"

"No, but I am your boyfriend and you should respect my wishes," came the irritable response before he adjusted his tone to pleading. "Trust me on this. Please."

"This isn't about trust, Josh. This is about you controlling my life, and I won't be told what to do. If I want to talk to Jay and text him every day, I will. And don't you dare demand otherwise."

"Why is he so important to you? Are you in love with him or something?"

"What the fuck is wrong with you? I just finished saying I've known the man since we were children—practically my whole life. He's like a brother. Nothing ever happened between us and nothing ever will. Why can't you get that through your thick skull?"

"Because I see the way he looks at you. You are so oblivious, Marissa. He's trying to come in between us. And I know Bruce isn't my biggest fan, as I'm sure your mom told him I tipped you off about his divorce. So, maybe they are plotting against me."

"For goodness' sake, you are being paranoid and stupid right now. Josh, I love you. Nothing Jay or Bruce or anyone else says is going to change that. Except maybe *you,* if you keep this shit up."

"So, now I can't be concerned over your guy best friend, who you used to live with and practically walk around naked in front of? Who made you promise to keep in touch daily and then goes and suspiciously meets with your mom's boyfriend? I'm just asking for you to be cautious instead of impulsive."

"You can be concerned all you want. But I'm a big girl and can make my own decisions. And I'm not going to stop talking to Jay because your ego is bruised."

"You're impossible. How am I supposed to protect you if you are going to be so belligerent about everything?"

"Sweetheart, you haven't even seen belligerent. Tell you what. I'm going to go to bed, and you can take the rest of the evening to contemplate why being a Neanderthal is not the way to keep my heart. Good night, Joshua," I spat out, not giving him the chance to respond before hanging up the phone.

My fire was fueled—and not just over Josh. What the fuck was Jay doing with Bruce? True, he could've been doing just as I asked, but why didn't he tell me he had planned to meet him and keep me in the loop? Since I still had yet to text him today, I thought I'd do some investigative work of my own.

Just checking in. All quiet here. Incredible museum tours. How was your day?

Can't wait to hear about it. Day was normal. Work, gym, eat.

That's it? Sounds like an uneventful day. Nothing exciting to report?

Nope. Same old. Gotta run though. BNO.

K. Have fun.

You too. Stay safe xo

Same old, huh? Now I was truly pissed. Why didn't he just tell me about his little rendezvous with Bruce? What was he hiding? Even if he was going out for a "boys night out," he could have said he had to run, but that he'd fill me in later.

Now I understand why Josh was so miffed. Why would Jay lie to me?

Jay's omission was a lie. Josh's demands were juvenile. I was dealing with two little children.

That was it—I had enough of this stupid boy battle between them and now they were going to face the consequences. I wasn't going to contact either of them for a few days. See how they'd like that. No one tries to control or fuck around with Marissa Rossi.

The next morning, Meg was feeling a little bit under the weather, so we delayed our trip to the beach for a few hours so she could get some more rest. Still angry at the men in my life, I took the opportunity to close myself off in my little studio.

But I didn't want to finish painting my hostess gift or continue on with my Italian-inspired intentions. No, I wasn't feeling flowery at all.

It was darkness that consumed me. Anger, mistrust,

betrayal, lunacy even. Not knowing who or what to believe, and quite possibly overreacting like I tend to do. It didn't matter. I picked up the dark colored palette and began drawing from deep within me.

The dragon popped into my mind. Not a cute little *Puff, the Magic Dragon.* A sinister, dark gray, scaly, green-eyed, pissed off beast breathing fire onto a red heart, turning it black. The sky was ominous with rain clouds and lightning in the background.

I painted for hours, frantically pouring out how I felt. How betrayed and annoyed I was by the two men in my life. How my tender heart inevitably was going to be consumed by the evil creature representing man.

Like the man who changed me for the rest of my life.

Oh no, I would never forget Mr. Terrance, my high school English teacher. The man I trusted, who promised he would help me pass the course so I could graduate—who wanted nothing more than to seduce the innocent child that I was.

It started all so innocuously. *Stop by after school and we'll go through the lesson,* he said. And so, I did. It just so happened to be a lesson in poets of the Romanticism Movement, where he'd first seductively read the words of Keats, Hugo and Lord Byron, and then engage me in deep conversation about their meaning.

He'd increasingly move in closer each time, and my teenage hormonal body became confused with the rush of lustful feelings and wetness building down below. *Was that normal?* I had the courage to ask him, as he made discussing sex such an easy topic to open up about. *Oh yes,* he would reply, and simply smile.

Paint, paint, paint. Darken the dragon scales and deepen the evil green eyes of the demon centerpiece.

It was Robert Burns' *A Red, Red Rose* that tipped the scale between conversation and physical touch. I could feel the love he "declared" for me as he demonstrated what that love did to his body as he cited the poet's words. I could see the hardened outline under his pants. I felt the curiosity as he encouraged me to touch…to open his pants and allow an exploration. He let me take a taste before he took my lips in a heated, twirling tongue kiss that sent electrical pulses through my young body.

He then took it upon himself to remove my skirt and panties, ever so gently inserting his fingers inside of me. I had only read about what happens between a man and a woman, but nothing told me about how it felt. Not even stealing a first kiss and a boob grope from a kid named Joey in my freshman year prepared me for this. I could feel a weird pressure building inside, and yet, it felt so good. It must have been right, I thought. He was my teacher, and I trusted in what he was teaching me.

He kept telling me how beautiful I was, confessing how he would think of me at night as he touched himself. He twistedly quoted Burns, *"And I will come again, my luve,"* as he finally overpowered me onto the cold, hard classroom floor and inserted his hardened cock into my virginal center. My feelings were mixed with shame and curiosity and confusion, but it felt so good that I didn't make him stop—even if it pained me in the beginning; it quickly turned pleasurable.

Whatever he was doing made my body rise and shudder into a maddening explosion. He then moaned my name— he really loved me!

And yet, as he pulled out of me and zipped up his pants, he simply congratulated me on getting an "A" in his class, and threatened if I ever told anyone, he would make certain

I would never graduate high school and that my parents would learn how much of a seductress whore I really was.

Deepen the black around the heart—the fire to singe an outline of the gentle love it's supposed to represent.

He left me on the cold floor in a panic, half of my clothes crumpled in a sinful ball in the corner. I feared him and believed him. I knew I couldn't breathe a word or he'd make good on his promise—the danger in his eyes told me so.

How could I possibly have told anyone, anyway? At that moment, the whole family was rallied around Meg, whose heart had just been completely shattered by the cheating Scotty. Scotty, who was like a brother to me. Who I confided in about everything, who promised that he would always be there for me. "I'll always watch out for you, little sis. You can count on it."

But no, when he abandoned Meg, he abandoned me, and I was left with no one to guide me through this confusion and degradation of my body and soul.

It became all about "poor Meg;" I didn't exist. *Meg, Meg, Meg.* We had to be gentle with her and kiss her ass until her heart healed. Mom and Dad and even Granny and Pops had to keep checking in on her and walk on eggshells while she transformed from sweet and creative to ambitious and selfish. All the while, I was invisible.

Mia had hopelessly been in love with her high school sweetheart, Kevin, and life was working out swimmingly for her, so she didn't need any support. She gave all her attention to Meg, too, trying to save her from herself. But me? Nothing more than, "How's school going, Marissa?" and a blank stare as they all barely waited for my response.

I had no one to unload my burden on, and so, I internalized it and never spoke a word. Thank God he didn't get me pregnant that day. I was grateful for that small miracle, though it took two period cycles and countless false home stick tests before I could breathe a sigh of relief.

I did graduate, however, with the sick irony of Mr. Terrance being the chosen one to hand me my diploma.

Let's crack open a bit of the sky…

So, between the ill-intended poetry readings and the bastardized brother, my heart hardened to the concept of romance altogether. It was then that I spiraled into a world of sex, drugs and booze. It was then that I decided I would use my body for power and be the one in control of who, when and how. No one would ever use me again.

And I, along with my descent into trouble, went completely unnoticed. Eventually, I got my act together before I needed rehab or offed myself, but I never completely converted to "good girl" status, if you know what I mean. It wasn't until a few years later that I confided in Jay about all that went down, and he swore that my good old teacher was lucky he had already tragically passed away from a car accident, otherwise, he would have gone after him. But karma got to him first and spared Jay the lifetime prison sentence.

What made that old, stuffed down memory resurface? I wondered, recovering from the bitter reenactment in my brain.

Finished, I stared at my canvas in disbelief. It was hauntingly disconcerting, and yet, the best creation I thought I had ever imagined. It wasn't some prissy little landmark scene that people would smile at and wow over. It was raw and purely from me. Unfiltered.

I never heard him come in.

"Did you just make that? It's—disturbingly stunning," gasped EJ, moving in closer now that I was aware of his presence. Embarrassed that my work had been seen by someone who owned his own art gallery, I quickly made up a few excuses to preserve my artistic dignity.

"I—I was just playing around. It's not what I usually do. I was just upset and venting it out with paint," I explained.

"Just playing? Maybe you should just play around more often. Tell me—what do you usually design?"

"Landscapes. Buildings. A few sculptures of creatures or symbols of where I've been or memories that mean something to me. Something that moves me."

"Sounds positively ordinary," he mock yawned. "Are you happy with that work?"

"Everyone seems to think it's pretty," I admitted.

"Marissa, the first rule of art is that you don't make it for others. You make it for yourself so that others can see themselves through you," he enlightened. "This piece is phenomenal. This is exactly what I would love to feature in my gallery. I don't want your Ireland drawings," he decided emphatically.

"I want more of this. I want more primal passion and emotion. This isn't just heartbreak—this is the destruction of love that forever changes our hearts to black. It's not the sappy love song we sing to ourselves to make us hopeful— it's our real pain and loss portrayed in a way that pulls at us. This is brilliance, Marissa."

I only sat there looking at him in stunned reverence for his words. I never thought in a million years someone could see into me and accept that I had a darkness. Or that expressing that very darkness through art would be worth anything.

"Thank you," I replied meekly.

"Now that I have given my blessing for you to be the artist you are meant to be," he said in a softer, more conversational tone, "do you want to talk about the inspiration behind this painting? Are you all right, cuz?"

"I am, thank you. This helped. Sometimes I tend to overdramatize situations in my life," I laughed, pointing at the drawing. "I had a stupid fight with my boyfriend and best friend last night, and they pissed me off. Nothing life shattering, either." I wasn't about to go into the much deeper wound that breathed the real darkness into the dragon's life. Even in death, Mr. Terrance's threat haunted my truth-telling abilities.

"Well, they should piss you off more often," he joked, giving me a light kiss on the forehead as he left me to my finishing touches and went off for his final day of business. "Take care of yourself, young one. See you tomorrow."

After enjoying a light lunch with my sisters at the villa, we packed up our bags for a day at the beach. Meg was feeling much better, and Mia had our whole itinerary planned. I was feeling lighter as well, as if all the anger had been pulled out of me and onto the canvas. Had I discovered a new kind of therapy?

Our destination was Puerto Olímpico, where the 1992 Olympics were held. Before settling down onto the sandy beach, we checked out the famous "recent" addition; evidently, the games revitalized the economy and changed the culture of the city by opening up its heart to its oceanic roots.

A new skyline was built, marked by two new skyscrapers, a sports marina, several docks and the now famous golden fish. Restaurants and nightclubs lined the strip—something we were game for checking out as evening fell.

But first, it would be a day of sun and sand—and apparently, topless old ladies and speedo-wearing men. Even Mia laughed that she felt more confident about herself after witnessing sagging, aged boobs and beer bellies strutting their stuff without care.

The water was sparkling and colder than I expected. The saltwater revitalized my body, washing away the residual anger and frustration over my current dilemma. I had several texts from Josh that I ignored, eventually turning off my phone completely to avoid any further annoyance. Thankfully, Jay had no idea he was on my shit list, too—he'd figure that out tomorrow when I stopped responding to him tonight, though.

They both wanted me to have a sister trip—so that's exactly what I planned on doing.

We spent the afternoon laying in the hot sun, people-watching (we even stopped covering our eyes at one point) and swimming. We just talked and laughed like we used to—no heavy conversations, just fun sister chats that made it feel like we were young kids again. I needed this uninterrupted time with them more than I realized.

The evening continued with an incredible dinner at one of the seaside restaurants. We couldn't resist each ordering different dishes so that we could try as much as possible— pan-seared monkfish with braised kale, roasted garbanzo beans and spicy tomato sauce; sea scallops topped with a creamy bacon and mushroom sauce with baby lima beans; and of course, Mia had to go all weird on us and order the grilled octopus with fried potatoes and salsa verde.

I was game to give it a try (gross) but Meg wanted nothing to do with it, claiming the smell of it was making her sick to her stomach. As an alternate, we selected grilled lamb chops in a walnut cream sauce, which was a fabulous choice. The waitress insisted that we also try the legendary crema Catalana for dessert: a variation of crème brûlée but infused with hints of orange, lemon and cinnamon.

I might even dare to say it was better than the traditional French classic.

Feeling the heat rise up from the wine intoxication over dinner, I coerced my sisters into letting me dance off my alcohol at one of the nearby clubs.

Ah, now this felt like home to me. The bump of the beat and the sizzle of the salsa. Losing myself in music was the only way I could release stress in a non-sexual manner. Okay, well, I still was sexual about it, but kept my clothes on at least.

I kept downing the drinks, as the Spanish men were ever so generous in buying me them…much harder cocktails than dinner wine. My sisters were evidently becoming impatient waiting for me to get my fill of the evening so we could head home. Maybe if they loosened up a bit and accepted a drink offer themselves, they wouldn't be such old ladies.

Besides, my new dance partner, Santiago, was great company to keep; they were free to leave. I was in good hands. Literally.

He pulled me in close gyration, his hands planted firmly on my ass as I grinded into his under-the-pants hardening cock. I loved the feeling of knowing I was turning a man on and encouraged the seductive dance. I soon felt his hot breath biting at my neck and his hoarse invitation to take me home.

Josh, who?

But of course, dear old Mia had to ruin my fun by pulling us away and telling my never-to-be lover that I was in a serious relationship and that it was time for us to go home. Ugh, I was so pissed at her.

The whole cab ride back I remember I was yelling at them. I'm not exactly sure what I was saying, but I think I let the secret out that I thought Meg was a condescending, pretentious bitch and Mia was a nosy goody two-shoes and that I was tired of their constant belittling of me. Or something like that.

I believe I also proclaimed I was pissed at both Josh and Jay, though I'm not sure if I told them why exactly. I did let them know I wasn't pleased with how they pulled me off of Santiago, and that if I needed to have sex with a Catalonian stranger to get back at the jerks, it was my call to make and not theirs.

Oh, and I think I may have also admitted that I was not alone in Ireland and Italy, like they thought, before I passed out.

7

My head fucking hurts, I thought as the sun's beams stung my eyes. *How did I even get here?*

Oh, right. My sisters put me into a cab and must have tucked me in quickly. I was still in last night's clothes and the remnants of mascara were all over the bleached white pillows. Cleaning that wasn't going to be much fun.

Neither would returning the texts from a frantic Josh and Jay, although both seem to have settled down shortly after two a.m. when I saw the group text from Mia saying I was fine, just having too much fun. I'll have to remember to thank her for covering for me later.

Although I don't recall much, I figured I'd have some apologizing to do as well. I was not looking forward to the aftermath of my drunken stupor. I decided to prolong it as much as possible by hiding under the covers until the throbs went away. I could really use a joint right about now.

The peace didn't last long, as both of my sisters showed up at my bedroom door—one with a bottle of aspirin and the other with a huge jug of water.

"How's the hangover?" asked Mia.

"Terrible. I guess I deserve it after last night," I looked up apologetically.

"Oh, you do," replied Meg. "Sorry. I figured it would be okay for me to point it out since I'm the insufferable bitch of the family," she jabbed.

"Yeah, about that. There's a lot that is a blur, but I know I said some things I shouldn't have. I'm sorry."

Mia shot Meg a look that said "quit it" before turning back to me.

"We'll talk. Why don't you take a shower and then meet us at the pool when you're ready? EJ will join us later this afternoon, but us girls can have a little chat beforehand. Okay?"

Nodding my head in agreement and humiliation, I drank down three pills before getting out of the bed. I wasn't looking forward to the impending lecture from my sister-moms, but being stuck in a foreign country with no way out, I guess I couldn't run away from my own mouth this time.

"I am really sorry for everything I said last night," I began, approaching my two sisters sitting on the deep-cushioned lounges, leaving one in the middle that obviously was meant for me. Great, a Marissa sandwich. This was going to be hell.

Thank goodness Meg seemed to have cooled down a bit, probably thanks to Mia's interference—though my level-headed sister wasn't exactly in a happy-go-lucky state of mind herself.

"First, let's start with how you really feel about us," prompted Mia, like a damn kindergarten school teacher starting her lesson after morning circle time.

"I know I said mean things, but I don't know exactly what I said. I'm guessing from your comment this morning, Meg, that I was pretty nasty to you," I began.

"I didn't realize I was such a horrible sister, always making you feel bad about yourself," she answered in a saddened, remorseful voice.

"I know I can be challenging," I admitted. "But yes,

sometimes you make me feel like I am not good enough to even be your sister. I should have come to you about this before, and not waited until I was drunk."

"There are a lot of things we should have talked about before, but yes—having an open and honest relationship with each other would be a great start," she acknowledged. "I accept that I am not the kindest or most sensitive of sisters. I haven't always been there for you, and I'm sorry if I've ever made you feel like I didn't love you.

"I do love you with all my heart. We may not always see eye to eye little sis, but make no mistake that my intentions are never to hurt you. My job is to protect you and look out for you. But I promise to make more of an effort to listen instead of judge."

"Deep down, I know that. And I know how impossible I can be sometimes. I promise that instead of reacting or getting all jealous, I will try harder to open up about what I am feeling. I don't want us to always be fighting, Meg."

My eldest sister moved to pull me into her arms with tears in her eyes. "Me neither, Mar. Let's start over?"

"Absolutely," I smiled big and squeezed her tighter.

"And I can't help being the peacemaker of the family, but this is why," Mia pointed out.

"I know you mean well, too. I just wish you weren't so cynical or question everything I do," I shared.

"I guess we all have parts of our nature that we can't help," she chuckled. "But if we just accept these parts of each other, and respect how we feel, I think we can navigate this sister thing much better. We have a wonderful bond—one that I never want to break."

"I agree," said Meg. "I don't ever want to lose what we have. You both mean too much to me."

"To me, too. I'd be lost without you. Thanks for being

so understanding. My big mouth and impulsive actions have a habit of ruining a lot of things in my life."

"About that," Meg initiated. "You said a lot of inaudible things last night about being angry at both Jay and Josh. And you also mentioned confiding in Jay about some note. What's that all about?"

Fuck. I really do have loose lips when I drink. No use in hiding it from them now.

"Okay, but please don't get mad at me."

"We won't," Mia reassured me as she tossed a glance over to Meg to beg for her new oath of patience with me.

"A few days before we left, I received a new threatening note in my mailbox that said 'Watch your back. I'm not done with you bitches yet.'"

"Why didn't you tell us?" Mia gently asked.

"I was afraid that you both would cancel this trip and I'd never get my statue." I had to be honest. This wasn't a game and they did have a right to know what was going on. I couldn't choke down the truth anymore. It's never served me well before.

"It was wrong of me. I get that now."

"Does anyone know except Jay?"

"No. I lied to Josh and said it was just a thank you note from EJ and Rodney. In that moment, I didn't need him jumping to conclusions and freaking out on me. He's so overprotective. I didn't want to tell you and worry you both, either. It was only the one note, and I haven't gotten anything else since. Except—"

"Except what?" probed Mia.

"Except at our last family dinner, when Bruce was alone with me in the kitchen, he said those same exact words to me: 'Watch your back.' It threw me off, wondering if he was behind the note. Knowing that Josh and Bruce already had their reservations about each other, I didn't want to tell Josh just yet.

"I happened to be over at Jay's and we were talking, and something made me want to tell him. I knew that he would keep an eye on our family while we were away, in exchange for me keeping him posted every night." I saw Mia hold up a hand to Meg, who I could tell wanted to make a comment about my loose lips with Jay about our personal family business.

"So, nothing else has happened except the note and cryptic conversation with Bruce? Nothing at all in Spain?" Mia wanted to clarify.

"Absolutely nothing. I promise you."

"Okay, that's a relief. We'll still want to alert the guards and let them know of potential danger. I think just to be safe, Mia should call Kevin and let him know about your exchange with Bruce. Let's have him casually keep an eye on things. He can be discreet." We all nodded in agreement.

"I understand why you didn't tell us before, but if anything else happens, will you please, please let us know?" Meg pleaded.

"I will. I shouldn't have kept it from you. I'm really sorry."

"Now, why are you fighting with both Josh and Jay? Does it have to do with any of this?" Meg continued her questioning. Wow, I really did say a lot last night. What else did I divulge?

"So, Josh saw Bruce and Jay at my regular coffee shop the other day. He thought it was suspicious and informed me that I was not to talk to Jay anymore until he figured it out. Like I would do that," I rolled my eyes in remembrance of his stupid demand.

"And then I tried to find out what Jay was doing

that day, to see if he'd just tell me and give me a logical explanation—especially since they've never met before. But he never admitted to being with Bruce, so now I know he is keeping something from me and that ticks me off."

"Men," Meg mused. "They really are primeval creatures."

"Well, maybe after today, you can smooth things over with them. You are going through a lot right now—these journeys are more intense than you can even imagine. You are in a foreign country, and not only is it physically tiring, but mentally and emotionally challenging.

"As frustrated as you are with both of them, try to keep things balanced until you get home and can have one-on-one conversations with them both—like you just had with us," Mia suggested.

"You're right," I conceded. "I'll make peace by the end of today. But first, I'm starving. I need to eat something and then I would really love to talk to EJ—about anything except my life and drunken blabberings."

"Okay, we'll reserve the 'I wasn't alone in Ireland and Italy' conversations for another time then," winked Meg. My God, I was never going to drink again.

EJ's entrance to the rooftop pool was nothing short of ostentatious, with his loud flamingo shirt, khaki shorts and wide-brimmed sun hat announcing his arrival before his booming voice did. Someone was ready for a fiesta with his tray of delicious snacks and refreshing drinks (non-alcoholic, mercifully).

"Who's ready for a little mid-day grub?"

"Perfect timing, EJ. I'm absolutely starving," I proclaimed with gratitude as I grabbed some ham and cheese and a few pieces of bread and started shoving the food into my mouth.

"Mmm-hmm. I thought you would be, little señorita salsa."

"Does everybody know?" The red rushed right to my cheeks.

"Well, honey, I was here when they brought you in. Who do you think was able to carry your plastered patootie into the bedroom?"

"Oh. Thank you."

"Not a problem, cuz. You are turning out to be quite entertaining. I like you," he said as he poked my nose with his finger with a little "boop"-like noise. I couldn't help but laugh at this character. Should I tell him he was equally entertaining?

"Now then. Everything has been set up with your statue. It's currently going through an appraisal and validation and it should be ready for you to claim the day after tomorrow."

"Wow, that was fast. Usually we have to jump through multiple hoops to get there," said Meg.

"Well, I've been doing the hoop-jumping, so you're welcome," he responded with a smile and mimicked the scoring of a basket. "Marissa will just have to show her identification and get fingerprinted, but it should be relatively easy after that. I'll take you down myself to make sure it's smooth as peanut butter."

"Thank you for everything you have done for us," Mia said gratefully.

"Aw, shucks, it's nothing. I'm tickled y'all are my cousins. I've enjoyed getting to know you. I don't have any other family, other than Rodney and his kin, and this new cousin Teresa here. It's nice to know I actually have local relations."

"We feel the same way," I promised him. "So, how is it that we are so intimately connected when our lines are so many generations apart and scattered? It makes sense to us about the O'Sullivans and Bianchi families, but how is it that our Rubio roots are so easily traced?"

"Ah, that my dear, is a wonderful story. You see, when Elena went off to marry Banan, that was not the end of her family ties with her brother and mother. Quite the contrary," he began.

He proceeded to explain how Elena and Eduardo kept in touch, and how while James O'Sullivan was still alive, he would make arrangements to bring his daughter-in-law back to Spain to see her family at least once or twice a year. He really embraced Elena into the family, and by extension, her family.

Their mother had fallen quite ill, and with Eduardo a struggling middle class fisherman trying to provide for his own family of four, James had sent money over for her care. Eventually, he brought their mother to Ireland where Elena could care for her herself until her passing.

The Rubios never forgot the kindness of the O'Sullivans, and so, EJ's grandfather, Juan Tomás (and to some extent, his brother, Miguel), continued the kinship down the line as Cian and Banan Junior's cousins.

Junior didn't care so much for this Spanish family, but Cian was always welcoming and kept in touch. Juan Tomás made a trip out to Ireland upon Lena's birth, bringing along his only son, Matteo, who was nearing adulthood.

Matteo had big dreams of moving to America, as did Cian. And so, Cian and Juan Tomás forged an agreement that Matteo could indeed make a life for himself in America, under the care of Cian and Alessia. When the little O'Sullivan family departed, Matteo hugged his parents goodbye and set off to fulfill his dream.

After only two years, Matteo was then of age and ready to move out on his own. He had grown quite fond of his baby cousin, Lena, and was the one person in the entire country who looked out for her welfare, even years after her parents died and she was stuck in a loveless marriage with Antonio Marino.

Lena and Matteo kept in touch, though time and circumstances widened the distance between them, most of it due to the controlling nature of the Marinos. But of course, the spirit that resided in Lena wanted to continue honoring the only family connection she had, and so her son, Leigh, and Matteo's son, EJ—a few decades apart in age—knew of each other from brief visits and a few stories passed down.

It's why it was so easy for Leigh to track down EJ after Lena revealed all of this family history.

"So, how does the dragon statue come into play?" I was dying to know more.

"Okay, little minx, I will tell you a little bit about it since you have very little patience," he chided. "Forgive me, cousin Leigh, but I'm going to have to bend a few rules for this one over here," he continued as he raised his hands in prayer to the clouds.

"As I mentioned the other day, when Horace disgraced the family, all that was left to him was this dragon statue from his mother. Well, when he killed himself and it was found among his possessions, it naturally went to his only son. Although my great-uncle Miguel was better suited for it philosophically—God rest his soul, the manipulative philanderer—Eduardo thought it would be in better hands with my grandfather.

"Miguel really couldn't care less about it, so gratefully,

there was no objection to it continuing down the line to my father as he left for America, so that he would have a piece of his family with him always. He then granted it to me as his only child, where I held it in high regard at my gallery until I received the call from Leigh.

"Lena had told him about the relic, and he wanted to know if I would be open to passing it across the lines to his youngest granddaughter. Being that I have no children of my own, and I hadn't known about Teresa at that point in time, I had no qualms about handing it off—especially after hearing him talk about you. It was meant for you, darling," he added.

"I'm not sure I understand why," I said, rather offended by the whole idea of it.

"My dear, why is that?"

"You just said it was passed to your grandfather, but his brother, who was not quite so upstanding, was actually more deserving of the statue? That doesn't exactly make me feel like my grandfather had a high opinion of me."

"Oh my. Oh, no, no, no. You have me all wrong, cuz. I can't get into the meaning behind the statue just yet. But I can tell you there was more to Miguel that made him a better match. Let's just say passion is involved, and a wonderful life lesson. Do not jump to lopsided conclusions just yet, until you hear the whole story," he gently lectured.

"Once you learn about the dragon in a few days, it will all make sense to you. But little one, you must know that your grandfather was quite taken with you. I assure you, this was skillfully coordinated, and after meeting you, I can attest that the man knew exactly what he was doing."

"Okay. I guess I will just have to wait, huh?"

"Indeed," he affirmed. "But—I do have an idea that I think will help you pass the time. How would you like to take a trip to Madrid?"

"That would be incredible!" exclaimed Meg. "Can we go see some flamenco dancers?"

Mia chimed in. "Oh, I'd love to see the Buen Retiro Park if we could! I've read so much about it."

"Yes, yes," he laughed as we all came at him. "We can do all that. But the main attraction will be the Prado Museum. A little birdy told me that Marissa's favorite artist is Goya. Now, how can she come to Spain and not see the grandest displays of his work?"

"Are you serious? Are you freaking serious?" I couldn't believe it. EJ was the best cousin ever!

"I'm serious! It's a 3-hour train ride, so to make the most of the day, it's best that we're ready to head out by three o'clock. If we plan this right, we can arrive in time to check into our hotel and then grab a flamenco dinner show this evening."

I ran over to him and embraced him with the biggest hug I had ever given someone. "Thank you from the bottom of my heart."

Before we left, I decided to follow my sisters' advice and restore peace to my relationships with Josh and Jay. I texted them both individually, letting them know we were doing well, had no troubles and were headed on an overnight trip to Madrid. I figured this short exchange would be enough to patch things up temporarily.

Well, with Jay, it was easy, because he never knew I was mad at him to begin with, thanks to Mia's intervention last night. As for Josh, his response was a cool *"have fun"* and not much else, but he did sign it with his signature *"J xo,"* so that was at least promising.

Guess he knows I need time to cool off, yet appreciates the fact that I reached out and acknowledged him. I'll deal with my relationship issues another time.

Tonight, we were going to leave everything behind us and enter into the exotic world of flamenco. Happening upon a local Madrid hotspot for both dinner and a show after checking into the hotel, the music took control and I immediately felt alive again.

The food was outstanding as we dined on a tasting menu of scallop carpaccio, wild sea bass, roasted pigeon and lamb with pumpkin purée and a side of buckwheat risotto and roasted vegetables. I refrained from drinking, as did Meg, but EJ and Mia certainly enjoyed their share of the wine pairings that accompanied our gourmet cuisine.

Watching the flamenco dancers was a complete sensory overload in the most wonderful of ways, from the vibrant costumes and masterful movements of the dancers, singers and guitar players, to the mesmerizing music that simply moved our souls. Our Spain experience certainly would not have been complete without this cultural extravaganza.

I'm not sure what it was, but I felt the pull to Madrid to be even stronger than that to Barcelona. The coastal town—and especially its outskirt town, Sitges, where we were staying—were both truly magnificent, no question. But there was an aura, a magnetism that was luring me into the core of Madrid's very existence.

Even the Buen Retiro Park we went to in the morning felt different from the other natural landmarks we've seen over the last few months. There was a magic and grace to it—even though, yes, it had lakes and monuments and gorgeous fountains like all the rest, but the ambiance was unexpectedly enticing.

The walkways were expertly manicured with the

brightest symmetrical greenery. I even found myself enamored by the Crystal Palace, with its unique metal and glass architecture that self-reflected into a lake.

But what I loved most were the daring sculptures—one in particular called *El Retiro,* or Fallen Angel. It is said to be the likeness of Satan, the only one of its kind, his fall depicted as he is surrounded by demon heads. It was defiantly fascinating.

We elected to sit among the open-air gardens for a fun picnic lunch, which Mia, of course, had arranged for us on her early trip to a local market with EJ. She hadn't been able to do as much cooking on this trip, so we indulged her request to pull together a special meal for us. She didn't disappoint.

The morning was light and relaxing, yet my nerves were getting worked up. I felt butterflies in anticipation of finally getting to seeing Goya's work in the flesh—or stone, as it may be.

The experience was more than I could have ever imagined.

I have to say, even as magnificent as my art experience has been so far on these three trips, nothing was as dreamlike as finally being able to see the works of my favorite artist of all time.

Known for capturing the darkness of mankind, I couldn't help but be drawn into the realities of his vision and feel his pain. It was as if I somehow related to the misery he exposed, wishing he could bring the internal darkness within me to such beautiful, expressive light.

Sure, some find him sadistic and crazy. I admit that there are some disturbing pieces, and yet, what he depicts is truth. Even in his *Black Paintings* of other worldly gods and creatures, they represent the human plight and angst.

Why did I feel so guilty for being fascinated by the darkness? For hearing the call? Sensing my internal dilemma, EJ found a way to my side where he could speak without my sisters overhearing.

"I see you are completely captivated, my cousin. Does that trouble you?"

"Yes. I mean, so much of his work depicts violence and brutality, and yet, I feel like I truly *get* it; that I live it. Like it's not that I just understand the artist's interpretation, but also the subjects within and their own drive to commit such savagery. Does that make me, I don't know, evil?" I looked at him with imploring eyes, surprised at myself for revealing such a personal inner secret to someone I barely knew.

"No, cuz, it does not. It makes you emotionally connecting and passionate. Tell me—what is it that moves you so much about his work?" he asked, genuinely interested and non-judgmental.

"Human beings can be ugly and cruel, and it doesn't make the world a better place by living in denial. At least, not in my opinion. Sex, drugs, war, crime—we are that as much as we are hope, faith and love. When we embrace the very idea that we each have a dark side to us, we are that much closer to living in our own truth."

"Indeed. And, therein, lies the beauty of *el dragón,*" he cryptically hinted and walked away to join the others, while I pondered what he could possibly mean by that.

8

The trip back to Sitges was uneventful; mostly a foursome of sleepyheads finally getting some rest after a long day's excursion. We all instantly retreated to our bedrooms to continue the slumber, knowing that tomorrow was the big day. I'd finally have my hands on my statue, and hopefully the reveal of my connection to it.

Of course, I couldn't sleep. I stared at the ceiling for hours trying to figure out what the dragon meant, and what the "theme" of this journey would be for me. Love for Meg, dreams for Mia. So far, all I experienced was a fascination for obscurity and fighting with a whole bunch of loved ones.

Simply confirmation that I was a black sheep? Or rather, a flame-breathing dragon?

This shadowy ewe knew she had to make some kind of amends with Josh, so I called him. It was just approaching evening back in New York, so I knew he would be awake. As expected, he was colder than a polar bear in the Arctic Ocean.

"How was your trip to Madrid?" *Great,* I thought sarcastically. We'd go the small talk route.

"Unbelievable," I barely answered. "Listen, Josh—"

"No, wait Marissa," he cut me off. "I've had a lot of time to think, and I realized it was unfair of me to ask you to stop speaking to Jay. I just get so jealous of the guy," he admitted, melting his iceberg tone as he got right to the point.

"Thank you for saying that. But you have no reason to be jealous of him, Josh. I love *you.* "

"I love you, too."

"I'm sorry, too, for overreacting. I know you are just trying to protect me. I'm trying to accept that there is someone in my life who truly loves me. It's a struggle, like I'm waiting for this 'too good to be true' scenario to fall apart in my face and it scares the fuck out of me. So, I default to pushing you away before you can do it to me.

"Classic Marissa," I explained, feeling the need to pour my heart out instead of shut him out.

"I know, and I tried to give you space without being angry. But I'm a hothead, too," he laughed. "I guess we both just need to accept that about each other—but also learn how to trust and communicate better instead of blow up. Can you forgive me for being a caveman?"

"If you can forgive me for being an unrelenting firecracker, then sure," I giggled. "But please, don't give me masked ultimatums like that ever again. We may be together, but I will always be an independent woman and I won't do well to be controlled."

"Understood. I will not chain you up like that again," he said sincerely.

"Well, I didn't say you couldn't chain me up," I replied seductively, leading us to a more pleasant bedtime conversation.

After a sexually releasing make-up video chat, I thought I should quickly text Jay as promised before I fell asleep. Maybe now that a few days had passed, he might be more willing to offer up the information about seeing Bruce.

And I knew exactly how to get it out of him.

Just got back from Madrid. I might need to live here. All is quiet though. How are things over there?

Hey beautiful. I had a feeling you would love Madrid. Things here are great but lonely. I miss you.

Miss you too. How's my family? Been keeping an eye on them and Bruce?

Everyone is fine. Just like I promised.

Have you seen them?

Kevin had questions so I stopped by Mia's house to check on them. They suckered me into tea time lol. But they are doing great. No worries.

Is that all?

Yeah. Why?

No reason. K TTYT.

Okay...good night Riss. xo

I didn't even bother to respond. He just failed my little test. No mention of meeting up with Bruce. Either something was wrong and he wasn't telling me, or he was up to something. I hated being across the ocean because typically, I'd show up at his doorstep and demand an answer.

But as my sisters suggested, I'm trying to keep a cool head and bide my time until I can confront him in person and get the real truth. Easy for them to say, but I knew I wasn't going to get it over a text or even a phone call. We all group chatted with Mom, Granny and the kids while we were at the park, and everyone was sincerely well, so I could believe that at least.

Finally feeling the sleep set in, I allowed my body to sink down into the soft covers and enter dreamland. Though, with visions of bloodshed, dragon fire and destruction, I'm not exactly sure I could call it that.

Needless to say, I did not wake up refreshed and perky like Mia. The remnants of the nightmares were disturbing as I adjusted to a new day. Instead of joining my family for breakfast, I snuck a cup of black coffee and a piece of toast on my way up to the studio. I had some images that wanted to leave my head and fill up a canvas. I guess there were more wounds that needed artistic therapy.

This time, the sun was the victim. Set amongst a picturesque, bright blue sky with cirrus-type clouds above a sparkling waterfall, it was torn. Claws from an unidentified creature's scaly hand had ripped through its fiery surface to reveal drippings of black blood that melded with the flow of the natural water source, creating alternate waves of sparkle and dullness.

I wanted to scar the fake brightness of its omnipotent beams, representing the idea that everything has a dark and a light side. Not even the most perfect object in all the universe is immune to the grasp of the shadows.

No, not even the flawless Megan Rossi or sugary sweet Mia Logan. I saw their hidden darkness, yet others just saw them as perfection. I'm not sure why these feelings resurfaced when we had all just bonded and reconnected. Where were these emotions coming from? I thought we had come to an understanding, and yet, I could still feel the resentment over the attention they got while I was always pushed to the side. I had to do my feelings justice and let them be drawn.

The conversation with EJ about how we are all light and dark kept coming back to me as I poured my soul into the painting. I felt driven to convey the message that alluded me in words but found its place in color. The madness had to have its say.

Looking at the hasty work I just procured within only an hour, I was stunned at how pleased I was with it. Like I had channeled the madness from somewhere beyond my consciousness, even as thoughts ran rampant. That idea terrified me—*am I possessed by some wicked power somehow?*

Knowing my imagination was sprinting a marathon, I covered up the canvas with a sheet and headed down the stairs to get ready for the day. I took a deep breath, feeling some relief that my sisterly competition in my mind had been released onto the canvas. I had more important emotions to confront.

Today, EJ was going to reveal more details about the statue and how to get it. By evening, it would be in my hands.

With guards in tow and back at the villa to protect us, we traveled into Barcelona to a small alleyway antique store, where a fat, balding, jovial old man came waddling over to us with a big, silly grin for EJ. He signaled to wait a moment until he was done with the only customer in the store, and then locked the front door and put up his "closed" sign.

"*Bienvenido,* Eduardo," then turning to shake each of our hands, "*Es maravilloso conocerlas señoritas.* I am honored to finally meet you. I am Señor Guarez. Please, come sit down."

We sat upon the red velvet-like cushioned couches in a small lounge area of the store while he disappeared into the back to retrieve a stack of paperwork and a black wooden box. After checking my identification and fingerprints, he motioned over to EJ for a final confirmation.

"For you, Señorita Rossi," Señor Guarez said as he finally handed me my intended heirloom. Inside this box was what I'd been waiting for, for close to six months. I couldn't breathe; the anticipation was building up like rising ecstasy not wanting its release just yet.

I had an image in my mind, but nothing prepared me for the grandeur that was placed into my hands. This had to be the greatest orgasm of my life.

Possibly about a foot or so in height, the double-headed black dragon stood proudly defending its mountainous post upon a base of clean, solid black marble. Its single body twisted with smooth, yet edgily defined body scales with swirls of white embedded within the natural stone. The tail majestically lay curved upon the base, a single sparkling diamond upon its pointy tip.

The right head—the demon side I supposed—had a red eyeball and a gorgeous matching blaze of fire spewing out, as its corresponding hand reached out to grab something within the ethers in front of it. The left side possessed a dark, but lovely blue eye that looked towards the sky with a less intimidating light yellow flame and its claw reaching upwards.

The appraiser stopped me mid-thought to explain some of its unique composition.

"The dragon itself was sculpted entirely from black onyx. You can see here the natural white and gray hues buried within it. Stunning piece of rock. This here is a rounded ruby eye and his flame was shaped using a red fire opal. The artist had a love of rich colors and materials," he illuminated, happy to show off his historian expertise.

"If you look closely, you can see the way this piece was created, that it was shaped and intricately bonded into layers. Underneath here is a solid copper tongue. Blink and you'd miss it! The other side has a princess cut sapphire eye and her flame is made entirely from citrine with a gold tongue underneath."

"That's my birthstone," I recollected as I explored every inch of the statue, lingering on the yellow stone flame that I knew so well. Thoughtfully, I considered what he had just said. "Him and her?"

"Yes, him and her, simply like yin and yang, light and dark. Polar opposites that can come together as one. It is how the creator himself described it," he explained.

"Goya?"

"It is believed to be so, yes. Legend has it that when the art world was creating sculptures of people and religious symbols, his work was way too ominous to be accepted— at first. A double-headed dragon? Blasphemy, as it represented pure evil in a timeworn Spanish era. Society was not ready for such things.

"Eventually, as we all know, Goya made his name anyway in the world. But this being his first sculpted piece, as it is said, it held such a special significance that he never again offered it up as part of his collection.

"It originally did not have this detailed gem work; only solid bronze and brass flames, from what I have been told. He crafted those exquisite gems later in life as he made his fortune and perfected this magnum opus of his heart," he added as an aside.

"There is a deep story behind its creation, and how it came to be passed to your family, but your cousin is the one with that information, not I. But after studying this, I can assure you, it is very much in line with his beginning personal stylings. It is a Goya," he confirmed.

We all turned to EJ at that moment, who aloofly gave his "not now" look, I think rather relishing the fact that he was keeping us in suspense. We thanked Señor Guarez, placing the statue gently back into its case as I signed off on the paperwork and made our way to the car.

"It's gorgeous, Mar. The whole piece seems to suit you," Meg commented on the drive back.

"You think so?"

"Absolutely. It's got that edginess that's uniquely you, yet sparkles with beauty. I think a boring ring or wooden box would not have spoken to you the way this did today," she considered. Wow, I was beginning to realize my sister did understand me after all.

"Is that how you see me?"

"It's how I've always seen you," she smiled. "It's a good thing," she added, I think hoping that she wasn't offending me. She didn't at all, though.

She was one hundred percent right. It did speak to me, just like Goya's other paintings and sculptures, but more on a personal level as I held it in my own hands. I let my eyes wander through its complicated details as my fingers moved across its multi-textural terrain.

"So, what does this all mean for Marissa?" asked Mia on my behalf.

"That has yet to be revealed," EJ gently cautioned. "I know you are anxious to know the story, but the dragon will reveal itself to you first."

"What do you mean?" I asked, puzzled.

"Well, I think you should take some time to sit with it. Ask it what message it has for you," he offered.

"You want me to talk to a statue?"

He burst out laughing at my sassy tone.

"Yes, I want you to talk to a statue. Actually, better yet—just like your sisters did for their adventures, I think it would be a good idea for you to take a few days to yourself to really reflect on your journey and what you've learned.

"You are to embark on a quest of self-discovery. Sitting in the presence of this superb piece of art might give you some of the answers you are seeking." *That's funny,* I thought to myself, *I wasn't aware I had any questions, other than the symbolism of this dang thing.*

"Where would I go?"

"You can stay here," Mia proposed. "Meg and I were talking about this after we tucked you in the other night. We are so close to France that we thought we could hop on the train and visit some of the southern areas while we are here.

"And even though you'd have time to yourself, we'd also feel more comfortable knowing at the end of the night, EJ was still in the house with you. You know, just in case."

"And the villa is big enough for me to stay well out of your way," he agreed. "I could use some downtime myself for a few days."

"Okay," I relented, knowing how much I hated being alone. At least I'd have the presence of EJ if the solitude got to be too much. Josh wasn't due to arrive for a few more days, and I would've liked that time with him, but with the speed in which my sisters planned their escape, it looked like I wasn't being left with a choice.

"There is one more thing I would like to share with you all first, though, if you have a moment this evening," he said as he pulled up to the villa. "Meet me for dinner on the second floor terrace in about an hour and we can discuss," he directed.

We did as requested, walking into a neatly set table for

four featuring gazpacho soup bowls and a Mediterranean mixed green salad that EJ picked up from a local takeout eatery. He took no time getting down to business.

"The reason I have called this little assembly this evening is to give you some insight into the grand finale," he previewed.

"Although Marissa's journey is not over quite yet, there is a bigger picture that has yet to be unveiled. I believe Sorella Maria alluded to the jewelry box being more than it appears?"

"Yes," Mia responded. "She mentioned something about needing to figure out how to unlock it, but I have yet to discover how. But I do hear the rattling inside, so if something got in there, there's a way to get it out."

"There is indeed," he shared. "This is your final task. You must find the map that gives you the instructions on how to locate the keys and where to insert them."

"A map?" Meg inquired. "Where would we even look?"

"That part I can tell you," he grinned. "It is within the dragon statue. Find the map, and you can unravel the mystery."

"I thoroughly inspected every inch of that statue. Nothing is hidden in there," I protested.

"Just like life, not everything is easily accessible at our fingertips. It will take clever thinking and determination to find the loophole," he advised.

"Do you know where it is? I mean, I know we are the ones who have to find it, but were you told?" asked Mia.

"I was," he acknowledged. "You see, a lot of planning went into this whole legacy journey than you even realize," he began.

"When Leigh conjured up this plan, he left no stone unturned. He began with what he knew from his mother and went to work to contact each of us—Colleen, Sorella Maria and myself. His first step was to actually make sure the heirlooms existed and that they were safe, preserved and contained their original heritage letters."

Sensing my next question, he added, "I do have yours, Marissa. But my instructions were to wait for the right time to give it to you. And I will, I promise."

"After I talk to the double dragon head," I replied sarcastically, causing him to guffaw grandly.

"Yes, yes," he replied. "Oh, how I adore your sass, young one."

"Continuing on. Once the three of us confirmed that the pieces were all intact as desired, he summoned us to meet in Florence—Francesco as well. Leigh chose this location because of Sorella Maria's inability to travel far, and also because that's where the jewelry box, with all its intriguing secrets, was held.

"We were just as enthralled by the mystery of it all as you were—unending questions and desires to know the scandals and riddles behind it. He indulged us, sharing every last juicy detail. Admittedly, we each knew pieces of it already; but Leigh had the links that connected it all together.

"Even though the three of us do not have our own lines to pass it down to, the fact that we were included and learned such a robust, magical, inspiring family tree was worth more than the riches these tokens we bestow upon you bring.

"It was his hope that through the three of you, the full stories would be carried on. In fact, Meg, he wished for you to author the complete legacy, you being the writer of the family."

"What? But I thought this was to remain a secret? For

family only?" she disputed.

"And that is where the ingenuity of your grandfather comes in. You weave the story of truth and present it to the world as fiction. Only within your bloodlines will they know the fairy tale is a reality."

I saw the epiphany dawning upon my sister's face, and an excited glow about her. Like a life purpose had just awakened within her soul. I could tell she couldn't wait for time alone to begin writing it all out; it wasn't unlike my desire to paint at the exact moment of inspiration. Another likeness I hadn't considered.

"The jewelry box can in fact be opened, my dear hearts. I have seen it. That is why Leigh brought us all together. Leigh had the map from his mother, who held it in her safekeeping. No one could come across that map and have any idea what it was or where to find the pieces—that is the deliciousness of it all.

"It was so strategically planned by your great-grandmother, to be carried out by your grandfather in the end. In fact, it was Lena who created the chest as a puzzle box; it was not designed that way originally. She took great care in converting it from the traditional open box format—which is why you can see the seal along its side, but it is welded shut."

Mia nodded her head in awe and acknowledgment, knowing she had painstakingly scrutinized that chest even more than I did the statue.

"Lena worked with an expert lockbox maker in Florence—when she was off on a 'ladies retreat' upstate, or so her husband thought. She made sure her actions could not be traced for fear of the Marinos uncovering the truth of her wealth.

"Before heading to Florence, she had already started

making the plans to reclaim the family treasures and ensure their authenticity and legacy preservation. She then headed to Florence where a trusted woodworker, an old friend of Sorella Maria's, took her creative vision for the puzzle box and brought it to life.

"She had him draw the map, which he also carefully built into the dragon statue, and then she clandestinely returned all of the different tokens to the current owners—Colleen, Sorella Maria and my father, Matteo—with the prediction that her son or his heirs would one day be the ones to carry on the legacy.

"She planted the seeds. It was hard for any of us not to help Leigh harvest the crops when he finally reached out. To this day, it amazes me the foresight that Lena had. But then again, growing up with a mother who practiced 'witchcraft,'" he said playfully, gesturing with quotation mark fingers, "none of us should be surprised by her intuitive abilities."

"That really is something," Meg said softly, just as taken aback by the story as we were. But EJ had more to say.

"When Leigh was with us, it was the first time he or any of us was able to see how the box opened, and it was flawlessly inspiring. Lena, for all her broken-hearted faults, was a genius. We found a beautiful note written in her handwriting to her future generations, which we read with tears in our eyes before placing it back inside.

"That is also when Leigh added his own surprise inheritance gifts that would await his true family, as he called all of you, upon its grand opening.

"That is why we have summoned all of the cousins and your mother and grandmother and children to come join us, because it is about more than just you three. It is about family and a woman who loved so deeply, she deserved a distinguished affair in her honor.

"I hope that I have left you inspired enough to find the map. For once you find it, it will be up to you to decode the different keys and figure out how to solve the puzzle. This mission, should you accept it, will unlock a life-altering future for you all."

9

After our dramatic evening of storytelling, we decided to postpone the map search for a few days while we went on our own; we'd reconvene when my sisters returned, though I'm not sure I could be patient enough to avoid looking for it in their absence.

Meg and Mia were traveling before daybreak and early bird EJ decided he was headed to the beach, leaving me to figure out how in the hell I was going to spend my day alone.

I figured I could go back to one of those museums and enjoy the artwork without pressure. But then I realized that nothing would compare to the greatness I experienced in Madrid, so visiting a different kind of landmark in Barcelona might be a better idea.

I started out at the Boqueria Market, famous for its hundreds of fresh fruit and vegetable stands and more. *Mia would love this place,* I thought to myself as I sipped on a freshly squeezed juice smoothie. I could only imagine the meal she would concoct for us from the colorful ingredients that lined the street.

Walking around the area, I came upon the Gran Teatre del Liceu, where they just so happened to have a rare morning opera performance. Although I figured this was more of Meg's thing than mine, I decided to give it a chance. After all, I was here to experience as much as I could on this journey, and I really didn't know how else to spend my time.

I did not expect the show to move me so much; I couldn't understand a word, and yet, the emotions made their way into my heart and my eyes. The tears streamed down my face as I tragically watched the actress's love of her life die in her arms. Was I becoming a—gasp—*romantic?*

Shaking that scary notion off, I continued to wander down Las Ramblas, the bustling boulevard EJ had taken us to on our first night. *Oh yeah*, I remembered, as I walked towards the Erotic Museum. *Now, that's more my style.*

It wasn't at all what I expected—not lewd or distasteful in the least. And it wasn't full-on pornography-laden like a strip club or sex store, either. Rather, the museum was a historical depiction of sex throughout the centuries. Quite fascinating to enter the worlds of Kama Sutra and Japanese sculptures—even Picasso works were on display!

The visuals, although treasured pieces of art, did arouse me as I walked through the nude photos, sculptures with oversized penises and orgy-like paintings. Fuck, why couldn't Josh be here right now to take care of my sexual needs?

I wandered into a less crowded alleyway to give him a call, but received his automated text that he was in court for the day and would return my (anyone's) message at his earliest convenience.

So much for that idea, I pouted. Knowing I needed to distract myself, I strolled on down to a nearby café for a pitcher of sangria and some tapas. At least if I got myself into trouble, my sisters weren't there to rat me out.

No such luck. Turns out, there weren't many prospects— at least, not mid-week—as many Barcelonans were set to return to their jobs for the afternoon. A bit tipsy, I boarded a train back to Sitges to end my day poolside. Maybe EJ was back and could entertain me.

Bored and restless on the train, I did the only thing I could do—text Jay.

What r u doin?

Finishing up work. What are you up to?

Went 2 erotic museeeem. Totes hotttt.

Oh boy. Shorthand and typos can only mean one thing haha How are you feeling over there?

Fuckin lonely. WTF. Why does Josh have a case?

LOL I don't know, Riss. Had a few drinks?

Dont judge me asshole. At least I dont lie to friends.

Whoa. Easy killer. What are you talking about?

Like u dont kno.

I don't. So why don't you tell me what's up.

Hows ur buddy bruce?

Uh, fine I guess. He's not a threat to your family, if that's what you're asking. I've been keeping an eye on everyone like I promised. What's the problem?

The problem is ur a liar. I kno about ur little date w him at the coffee shop.

How do u know about that?

Josh saw u so dont deny it. WTF Jay. I trusted u.

Riss, I have my reasons for meeting with him.

And?

I'm not getting into it with you like this. We'll talk later.

Sorry, no can do. Im done w u. have fun with ur new coffee buddy. byyyyeeeeeee

Whatever. Just be careful, Riss. Now that you have the statue in your possession, anyone could be lurking about. Watch your back, remember.

What the fuck? Is there a reason he used those specific words? And how in the hell did he know I had the statue already? Did I tell him? Fuck him, I'm not responding.

The room started to spin as I thought about how oddly ominous his words were. It wasn't like him to be so melodramatic; then again, I was text-bitching at him, so maybe he was just being defensive—or wanting to verbally slap me back in the face.

Still. I felt the goosebumps crawling up my back and down my arms. There was something unsettling about him and Bruce meeting, and now him not telling me why.

What if Josh was right? What if Jay had something to do with this, or was helping Bruce or someone else? Even Kevin had mentioned the possibility that someone on the outside could be trying to set the Marinos up. Could he possibly…

No, not Jay. He wouldn't hurt me or my family. Would he? I mean, he had me slammed up against that wall and could have pummeled me if his body allowed him to do what his facial language wanted. Maybe I got out just in time before his psychopathic tendencies revealed themselves. You don't know a person until you live with them, they say.

I pulled up to the station and managed to get myself into a taxi and back to the villa before completely passing out. I might've had more sangria than I realized. It wasn't even four in the afternoon, but I fell onto my interim bed and didn't wake up until the middle of the night.

I missed a few calls and texts from Josh and some pleading texts from Jay to please respond that I was okay. I ignored the Jay texts but thought I would at least send Josh a quick apology text that I fell asleep early, loved him and would talk to him in the morning. I figured by now he'd definitely be asleep in bed. Not getting a response confirmed that.

A bit hungry, I made my way to the kitchen where I was relieved to find some leftover ham and cheese and a few crackers to nosh on. The house was eerily quiet—even the snores coming from EJ's room weren't loud enough to chase away the sound of solitude.

Ugh, I really hated being alone.

I tried falling back to sleep, but when that didn't work, I found myself in the studio. And there, in that space, was where I finally felt comfortable in my isolation. No one to walk in on me or ask questions about what I was working on. Perhaps this was solitary bliss after all.

I picked up the coveted paintbrush and went to work on my latest inspiration—thank you, Erotic Museum and endless sangria.

She was a gorgeous silhouette, laying there naked on the canopy bed, her arms above her head in leather-bounded chains, her legs spread out in an exasperated 'V' and her chest turned slightly to the left.

A man knelt beside her by the bed, taking her one breast into his mouth, while he caressed the other with his fingers. In his other hand, he held a small whip raised in the air—ah, yes, and across her belly were the remnants of a red marking from the last strike.

His hardness was evident and on display, though untouched. He hungrily yearned for her, but he was not to be satiated; this painting and moment was all about her. Finally, about *her* and *only her.* And there was more.

There, at the base of her womanhood was the backside of a voluptuous blonde, the side of her face visible only enough to see her tongue reaching out towards her openness, her hands firmly keeping the silhouetted woman's legs in place.

Now with the scene set, I could more clearly define the receiving woman's carnal face, mouth gaping in rapture while a single tear from the pain-pleasure dichotomy fell from her closed eye.

Or, was it confusion over whether she wanted this kind of life anymore? Was it finally time for her to realize that sex was more than a game? Perhaps the tear beckoned her to relinquish the incessant need to feel worthy by giving her body to others for empty pleasure. Wishing the lash of each whip could slap out the feelings of shame left behind by a twisted high school teacher.

Where does the boundary between indulging in healthy fantasy and tawdry, scar-induced body abuse lie?

A question I'd face another time. My soul did not want to be bothered by such mental inquiries; it just wanted to feel. I wanted to express how okay it was to feel so satisfied with personal pleasure, right or wrong. How its escape is what I needed to get me through trying times, and I refused to apologize for it.

But all of the passion behind my painting, the memories and wounds they stirred up, were depleting my energy. Lost in exorcising what had been hidden within me for so long, I had no control over my own hands and heart to stop the flow of art or emotions.

I sat in the room painting for hours, not realizing how quickly time had passed until the sun peeked in from the window. Completely expelled of all creation, I decisively left my work of art to grab an orange juice and sit up on the rooftop to watch the sun rise over the glistening sea.

Now that I liberated the dark within, I could welcome in the beauty of the light.

The colors of red, orange and yellow ran together in a chaotic harmony as they fought their way to their proper place in the rising. Quiet, wondrous, peaceful.

I didn't resist the stillness.

Instead, I let my mind wander in this meditative moment to places that caught me off guard. Tears formed and forced their way out of their usually contained chocolate-colored cages.

I felt truly alone.

I didn't mean physically. I meant existentially.

I no longer knew who I could trust. Betrayal had been my only ally, alluring me into its web of suspicion. Jay was a lifelong friend, and yet his cryptic warnings and refusal to be straight with me made me question our 30-year history.

How about this new man of mine who promises me the world; the love of my life? Could I really believe that Josh could keep his jealousy in check—or better yet, honor his vow to love me exactly as I am and not abandon me like others had?

I questioned if my newly strengthened bond with my

sisters would truly last beyond this trip. With all those unresolved hurts swirling around my heart, I feared that we would fall back into our individual lives once we hit American soil and I'd be the unimportant baby sister again.

Would Bruce completely win my mother over and take her away from us?

Would whoever sent that note come for me now that I had the statue?

Would I ever find true happiness? I never dared to allow myself to dream that I could ever have love, artistic success and a bright future. Am I deluding myself that just because I got a statue from an estranged grandfather that my life would actually change?

Questions—so many questions. And no answers.

Oh, hell no, brain. You're not going there. I'm not going to go talk to some bejeweled dragon. You're insane, I told myself.

Ignoring the curiosity within, I left the rooftop pool to brew a pot of coffee when I discovered EJ had already beat me to it. I was grateful for the company and the break in intense self-reflection.

"Well, good morning, sunshine! I don't ever think I've seen you up at the same time as the sun," he quipped a little too gleefully.

"I fell asleep early and then couldn't go back to bed. I've been working," I answered, trying to match his pep but failing.

"How wonderful! I hope it is more of that greatness you started with the dragon piece. I should like to see your work later," he remarked.

"Sure," I said nervously.

"Now tell me, what do you have planned for the day?"

"I don't know. I haven't thought that far ahead. I don't

have the foggiest idea what to do with myself," I admitted.

"Well, how would you like to join me at the races today? Señor Dominguez down at the barber shop hooked me up with tickets to the Circuit de Catalunya racetrack in Montmeló, not too much more than an hour's trip away. I have an extra if you are interested?"

"Actually, that sounds perfect! What time's the train?"

"Oh, my dear, we are not going by train; we are going by bike. Meet me downstairs in two hours and we'll ride off in style."

The motorcycle EJ sat upon was stunning. A first class BMW® K 1600 GTL with an inline six-cylinder engine rumored to be smoother than silk on the road. Jay would absolutely die to get his ass on one of these babies.

Wiping the imaginary drool from my mouth, I walked up to the Godly machine and ran my hands along its steering. I was getting all warm and tingly inside just touching it.

"Should I leave you two alone and come back later?" EJ quipped.

"What? Oh," I reddened, realizing I had blocked him out to focus on this beauty. "Have you ever ridden something like this before?"

"Have I ever? Girl, I own one of these. Now, put on your helmet and hop on. We're about to go on the ride of a lifetime."

He wasn't kidding. This was no U.S. Highway thrill ride with a broody man. It was a fully immersive experience along the coast of the Mediterranean Sea. We practically drove up the edge of the beach as we made our way towards Barcelona, passing its many ports, marinas and even its own World Trade Center.

EJ was a natural rider, braving the curved roads with

exhilaration and speed. I smartly wore my hair in a long braid, yet the escaped tendrils couldn't help but surrender to the gusts of wind.

Freedom. I could feel it once again, where there were no questions, no expectations, no conversations. Simply, freedom.

When all was said and done and this multi-country journey was over, I planned on buying my own freedom so that I could ride whenever I wanted to.

The raceway was packed with fans from across the nation and every kind of tourist you could imagine. We made it just in time for the opening ceremonies of the 24H Series, featuring both sports and touring car racing.

The crowds were lively, sporting the flags and colors representing their favorite driver. Cheers, hissing and chanting made the announcers almost inaudible, but it was hard not to fall into the spirit of the game. I had never been to a track before, and I was mesmerized by the adrenaline-pumping speed through the circuit and the edge-of-your-seat, near-miss crashes.

How terrifying and invigorating all at the same time. I made a mental note to look up nearby racetracks when I returned home; this was a spectator sport I could undeniably see myself getting into.

With many, many hours of racing left, EJ persuaded me to leave so we could enjoy some more of what Spain had to offer. I reluctantly agreed, not wanting to leave my newest addiction after a 6-hour viewing obsession. I was starting to get hungry, after all—for something more than a hot dog and alcohol-free beer.

We stopped at a small coastal town café, where we sat outside underneath a tiny umbrella with a magnificent view. As I stared out into the intoxicating water, I felt EJ watching me with a smirk.

"This is the first time I have seen you relax since the moment I met you, cuz. This suits you," he commented.

"I love riding. There is just something about it that liberates me from life."

"I can tell," he smiled. "I like this version of Marissa very much. It gives you balance."

"Balance?"

"Yes. We all need balance. I've witnessed your intensity in so many ways. This brings you to the opposite, more tranquil state of your being. Don't forget to nurture this side as well," he advised with a kind, caring tone before taking my hand and leading me back to the bike.

The rest of the way home was quiet, any sounds seized and carried away by the winds that hit our faces as we dared into the setting sun. Before long, we were back at the villa, refreshed and spent.

"Would it be all right if I came up and saw some of your paintings?"

"Okay. I—I'm not sure if I'm finished with them just yet."

"No, an artist's work is really never done. Even when completed, we always find something else that could've been done differently. We'd go on forever if we had the chance," he observed. "You don't need to be ashamed to show me. I already find you quite talented."

Begrudgingly, I escorted EJ to the studio where I unveiled my four paintings (including the completed blown glass one for Teresa).

"My, my," he spoke reverently, "How fast you work when inspired. And I don't mean as in rushed...I mean as in channeled, focused. Raw imagination versus planned perfection. I love them. Truly."

"Really?" His acclaim of my work meant the world to me as a fellow artist and renowned gallery owner.

"Yes. The use of colors isn't the captivator—it's the messages. How effortless and undiluted. I love how you reveal the sun's core to be less than perfect. And over here, what a marvelous expression of sexual decadence. They are daring, and I like that in an artist. I truly believe you have a vision, Marissa; one that needs to be seen."

"I don't know what to say. Thank you," I was speechless. Tears formed in my eyes.

"What's the matter, cuz?"

"Just—no one has ever expressed this much passion for or approval of my art. It's like for the first time, someone sees me and acknowledges me. It feels—unreal."

"Come, cuz. Let's go grab some cava and talk out on the balcony. I think there is much more to say," he said gently. Usually I would put my defenses up, sensing a lecture, but with EJ, we had this kindred connection that made me feel safe and unjudged.

Settled down deep into the cushioned chairs with glasses of the ticklish bubbly, we took in the view before breaking the silence with what was sure to be a heavy conversation. But I think I was ready for it.

"Where to begin?" he pondered. "Tell me, what were the motivations behind your recent paintings? It's more than just an impulse—there is history there. Talk to me—artist to artist, blood to blood."

"Okay," I started, not sure what to tackle first. "So, the dragon blackening the heart—I kinda told you that I was fighting with both my boyfriend and best friend."

"Yes, I remember. Go on," he encouraged.

"Well, there was more to it," I confessed. And then, after so many years, I was able to share my story to an open ear who was both sympathetic and respectful of my privacy. He said not a word but held my hand as I bravely recounted the memory that pushed me to create.

"In that moment, when the brush touched the canvas, I felt like love was impossible. That it wasn't all sonnets and flowers, and as much as I wanted to love and give of my whole heart, there was always this darkness that betrayed it. Lies, abandonment, lack of trust. That my heart, or any heart I tried to love, was not pure like they claim love is. That there is always something waiting in the shadows to darken it."

"And yet, there is still hope."

"Yes, exactly. I guess it's just my way of wrapping my head around the fact that love's not perfect, but it's still worth it. That the dragon, so to speak, can come for it, but it cannot—will not—have it all. That the heart's resiliency can win out after all."

"I can see how this mirrors your teenage experience, and I am so sorry you had to face that alone. But I also have to ask—does this reflect your current love life as well?"

"It does. I love Josh with all of my heart. He's the one; I know it. He is handsome and understanding and him having money doesn't hurt, either," I admitted. "He's been so supportive throughout this entire year, ever since we found out about this secret grandfather."

"And how does he feel about you?"

"He says he loves me, and I believe that. I think." I saw EJ raise an eyebrow. "Well, I'm slow to believe any man could love me, because no one has ever done so before. So, I am treading lightly."

"Treading lightly, or blocking intuition?"

"What do you mean?"

"There is a very thin line between fear because you are

trying to protect yourself and fear because it's a warning signal. What keeps you so guarded?"

"I'm not certain."

"He is the first man you think ever loved you, you say?"

"I know he is."

"Hmm. And don't get angry for this question, it's just a question—are you finding yourself more drawn to the idea of love, or to Josh himself? I ask because sometimes when we get a glimmer of what we have always so desperately wanted, we cling on to it for dear life and never see the red flags."

"I mean, no one is perfect, right? We do have some differences, but I'd like to think we are working on them and that our love is real."

"That's not what I asked," he gently delved. "You don't need to give me an answer, dear heart. But you do need to ask and answer it yourself," he added. "Now, how about this Jay fellow? What about him and your relationship?"

"We're just friends. I've known him since we were kids."

"Okay, but you were also angry with him. Why?"

"He lied to me. Well, not that he lied, but he withheld something important from me, and when I confronted him, he wasn't forthcoming."

"I see. And how did that make you feel?"

"You know, for an artist, you certainly would make a great therapist," I remarked, as he laughed.

"Why, thank you. I'll consider that for my next life. Now, continue. Unless you would be more comfortable on the couch?" I loved how this crazy cousin of mine matched my sarcastic wit. I realized then that I was so glad he lived close enough to visit on occasion. Absolutely hands down, my favorite person, probably on this entire planet.

"Fine," I laughed with him. "I have known him my whole life, and we never kept secrets from each other. And now, it feels like he is. Ever since our big fight and he moved out, he has been distant and unreadable. Like I don't know who he is anymore."

"Ah, well that happens sometimes in life. But now I can see where the dragon painting came in. Your fears, anger, sense of betrayal, confusion, yet wanting to hold on. Thank you for sharing all that."

"You're welcome. I actually feel like a weight was lifted off me, getting it all out in the open. Thank you for listening."

"Of course. But we're not done yet," he smirked. "The torn sun picture."

"So, with that one, I had some really disturbing nightmares—which are happening more and more frequently while I am here, by the way." I shuddered at the thought of the blood-dripping scaly monsters chasing after me and images of loved ones turning into demons with black hearts.

"You know, dreams and nightmares are messages that our subconscious is trying to send to us. There is powerful symbolism that if captured, can unlock your own mysteries."

"Well, if that is the case, then I have pretty twisted insides," I lamented.

"Take notice of who is in them, what is happening around you and how it resolves—if at all. You may get a pattern. Just something to think about offline," he suggested.

"Okay, I will. So, the torn sun. Oh boy, if I am being honest—" I had to pause and take a deep breath.

"That was me, tearing apart my perfect sisters to show

they are not really all that perfect. I am tired of living in their shadows when they have plenty of their own. I'm not the only one with darkness and I wanted to expose them as frauds." Silence. "Oh my God, I can't believe I said that out loud."

"Honey, I told you, I would never judge, and I am not. My lack of response was allowing you to absorb the enormity of what you just said for yourself. You are the one judging, sweetie."

"So, you don't think I am completely depraved for thinking this?"

"Not at all. When people do not understand each other, and it's not communicated, it can sometimes fester into this heightened sense of bitterness. I know you love your sisters and would never hurt them. If I thought that, I'd have you committed," he joked, though I'm pretty sure he meant it.

"But the problem is, I had just had a wonderful conversation with both of them to clear up all of our repressed feelings. I felt our bond restored. I'm not sure why I still felt compelled to create this."

"Conversations are healing; but even after the words are said and apologies accepted, remnants remain that need to be worked out and healed. The scars still need to be addressed so that you can become whole again. Tell me, after painting that, did you feel more at ease with them?"

"Come to think of it, I did," I was floored to admit that.

"Wonderful, then well done. I won't tell them they are the subjects," he teased. "And now for this exquisite *ménage à trois?"*

"Yeah, about that one. Um, I'm not sure I want to talk about it."

"Girlfriend, I'm an openly homosexual man and I ain't got anything against the kinky. Spill it."

Nervously chuckling, I relented. Why the hell not? He was learning everything else about me.

"I have always been the black sheep of the family—you know, the one drawn to experiment with drugs and sex, and I even have this obsessive attraction to crime. Not committing them, but watching those suspense shows and hearing about real life stories. I want to know what makes those animals tick and how clever they must be to get away with that shit.

"Maybe that's why out of the three of us, I'm the least freaked out by all of the drama following us. It enthralls me to be a part of something like that.

"Anyway, I'm what someone politically correct would call sexually fluid. I love men first and foremost. But I also love the touch and scent of a woman every now and then. I love multiple lovers at once, and some light bondage and—I don't know, a little bit of pain heightens the pleasure for me."

I looked down, beet red, utterly embarrassed that I was exposing all of this to a 50-something-year-old gay man I just met a month ago.

"It's all right," EJ assured me. "I'm listening. Why do you think it appeals to you so?"

"I—I think it's freedom. I don't like to be told what to do or be limited by society, so I think I act out against it. It also, well, keeps me safe from commitment. Josh enjoys it and indulges me—but as I watch him with another woman and I'm with another man, I wonder if it's the safe zone that lets us love without obligation. Or, that I let myself be used in this way to hold on to what I am so afraid to lose, when what I should really be afraid of is losing myself.

"Holy crap. I never thought of it that way," I surprised myself with my own insight. "I wondered why her tear felt so powerful to me. Now I see it tells a bigger story than I even imagined."

"Well, my sweet cousin, seems to me you have uncovered a lot and have some feelings to sort through," he said, rising up from his chair to give me a kiss on the forehead. "Might I suggest that conversation with your dragon statue now, and a day at the beach tomorrow to ponder it all?"

"You really think me talking to that thing will help?"

"I do. There are some things that, even as open as you were with me, you held back from. The dragon for certain will not spill your secrets—and someone should listen if only to let you hear them for yourself. Ask yourself what it is you truly want in life, Marissa. Let the answers come to you like they did tonight."

"I'll think about it," I obliged, as he smiled warmly and wished me good night.

I couldn't yet bring myself to talk to some onyx stone, and even with questions driving down the roadways of my brain, I needed to check in with Josh before I fell asleep. I missed him and just wanted to hear his voice.

"What's that noise?"

"Oh, just the courtroom. Lots of people here today. Been a hectic day."

"At this time of night?"

"Yeah, um, big murder trial going on. Lots of press. Listen, Mar, I gotta go. I just wanted to pick up and hear your voice."

"Only three more days," I pointed out.

"I know. I can't wait to see you, babe. I've missed you so much and have hated all this fighting."

"Me too."

"Hey, I've been meaning to ask you—did you get your

statue yet?"

"Oh, I thought I told you. Sorry. I did. It's beyond incredible, Josh. It's a double-headed onyx dragon laced with rare stones and crystals. Wait until you see it."

"Soon, my love. Soon, you will be in my arms and you can tell me everything."

Deciding to ignore my cousin's advice for one more day, I chose to let myself fall into a deep sleep instead of chat with an ancestral heirloom. There was always tomorrow for that one.

10

I spent a great deal of time looking at my reflection in the mirror the next morning. At times, I knew exactly who Marissa Rossi was. At other times, the girl looking back at me was just a stranger.

The question replayed over and over in my mind like a skipping record. *What do I want in life?*

It would haunt me for most of the day.

I did take EJ's advice to go to the beach—but not just any beach. With my sisters and their rather prude outlook on life (at least publicly), I couldn't exactly suggest that we experience the nude beach together, so I was going to jump on the opportunity to check one out while they were gallivanting through France.

Grabbing my suntan oil, a light lunch, my phone and my headphones, I headed out to Sitges' local Playa de las Balmins.

Being midweek with school in session and summer winding down, it wasn't especially crowded. Though predominantly gay, it was welcoming to all walks of life— surprisingly, even to families with young children. Not everyone chose to strip down, but those that did must not have had a care in the world.

They certainly weren't the buff, hot volleyball players I expected, that's for sure.

But I was game, sinking down into the sand and

removing every last article of clothing that restricted me. I made sure, however, to put extra sunscreen on my most sensitive areas—a burn there must be excruciatingly painful.

Turning on my tunes to the welcome alternative rock sounds of Foals, I soaked up the sun, feeling the warmth penetrate my cells and create that glistening moisture of sweat all over.

After a while, I sat up to enjoy people watching while grabbing a snack. Couples were rubbing lotion on each other's backs. Kids were playing tag with the waves that crashed onto the sand, trying to pull them in. Girlfriends were gossiping in Spanish with drinks in hand under their shady umbrellas.

Everyone seemed so—content.

And I did, too; temporarily.

What would make me this blissfully happy all the time? Would it be to marry Josh? Maybe I could buy a house. Own an art gallery. Get a motorcycle. All of the above? What *did* I want?

I tried to make a mental checklist of the things I thought would make me happy, but at the end of the day, they all seemed empty. I was missing something but couldn't put my finger on it. Not wanting to get lost in my over-analyzing and burn to a crisp, I packed up my things and headed back to the villa.

I laid there on my bed, still confused as to the purpose of my life. It prompted me to text my mom, sisters, Josh, Jay and even some random friends just so I would not have to feel this sense of loneliness amid the deep white comforter.

Of course, most everyone was busy, some not even texting back. Mom and Granny were out at an end-of-summer day fair while the kids were at camp. Meg and Mia were sending pictures of themselves in berets eating crepes at a cute little outdoor café. They looked like they were having the time of their lives—together. Without me.

Josh quickly replied that he was still in court. Jay never responded (probably working or on his bike). My best girl friend, Jenna, was getting ready to go on a hike and another friend, Em, was getting her nails done. Even EJ wasn't around, off enjoying some more sights—though, of course, his response was a prompt to remember what we had talked about.

Ugh, as if I could forget our heavy conversation last night. I've been trying all day to block it from my brain.

My confusion over whether I was just settling for Josh because someone finally loved me. Or, if I was being too quick to judge Jay's trustworthiness just because he didn't tell me the whole story yet. Why on earth did EJ have to plant those contemplations in my head, like I don't question my life enough?

I thought about how I lived in the shadows of my sisters, noticing how different and how drawn to the "bad things" in life I was. How I kept comparing myself to them and never measuring up.

I remembered EJ's observation, and my own revelation, that I needed to find that equilibrium between intensity and peace. Staring at the exquisite double-headed dragon on my dresser, it occurred to me that it represented balance.

Balance. That's what my life was missing. Either I was independent or co-dependent. A workaholic or a bum. Successful or caught in the daily grind. Accepted or outcast. Black sheep or proud daughter.

It's how I've always been, though. But he was right—I had to find a way to bring all these parts of me together.

I erred on the side of passion; whatever could give me a thrill. I was ignoring the softer parts of me to protect myself from being hurt again.

I picked up the statue and gazed at its two sides. Light and dark. Both parts of one body. A united front. Him and her, as the antique shop owner had said. Yin and yang. Life. *My* life.

Holy crap, was this really the answer to everything?

My epiphanies took off like a race car on the Circuit de Catalunya racetrack.

Through reckless riding, drugs or even push-it-to-the-limit sex, I was numbing the part of me that craved security and love. If I put myself in the danger, then I was in control. I would be the one to hurt me—not anyone else. It was a choice I made a long time ago when I thought I couldn't live up to family expectations; when I believed Mr. Terrance's assessment that I was nothing more than a body to use. Might as well give the world what it thinks I am.

But I am more than that, I asserted, fighting back a few tears. I am just as intelligent as Meg and just as kind as Mia. I am much more than a pretty face. I have the drive to make my dreams come true and a heart that deserves true love. Real, genuine love.

Even with Josh, I knew I was still guarded. I used sexual fantasies to keep him lured in; content, aroused and entertained enough so that he wouldn't want to leave me.

But what if I didn't indulge? What if I removed the mask and let vulnerability shine through?

Sure, I enjoyed a kink every now and then. But what surprised me was how powerfully affected I was that night Josh and I actually made pure love, without the extravaganza. How he moved within me slowly, deeply, connecting with me—rather than enjoying some fantastical game.

That night together sparked something within me I hadn't known was there. A desire for affection and gentleness over rushed and rowdy. A completeness. I wanted more of that kind of love, that kind of touch, that kind of deep bond. I yearned for it.

I want to be more than just this temple of pleasure. To find more depth in life than to escape into moans and orgasms. To find a balance between sexual expression and meaningful intimacy. That is what I wanted—no, that is what I *needed*.

Would Josh be open to shifting our sex life to be more intimate like that night? Or would he run for the hills? Bigger question: am I brave enough to find out?

My reflections then shifted over to my paintings— another soul awakening revelation. I didn't have to paint the pretty; I didn't have to produce something just for others' approval. I desired to reach people's innermost repressed feelings to give them permission to embrace their murkier stirrings without guilt.

Honoring our forbidden notions doesn't make any of us "bad" people. We all have a bit of anger that darkens our hearts when love burns us; but it doesn't turn our heart to complete black. We can heal from it.

We all have that contrasted core of brightness and obscurity, and it shouldn't take someone ripping at us to accept that we are still whole, with both sides a strong part of us. We can shine and depress like the ebb and flow of the ocean. It's an innate part of our human psyche to rise and fall.

And we all have those sexual fantasies—perhaps not exactly as depicted in my painting, with multiple sexual partners or erotic pain—but we do all have that desire to receive pleasure in the way that arouses us without shame. Whatever those fantasies are for us as individuals are perfectly natural.

Interesting—it is in my art that I can see my own balance. Just like this two-headed dragon. Both sides of me can come together and be expressed. Though I do feel compelled to finally add more illumination to even it out, the dark does not need to "win." It just needs to be seen and acknowledged and loved just as much as the light.

It's not supposed to be a fight; it's a mutual compromise. Not one or the other. Both.

And it all starts within me. I can be a more vulnerable person if I accept that love can sometimes hurt but never destroy—unless I let it. It may or may not work out with Josh, or in my friendships, or even with my family. But to have that feeling of being loved is worth the risk, more than protecting myself and shutting out the potential.

I can be a better sister by not judging Meg or Mia for what I deem to be their worst sides, and not projecting my jealousy onto them when they shine. I just need to honor my own capacity for the spotlight and strive for it, knowing I am imperfect and so are they. I can transcend this pettiness and embrace the love that they offer me and give it right back to them.

I don't need to use my body in exchange for love and attention. I can enjoy sexual carnalities that truly entice me, but not the constant theatrics I feel are necessary to keep someone interested. That is not love; that is desperation to fill a hole in my heart.

I am *not* a broken young girl any longer.

I want to receive pleasure that is given freely and without condition. Josh could be that man, but it was a test I would have to give him. We had to be more than outstanding sex. I deserved the whole package.

Wow. If Meg were here, she'd say something about how these trips really bring out my "uncharacteristically deep" thoughts. It's a comment I would've usually gotten mad at. But now I'm saying the same words to myself, recognizing that my thoughts are more golden than I give them credit for.

That's when it hit me. I knew exactly what I wanted in life. Like I said to Josh, I wanted respect. I wanted respect, acceptance *and* love.

But I had to give those to myself first before expecting others to give them to me.

I let the awakening wash over me in the shower as I inhaled the lavender scents of my shampoo. The cleansing bubbles and warm water washed away the world that was holding me back; releasing me from the cage I put myself in.

I felt refreshed and vibrant; alive with new purpose and a determination to make the best out of life. I had conquered my demons by embracing them, and by finally allowing myself to be reflected in my art. I now get how crucial this time alone was for me—for each of us on our respective journeys. It gave me a whole new perspective on my sisters and their individual battles, and their wins. I couldn't wait for them to come home tomorrow so I could share all that I learned.

Oh, how I wished EJ was in the house so I could tell him about my powerful revelations—and then maybe he would divulge the mystery of the dragon to me!

The wait would be torture, but there was one thing I

could do while I waited for everyone: I could try to find that hidden map. I turned the sculpture every which way to see if I could find an inkling of an opening. Not under the base, not in the flames—though I did find the two tongues to be quite loose. I'd have to see someone about getting those tightened up.

Where could it be, damn it? I thought I might have stumbled upon the secret when I saw an envelope sticking out of my purse by the door.

Strange—has it been here this whole time?

Reading it, I could feel the color drain from my face. On instinct, I dialed Jay's number. Straight to voicemail. I tried calling his work but they said he had abruptly taken a few days off for a family emergency. I called his mom, but there was no answer there, either.

Where the fuck was he?

Ready or not, here I come. For what is rightfully mine.

I looked at the note again. Same font as the last one. But how on earth did it get into my purse? Did someone slip it in there while I was at the beach?

The thought of some creep sneaking up on me as I laid naked on the sand sent chills down my spine. I felt violated, like I needed to take another shower to wash away the disgust I was feeling.

Come on, Jay, I begged as it went to voicemail yet again. I began to panic. I didn't know what to do. Should I tell Meg and Mia? Should I call EJ? Should I tell the guards, or call Kevin?

I regretted my previous decision to follow jealous impulses instead of protecting my family; this time, I wasn't going to keep the note a secret. But first, I had to get ahold of someone—anyone at this point!

I had to clear my head. I needed to go for a walk so I could figure out my next steps. I planned to alert one of the guards that I needed surveillance, and would instruct the other to safeguard the house.

I left a message with the note on the kitchen table for EJ to find, so that he knew what was going on and could stay safe until I returned. I let him know I was with one of the guards and that I would be back soon—to call me if anything else happened.

Before I could make my way out, there was a knock at the door. Petrified and no longer enjoying being in a suspense thriller, I carefully peeked out of the bedroom window to see who it was first.

Josh!

"Oh my God, I am so glad to see you," I cried, rushing into his arms and squishing the beautiful bouquet of lilies he had in his hands.

"Marissa, what's wrong?" He pulled me away from him with concern, wiping my tears with his fingers.

"I—I got another note. Someone is still out there, Josh. Someone is still trying to hurt us," I spit out, rushing right back into the safety of his arms. He gently moved us so that we were inside the lobby and closed the door.

"What are you talking about, babe? I can barely understand you," he said, guiding me to the bright blue armchair before I passed out from panic.

I finally admitted to him about the first note, begging for forgiveness for not telling him or anyone else sooner—and how I was afraid he would be so overprotective that I would never get to come here and get my heirloom. I told him about my interaction with Bruce, them rambled about how selfish I was, and how I have now put everyone I love in danger—in between gushing repetitions of relief over seeing him.

"Does anyone know about these notes?"

"I told my sisters a few days ago." Then with a guilty look, I whispered, "And Jay."

"You told *him* but not me?" His fury began to rise, but quickly dissipated as he saw me in such angst over it.

"I knew he couldn't stop me from going. Plus, he was level-headed enough to keep an eye on Bruce for me. But I can't get ahold of him."

"I might know why. This explains a lot, Marissa. I wish you had told me sooner."

"Explains what?"

"Jay and Bruce meeting. Me not being able to find Jay the last two days. I had a suspicion something was off, so I did some investigating. I don't know how to say this, but I found out something unsettling about your best friend. One of his closest pals from college was Thomas Marino—Peggy and Patrick's son."

"What? That's not possible," I said in disbelief. "He would never—I've known him forever, Josh."

"I know. I'm so sorry, sweetheart. But as soon as I found that out, I needed to get here to you. Since no one can reach him, I can only assume he has made his way to Spain. Turns out my instincts could be right—I need to protect you myself. And I want no arguing this time," he insisted.

Stunned and heartbroken, I nodded my head and awaited his direction. He immediately was on the phone booking a private cottage for us; somewhere Jay couldn't find us until everyone came back tomorrow. I forgot to tell him about the message I left for EJ, but we didn't have time for me to revise it with further details. I'd just call to check in later.

Grabbing just enough for an overnight bag, I moved in a daze as he barked orders at me to hurry. So much to process. How had I never known Jay was best friends with a Marino? How naïve could I be?

"Mar, we have to get going before anyone finds us. Do you have the dragon?" I nodded.

"Good. Let's go," he rushed, stopping briefly to convince the guards that we were in no danger and that he would keep an eye out for me. They looked at me for confirmation, and I nodded and smiled, asking them to please watch over the house and I'd be back later.

It was seamless, rehearsed and believable, just as we had conned the guards before when we were in Ireland and Italy to have some alone time together. We had this scheme down to a science.

About fifteen minutes later, we arrived at a quaint little cottage somewhere in between Sitges and Barcelona. Nestled into what appeared to be a national park, there was nothing and no one around except hiking trails, a stunning view and perhaps a few wildlife.

"We'll be safe here tonight," he assured me. He wrapped his strong arms around my back and held me as I broke down in sobs. He stood quiet, letting me emote and ramble and slobber all over his cashmere sweater without flinching.

He brought me over to the queen-sized bed and sat me down, removing the wet strands of hair from my face and lifting up my chin.

"Promise me you will never keep anything like this from me again," he pleaded.

"I promise. I am so sorry," I replied.

"If anything were to ever happen to you..." he broke off

mid-sentence, choking back his own sobs that threatened to take over.

"I love you," was all I could muster up. I looked at him with my tear-stained face, and he brought me in for a passionate kiss. He instantly had me on my back, tearing off my clothes with the hunger of a man who had not eaten in weeks.

But I had to stop him. I didn't want savagery right now. I needed his pure love and protection.

"Please, can we be gentle tonight?" I implored. He smiled and obliged, slowing down his passionate fury to kiss me more delicately. Not as much tender foreplay as I was hoping for, as his hands still anxiously went straight for my swelled opening.

My phone rang—I stopped him enough to see that it was Mia. He groaned in agony.

"Please, Marissa, I've missed you. You can call her back after we make love. I need you," he groveled as he continued to play with my breasts and finger my insides. I conceded, turning my ringer to silent and letting him devour me with as much patience as the man could find to somewhat honor my request for slow and steady. I needed him as much as he needed me.

His tongue traveled from inside my ear, down the curve of my breasts, over my tightened stomach and down into me. He squeezed my ass as he impeccably flicked his tongue against my clit, causing the heat to rise within me. Sensing my pre-orgasm arch, he stopped to move his kisses up to my mouth so that he could slide inside me instead.

Rhythmic throbs as his drenched body rubbed up against mine, the fire between us burning even hotter. He kissed me like there was no tomorrow, before swiftly moving his mouth to take a hard bite of my nipple, making me scream as his final plunge nailed me hard. He knew all too well that this would make me explode simultaneously.

Part of me loved when he did that, so that we released together. But I didn't want that tonight. I freed the disappointment from my mind, as I felt him pull me into a spooning caress, stroking my hair with deep affection and placing a kiss on top of my head. I could hear his heartbeat, and before I knew it, I was sound asleep in his arms.

His hardened cock woke me in the middle of the night, finding its way into me for another round. Groggy, I didn't put up a fight, and just let him pleasure himself without bringing me to orgasm. I'd save the conversation about a new way of lovemaking for another time. I didn't want to fight; I just wanted to remain safe and protected here in his arms.

In the morning, I found him standing over the bed, naked but holding a tray of blackened coffee and a pastry, complemented by a small white vase with a single red rose.

"Good morning, beautiful," he said cheerfully.

"Good morning," I cooed back. "What's all this?"

"I figured you could use some sustenance. We have a few hours before I take you back and I thought we should take advantage of this private time," he suggested.

"Thank you. I'm starving," I replied as I bit into the flaky croissant with decadent chocolate inside.

"Hey, where's that statue by the way? I'd love to see it."

"Oh, of course. It's over here in my bag," I said as I went to retrieve it and carefully remove it from its protective wrapping. There it was—I could look at it a million times and still be in awe of it.

"It's as splendid as you claimed it was," said Josh in matching awe. "May I?"

He took it into his hands and ran his fingers over it with the same softness I did, taking in every inch of its rich features.

"What have you learned about it?"

"Not much," I admitted. "Its composition is black onyx with a marble base, and it has ruby and sapphire eyes and red opal and citrine flames. Goya is confirmed as its creator, one of his very first pieces. EJ hasn't told me yet what it represents, but I think I figured it out. One head represents good, the other evil, but they are made from one body and part of each other. Just like I am."

He looked over and smiled at me. "Though I must say, I like your evil side a little better," he joked. I bashfully grinned, not knowing if I should take that as a compliment. I heard EJ's voice of warning. Red flags were popping up; I was starting to get the feeling that as much as he supported me, the sex was more important to him. But I'd save that investigation for another time, when we were safe back in the states.

"Oh, I almost forgot. There is also a map hidden within the statue. It's a guide to the keys that open the jewelry box, where EJ said there is a greater inheritance awaiting us."

"Is that so?"

"Yes. Once everyone arrives for the party—and we find the map—we will learn how to open it all together as a family."

"Interesting. But you haven't found the map yet?"

"Not exactly, but before I got that horrible note last night, I think I stumbled upon a crack in the tail...perhaps if I twist it, it will open."

"Clever girl," he said slyly, making his way over to the bed, trailing kisses down my neck and removing the coffee cup from my hand. His tongue thrust into my mouth, pulling me into a heightened arousal that made me want him to touch me endlessly.

He stepped back with a smirk, reaching into the drawer beside me and pulling out four sets of handcuffs and bonds.

"We played it your way last night. Indulge me, would you?" he asked so sweetly, yet seductively. I acquiesced by raising my arms above my head so he could strap each one to the bedpost, and then spread my legs apart so he could tie them up as well.

He took an ice cube from the bucket and ran it down the length of my body, concentrating it around my nipples to create stinging sensations before biting them hard.

"Ow, Josh, you're hurting me," I whimpered. "Take it easy."

He ignored my pleas, biting harder and moving the ice cube all the way down and into me. The sensation was at first unbearable, but as it melted with my heat, the pain eased. He then taunted me with the sight of another ice cube, clearly wanting a repeat performance.

"Josh, stop it. Please." Throwing the block to the floor, he angrily straddled me until his face was only an inch away from mine.

"I'll do whatever I damn well please to you, bitch. You're mine, and if I want to stick ice cubes up your pussy, I will. Lucky for you, I'd much rather fuck you hard and senseless. You should have watched your back like I warned you to. Stupid whore."

The evil smile spread over his face and his maniacal laugh sent chills colder than the ice throughout my body.

Joshua Perkins was the mastermind all along.

11

Mercilessly, he didn't come near me—yet. Instead, he seemed disgusted at the sight of me.

"What's wrong, Marissa? Perk up, you kinky slut. You're no fun to fuck when you're lifeless."

"Why are you doing this?" I furiously hissed, traumatized enough not to cry but embarrassed enough to realize I was locked up and spread eagle, unable to move or get away from this psychopath if he chose to touch me.

"Because I can," he spat. "Because finally, I am the one in control. I knew you would be my ticket," he sneered, dancing around like a crazy Christmas elf.

"All I needed to do was make you believe I loved you, and you'd spill your guts to me. Fuck, you were so predictable. Oh, and it was a bonus that you happened to be into all this bondage and orgy shit. Had you not gone sensitive and wanted 'gentle lovemaking,' I might have even put up with you for a while longer.

"But now you're making my dick soft," he grumbled in disapproval, playing with himself to try to get erect again.

"So, you've been lying this whole time?" I asked incredulously. How could I have been so blind? What was wrong with my internal warning system that I didn't see this coming?

"Yes, sweetheart. How else could I get close to your sainted family? I knew prissy Meg would be too smart and catch on, and well, I wasn't really into the roly-poly married one with the cop up her ass. You were dumb and desperate, so I went for the baby of the family and hit the jackpot."

"I don't understand why?"

"Why, princess? Because that's *my* fucking fortune. MINE," he spewed in intense anger.

"I'm sorry, how is this yours?" I was beginning to feel the fight rise back up in me. This man that I thought I loved lied to me, betrayed me and possibly intended to rape me—or worse. No way was I backing down now. If he was going to violate me, I was going to get some answers first.

"That's none of your business, bitch. All you need to know is that this little gem is stolen property, and I intend to claim it back. All of it." He grabbed the dragon statue and kissed it, hugging it to his chest as he laughed in sinister relief.

"You won't get away with this, asshole. Someone will find me, and you'll go down."

"Like who? Like your sisters who don't care about you? Some fag who is off at a nude beach getting his jollies? Some biker dude you cut off because I persuaded you that he betrayed you? The guards we slipped by? I don't think so, sweetheart. No one knows where you are. I'll be long gone by the time anyone finds your rotting corpse."

"You wouldn't dare."

Now fully dressed in his clothes, he walked up to me and stuck his face in mine again, practically spitting on me with his hateful vengeance. "Watch me."

Oh my God, he meant it. I saw it in his possessed, raging eyes. He was going to kill me.

Way to go, Marissa. You've finally gotten yourself into a mess you can't get out of. All because of your selfish desires for a dragon statue, a fortune and all the joy money promised you.

Against my better judgment, I began to cry.

"Oh, knock it off, you baby," he said as he slapped me across the face. As I recuperated from the sting, I felt the slightest hint of blood drip down from the corner of my mouth.

"Maybe baby wants to hear a little bedtime story before she goes bye-bye?" he chided with a cold, childish mock. "Want to know how I did it?"

I looked defiantly at him, trying to find whatever dignity I could muster. If these were my last moments on earth, I'd go down demons blazing.

"I'll take that as a yes?" He strolled over to the red high back armchair in the corner of the room and crossed his legs, a smug look of satisfaction upon his face as he played with a box of matches he picked up from the nearby table.

"Once upon a time there was a hypocritical old man who betrayed his family, first by lying about his bastard child and then by leaving a fortune to a bunch of lower-class nobodies.

"One by one, his adopted and blood family members received grand gestures—houses, riches, estates—while the one grandson who was there for him, who served him until his dying day, got a damn Rolex watch and a pat on the back. The least the fucker could have done was reinstate me to the family," he said, breaking from his singsong storytelling to expose the secret behind his wrath.

"Reinstate you?"

"Yeah, sweetheart. I was born Joshua Marino, youngest son of David and Bethany, brother to sainted Patrick and Colin. But I never measured up to the prides and joy of the family, and one wrong move landed me in jail.

"Tarnished the family name they said, so they excused me from it, as luck would have it," he said bitterly, reliving his personal nightmare.

"Then how did you end up as my grandfather's lawyer? If everyone knew you to be the rotten son of a bitch you clearly are, then why would he bother with you?"

I relished in the opportunity to pour the salt into his wound. *Maybe I shouldn't instigate him,* I thought to myself, *but what did I have to lose at this point?* It seemed the more I angered him, the more he wanted to reveal. And I wanted to know every last detail.

"The dumbasses underestimated me. When they were all at a little family party—one where they seemed to have lost my invitation—I broke into good old Grandpa's study and found a damaging tell-all journal and an old photo of him with a sexy little minx and a bratty kid, the words 'Lillith and Alissa' scribbled on the back of it.

"I confronted him about it, bringing him to his knees. All I had to do was threaten to expose him or hurt them, and he was putty in my hands."

"You blackmailed him."

"If you want to call it that, then technically, yes. I saw it as finding my way back to my family's loving arms," he said in defense of his actions.

"I asked to be made a Marino again, but he said the rest of the family would never accept it; it would be too much and they'd never go along with it. Pissed and weak, I compromised and agreed to take Perkins as my last name, be dubbed his lawyer and receive a piece of the inheritance when he croaked.

"The family was resistant to his decision to name me as his lawyer, but as the patriarch, they believed his claims of wanting to keep the family intact due to honor or some shit. Whatever, they bought it. I tried to push repeatedly to be let back in, but he got the upper hand when he softened and came clean about his bastard family to everyone. Sentimental asshole," he spat.

"I was irate. I had nothing left to hold over his head, with them being all forgiving and shit. He met enough stipulations that would satisfy the wishes of dead Uncle Rocco, so they allowed him to remain as head of the family.

"He lost nothing. He betrayed his word and the ancestral wishes, and he lost NOTHING. Yet, I couldn't be forgiven for one little accidental murder in my teens," he muttered bitterly.

"I guess I should be grateful to the geezer that he never ratted me out to the family for 'blackmailing him,' as you called it. I confronted him about it and he said that I was in enough trouble with the family and he wanted to leave it all behind us. Too much family disruption as it was, the pussy said.

"Anyway, to keep peace, he kept me on as his lawyer and made me jump through hoops to prove myself as worthy of staying that way. It was complete torture. I had to pretend my ass off that I was rehabilitated and trustworthy—no small feat, but that practice certainly came in handy with you, princess," he leered with self-gratification.

"Of course, after all that hard work, he still stiffed me in the end and left me nothing. Nothing but instructions to carry out a plan he had for his 'dear Lillith' and 'little diamond' and gag me with the rest."

"But you weren't even mentioned in the will," I pointed out.

"Yes, I was. Are you even paying attention? I got a Rolex watch. One goddamn watch," he yelled irritably. "But since you are so stupid, I guess I should remind you that I'm the one who read the will to you. I conveniently left out reading my name so you didn't catch on. I counted on you never reading the will in detail after that, which was something else that worked in my favor. You were all so emotional about Grampy's farewell letters that you missed what was right in front of your face."

"And so now you think that because of all this, you are entitled to our heirlooms?"

"Yes, damn it, I am. My father was the one raised by him and took his name. Not your slut Mahoney, Rossi, whatever of a mother. My brothers got their share from the Marino side. It would only be fair for me to receive equivalent value, so I thought instead of fighting my brothers and worsening the family feud, I could hoodwink great-grandmother Lena's side and make a killing for myself." He was so damn proud of himself and his smug treachery. If I could kick him in the nuts…

"*'These letters are not to be opened by anyone except the Rossi family,'* he warned me. Like the good little puppy dog I was, I promised him with every repentant cell in my body that I would honor his final wishes. Ha! The fool.

"Like I wouldn't steam open the envelopes, read the letters and then reseal them before delivering them to you. Like your old bat of a grandmother would remember Leigh's real handwriting versus my forged one on new 'sealed' envelopes."

"You're such a creep," I couldn't help but comment.

"Yeah, but a smart one. My plan was brilliant—and clearly, it worked. The moment I met you, I knew I would get everything I wanted. It was so easy to penetrate you— literally and figuratively," he laughed, rising from the chair to run a finger down my body and tweak my nipple.

He stood there and toyed with the idea of touching

me more as he continued his diabolical monologue. I cringed at the feeling of his finger circling my stomach and suggestively moving lower.

"You were so desperate to be wanted that you went along with all my ideas, believing my lies about needing information every step of the way to protect you. You sang like a canary, sweetheart. Where everybody was, about the decoys, about the warnings and about your plans for security. You made it so fucking easy, doll face.

"It makes me almost sad to kill you when I should be so grateful," he taunted as his breath drew to a whisper near my earlobe, taking a prolonged nibble and licking my neck. Thankfully, he was too engrossed in his own story to continue his sexual torment.

"I worried about you catching on all those times when the break-ins and notes happened, but then you so innocently believed my whereabouts every single time. Didn't you once consider me a suspect when I was in each country every time something happened?"

He watched me as I hung my head in embarrassment, knowing that the signs were all there and I missed every single one of them. He was painfully spot-on about me being so captivated by the thought of true love that I turned a blind eye to what was happening around me. I did this to myself—to my family.

"God, are you so inept. No wonder your family has no faith in you," he said to degrade me.

He continued to walk through all his treachery, step by step, delightedly pointing out how I went along with it. Like the time I danced with the Irishman and told my sisters I was leaving with a stranger for the night, when I was really meeting up with Josh. Or when I snuck him into my room on Clare Island while Mia was in the library—

after he trashed the house looking for clues about the ring, he just informed me.

I believed him when he said he was at the beach processing his feelings for me right before he hopped on the ferry to the island. He claimed he was so overwhelmed with how fast our relationship was progressing, that he needed time for himself. When he heard about the break-in, he rushed to my side without the others knowing, swearing to protect me. And I bought it all.

Oh, he could tell I had an initial doubt in my mind since it was all so coincidental and our budding romance was still so new—but how persuasive he was. The lawyer in him convinced me that it would be insane of him to be so blatantly obvious, with me knowing he was in Ireland.

If he was going to be behind something like this, he wouldn't have ever shown himself to me, he said. Plus, since I thought he was back in the states when the Dublin hotel break-in happened—it was "proof" that he couldn't have possibly been behind it. So, I dropped the suspicion.

I was such an idiot to believe him.

But he hooked me good in Ireland with his leprechaun trickery. Especially after presenting me with my own Claddagh ring, declaring that even though Meg had some old family heirloom, that this would mean more because he had it created just for me, to show me how much he cared for me; how much more he cared for me than "obviously" my sisters did. He knew my Achilles heel and exploited it.

I was falling quickly for his love and his lies, that I never saw the rest coming. I felt so comfortable that I betrayed my family's secrets time after time, making it incredibly effortless for him to keep up his plan.

"Except when your bitch of a sister pulled one over on me with that decoy ring," he fumed. He reaffirmed his vow to get it back before continuing on his journey of deceit.

He thought he could make things a little easier on himself by scaring us with the notes before Italy, but we didn't take the bait, so he had to kick his strategy up a notch. He disclosed that he partnered with Dominic Moretti, who was more than happy to help a fellow con man out.

Moretti had no desire for some old jewelry box himself and thought the idea of revenge against an ancient feud line was deliciously fun, so he provided Josh with all the resources he needed to get the box back. Moretti's henchmen came in handy—as did his verification that the box was not in the attic after Josh had overheard us divulging the details in the garden cafe.

"It *was* you at the Bianchi house that day," I deduced. I knew I had seen him but told myself I was crazy; he didn't visit until a few days later when we went off on our alone time. If only I had shared my suspicion with my sisters then, instead of blowing them off, maybe this all would have turned out differently.

"I came earlier than you expected, but made you believe otherwise," he declared with glee, the sneer never leaving his face.

"Even when you questioned me, asking me if I was there, I was able to assure you that you were just seeing things—after all, you came two days later to pick me up yourself right from baggage claim at the airport," he reminded me. "Ah, that Dominic and his connections. I promised to return the favor whenever he needed it."

"So, when I called to tell you that my sisters and I were going our separate ways for a few days and I asked you to come visit, you were already in the country?" I inquired angrily, more so at myself for how gullible I had been this whole time.

"Yup," he snickered, quite pleased with himself. "It was so easy to pretend I could book a last-minute flight there. And after your little investigative questioning, I distracted you with some hot sex. Remember that beautiful 20-year-old Italian girl we picked up at the club? You gave such great head while she dined on you for dessert," he recalled wickedly.

The more he spoke, the more I was repulsed about my entire relationship with him. Every time he touched me, every lie that dripped out of his conniving mouth. If I wasn't tied up, I would beat the living shit out of this fucker. I think he sensed my fire rising, undoing his pants and bringing his hand to his cock to help it harden.

"There's the feisty spirit that gets me all hot. Do you want a little break in story time? Want some more of this?" he asked, moving towards me on the bed.

I panicked but pulled myself together to snarl at him and hit him verbally where it hurt.

"Are you so pathetic that you have to chain a woman up to have sex with her? Are you the type of gutless man who gets off on rape? That's sad."

"Rape? Fuck you, Marissa. I don't need to beg a woman for sex," he replied, clearly pissed off and backing away, his overdrawn ego evidently insulted. I hit the right button, thank God. But then he turned around to me and stuck his half-stiff dick in my face as if to put it in my mouth.

"Though I do wonder if the rush that comes along with taking a woman by force is as orgasmic as they say it is," he hinted, standing his ground. "I could always pretend we are playing dom and sub and that your begging to stop is code for fuck me harder," he said viciously.

"As if I would ever want to touch you again willingly. Fuck me if you want, but it's just my body. It means nothing to you without my resistance or my consent, because you'll get neither. It would be like doing a corpse, if you're into that sort of thing."

He considered his options for a moment before deciding to walk away, zipping his pants back up.

"So, how does your sister-in-law and her brother factor into all of this if you're estranged?" I urged him to continue, wanting to know the depths of his destructive plot.

He snickered heartily and deeply. As he unraveled more of his saga, he was becoming increasingly joyful over his great sham.

"Just collateral damage like you, sweetheart. Peggy's idiot brother had a record and I knew if I played around with his name, eventually everything would be traced back to him. I also realized that Mia's damn cop husband was good and getting too close, so I had to set someone up for the fall—and be careful about it.

"So, I kept my ticket out of Florence to New York to throw the Feds off my scent, while paying cash and hopping a plane in Pisa to Boston. I still knew that it was traceable, but by the time I had gotten through customs and hightailed it over to my nice, cushy home in Manhattan, no one would ever know it was me setting him up.

"I even gave the heads up to my stooges to reveal my 'name' on purpose if they were ever caught, knowing that it wasn't my identity the authorities would go after. In fact, that goosechase gave me the opportunity to take the fake jewelry box—thank you for spilling the beans, yet again—wrap it up as if from Jorden to Peggy and tip the cops off anonymously.

"Knowing that bitch couldn't resist a bauble, I had hoped she'd be wearing the brooch when they showed up to question her. Jesus, do I know people or what?" he snorted with triumph.

"The dumbass elitist took her sweet time thanking her brother for the gift—giving the police enough time to detain Jorden before he spoke with her. It was the perfect setup. She had no idea her brother didn't give her the box, and with his record, she thought he went way too far and was happy to give him some tough love by throwing him under the bus.

"For all his detesting that he had nothing to do with it, his past spoke for itself and he was arrested. The family foolishly confirmed her comments at the will reading, keeping her locked up as well. All that time gave me the opening to slip in the matching notepaper and have my hacker buddy craft some damning emails between them. So sweet," he uttered as he kissed his fingers Italian-style, as if every move he made was a delectable masterpiece.

"I wrote those fucking emails, yeah," he said with arrogant pride. "I planted everything. I'm a goddamn genius, Marissa; a genius that everyone underestimated.

"Oh, and I threatened to kill Peggy if her idiot brother didn't confess—but he didn't know it was me at the jail he was talking to because we never met, thanks to me being disinherited and all. You should have seen him squeal like a pig. He begged me to let Peggy go, and I agreed—if he would take the fall to clear the way for me to claim everything and get away with it.

"He knew that if he reneged or tried to claim someone else was behind it, her neck would snap like a pencil and my buddies on the inside would fuck his ass well into Tuesday.

"But the best was implanting the idea in your gullible head, little by little, that Peggy could do something like this. By the time she was arrested, you were all so eager to accept that she was the one behind it, along with her rap sheet bro—just as I expected.

"Of course, after they were detained, I realized my plan hit a snafu," he admitted with a twinge of regret. "I only had the fake ring in my possession and lost the valuable decoy that Mia set up—clever, clever, girl by the way. I have to give her props because she was hard to outsmart and made one hell of a convincing work of art.

"I had a plan to get the real ring and box like she promised in her fake note, but your damn sisters fucked that up on me again, with Meg staying in Ireland and Mia in Florence. Then when she returned, her ex-husband playing hero watching over her made it hard to get past security at her house.

"That's when I figured that I might as well wait until I get your statue from you, then while the family was in mourning and distracted, I could lift the others."

"So, with Jorden in custody, why send the threatening notes and let me believe someone was still out there? Why not let that go and just take me here and now like you planned?"

"I did consider that. It would have made things easier to lull you into a false sense of security, but that wouldn't have been any fun. I knew how selfish you were, Marissa. I knew you would keep it a secret from your family because you wanted to come here so badly, and if you told them, they would call it off. And you couldn't have that, could you?"

He laughed as my face gave away how he was on the money.

"Told you I'm good at figuring people out," he jeered. "Oh, it was so much fucking fun to play with you. To mindfuck you. Even after I physically handed you the note, you didn't even tell *me,* your boyfriend. Classic move, Marissa. But I didn't expect you to tell that prick, Jay, by the way. Your loyalty to that jackass almost cost me everything."

"Jay…you made me believe he was behind this. But he wasn't, was he?"

"Of course not, but I had to deflect suspicion to someone, and I had it out for that meddling moron who couldn't keep his eyes off you. It gave me a hard-on to watch you tear that friendship apart. And pitting you against Bruce and causing conflict with your mom? I kept you looking everywhere but straight at me as the culprit.

"Oh, just for the record, that loser couldn't hurt a fly, he is so weak and pathetic. I'll be taking care of my buddy Bruce when I get back to the states, because he is getting a little too close for comfort for me," he noted as if making a checklist of things to do after he murdered me.

"So, what now, huh? What's the big plan now that you've got the dragon?"

"Wouldn't you like to know?"

"You're right. I don't give a fuck. You can take the statue and shove it up your ass for all I care."

Within seconds, his face was in mine again. "You should care, bitch. Because when I'm done with you, I'll be going for the others," he threatened.

"Jesus, that mouth of yours. Haven't you figured out that *you* are the reason all this is happening? If you had just kept your mouth shut and your legs open, I might have even let you go unharmed and staged some kind of break-in at our house before I dumped your ass legitimately. I would have made it work.

"But you had to push me, didn't you? You had to cross the line and bring love into this, forcing me to pretend I loved you. And now you want to do away with the kinky sex and make love.

"Moving in with you was nauseating. The only thing that kept me sane was the great sex—it's what has kept you alive all this time. You're the best little whore I've been with, and you were free," he laughed maniacally. "Well, maybe not completely free, because these trips and henchmen and strategies cost me a fortune. But now that I have the one piece, I can start making up for it."

He went over to the dragon and lifted it up, packing it into his suitcase as he gathered all his things and placed them by the door. He then brought out a red gasoline container and began dumping the fume-laced contents all over the room, concentrating by the bed.

Oh my God. He was going to light me on fire.

"You should have played nicer, Marissa," he scolded. "This all could have ended differently. But now you will burn up like the dragon you think you are. I'll just use your phone to text your location to your sisters, and then send a suicide note by email, so by the time they find you, you'll be ash in this accidental fire and they'll think both you and the damn dragon went up in flames."

"They'll never believe I killed myself, you idiot. I may be a lot of things, but I'm not suicidal. Plus, with Jay knowing about the notes, it wouldn't take long to figure out my messages were fake."

"Then I'll just have to call in another favor and make sure he has a terrible motorcycle accident before he even finds out you're dead. And then I'll have Meg mugged for her ring and tragically killed when she struggles. Unfortunate accidents. Purely coincidental.

"Oh, and my buddy in New York is ready to bound, gag and kill anyone who gets in the way of lifting the jewelry box out of Mia's hands once she gets back—maybe he'll even get to ride that ripe 16-year-old niece of yours. She's a fine piece of ass. I wouldn't mind tapping that myself," he mused.

"You're a sick bastard. I hope you rot in hell," I spat at him.

"Oh, there's that fire again that gets me hot. Yeah, that's it. Make me harder, baby. For old times' sake," he cooed, stripping down to nothing and hardening with every inch as he drew closer to me.

"You think you've won, but you haven't."

"I haven't? Tell me, Marissa—are you broken yet? Have I not obliterated every last ounce of respect you had for yourself? Destroyed your faith in men and the ability to love? Ripped your heart out of your chest?

"Think about this as you take your last breaths. Your selfish betrayal of your family has now led to your and their demise. You should be grateful that I am putting you out of your misery; you'd never be able to live with yourself. The shame, the humiliation, the grief of knowing this is all your fault."

"No, this is all the fault of an entitled psychopath. And just for the record, you didn't break me, asshole. All you did was teach me a life lesson; to listen and trust my own instincts better."

As I reviewed the flash of life before me—all the mistakes, challenges, heartaches, pain—I had never been able to see my life or myself so clearly. In my last moments, I finally understood who I was and what life was about.

"With your every attempt to bring me down, you built me up. You think your words can hurt me? You think your deceit has ruined me? You don't have that kind of power over me." It was my turn to laugh like a lunatic as he looked at me in shock.

"Sorry, buddy, but you failed. Because I still believe in love. I still believe in the goodness in the world. I still have faith in my family's forgiveness and acceptance of me for who I am—and whether they think this was suicide or murder, I know in their hearts I'll be remembered for the amazing human being I am. I am unconditionally loved by them.

"The best part? I finally respect myself, because mistakes and all, I know I am a good person. I am both the dark and the light, and I accept all parts of me. The naïve and the trusting, the vindictive and the passionate. I'm fucking fantastic just as I am. So, try as hard as you can, but you will never destroy me.

"The problem is, I was too much of a woman for you to handle. And truth be told, your dick is too small. The only reason I had to invite other men and women and fantasy tactics into our sex life was because by yourself, you didn't have what it took to pleasure me. I faked it," I revealed, knowing that if I was going down, I'd take his ego down with me.

Uh oh, that did it. I went too far, as the fury rose in him like the flames he threatened to perish me in, mounting my chained up body. I tried to resist him positioning himself to enter me, but the restraints were so tight, they almost cut off my circulation. There was nothing I could do to stop what was coming.

Deranged and lustful, with matchbox in hand, he readied himself to take whatever he wanted from my already dead body before lighting the torch.

All I could do was close my eyes and wait in agony until this nightmare was finally over.

12

"**D**on't even think about it, asshole," came the voice barreling through the cottage door, placing a 6mm gun next to Josh's head, cocked and ready to fire. "Touch her and I'll blow your fucking brains out."

"Well, well, well. Look who it is," Josh sneered as he froze in place, the cold metal pressed against his right temple.

To our absolute astonishment, there Jay stood, fierce and protective. And he wasn't kidding—he was ready to pull the trigger.

"Get off of her. Slowly," he warned. "One wrong move and I'll gladly take the electric chair in exchange for the pleasure of your death."

Josh had no choice but to concede, carefully removing himself from the bed as instructed. Jay was in soldier mode; he didn't even look at me or ask if I was all right. He was solely focused on getting this terrorist away from me.

"You think you can stop me, Boy Scout?" Josh asked in an attempt to intimidate Jay. "I have the entire cottage laced with gasoline and this match in my hand ready to strike. One wrong move and either this match—or your stray bullet—will ignite this volcano," he forewarned.

"I'll take my chances," Jay replied from behind gritted teeth. "Now move over to the door."

"And what are you going to do? Hold me here forever?

You move from your position to free her, and I'll light you up and get out unharmed. You stay here like a homo up against my bare body, and she stays there, naked and chained up for you to drool over what you can't have.

"Gorgeous, isn't she? Look how perfect her breasts are. Not an ounce of fat on her toned stomach. That tight ass, man. It's everything you'd dreamed she'd be like underneath those silky nighties she wears. You should see how she writhes with pleasure when you bite her tits or ride her when she's dripping wet," he taunted.

Jay then looked over at me, trying not to notice all that Josh had pointed out as I lay there in a humiliating position.

"Shut your mouth," Jay demanded, keeping his gun on Josh's head while being careful to only look at my face and make eye contact as he spoke to me.

"Are you okay? Did he hurt you?"

"No. You got here just in time. How did you find me?"

Before Jay could answer, Josh took the distracted opportunity to move away and light the match, threatening to drop it near me.

"Looks like we're at a draw, partner," Josh teased condescendingly.

"No, we're not," Jay countered, and in an instant, the battle was over.

Jay fired a single, perfect shot to Josh's groin, dropping him and his match to the ground—thankfully in a spot where the idiot had very little gasoline. Some kind of angel had to have stepped in to make sure of that. Jay was able to swiftly stop the spark of fire that started in the carpet as his victim lay in a small pool of blood, grasping his damaged penis in groaning agony.

Knowing he didn't have much time before Josh could possibly get up, Jay moved to the bed to first cover my exposed body with a sheet, and then released me from the chains. Keeping the gun pointed at Josh with one hand, he brought me against his chest with the other.

"I'm so glad you are okay," he murmured, placing kisses all over my face and leaning his forehead into mine with a deep sigh. "I would never have forgiven myself if anything had happened to you." He hugged me tighter, then released me when he felt some of the sheet slip away; my bare breasts pressing up against his chest.

"You should put some clothes on. The cops will be here soon," he said, blushing and turning away to give me privacy.

Everything that happened afterwards was a blur. As promised, the authorities were on the scene within minutes, as well as an ambulance and armed escorts to take the injured Josh to the hospital. Unfortunately, the scumbag would live; not so sure his cock would, though. The thought of him never being able to have sex again brought an evil smile to my face. *Way to go, Jay.*

The next few hours were spent being interrogated by the police, as I reiterated Josh's list of crimes and motives verbatim to them, as well as to Jay and my sisters, who met up with me at the station with hugs of relief. The police also questioned Jay in a separate room before clearing him of all charges, ultimately declaring the gunshot was in self-defense. He wouldn't have to spend a single day in international jail, thanks to Bruce's calls and connections.

EJ came storming in shortly after, and gratefully, my sisters took on the job of bringing him up to speed so I did not have to relive the nightmare again. I was in a daze, drinking down glasses of water shoved in my face, accepting embraces from everyone around me and repressing the trauma I had just been through. I didn't even notice that we were back at the villa, and I was in my room.

I can't believe I survived that. It was a miracle.

A light knock at my door brought me back to the present. Meg and Mia quietly entered and sat down on the bed beside me.

"How are you doing, honey?" Meg asked.

"I'm okay, I guess. It's a lot to process," I said stoically.

"You've been through quite an ordeal. Is there anything we can do for you?" Mia asked, grabbing my hand while Meg rubbed my back.

"Do you know where my phone is?"

"It's right here on the night stand. Jay grabbed all your stuff when you left the cottage. The police currently have the statue from Josh's bag in evidence right now, but they assured us they would return it in the morning."

"Okay," I answered, looking at my phone to see the countless missed calls and texts from my loved ones trying to track me down.

"How did you know I was in danger?"

"It all happened so quickly," Mia began. "After Jay wasn't able to get in touch with you, he called to alert me about Josh, hoping that I was with you and could watch over you until he got here. I tried to reach you to warn you, but you must have turned your ringer off.

"Not even five minutes later, EJ called to tell me about the note you left behind for him, and how the guards said you went off with some guy matching Josh's description with the promise you would be safe, and it took me all of one second to figure out that he got to you before we did.

"We were so terrified that we lost you," cried Mia.

"I'm so sorry," I broke down, allowing the sobs to flow out of me. My chest hurt as I heaved, the excruciating pain of betrayal and disbelief over being rescued consuming me. My sisters sheltered me in their bear hug sandwich, the tears also pouring down their faces as we wept together.

"I should have been honest about Josh all along. If I had, one of you would have been smart enough to catch on to his plan long before this," I confessed.

"If you had only known he had snuck on our trips to Ireland and Italy to spend time with me, and that I was spilling my guts to him more than I let on, we likely wouldn't even be in this mess. I should've told you about the recent threats. I shouldn't have been selfish, putting us all in danger over some stupid statue," I admitted in defeat.

"Don't do that to yourself," Meg hushed. "Don't blame yourself. You did what you thought was right at the time. We're just relieved that you weren't hurt. That's all that matters."

"Besides," Mia added, "we might have done the same thing in your shoes. But I will say I am glad you confided in Jay about everything. He's the one who figured it all out, and the reason you're breathing right now."

"Where is he?" I asked, wanting to see my dear, brave friend.

"He's patiently sitting with EJ by the pool, waiting to see you. He wanted us to make sure you were up for a visit before he bothered you."

"Bothered me? He saved my life. How could he even think that?"

"That's what we said," Meg chuckled. "Should I let him know that you'd like to see him?"

"Yes, please," I smiled up at them. Before they could leave, I stopped them and gave them each a hug. "Thank you for being the best sisters in the entire world. I love you so much and promise to never let another day go by without telling you again."

"We love you, too," they replied in unison.

I stood up to look in the mirror. I aged about twenty years from lack of sleep and stress. I must have looked like a horror film with my gaping zombie eyes and drooping cheeks. My dirty, unwashed hair and the thought of Josh's DNA still on and in me almost made me vomit in my mouth.

I had to get into the shower and wash away the filth; scrub the horrific memories off my body and out of my mind. By the time I was done, my skin was almost raw from panicked exfoliation. I was grateful he never got to rape me, but he was still a part of me—a part I needed to flush and forget.

Stepping outside into the bedroom in a towel, I had forgotten that Jay was on his way in. He swallowed hard in embarrassment, excusing himself towards the door and promising to come back at a better time so I could get myself dressed.

"No, wait," I said. "Stay. I'll get changed in the bathroom and be right out."

Like a nervous teenager, Jay sat in the corner in the oversized lounge chair, his hands wringing together as his leg bounced up and down in his classically anxious way.

"Hi," I started, alerting him that I was fully dressed and present.

"Hi," he simply responded, not knowing what else to say. I motioned for him to come sit on the bed next to me, so we could talk. He reluctantly settled beside me, finding it difficult to look me in the eyes.

"Thank you," I managed, reaching my arms out to him, bringing him close to me as he let out his own cries of relief now that the nightmare was over.

"I'm sorry I didn't get here sooner. I'm sorry I failed to protect you like I promised."

"Jay, look at me," I said lifting his chin up so that we could be face-to-face. "You did exactly as you promised," I assured him. "I am here, alive and unharmed, because of you. By the way, how did you find me?"

"Location tracker," he confessed. "Remember a few months ago when we went to the Coldplay concert and we shared our locations on our phones in case we got separated?"

I nodded in recollection—that was a kickass concert, too.

"Well, you never turned your location sharing off from me. Once I landed and learned you were missing, I checked my phone and miraculously, wherever you were had the reception I needed to find you."

"So, how did you figure out Josh was behind it all?"

"It's a long story."

"No time like the present," I responded, sitting back onto the bed and pulling him to me into a comfortable position, my head on his familiar and safe shoulders. "Let's hear it."

It all began when I asked him to keep an eye on Bruce. Well, actually earlier than that, because Jay had always had his suspicions that Josh was up to no good, but didn't have anything concrete enough to prove it. He only had the information (lies) Josh told me to go on, and since it was agreed that he had plausible alibis the whole time, there was no need to question the "facts" and accuse him.

Knowing that I was way too into the guy, Jay didn't bring up the subject anymore and privately kept notes on what I told him in hopes of figuring out what my boyfriend was really up to.

Wanting to find out the truth behind Bruce's ominous 'watch your back' warning, Jay reached out to him to set up that meeting at the coffee shop.

"I'm sorry for not telling you about that, Riss, but I knew you kept feeding information to Josh. It's not that I didn't trust you. I just couldn't risk you tipping him or anyone else off about what I was up to," he reasonably explained.

"Given the circumstances, I get it now. I'm glad you followed your gut—at least one of us did. I'm just sorry you had to endure my wrath," I offered apologetically.

"It was worth it to see you safe," he said, and meant it. But there was much more to the story he had yet to reveal.

When Jay and Bruce talked, they ended up exchanging information—Jay about my threatening note and Bruce's ill-timed wording, and Bruce about his investigative file on Josh and the Marinos. Turns out, my mother's man had his own antenna up in protection of his love and her daughters.

Since they did, in fact, move in the same professional circles, while Josh was trying to discredit Bruce in my eyes, Bruce was diligently gathering intel on Joshua Pekins. So far, he had only learned that Josh was on probation for attempting to bribe a judge, getting off with a warning. That wasn't enough for them to lynch him just yet.

Bruce then approached Kevin one night while helping with a security camera installation, triggered by a gut feeling that something was awry about Jorden and Peggy being arrested. It just so happened that Kevin was suspicious all along as well—too clean of a capture to not question if it was a setup.

But for our safety and peace of mind, both men agreed to play along with the scenario that the duo was guilty, while hatching a plan to have Bruce represent Peggy. Kevin thought that if he could earn Peggy's trust, he could investigate the skeletons in the Marino family without tipping off the real perpetrator.

But Peggy was released before Bruce could learn anything new, and we were already en route to Spain, so there was nothing he could do to stop us—except try to warn me to be careful, which I mistook for a threat.

Bruce was glad to receive the call from Jay, as he had hit a dead end. After their coffee shop meeting and Jay's brilliant idea to go back to the Marino drawing board, Bruce requested a meeting with Peggy, who was more than willing to open up to her new lawyer once she found out he could help free her innocent brother. Apparently, she had a change of heart about the scoundrel and didn't believe he would be more than a "harmless" drug dealer.

It didn't take long for Peggy to reveal that Patrick had an estranged younger brother who changed his last name to Perkins. At the same time, Kevin learned that a blonde-haired lawyer type visited Jorden in jail—igniting the lightbulb that prompted the connection between my boyfriend and the disowned heir.

That's when Jorden finally revealed the threat against his sister and proclaimed his innocence once again. But since Josh had never revealed his identity to Jorden, the police still had more work to do to tie him to the crime and make an arrest. The cameras never caught his face, so they had no hard evidence that it was Josh who really visited Jorden.

Shortly after, one of Kevin's associates tracked down the closed juvenile records of Joshua Marino, which uncovered his allegedly accidental, drug-related stabbing that killed another young boy, for which he spent time in a correctional detention center.

Even though this was an underage crime with sealed records, Josh didn't mind the forced family name change and brand new start as a Perkins, enabling him to become a dirty lawyer with access to all kinds of underground resources to support his criminal pursuits—including a fake identity passport procured with Jorden's altered name, using Josh's photo, and then a second one with Jorden's real photo to plant as dummy evidence.

"Josh really did think of everything," I mused solemnly.

Once Bruce filled Jay in on this newly revealed information, my best friend booked a red eye to come find me. They knew time was of the essence, seeing as the tail Kevin had put on Josh lost him earlier in the day, and Bruce confirmed he had no court hearings on the docket. Then, panic set in when no one was able to get ahold of me.

"That's when all the pieces were starting to come together that Josh was truly behind it all, and that you were in grave danger. By the time I landed, he had already kidnapped you and we feared it was too late."

I shook my head in disbelief.

"All the signs were there," I admitted. "Not just the obvious ones, like him being in the countries when the break-ins happened. I mean, the subtle signs. Who else would know that Meg's ring was hidden in a Fabergé egg in the little church where the priest was called? That we had a feuding line of Bianchis who could have possession of the jewelry box and be the perfect accomplices? That there were real items versus decoy items, for heaven's sake?"

"Technically…me. You did share all of that with me, too."

"Oh, you're right. I did have loose lips," I confessed,

embarrassed again that I fell into the trap and endangered everyone I loved. "Huh, all this time, he had me thinking you or Bruce were in cahoots with the Marinos, when it was him all along. He actually had me doubting *you*," I looked at him apologetically.

"It's okay, Riss. The guy is a master manipulator. He had your heart and your trust. I don't blame you for wanting to believe your boyfriend. Even though I've known you your whole life," he joked to lighten the mood. I had to laugh along with him.

"So, what did he say that made you doubt me, anyway?"

"Well, first it was him spotting you with Bruce—and then when you failed my little tests to get the information out of you, it made his whole story more believable about me not being able to trust you. I thought it might have something to do with the scheme you were hiding from me when we got into our fight."

"Oh that? I, uh, was ashamed that I got involved in some pyramid sales funnel thing that almost wiped out my savings and was freaking out that I wouldn't be able to pay the rent and let you down. Plus, I got some of my buddies involved who were on the verge of losing money as well, so I had to set things right."

"That's it? *That's* what you were hiding from me? Are you kidding?" I asked disbelievingly.

"There's a lot more to that story, but we don't need to get into that right now," he said, shifting nervously with body language that begged "not now," and yet, nothing that screamed anything more than poor, impulsive decision making on his part. Definitely not sinister or malice; just stupidity.

"Okay, fine. But you're not getting out of it, mister," I warned with a light finger wave. "Oh yeah—he also told me he investigated you and found out you were college best friends with his nephew, Thomas Marino."

"Thomas Marino? Dude, I've never even heard of the guy."

"Well, I believe that now," I said groggily, feeling the weight of my eyelids bog me down.

"Okay, Riss. You've had enough. I should go and let you rest now."

"No, please don't go," I pleaded. "I don't want to be alone."

"Okay," he said hesitantly, as I snuggled into his warm, comforting, trusting arms and fell fast asleep.

Jay must have been as tired as I was, because we woke up side-by-side, still in each other's arms, on top of the bed covers as the morning light snuck in through a crack in the blinds. I looked up at him, feeling loved and protected, finally seeing what everyone has been trying to tell me for years.

No one has ever loved me the way Jay has.

But I couldn't think about that now, coming off a long ordeal with a few more days ahead of me until this was finally over.

Today, everyone was somber, the gravity of these last few months finally taking a toll on all the game players. Ever the spirit-lifter, a loud, Hawaiian shirt-wearing EJ swung into the kitchen where we all sat drinking coffee and announced that he had the perfect day planned for us—a quiet day at the beach.

At first, we started to resist, but he insisted that the moping would only get worse if we confined ourselves to this stiff little villa. Knowing that none of us could successfully talk him down off the pep squad ledge, we gave in and let him take us to a quiet little seashore on the outskirts of the city—with fully dressed beach-goers, thank goodness.

The fresh air did us all some good. With our family slated to fly in tomorrow, it really was a smart idea to soak up what was left of the peace.

I welcomed the burn of the sun on my back, enjoying the heat and stillness. Meg, Mia and EJ preferred to dive right into the water, but I wasn't quite in the mood to move from my secluded spot. Jay opted to stay behind to watch over me like a guard dog, despite my protests that he should go enjoy himself.

"Go. I'm fine. I promise."

"So am I. The view is spectacular. With everything that went down yesterday, it's just hitting me now that I'm in Spain. I'm actually on the Mediterranean coast. How wild is that?"

"Pretty wild," I indulged him, twisting my neck back and forth as I felt a cramp creep in.

"You okay?"

"Yeah, it's just my neck is so stiff."

"I'm not surprised with how long that lunatic kept you chained up in that awkward position. Here, let me help," he offered, sitting up so that he could rub out the tension that plagued my neck.

I'm not going to lie, it felt incredible. His hands skillfully and deeply massaged the knots of my neck and I encouraged him with my body language to continue down to my equally locked up shoulders and back.

He poured some of the sunscreen onto his hands as a lubricative buffer, gently and methodically pressing along my tightest areas to relieve the pent-up stress. If he didn't make it as a musician, he could definitely make a killing as a massage therapist.

Although he was being quite professional about it, I could feel the sensuality behind each stroke; an affection behind each healing motion.

"That feels incredible," I said, not realizing it came out as a sexually-induced moan. I felt his hands instantly freeze up, their fluidity becoming rigid as he quickly finished up.

"There. That better?"

"Much. Why did you stop?" I turned to ask him.

"Oh, I was getting a cramp in my hand. Sorry," he said, lying unsuccessfully. How respectfully cute of him. I'd let it go for now.

"I'm going to just run up to the bar. Want me to grab you a drink?" I nodded emphatically, knowing I could use something more to keep the nerves at bay.

A few minutes later, he was back with a few bottles of beer and a plate of nachos.

"So, your mom and everyone is coming in tomorrow, huh?" he said, sadly trying to make uncomfortable small talk. He was even more adorable when he was geeky.

"Well, Mom, Granny and Bruce get in tonight after dinner—oh, and EJ's husband, Rodney, too. Colleen and Kieran fly in together in the morning and will probably meet up with Francesco at the airport arriving around the same time."

"So, what's the plan? I know the big party is at night, but what's going on during the day?"

"I don't know exactly. I'm pretty sure Meg and Kieran will want some alone time, and I have a feeling that Mia might end up in Francesco's hotel room for a little catchup rendezvous," I giggled. "With all that has gone on, just to be safe, the kids are going to stay behind with Kevin in New York. So, she'll *carpe diem* the hell out of that opportunity."

"What about you?"

"Well, EJ said something about taking Rodney, Mom, Bruce, Granny and Colleen on an expedited tour of Barcelona while the party planners decorate the house and set up the feast. I was thinking I could join them and spend a little time with my mom. You wanna come?"

"Sure," he said, hesitation masking his feigned excitement.

"Okay, what's wrong?"

"Nothing. Sounds great."

"Jay, I know you better than that. What is it?"

"Well, I was just thinking…maybe you might want to take a ride with me at some point. I reserved a bike for the morning and was going to ride the countryside. I thought, I don't know, possibly we could go together? But I get you want to see your mom, so maybe some other time."

"Are you joking? I love that idea!" I exclaimed. "EJ took me on a ride up to the raceway circuit the other day and it was unbelievable. I'd love to explore some more of the country with you."

"But what about your family?"

"You can't dangle a motorcycle carrot in front of me and expect me to turn that down! Besides, I'm not sure how much family togetherness I can take once everyone arrives," I chuckled—but meant it. "We can plan to spend the morning on our own tour and then meet up with everyone for siesta in the afternoon. Best of both worlds. How does that sound?"

"Great," he beamed like a little kid, sitting back into the sand with the first genuine smile I've seen on his face since he arrived. After that, we both were ready to jump up and join the others in the water and spend the rest of the afternoon lounging amidst relaxed chatter.

Dinner was a magnificent fanfare overlooking the water, as EJ, of course, had to show off his now polished Catalonian culinary expertise for our newest guest. Tapas galore lined our table, along with pitchers of sangria.

"A toast," he began as we raised our glasses in anticipation of what our cousin had to say. "To three very brave, extraordinary women. You are all gutsy, inspirational and an absolute pleasure to be around. It is an honor to call you family. Cheers."

"Cheers!"

"And to two incredible men, without whom I would not be here today. I love you both so much," I added.

"To family and friends," Mia summated.

"To family and friends," we echoed.

13

Ihad never been so happy to see my mother in my entire life. The moment she walked through the door, I ran straight into her arms.

"Oh, my baby girl," she cried, holding me as tight as I held her. "I'm so happy to see you. How are you doing, sweetheart?"

"Much better now that you're here. It was so awful, Mom."

"I can't even imagine," she said as she took my face in her hands and stared as if she needed to memorize every inch of it. "I'm so sorry I wasn't there for you."

"Don't be silly. You couldn't have known," I replied.

"But I should have," came the mousy, fragile, tired voice of my beloved grandmother. "I shouldn't have fallen for his cheap charm. Guess old dogs can't learn new tricks after all."

"Oh, Granny." I left my mother's arms to tightly squeeze and kiss her. "I love you. But it wasn't your fault either. It wasn't anyone's. He swindled all of us."

"Not all," interjected Bruce in a playful tone, who came out from behind Granny, his hands full of luggage. He stood there awkwardly smiling, unsure of how to greet me given the aloofness of our past interactions. I ended the doubt as soon as I walked over and threw my arms around him.

"Thank you," I whispered in his ear.

"It was nothing," he gushed, showing his shy side. "I'm just glad it all worked out in the end. How are you holding up, kiddo?"

"I'm better. It's still surreal to me. But knowing that son of a bitch is chained to a hospital bed and headed to jail helps."

"And if I have anything to do with it, he'll be there a very long time," he added. "In fact, he's already been extradited back to the U.S. and Jorden has been released. Which reminds me—thanks to your statement and permission, we got the search warrant for Josh's house. Guess he didn't realize that living with you would give us the access we needed to take him down.

"We were able to locate his hidden desk drawer in that studio he set up for you. In it was a black leather-bound book filled with his intricate plan that corroborated your story and every person he had contact with, including their role. Kevin and his team were able to track every single one of them down, get a statement and diffuse them. No one will be coming after any of you anymore.

"Including Dominic Moretti, who is also now in custody on several counts, thanks to Josh's written elaborations of his corruptive history and a paper trail to follow. Everyone's crimes were wrapped in a neat, thorough little package. Right down to the tax evasions and drug smuggling," he beamed.

"How could we ever repay you for helping us, Bruce?" Mia asked.

"Mia, you don't ever have to repay me. That's what family is for. Besides, Kevin and Jay played a big part as well. I think we make a very good Three Musketeers," he said with pride.

"We certainly do," agreed Jay as he walked into the room, along with Rodney, who was the last to enter. "EJ's been busy in the kitchen and asked me to come welcome you all. Who's up for some tea?"

We gathered in the living room, a renewed energy with the entrance of our special visitors. We took turns catching up: I filled them in on the details of what happened with Josh; Mom gave Mia an update on the kids; Granny told us all about her casino winnings from her last trip; EJ and Rodney shared an adorable reunion talking about Muffy, their dog; and Meg and Mia finally had the chance to regale their stories about their quite entertaining journey through France.

As we wound down for the evening, we realized we needed to figure out the best sleeping arrangements for our newest guests, though of course, our "host with the most" cousin already had it mapped out.

Meg would move in with Mia for now, giving Mom and Bruce the privacy of her room. EJ insisted that Granny have his room; the futon he had set up in the art studio was more than adequately comfortable for him and his love, he declared. Jay was going to create his own man cave on the couch, but I insisted that he stayed with me.

"No, Riss, it's fine. You need your own space. I'm totally okay here."

"What's the big deal? We slept together last night."

The whole room turned and looked at me, as I realized what I said didn't come out right. It didn't stop Jay from turning fifty shades of crimson though.

"Oh, no—not like that," I back-peddled. "I just meant—we just happened to fall asleep together. I—I don't want to be alone," I looked at him and knew he couldn't say no to my pleading eyes—the same ones that reluctantly earned me a ride on his bike that final morning as roommates together.

"Fine. But I'm sleeping on the floor," he insisted.

He didn't. I manipulated him into joining me in bed. I needed to feel the safety of his presence beside me. Even though I knew Josh was locked up, I hadn't quite released the fear that he'd come back for me. Telling him that had him snuggled up and ready to protect me in an instant.

Men really are so easy to figure out at times—now that I had a clue that this particular man was legit.

Waking up in his arms for the second morning in a row felt so natural that I didn't even notice I kissed him good morning until he jolted up after a sensuous response.

"Wait—what are you doing?"

"Oh my God. I am so—sorry. Force of habit I guess," I suggested, embarrassed beyond all belief.

"Oh. I, um, I'm going to grab a shower before everyone gets here," he croaked out, rising from the bed and avoiding any further talk about what had just happened—or how his morning wood was standing at attention.

Damn, he really was a fine-looking man, even with his facial scruff and disheveled head of thick hair. *Stop it, Marissa,* I scolded myself. *You just ended a relationship with a serial narcissist not even two days ago. Must you always think about sex?*

The morning was bustling, as one by one our cousins arrived. First came Francesco, whose flight landed earlier than expected. After greeting the family, he unapologetically whisked Mia away for a day at the Gardens of Mossèn Cinto Verdaguer, promising to have her back in plenty of time for the party. I loved the way my sister glowed with anticipation of a heavenly day in nature with an old, sexy beau.

Next came the raucous arrival of lovable Colleen, chattering up a storm in her adorable Irish tongue. Entering behind her was dear Kieran, courteously greeting us all hello before running to his love and lifting her off her feet in a sweeping circle. Seeing them together after all the heartaches she's endured gave me hope that one day, I could find that kind of true love.

It was now Kieran's turn to steal Meg away for a romantic Spanish getaway, with another oath that they would be back in time for the festivities.

That left Colleen and EJ to happily reacquaint themselves after their introductions last year when Leigh set his whole plan in motion. Hugs abound as Colleen greeted her other American kin, inviting them to come to the O'Sullivan house anytime they pleased.

"Thank you so much," Mom replied. "We would love that."

"Ah, sure look it. It'd be grand to have you there," our cousin beamed. "So, what's the story?"

Since I was the only one left who was most fluent in "Colleen," I took the lead.

"EJ wanted to take you all on a master tour of Barcelona, to some of his favorite spots. If it's all right with you, Jay and I are going to take a morning motorcycle ride and will meet you around lunchtime."

"Of course, sweetheart," permitted my mother graciously. "Enjoy your ride."

"Fabulous," exclaimed our tour guide cousin. "I'm figuring we'll be by Las Ramblas by one-ish. You know, I thought I'd take them to our fave little tapas place."

"Sounds perfect, cuz. We'll see you then," I said, giving everyone a big kiss goodbye and grabbing Jay by the hand to start our adventure. He looked smoking in his blue jeans and black leather jacket—funny how we ended up twinning with the same exact outfit, right down to the white button down shirt and black boots.

"Hop on," he said, handing me a black helmet with pink stripes after I pulled my hair back into a messy but effective braid.

"Duh, aren't I supposed to get on after you?"

"Not today," he grinned. "Today, you'll be doing the driving."

"Are you serious?" I squealed, unable to contain my excitement.

Always the companion, never the rider, it killed me that I could never take the lead. No way would Jay ever let me on his baby, just like every other man who denied me the opportunity.

I couldn't believe he was actually going to let me drive. Me. Marissa Rossi. I was going to steer us along the Spanish coastline.

After a few quick lessons and practice runs around the villa driveway, he gave me the green light to take off to anywhere my heart desired.

I don't think I will ever be satisfied riding as a passenger again. The power of holding on to the Harley's love handles electrified all the cells in my body. The thrill of rolling the throttle fueled both me and the bike as we cruised away, hearing nothing but the symphony of the grueling engine. Clutching the bike with my legs as they molded perfectly to my thighs gave me a whole new appreciation for being on top.

Some people find their center in a twisted yoga position; I meditate on the open road. All the tension and fears from the terror with Josh blew away in the gusts of wind that carried us on paved clouds.

My genetic code was programmed for this kind of life.

After an hour of riding without a single word spoken, I pulled over to this small, secluded park overlooking the water. We dismounted, remaining silent, as I took his hand in mine and led him to sit on the dry, browning grass beside me.

"That was the best PTSD therapy I could have ever received," I sighed, knowing that when I returned, I did need to make a real appointment to talk through and heal my trauma with a professional. I couldn't resolve this one on my own; I owed it to myself and to my loved ones to get the care I needed to move forward with my life. But this moment right here was certainly a good start.

We continued to watch the glistening waves in the distance, the birds flying in and around a clear sky, not needing to say anything further.

My chest was lighter, and I could feel my breath restore to its natural state. I absentmindedly leaned back and into Jay's chest, closing my eyes and letting our lungs work in rhythmic unison. A few moments later, he shifted his body and my head ended up in his lap, his fingers mindlessly stroking my hair. I could feel him progressively tense with every relaxed touch.

"Riss, I need to talk to you about something." His legs started to tremble as I lifted my head and body to sit up and give him my full attention.

"It sounds serious."

"It is." He was struggling to formulate the words, taking three deep breaths to calm his erratic nerves.

"I'll never forget what I walked in on the other day. Seeing you like that. Degraded, abused. It took a lot of restraint not to instantly pull the trigger," he admitted, holding his finger up to my lips before I could respond.

"Please, just let me get this out.

"It made me think about how I pinned you up against the wall the day I moved out. How I could have hurt you just because I was angry. I haven't forgiven myself for that," he said, hanging his head in shame. "But I thought you deserved to know what triggered me that night."

He was finally ready to talk, and I was ready to listen.

"We've known each other since we were kids, Riss. From the moment we met, we were like these badass kindred spirits."

"Peanut butter and jelly." I couldn't help interrupting, fondly reminiscing what we called ourselves in our youth. "You, of course, being the smooth one, and me the sweet and flavorful one."

"Flavorful I'll give you; sweet—let's circle back on that one," he teased as I good-humoredly pushed him away before resuming my attentive state.

"Anyway, back then, we were just these dorky, troublemaking PB&J kids. I was drawn to your feisty, free spirit, but I've always known you to be more than that. I've watched you compare yourself to your sisters your entire life, and it bothers me that you don't see what I see.

"You have intelligence and ambition in spades. You're the girl who when she got an 'F' on her history essay in the eighth grade for not responding to the question correctly, confronted the teacher and persuaded her that an alternative perspective was absolutely acceptable. You got your 'A' because that's what you do—you never back down.

"You're the girl who saw an awkward little classmate cornered by the swing sets near a bunch of bullies and fearlessly knocked each one of them on their asses with your fist, but then took that sweet girl by the hand and started skipping with her. You and Em are still friends today because of that moment.

"You helped a lost little bird find its nest; were the first in line to help care for your dying Pops Mahoney after his stroke; and you took your wool coat off in the middle of a frigid New York City afternoon to give it to a cold homeless person. You have one of the biggest hearts I know.

"You have this passion that is unsurpassed. Sometimes it's sassiness; sometimes it's sexual confidence; and sometimes it's artistic brilliance. You have been this way ever since I've known you as a spunky little brat with an overbite, and I've admired and respected you for it every single day of my life."

"You saw me before I was beautiful," I finally grasped.

"Correction: I *always* saw you as beautiful."

"Why are you telling me all this now?"

"Because I wanted you to know why you were impossible to live with."

"Wait, what? You pretty much told me how fabulous you think I am, but not as a roommate?" He laughed as I looked at him puzzled. That had to be the worst backhanded compliment anyone has ever given me.

"Oh, you silly, sensitive girl," he teased, finding great amusement in my perplexion. "You are fine as a roommate—except when you walk around in your see-through lingerie and make me listen to hours of you having sex with your boyfriend."

"Oh. Well, if I promise to be more considerate, do you think we could be roommates again?"

"You really are daft sometimes, girl. Why do you think I got so angry that night?"

"I honestly don't know."

"Marissa Rossi, I have loved you since I was eight years old," his confession began. "We've spent our formative years screwing up our love lives with all these awful relationships. Somewhere along the way, a few years ago, I realized that the woman I've been searching for all my life was *you*.

"The girl I told you about, the unavailable one who treated me like just a friend? The one you would tell me wasn't worth it and that I should get over her? It was you all along, Riss. My jealousy had reached its breaking point and I couldn't torture myself anymore by seeing you day in and day out as just my best friend.

"Don't get me wrong—I can accept you as my best friend, if that is all you will ever see me as—but I just can't live in the same space with you anymore without giving in to temptation and ruining almost thirty years of friendship.

"Being here with you, waking up with you, has been both wonderful and painful. Even right now, as I'm spilling my guts out to you, all I want to do is kiss you and never let you go.

"But I know you have been through a terrible ordeal and you have a lot of healing to do. I'm not pressuring you to react or love me back or any of it. I'm not trying to dump this all on you with an ulterior motive.

"I just needed to come clean because I don't want there to be any more lies or secrets between us. You mean the world to me, Riss. You need to know that I am right here for you, however you want me to be, to get you through this and any other challenge that comes your way."

I didn't know what to say. I felt like I should respond, but words escaped me. Like, part of me deep down knew how he really felt all along, especially when my sisters pointed it out. I denied it, but I knew why he had to move out of our apartment, and it broke my heart.

It broke my heart because I think I was feeling the

same way all along, but pushed it down because I was committed to Josh.

I started to speak, but he just shook his head.

"You don't have to say anything," he reassured me, relief washing over both of us that this was finally out in the open and no longer tearing at us. "I'd rather you not force a nicety out to spare my feelings or say something you might not mean. When the words want to come, I'll listen."

And with that, he kissed the top of my forehead and led me back to the bike.

Lunch at Las Ramblas was quite the spectacle, with EJ and Rodney hooting and hollering over drinks, Colleen getting up to dance and my family laughing heartily in response to their antics. What a crazy family I had accumulated over this last year—and I wouldn't trade a single one of them.

Since we arrived separately by motorcycle instead of the clown car the rest of the gang traveled in, Jay and I were able to weave in and out of traffic and arrive back at the villa much sooner than everyone else. Even though it pained me to give up control, I thought Jay could use some reflective driving time of his own on the way back. I'm sure it couldn't have been easy on him to share his feelings with me and not get a response.

The party planners were hurried little carpenter ants, bringing in tables, floral centerpieces and Lord knows whatever other over-the-top ideas EJ had in store for us. Not wanting to get in the way, I thought it would be a good time to show Jay my latest paintings.

"They are fantastic! They're so—you!"

"Really?"

"Of course. They've got your fiery passion and are unapologetically bold and honest. I love these so much more than your landscapes—no offense," he quickly added.

"Wow, thank you. EJ said the same thing. He wants to put them on display in his gallery when we get back."

"For real? That's amazing! I'm so proud of you!" he screamed as he picked me up and spun me around. "My girl's an artist!"

"Your girl, huh?"

"Well, you know what I mean. My bestie girl," he covered nervously.

"That's not what you meant." There was no use in playing games. I couldn't help but see him in a different light since his confession—no, since his rescue. It made what happen next feel so right.

I leaned up to kiss him, wrapping my hands around his neck to bring him closer to me. Surprised and slow to respond, I urged him with my lips to open up to me, finally granting him the permission to cross that line from friend to lover.

I never knew a kiss could be so gentle, so sweet, so endearing. Even when our tongues met, he was tender and soft, even reserved—wanting to cherish this moment as if it would be the only time our lips would ever meet. His hands cupped my face as we explored, tasted and delighted in the coming together of the old friendship and the new possibilities.

"Riss..." He searched my face, still so unsure if what we were doing was the right thing.

"No. My turn to talk," I commanded lightly. "Before the incident with Josh, I had an epiphany—well, a number of them, actually. These paintings reflect what has been hidden in me for so long. EJ helped me see that, and so did my dragon statue and so many other people in my life who love me, including you.

"For as long as I can remember, I've been in a one-way competition with my sisters, always wishing I could 'one-up' them. But we are all the sun and the shadow; each one of us has our own strengths and weaknesses—and together we are stronger.

"I will no longer deny that I have both darkness and light within me; I am not afraid to be who I am, and I will not change for anyone. But what I will do is free my gifts from their chains and honor the goodness in me. I have so much potential to unleash upon the world, and it's ready for me."

I moved on to the next painting, demonstrating to Jay that I had a story to tell for each one and needed a captive audience. He respectfully stood in silence, following my lead.

"In trying to use sex as a weapon to control men, it backfired on me, giving men the power to use sex against me. Men just wanted one thing from me, and the only way I could get approval or acceptance or work my way up the artistic ladder was through my body instead of what I really had to offer.

"I no longer want that kind of game in my life. My body is a temple and a gift, and I won't be giving of it lightly," I hinted. He smiled in obvious respect for my decision as he moved back around me, his arms enveloping my waist and his chin lightly resting on my shoulder.

"Love," I sighed, running my fingers around the dragon-burnt heart. "I used to think it was impossible for me. That I was never good enough to deserve the love of a good, honorable man who would want more than my physical beauty.

"You would think that what Josh did to me would have scarred me for life; and in many ways, it has. I won't easily forget that betrayal or walk confidently without looking over my shoulder. At least, not for a while. But he did not destroy me. I will not give him that satisfaction of burning my heart to a crisp.

"Quite the contrary; his attempt to break me made me even more defiant. I don't want to shut down, Jay. I want to keep my heart open and loving and completely vulnerable. You make me feel safe, protected and cherished." I turned around to face him, meeting him eye-to-eye with a depth I never allowed myself to express.

"I have loved you for as long as you have loved me. But, I'm not ready to walk down that path just yet. I want—*need*—to take things slow. I don't know when I will be able to share my body so intimately after what I just experienced. I can't make you any promises, Jay, other than to take it one moment at a time."

The way he looked at me crushed my soul…in the best of ways. Real, raw, true. My musical poet.

"I have waited decades to be with you, Riss. I can wait decades more, because you are so much more than a body. You are my soulmate. I want you to be my forever," he replied, bending slowly down for a short but deeply affectionate kiss to assure me that he accepted my terms and wasn't going anywhere.

I was tempted to dive deeper into this moment when the noise level of the house hit the roof with the entry of my boisterous family members—Colleen taking the lead.

"Shall we get ready for the party?" Jay asked as he regretfully removed himself from our romantic hold to be honorable.

"Let's do it."

14

An arc of gold and silver balloons lined the entranceway to the rooftop pool. Tables were laced with glittery cloths and chairs with sparkling bows. Centerpieces of bright red carnations and Catalonia's national golden weaver's broom flowers burst out of clear glass vases.

Waiters in contemporary tuxedos with red bowties stood in stance with trays lined with doilies—some with glasses of cava, others with assorted tapas. Flamenco-style music escorted us back to our evening in Madrid as hired dancers glided across the far side of the pool.

"You've outdone yourself, EJ. This is extraordinary," Meg said.

"Only the best for my favorite cousins," he declared. "So, who's ready for the grand finale?"

He brought us over to a beautiful altar-like display, with large framed photographs of who I rightfully assumed were our grandfather, Leigh, and great-grandmother, Lena. He gestured to Colleen and Francesco to join him in front, presenting them each with our heirlooms that he had gathered back for this evening.

"I would like to start off by saying when Leigh first approached me to fulfill his wishes, I thought he was battier than Robin," EJ began. "But as time went on, and I saw his plan unfold, I have never been more in awe of a man's vision before in my life. He truly was a genius whose heart was used for good in the end.

"As we stand here in honor of your great ancestry, I thought it would only be appropriate to bring this quest full circle by presenting you with your heirlooms, once again, while reliving the legacy that brought them here," he said, gesturing over to Colleen to begin.

"Ah, our lovely Megan. You are indeed a treasure to behold, that you are. You boldly took on this challenge to not only claim this here ring, but to discover your heart. It was your Granda's wish that you remembered who you really are: a writer, a romantic and a believer in true love.

"In opening yourself to the journey, and your heart to my dear Kieran, you have honored the *Legacy of Love Claddagh* ring, and it is with pride that I grant you its everlasting blessing," she said, placing the ring in Meg's hand and pulling her in for a tearful embrace.

"Mia Bella," Francesco began solemnly, saddened that he had to take our dear Sorella Maria's place. "Your cousin is looking down on you today as I present this cherished chest to you on her behalf. For you, this gift was destined to remind you that if you believe in yourself, anything is possible.

"As I look at you today, I see a transformed woman who has restored her faith in herself, and in her dreams. You will be an amazing restauranteur, but do not let that be the end of your passionate endeavors. As you take this hand carved jewelry box back into your possession, may it continue to inspire a lifelong pursuit of inner peace and happiness."

Mia proudly accepted her treasure, along with an affectionate kiss to the forehead, from a man I know she will hold dear to her heart for the rest of her life.

"And you, my firecracker of a cousin," EJ commenced,

"have finally come to the end of your personal mission. But before I hand this handsome devil over to you for good, I do believe I promised you a full history and symbolism.

"According to Iberian mythology, the dragon was a cave-dwelling, treasure-hoarding louse who imprisoned nymphs—kinda like Josh," he attempted to kid, but failed as we groaned and shook our heads.

"Too soon? My bad. Anyway, to be identified with a dragon in European culture was to be outcast as destructive, manipulative and evil. The only way to defeat such a force was to reflect its spell-casting eyes back at him with a shield.

"Now Goya, being a man of worldly intelligence, was equally enthralled with the east Asian philosophy that held the dragon in high reverence. They believed it symbolized inner strength, good fortune and the doorway to our intuitive guidance.

"So, when Goya designed his masterpiece, he wanted to blend the ancient Spanish mythology with the eastern world's more promising interpretation, as he believed both theories held truth. In creating the two heads, he wanted to represent the evil dragon that haunted him—his jealousy, greed and illicit sexuality. Something you might know a little bit about, huh honey?"

My cheeks reddened at his implication, but I assented with a shrug of the shoulders and a nod.

"The other head signified something much more formidable—his strength, valiance and pureness of heart. When he unleashed this side of him, it allowed his passions to turn to power instead of pain; prosperity instead of defeat.

"But in the end, he knew he had to embrace both sides of him as one, with the understanding that whichever side decided to rear its head at any given moment was still worthy of his love and happiness. As I believe, sweet child, you have finally come to accept this within yourself."

"I have," I acknowledged.

"That being the case...Marissa Rossi, you have fulfilled your grandfather's dying decree that you live in harmony with both your strengths and your weaknesses, allowing them to catapult you into greatness. I hereby bestow upon you...oh wait.

"Before I do that," he said dramatically, taking the statue back before I could even touch it. "I have another story to tell."

"Now who's being a wicked dragon?" I goaded.

"Oh, I love how cheeky you are, cuz. But since you asked—how did the statue come to be in our family's possession? Fabulous question, Marissa.

"According to a letter that unfortunately has long since been lost and become hearsay, Goya was in love with a Rubio. Of course, to the world he was married to Josefa Bayeu and was thought to possibly have a young maiden lover somewhere along the way.

"But according to this letter—which I paraphrased in this little notebook for you so that you can remember the full story—she may not have been the only one to grace his bed.

"As I mentioned, he had first designed this dragon to represent the two parts of himself, but not just of good versus evil—of the one he presented to society and the one in his heart.

"When he fell in love with Marco Rubio, he had further embellished the statue with great riches for his paramour, the only man he said at the time knew the truth of his double-edged heart and yet accepted him for it with love.

"So although it was given for a forbidden love, the true meaning behind this legacy is to respect the duality of our souls and free ourselves from these societal chains that dictate we must be one or the other; when in fact, we all are both at our cores.

"It was then passed down to Marco's nephew, and years later down the line to the horrific Horace, his honorable son, Eduardo, and so on, finally leading to this moment.

"In the presentation of this rather magnificent creation to you, Marissa, it is done with the greatest pride and the deepest admiration. You have heroically and brazenly shown us the beauty of who you are, in every way, and we love you for it."

I lovingly removed the meaningful sculpture from his hands, granting him two cheek kisses before letting a few tears fall.

His speech and profound words will live on in my heart forever.

"Now for the fun part," teased Colleen. "I reckon you'd all love to know what other secrets the ol' cod had in store for ya."

"Indeed," agreed EJ. "Now Marissa, did you happen to uncover the hidden map?"

"Well, somewhere in between me being held hostage and almost torched to death, I think I might have stumbled upon a clue," I mocked with sarcasm as he shook a naughty finger at me.

"I believe—" I said, giving the dragon's tail a mild twist to separate the tip from the body, "it is in here." Out came a small, weathered scroll tied with a thin blue ribbon.

"What does it say?" urged Meg. I opened it up as my two sisters gathered around me.

When three join as one
The seal can be undone
By fork in vine
The treasure be almost thine
By heart in center
You may finally enter

"Well, that's a riddle if I ever did hear one," murmured Mia. "I wonder what it means."

"When three join as one...must have to do with all three of these pieces, since Lena wouldn't have known about us as the three to go on this journey."

"Good call," approved Mia. "By fork in vine? I get the vine...that could be the ivy around the jewelry box. But what is the fork?"

It didn't take long for me to make the connection. "Oh! The tongues! The forked tongues of the dragon!" I exclaimed, excited to have a piece of the puzzle figured out so quickly.

"Heart in center...could it be the jewel of my ring, since it is shaped like a heart?" Meg offered.

"Boy, are you three smart, I reckon!" proclaimed Colleen.

"Yeah, but how does it all work to open this thing? There are no holes from what I can see," said Mia.

"Uh, how about you turn over that there piece of paper and look at the dang map?" teased EJ.

"Oh," I blushed, not considering that it could be two-sided. And there it was. An actual drawing of how all the pieces worked together to unlock the puzzle.

"Wow! I never would have figured this out, and I spent

a lot of time examining that box," Mia professed.

"Leigh had quite the stir watching us trying to figure out this wretched box before he showed us the trick," confessed Colleen. "We didn't see the backside, neither."

"I can only imagine our grandfather's fun," I chuckled. "So, let's see the box. If we remove the tongues—forks—from the dragon's fire like this—ah, that was easy. No wonder they were wobbly. Glad I didn't get the chance to glue them in yet!" I handed over the two double-forked metal pieces to Mia.

"According to this diagram, they are supposed to be inserted into these tiny, little grooves hidden within the grapevine carving on both sides. Clever—so small that I missed them," said Mia, impressed over being so stumped.

Click, went the first key. *Clack,* went the second.

"In the spirit of full disclosure, those tongues are not actually part of the statue," EJ explained. "They were inserted later by Lena after she designed the puzzle box. Thought it was the best way to keep them safe."

"That actually makes a lot of sense," I responded. "I think we should keep it that way for now, until we know how our futures unfold. I'll arrange to have them placed more firmly so they don't fall out, though. So, what's next?"

"It looks like the stone of my ring is the other key— Kieran, are you able to remove this?"

He took the ring from Meg and examined it. With a small, delicate pop, it was released from its setting.

"We'll get it all nice and secure again when this is through," he promised her.

Mia then took the stone and placed it inside the center groove of the rose—another secret lock that none of us had seen before. With a press and turn of the gem and another unlocked sound, the top of the box snapped open.

"Holy crap, look at all that loot!" I couldn't believe the paperwork, jewelry and trinkets that filled the intricately carved wooden box. "What is all this?"

"I'm afraid we weren't privy to all the contents, *cara,*" said Francesco. "When we came together, Leigh explained his plan about each heirloom and how we all were to tell each story, and then showed us how the box opened. He shared nothing about what he intended to place inside.

"His grand scheme required a contract of silence on our part, which we eagerly signed. In return, to our surprise, he gifted us with a generous payment and a token of gratitude each. We all tried to refuse, but he would have none of it.

"It is a pity that none of you got to meet him—or that you didn't get to see him again," he addressed my mother and grandmother. "In the end, he really did want to do right by his family and shared his deep regrets with us. He wanted to be the man you fell in love with one last time."

Tears came to my grandmother's eyes but didn't dare to fall.

"It makes me happy to hear that," she said genuinely. "But there is something that I still don't understand about all of this. If he was forbidden to use any Marino money on our side of the family, how was he able to do all of this?"

"Ah, so Lena had an inheritance that Cian and Alessia had hidden in an Italian bank account set up by my father, the protection of which was passed down to me upon his death," Francesco continued. "Lena purposely never told her husband about it—it's how she was able to expense her overseas trips without being traced.

"Upon her death, she had it signed over to Leigh, confiding about it when she disclosed these legacies. When we met up in Florence, he went down to *la banca* to arrange for Colleen, EJ and I—knowing that Sorella Maria would not be the best choice given her age, rest her soul—to take ownership of the account to fund your three trips and all expenses.

"Now that the quest is complete, we will be signing it over to the five of you women to withdraw and distribute however you see fit."

"How much is in there?" I couldn't help but ask.

"A whoppin' twenty mil!" hooted Colleen. "Well, give or take, since we did have to set up your little travel funds and whatnot."

"Twenty million dollars?" I thought my mother was going to pass out. *I* was going to pass out. Was this for real? What kind of scam was this?

"You can't be serious," Meg insisted.

"It's true, I've seen the ledger," EJ admitted. "Leigh had hoped that you would all dissolve the Italian account and each open your own in the States and begin your own legacy lines with it."

"Wow. Just wow. This is all so overwhelming," Granny said, needing to grab a chair and sit. Thankfully, Kieran was there to help her settle down.

"Now, don't get me wrong—I am extremely grateful for this gift. It just saddens me that what he leaves behind is money. I would have given anything in the world for him to turn his back on it and just be a family with us. To see him one final time. We lost so many years," she thought wistfully.

"Well, Granny, I intend to help a lot of people with this money," vowed Mia. "Maybe we'll never get the years back, but we can use this blessing to make other wrongs right in this world."

We all nodded in agreement; there would be no better

tribute to our ancestors than to pay forward their kindness.

"So, if we were left these amazing treasures and all this money—what else could we possibly need from this box?" I asked.

"Might as well take a look," Meg suggested.

On the very top was an old white notecard with a blue rose. Within it was a folded up piece of paper that fell out to the ground. While Meg picked it up, Mia read the handwritten note inside the card.

Darling Leigh,

Always remember that you are just as much an O'Sullivan as you are a Marino. I am trusting you to honor our family legacies and find a way to keep the stories alive. Blessed be those who receive such rich keepsakes. I will be with you always.

Love, Mama

"How sweet."

"What does the letter say?" Meg unfolded the crinkled piece of paper to reveal a personal note from our grandfather wrapped around what appeared to be a computer USB.

My Final Legacy Letter

I thought you deserved to see me face-to-face as I revealed the final part of your lost legacy. I have recorded my last words to you on this drive. I only wish we could have met in person; I would have given anything to have hugged each of you at least once as I said goodbye so that you could feel my love for you. So that I could leave this life with warmth. Perhaps in my next life, I will be a braver man. Beyond what I gift you now, I leave my heart and my pride *with you, the beautiful family that you are.*

With Love and Blessings Forevermore, Leigh Marino

"Does anyone have a laptop?" Meg asked. As if on cue, Francesco easily pulled one out of his leather briefcase and set us up so that we could watch the video Grandfather Leigh left for us.

As the screen faded from black to color, the image of our long-lost grandfather came into focus. Weathered and noticeably ill, we couldn't help but see the handsome face behind the wrinkles and the striking resemblance to each of us. We knew this man. We may never have met him, but we knew him.

Granny choked back a sob as the love of her life appeared before her on the screen. Her eyes wistfully gazed upon the kind aqua eyes of a man who had so much left to say, and no time to say it. Mom was less restrained in her tears, seeing her father for the last time. Protectively, Bruce brought her into a side embrace and held her with obvious love and respect to comfort her as she grieved once again.

With their blessing, we began his message.

Greetings my beloved family. I am Leigh Marino, son of Antonio Marino and Lena O'Sullivan. Ex-husband to the beautiful Lillith Mahoney; father to my diamond, Alissa Rossi; grandfather to Megan, Mia and Marissa Rossi; and grateful cousin and friend to Colleen O'Sullivan, Sorella Maria Bianchi, Francesco Marchesi and Edward John Rubio. This message is for all of you.

If you are watching this, it means my darling granddaughters have traveled to all three countries, met their wonderful cousins and successfully retrieved their inheritances. I am so proud of each of you—I hope that you found your journeys to be life-changing and more rewarding than you ever expected.

Now that these charms are in your possession, I must beg you to preserve our legacy and only pass them on to future generations who are worthy of the honor.

If your cousins have not yet revealed the Italian bank account, now would be the time to learn about it. It goes without saying, but to repay them for their kindness, I would hope that you would willingly present them with at least a million dollars each for their troubles.

We all looked at end other and nodded in agreement as our cousins started to protest. Even our virtual grandfather anticipated their resistance as he paused with a look as if to warn them not to object.

"We can argue about it later," Mia warned before gesturing for Francesco to resume playing the video.

But that is not the end of it, my dear family. Yes, there is more. It may seem like too much, but what else would a dying man do with the rest of his treasured possessions? These you are free to keep, sell or share as you'd like; only the ring, box and statue I request that you conceal and protect.

He stopped to gather his thoughts, a single tear escaping down his tarnished cheek. Seeing him like this made him real. His emotions, his gestures, his honesty. He became so much more than words on a piece of paper, and it moved us all. After a moment of silence, he began his words of farewell to each of us.

Mo shíorghrá Lillith,

In this box, you will find a few of our love letters and my most treasured photo of us. I looked at them daily, and though they may mean nothing to you at this point, I wanted you to have them. I hope that one day you can remember us fondly. You are the love of my life. Please remember that always.

I have also made arrangements with the matriculation office at Pace University to enroll you and have your tuition paid in full. It is one promise I can finally keep to you. My dear, it is never too late to fulfill your dreams. Go get that criminal justice degree you always wanted and fight for those underdogs. The world is a better place because you are in it. I know mine was.

I loved you. When I met you. When I married you. When I left you. And now, as I die. I will take my love for you into my eternal grave.

His words ended with shaky hands that blew a kiss through the screen as he mouthed "I love you" once more. Equally shaken, Granny gestured to the man on the screen with her own kiss goodbye and words of gratitude and love.

My little diamond, Alissa,

I have also left you quite a few photos of us, along with the card you had made me for my birthday the first year I left. I treasured everything about you. You will also find a rare, original edition of your favorite childhood book, "I Will Love You Forever." Because that, I will.

He then proceeded to read a few lines from the book, moving my mother to deeper tears and a hidden smile—

her last memory of him can now be a happy one. No longer will it be the moment he left; it will be his recitation of a book she held dear to her heart. He continued his message to her, though we all struggled with the poignancy of his video. Not a dry eye sat on that rooftop.

If I am correct, you have not yet visited the refurbished home I set up for you and your mother. I know it must hold many painful memories and I cannot blame you for hesitating. However, I ask that you go at least once. There is something more I added to it for you—a new wing that serves as an Elizabethan Library, fully stocked with every book, novel, play and poem from every era you can imagine. There is also a classroom; share your passion with children and keep the love of the classics alive. Teach them and start a new generation of literature lovers.

There is nothing I would love more than to see your wisdom spark a revolution—except to see you fall in love again. Open your heart, sweet diamond. As I wished nothing but a happy future for my Lillith, I know Joseph would have wished the same for his beloved. Your heart is too good and too pure to go unshared. But I shall warn you—if you find a devil like me, I will use my heavenly superpowers to punch his lights out.

It was a much-needed joke to lighten up the crowd, before Grandfather Leigh signed off with his last words of love for his little girl. Bruce fondly looked at my mother, who kissed him gently and assured him that her father would most certainly not be coming after him. After all the times I misjudged him, I could finally see he was the perfect man for her. I gave him a wink of approval to let him know he had my blessing as well.

Video resuming, we knew it would be our turn. With such extraordinary heirlooms in our possession and a multi-million dollar account, I couldn't imagine what else he could possibly want to give us.

My bold Megan,

I have a feeling that Ireland will call to you, and as such, Colleen and I have already arranged to turn the deed to the O'Sullivan family home over to you. It will now be yours: live it in, visit it, turn it into a home exchange or timeshare for the rest of the family or sell it—the choice is yours.

My only request of you going forward is that you write and publish our story (as fiction, of course) and embrace the author inside you. Let your words speak your truth. If there is anything I can share from my life's mistakes, it's that love is much more important than power. Find it and hold on to it.

A kiss from Kieran sealed that deal.

My sweet Mia,

I hope you have discovered that happiness is more than serving others; it is also honoring your own dreams. That being said, I have purchased for you a beautiful abandoned building in a prime location along the water for your restaurant. If you do not like it, you are free to sell it and invest elsewhere, of course.

In an envelope is a list of contractors I have already vetted for you—good, honest workers who can oversee the entire construction of your dream. Do me a favor, please. Even though I am sure you will offer much more sophisticated cuisine, can you always keep your grandmother's sausage and peppers on the menu? It is my *favorite, and no other recipe has ever come close. And don't let this be the end of your dreams—always keep believing in whatever your heart desires.*

Mia laughed as she promised the man on the screen that she would wrangle the recipe out of Granny's hands somehow. Granny, of course, lovingly teased Mia that she'd leave it to her in her own will. What a wicked sense of humor my grandmother sometimes had.

I took a deep breath in, wondering what was in store for me.

My fiery Marissa,

I have never seen your work, but I have witnessed your passion. I have no doubt that you have a successful career ahead of you. And every artist deserves a proper studio and gallery to exhibit her artwork.

That's why my final gift to you is the purchase of the Rubio Art Gallery. I have other plans for EJ and Rodney, and the transfer of the deed shall be complete upon your viewing of this video. It will be your space, and your cousin has promised to mentor you along the way. Never stop creating from your heart. And always keep an eye out for those struggling artists like yourself; give them the chance to shine as you have been given. Everyone deserves to express themselves and be accepted for who they are, as do you. Never forget your perfection.

"EJ, you knew about this?" I asked incredulously.

"Mmm-hmm. Now hush and let the man speak," he warned playfully. Grandfather Leigh concluded with addressing each of his trusted cousins.

Darling Colleen,

Words cannot express my gratitude for all you have done for me and our family. There is not much I can give you, except this: your dream of traveling around the world. Enclosed is an envelope with travel agent information; they have the plans lined up for a cruise around Alaska, a spiritual retreat in Bali and a vay-cay on the sunny shores of Fiji. They just need dates that you can go and any companion of your choice—perhaps your cousin Mary? Enjoy seeing the world. And thank you from the bottom of my heart.

Dearest Sorella Maria,

I know your vows forbid you from extravagant gifts. However, in gratitude, it is my wish for you to have this treasured ivory angel statue and rosary my mother prayed with daily. I know your cousin would want you to have them. You are a blessing, and I humbly thank you. It was an honor to have spent time with you listening to your stories. I am forever changed by your wisdom.

Francesco,

My deepest appreciation to you for your discretion and support. I could not have done this without your guidance and resources. I have one final favor to ask of you. As Sorella Maria cannot accept grand gestures, I am hoping you will accept this gift on her behalf.

Her old convent, now a hotel, will be undergoing renovations upon your presentation of the enclosed contract. The owner was looking to retire, and I have set him up handsomely. The intention is to convert this building into a home for single mothers and abused women who have been turned away from their families, in honor of Concetta and Maria's struggle—The Maria Bianchi Women's Center.

Though I must admit, it is also in acknowledgment of how I left my beloved Lillith and Alissa behind to suffer on their own. I cannot make it up to them, but I can help others who were equally abandoned in retribution.

All plans are set; all I ask of you is to oversee that my wishes are carried out and that you accept ownership of the deed. To thank you and your brother for your kindness, a wing is being built in the Marchesi name. May your legacy live on as ours does.

My American cousins EJ and Rodney,

You light up my life with your kind hearts and generosity. I know you think it is too late to raise your own children, and I respect your wishes—but I have a greater plan for you. As you retire from the art community, it is my wish that you find purpose in my final project—a new Rubio Community Center for foster children. Although you will not have any children of your own, there is nothing stopping you from caring for those without a family and filling that void in your life and in theirs. Give them the love and guidance they deserve and I promise the love you get back will astound you.

The three cousins just stared out in reverence for a man they actually had the pleasure of meeting. None of us wanted the video to end; it felt so cruel to finally see the man behind the letters, to get to know our grandfather on sight, for it to just end like this forever. But this was all we had, and we needed to cherish what little bit of him we did get to hold on to as he left us with parting words.

And now I may rest in peace, knowing I have taken care of my loved ones and attempted to make a difference to those who suffer through my death. While I have learned that money will never buy happiness, my wish is that you use the resources at your disposal to follow your hearts, do some good in this world and always, always remember that family and love come first.

I love you all. Thank you for allowing me the chance to right my wrongs. I promise to love and protect you from above.

"This is unbelievable," murmured Francesco, finally breaking the revered silence. "I am so honored to be a part of this, and I know Sorella Maria was, too. I will take the angel and rosary and lay them on her grave, so that they will be with her forever. And I will make sure that shelter helps hundreds of families."

Mia grabbed his hand in gratitude. "Thank you, Francesco. For everything. I'm inspired to build a sister center in the heart of New York. Perhaps you can help guide me with another dream." He looked at my big-hearted sister and simply kissed her and replied with an "of course."

"I can't believe I'm going around the world," said Colleen in a rare moment of speechlessness. "Bless his soul."

"I can't believe we are going to have a family like we always wanted to," said Rodney, hugging his love. "I never considered fostering as an option. Think of all the kids we can help and love," he beamed as EJ sentimentally kissed his husband in great joy.

"And I'm getting your art gallery. I don't know what to say, EJ."

"There's nothing to say. I'm leaving it in great hands, and I couldn't be more tickled to move on to a new chapter in my life. On that note, I have something to show you."

He brought us over to the right side of the rooftop, where a glass top table stood with three easels and golden leaf title cards displaying my paintings: *Fire Resistant, Shadow of the Sun* and *Pleasure Conundrum.*

"You remembered," I said, astonished that EJ recalled the names I had lovingly given them during our conversation in the studio.

"Honey, these are wonderful," my Mom said with pride.

"This is how it will look in three weeks when I add them to my Fall exhibition—before we transition the gallery over to you," EJ announced with honor and commitment. "Although, they will be hanging on a wall and not on a table."

"I'm so proud of you," proclaimed Granny. "I told you this would happen. I knew once you let your heart do the work, you'd become the artist you were always meant to be."

"Thanks, Granny. I think each of us got exactly what we wanted—even if we didn't know what that was," I said, looking at my two sisters and taking each of their hands and sending a wink to Jay.

"That's for certain," Mia agreed, smiling big at Francesco, the man who opened the door to loving herself. "I had an appointment with a real estate agent next week to find the best place for my restaurant, but I think I'll check out my new building first.

"I'll have to look into these contractors and make sure they align with my vision, but if all goes well, I can start construction in a few weeks and have a grand opening in the spring. I would love for you all to be there. If I send you an invitation, will you come?"

"Will the meal be free?" EJ joked. "I'm just joshin' ya—of course we will be there, honey!"

"You can count on it," smiled Francesco. "And perhaps we can use the real estate agent for your new family center while I am there."

Colleen gave a big thumbs up as I threw table confetti into the air in congratulations.

"It's so unreal that this is finally going to happen," Mia reflected. "In a weird way, I feel like life is finally where I've always wanted it to be. I have a great family, amazing kids and now a dream come true. What else could a girl ask for?"

"It certainly is a gift," Granny agreed. "I'm still in shock that he fulfilled his promise to send me to college. I'm going to finally get my degree," she said giddily like a little girl.

"And I can't wait to explore my new library," Mom added. "I know it might be hard at first, Mama, but I think I am ready to forgive and move on. Yes, what Daddy set up for all of us was built from his fortune. But all the good he is putting in place eases my personal pain of abandonment. Think of all the families and children we can teach, help and heal because of his generosity. It's comforting to know that after everything, the heart you fell in love with—that created all of us—is who he chose to be in the end."

"I couldn't have said it better myself, my sweet girl," agreed Granny. "It is time to put the anger and resentment behind us and start living again. To remember who we are and to use our gifts to make a difference in this world. Time to create new life."

Catching a glance at Meg and Kieran staring into each

other's eyes and suppressing a giggle like they had a secret, I prompted them to speak.

"What's up with you two?" I asked as Kieran nodded at his beloved.

"Well, we were going to wait until after the party to tell everyone, but since everyone is here…" She lifted up her left hand to uncover a stunning princess cut diamond ring. The boy had some taste!

"You're getting married?" Mia screamed in excitement. "When?"

"Well, we're thinking by Christmas," Kieran responded. "A small, intimate wedding in Ireland where my mum can be there and then a bigger reception later in the summer in New York."

"Why so soon and spread out?" asked Mom curiously.

"Well, like Granny said, it's time to create new life. Looks like I'm ahead of the game–because I'm pregnant," Meg answered shyly to shouts of excitement and well wishes. "We just found out last week. It explains why I've been so tired this trip."

"How wonderful for y'all! So, how will this all work with the across-the-ocean thing?" EJ asked, addressing the obvious.

"The plan is to live in the States September through June—the school year, essentially. Then, we figured we'd live in Ireland during the summers and go back as often as we can to visit Kieran's mum with the baby."

"Sounds like a great plan," Mom supported.

"This is absolutely amazing. To be here with all of you like this, and so happy," I teared up, never so content in my entire life. "I never want to forget this night."

"I think we should have a reunion every year," suggested Mia.

"Yes! What a splendid idea! Absolutely!" cheered the rest of the group.

"Shall we have one final toast?" Jay prodded, and we all gestured for him to lead the way.

"To five incredible women, who I have known and loved my whole life. And to their extended family of generous, kind cousins who have made their lives complete. May you all always have the love and joy you have now and be blessed for the rest of your days."

"Cheers! Here, here!" came the group shouts and clinking glasses. With the final reveal at its conclusion, our tormentor behind bars and no more mysteries to solve, we were all free to eat, drink and be merry. As I stood looking at my art with great pride and hope for the future, I felt Jay come up behind me and wrap his arms around my waist, putting his head on my shoulder.

"So, how does it feel to finally get everything you ever wanted?"

"It's more than I ever expected. I never thought I would see a day like this. I mean, look around. I'm at a family gathering and I finally feel like I belong instead of being the black sheep. And yet, nothing has changed except the way I react. There's no jealousy, no resentment—just genuine love for everyone here.

"And I look at these canvases—these rather dark visions I created, and am amazed at how accepted they are, just as they are. How accepted *I* am. I feel—free."

"I, for one, would change nothing about you. I'm glad to hear that you finally feel the same way about yourself."

"I do. The only demon I had to face was my self-judgment. That part of the dragon is now gone, and I'm ready to let the bright one lead the way."

"I hope that other dragon is not *all* gone," he said

suggestively, with a slight smirk on his face as he turned me around to face him.

"Oh no, not all of it," I swore with my own alluring look. "There are parts of me that will never change. You can count on that, lover."

I leaned up to kiss him passionately with the promise of forever, knowing that with Jay, I can be both the dark and the light. And there is no other way I would ever want to be.

Rubio Family Tree

Rubio Family Line

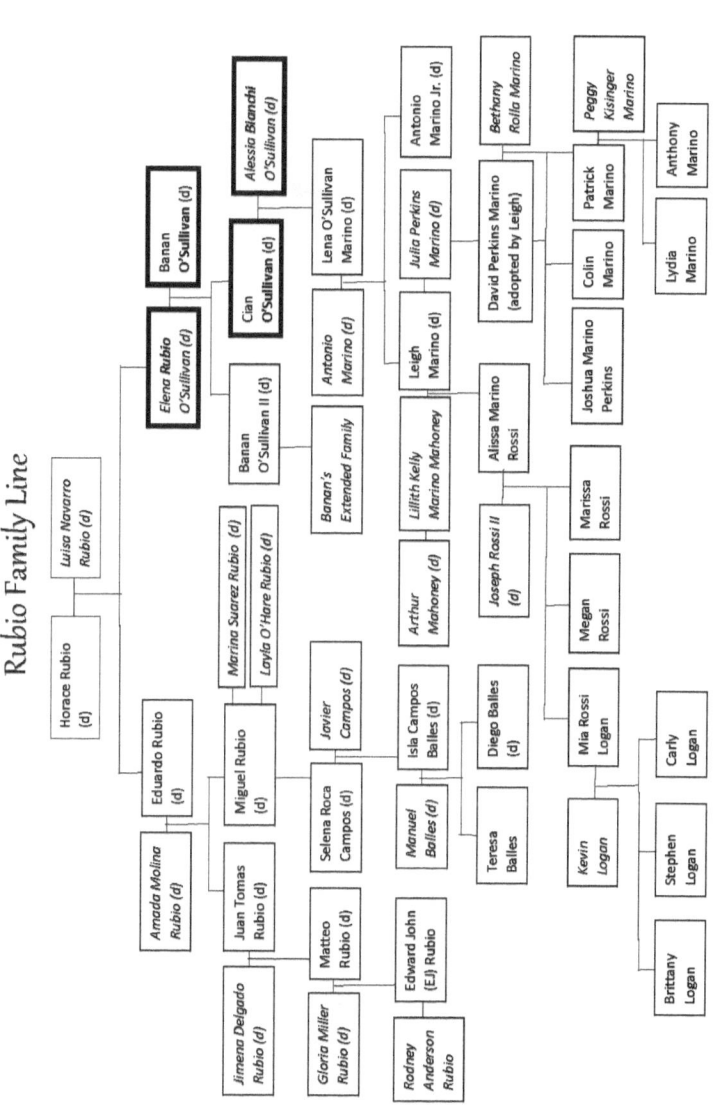

Other Books by Jenny Dee

Autobiographical Memoirs

Butterfly Travels

Butterfly Travels 2

The Cosmic Kids Club Series

Meet the Z Team

Planet Personalities

Stars Live in Houses, Too

Cosmic Kids Astrology

Numerology for Kids

Independent Titles

A Cali Christmas

Beat Me With Your Words: An Inspirational
Story of Survival and Hope

About Jenny Dee

 An avid writer since childhood, my career in professional writing anchored my passion and encouraged my dream to become an author—my first book, *Butterfly Travels,* was published in 2014. Five years later, my children joined me in both my physical and literary journeys, and we are delighted to share our family adventures with the world through *Butterfly Travels 2.*

I've never been a "one size fits all" type of girl. I like to connect to all kinds of people and share my stories and experiences in hopes that they touch a life. I don't ever want my inspiration to be limited to a single genre, so it is with a great love for writing that I offer a multitude of styles to strike your fancy, from travel memoirs and children's books to empowered women's literature and traditional romance.

To learn more about me or to subscribe to my publications, you can find me at www.jennydeeauthor.com or simply scan this QR code.

~ Find Yourself in a Character ~

www.ingramcontent.com/pod-product-compliance
Lightning Source LLC
Chambersburg PA
CBHW030838030726
47495CB00005B/1277